BEYOND the FIRE

A TRILOGY

Dewayne A Jackson

Copyright © 2017 Dewayne A Jackson.

All rights reserved. No part of this book may be used or reproduced by any means, graphic, electronic, or mechanical, including photocopying, recording, taping or by any information storage retrieval system without the written permission of the author except in the case of brief quotations embodied in critical articles and reviews.

WestBow Press books may be ordered through booksellers or by contacting:

WestBow Press
A Division of Thomas Nelson & Zondervan
1663 Liberty Drive
Bloomington, IN 47403
www.westbowpress.com
1 (866) 928-1240

Because of the dynamic nature of the Internet, any web addresses or links contained in this book may have changed since publication and may no longer be valid. The views expressed in this work are solely those of the author and do not necessarily reflect the views of the publisher, and the publisher hereby disclaims any responsibility for them.

Any people depicted in stock imagery provided by Thinkstock are models, and such images are being used for illustrative purposes only.
Certain stock imagery © Thinkstock.

ISBN: 978-1-5127-9557-8 (sc)
ISBN: 978-1-5127-9559-2 (hc)
ISBN: 978-1-5127-9558-5 (e)

Library of Congress Control Number: 2017911232

Print information available on the last page.

WestBow Press rev. date: 09/28/2017

DEDICATION

This story is dedicated to both my heavenly Father, who gives hope to a troubled world, and to my wife, who has endured me for a long time.

I want to thank everyone who has encouraged me along this journey, but special thanks go to the staff at Westbow Press for including this story in their labors.

I also want to express my heartfelt gratitude to David and to those like him who are willing to step into harm's way to keep us safe.

To my children, grandchildren, and readers of every age: let us do justice, love kindness, and walk humbly with our God. Incredible things can happen when we yield completely to our Creator's plan and purpose.

CONTENTS

Preface xi

Book 1   A World in Conflict: Sparks in the Tinderbox

Prologue xvii
Chapter 1   A Test of Faith 1
Chapter 2   Trial by Fire 15
Chapter 3   Walking by Faith 20
Chapter 4   Judgment 22
Chapter 5   Turmoil in Amity 29
Chapter 6   Problems at Home 34
Chapter 7   A Gathering of Leaders 44
Chapter 8   The Council 53
Chapter 9   Decisions 67
Chapter 10   Call to Arms 78
Chapter 11   The Road to War 93
Chapter 12   No Place to Hide 108

Book 2   Facing the Defiler: Enduring the Flames

Chapter 13   Christmas Morning at the Cottons' 123
Chapter 14   The Plot Thickens 139
Chapter 15   Breaking Point 146
Chapter 16   Realization 152
Chapter 17   One Final Mission 160
Chapter 18   Last Rites 167
Chapter 19   A Quest Begins 173
Chapter 20   Perilous Choices 182
Chapter 21   Into the Unknown 190
Chapter 22   Captivity 197
Chapter 23   The Interview 216
Chapter 24   Condemned 223
Chapter 25   Detour 230
Chapter 26   Enemy Territory 245

Chapter 27	Regrouping	249
Chapter 28	Into the Jaws	251
Chapter 29	Escape	268
Chapter 30	Deliverance	280
Chapter 31	Healing	297
Chapter 32	Evil Spreads	301
Chapter 33	The Doors of Endor Open	304
Chapter 34	Making Plans	315
Chapter 35	The Road to Freedom	322
Chapter 36	Plans Unravel	328
Chapter 37	Quelling the Rebellion	340
Chapter 38	Dispelling the Darkness	344
Chapter 39	Change of Regime	348

Book 3 Restoration: Beyond the Fire

Chapter 40	Nighttime at the Cottons	355
Chapter 41	Reunion	362
Chapter 42	Unsettling News	365
Chapter 43	Amity	370
Chapter 44	Jennifer's Hospital	386
Chapter 45	The Cotton Household	400
Chapter 46	Dark Days in Capri	411
Chapter 47	A New Beginning	425
Chapter 48	A Daring Escape	429
Chapter 49	Stonewall	433
Chapter 50	New Faith	443
Chapter 51	Choices	449
Chapter 52	Taking a Stand	454
Chapter 53	A Different Battlefield	463
Chapter 54	Mercy	465
Chapter 55	New Revelations	467
Chapter 56	The Tide Turns	477
Chapter 57	Darkness Covers Green Meadow	483
Chapter 58	A New Day	486
Chapter 59	New Challenges	489
Chapter 60	Starting Over	497

Chapter 61	Change	500
Chapter 62	Journey Home	512
Chapter 63	Stonewall	521
Chapter 64	Bill Cotton's House	525
Chapter 65	Life beyond the Fire	534

PREFACE

In John 16:33 (King James Version), Jesus tells His disciples, "In the world ye shall have tribulation: but be of good cheer; I have overcome the world."

This story began back in the early 1990s when our nephew was called to serve in the Persian Gulf during Operation Desert Storm. I wanted to write him on a regular basis while he was deployed, but our quiet farm life didn't yield much interesting news. I tried instead writing him chapters of a story, much as J. R. R. Tolkien had done with his son during WWII. At the time, we did not know the actual fighting to free Kuwait would take four days.

Our nephew was home long before the story was completed, but my sister-in-law read the chapters sent to her son, and her comments triggered thoughts in my mind that would shape much of the rest of the story.

We live in a world that is polarized and angry. Everywhere we look, embers of turmoil smolder around us, and we do not know if it will be a choice we make or the belief of someone else that will set our world on fire. Though the characters in this story are fictional, many of the circumstances they face are very real. We, like the characters in this book, tend to underestimate the power of prayer and the unusual things that can happen when the Word of God mingles with the world of mankind. I hope *Beyond the Fire* will strengthen your faith and encourage your walk with God.

Northlands
Gray Haven
Graylands
Great River
Jeshemon Ridge
Peom
Hesron
Fords
Western Wilds
Western Slopes
Green Meadow
Great Bend
Emancipation
Freedom City

Great Desert
N
W
E
S
ashan
Sundering Sea
tains Despair
Lashish
Guardian Range
Range
Orchard Creek
Miners Creek
North Glen
Amity
Waterfront
Zarapheth
Deep Delving
Stonewal
Capri
Sebring
Highland
Cresent River
Southglen
Independence Mountains
Great Sea

BOOK ONE

A World in Conflict: Sparks in the Tinderbox

PROLOGUE

An icy wind nipped her cheeks, and snow cascaded from the towering trees. A swirl of white encircled the sleigh. Destry peered anxiously over her shoulder to see if Robbie was still covered.

Why must we make this trip? she fumed inwardly. *Robbie should not be out in weather like this. Besides, we've survived this long without spending Christmas with Philip's family.*

She stole a glance at the handsome man beside her and wondered why he had been so moody of late. Why should he have this sudden urge to see his family after so many years? Destry bit her lip. She resented this trip, and doubly so at this time of year. But she had said too much already; Philip was barely speaking to her. Staring straight ahead, she thought, *All right, we will have Christmas with his family, but I don't have to like it!*

Angry thoughts melted as the walls and gates of Amity suddenly appeared between the trees. Philip slowed the team and brought the sleigh to a halt.

"I'll have to get clearance," Philip said stiffly. Clambering from the seat, he plodded heavily through the snow.

"Formalities," Destry whispered, wishing they could hurry to the warm lodgings of the Stafford House Inn. She loved the great stone cathedral that served as a refuge for travelers, rich and poor alike. Mentally, she compared her own headstrong husband with the friendly old man by the same name in Stafford House Inn. Why was Philip acting like this? Checking behind the seat again, Destry noted with satisfaction that Robbie was still asleep beneath the bundle of blankets. She was grateful the stop had not awakened him.

"Oh, good," she sighed. Philip was returning. There would be a hot meal and warm lodging on the other side of this wall, and she was more than ready.

Christmas Eve at the Cottons'

"I want to be Stafford!"

"No fair! You were last time! You have to be Jabin this time!"

"No, I don't!"

"Yes, you do!"

"Boys, boys!"

Destry watched her sister-in-law corral the larger of two boys and soundly twist his ear.

"Ouch!" the lad yelled. "Mom, you're hurting me!"

"Not as bad as I'm going to if you don't stop fighting."

"But he started it!"

"Did not!"

"This fighting has to stop!" Kelsey's voice carried a no-nonsense tone. "Why don't you go ask Grandpa for a story?"

"Will he tell us about the origin of Amity, Mom?"

"Not if you don't ask him."

Just then, more children dashed into the dining room. The first in line collided with the table and immediately set up a howl.

Destry was the first to reach the injured child. "Kelsey," she said timidly, "could you bring a cold cloth? Joshua bumped his nose pretty hard."

"Sure," Kelsey said, giving her son a motherly shove toward the parlor where the men were stoking the fire and telling stories.

A slender woman with snow-white hair stepped from the kitchen. In her hand was a damp cloth. Promptly she knelt beside the whimpering boy. "What happened this time?"

"Just running, Mom," Kelsey explained. "Boys!" she called, leaving her mother-in-law, Mary Cotton, in charge of the whimpering child. "Grandpa is about to tell a story. Better go to the parlor quick."

The wounded child suddenly squirmed from his grandmother's arms and raced into the parlor, shouting, "Oh, boy!"

Mary smiled at Kelsey. "That was a quick cure! Does Grandpa know he is about to tell the children a story?"

Kelsey grinned. "He's about to find out."

Both women laughed and returned to the kitchen to finish washing dishes. Destry sat bewildered on the floor, wondering what had just happened. Philip's family was so strange. Looking about, Destry spied her own son still sitting quietly at the table, drawing pictures on a scrap of paper. He was such an obedient boy. Her heart twisted within her breast.

"Robbie," she called, "all the other children are going to the parlor with Grandpa and Daddy. Would you like to go too?"

A smile brightened the tiny boy's face. "Oh, may I, Mama?"

"Yes," Destry said, stooping to hug her son as he hurried past, his cast bumping clumsily on the floor. "But don't run," she warned.

"Yes, Mama," the lad said, wiggling from his mother's embrace and noisily scraping his cast across the floor.

Destry's heart swelled as he passed. How fortunate she felt to still have him.

Kelsey soon had all the children corralled, sending each to the parlor where the men had gathered. The noise level lessened for the first time since the children had been excused from the Christmas Eve meal.

Bill Cotton grinned at the children dancing around their fathers in the parlor. "So, you want to hear a story?" he asked.

"Yes, Grandpa! Will you tell us the story of how Amity came into being?"

"Please, oh, please!" chimed a chorus from the rug before the fireplace.

The old man quietly surveyed the little mops of blond, brown, and red hair before him. *I am blessed,* he thought. He glanced at the others who had drawn near the pleasant crackle of the flames. Ned, his only son-in-law, was nearly asleep in an oversized chair, while Thomas and Philip appeared as eager as the children for the story to begin. James was not present. It was snowing heavily, and he had slipped outside to check the livestock and make sure everything was all right.

"Shouldn't we wait for the ladies?" The long ends of Grandpa's mustache danced as he spoke.

"Oh, Grandpa, they know the story anyway! They won't mind if they miss the first part."

"Well, you might be right about that." Grandpa laughed. "Where should we begin?"

"With Josiah Stafford!" was the overwhelming response.

"Very well. Here we go."

The clink of dishes and soft laughter of women's voices drifted in from the kitchen. The fire crackled pleasantly in the hearth, and every child was stretched out on the floor at Grandpa's feet—all except Robbie. He had crawled into his grandpa's lap and was nestled against his broad chest. Grandpa's arms cradled Robbie gently, wrapping him in love. Everyone watched Grandpa expectantly as he stared into the flames on the hearth.

"Long ago when I was a child," Bill Cotton began, "my grandfather told me of a land beyond the mountains. If you would climb to the top of the Guardian Range today, all you would see is a great body of water. But long ago, there was a land of wealth and power to our north. Protected on the south and west by mountains, on the east by the sea, and to the north by a great desert, Shingmar was a land blessed by heaven. Its people lived in peace and prosperity, for rain fell abundantly upon the deep, fertile soil of that wondrous land.

"But time passed, and the people of Shingmar forgot the Creator of heaven and earth. They began to believe in the sun, the moon, and their own sense of power. They became futile in their thinking and exchanged the wonder of heaven for a figment of their own imagination. Slowly, Shingmar slipped into idolatry and they began to worship creation rather than the Creator. This was true of many people, but not everyone. One man stood against the growing tide of popular idolatry. His name was Josiah Stafford."

CHAPTER 1

A Test of Faith

King Shinar looked at the man standing before him. His eye was swollen, and his lips were split and bleeding. A deep cut on his scalp sent blood dripping down his face. The king wrinkled his nose at the smell; sweat and blood mingled in a most disagreeable way. "What are the charges against this man?"

A man stepped forward, his shoes clicking on the marble floor. "Treason, Your Majesty."

"What has he done?" King Shinar asked.

"He refuses to worship in the Temple of the Moon."

Shinar scratched his fat chin. *That isn't treason,* he thought. *That's foolishness. People should enjoy life.* Turning to the man before him, he asked, "What have you to say for your actions?"

The battered man looked straight at King Shinar. "Sire, I cannot worship a woman who pretends to be God!"

King Shinar heard a murmur spread through the men in his court. They believed that the goddess of the moon was, in fact, divine. She was the source of all fertility, and she could bless the nation with prosperity. Without her, rain would not fall in its proper season, and famine would ravage the land.

"These are the words of a traitor!" shouted one councillor.

"He deserves to die!" screamed another.

"He leads people into rebellion! He should be stoned!"

Others took up the cry as the council sought the man's life.

"Silence!" Shinar roared. He seldom raised his voice, but his council was getting out of hand. He turned again to the man before him. "What is your name?"

"Josiah Stafford," the man answered.

King Shinar noted that the man was humble. There was no belligerence in his tone or action. "Stafford, do you lead a rebellion as these men say?"

"No, sire. I merely speak the truth. Others might listen, but we are not rebelling against your kingdom."

"We? So you are a leader."

There was no reply.

"If you are not rebelling against my house, why do you not worship the goddess of the moon? Are you aware that the law decrees that you must worship her?"

"I honor you as my king, O Shinar, but I will not worship anyone but the Creator of heaven and earth."

"Kill the traitor!" shouted one of the men in Shinar's court.

"He would have us starve!" Shouts began again to fill the hall of judgment.

Shinar signaled for silence. When order was restored, he spoke to the bold man. "Do you not realize how much we honor the queen of heaven?"

"I do, Your Majesty. But to worship her is to deny my allegiance to the Creator of heaven. If I honor Him and Him alone, I will in no way bring disaster upon the land."

Shinar pursed his lips. He didn't believe that the goddess could bring rain, but he did like the worship services. *Why wouldn't anyone want his fill of pleasure with the most sensual women in the land?* he thought. *This man is a fool.*

King Shinar remembered many years earlier when a drought had come upon the kingdom. Some people had thought that mandatory worship of the goddess would break the drought. Shinar had passed a law, and rain had soon fallen on the land. Shinar didn't believe the goddess had brought rain, but many people did. However, since Shinar enjoyed the worship services, he had kept the law in place.

Today, King Shinar was troubled by the man before him. He seemed like an honest man with no trace of treachery. Yet he had defied Shinar's law.

"By what authority do you defy this court?" Shinar demanded. "Why will you not worship our deity?"

"It is written in the Book of the Almighty," Josiah Stafford declared. "The Lord our God is One. You shall have no other gods before Him. The Lord is a jealous God, visiting the iniquity of the fathers upon the children to the third and fourth generation of those who hate Him, but showing steadfast love to thousands of those who love Him and keep His commandments. I dare not worship any other but the Creator of heaven and earth."

Shinar shuddered. He hadn't heard about the scriptures since he was a child. This book was hardening good people into rebellious traitors.

"Do you have a copy of the scriptures?" Shinar asked.

"No, sire. Copies are rare."

Shinar's dark eyes nearly vanished under his furrowed brow, and his thin lips turned down as his shoulders slumped. *They are rare indeed*, he mused. *Maybe I could crush this rebellion if I could get my hands on the book.*

"Do your followers have a copy?"

Stafford made no reply.

Shinar's face grew red with anger at Stafford's silence. "You refuse to speak? You are a fool!"

Shinar turned to his council. "Do you know this man's followers?"

"We know some of them," they answered.

"Seize them! Bring them in chains to this court, and find their book!"

"To hear is to obey, O King," they fawned. "Now the Queen of Heaven will bless you and this land richly for your devotion."

Shinar smiled at their praise but turned his attention back to Josiah Stafford. "Send this man to the dungeon until I call for him."

"Yes, sire."

So began a great purging throughout all of Shingmar. Men were gathered from every walk of life. Homes were entered and searched. Every book and paper was examined as King Shinar sought to find this book of rebellion and trouble. His search affected every class of people in the land.

However, months later, Shinar shook his head at the report. The number of dissidents had grown. Nearly fifty rebels were scheduled for court that very afternoon. Sometimes Shinar wished he could call off his search for the scriptures, but how could he explain that to his council? Maybe he could still get to the bottom of it.

"Grekko! What is the schedule today?" Shinar asked.

"We have more traitors to the crown, Your Highness."

Shinar groaned. "Why can't someone capture the book that is causing all this grief?"

"There is a conspiracy, sire," the king's chief aide responded. "The men and women of this movement are so careful of their document that whatever plan we devise to obtain it seems to be known to them in advance. The book shifts from one to another so quickly that we have not caught up with it."

"Women?" Shinar asked. "Are there women involved in this movement as well?"

"Yes. The wives of many men we now hold in prison continue the movement."

"What is being done to quell their activity?"

"Nothing, sire. We've had no direction from your throne."

"Good heavens." Shinar sighed. "Do I need to hold your hand? We are trying to stop a rebellion here."

Grekko didn't reply at once. "What is your desire, Majesty?"

"The women who are actively involved with the movement shall be sent to the work farms. There they can grow food for themselves and for my court."

A sly smile spread across Grekko's impudent face. "There are some lovely women among those involved, sire."

At first Shinar was irritated by what seemed to be a needless statement. Then slowly a grin spread across his fat face. "I think I understand. Bring the loveliest women here to the Temple of the Moon." His smile spread to a low chuckle. "So they don't want to worship the Lady. They will worship the Lady, all right!"

The Building of Stonewall Prison

"Put that stone over here, you swine!" A whip cracked harshly, and an old man winced as a red welt raised upon his back.

King Shinar had ordered rebellious traitors removed from Shingmar, and forcing them to build their own prison on a distant island seemed a perfect punishment. Men who believed in the Holy Scriptures had been rounded up and shipped either to quarries to cut stone or to the island to build their own prison. Some men who were not even in the movement had been arrested and sent to prison if their wives were attractive enough to serve in the Temple of the Moon.

The king's chief aide, Grekko, came and went at will, and today he strode with cocky confidence before King Shinar. "The building of our island prison progresses nicely, Your Highness."

"Good! Good. How many prisoners are under your care?" Shinar asked.

"There are five thousand at the island, sire, not counting those cutting stone in our quarries."

"Five thousand!" Shinar exclaimed. "Has the whole world gone mad?"

Grekko wisely refrained from answering.

"How many women and children work on our farms here?" the king asked.

"There are at least ten thousand." Grekko smiled.

"Are they productive?"

"Their labor fills our larders with abundance."

"Are we quelling the movement?"

"No." Grekko shook his head. "The harder we repress this movement, the more people get involved."

"Have you obtained the Holy Scriptures?"

"No, sire."

"Get that book! I'm going to destroy it, if it's the last thing I do!"

There was no opportunity for prisoners at Stonewall Prison to openly worship God, but at night when they were chained to the walls of their cells, the guards could not stop them from reading or discussing the few pages of scripture that had been smuggled in and were carefully hidden from the guards during the day.

One night the prisoners in one particular cell were preparing to listen to the Word of God when someone hissed a warning. "Someone is coming!"

The men in the cell grew quiet, and footsteps could be heard in the corridor. Guards were the only people free to roam the hallways at night. Suddenly, a door opened into the cell, and Commandant Gaff stood silhouetted in the light.

"Gentlemen," he said, and everyone relaxed. Gaff was the only guard who treated the prisoners as though they were human and deserved dignity. Though the prisoners loved Gaff, the other prison guards hated him and wanted to overthrow his authority.

Closing the door behind him, Gaff whispered into the darkness, "Are the scriptures being read here tonight?"

"Yes," Josiah Stafford whispered. "Would you care to join us?"

"Please."

The moon shone through a tiny gap between stones in one wall, making a dim light in the darkened cell. Stafford studied the page before him and then spoke in little more than a whisper. "In the beginning was the Word, and the Word was with God, and the Word was God."

A slight movement outside prompted a quick "Shh!" Everyone held their breath.

"Commandant?" It was the night watchman.

Gaff spoke from inside the cell. "Yes, watchman. What do you need?"

"Are you all right, sir?"

"Yes," Gaff answered. "I was just checking on the prisoners."

"Very good, sir."

They heard footsteps move farther down the corridor, which connected with the other cells deep inside the building.

"That was close!" someone whispered.

"Too close," Gaff breathed. "I've got to stop coming like this. Will someone tell me where I can find Josiah Stafford?"

A long silence ensued. The man who had been reading finally spoke. "I am Josiah Stafford."

The commander stepped toward the man who had spoken. "Sir," Gaff said, "forgive me." Though it was too dark for most in the cell to see, the commandant knelt before the most hated of all the prisoners.

"Forgive you of what, Commandant?"

"I need to be forgiven for the chains you wear and the scars upon your back. I feel responsible for the hatred among the guards and the wrongs done to everyone imprisoned here. Your only crime is trusting in the hope the scriptures give."

"My friend, you are the one ray of hope many of us have. If it were not for your gentle hand, many of us would have perished at the hands of the officers long before now."

"Maybe to perish would be better than to rot here."

"It may seem that way, but the Almighty One has given us life and hope. He will not leave us or forsake us."

"Josiah," Gaff began, "I have come to inform you that I will no longer bear the responsibility of your confinement and hard labor. I am leaving my post."

A low murmur filled the room. The men knew their conditions would worsen as soon as Gaff was gone.

"I wish you would reconsider," Stafford said quietly. "Our burdens will surely become harder if you leave."

"Resentment grows daily among the guards," Gaff said. "I feel that soon I shall be one of you, confined to these walls and unable to lessen your burden anyway. Tonight I plan to stroll outside the fortress walls. When I'm out of sight, I'll swim the river and make my escape. But before I do, what last favor can I do for you?"

Josiah remained quiet for a long while. Finally, he broke the silence. "Master Gaff, I respect your decision. There is one thing that troubles everyone here, and we are powerless to change it. Our latest arrivals tell us that our wives and children suffer terribly at home. King Shinar has driven them from our homes, and they labor long and hard in work camps. In these camps they produce abundant food for the castle, but the women and children live on barely a morsel themselves. Will you return to Shingmar and help them escape their bondage?"

"Sir, I have no ship, and the mountains are impassable. I will be an outlaw, marked for desertion of my duties, and if I'm caught, I'll be executed!"

"You have planned your escape. Maybe you can devise a plan for our families as well. We will not bind you with an oath to help them, but we pray you will remember us always and travel in the power of the Holy Spirit."

It was a hot afternoon in Shingmar, and Suzanne was hoeing weeds in long rows of corn as she watched a ragged man slowly approach the field where she labored.

"Madame?" The man tipped his hat to Suzanne. "Might I inquire if this is a labor camp of King Shinar?"

"You might, but I'll not be telling," Suzanne responded, even though she knew her saucy remark would have incurred a beating in some circles.

"Madame," he began again. "I don't blame you for not wishing to speak to a stranger, but I have a duty to fulfill for some men I once knew. I think you might be able to help me."

Suzanne made an ugly face and said, "I'm not pretty at all. You needn't take me to your precious altar to serve in the worship of the Lady!"

"What are you talking about?" the ragged man asked.

"Oh, that's right!" Suzanne retorted. "Pretend you do not know!"

"I have no idea what you are talking about. The men I spoke of are in Stonewall Prison."

The young woman's face blanched at the name of the prison. Its fame was spreading across all Shingmar as the vilest and most oppressive place dissenters were sent. "You know people there?" she asked incredulously.

"I do. They asked me to help their wives and children."

"How do I know you aren't one of the king's men trying to trick me into revealing our leaders and our books?"

"If I were indeed your enemy, you've already said too much."

Suzanne's dark eyes flashed angrily.

"Back to work!" the ragged man said loudly. Then whispering, he said, "Your foreman is watching."

Suzanne blushed deeply, knowing a whip could soon be on her back. It was forbidden to talk to strangers.

Having seen the hovels in the distance, the man whispered, "We'll talk more tonight."

Suzanne glared angrily at the man as he walked toward the foreman, but she did not expect to see the stranger again.

Later that night, after Suzanne had put her children to bed, she heard a soft tap on her door. These homes had no locks, so Suzanne had propped chairs against the doors before going to bed. Now she slid a chair carefully to one side before lifting the latch.

She gripped a broom handle tightly. It would be her best defense, she assured herself. Easing the door open, she was startled when a hand and foot shot through the opening. Despite her efforts, she couldn't hold the door shut. *The children*, she thought in horror. *What if the children should awaken?*

She jabbed savagely at the growing shape of a man slipping through her doorway.

"Stop it!" the man hissed.

It was the same man she had seen during the afternoon. He wrenched the broom handle from her hand. Angered, she pummeled him savagely with her fists.

He finally had to wrestle Suzanne to the floor, pinning her beneath his considerable weight. "Stop fighting me! Are you going to listen or not?"

She was exhausted and pinned so effectively that she could not move.

"I was hoping I could talk to you again," the ragged man said.

"All right." Her breath came in puffs. "Talk."

Talk he did, and in the days to come, not just with her. Gaff spoke with many of the women in that particular work camp.

Some days later, while Suzanne hoed in the fields, she eyed the snowcapped peaks of the Guardian Range in the distance. She could scarcely believe that one day soon she would take her children over those peaks.

"It's impossible!" some had cried.

"Don't be a fool," others had exclaimed. "The man is leading you to your death."

Suzanne's decision to follow Gaff might have been wrong, but she wasn't alone. The number of people going with her was astounding. How could one man make such arrangements? How could he have all the right connections?

Liz hoed nearby in a long row of corn. "You'd better keep hoeing, Suzanne. The foreman is watching." Her voice was low and tense, but her eyes understood. Suzanne rubbed her back as if to soothe an ache and then bent over the hoe again. The two women worked silently side by side until the foreman had passed.

"Do you think it will work?" Liz asked.

"I hope so."

"But what is to keep the authorities from chasing us down and bringing us back here—or worse, to the Temple of the Moon?"

"Gaff says we will be hidden along the way."

"It will be hard to hide that many people."

Suzanne shrugged. "Gaff thinks he has the connections. Besides, it's only forty miles to the foot of the pass. He's sure the authorities will never think of looking there. They think it's impossible to cross those mountains. It is impossible to live there. That's why we have to pack so much."

"Do your children understand?"

"They think it will be fun. I hope they'll still think so after a few miles."

"Look out. The foreman is coming back. See you this evening."

"Right."

It was the dark of the moon three nights later when Gaff's first pilgrimage began its journey. Having worked all day and walked all night, women and children were silently herded into a large barn. Two more nights and they would begin the greatest challenge they had ever faced: scaling the impassable Guardian Range. They spoke little as they dropped into soft piles of hay.

"Cover up!" Gaff's voice was soft but urgent. "You will be missed when you do not show up to work this morning, and they will come searching for you."

He helped tuck a youngster into a hollow part of a fresh stack of hay. "There you are. Everyone, listen! I'm going out, but I will return near sundown. Stay silent! If someone should come into this barn, remain calm. Don't speak, cry out in fear, or move. Not only are your lives in danger but so is the man who owns this barn. Take courage. We've made good progress. Rest, for tonight we move nearer our goal."

With that, he was gone, and the people drifted silently into an exhausted sleep. Only a few hours later, voices startled the pilgrims into wakefulness. Daylight filtered between the boards covering the barn, and they could hear a voice outside: "Have you seen any women or children passing by?"

"No, sir." The farmer spoke the truth, for Gaff had arranged many escape routes and no one knew which route he would take.

"A number of prisoners fled with their children during the night, and we believe they are hiding somewhere in the area."

"Have a look around if you like," the farmer said. "I'm not aware of anyone passing during the night, and I haven't seen anything today."

The heavy barn doors creaked upon their hinges, and light poured into the barn's dark interior. A group of six armed men strode into the cavernous building. Mounds of fresh hay covered the floor.

"It looks like you've had a good crop," said one of the men.

"We've had good rains."

"The Lady has blessed us."

"Ah." The old farmer choked on something and began to cough.

"Are you all right, old man?"

"Yes," the farmer said. "Just a bit of dust, you know." He turned and left the guards inside the barn. He hoped they wouldn't see the small foot sticking out of one pile of hay.

The men searched the corners of the barn briefly, and satisfied with their search, they came back to the old man outside. "Thank you. If you see anything, report it to us immediately." They mounted their horses and rode on down the road.

Breathing deeply, the old man turned and swung the heavy barn doors shut once again.

The rest of the day was uneventful, and that night the group traveled many more miles. Within two days, they reached the foot of the Guardian Mountains.

After several hours of hard climbing, the group paused at the edge of a sheer cliff. "Everyone must stay together," Gaff ordered. A chilly wind bit through their clothing, numbing their fingers and chilling their souls. The group huddled tightly together seeking warmth for their first night under the stars had been bone-chilling as winds swept off the permanent caps of snow above them.

"We must tie ourselves together," Gaff continued. "If anyone should fall, the others can pull them back to the trail." The path they were following disappeared into a smooth, vertical plate of stone.

"Tie a child between each adult, and when we run out of adults, substitute a larger child for an adult," Gaff instructed.

"We can't cross this!" said a man's voice. Several men had joined the expedition, hoping to settle a new land that was free from the worry of a corrupt court.

"It *can* be done," Gaff replied. "I have crossed it, and we can go back the same way."

"But I can't see any handholds or footholds."

"They are only visible as you climb out upon the rock," Gaff said. "Hurry! We must cross before night falls or a storm comes."

All eyes turned toward billowing clouds on the horizon. They had weathered one thunderstorm already, and they didn't want to be on an open-faced rock during another.

"Please hurry! Tie yourselves together with these ropes!"

The pilgrims fumbled with the ropes. The rough climb had taken its toll upon the ill-clad travelers. Their bare feet were cut and swollen, and their fingers shone red in the late afternoon sun.

Constant urging finally motivated the group into action. "Follow my moves exactly," Gaff said. "There is no room for error. It is a long way down. Don't look, just take my word for it. Place your hands and feet exactly where you see your neighbor leave his or hers. We will go slowly, but it will not take long. It is not far."

Gaff began with one hand, and then one foot. Hearts pounded as each pilgrim in turn, even very young children, swung out over the edge of the mountain.

Heavy packs filled with food, clothing, seeds, and other necessities burdened each back. Lashed to the packs were hoes, shovels, axes, and other such tools as would be necessary in the days ahead.

It would have been comical to see the packs bobbing along the face of the mountain had their plight not been so serious. Fingers and toes, numbed from the cold, sought tiny cracks and gouges in the sheer wall of stone. Clinging to the rock, these people were willing to risk their lives for a new beginning free from the terror of tyranny. Hope spurred them on.

Gaff had reached the other side, and nearly half the people had made that first daring step into nothingness, when a cry echoed in the clear mountain air.

"I can't! I just can't!" When it was her turn, one woman could not make herself step over the edge, though she had seen her little daughter do so only seconds before.

The line stopped moving. Frightened eyes on the cliff peered back. Fervent prayers were offered for the woman. Some cajoled but most spoke words of sincere encouragement. No one could move without pulling or pushing the frightened woman over the edge.

A small voice came from behind the terrified woman. "It will be all right. I'll help you, Mother." The lad's quiet confidence calmed the woman's heart. With a quick prayer, she fearfully reached out, grasped the first fingerhold in the rock, and swung over the edge.

The group moved successfully beyond the towering cliffs, but soon they encountered the permanent snow line. Inadequate clothing and rations were taking their toll. Barely a night passed without someone freezing to death in the cold.

The ground was always frozen, and though Gaff did his best to cover those who died, he could not risk delaying their journey. "We have to keep moving," he insisted. "Our heavenly Father will care for them now."

Some people were angered by Gaff's seeming insensitivity, but everyone turned back to the path leading over the snowcapped peaks. They paused only briefly as they passed the mounds in the snow. Most wondered if anyone would wake in the morning.

But the snowcapped peaks claimed no more lives on that journey, and two days after they came to the forests on the other side, they held a feast. They spent some time gathering wild berries and firewood, and they tended the cuts and bruises they'd suffered along the trail. Everyone was thankful to be out of the mountains, and they knelt before the Lord and thanked Him for His mercy.

The grass was green, and wild berries flourished on branches. Wild rice grew along the stream, and children gathered as much of it as they could.

Everyone worked hard. Winter would come soon, and they had little to live on. The food they had carried with them was nearly gone, and they had few clothes and no shelter.

Men who had come with them across the mountains felled trees and split the great trunks into lumber for housing. Women dug small patches of earth to plant beans, hoping winter would delay. Children collected nuts and berries and caught small rabbits in snares. Fish were abundant in the streams. Their small community felt its first real hope.

Summer melded into fall, and fall into winter. Gaff's small community had shelters for everyone and a large meeting house for group meetings. One of the best parts of that winter was when everyone gathered in the meeting house around a roaring fire to listen as the Holy Scriptures were read.

The long winter nights gave the people time to think of the conditions they had fled in Shingmar—and about those still living there. There was freedom here without fear that soldiers would break in to drag people off to prison.

The hunger for freedom was strong among believers in Shingmar, and Gaff recruited others of his community to return with him year after year to lead pilgrims over the mountains to settle in the new land. Every summer the little colony of Amity grew as more people escaped Shinar's tyranny in Shingmar. After four years, the colony in Amity had grown so large around Orchard Creek that many were looking to expand into new areas.

CHAPTER 2

Trial by Fire

Shinar paced the floor impatiently. "Can't you get anything right?" he bellowed. "We have the best army in the world, and you can't tell me where these people are going?"

His chief aid, Grekko, fidgeted nervously. "No, sir! The northern borders are guarded very closely, and we have searched every house in Shingmar. No one can escape over the mountains, and our navy watches for vessels on the water constantly. It's like they simply disappear!"

"Don't you realize our work farms are short of labor?" Shinar shouted. "We fear a lack of rain, but I tell you, we'll be hungry for lack of labor if things don't happen soon. This is the fourth year since these people began disappearing! Are there no more leaders in the rebellion of Stafford?"

"The leaders and active followers were rounded up long ago, sire."

"Are there any sympathetic to their cause?"

"Oh, yes. A great many are sympathetic to their cause, sire."

"Well, don't just stand there. Round them up! Fill the prisons! Man the work farms! Shingmar must eat!"

Gaff had just returned to Amity with another expedition over the mountains and was enjoying a time of quiet reading in his study when a young girl with curly blonde hair knocked on his door and entered the room. Timidly she asked, "May I bother you, sir?"

Gaff looked up and gestured. "Come in." He recognized her as one of the children who had recently come across the peaks. "What can I do for you?"

"Sir, my heart is broken for my mother."

Gaff stood and motioned the child in. "Did she die upon the pass?" he asked softly as he motioned her to a wooden box that served as a chair.

"I could bear that better. Oh, sir, she was taken to the Temple of the Moon!" The girl began to sob.

Gaff had heard whispers of this fear among the women before, but he had never known exactly what it was all about. He was about to learn.

Within two months, Gaff was back in Shingmar with some of his closest friends. He had learned about women who were forced to serve in the Temple of the Moon against their will, and he had developed a plan to facilitate their escape.

Gaff had changed so much in appearance that now as he stood before King Shinar he had no fear of recognition. "I have heard it said, O King, that you seek a copy of the Holy Scriptures."

Shinar studied the roughly clad man. "It is true. I have long sought the Book, but it has always been denied me."

"I think I can get you a copy—for a price." Gaff smiled.

Shinar studied the man suspiciously. "What is your price?"

"I propose you establish a ritual of purification among those who serve in the worship of the Lady. You know we have suffered through several years of drought, and rain will only return to Shingmar if the goddess of the moon is pleased with our sacrifices."

Shinar had heard this argument before, and he nodded his head.

"There are women serving the goddess who do not believe in her power or deity," Gaff continued. "Do you think the goddess is pleased with their worship? I propose we sacrifice all these women to the goddess on the thirteenth of next month in a special worship service to cleanse the temple and purify the worship of the Lady. Then, and only then, will rain return to the great land of Shingmar."

Shinar pursed his lips. "I get the Holy Scriptures if we hold this special worship service?" he asked.

"Yes," Gaff replied.

Shinar raised his eyebrows. "What do you get out of this?"

"I will have done my part to purify temple worship." Gaff smiled.

This is too easy, Shinar thought to himself. *The council will jump at the chance to have an extra worship service to please the goddess.* "I will see what I can do," he said with a smile.

Gaff and his men hurried to prepare everything before the thirteenth of the following month. The house of Josiah Stafford was chosen to be the site of the sacrifice. The Stafford rebellion, as it was known in Shingmar, had begun in that house years earlier, and for some it seemed fitting that the house should be burned to signal the end of the rebellion. Though it was not known to many, one of the ladies scheduled to be sacrificed on the thirteenth was the wife of Josiah Stafford.

Men attached chains to the benches that lined the walls of the Stafford house. These benches had once been used as people gathered to hear the Word of God, but now they would hold women firmly in place until fire consumed them. At least that was what many thought. However, the chains were actually designed to allow men to free the women quickly and without confusion once fire began to lick at the walls of the house. A tunnel had been dug underground from the house to a cluster of trees behind the house. While the worship service drew people's attention away from the fire, the women would escape through the tunnel and gather in the trees outside. The thirteenth of the month had been chosen because it would be a new moon, and darkness would aid the flight of the prisoners.

Gaff was reviewing the details of their labor several days before the scheduled sacrifice. One of his men asked, "Will this plan work?"

"It has to work," Gaff answered. "We have to rescue these women."

"How will you get away after you present the scriptures to Shinar?"

"I'm willing to leave everything in the Almighty's hands, but I will have a horse to ride."

"So will the king's men."

"Don't worry about me. Are all the preparations ready for the sacrifice?"

"Yes, the tunnel is complete."

"Including the wall of dirt to dump after the last person is out?"

"It is just as you ordered."

"Remember," Gaff said, "don't take one woman out of her chains until they set the house on fire. You'll have to work fast, but people must think everyone died in the flames. Hopefully, I can draw them off while you make your escape."

"It's too risky!"

"We have to take a chance," Gaff said. "We have to free those women!"

"All right," the man responded. "Peace to you, my friend."

Dusk began to settle around the Stafford house on the evening of the thirteenth. Gaff watched from a distance as nearly seventy women were herded into the building and fastened to the benches.

"Is that the last one?" Gaff heard one guard ask.

"Yes," said another guard.

"It seems a shame. These are some of the most beautiful women in the country."

"I know."

The first guard shook his head. "And we are going to burn this building down with them inside."

The second guard only nodded.

"Wait!" said the first guard. "I hear trumpets. The Goddess must be arriving!"

Near the road, an elaborate altar had been constructed for the worship service. The priestess and her retinue were to gather before Stafford's house during the dark of the moon, and there before the roaring flames of their great sacrifice, they hoped to appease the gods, and bring happier times to Shingmar.

It was nearly dark as the players began to assemble. The priestess arrived in a litter carried by men dressed in crimson and white. Incense for the fire was carried by two priests in white robes. The finest wines and goblets to serve it in came in covered wagons. Soft cushions covered beautifully woven carpets lying on the ground. Silks rustled and jewels glistened as courtiers and courtesans walked to pillowed seats occupying the best view of the ceremonies. This was the first time such worship had been performed away from the temple.

Maybe it was the night, or maybe it was knowledge of the sacrifice, but very few people other than the king and his court came out for this service.

It began as most services did, with incantations and erotic dances. Drums throbbed. Flutes and pipes moaned sensuously. Wisps of smoke from the incense added ghostly movement to the dancing of the firelight. King Shinar breathed deeply, warming to the services as the first flames began to flicker about the former home of Josiah Stafford.

Frightful screams from inside the house seemed to intensify the lust running through Shinar's veins. The thought of all those lovely women dying for the goddess aroused his warped mind. The priestess progressed slowly and seductively around the circle. Whom would she choose tonight? The woman drew near King Shinar.

Suddenly, a voice called from the dark side of the clearing. "King Shinar!"

The ritual stopped, and all eyes turned toward the voice. "Who goes there?" Shinar responded, irritated by the interruption.

"I promised to give you the scriptures!" Gaff shouted. "They are here on this stump."

Shinar tore his attention away from the beautiful woman before him and looked toward the voice that was speaking. "You have the Book?" he asked.

"Let me warn you, O King. This book is a dangerous possession. If you humble yourself to obey its teachings, you will find grace and mercy, but if you despise its teaching, it will turn upon you and destroy you like a two-edged sword. Beware, King Shinar, of how you handle the Book!"

"Seize that man!" roared Shinar. "He has the scriptures. He's clearly part of the rebellion!"

Armed guards raced across the clearing.

With a laugh, the lone man turned, mounted a horse that had been standing in the shadows, and shouted, "Catch me if you can! I'm Gaff, your disappearing man!" And with that, he raced north down the road toward Shingmariton.

Anger filled the clearing. The army wanted Gaff for desertion. They would stop at nothing to catch this rebel and see him hang. Men swung up on their horses, and with a cry, they thundered into the night.

Once the flames had begun to lick the sides of Josiah Stafford's house, men inside leaped into action. Long chains were unlocked and pulled from the rings holding the women in place. One woman after another was led to a trapdoor and the escape tunnel. Even though the women were terrified, the plan worked, and in less than two minutes, every woman was rushing through the tunnel.

"Is that the last of them?" a man asked anxiously as another man emerged from the tunnel.

"Yes! Gaff's plan has worked so far."

"Good! Gaff has just interrupted the worship service. We'll have to move quickly!"

The women were each given a black cloak to wear and were encouraged to remain silent. "We will be heading south while Gaff leads the soldiers north," the rescuers told the ladies. "You are going to be all right."

CHAPTER 3

Walking by Faith

Gaff ran his fingers through his thinning hair and surveyed the thriving community. Homes and fields dotted the verdant valley at the foot of Guardian Range. This was a picture of peace and prosperity. Every woman who had been forced to serve the goddess had been rescued, and they had escaped Shingmar to rejoin their friends and family in this new land.

I've fulfilled my promise to Josiah Stafford, Gaff thought, but he knew that wasn't quite true. Yes, he had rescued many women and children from the work camps of Shingmar, but he had not reunited those women with their husbands in the prison at Stonewall.

Gaff knew how to reach Stonewall; that was not the problem. The survivors' community was built around Orchard Creek, which flowed down the valley into the main river meandering through Amity. The Crescent River slowly churned its way through Amity until it flowed around the walls of Stonewall and drained into the sea. Gaff knew they could easily float the entire community downriver to the prison, but what would happen then? Would King Shinar send troops to recapture the women and ship them back to Shingmar? Would they be captured and put to work there to feed the men in prison?

Though discussions had raged for months, Gaff still had no answers to these questions. It was finally decided that a small number of men and women would build rafts and float downriver to the prison. They did not know what they would do when they arrived there, but they would trust God to do for them what they could not do for themselves.

As the day for their departure approached, supplies were loaded onto rafts, and farewell parties were held. Six men, including Gaff, and nearly thirty women prepared to set sail. Since no one knew what their reception at Stonewall would be, no children were allowed to go.

When the day finally arrived, hugs were abundant and tears were shed as the pilgrims set sail. Things ran uneventfully the first day, but on the second afternoon, black clouds began to build over the Guardian Range.

An eerie sense of doom hovered over the travelers. The day had been uncommonly still, and birds forgot to sing as the rafts drifted lazily along the river. The air was filled with expectation.

Listening for sounds of wildlife along the river and hearing nothing, Gaff's boatswain commented, "It's the calm before the storm."

"I think you are right. We'd better get to shore and try to set up some kind of shelter."

"Sure glad there aren't any children with us. It looks like it could be a rough one!"

After guiding their rafts toward a clearing along the river, the women scrambled ashore and began to unload supplies while the men anchored the rafts and began cutting trees for makeshift shelters. Supplies were brought into the shelters, and limbs were gathered for firewood.

The sky grew dark, and though it was the middle of the afternoon, the light of the sun could not penetrate the thick clouds. An eerie quiet settled over the land.

Everyone ate sparingly and then covered the supplies as best they could. Without warning, a sudden blast of wind swept hot ash and dust into their camp. Lightning smote the trees in the forest. Thunder roared, and the wind rose to a scream.

Dust clogged everyone's nose and eyes. They huddled together tightly under what shelter they could find. Trees toppled, and limbs crashed around them.

Soon the wild wind brought driving rain. Each drop splashed like mud upon the earth, and in moments everyone was soaked to the bone. Lightning lit the sky in a dizzying display, and the roar of thunder kept the group paralyzed with fear.

The rain-soaked earth began to rise and fall. Even the hardiest trees lost their grip on the soil and with sickening groans toppled over. An ancient oak towering over one of the shelters suddenly came crashing down. Screams filled the air between the terrifying claps of thunder.

CHAPTER 4

Judgment

The black clouds filling the sky could not compete with the dark mood among the prisoners at Stonewall. Ever since Gaff had escaped, things had gone downhill. Food and water were routinely denied the prisoners, and a misspoken word would incur a beating. Prisoners were executed for the slightest infraction of the rules.

Chained to the wall, the prisoners watched as an old man was beaten for asking for food.

"Stop it!" Eli Cotton screamed. "He's just an old man! You're going to kill him!"

"Shut up, or you'll taste the same!" a guard ordered and then spat at Cotton.

The club rose and fell again. This time the old man did not move.

"No!" Cotton screamed. He twisted his arms frantically, trying to get free.

"I told you to shut up!" The guard whirled about to face Cotton. "Do you want of a taste of this?" he said, leering as he raised his club for all to see.

"You wouldn't be so brave if you unchained me from this wall," Cotton taunted the guard.

"I told you to shut up!" the guard yelled, and he swung his club at Cotton's head.

The room was nearly black when Eli Cotton began to stir.

"Cotton, are you all right?" The voice of Josiah Stafford came from somewhere in the room.

Cotton groaned. "I think so. How's the old man?"

"He's dead," Stafford responded.

"It's a wonder we ain't all dead!" another voice chimed in.

"Where are the guards?" Eli asked as anger fueled new life into his limbs.

22

"The storm sent them running for the guardhouse." Stafford chuckled.

"What storm?" Eli began to ask, when a sudden flash of lightning lit up the sky.

Thunder crashed, and the floor began to sway. The walls began to shake, and the chains anchoring the men began to rattle. One man suddenly shouted, "I'm free!" Others yanked on their chains, and most fell away from the wall.

"I'm free! I'm free!" voices cried from nearly every corner of the prison. "Hallelujah!"

Just then, the stones along the wall shifted dangerously, and shouts of joy turned to cries of fear. Stronger men pulled weaker comrades from the walls while others searched for a way out into the courtyard. Great drops of rain began to fall from the sky, and those who had wanted to flee the stone prison now cowered in its relative safety.

Peeking through doors that had been shaken open by the earthquake, the prisoners saw the lanterns in the guardhouse dim and then disappear behind a wall of rain. Water poured into the cells.

All that night, men were torn between fear and rejoicing. What would the guards do to them in the morning? What should the prisoners do with their new freedom? Debate raged as the sea crashed against the heavy gray stones surrounding Stonewall. But for those stones, not one man would have survived. However, if the storm didn't abate soon, even the stones would not see the light of a new day.

It seemed that morning would never come. Heavy-laden clouds poured their contents upon the earth in an unending torrent. No guards came when night's black turned deep gray at dawn. No one appeared all that day or that night—or the next day.

Though the prisoners were free to move about, they became restless. They were hungry, and anxiety mounted as the rain continued. They collected water in basins as it poured off the roof, but it was so black that none even tried to wash their wounds in the liquid.

After six days of pouring rain, despair crept into men's hearts. But with the dawn of the seventh day, the rain eased to a steady drizzle. The water running off the roof was clear, and men drank deeply from the collection bowls.

A discussion arose over what should be done next, and debate raged for some time. Josiah Stafford grew weary of the bickering. He was hungry and knew that there was food stored in the guardhouse.

"Gentlemen!" he called out. "Who wants to go with me to the guardhouse?"

There was a brief silence followed by a chorus of dissent. "You can't go. They'll kill you on the spot. They hate you more than anyone."

Gesturing for silence, Stafford reassured them. "The Lord has saved me this far. I can trust Him for the next step. Will anyone go with me?"

He did not go alone. Nearly thirty daring souls followed their intrepid leader across the courtyard. The area inside the great gray wall stood partially under water. It looked like a devastated swamp.

Sloshing across the water-laden earth, the prisoners became aware that there was no activity inside the guardhouse. When they reached the doorway, Stafford turned and glanced at the men who had followed him. All were nearly naked, gaunt, and weaponless. Looking into the sky, he offered a prayer: "Help us, Lord Jesus." And then he lifted the latch.

The room inside was dark except for what light filtered through the windows. Nervously, the prisoners started across the room but stopped when they became aware of movement in one corner. Three guards stood with their backs to the wall, swords drawn.

"Stay back," one guard yelled, "or we'll kill you!"

Stafford walked forward until the tip of the man's sword rested against his chest. "We've come looking for food, not a fight. Put your sword away."

"Stay back!" the guard yelled again. "I'm warning you!" His sword brushed against Stafford's hairy chest.

"Kill me if you wish," Stafford said, "but you cannot overpower all these men who have come with me. Why not lower your weapons, and lead me to your master?"

At this, the young guard dropped his blade and his head. "Alas, we are without a master."

"What?" A chorus of voices broke out.

"It's true," said another of the guards.

"What happened?" Stafford demanded.

"Come and see."

The guards led Stafford and the prisoners into a large room that served as the guard's dining hall. Bodies of prison guards and officers lay scattered about on the floor. Some looked as though they had fallen in battle, and some might have killed themselves. The scene was grisly enough, but it was worse for being seven days old.

"When did this happen?" Stafford demanded.

"We found them like this the night the storm hit. We rushed in from the cell block, and this met our eyes."

One guard suddenly knelt before Stafford, laying his sword at the startled man's feet. "Please, sir!" he begged. "I have been harsh with you and the prisoners. Please forgive me and treat me with mercy."

The other guards knelt in like fashion, each laying his sword at Stafford's feet and asking for forgiveness.

"All right," Josiah Stafford said. "You are forgiven. Now, leave your swords and show us the larder! We'll bury these men after we feed the others."

To everyone's relief, most of the goods in the larder had survived the storm. Food was rationed out with care, and after the needs of everyone had been met, the cleanup began.

It took several days to restore some sense of order within the prison, and sentries were posted on the walls. The prisoners feared that fresh troops from Shingmar would arrive on the next ship and they would lose their newfound freedom.

The river that separated Stonewall from the mainland was still overflowing its banks, and though sentries watched for ships from Shingmar, they kept their eyes on the river as well.

One afternoon when the sun was trying to peek from behind thick clouds, a lookout on the western side of Stonewall shouted, "There is something on the river!"

Men ran from every corner of the courtyard to investigate. Two large rafts rolled and swayed upon the raging river current, and as the rafts neared the prison, someone shouted, "There are women on those barges!"

Men threw open the gates of Stonewall prison. Muddy water lapped at the prison's foundation, but men ventured into the current to get a better view.

"Catch hold!" boomed a voice as the first raft approached, and a rope sailed toward shore. Eager hands pulled the raft to the prison gate and tied it tightly to the wall. Soon both rafts were secure.

"It's Gaff," Stafford whispered. "He's fulfilled his promise."

Though supplies at Stonewall were running low, there was a celebration that night, which continued into the early hours of the morning. Everyone knew there were many things which must be decided, but for a few hours, they did not deny themselves the chance to rejoice.

It was late the next morning when Gaff, Stafford, and a few other men gathered in the guardhouse to discuss their next move.

Gaff surveyed the men gathered in the room. "As you now know, we have a fairly large colony several days upriver from here. Many of these men's wives and children are there. The land we have seen coming downriver appears beautiful and unsettled. I think we should empty the prison, reunite our families, and then settle this new land."

"Shouldn't we return to Shingmar and demand what is ours?" one man countered.

"How would we get there?" another asked.

"Maybe we could build boats," another suggested.

"What if Shinar should send troops to control this new colony you propose, Gaff?"

"Gentlemen!" Stafford said. "I fear that much of what we once knew is no more. Does it not seem that the storm we endured was from the hand of God? We are reminded in God's Word that the sins of Sodom and Gomorrah became so great that the Lord finally sent judgment in the form of fire and brimstone to destroy them. Is it possible that God has sent His judgment upon the land we once knew as our home?"

The room grew silent, and Stafford watched as men looked from one to another. Many turned their eyes upon the floor as they pondered his statement. Finally, Gaff looked up and nodded. "I have wondered the same thing."

"All right," said another, "but how are we going to know? We have no ships to sail back to Shingmar, and the Guardian Range blocks our view."

The room grew quiet. Josiah Stafford said quietly, "There is a man sitting right here who has explored the Guardian Range extensively. What if Gaff leads some of us to the top of the mountains where we could survey what has become of our home?"

Heads began to nod as people considered the idea.

A small expedition soon set off from Stonewall to follow Gaff into the mountains north of the Crescent River. As they traveled, Gaff told them of his wanderings and the first time he had stood at the top of the Guardian Range and observed Shingmar shining like an emerald, lush and green below him.

They climbed for several days, and as they neared the top of the Guardian Range, Gaff rounded one final turn only to stop in disbelief. He knew this was the right place. He'd marked a stone on his first visit here, and that mark remained. He remembered the lush green beauty of Shingmar, but all that met his eyes was water.

Stafford and the others struggled up the slope to join Gaff. Everyone stood in silence, surveying the scene below them as an icy wind tossed their hair. There were no pastures, no fields, and no lush green forests. All they saw were whitecaps dancing on a sea of water.

Turning his back on the ocean, Josiah Stafford surveyed the mountains, hills, and valleys through which they had climbed. Far below them he could see Stonewall Prison surrounded by the muddy water of the Crescent River. A smile touched his lips. "Gentlemen," he said with a sweeping motion of his arm, "let's make this new land our home and call it Amity."

Back in the Cotton Home

"But, Grandpa, how could that be? A whole nation can't just disappear, can it?"

"Well, I can't explain it, Grandson, but nothing is impossible for the creator of heaven and earth!"

"So that's why we live in Amity?" another grandchild asked.

"It is!" Bill grinned.

Robbie sat up in Bill's lap and with wide eyes looked full in his grandpa's face. "Was Eli Cotton your father?"

"No, Robbie. Eli Cotton was my great-grandfather. I was very young when he died, so I didn't know him very well."

"Was he a hero, Grandpa?"

Bill stared at his grandson. "I don't know, Robbie. I always thought of him as a good man because he loved God and wanted to do the right thing, but I never thought about him being a hero."

"Aren't heroes people who do the right thing?"

"I guess they are." Bill smiled and ruffled Robbie's curly hair. "You're a thinker, aren't you, young man?" Bill could see Robbie's mother trying to hide her embarrassment, but he feared things were going to get worse for Destry.

"You're a hero, aren't you, Grandpa?" Robbie asked.

Bill laughed. "I don't think so. Why do you ask?"

"Didn't you lose your hand trying to do the right thing?"

"Robbie!" Destry exclaimed, her face aflame. "How could you ask such a question?"

"It's all right," Bill said, waving Destry's concern away.

"Hey, Grandpa," another grandchild said, "tell us how you lost your hand."

Destry hid her face in her hands. This was one of the many reasons she had not wanted to make this trip. She was embarrassed for Bill and was horrified to think that the children, especially her own Robbie, would want to hear about something as grim as the severing of a hand from the body.

Bill studied the group settled in the parlor. "I could tell you my story, but I play such a small role that it's not very interesting unless I include some of the others involved at the time."

"That's all right, Grandpa!" several children chorused. "Tell us the whole story."

Bill glanced toward the fireplace where his lovely bride of many years sat. Her head was bowed, and her knitting needles clicked furiously. Mary looked up, met his gaze, nodded her head, and returned to her labor. Bill smiled and heaved a great sigh. "Well, it began like this …"

CHAPTER 5

Turmoil in Amity

"I was a young man," Bill began, studying the grandchildren in the room. "Your grandmother and I had not been married very long, and we lived on a farm not too far from here. Some good things were happening to us, but we were young and unsure of what we wanted from life. We were also a bit naïve and thought that the world revolved around us. We did not know about the terrible things taking place far away, and we certainly did not think anything so distant would ever affect our lives. But I'm going to start this story by telling you about a man I came to know and love during that time in my life. His name was John Stafford, and he lived at Stonewall."

"Is that the same Stonewall that Josiah Stafford and the prisoners from Shingmar built?" one grandchild asked.

"Yes, it is." Bill smiled. "But it wasn't a prison anymore. It had become the home of the Stafford family. The people who escaped Shingmar and came to Amity looked to the Stafford family for leadership, beginning with Josiah Stafford and following through to Josiah's grandson John. Though Amity had no king, John Stafford was widely recognized as its leader.

"Just close your eyes and let your mind imagine back to the days before your parents were born. Picture a man standing by the eastern window of a room up high in a castle. That castle sat beside the sea, and the man kept looking into the darkness over the water.

"That man was John Stafford, and he could not sleep. He paced the floor of his room, only to return again to the window. John Stafford was unsure of a decision he had made months earlier. He'd sent his two oldest sons and a thousand men to Green Meadow to provide protection on Amity's western border. He knew that the steward of Green Meadow, Master Devia, had not wanted the army of Amity on his doorstep, but a battle had been fought the summer before only miles from Amity on the Great River in the land of Emancipation. John had felt he could not leave Amity unprotected on the western border, but tonight he was no longer sure he had done the right thing. *Will this night ever end?* he thought, looking out the window for the hundredth time. Finally, he saw a faint glow in the east, and before long he could discern a definite line between sea and sky."

John opened his window and felt the breeze as it blew in from the sea. Suddenly, he heard a voice shouting from one of the many watchtowers at Stonewall. "Rider coming!"

John hurried down the stairs and out into the courtyard. People were just beginning to stir in the kitchen and the stables, but things were already busy down at the ferry.

Being located on an island, Stonewall was completely separated from the mainland. The Crescent River ran its course through nearly all of Amity, cutting the country into north and south, but at Stonewall it split and poured into the sea around both sides of the castle. The towns of Sebring and Waterfront were on either side of the river, and large wooden rafts were used to ferry people and goods across the river.

Two men hurried from one of Stonewall's guardrooms to man "the tug," a name people called the ferry. On either side of the river, there was a large wooden spool of heavy rope, with the free ends attached to opposite sides of a large wooden raft. Whenever people wanted to pass from Waterfront to Stonewall, they used the ferry. Stout young men on either side of the river pulled the raft toward Stonewall or back toward Waterfront.

John noted unusual haste this morning. There was a horseman on the far side of the river, urging the lads and saying, "Pull, Dick! Harry, put your back to it, lad. I must see John quickly."

The young men on Stonewall's bank pulled heartily to turn their wooden spool and slowly draw the raft to their side of the river.

Reaching Stonewall's shore, the man urged his lathered mount up the slope and through the gate. "Thank you, lads. That was a good pull so early this morning! Is the master of the house up?"

"I think so," Harry said. "He told us to be on the lookout for a messenger, though I'm not sure he knew it would be today."

"May I take your horse?" a stable boy asked, running to meet the man riding a huge black mare. Horses were not plentiful in this region of Amity, and this great steed rivaled any horse in the master's stable.

"Aye, but give her a good rubbing! She's had a bit of a run. She could use some oats, if you have any to spare."

"Yes, sir!" the lad said, leading the heaving horse toward the stables.

John saw the man turn toward him as he hurried up the path.

"John Stafford! Bless me, if it isn't good to see you."

John grabbed the rider's hand and gave it a hearty shake. "Greenwold, what are you doing, waking the countryside? Have you news? Come, man. Let's get a bite to eat, and then we can talk."

Leading the messenger to the house, John Stafford entered the kitchen and called to his cook. "We'll have breakfast in the private room, please. Bring enough for two!"

The men passed through a large dining hall with rows of tables flanked by benches. Opening a rough, wooden door, they entered a small room where a fire blazed in the hearth. Settling at the table, John studied the clear blue eyes of George Greenwold. "Is there trouble?" he asked. "I don't suppose you've ridden this far just for a cup of coffee."

"Aye! There is trouble at Green Meadow. Jabin is encamped on the Western Slope."

John carefully maintained his calm countenance. "George, maybe you should start at the beginning," he said quietly.

Greenwold cleared his throat and stared into Stafford's eyes. "Jabin and his cronies have pillaged farms west of Green Meadow. We don't know how many villains are with him, but old Stanley got about twenty men together to investigate, and none of them returned. It was Stanley's wife who told us. She and some other women came to the garrison to let us know. They were afraid to go home."

John felt the hair rise on the back of his neck. "I know Stanley, and I've met his wife," he said. "Fear is not common among families on the Western Slope. The people who live there are tough and prepared. This is not good news."

Greenwold continued, "We'd seen smoke a few days before the ladies came, and when we checked it out, we found the Billings farmstead burned to ashes and the livestock driven off. But when Stanley's wife made her report, we decided we had real trouble."

John sighed and stroked his graying beard. "Are you sure Jabin is behind this, or could it be the work of bandits?"

"Jabin's work or bandits, it's all the same," Greenwold growled. "You know Jabin is a thief and a liar."

"Wait!" John held up his hand as a servant carried a large tray into the room. "Thank you," he said, but as an afterthought he motioned to the servant. "When you leave, will you tell a messenger to stay near our door? We may need him to run an errand soon."

"Yes, sir," the girl responded as she set out plates filled with eggs, bacon, and huge slices of bread smothered in butter. Finally, she set two mugs of coffee before the men and asked, "Will you need anything else?"

"I think not," John said as he watched her leave the room. Turning his attention back to Greenwold, John spoke quietly. "Have you told me everything there is, or do you have a message from my son?"

"I do," Greenwold said. "James requests a council of all Amity, and he also asked for reinforcements. Only a few days ago, Gaff's scouts reported a vast army moving south from Bashan, departing the Mountains of Despair and following the Great River. Gaff fears that if they stay on the river, they will hit Great Bend again. But if they leave the river at Deorn and travel south, they will hit Green Meadow."

"Have the members of Amity's council been informed of James's request?" John asked.

"Aye! I have ridden hard and tarried little since leaving Green Meadow, but I stopped in each village along the way. Every town's master has heard the summons to council. Representatives should be coming this very day. Your son wanted me to represent Green Meadow."

John's eyebrows arched in surprise. "What about Master Devia?" John asked.

"He may come, but your son and I feel his council is no longer to be trusted."

"That's a bit harsh, isn't it? Devia is twice your age, George. Why do you feel so strongly about a man who has weathered some hard times?"

"If Master Devia does make an appearance, you will understand. Oh, I nearly forgot. I have not ridden through Northglen, Sebring, or Southglen. Could you send word for them to prepare for council as soon as the sun sets tomorrow? By then your son may already be at war."

John rose and walked to the door. He spoke briefly with the man stationed in the hall and then closed the door again. He returned to Greenwold. "You know more, don't you?"

"Aye," George replied and leaned back in his chair. "I'll share it all with you, but maybe we should eat this food before it gets cold."

The sun grew hot before the two parted company.

CHAPTER 6

Problems at Home

Young Bill Cotton typically milked his goats so early in the morning that he carried a lantern to the barn. It was during this predawn darkness that he heard hooves thundering down the greenway. Barely able to see the rider, Bill thought he resembled a phantom in the darkness.

After the rider had passed, Cotton milked his goats and hurried to the house. Slipping into the kitchen, he was surprised when Mary called, "Bill, is that you?"

"Yes, Mary. You didn't need to wake so early."

"I'm frightened!" Mary said, peeking from behind the curtain that separated their bed from the main room. Her eyes were large, and her slender shoulders quivered in the cold.

Bill set the milk pail down and crossed the room. Taking her shoulders in his hands, he gently asked, "What's the problem?"

"I dreamed there was a rider."

Bill could feel his wife shivering, and he held her close in his arms.

She seemed to relax in his embrace. "I thought the rider was death. He came to our window and called my name. I tried to scream, but I guess I just woke myself up. Then I thought I heard hooves racing away. Was there a horseman, Bill?"

"Yes. A horseman did pass earlier this morning. I think he may have been headed to Stonewall, and I don't feel good about this."

"What do you mean?" Mary asked, pushing Bill's protective arms away, the terror in her voice ebbing. She rose and moved to the blazing stove to start the coffee. "How could one rider cause trouble for anyone, especially for us?" She tossed her auburn locks and gave her husband a teasing smile. "You know, I think the baby could come soon now."

A worried look came over Bill's face. "Do you really think so? Should I get your mother?"

"Not yet," Mary said with a laugh. "Let's have breakfast and talk.

Tell me how my dream and this early-morning rider could cause us any trouble."

Bill didn't answer. He strained the milk into crocks and carried it to the spring where it would remain cool. Mary busied herself with breakfast.

When preparations were made, Mary eased herself into a chair and smiled at her husband. "Now, my worried man, how could this early-morning rider affect our lives?"

Steam billowed from the mug between Bill's big hands. "I don't know, but there have been rumors of trouble in the western land."

"Oh, those rumors again! Bill, we've heard of trouble over there for years." Mary waved her hand vaguely in a westerly direction. "Nothing has ever come of it in my time or my father's time. Why should rumors affect us now?"

"I don't know, Mary, but I feel like something huge is about to happen to change our lives forever. I don't want anything to happen. I'd like to go through life without a care, raise our children, grow old together, and pass quietly, but somehow I don't think we'll be able to do that."

"But why should rumors from the western lands affect us?" Mary asked, lightly touching her man's big hands.

"I've joined the army," Bill said quietly.

Mary recoiled, her eyes sudden balls of fire. "You did *what*?"

Now it was Bill's turn to get defensive. "I did it for you and the baby. If war should threaten our borders, I thought maybe I could help keep it away from you and our baby!"

Fear edged with anger laced Mary's words. "Bill, what if you are called away? The baby's due anytime. Where will I go? What will I do? I can't stay on the farm!" Tears filled her eyes. "Bill, please say you're not serious, that you are only teasing me!"

"I am serious, Mary. The sergeant of arms spoke to me three weeks ago, and I signed up. That's why I've been going to town so often. They have drills for the new recruits. I've been—"

"Three weeks!" Mary exploded. Her tears disappeared in a wave of red-hot fury. "Bill Cotton, do you mean to tell me you have been playing army for three weeks behind my back? Just when were you going to tell me of this foolishness? I cannot believe you would deceive me this way!" Her chair clattered across the floor as she leaped to her feet. "Get out of this house!" she stormed. "Get out! Do you hear me? Go to town and play army! Just get out!" Grabbing a small skillet from the stove, she hurled it in Bill's direction.

In one deft movement, Bill dodged the skillet, grabbed his hat, and slipped through the door. He grabbed a hoe from the toolshed and headed for the cornfield while the banging of pots and pans resounded inside the cabin walls.

"Dear Lord, forgive me," he whispered. "I really messed things up. I should have talked things over with her first."

His hoe struck the earth. *Who am I kidding*, he thought. *I'm no warrior.* He liked the feel of the hoe in his hands. It certainly felt better in his hands than the old sword he'd been practicing with in town.

The sun grew hot by midday. Bill wiped sweat from his brow and looked back at the cabin. "Guess I'd better face the music," he muttered to himself. "Sure hope she's calmed down."

After placing the hoe in the shed, Bill eased open the front door of the house. It was cool, dark, and silent inside. "Mary, are you all right?"

"Bill, come to me," a small voice called from behind the curtain. "Bill!"

As he pulled back the curtain, he could see Mary reaching for him. Her cheeks were damp, and her eyes were large. "I need you!" she whispered.

His big arms wrapped around her tiny figure.

"I've been thinking," Mary continued. "I think everything will be all right. Do you remember the dream I told you about this morning?"

"Yes." Bill nodded.

"I felt so threatened in my dream, but the rider turned away at the last moment and sped away. I think that's a good omen. Evil will turn away from me, Bill. The baby is due soon, and I can stay with Mother. We will be fine. But your lovely crops ... what will become of them without you to care for them?"

Bill hugged his wife tightly, and she buried her head on his shoulder. "Mary, I love you so much! I'm sorry I didn't talk this over with you. I'm no hero! I don't want to go to war. I just want to protect you and keep you safe. Say," he said suddenly, "why don't you come and watch our unit practice in the town square. Quite a few women do."

"Women?" Mary's eyebrows arched as she pulled from Bill's embrace. "What kind of women?"

"I don't know," Bill said absently. "They come to watch their husbands and sons march and practice. I'd love to have you there. Some say our unit looks pretty impressive, but being in it, I can't tell."

"Oh." Mary turned away. "I can't do that yet. I'm a little concerned about the walk, and I still don't like the thought of you being in the army. Go if you must, but I'm not ready to give you up yet, Bill Cotton. I guess that will take more time."

"And prayer," Bill said softly.

"You keep God to yourself, Mister Cotton," Mary snapped. "I have enough to think about without adding that to the list."

They went to the kitchen and ate in silence. After dinner, Bill stood to leave. "I love you, Mary," he said softly. "I'll be home as soon as I can."

She brushed her tousled hair back from her reddened face and rose to wrap her arms around Bill's neck. "I love you too. Hurry home to me."

He smiled and kissed her gently. "I will." His heart was lighter than it had been in days. He donned his old hat and stepped into the bright afternoon light to begin his walk into town.

Sweat trickled down his face in the bright sunshine, but he didn't even notice. His mind was full. He hoped his neighbor Bob Walton would join him for the journey into town.

Though Bob lived over the hill from him, they saw each other quite often and traded work back and forth. Bill had helped Bob dig a well last winter, and this spring Bob had helped plow the cornfield in return. Their wives enjoyed each other's company, and the couples got together as often as they could.

The Waltons were religious folk and attended church regularly. They invited Bill to go with them, and even Mary had attended once out of politeness but she refused to go after that.

Bill pondered his recent change of attitude. As a youth he was talented and confident, and when he set a goal for himself, he attained it. He had even won the hand of the lovely Mary Trumbell when others far wealthier had failed. Still, church had troubled him. He had thought of himself as a good, honest, moral man, but he knew something was missing.

Bill knew there was a creator. There had to be. A person had only to look around at the beauty of the earth, the soaring mountains, the towering trees, and the rushing water to see it. Being a farmer, Bill never ceased to be amazed that he could plant a tiny seed in the earth and that with the proper conditions; the seed would sprout and grow. Who brought that seed to life? And the animals of the field were designed not only to survive but to thrive in their environments. And who had placed the stars in their never-changing courses or caused the sun to rise each day?

Yes, there had to be a creator, but the pastor spoke of God as a friend, not just an all-powerful deity. How could someone have God for a friend?

One Sunday the pastor had quoted the Bible, saying, "No greater love hath a man than this, that a man lay down his life for his friends." He had gone on to say, "God so loved the world that He gave His only begotten Son, that whosoever believes in Him should not perish, but have everlasting life."

The pastor had said that Jesus loved mankind so much that He had come to die in our place. God had showed His love for His friends when Jesus lay down His life for us.

Bill understood that love could serve others to the point of death. His mother had cared for many of her neighbors when fever ravaged the land. She had sought to ease their suffering, until one day she too had fallen prey to the dreaded disease and died.

Bill reasoned that the grief he'd felt when his mother died was similar to the grief God felt at the loss of His only Son. Considering their similar losses, Bill began to feel a kindred spirit with God. He'd begun to look at things from the heavenly Father's point of view. How would a father feel? What would a father think?

It was this outlook on life that had prompted Bill to join the army. Bill's life was no longer his own. He was responsible for a wife and a child. However, his world had grown even larger than that. If the heavenly Father felt awful when evil men plundered the innocent, raped the earth of its resources, or spread slavery and fear across the land, then shouldn't Bill try to do something to stop these things?

"Bill, wait up!" a voice called.

Bill's thoughts vanished. Turning, he saw the lanky Bob Walton running up the path. He could always share his thoughts with Bob, and he had plenty on his mind.

"Did you see the rider early this morning?" Bill asked as Bob caught up with him.

"No, I didn't," Bob admitted. "Do you suppose he brought tidings of war?"

"I don't know, but I think it's likely," Bill responded. "I was so disturbed that I shared my thoughts with Mary."

"Did you finally tell her about joining up?"

"Yes, but I'm afraid I did a bad job of breaking the news to her."

"Was she upset?"

"She threw a skillet at me!"

"Whew!" Bob whistled softly and then pointed down the road. "Isn't that Master Johnson?"

"I think you are right." Bill nodded, and the two hurried on in silence. They came upon a huge man driving an ox cart heavily laden with produce.

"Better hurry, boys," the jolly giant laughed. "There's news aplenty in town. I warrant you'll have some business to take care of as well." Saying no more, the steward of Capri waved and continued his journey east toward Stonewall.

The men found Capri a mass of confusion and talk. Some said, "Green Meadow is at war," while others said, "No, Master Johnson is just going to a war council at Stonewall."

The recruits assembled amid the bedlam, and a trumpet blast brought order to their ranks. They executed marching and weapon drills with precision. Finally, the troops stood for inspection.

Commander Barker spoke emphatically to his men. "Gentlemen, we must be ready at any moment now. A council has been called for tomorrow evening at Stonewall. If the verdict is war, as I expect it will be, there will be a mustering of troops and a hard march west very soon. I have instructions from Master Johnson to inform you of this. Make provisions for your families in the event of our departure. There may be little time, so I urge you to act promptly—today, if possible! Make sure your affairs are set in order and your families know what they are to do."

Bill scratched his head and wondered, *What should I do?*

The men were dismissed, and Bob found Bill among the milling men. "Was Mary coming to town this evening?" he asked.

"No," Bill said. "She said she had more important things to think about right now. I do wish she had come."

"Hey, there's my Ella," Bob said, waving at the crowd. "Come and say goodbye to her, Bill."

"Goodbye? Where is she going?"

"She has an aunt in Waterfront, and we thought she would be safer there. Her aunt has plenty of room. Do you think Mary would want to join Ella?"

"I don't know. I'd feel better if she was nearer Stonewall, but I think she was planning on staying with her mother."

"Here in Capri?" Bob exclaimed. "But I've understood that the women are to be evacuated if the men leave for war."

By this time the men had reached a gathering of women who had been watching their practice. A plump little woman with soft brown hair swirling about her rosy cheeks ran to Bob and threw her arms around his neck. "Oh, darling, I was afraid we would leave before you were finished with your drills."

"And I was afraid your papa would whisk you away before I could say goodbye," Bob said, laughing heartily and swinging his wife in a grand circle. "I was sure he would want to start right away."

"I know, but we don't even know what the council's decision will be yet." Ella pouted.

"John Stafford will never stand for an invasion of Amity. He loves this country more than anyone else. I am sure he will call for action. Obviously your father thinks so too."

Ella suddenly noticed Bill standing discreetly to one side. "Bill Cotton, bless you," she said as she came and gave him a hug. "I wanted to ask Mary to come with me, but Bob kept telling me you hadn't told her about joining the army. Does she know yet?"

Bill blushed deeply as several women turned disapproving eyes in his direction. "I … I told her this morning," he stammered.

"Bill Cotton!" Ella scolded. "The poor girl hasn't had time to accept that yet, and you may need to leave anytime now."

Bill turned a deeper shade of red. "I didn't want to upset her, in her condition."

"Her condition is exactly why you should have told her sooner. She should have moved before now," Ella chided. And then suddenly she changed her tone. "I'm sorry, Bill. I didn't mean to scold. Do you think she would stay with me?"

"She plans on staying with her mother," Bill said uneasily. "I haven't spoken to her mother about it yet. I really should be getting over there."

"They wouldn't stay here, would they?" Ella asked with growing concern.

"I don't know," Bill croaked.

"You will let them know about my aunt in Waterfront, won't you? They would both be welcome to stay." There was a soft pleading in Ella's voice.

"I will," Bill said heartily. "I'd best be off, but you have a safe trip. You won't go all the way tonight, will you?"

"No, I think Father will stop at the Canterbury Inn. He hopes to get that far before dark," Ella said reassuringly.

Bill nodded his approval and turned to leave. Waving to Bob, he called, "See you tomorrow."

Bill's walk across town revealed many people packing carts and wagons hurriedly in preparation to leave. A sense of urgency crept into his heart, and he began to run. Mary's mother lived above a store named Tinker Trumbell's Toys. Mary's father had been a toymaker, and his shop had been the joy of every child in town. Since Tinker's death, Dolly, Mary's mother, had kept the shop open and had allowed others in town to display their wares on her shelves.

Trumbell's store was in a lovely location, set on one of the few paved streets in Capri. Huge cottonwood trees along Orchard Creek lined the street and shaded the houses, from early afternoon until sunset.

Upon reaching the store, Bill lifted the latch and pushed the door ajar. A tiny figurine rang a bell, announcing his arrival. Matronly and well-dressed, Dolly bustled into the room from stockrooms behind the counter.

"Bill Cotton, bless me! Where have you been?" The voice was pleasant but demanding. "I've been expecting you to bring Mary for weeks. Is she all right? Is the baby about to come? Well, speak up."

"I will," Bill said, laughing, "if you give me a chance. Mary is fine, but she thinks the baby could come very soon. I asked her to come in with me today, but she didn't feel up to the walk." Bill's voice grew serious. "Mother, a lot of people are planning to leave Capri. What are you going to do?"

"Leave!" Dolly said in surprise. "Why?"

"Haven't you heard? There is trouble at Green Meadow, and there are rumors that Amity might be invaded."

"Green Meadow." Dolly snorted in disgust. "That place is always in trouble. I wish it had never been founded. If there is going to be trouble, it will be at Green Meadow. But why should trouble there affect me?"

"Mother, if Green Meadow is invaded, the enemy won't stop there. They'll probably come down the Crescent River and steal or destroy everything in their path. I've heard rumors that farmsteads on the Western Slope were robbed and burned to the ground. If Amity is invaded, every person, every building, and every animal is in danger. The safest place to be is near the fortress of Stonewall. That's why Master Johnson may order an evacuation."

"Who does that bullheaded busybody think he is?" Dolly stormed. "Why should Master Johnson tell me or anyone else where to go? I don't know anyone in Waterfront, and I have no intention of going there, either. If I must leave town for some strange reason, I'll just come stay with you. Mary is about to need my help anyway."

"That won't be possible, Mother," Bill said firmly. "I won't be there if the army is called out. I've joined up."

A long silence ensued as Dolly eyed her son-in-law with a mixture of shock, disbelief, and anger. Finally breaking the awkward silence, she huffed, "Whatever possessed you to do something so totally irrational? Don't you know you have a wife to care for? And she is about to have your baby!"

"I'm sorry I didn't tell you sooner," Bill apologized. "I thought I was doing the right thing, but I might have been wrong. Mary's not happy with me, and neither are you. I truly am sorry!"

Just then the tiny figurine at the front door rang as the next-door neighbor opened the door.

"Hello, Bill," the old man rasped as he shuffled across the floor. "Have you come to help Dolly move?"

Before Bill could answer, Dolly said sharply, "He has not! This moving idea is ridiculous. We will be perfectly safe here. I, for one, am not going to run scared of a little rumor. If trouble comes—and mind you, I said *if*—then we will face it head-on."

"Those are brave words spoken in the comfort of your home, but what will you say when soldiers break in and hold you at the end of a sword?" the old man asked. "Don't be foolish, Dolly. Master Johnson is wise to request all who can, to leave."

"But what makes Waterfront safer than Capri?" Dolly asked. "Besides, I don't know anyone there. Where would I stay?"

Bill answered this time. "The protection of Stonewall is only a ferry ride across the river. Here we have no fortress of stone to slow an attack. There they have both a river and stone walls to keep the enemy out. When under attack, one should always seek the safest shelter. Besides, I just spoke to Ella Walton. She and her mother are going to stay with an aunt who lives in Waterfront. She invited both you and Mary to join them. She said they have plenty of room."

"That was very kind of Ella to offer her aunt's home to a total stranger. She shouldn't be so generous with others' goods, although it does sound tempting. But I doubt Stonewall could hold everyone." Dolly now spoke without anger.

"Stonewall will be a good refuge for old folks like us," Dolly's neighbor said. "I think you should go."

Dolly Trumbell's features hardened. "Old folks like us, you say. Thank you for your opinion, but Mary and I will be staying. Bill, bring Mary with you tomorrow. We ladies will just have to make do without you brave gentlemen, since one of you is running off to war, and one is just running." With that, she turned and passed quickly from the room.

With nothing more to say, both Bill and Dolly's neighbor turned to leave. *Well, that didn't go very well*, Bill thought. *I haven't done a very good job preparing either of these women for what might come next.*

All the way home, Bill felt growing frustration as he watched countless families pack their belongings into carts or wagons. *I should have made plans weeks ago. Now I don't know what to do.*

CHAPTER 7

A Gathering of Leaders

Only hours after George Greenwold brought news to John Stafford of trouble at Green Meadow, the stewards of Sebring and Waterfront came to the ferries for passage to Stonewall. Now, Stonewall had no particular beauty, but it was very strong and functional. It was built on a small island at the mouth of the Crescent River, and it could only be reached by boat or ferry. The fortress's great wall encompassed the entire island and appeared to rise straight out of the sea. Centered at the height of the island rose a large, towering house made entirely of gray granite.

That house was now the destination of emissaries from all over Amity. The travelers brought an air of excitement that had not been felt in Stonewall for a long time. Such gatherings were few, so food and supplies were pouring in for this one.

The stewards of Sebring and Waterfront each brought a group of men and boys. Few refused an invitation to Stonewall. It was well known for its good food, hospitality, and song. There were no banners flying or horns sounding to announce the entrance of either steward. They came quietly and on foot. John greeted each at the gate and showed the boys to the stables and archery range.

Rolph Gammel was not only the steward of Sebring but also a sea merchant, and he had sailed all over the world. He laughed easily and told a story a minute. Handsome and likeable, Rolph was soon located on the shady side of Stafford house, carving an apple from the larder and telling stories of lands far away.

Not only were John and Rolph good friends but their children were friends too. John's youngest son, Philip, was seeing Rolph's only daughter, Katherine, in a regular way, and John secretly hoped the two would wed someday.

Coming to Stonewall about the same time as Gammel was Peter Simone, a large, rawboned famer and steward of Waterfront. Simone was a quiet man, but he loved listening to Rolph's stories as much as anyone.

Late in the afternoon, Jeff Cotter, an old cotton farmer from the Southglen district, rode in on a mule. Cotter was turning gray, but he was still as strong as a bull. Most people had a deep respect for his years of knowledge and labor. Though he was not particularly interested in Gammel's stories, Cotter joined their group and did not dampen their spirits with his presence.

Ronald O'Towle came soon after Cotter. He joined the storytelling with some of his own. Ronald raised the very finest dairy goats on his farm in Northglen. He traveled widely throughout Amity, promoting and selling his goats. He was young and ambitious but honest in his dealings with people.

The aroma of fresh bread and roast lamb began to fill the air as the evening meal drew near. Raymond Johnson became the focus of much mirth as he pulled his cart laden with garden produce into Stonewall. "Good old Ray!" people shouted. "He always knows when there is food on the table." And the charge appeared to be true. The jolly man had an oversized paunch and heavy cheeks hanging down to his double chin. But for all his size, Raymond Johnson was not defensive about it.

Laughing as merrily as any schoolboy, he shouted back, "Years of practice make a man's nose keen." Then he pulled his cart next to the larder and unloaded produce that would be needed the next day.

John was glad for the festive mood. Nearly twenty men gathered around a table in the great dining hall. They ate spring peas, roast lamb, and freshly baked bread while they swapped stories.

The relish of good food and story did not diminish, but it moved from the table to the hearth. Chilled cider was replaced with hot cider, and talk continued deep into the night.

Laughter was still roaring in the great hall when John was informed of a new arrival down by the river. He slipped away from the rowdy group and hurried toward the tug. Even in the dim light, John could see that the rider being pulled across the river had not dismounted. When the ferry touched land on Stonewall's side, the rider urged his mount through the gates and into the fortress. John could hear the clatter of hooves pounding up the path.

"Easy there," John called to the rider. "Who have you come to see?"

The rider reigned in his horse and looked about in the darkness for the voice. The dim torchlight at the tug had revealed little in the vast courtyard.

"Do you come for the council?" John asked as he stepped from beneath a great oak tree.

"I represent James Stafford, son of John Stafford, master of this house," the rider called briskly. "I've a message from James to his father. Haste is needed. May I have an audience with the lord of Amity?"

"You may, for it is John to whom you now speak." John stepped onto the path near the motionless rider. "Speak, if you please. Or would you prefer a private setting?"

Quickly dismounting, the rider dropped to one knee and said, "Forgive me, my lord, I didn't know to whom I was speaking."

"You may rise," John said softly. "Bring your horse; a lad will look after it. Let's go inside. You've ridden hard and come only hours after Greenwold brought his tidings."

A stable boy met the two walking up the path and took the horse to the stables. John led the messenger into the house and slipped through the darkened hallways to a private room. A small fire blazed in the hearth, and its warmth felt good.

Settling into a chair near the fire, John motioned to the messenger to sit as well. He was surprised to see that the envoy was no more than a youth, but he said nothing about that. "Now, tell me the news."

"Sir, Master James expects Amity to be invaded. He has ordered the evacuation of civilians from Green Meadow and urgently requests reinforcements. I would like to start my journey back to Green Meadow yet tonight. What message am I to give your son, my lord?"

John was silent for a long moment. James and Thomas had both volunteered for duty on the western border, but now it seemed that James was exercising more authority than he should. Stewards were responsible for the people in their district, not some commander of a garrison of soldiers. However, if battle were eminent, the commander of a garrison could exercise martial law and evacuate women and children from a war zone.

John shook his head. What was happening here? Why would James exert this much authority? John considered how Master Devia had opposed Amity sending troops to aid Gaff at Great Bend last year. That had been a battle with rogue bandits, but many had felt that Jabin was behind the attacks upon Emancipation. With the threat of Jabin in the area, the council had approved sending a garrison to Green Meadow to protect the western border. Devia had objected. He hadn't seen any need for extra protection.

John began to wonder, *What is Devia thinking? Why wouldn't he want extra protection? Didn't he want Amity to be secure? Did Master Devia have a reason to allow an enemy like Jabin to camp on his doorstep?*

Finally, John spoke. "A council has been called for tomorrow evening. The representatives from each major city and village will decide the direction Amity must take. If I could, I would leave tonight, but duty requires that I stay for the council. Will you rest tonight and return to my son with the verdict of the council?"

"With my lord's permission, Master James needs to know what you plan to do about reinforcements. The sooner I inform him that he is not alone, the sooner he will be encouraged."

It was hard for John to control his emotions. "You have a loyal heart, my lad, but you will not leave alone tonight."

A look of dismay crossed the youth's face. He was about to protest when John held up his hand and smiled. "Fear not. You will be able to leave tonight, but you will not leave alone. I will send the mounted bodyguard with you. You should eat and rest while preparations are being made."

John laughed at the relief displayed on the youth's face. "Come! Let's find you something to eat in the kitchen while I set the guard in motion."

They walked through dark hallways until they reached the pantry, where John located cheese, bread, butter, and milk. "There are apples in that barrel," he said, pointing. "I'll leave you in charge of these while I make other preparations. There is a cot in the adjacent room. Get some rest after you've eaten your fill and packed food for your return journey. We will prepare a fresh horse for you. Now, get some food and rest. Don't worry about missing the ride. My men will come to the larder before they leave, and you will never sleep through that!" John laughed as he left the bewildered youth at the pantry table.

Stepping into the brisk night air, he walked quickly across the courtyard to the barracks. The sentry on duty snapped to attention when John approached.

"Young man, fetch Seagood, please. I'll watch your post while you are gone."

The young man disappeared and soon returned with the captain of the guard. John motioned Seagood away from the barracks and kept his voice low. "Seagood, I want you and a strong body of men to ride to Green Meadow, starting as quickly as you can. James is in trouble! I will come as soon as I am able. If the council calls for arms, it will require time to assemble the troops and move west, but James needs help quickly. Choose your men and then come to the pantry to pack your victuals. James's messenger is waiting for you there. Get ready, and I will see you off."

Seagood nodded and disappeared. Left alone, John strayed toward the cemetery located behind the chapel. Helen was there. Seagood always reminded John of his own wife. She'd been gone twelve years now.

Gazing beyond the nearly invisible stones, John was oblivious to the cold mist beginning to whip his hair. His mind began to relive picnics, rides in the meadow, and little boys bouncing around their mother's knees.

A strange thing had happened when James and Thomas were young. A sea captain had docked in Sebring, bringing a tale of a rescue and lad who could not speak. Shipwrecks at sea were not uncommon, but this lad was unique. The first time Helen laid eyes on him, he captured her heart. Without a home and no ability to speak, the lad had come to Stafford House and had become part of the family. Helen had named the lad Seagood, saying, "I know the sea has given him to us for our good."

Being somewhat older than James or Thomas, Seagood had tried to hold himself aloof, but the boys included their new "brother" in every rough-and-tumble game they knew: wrestling, foot races, horse rides, studies, and even exploring the underground sewers of Stonewall. The last would have horrified their mother, had she known, but John had found the boys, whipped all three, and never said a word to his wife about the incident.

Seagood had grown to love horses and weapons. The rough-and-ready life of a soldier was to his liking. Not to be outdone by their older "brother," James and Thomas had followed suit. They had all become skilled in the use of sword and spear, and only last year they had helped Gaff defend Great Bend, proving their courage in battle.

The wind moaned through the trees and stones, but John thought of the twinkle in Helen's eyes. She had been expecting again! Thus, Philip had joined the family. He grew and learned to handle the sword and spear, but he had no desire for such things. His joy was in books and plants and the nurturing of heart and mind.

Then had come the fateful year when fever had raced across the country. Helen had cared for the sick daily, until one morning she'd been too weak to rise. John had felt her brow; she too had the fever.

They'd carried her back to Stafford House and placed her near the window in her bedroom. The house had grown quiet as the cool sea breeze whipped her hair. John had watched her listless eyes struggle to focus on the gardens below. Three days later, she was gone. Only her memories remained.

John liked this place where memories of her were strongest. Even now, he could almost hear her saying, "John, what are you doing out in the cold? You have guests inside, and the boys will be leaving soon. Pull yourself together, and see the boys off."

He became aware of horses crossing the courtyard. Turning, he saw the silhouettes of men and animals headed for the great house. The dim torchlight caught the faint glitter of spear tips.

Reluctantly, John reined in his thoughts and turned toward the house. Brushing cold moisture from his face, he strode quickly to the kitchen, where his men were quickly packing food in their knapsacks. All these men had grown up with Seagood, James, and Thomas. Most were sons of staff who had worked at Stafford House for years. Some were James's and Thomas's friends from Waterfront and Sebring.

John remembered good days gone by when all these boys had romped through the house and around the grounds. Now they were grown men, preparing to ride to war. What if they never returned? A shadow passed before his eyes as he thought of their mothers and fathers learning of their child's death. These men knew the danger of war, yet he knew they would go, regardless of the peril.

John entered the pantry, and every man stiffened to attention. "At ease, gentlemen," John said. "Finish packing your victuals while I get James's messenger."

He stepped into the adjacent room where the lad lay curled tightly upon a meager cot. John had to shake the boy several times before he opened a sleepy eye. Suddenly the lad bolted to his feet, stammering, "I didn't miss them, did I?"

"No, but you nearly knocked me down," John said with a laugh as he led the boy into the pantry. "Gentlemen, meet your new comrade. He will ride with you tonight."

There was an awkward moment as the boy, much younger, stared in awe at the grown, fully-armed men. Seagood moved to the front and eyed the boy closely. The lad sensed he was on trial. Intimidated but unflinching, he stared back into Seagood's clear sea-green eyes. After a long moment, Seagood's face softened, and he offered his hand. No words were spoken, but the boy had officially joined the guard.

Scanning the room, John saw that the men were fully outfitted. Each wore a dark, hooded cloak, and underneath was a wide belt containing a sword, dagger, double-bladed hatchet, and quiver filled with arrows. A small spade was packed inside a knapsack, along with a blanket and three days' provisions. A small water pouch hung on each belt, nearly rounding out their gear.

Outside, a small, sturdy shield hung over the horn of each saddle. It was black with a single golden cross in its center. Underneath, securely attached to the shield, was a strong wooden bow. Spears methodically lined the pathway, handles planted firmly in the earth, tips pointing to heaven. To finish the gear, each man wore a leather helm. It had a bronze strap running from front lip to rear lip, and from right to left ear. When the bronze was polished, it shone like gold against the black helm.

"Seagood," John said, "this lad has come in peace with little or no armor. I am afraid he returns to war."

Seagood nodded and pointed to the far end of the table where a belt of weaponry and a cloak were neatly stacked. A huge man brought them to the lad, quickly fastened the belt in place, and handed the lad the cloak. "Do you know how to use these?" he asked.

"Well enough in practice, sir," the lad said timidly. "I don't know about in real combat."

An understanding smile crossed the big man's face. Putting an arm around the boy's shoulders, he said, "No man knows what kind of metal he's made of until he goes through the fire. You'll do fine. Remember—you are not alone."

The men quickly finished filling their knapsacks with provisions and shouldered their packs. Armed and supplied, the company filed into the darkness. Each man chose his spear and untethered his horse. The same huge man led the young messenger to a black mare. "Wart, this is your horse."

"That isn't my na—" the lad started to say.

"I know it isn't the horse you rode in here. That poor nag was half dead. Treat this lady well, and she will carry you a long way."

"I know how to care for a horse," the lad mumbled under his breath. "And Wart isn't my name."

"What's that?" the big man queried.

"What's your name, sir?"

"Rudy. Why do you ask?"

"I was just curious."

The men passed silently down the hill toward the tug. Across the river they could hear a whistle announcing that the ferry was ready to be pulled away from Stonewall.

John led the men to the ferry, but as the first group boarded the raft, he pulled Seagood aside. "James may have overstepped his authority in Green Meadow. He ordered the evacuation of the city without Devia's input or consent. He may have enemies among our own people as well as from the outside."

Seagood nodded as the tug returned. He saluted and led his black gelding onto the raft with the remainder of his men. The dull clump-clump of horses' hooves on heavy wooden planks was barely audible above the moan of the rising wind.

Through the black mist, John could see dark silhouettes on the distant shore. At a signal, all mounted and turned west on the Greenway. The horses soon caught their rhythm and thundered into the night.

It was dark when Bill got home, and Mary was frantic with worry. "Bill, are you all right? What took so long? Why are so many people going east in carts and wagons? What is happening?"

Bill realized how disturbing it would be to see all the traffic on the Greenway and not know why. Taking Mary in his arms, he kissed her and held her close. "Master Johnson has asked all women and children to leave Capri if the army is called out. Would you consider going with Ella Walton to Waterfront?"

"Is Ella leaving?" Mary looked surprised.

"Yes, her father is taking her and some others to stay with an aunt in Waterfront. She wanted you and your mother to join her there."

"Did you ask Mother?"

"Yes."

"What did she say?"

"She won't leave Capri."

"What do you think I should do, Bill?"

"I'd really like you to go with Ella."

"When will she leave?" Mary asked.

The problem of getting Mary to Waterfront suddenly hit Bill. With Ella's family gone, who would take Mary and her mother? He would have done it himself, if he didn't have to report for duty every day. Most of the men in the community were in the same predicament.

Bill groaned. "They left this afternoon."

"Why didn't she ask me?" Mary asked, confused and hurt by the oversight.

"Because I was too slow in telling you about joining the army," Bill growled. "She didn't want to be the one who broke the news to you."

Mary bit her lip, clearly holding back angry words, and her eyes flashed, indignant. "I'll just stay with Mother," she said. "At least she will take care of me." Her auburn hair whirled with an angry toss of her head, and she stomped to the curtain that divided the bedroom from the kitchen. "Good night!" she stormed and yanked the curtain shut.

Bill slumped into a chair. *What have I done?* he thought. *Why didn't I tell her sooner? Why didn't I make preparations? What do I do now?*

Head in his hands, the big, confident man sat at his table and sobbed like a baby. A candle burned late in the Cotton house that night. It was some time after Bill had finally gone to bed that he heard horses thundering down the Greenway, passing westward into the night.

CHAPTER 8

The Council

Morning at Stonewall dawned cold and gray. A roaring fire in the hearth did little to cheer the stewards of Amity who had gathered the day before. Everyone dreaded the decisions this group would have to make. Gammel tried to ease the tension by telling a story, but no one listened. Breakfast was served, but few ate.

It was late when John came into the room and joined the stewards. He'd slept little, and his eyes were bloodshot. Trying to sound cheerful, he addressed his guests. "Gentlemen, I trust you slept well."

Only a few men bothered with a response, but John overlooked it and continued. "As you know, council is called for this evening. You have been gracious to come so early. There are six members of the council yet to arrive. Until tonight's meeting, you may have access to the entire house and grounds. The fireplace will be stoked for your comfort, and our cook will keep apples and cheese on the table during the day. We will sup late this afternoon to accommodate late arrivals. Please make yourself at home."

John cleared his throat. "If anyone has a question, I will try to answer it at this time." The silence was deafening. John could see men watching him through wary, guarded eyes. He could only imagine what they had heard about the mounted guard leaving during the night. All around the room, John could see men watching him the way a lamb might observe a lion. He could see fear in their eyes, and it seemed they were all afraid of him.

"Ahem." John cleared his throat. "I have a few things I need to complete, so I will now retire to the study. Please make yourselves at home." Grabbing a small loaf of bread and an apple, he made a hasty retreat.

There was an uneasy stir in the room. Eyes shifted nervously from one to another. Rumors spread and grew rapidly. "John is for war. We are here solely to approve his plans to take this nation to war. Didn't he send troops to help Gaff last year, even when not everyone thought it was prudent?"

Someone had checked the stables and reported that the mounted guard was gone. Rumor had it that they had been sent west last night. That, coupled by John's appearance and reluctance to remain in the room, caused the rumors to grow and flourish.

Not everyone believed the rumors. Gammel and Simone knew John better than most and were outspoken in his defense. However, they soon found themselves excluded from the little groups that were forming.

A young man slipped unnoticed into the room, listened to the talk for a few moments, and then vanished through a side door. Finding the stairs, he climbed to his father's study. Stepping noiselessly to a heavy door, he stood and listened for a moment, assuring himself that the master of Amity was inside and without company. Without knocking, he opened the door and said, "May I come in?"

John looked up from his reading and smiled broadly. "Philip, it's good to see you, my boy! Where did my man find you: at Rhoop's or Gandrel's? Or were you off to see your young lady in Sebring?" John laughed heartily at the thought of his messenger calling on a lady to find his son.

"Not the latter, Father, but you were right about the former," Philip said easily, pulling his wet cap from his head. John watched his broad-shouldered son easily swing a chair over the grate that allowed heat to pour into the room from the fire downstairs. He stepped behind the chair and sighed as the heat warmed his damp clothing. "Ah, that feels good. Why did you call me, Father?"

John smiled at Philip's casual question. He was so unlike James, who would have had a sword in his hand when asking the same question. To James, life was a battle to be won; to Philip, life was to be lived. They were so different, yet both were natural leaders of men.

John turned to Philip. "I wanted you to know that James has asked for help. Jabin is poised in the forest just west of Green Meadow."

The color drained from Philip's face, but he asked no questions.

"I sent Seagood and the mounted guard out last night," John continued. "They will help James all they can. You have probably heard that a council has been scheduled for tonight. Amity lies in the balance." John looked directly at Philip as he spoke. "I do not know what action the council will take."

Philip suddenly came to life. "Is there any question what must be done? We must mass troops and defend Amity. What other action can be taken?"

"I once would have thought the same," John said sadly, "but I have heard many things in the last day or two that make me wonder. The group downstairs is not cohesive in their talk. There is talk of peace at any price. Rumor has it that the Stafford family is opposed to peace. They think we want war."

"Do they know that Jabin is just west of Green Meadow? Do they know of James's request?"

"No, I've shared that with no one but you. It might bias certain members of the council before the meeting ever begins. That news will come out tonight when everyone can hear it and have their say."

"But what will you do if the council should say no? Will you leave James and Thomas to fend for themselves?"

There was a long silence. Finally John spoke, but he didn't answer Philip's questions. "I would like you to be present at the council this evening."

"But I can't vote—" Philip began in protest.

"I didn't ask you to vote," John interrupted, "but, debate is open to everyone. We will withdraw for the actual vote, but I think you should hear all sides in this matter as each district speaks its mind. I really want you to be there."

"Then I will be, if the Lord is willing," Philip said, rising from the chair. "Thank you, Father. This conversation has warmed me, inside and out."

John smiled at his son and realized that the tension was ebbing out of his own body. "Thank you for coming, Philip. Say, you never said where my man found you."

"I was with Rhoop," Philip responded. "We were going over some of the old books he has at his house. It grew late, and I spent the night there." Philip grinned, grabbed his hat and coat, waved, and said, "Until tonight!"

"Thank you again, Son."

Philip nodded and stepped from the room.

John hadn't felt this good in days. Knowing that Philip would be at the meeting tonight, he no longer felt so isolated and alone. Crossing to the door, he decided it was time to mingle with his guests.

In John's absence, Jan Vanderwick of Highland had arrived, and with his arrival, the tension had eased somewhat. By the time Steele and

Coalman arrived from Deep Delving and Zaraphath, things had become almost jovial.

It was not surprising that Coalman and Steele had arrived together. Their communities were tied together by their trade. Deep Delving was a mining community nestled in the foothills of the Guardian Range. Coal and iron ore were pulled from deep in the earth. Zaraphath, only a few miles away, was where the coal was burned in huge furnaces to smelt the iron from the ore and turn the liquid metal into tools and, more recently, weapons of war.

Gaff had ordered a large shipment of war supplies after the battle of Great Bend last year, but recently there had been other orders for new weapons, though no one seemed to know where they were going. Wherever those weapons were going, someone was paying a good price for them, and these two communities were prospering greatly.

Conversation shifted to include each new arrival, and John, in an effort to be a good host, led each man to the table laden with bread, cheese, and fruit. Nearly everyone ate a bite with each new arrival, and by late afternoon, few were feeling anxious for a meal.

The sun was dipping low in the western sky when the last two members of the council arrived. Andre Barleyman of Headwater and Master Devia of Green Meadow made their way across the river and into Stonewall. Headwater had a large brewery and supplied much of Amity with their brew. Due to the large number of orchards near Sebring and Waterfront, cider was the preferred drink closer to the sea, but Andre Barleyman had enough business up and down the river to have become quite wealthy.

Short and excessively fat, Barleyman loaded his hands with more food than two men would normally eat and then stood near the fire to be warm while his companion garnered nearly everyone's attention.

Master Devia was a thin, bony man with long white hair. His long crooked nose matched his gnarled hands. The wrinkles in his face betrayed years of rough living. Born the son of a preacher, Devia had soon learned that a pastor did not make nearly enough money to wield much power in the political world. So, at the age of ten, he had begun a delivery service. Some years later, he'd added a horse and cart to assist in his deliveries. He was shrewd in business and had become quite wealthy, adding horses, wagons, drivers until late in his life, he gave the business to his only son, Samoth.

With over a hundred wagons, four hundred horses, and ninety men in his employ, Samoth moved more merchandise outside Amity than many sea merchants could boast. He began to monopolize barge traffic on the Crescent River as well. Purchasing rafts and hiring men to work them, he often underbid long-time rivermen on loads, garnering much of that business as well. Though Devia Freight was a respected company, resentment had grown among many raftsmen, as loads were reduced and incomes were threatened.

After leaving the freight business, Devia had returned to his father's occupation as a minister. He'd spent many hours studying the Holy Writings and had given large sums of money to build a huge cathedral in Green Meadow. His respectability had grown since his retirement, and many people came to hear him speak each Sunday.

Here at Stonewall, Master Devia was in his element. Bending low over his cane, he garnered every tidbit of courtesy to be found among the council. One would say, "Master Devia, let me help you with that platter of bread?" Another would add, "Here is a place near the fire. Come and warm yourself."

Smiling, Devia would cackle in his high, broken voice, "You shouldn't bother with an old man like me" or "I'm really too much trouble."

This would bring a chorus of, "No! No! It's no trouble at all!"

After everyone had joined the new arrivals in another round of food and drink, John called the meeting to order. "Greetings, gentlemen. I'm glad you all could come so promptly. Some have traveled a long distance and have endured a cold, miserable day to get here. I hope you are fed and warmed sufficiently that we might begin." Looking about as he spoke, he noted Philip near the edge of the room among the onlookers.

Encouraged, he continued. "We will meet here in the great hall. A table has been prepared for the council members, and the rest of you are welcome to make yourselves comfortable. This portion of the meeting is open to all, and debate or comment is welcome from anyone, not just council members. Later, the council will adjourn to make final debate and vote on the direction Amity should proceed. Are there any questions?"

No one spoke, and when John motioned, there was a general hubbub as men chose their places around the table and the room. John noticed that old Rhoop was beside Philip. *Well, I'm not surprised*, he thought. *Sometimes I think those two are inseparable.*

Once everyone was seated, John studied the faces of the men around the table. He knew these men represented the people from their districts. All of them wanted what was best for their people. No one wanted a tyrant to invade this peaceful land or to enslave these wonderful people. *Lord*, John prayed silently, *help us do Your will.* Then he spoke aloud.

"I'm sure you have all heard rumors of why we are here." Some council members glared at John, others looked worried, and some would not even meet his gaze. "All spring we have heard about evil deeds near our western border. Yesterday, Mr. George Greenwold came from Green Meadow. He has reported seeing enemy troops near Green Meadow. George, would you like to share your news with the entire council?"

"Aye, I would." George stood and told the group that only five days prior, he and James Stafford had ridden out three miles west of Green Meadow to see four to five hundred men camped among the trees. James and George had been spotted by enemy sentries and had fled. No sooner had they returned to camp but Gaff had sent a man to report that an army much greater in size was making its way south along the Great River.

A murmur of dismay ran through the room, but Devia cackled, "Gentlemen, be not alarmed. It is true: there are many men encamped west of Green Meadow. But they have no business with Amity. My son's trade is unhindered in the western lands. These people have a disagreement with Gaff over the use of the Great River, and they are circling wide, looking for another route to the sea. If these people hold anything against Amity, it is because you sent troops to assist Gaff last year as he tried to retain his control of the Great River. If you will remember, I tried to warn you not to interfere."

He smiled to give reassurance to his words. "We have nothing to fear from these men," he said, and then he began to wag his finger. "We need to stay out of this business. Gaff wants to control all shipping on the Great River, and these men merely want to move their own cargo downriver. Access to the sea is their goal, but if we meddle as we did last year, it will not be so graciously overlooked this time."

Rolph Gammel shifted in his chair, clearly uncomfortable. It was well known that he frequently docked at Freedom City located at the mouth of the Great River. He knew many of the rivermen personally. Clearing his throat, he began to speak. "Some of what you say may be true, Master Devia, but I know many rivermen who make their living on the Great River. Not all are in Gaff's employ."

John noticed Devia stiffen as the hollows of his cheeks turned red. "You sound as though you have never dealt with Gaff," Devia scoffed. "He is a hard man. He rules with an iron will. Only commodities he approves may be shipped down the river, and everyone must answer to him for their business dealings."

Barleyman spoke. "Listen, everybody." His speech was slurred as if his tongue was too thick for his mouth. "Master Devia speaks the truth. I have tried for years to sell my beer on the Great River, but Gaff has prevented me. He allows no one to buy or consume it on the river. He says it causes more trouble than it's worth. I resent that! I see no trouble with drowning a man's thirst in a mug or two. We have no trouble on the Crescent River."

Coalman suddenly spoke. "You may have no trouble, but we have plenty. Our barges move coal up and down the river, and usually we keep a good schedule. But if my lads get too much of your brew, I may not see them for a week or two."

Clearing his throat, John said, "Gentlemen, shall we return to the issue at hand? There are enemy troops located outside Green Meadow. What response are we to make?"

Devia again stood and motioned for silence. "You say we have enemy troops outside Green Meadow. Did I ask the council last year for protection? No! But after your Gaff scandal, you felt it necessary to leave a thousand brawling, lazy, unprofitable men in my city for us to feed, house, and put up with. I ask you, gentlemen, who is the real enemy: those encamped west of the city who have not cost us a dime nor brought any harm or those sent to protect us by this very council?"

George Greenwold nearly jumped out of his chair. "You say they have brought us no harm. What about old Stanley? He's missing, as are others on the western slope. The Billings farm was burned to the ground and his stock run off. If that isn't trouble, I don't know what trouble is!"

There was an uneasy murmur in the room. Jarod Steele looked at

Devia. "I have family on the western slope. What about it, Devia? Are there people missing and homes burned?"

Devia's face had gone expressionless, but he licked at his lips as though they were dry. His voice became cool and steady, sending a shiver down John's spine. "It can't be true! This is the first I have heard of it."

George jumped up again, shouting, "I'm not surprised you haven't heard of it. Old Stanley's wife is afraid of you. She came to James for help."

John noticed a streak of red creeping up Devia's neck as he asked, "Who is the master of Green Meadow: James Stafford or me?" Suddenly he turned his venom on John Stafford, but he continued to address the entire group. "What is the real reason for this council? Is it not to strengthen the Stafford hold on Amity?" Devia pointed his bony finger at John. "Do you not see his method? First he picks a fight in which he has no business. Then he claims he is protecting Amity by placing a large garrison of obedient soldiers in my city. Finally, he brings unsolicited friends to the council to support his evil designs."

"That is ridiculous—" George began, but John cut him short.

"Peace, George."

The room was silent. Members of the council recalled their last meeting when John had pushed hard for helping Gaff and leaving troops in Green Meadow—all against Devia's vocal opposition. Uneasy suspicion filled the room.

John could see that Devia had regained his momentum. His demeanor softened, and his voice became less shrill. "You know I objected to sending troops to aid Gaff. You know I did not want a garrison in my backyard. If you will remember my reasoning, it will help you decide what action should be taken tonight."

Devia's voice fell into the singsong pattern often used when giving a well-rehearsed speech. "I am diametrically opposed to war. Such violent action is perpetrated by men of weak character who have no regard for human life. Why should anyone send young men to die a senseless and premature death? Those who push for war desire only the wealth of other nations or victory in battle. They are a base and depraved people, promising much but delivering only destruction. Too long I have lived among those who hate peace. I am devoted to peace, but when I speak, they are for war."

John sensed the power Devia was exerting over everyone in the room. Still Devia droned on. "There are strong reasons to oppose war, such as loss of life, broken families, thwarted business, and orphaned children. Young women will suddenly find themselves widows, and society will begin to crumble."

The room remained silent, but Devia went on. "The economy will suffer, factories will close, crops will remain in the fields, boats will remain at their moorings, and produce will cease to flow into villages and towns. Hunger and famine will appear. Fear will replace joy; want will replace plenty; despair will replace confidence! The wages of war are far too high. Besides, it does not solve man's basic problem. We must learn to deal in a positive fashion with man's great lust for power."

Devia stood tall and spoke with growing enthusiasm. "My friends, consider the futility of war. Grown men should be able to sit at table and reason together. In my study of the Holy Writings, I find that war is morally wrong. This, though I have listed it last, should be the most important reason to avoid the evil of war. Considering the Holy Writings, are we inspired to make peace or war? Blessed are the peacemakers, for they shall be called sons of the Divine. In another place it is stated, 'They shall beat their swords into plowshares; and their spears into pruning hooks; and nation will not lift up sword against nation, neither will they learn war anymore.' Also, when the believers in the garden drew their swords to save their Lord, Jesus said, 'Put your swords away, for all who live by the sword will die by the sword.'"

John had heard these arguments before. Everyone in the room had heard them, but Devia looked as if he had won a great debate, standing with his arms spread wide and a radiant glow upon his face. John cleared his throat. "Thank you, Master Devia. You have given us much to consider as we decide what we must do."

Devia glared at John. The two were at opposite ends of the table, locked in a battle of mind and spirit, but with firm resolve, John continued. "If peace could be achieved by talking, it would be far better than war. I would favor that approach, but no envoy has been sent, only troops."

"There you are uninformed," Devia said, almost gloating. "There is a parley scheduled two days hence. The Lord Jabin will meet with your son James. This would not have been necessary if James had not declared Green Meadow a war zone precipitously, ordering the evacuation of my people from their homes. This order alone has brought untold hardship on families and has created a dangerous tension with his lordship, Jabin. I have sought to bring about peace through dialogue, not arms."

Jeff Cotter rose. "But you can't possibly host that meeting, since you are here!"

"I have made all the necessary arrangements, and my son, Samoth, will host the parley in my stead."

"Do you know the provisions Jabin has set forth in this parley?" Peter Simone asked hopefully.

Devia continued to watch John as he addressed the group. "Gentlemen, Jabin is a generous and gifted man," he said with a flourish. "He asks so little when befriending people. There are but three things he desires. First, that all nations have one governing body. They will retain their own identities, of course, being governed by appointed officials. These men would answer directly to the central government. Second, all communication would be carried by the government's own couriers. This act will reduce the threat of war by intercepting subversive activity before it can spread. Third, commerce will be directed through the central government. This will open heretofore closed markets to your products!"

Devia turned to Steele. "Your factories are the best known to man. Wouldn't you like to ship your goods all over the world?" He turned to Coalman. "And you are sitting on rich coal and ore deposits. Wouldn't your miners enjoy working the most coveted mining center in the world?"

"Isn't it just too good to be true?" blubbered Andre Barleyman. "Imagine my beer being marketed all over the world."

"Is that all?" Jeff Cotter asked. "There must be more restrictions than that?"

"Is that *all*?" boomed George Greenwold. "Isn't that enough? Jabin clearly indicates his desire to control the entire world."

Unruffled by Greenwold's outburst, Devia addressed Cotter's question. "There are a few minor details to cut the risk of war."

"Such as?" asked Peter Simone.

"All weapons will be banned. As indicated by the Holy Writings, swords shall be beaten into plowshares and spears into pruning hooks. Does this not fulfill the scriptures?"

"Does this ban apply to everyone, or will some keep a sword while others are not allowed to defend themselves?" John asked coolly.

Devia glared at Stafford. "Why do you ask that question? Are you afraid of tyranny? Are you afraid of people imposing their will upon you as you have imposed your will on others?"

"Now, just a moment—" Greenwold began, but Devia cut him off.

"If it's not true, why is there a garrison of soldiers stationed in Green Meadow with James Stafford in their command?"

The room fell silent.

"There are other reasons for defending oneself besides tyranny," Gammel said. "Thieves respect a well-armed man and leave him alone."

John watched as Devia turned on his charm. "Gammel, you are an astute man, but your fear is unfounded. Crime will likely disappear, for there will be no need. A tax will be levied on all goods and services, so the central government will have funds to care for the poor, the needy, widows, and orphans. Thus, with all needs met, crime will disappear."

Gammel frowned. "Most pirates at sea are not in need. They simply want to steal that for which another has labored. Providing for their needs would not eliminate their desire to obtain unmerited riches."

"There would be prisons for such people, though I guarantee that there are very few such men in the world," Devia stated quickly. "Most crime is driven by need."

John noticed the smug look on Devia's face as he continued. "It is imperative that all men learn new and better ways to live. Prosperity and peace are attainable, if men work together."

"Would those prisons be designed strictly for criminals, or would those who disagreed with the central government be confined there as well?" An unfamiliar voice posed the question from the far side of the room.

Devia craned his neck to see who had spoken. Seeing Philip Stafford step from the shadows, he smiled. "Here is a clever young man. However, your concept of this new government is misconstrued. This will be a fair, equitable, and just governing body. Few, if any, would find reason to disagree with its policies or principles. I suppose those who did would be dealt with, for it is in such disharmony of thought that rebellion and war is created."

"I credit you, Master Devia," John spoke up. "You seem genuine in your desire to avoid war. But the price of peace seems very high." He looked about the room. "Are there any other questions for Master Devia? If not, I would like to retell a story familiar to you all."

Devia had settled into his chair with a satisfied smile on his face, but at John's request to tell a story, he leaped to his feet. "You want to tell a story. We haven't time for that! I didn't come all this way to hear a story, especially one I already know!"

"Aw, come on, Devia!" The protest surprised everyone, but especially Master Devia. Andre Barleyman lumbered to his feet and looked Devia in the eye. "I want to hear a story! I am tired of all this heavy talk!"

"Me too!" someone else in the room echoed.

John felt Devia's control slipping, so he hurried on. All eyes in the room turned to John, for there was no greater pastime in Amity than storytelling, and John Stafford was nearly as good as Fredrick Gammel. All but Master Devia sat up with heightened interest.

"Gentlemen," John began. "I should like to recount for you the founding of Amity."

Indeed, everyone knew the story, but few tired of hearing it again and again. Smiling, the group relaxed and leaned back to enjoy their favorite story.

At Bill Cotton's Household

"Grandpa, did he tell the same story you just told us?" Joshua asked.

"Yes he did, Grandson," Bill said. "But John Stafford was a very wise man. He made sure to mention the ancestor of each council member present. Names like Gammel, Vanderwick, Coalman, Steele, Simone, Johnson, and others were very prominent in his story. He told of their courage to stand up for what they believed, even though hardship had been the only result. In fact, the only council member who was not mentioned by name was Master Devia."

Bill scratched his head thoughtfully. "Where Devia had come from was a mystery. Some thought his father had come from Emancipation. Others said his family had drifted south from the Mountains of Despair. No one knew for certain where he had come from, or why. They only knew he was there."

"How did the meeting turn out, Grandpa?"

"Well, it's a long story. Shall we ask Grandma if there is time for it yet tonight?" Bill winked at the grandchildren and cast a mischievous grin toward Mary. She sat near the fire, her knitting needles clicking softly. Their steady rhythm added a quiet charm to the setting.

Mary noted a lull in the story and glanced up. Bill was smiling, and a roomful of anxious eyes were pleading for her approval. Glancing at the clock on the mantel, she nodded—and quickly returned to her labors.

Bill grinned at the grandchildren. "Well, let's find out!"

The Council Continues

John looked around the room as he concluded. "That is how Amity was discovered and settled. We have a colorful history, and our future has yet to be written."

People began to stir as they considered the founding of towns and villages—and their own families' roles in the unfolding history of Amity.

The silence was broken by Devia's high-pitched voice. "Well, that was a very pretty story indeed! I hope you are satisfied that a great deal of time has been wasted?"

"I was hoping we would all remember what our ancestors fled when they came to this place," John said quietly. He addressed the entire group. "Gentlemen, we are in a serious position. A large army is encamped on our western border, and they request a merger of our governments to avoid war. Master Devia is apparently their spokesman, for he alone seems to know the mind of this group. We have two choices: either we agree and become vassals of Jabin, or we oppose Jabin and risk going to war. Those of us who vote on this matter will involve others besides ourselves. Everyone has family, friends, or loved ones at home. Those people will be affected by your decision tonight."

John looked thoughtfully around the room. Many were old, and some were young, but most had honest hearts endowed with purity and innocence. How he loved these people! If only he could spare them the heartache that would accompany either decision.

"We will adjourn for fifteen minutes," John stated. "You should meet with members of your party to reach a decision. I encourage you to talk, but please spend some time in prayer as well. Ask the Lord what course of action He would want us to take. When we regroup, we will meet in the private room to my left. Only the representatives of each district will be allowed in that room for the final discussion and vote."

John paused, looking the group over. "Are there any questions?" When there was no reply, he added, "You are dismissed for fifteen minutes. Return with your decision."

As men began to sort themselves into various groups, John searched for Philip. Locating him, John gave Philip a great hug and whispered, "Thank you for coming tonight. It was your question about the prisons that prompted me to tell that story."

"It was a good move," another voice added.

John turned to see an old man to his right. "It's good to see you, Rhoop!" The men clasped hands firmly. "I'm glad you are here."

"I think you have won the first round, John, but I do not think your opposition is over. Look over there." Rhoop pointed to where Master Devia and Andre Barleyman had withdrawn and were in deep conversation.

After watching the exchange between Devia and Barleyman, John turned again to Philip and Rhoop. "I know you already have, but continue to pray for the outcome of this meeting. Many lives are at stake, regardless of the choices we make."

Both Philip and Rhoop nodded, and John turned to seek a quiet place for prayer. Instinctively, he was drawn to the cemetery behind the house. Quieting his mind, John began to consider the men and women of Amity. He'd seen them in the markets, in the fields, on ships, and working rafts of the river. These were people who trusted him to guide them and protect them. What would become of them in the days ahead?

In the darkness behind the house, John lifted his eyes to heaven and prayed, "Lord, I know what I must do, but is it right for everyone? Guide our hearts that we might do Your will and honor You with our actions. Strengthen the people of Amity to face the coming days with Your grace. Protect us, I pray, in Jesus's name, amen."

Knowing time for prayer was over; John turned back to the house and made his way resolutely to the meeting room where the future of Amity would be decided.

CHAPTER 9

Decisions

The men returning to council formed a much smaller and quieter group than before. Everyone sat around a large table in a private room. Some quietly eyed the floor, while others searched the eyes of their neighbors, wondering what choices would be made this night.

When everyone was seated, John stood and opened the meeting. "Gentlemen, how will we respond to the army on our western border?"

Devia stood. "I have already said that a parley is set for two days from now! Why don't we wait to see the outcome of that meeting?"

"Discussion of such important matters should have come to us here at Stonewall," said Peter Simone. "It is not fitting that James should decide such weighty matters alone!"

"You apparently do not trust James any more than I do?" Devia said with a sly smile.

"Oh, I trust James, all right," Simone responded. "It is just that he cannot possibly know the entire mind of this council."

"I have no doubt he will be glad to decide for all of you," commented Devia dryly. "He seems to take delight in being in control."

Simone's only response was to shift uneasily in his chair.

"Do you mean that James could decide our fate without our input?" Cotter asked uneasily. He directed his question toward John.

"No," John stated quietly. "A parley with James is useless. He has no authority to decide Amity's fate. He has been assigned to defend Amity from invasion. This council has not even given him the authority to initiate battle unless he has been attacked. Once engaged in battle, he may or may not accept terms of surrender."

"I wonder if your son's time away from Stonewall has not made him a little headstrong?" countered Devia. "There is something a bit heady about commanding a division of armed men. He may respect the council's advice, or he may ignore it."

George Greenwold jumped to his feet. "I am incensed by your attack on James's integrity! How dare you attack the lad when he is not here to defend himself? I cannot sit here and let you defame his character."

"Peace, George," John soothed. "No one feels the sting of these accusations more keenly than I. Time will bear out the truth or folly of James's actions. Presently, I also trust his judgments."

"It is noble for a father to trust his son, but not to the destruction of a nation!" Devia turned angry eyes upon George Greenwald. "However, I doubt not that this horse breeder will share the spoils when James becomes the supreme ruler in Amity."

"Gentlemen," John said sharply. "This meeting will not digress into a shouting match. Currently we have one suggestion on the floor. Master Devia has suggested we wait for the results and terms of parley. Are there other ideas?"

Surprisingly, Richard Woolsey suddenly stood, and though it was unusual for him to speak in public, he began. "Master Devia says he has no fear of the army on his border. I am glad for him, but those of us in Shepherd are not so confident. Our men, women, and children are prepared to flee if Green Meadow is attacked. We have been grateful for James and the garrison stationed there."

Woolsey shifted uncomfortably. Every eye in the room was on him as he continued. "Our concerns have been growing for a long time. Many families have moved from the western slopes to our district in the last two years. They tell of bandits raiding homesteads and grabbing the oldest boys. The boys are then forced to join the bandits. If they refuse, their families are killed."

Devia hissed through his teeth, but Woolsey plunged on. "Some of the families that have come to us have boys in Jabin's service. They fear for their boys, and they fear for their own lives. That is why they have fled. They hope to be safe in Amity."

"Where did you dream up such a wild tale?" demanded Devia angrily. "I have seen no immigrants passing through Green Meadow over the last two years."

Woolsey suddenly turned to face Devia. "I'm sure you haven't. They thought you might inform Jabin." There was dead silence for a moment, and then Woolsey continued. "Admittedly, there is only one road crossing the pass, but the valley is fairly wide, and not all areas can be seen from the towers of your basilica."

Devia stood tall and proud. "Are you accusing me of treason? That is some thanks for all the grain and wool I have moved to market for you. Don't you understand that your well-being is because of me?"

The color began to rise in Woolsey's neck, and he clenched his fists. "You steal ten percent every year!" he shouted.

"Those are customary charges," Devia countered. "However, with such an attitude, your bales of wool in my warehouse may never find a market now."

"You are a cheat and a liar!" Woolsey shouted, nearly coming across the table to get at Devia.

"That is enough, both of you!" John roared.

Several men grabbed Woolsey and held him back while Master Devia merely brushed his sleeves and calmly sat down.

"We can settle these issues another day, gentlemen, but for now, let's get back to the business at hand," John said firmly.

Ronald O'Towle stood. "Gentlemen, in Northglen, we are few and far between, being shepherds and such, but if a bear wanders into our area, we band together to destroy the bear or drive it back into the mountains. No one is safe until he is gone."

He continued. "It would seem that Jabin is a predator lounging on our doorstep. If we allow him entrance, we may later wish we had not. Much can be tolerated, but this rounding up of boys and making them serve in a foreign army cannot be tolerated. It must stop. I say, if Jabin will immediately release all the boys he has pressed into service, leave these lands, and promise to never return, let him do so in peace. However, I do not think this kind of man will turn away so easily."

There was a brief silence, and O'Towle went on. "I do not wish for war, but I fear this tyrant even more. I hope we will band together and not allow each community to fall victim to Jabin's desire."

There was a murmur of approval around the room. Master Devia looked straight at Andre Barleyman as if to say, "It's your turn."

Slowly, the fat man elevated his ponderous bulk, grunting heavily. His chair squawked a sigh of relief, if only for a moment. This sent a smile around the room, but Barleyman was unaware of anyone's mirth.

Saliva trickled from the corners of his mouth and dripped from his chin. "Gentlemen, you are wrong to call Jabin a tyrant." He looked straight at O'Towle as he spoke. "This man is offering financial liberty to us all. With all nations bound together, the opportunity for economic expansion is unbelievable. The barriers placed by unenlightened people will be removed, and products we produce and market here in Amity will be purchased worldwide. The wealth and prosperity that flow into Amity will rival any on earth. Surely you would not call that tyranny?"

"We could produce more coal if we had a market for it," Coalman replied as Barleyman eased his bulk back into his groaning chair. "It would create new jobs, but everyone who wants to work already does. We would have to bring help from outside to mine and ship more coal."

"Shipping is no problem," smiled Devia. "We would be glad to assist you. Indeed, we have not hauled much coal yet."

Jarod Steele snorted. "I'm sure you would like to help. I sent a shipment of weapons to Gaff via your company, and he complained that they never received it. Not only that, but your shipping rate was nearly double the standard!"

"The cost was higher because you were shipping into a war zone. Gaff lives in a war of his own making, and the risks of cargo loss are greater in the turbulent arena of such unstable men." Devia sounded calm and matter-of-fact.

And so the discussion continued. Some seemed reluctant to confront Jabin, but most did not want to appease him. Through constant encouragement, John was able to weave a proposal together that he hoped most of the council would support. Amity would issue a call to arms and raise an army. This would not merely be a show of resolve. Amity would be ready to fight and even die to retain her freedom and her identity.

At long last, the council was ready to vote. "Gentlemen." John addressed the group, signaling them to once again be seated. "Shall we raise an army with the intent to keep Jabin from entering our borders? How do you vote?"

The room grew suddenly still. One by one, each representative from the districts of Amity stood and gave his reason for assent or objection. It was a lengthy process, but when everyone had had his say, only Devia and Barleyman were opposed to the plan.

Vanderwick summed it up the best when he quipped, "We're caught between a rock and a hard place, with no way to win. But I'd rather fall together than be picked off one by one."

So the die was cast, and though Master Devia objected strongly, the council began to plan for war. Representatives from each community offered varying numbers of troops, though no one committed their full strength. Although most communities had some weapons and protective armor, war was relatively new to Amity. If this newly formed army did not repel Jabin on the western border, these stewards wanted some defense left at home.

It was when neither Devia nor Barleyman offered any troops for the effort that Woolsey jumped up in frustration, "I do not understand why we make plans for war while members who refuse to assist are among us. If they want no part of this, then maybe they should leave."

"Aye," Greenwold growled. "Get them out of here!"

"Wait!" John cautioned. "These men are still members of this council. However, I agree that it will look bad if our plans are known by the enemy."

Devia glared angrily around the room. He remained silent, but his mind was working quickly. *I may have lost this round, but this is only the beginning. I will show these fools! They can't stop me. In a matter of days, James will be overwhelmed by Jabin's forces, and no matter how many men are raised tonight, they will come to Green Meadow too late. The battle will be over, and Amity will fall. Because I support him, Jabin will place me on Amity's throne, and I shall rule. And when I do, these men will pay.*

In the end, little more than fifteen thousand men would march west to Green Meadow. There would be twenty-five hundred from Sebring, three thousand from Waterfront, and five hundred from Stonewall who would begin the journey that afternoon. Northglen would send five hundred men as soon as they could be mustered, but they would be several days behind the others. Capri offered two thousand men, as did Deep Delving. Zaraphath was a large community, so it was glad tidings when Jarod Steele offered thirty-five hundred strong and capable men. Shepherd was a sparsely settled region, but it lay nearest the troubled area, except for Headwater and Green Meadow. Woolsey promised a thousand men to the effort and Vanderwick three hundred. Besides men, Vanderwick offered five hundred horses to be used for commanders, messengers, scouts, the injured, and any other needy personnel.

John summoned the messengers of Stonewall and made them available to each council member. By daylight, horses and riders were being ferried across the river. Each bore instructions to the communities to which they were being sent. Preparations were to be swift, for timing was essential.

The council was about to adjourn when Master Devia rose and signaled his intention to speak. After the long night, his voice was shrill. "Gentlemen, you have made a serious mistake. The world is changing, and you don't seem to care. Don't you see that the Almighty One has empowered the Lord Jabin to unite our world, not destroy it? Our heavenly Father desires that all should become equal in this life. There should not be rich and poor, affluence and poverty, wealth and want. These things cause envy and strife. People attack each other in an attempt to attain things they do not have."

Seeing that he had everyone's attention, he continued. "If you fight against the Lord Jabin, you may just find yourself fighting against the Divine One himself. I implore you; it may not be too late to avoid this disaster you have planned. The Lord Jabin, whom you describe as a tyrant, is doing the Holy One's work by making peace through unity. He wants all men to have their own homes and their own jobs. Under his plans of expansion, there will be many new jobs created. The homeless will be housed, the oppressed will have justice, the weak will be made strong, and the proud will be humbled. Why would you fight against one with such noble designs for mankind?"

John responded quietly. "There is no peace, except that which is found when we give ourselves to Jesus Christ. Avoiding war is a noble concept, but it is not the essence of true peace. Part of our calling in this life is to stand for truth, to fight injustice, and to protect the innocent. I appreciate your concern for Amity, but this is the path that most in this room feel is best for the people. Only our heavenly Father can determine the outcome, but for our part, we can place our trust and confidence in Him and ask that His will be done."

John watched Devia sadly turn to the messenger assigned to him and give his instructions. One by one the stewards of Amity bid John goodbye and gathered with those who had come with them, to begin their journey home. Not only were the men exhausted from the all-night debate but no one was certain how their decision would turn out. It was a very subdued group that left Stonewall that day.

Greenwold cornered John Stafford. "Sir, I mean no disrespect, but I fear Devia will spill the beans to our enemies when he gets home. We'll have no element of surprise."

"I understand what you are saying, George, but Master Devia doesn't know everything," John said softly. A sudden sadness filled his voice. "You know, I really think Devia believes Jabin is doing a good work. I don't understand why he is so blind."

Later that afternoon, John moved through the crowd that had assembled on the watchtower. He took a position near the left side and leaned against the cool stone wall. From his vantage point he could barely make out the ferries below, but he knew they were transporting men from Sebring to Stonewall and then to Waterfront. It was going as well as he could expect. With great interest, he watched as men hugged their families goodbye. Long rows of men issued from Sebring's armory; all were helmed in black with a sword by their side. All carried a shield in one hand, and most carried a spear in the other.

We might have a chance, he thought, and he hoped the cost wouldn't be too high. John tried to put himself in these men's shoes. Green Meadow was nothing more than the name of a town to most. Though Sebring was a large city and goods came to her from both the river and the sea, most of her people did not travel beyond the city limits.

There were notable exceptions. Rolph Gammel, the captain of his own merchant ship, was now a squadron commander. He had traveled a great deal and had experienced many adventures firsthand.

A swift movement caught John's eye. On the narrow streets of Sebring, a young woman dashed toward the departing tug, waving her arms and shouting wildly. Though the tug was already several feet from shore, the girl raced without hesitation toward the departing structure and leaped with all her might. Strong hands caught Katherine Gammel before she hit the water, and they were rewarded with a curtsy and a smile, which melted every heart on the ferry.

John smiled. Philip must be on the embankments of Stonewall, waiting. Had Katherine only known, she would not have had to hurry so quickly. Philip was not marching west today, for John had placed him in charge of Stonewall until this mess was over.

That decision had created a firestorm at the council last night. Many felt that Philip was merely a lad with no experience. Others felt that he was all schoolboy and no guts. Though words like *wimp* and *ninny* were left unsaid, they were strongly implied. It hurt John to think that people felt this way about his youngest son, but he was confident that Philip would prove them wrong.

John turned and descended the watchtower's long flight of stairs. He walked briskly to the stables to prepare his horse and then proceeded to Stonewall's armory. There he found his own men busy getting ready. Their faces brightened, and they snapped to attention as he entered. "At ease," he called, and each man returned to his tasks.

John selected his armor. He had no special weapons, and he preferred it that way. He claimed one special horse, but otherwise he was only a soldier of Amity. He packed his gear while listening to the general chatter of his men. It was rather subdued. He had hoped the men would take this task seriously, and they did.

Strapping on his weapons and hoisting his knapsack, John strode outside into the late afternoon sun. He was headed back to the stables to collect his horse when he spied Philip and Katherine walking hand in hand across Stonewall's courtyard. When Katherine saw John, she dropped Philip's hand and stepped behind him, but not too far.

"Father!" Philip said when the three met in the courtyard. "Won't you reconsider and let me go in your place? It is I and not you who should ride to war. You should stay here and govern Amity in her hour of peril."

Ignoring Philip's question, John leaned round his son to wink at Katherine. "It is always good to see you, young lady."

A happy smile brightened Katherine's face, and she curtsied low. "Thank you, my lord."

Feeling suddenly young again, John grinned and turned back to his son. "Now, what is all this noise about? I've given an order, and I expect it to be obeyed."

"But I am no leader," Philip protested.

"You underestimate yourself, Son," John said, gripping Philip's shoulders in his big hands. "You are intelligent, and you surround yourself with wise friends. A capable man needs only a test in order to be proven. This is your test. I know you will do well."

"But ... Father!"

"No buts! I expect you to stay here and assist people in any way you can. You are to maintain order if possible. I expect suffering will come to all, and I know of no one with more compassion for humankind than you. You will do an excellent job. Simply remember others. The greatest burden of leadership is that you must fight for others rather than yourself. You must never use the position of leadership to gain for yourself power or prestige. Now, are you ready to assume your position?"

"Very well," Philip sighed. "I will submit to your will, though I would rather march west with the men."

"So would I," John laughed. "Someone has to stay, and this task is best served by you!"

Turning to Katherine, John asked, "Will you watch us assemble?"

Eyes sparkling, Katherine nodded with such vigor that auburn hair swirled about her face. Brushing aside rebellious strands from her dark eyes, she asked, "May I?"

"Certainly!" John exclaimed and pointed to the watchtower. "Philip can take you up there where you can see everything and everyone assembling across the river." Turning to Philip, he said, "You will do that for me, won't you?"

Philip laughed. "Between the two of you, I don't have a choice."

John grew suddenly serious. "Philip," he said in a low voice, "not all counsel is good. Choose carefully to whom you listen. We have already spoken at some length about different policies you might employ. Do you have any questions?"

"No, sir."

"Base your decisions on good counsel, the Holy Writings, and common sense. Some distraction is healthy, Philip, but beware of too much." John tipped his head and winked in Katherine's direction, causing the poor girl to blush a deep shade of red.

John suddenly wanted his family to know he cared for them. Impulsively, he grabbed both Philip and Katherine, pulling them close. "Come with me to the stables, and then you can climb the tower." Striding toward the stables with Katherine on one side and Philip on the other, he sighed. "I'm so glad to have you both here."

Upon reaching the stables, John parted company with them for a moment, and on his return he led a dark-gray gelding. Though the mount was gentle, a fire still smoldered in his eye.

The three walked in silence to the foot of the watchtower. Standing in the shade of a great oak tree, they watched the movement all around them. Men from Sebring streamed through the southern gate of Stonewall and marched out the northern gate to be ferried to Waterfront.

They heard a trumpet blast and turned to watch the men of Stonewall gather and then march to the ferry.

John turned to Philip. "I leave you five hundred men for your defense, Son. I pray you will not need them. We do not know the future, but these are good men, and they will serve you well." Stepping out of the shade and into the late afternoon sun, John turned and said, "Now I must go. Climb the stairs and witness the mustering of Amity. I pray the Lord Almighty will guide your steps!" He turned, led his horse swiftly toward the ferry, and never looked back.

The Greenway was already crowded, and yet more men poured onto the rutted pathway. John pushed his way through the crowd toward a small, flat-topped building. Handing his horse's reins to a lad nearby, he found a ladder and climbed to the top of the building. He had a good vantage point and could see the gathering quite well. Signaling to a man below, a trumpet sounded, and the gathering grew quiet.

John raised his hand and began to speak. "Today marks a new chapter in our lives as we seek to defend our freedom in the face of tyranny. No one who sets foot on this path will remain the same.

"Join me as we yield ourselves to the Lord in prayer. Our heavenly Father, take notice of these, Your people. Forgive us our sins, and empower us to march forward in the strength of Your Spirit. Become our shield and our protection. Guide us with wisdom, and guard us from all enemies of truth and justice. Whether we live or die, allow us to glorify Your name. We pray these things in Jesus's most holy name, amen."

John turned to address the women and children gathered near the road. "To you I give a difficult assignment: trust God, wait, and pray!

There is no armed soldier on any battlefield as loathsome or dangerous as the demon of fear. He will haunt you and attack you at the least expected moment, but you must conquer him. And when you have conquered him twenty times, he will come at you again. He can be beaten, but only through the power of prayer and by trusting in the Lord who reigns on high.

"Pray always for your men. They will advance on foot, but you must advance on your knees. Your prayers will release the power of the Almighty upon the battlefield. So again I charge you to keep the faith. Wait and pray."

At John's signal, three sharp blasts from a trumpet transformed the men standing casually in the road into rows and rows of black helms and shields. For a few moments, John marveled at the sight of six thousand men standing shoulder to shoulder. Ten abreast, the rows of men stretched a long way in both directions down the Greenway. For one fleeting moment, a sense of power surged through John's veins, but the words of Master Devia brought him quickly to his senses. *It is a heady feeling to be in command of a large host of soldiers.*

Descending the ladder, John saw a tearful young woman holding an infant and restraining a toddler. Though the girl was trying to look brave, it was clear that her heart was breaking.

John's shoulders drooped, and a great heaviness fell upon his soul. Taking the reins from the lad who held his horse, John swung astride the great gelding. Making his way to the front of the line, he raised his spear and shouted with a fierceness he did not feel, "To victory!"

A great shout rose behind him as soldiers and families alike echoed the call: "To victory!" With the shout came a cadence call, and men began the long march to Green Meadow. Stepping in time, row upon row of men marched west into a beautiful sunset on the last day of peace in Amity.

CHAPTER 10

Call to Arms

It was still dark when Bill awoke. Mary had suddenly gone rigid in the bed beside him. *Help, Lord!* he prayed silently. He reached for his wife, and her skin felt cold and clammy. His heart hammered in his chest, and his voice cracked as he called, "Mary, wake up!"

Mary groaned, and as she opened a glassy eye, her face contorted with fear. Seeing Bill, she screamed, "No! Don't kill me!"

Bill was frantic by now. "Mary! Mary, wake up!" He shook her more vigorously.

The fear slowly passed from Mary's face as recognition took its place. "Bill!" she gasped. "What's wrong? I've never seen you so pale."

"Are you all right?" Bill asked cautiously.

"I guess so. Why?" Mary asked.

"You screamed. Were you having a nightmare?"

Mary closed her eyes and suddenly began to tremble. "Yes," she whispered. "I was with Mother, and I was in terrible pain. There was no one to help, and I felt so alone. We were at Mother's place, and we heard someone break into the store downstairs."

"What happened?" Bill asked.

"Mother and I were hiding upstairs, trying to be quiet, when I felt this terrible pain, and I screamed. That may be what woke you."

"Do you remember any more of the dream?"

"We heard a boot scrape on the stairs, and I felt someone grab my shoulder. I was so afraid, Bill!"

Bill began to breathe again. He drew the slender woman into his arms and held her tight. "I grabbed your shoulder, Mary," he whispered. "It was only a dream. You are safe here at home with me."

Mary buried her head in Bill's embrace, and the two were silent for some time. Her trembling body began to calm. Suddenly, she pulled from his arms and turned her tear-filled eyes toward him. "Bill, you won't really leave me, will you?"

Bill let out a long sigh and studied his wife, trying to determine the right words to say. "Even if there is a call to arms, I don't think they will take everyone. I may be chosen to stay here."

"You might not have to leave?" Hope lifted her spirits and added sparkle to her voice. "Oh, Bill, that would be wonderful!"

"There is a rumor that Master Johnson will leave some men here for the city's protection."

"Oh, I hope you can stay." Mary sighed, snuggling deeper into Bill's embrace. They lay in each other's arms until morning's light softened the deep shadows in the room. The half-drawn curtain became visible along with the footboard of their bed.

Bill and Mary's bed was one of the few "nice" items in their house. It was old, having been a wedding gift from Mary's grandmother Trumbell. It had four huge corner posts and heavy lumber connecting the head to the foot. The head and foot were huge planks, carefully carved with scenes of Amity's past. In one scene, a preacher was speaking from a pulpit. The next scene showed guards leading him away, and the next showed the same man in prison. The scenes continued until the final one showed a crown placed on the preacher's head.

Bill had fallen in love with the heirloom the moment he had seen it, so he was thrilled when Mary's aging grandmother had given it to them as a wedding present. Mary thought the bed was grotesque. She had covered the head and foot with quilts to hide the hideous little creatures who suffered hunger, thirst, and even death. It had remained covered until yesterday.

For some strange reason, she had pulled the quilts from the headboard and had begun to study the carvings carefully. Scene by scene, the story of Amity had begun to wrap itself around her, and strangely, it gave her comfort during the long afternoon while Bill was away in town. One scene troubled her because she couldn't remember it in the story: the crowning of the preacher. What did that mean?

She noticed the tiny figures in the growing morning light and suddenly stirred. "Bill, what does the crown on the preacher mean?"

Unaware of her thoughts, Bill stirred and looked at Mary. "What are you talking about?"

"The figures on our headboard, silly!" Mary teased, pointing at the tiny figures carved into the headboard. "Josiah Stafford was never crowned king, though his family has continued to live at Stonewall all these years."

Bill turned to look at the headboard. It was the first time he realized it had been uncovered. A slow smile spread across his face, and he asked, "Why the sudden interest?"

"Oh, I don't know." Mary tried to sound flippant. "I was just thinking about it yesterday."

Bill pondered it carefully and then responded, "Well, some feel the story is not over and that one day a man not unlike Josiah Stafford will be crowned king."

Though that did not answer all her questions, Mary decided to change the subject, and she clambered from bed to prepare breakfast and pack for her move into town.

The day was still very young when they heard the galloping of horses on the Greenway. Hurrying to the door, Bill watched as several messengers from the Stonewall livery pounded away to the west. Though neither he nor Mary spoke of the riders, tension grew between them until they nearly had a spat over whether to take Mary's mixing bowl. Mary finally relented, saying, "I know Mother has everything I really need. These will be here when I return."

It was midmorning when a lone rider came into the yard. "Cotton!" he called. When Bill appeared at the door, he continued, "You are to report for troop selection one hour past noon."

"Has there been a call to arms?" Bill asked.

"There has!" the rider snapped, wheeling his horse around. "Don't be late!"

Bill began to fret, as time was short. They would have to leave almost immediately if he had to tote their belongings into town, deposit them at Dolly Trumbell's house, and still make it to the assembly.

Once packed, Mary began to clean the house. "Mary!" Bill complained. "Why are you cleaning the house? No one is going to see it!"

"I don't care!" she huffed. "I'm not leaving a dirty house."

Rather than argue, Bill grabbed a rag and began a poor pretense of dusting the few pieces of furniture their cottage contained. A few minutes later, he was ready to leave again, but Mary was nowhere to be seen. He found her in the bedroom, lost in thought as her fingers slowly traced the crown on the head of the figure at the center of the headboard.

Bill's anger subsided as he watched his childlike bride. Gently he said, "Mary, we really must be going."

She turned and smiled. "I'm ready now."

They hadn't walked far when they began to meet people headed east: old men pushing carts, children playing tag, and women walking resolutely away from their beloved homes. Only Mary and her cart were headed west into Capri.

People were fleeing to Waterfront, Sebring, or Stonewall. Some of the people they met were from Capri, but many more were from villages farther west. Offers were frequent to take Mary and her cart with them to Stonewall, but with each offer, Mary grew more resolute. Her mind was made up.

She was shocked, however, upon her arrival in Capri. Hundreds of men were milling about the streets, but other than that, the town resembled a ghost town. Houses were empty, windows were boarded up, and people she had known all her life were gone.

When they reached Dolly's store, they were greeted by the old clerk, Peter. "So, you've come to stay with your mother a bit?" he asked.

"Yes," Mary said politely. "Is Mother here?"

"She's in the back, getting my pay." Peter gestured with his head.

"You're not leaving too?" Mary asked with alarm.

"Yes." The old man sighed. "If Jabin's men were to come to town, I'd only be easy sport for them."

Mary glanced at Bill but continued to address the old man. "But Peter, I had hoped you would stay with us. We could protect each other, couldn't we?"

"I'm sorry, Miss Mary, but I'm too old to ever handle a weapon again."

Just then, Dolly bustled into the room. Gliding over to Mary, she threw her arms around her daughter and exclaimed, "Gracious, child, I didn't think you were ever going to come! Peter has just dealt me such a blow." She looked coldly at the timid man. "He's not going to stay with us!"

"I know," Mary said softly. "He told us."

"Men!" Dolly said in disgust, eyeing first Bill and then Peter, and then

Bill again. "They up and run away at the first sign of trouble, leaving us women to fend for ourselves."

Bill knew it would be of no use to start a fight. Neither Mary nor her mother would change their minds. Instead he turned to Mary. "I've got to report for duty. Would you like to come along? I don't know how the selection process will work, but if you come, you'll know how it turns out as soon as I do."

Hope surged in Mary's heart. "What will I see?" she asked as they turned to leave.

"Nothing but men and weapons," her mother called behind her. "Be reasonable, child. Stay here and don't tire yourself."

"But Bill might not have to leave," Mary called over her shoulder. "I'm praying that will be the case." The words were out of her mouth before she realized what she was saying. Bill looked at her in surprise, but her eyes warned him not to say another word.

In silence they walked into the street and headed for the town square. Mary hurried to keep pace with her man. She knew Bill believed in God and wanted her to believe as well, but she didn't know why it was so important to him.

After about a block, she was nearly winded. "Bill, can you slow down a bit?" she pleaded. "I haven't hurried this fast for weeks."

"I'm sorry," Bill said, slowing quickly. "Are you all right? I'm afraid my mind was miles away."

They stopped beneath a giant oak tree, which blocked the sun and cooled the air. Mary looked longingly at the man she loved. "Where did your mind go, Bill?"

"I was hoping you had begun a relationship with the Lord."

There it was! Mary felt the old resentment and anger returning. Was she going to get a sermon today? Her words were sharper than she intended them to be, "I already have a relationship with you, Bill. Wouldn't you be jealous if I had one with God too?"

Bill stared at his wife in disbelief. "No! What on earth do you mean?"

Mary was angry now, and he'd asked for it. "I hate it when you spend so much time with God! You think more about Him than you do me. Last night I went to bed crying. Did you come and comfort me through my tears? No! You sat up half the night praying. And praying to whom? I didn't see anyone. Is God a figment of your imagination? Just think: a full-grown man talking to a figment of his own imagination. The idea is absurd!"

"But," Bill stammered, "only a moment ago you said you would be praying for the outcome of the selection process. What was that all about?"

Mary blushed deeply. "I don't know. I didn't know what I was saying. You seem to find relief when you pray. I thought it seemed like the right thing to say."

Bill's face softened. "Honey, if you had a problem too big to handle, where would you go for help?"

She eyed him suspiciously but answered, "To you or to someone who could help, I suppose." She searched his face for a clue to the reason for the strange question.

"Precisely." Bill grinned. "That is all I do when I pray. If I have a problem too big to solve myself, I go to someone stronger or smarter than I am. I take my problems to my heavenly Father."

They had begun to walk again, but they slowed beneath an old cottonwood tree. Bill clasped Mary's shoulders between his big hands. "Mary," he began. "I love you, and I've made some very foolish decisions lately. I've created some big problems for both of us, and I am so sorry. I don't really know where else to turn."

"But how does talking to thin air help you?"

"I don't talk to thin air." Bill led his wife to the trunk of the huge tree and placed her palm against its rough bark. "Who made this tree?"

Mary was at a total loss. "What are you talking about? I suppose someone planted it and watered it a long time ago, and it grew."

Just then, a woman came to the door of her house nearby and threw some water out the door onto a struggling garden. Bill pointed at the scene and asked, "Who thought of making water? It didn't just happen. Someone had to make the first batch."

Mary's patience was growing thin. Exasperation edged her voice as she asked, "Bill Cotton, what are you getting at?"

Laughing, Bill took his wife's tiny hand in his own and gently laid it on her burgeoning tummy. "Who made this?"

"I think you and I both had something to do with it," she said hotly.

"Sure," Bill said with a grin. "But who is making it grow, and who will give it that precious breath of life when it is born?"

"Isn't that just the way of nature?" Mary asked.

"Yes and no!" Bill answered. "It is the way nature works, but nature follows a carefully designed plan. Nothing just happens in life; everything follows a plan. Someone made a plan for each of us to follow, and that plan is not always easy. Look at this old tree. It is twisted and bent from enduring violent storms as it grew, but it still stands and gives shade to all who pass beneath its branches. Those hardships were part of our Creator's plan for this tree. He made a plan for you and me as well."

"A plan?" Mary asked. "What plan are you talking about?"

"You—" Bill started to say, but his words were cut short by a loud trumpet blast. He jumped. "Wow, I've got to report!"

They scurried toward the town square. Soldiers were everywhere. The number of women present surprised them both, for the town had seemed nearly deserted. Unknown to them, most of these ladies were already packed and waited only until the selection process was done before they left town.

Mary noticed that the men were all wearing a funny black hat that had two brass straps running across it. She'd laughed at Bill's when he'd shown it to her, but now, with all the men wearing them, they looked quite distinctive.

Bill gave her a quick hug and left her in the shade. Each unit had one hundred men, twenty abreast and five rows deep. Bill hurried to find his place.

Master Johnson had committed nearly all the soldiers in his community to the cause. He hoped to leave his town deserted so they could concentrate their efforts elsewhere. Out of twenty-five units, twenty would head for war.

Commander Barker strode through endless columns of men, pausing from time to time to look deeply into some man's eyes. Did he see eagerness? Dread? When Barker stopped before Bill Cotton, Bill knew that Barker could see a willingness to go—but a stronger desire to stay.

Finally the commander strode to the center of the assembly. "Gentlemen, we have been called to war! Twenty units will march with the army of Amity. The other five will remain in Capri and prepare for a possible invasion. I will number each unit, one through twenty-five, and each fifth unit will stay."

Bill glanced nervously at Mary as the numbering began. When his unit received number twenty-three, he wondered if Mary understood. He knew he was going to war, but how would Mary respond? There were further instructions about weapon selection and preparations to leave, but Bill thought only of Mary, standing there in the shade, worrying about the baby and the future.

Finally the men were released for their final preparations, and Bill slipped quickly over to where Mary stood expressionless beneath the trees. Slipping his arm about her waist, he said, "Come with me to the armory, Mary. I won't be able to walk you back to your mother's, but the armory is on the way."

As if in a daze, Mary turned and tottered silently along. Her silence bothered Bill, and he stopped and looked her full in the face. "Mary, are you all right?"

Mary's eyes suddenly flashed with anger. "Is this how your God answers prayer?"

Bill held her tight so she couldn't run away. "The Lord doesn't always say yes to our desires. Sometimes He asks us to do things we don't want to do. We must trust that this is His will for us!"

"Trust God?" Mary spat. "You're a fool, Bill Cotton! Why did I ever marry you?" She gave a violent tug and tore free from his grasp. Turning on nimble feet, she fled down the lane.

Bill watched in shock as his wife disappeared around a corner.

Mary turned the corner and found a bench near the street. Collapsing onto its shaded surface, she gasped for air. This little run and her sudden outburst had left her breathless. She hadn't done too much lately, for Bill had insisted on doing almost everything for her, including the laundry. He didn't want her to strain herself in her "condition," and now she was out of shape.

Flushed and hot, Mary swept hair from her brow and allowed the breeze to cool her face. The anger she had felt moments before was ebbing away.

The sun was still high, but the intensity of its heat had passed, and as she cooled, Mary's mind began to clear. Her first thoughts were of Bill. She felt a pang of remorse for the angry words she had spoken at their parting.

Bill would have no pleasure or comfort tonight, but neither would she.

Thinking of Bill's arms about her was too much. Her head dropped into her hands, and sobs shook her fragile body. She thought of all the hateful things she had said and done to Bill these last few days.

Is it my own fault? she wondered. *Did Bill join the army just to get away from me?* Suddenly, alarming thoughts entered her mind. *What if Bill should be killed and he never sees his baby? Why did I leave him that way? Will he know I really love him?*

Out of habit she began to rub her swollen tummy, a tune on her lips. "Hush now, baby, don't you cry. You need not worry; your mama's nearby. Hush now, baby, don't you cry." The lullaby had a calming effect on Mary, and her tears ceased to flow.

Gathering her wits about her, she began to plan her next move. Had she heard the instructions Commander Barker had given? Yes—and no. She had been so angry with God for not answering her prayer that she wasn't really sure what the commander had said. She thought the men were to collect their weapons, food, and supplies and then camp in the square during the night. The army of Amity would march from Stonewall late tonight and camp east of Capri. They would pass through town tomorrow morning, and the men of Capri would fall in behind them.

Maybe, she thought, *I can sneak down to see Bill tonight. No! Mother would never let me out of the house. But maybe I can come early tomorrow morning before he leaves.*

These thoughts buoyed her spirits, and she dried her tears with a handkerchief. "I mustn't look like I've been crying when Mother sees me. She hates weakness." She'd spoken out loud, and her voice startled her in the silence. The street was completely empty, and though she had sat there quite a long time, not a soul had passed by.

Slowly she rose to leave, but a sharp pain in her lower back stole her breath away and forced her to sit down again. The pain grew in intensity, spreading around her body and drawing her abdomen tight. She could not breathe! Then, as suddenly as it had come, it was gone. Gasping for breath, she sat perplexed, wondering what had just happened.

The next time she arose, nothing happened. She carefully brushed the wrinkles from her long skirt, straightened her hair, and turned toward her mother's home. Taking her time, Mary strolled down familiar streets, examining each house and dredging up memories of former playmates, now grown and gone.

She smiled as she reached the main road. It was paved with cobblestones from the creek and lined with large, beautiful trees. This was a lovely street anytime, but it was especially so in the fall when the leaves turned their vibrant hues of red, orange, and yellow.

Many businesses along the cobblestone street were now empty. There were no goats or cows at the butcher shop, and the carpenter's shop was entirely boarded over. She passed the silversmith's and the dry goods store. Further on there was a tailor shop, a cobbler's shop, and finally, Dolly Trumbell's.

Dolly lived in the rooms above her late husband's toy and craft shop. Mary noted that this was the first building she'd come to that was not fully boarded up. She smiled at the etching in the glass window: Tinker Trumbell's Toys. Her father had not been a big man. He'd been unable to do the heavy labor common to all industrious communities, so he had turned his hands to craftsmanship. Mary surveyed the laden shelves through the window. Most of her father's wares had been sold. The store now served as an outlet for others.

Memories surrounded her as she surveyed the handiwork of other craftsmen. She remembered how her father had delicately cut thin sheets of tin and twisted them into toy soldiers, tiny rocking chairs, or entire sets of tiny furniture. She remembered his painstaking labor while carving a miniature horse and cart. The rich smell of wood, paint, and lacquer filled her senses as she climbed the steps.

Lifting the latch, she half expected the same odors to fill the room. She almost anticipated her father's call, "Greetings, my one and only. Come see my new toy."

But there was no familiar smell, no laughing voice. All was silent, except for the door maiden's chime. Dolly called from the back, "I'll be there in a minute."

Bustling in, Dolly quickly transformed the quiet room into a vision of activity. Dusting the shelves and moving articles from one spot to another, she began an endless tirade of conversation. "Oh, Mary, darling, it's you. Thank goodness you're not late. Did your Bill get to stay? Of course not. I can see that in your face. I'm sure not many did. Our good Master Johnson thinks that when there is trouble everyone should pack up and run to Waterfront. Just go and leave all our things here. Well, not us! We'll show them. We can make it without men for protection. Now, I started some stew for our supper. Run back and wash up dear. My, you look dreadful! Have you been crying? Shame! Shame! You shouldn't cry over someone who would run off and leave you at a time like this. Well, don't worry. I'm here. Mama will take care of you now."

Without stopping for a breath, she gently took Mary's shoulder and pushed her into the hallway that led to the kitchen. Several rooms branched off this dimly lit corridor, and the first one Mary came to was her father's old work room. Pausing to glance into the darkened room, she half expected to see her father sitting behind his bench, wiry white hair flying about the fringe of his bald head, his long white mustache drooping nearly to his jawbone, his eyes twinkling with perpetual youth over his wire-rimmed spectacles.

That was how she remembered him. "Ah, my pet," he would call. "Come see what I've made today." Mary instinctively wanted to run to his embrace. Tears welled in her eyes, for she had not been here the day his heart had stopped beating.

Unaware of her daughter's thoughts, Dolly became impatient in the hall behind her. "What is the matter, child?"

"Nothing!" Mary dabbed at her eyes and turned toward the kitchen.

"Well, let's eat before it spoils," Dolly chided, hustling the girl on down the hall.

The smell of vegetable stew filled the kitchen. Pouring some water in a basin, Mary began to wash her hands and face. A charcoal portrait of her parents hung on the wall nearby.

The man in the picture was older, but with a black mustache and far more hair on his head than Mary could ever remember. The woman beside him was a beauty and much younger than the man. Mary wondered what had drawn the two together.

Settling at the table, she asked, "Mother, how did you and Daddy meet?"

"Gracious, child! What makes you ask that?"

"Oh, I've been thinking about a lot of things this afternoon, and I just saw your picture on the wall again."

Mary learned much that evening. Dolly, more patient than usual, spoke of her past. The time was ripe for the women to share intimate thoughts together.

"Tinker" had been an old and lonely man when Dolly had met him. Dolly had been young, beautiful, and orphaned. Raised by an overbearing aunt, Dolly had sought to escape her seeming bondage.

When Tinker showed the young Dolly kindness, she jumped. The two of them were married before either of them knew what was happening. It wasn't long, however, before Dolly became impatient with her husband. They seldom went to any social functions together. If Dolly wanted to dance, she went alone, though she was never short of partners. Men would bring her home late at night. This arrangement seemed to work quite well for several years, until Dolly became pregnant. Parties and dances were set aside to care for the new little girl.

Tinker doted on the new arrival, yielding to her every whim, smiling at her tantrums and peevish behavior. Dolly had been little better at curbing her daughter's behavior, for it mirrored her own.

Mother and daughter ate, chatted, washed dishes, and prepared for bed. Dolly opened her heart to Mary as never before, and when Mary finally slipped under the covers of her old bed, she was exhausted. She had learned so much, but all that information only created more questions. Dolly had remained silent about her pregnancy and Tinker's reaction to it. Mary struggled with a growing suspicion in her mind. Was that lovable, doting old man her real father? She slipped into uneasy sleep as outside the sky darkened around the tiny store on Orchard Creek Avenue.

The men with John Stafford put in a long march, even though they had not started until late afternoon. Finally they were allowed to stop for the night. They made camp beside the main road in Amity called the Greenway.

Camp was settling quickly when a voice rang out clear in the calm night air. "Great is the Lord and greatly to be praised, in the city of our God, in the mountain of his holiness." Many voices took up the chorus. One song led to another, until a trumpet brayed and silence fell. Still, a rich, sweet sense of peace settled among the tired men, and they slept soundly.

Bill Cotton and Bob Walton lingered over their meal of hard bread, cheese, and raisins and then talked until nearly dark. Upon rejoining their own units, they found their last night in Capri under the stars less than comfortable.

The men chosen to stay in Capri were not idle. While Bill slept, preparations were made to restock the troops passing through town early the next morning. Large quantities of cheese, bread, and raisin cakes were acquired and packaged. Huge containers were filled with fresh water. Extra water skins were collected. Everything was transported to a location east of town. Yet for many, the night passed slowly.

Light had not yet begun to tint the eastern sky when the men of Capri were roused for final preparations and inspection. They ate breakfast and checked packs and gear, and their units were repositioned.

The sun was barely peeking over the horizon as the men stood, row by row, unit by unit, awaiting the inspection of Commander Barker.

Barker was a likeable man but aloof to most. Short in stature, he was decisive and abrupt in his actions. He had wiry black hair, intimidating black eyes, and a thick black mustache that made him quite a spectacle to behold. The authority with which he spoke left no question as to who was in charge.

He paced up and down the rows of men, carefully checking their posture and weapons. Occasionally he would order a knapsack lowered to check its contents and the order in which they had been packed.

During inspection, Bill saw Mary out of the corner of his eye. She was pacing slowly around the town square, searching for Bill among the men. Her hair was loose and was tossed by the brisk morning breeze. She was wrapped in a shawl to protect her from the cold.

Finally she found Bill among the men, and she waved. He wanted to break ranks and run to her, but he allowed himself only a smile. Barker was nearing his unit for inspection.

Bill realized that Mary must have slipped out of the house quite early and without her mother's knowledge. Something about that caused a great peace to settle around his heart. He knew Mary loved him, and her presence here this morning was her way of telling him. If only he could assure her that he understood.

Bill's eyes strayed from Mary, and he was shocked to see Commander

Barker standing in front of him, staring into his eyes. Barker watched Bill for a moment, turned to look at Mary, and quickly looked back at Bill. Bill's eyes were riveted upon the black and gold helm of the man standing in front of him.

Barker opened his mouth as if to speak. Bill wondered if the commander had seen and heard Mary's angry display yesterday. Perhaps Barker could read the meaning of Mary's presence now. Maybe he was even thinking about allowing Bill to say a decent farewell to his wife, but considering all the others who would have liked to say goodbye one more time, Bill thrust aside any hope. As if reading Bill's thoughts, Commander Barker sighed and moved on down the line.

With inspection complete, the men were set at ease. Bill turned to gaze at Mary, and she could see the hunger in his eyes. She understood that the men could not leave their positions and that she would not be able to hold Bill in her arms, but the look in his eyes told her she was forgiven. Warmth flooded her soul, filling her with a joy she had not felt in many days. She was beginning to realize that although Bill felt driven to do his duty, he had no desire to leave her side.

It seemed like only moments before a rider dashed into town, dismounting at Commander Barker's side. The two men spoke briefly before the horseman remounted and rode swiftly into the sunrise.

At Barker's command, the men snapped to attention. A great gray horse bearing a large, gray-bearded man came into view. On his right was a horseman bearing the standard of Amity, a golden cross on a field of black, which fluttered freely in the morning breeze. The horses stepped lively, and close at their heels marched the trained and efficient men of Stonewall.

A rousing cheer broke from the crowd rapidly gathering along the streets. Mary found herself drawn into the emotion of the moment. Black-helmed men, smartly bearing shield and spear, marched rapidly past. Row upon row of leather-clad feet churned the street into a cloud of choking dust. The men farther back in the columns wore a cloth over their noses and mouths to keep the dust from their lungs. Only their eyes showed, giving them a fierce and impersonal appearance.

Mary shuddered. Would it require all of these men to hold back the threat of an invasion? The threat must be far greater than she had imagined.

The last row of men marched past. A trumpet sounded, and the men of Capri stepped into the street. Marching to the cadence call, they turned west into a cloud of dust.

She watched until the last row of men disappeared. The sun had climbed into the morning sky, dispelling the cold, but a chill pressed around her heart that no amount of sunshine could dispel. Turning toward Dolly's, she knew she was in for a scolding, but still she was glad she had come.

She walked briskly, the boarded homes and businesses bothering her less than they had yesterday. Her thoughts were upon Bill and the countless men she had seen marching through town. What could require so many men? What would they face? And would they ever return?

Mary wondered if all those men had left wives behind, and if those women felt as deserted as she felt. It had never occurred to her that others might be making a sacrifice too. Stung by this revelation, she began to feel very small and selfish.

Lost in thought, Mary found herself at her mother's door. Stopping for a moment to gather her wits, she grasped the handle, lifted the latch, and stepped inside.

CHAPTER 11

The Road to War

The monotonous march became hypnotic after a while, and though Bill was used to working in the sun all day, there was no escape from the heat, humidity, and dust. They made good time to Highland, which was only a few miles west of Capri. There they were joined by three hundred mounted horsemen and two hundred saddled horses. It was no surprise that the officers received the mounts.

The men from Highland formed a roughneck cavalry. They were untrained in warfare, but they were excellent horsemen and rugged individuals. They fell in behind the foot soldiers, though, for their horses stirred up a great deal of dust on the powdery road.

No clouds blocked the sun, and no breeze cooled their sweat. Doggedly the men of Amity marched on. They took short breaks every hour, sipping water from their pouches, trying to cool their throats and wash the dust from their mouths.

It was during these breaks that Bill became better acquainted with the men in his unit. Larry Chavez was at Bill's left. He had curly black hair and a thick black mustache that nearly hid rows of pearly-white teeth. He marched with undaunted enthusiasm. For Larry, this was just another adventure.

Chavez had been orphaned early and had grown up footloose and fancy-free. He had no father figure in his life except for a sea merchant by the name of Gammel, who had hired him while he was still a boy. Chavez had made a good sailor and stayed with Gammel for several years, but being as unpredictable as the sea, Chavez had left Gammel in search of adventure. Working flatboats on the river, he traversed all of Amity and much of the western wilds. Living in field or shrub, tavern or pub, Larry's love of Barleyman Malt kept him in brawls, out of work, and drifting from job to job.

Larry had been loafing in Capri, waiting for the wheat harvest, when he'd heard about the army's need for men. The next morning he enlisted.

Darren Ogilbe was on Bill's right. Tall and slender, no razor had touched his boyish face. His family lived north of Capri on Orchard Creek and tended orchards there. They also had a large cider press, and Ogilbe Cider was well known in Capri.

Darren was not adventurous like Chavez. He had joined the army because he thought the family should be represented, and his father and brothers were too busy with the farm.

Maybe it was the small talk, or maybe it was the miserable march everyone endured, but as the day progressed, the men seemed to grow closer. They had learned teamwork and maneuvers in training, but slowly they were being molded into a cohesive unit of men who cared about each other.

The afternoon became deadly hot. Water was running short, and though the river ran freely beside them, the officers would not let the men go near its inviting water. It was feared that the river contained "grip," and no one wanted that. Fresh water and food were at Zaraphath, though they wouldn't reach there until tomorrow. Everyone drank sparingly.

The cool of dusk brought a quicker pace, but when darkness shrouded them completely, they finally came to a halt. They were six miles from Zaraphath, and five miles from fresh water. They would have to make do with what they had until the next day.

There was little conversation as men prepared to sleep. Sentries were posted for the first time. The humid day, combined with the cool breeze, promised dew, so many men covered with their waterproof cloaks.

The camp had grown very quiet when a voice rang out. "Jesus helped me through the day, in life's toilsome weary way. Help me, Master, this I pray, to see the light of another day. Give me grace to make a start, help it come from Thy pure heart. Help me know within my soul, Your love so rich, Your grace so full. Fill me now so all can see that I'm in You and You're in me."

Chavez rolled over and tapped Bill on the shoulder. "That's a pretty song. Do you know anyone by that name?"

"What do you mean?" Bill yawned.

"Someone is singing a song about a guy named Jesus. Do you know Him?"

"No," Bill said. "I don't know who was singing."

"I don't care who was singing," Larry said. "I want to know about Jesus. It sounds like I should get to know Him."

Their conversation attracted others, and a small group gathered. Bill had never really shared his faith before, except with Mary, and that hadn't gone so well. He wasn't sure how to begin. "Jesus is the creator of heaven and earth, and He lives in my heart," Bill said awkwardly.

Larry cleared his throat. "Let me get this straight, Bill. The creator of heaven and earth lives in your heart."

"That's right."

"Did you get too hot today?"

That brought laughter from the little group. Bill grinned too and started to roll over.

"No, wait," Larry pleaded. "I really want to know about this Jesus fellow!"

"Are you serious?"

"Yeah, I'm serious!"

Bill lay back, resting on his elbows, and looked at the night sky. "Do you see those stars up there, Larry?"

"Sure."

"Jesus made those! He made the mountains, the rivers, the earth, and the food we eat; and He made us too. Do you believe that, Larry?"

"I don't know! I never really thought about it," was the honest reply.

"Everything Jesus made has a purpose, Larry," Bill said. "Your purpose and mine is to know the Almighty One and to fellowship with Him, but we can't, because God is holy, and we are sinners. Jesus died to wash our sins away, and by accepting what Jesus has done, we are made clean so we can fellowship with our Lord. Does any of that make sense?"

Larry shook his head. "I don't think so," he said. "This is a little deep."

"Sorry!" Bill said. "I've never really shared my faith with anyone."

The first song ended, and another began. The night air swelled with the voices of a thousand men. Bill's little group listened in awe until the bray of a trumpet brought silence ringing down over the camp.

"I would like to hear more about Jesus tomorrow, Bill," Chavez whispered.

"I'll try to fill you in," Bill responded.

Both men curled up under their cloaks and quickly fell asleep.

They would not have slept so soundly if they had known that far away Jabin was making his move. Thousands of foreign troops were set to pour into Amity. They would swarm like locusts around Devia's fortress and the four command posts of James's garrison tomorrow morning. Master Devia had just returned from the council at Stonewall and was safe inside his fortress. John Stafford slept soundly with his men, and young James Stafford was about to begin the greatest test of his life. Amity was on the verge of war.

The men of Amity were on the move before sunup. The snowcapped peaks of the Guardian Range turned deep red, then softened to pink, and finally glistened white by the time the soldiers reached the restock camp one mile east of Zaraphath. Gulping down water and refilling their water pouches, everyone wondered what the day would bring.

The elevation was changing rapidly—not that they were in the foothills, but the mountains were much closer than they had been when the men had started out that morning. A cool breeze off the peaks filled the day with expectation.

A quick meal and short break, and they were off. In no time they reached the outskirts of Zaraphath, the largest city between Waterfront and Green Meadow. The great smokestacks of the city belched smoke overhead, and the houses were pressed together more closely than in any village downriver.

The narrow streets of Zaraphath were packed with cheering crowds, for most of the population had decided to stay. Bill felt exuberant, until he saw the thousands of soldiers standing at attention in crisp, clean uniforms, looking fresh and ready for action. Bill glanced at his own dust-caked apparel and felt very common. Though he did not realize it, he was becoming a veteran of the road.

Bill groaned inwardly as Larry Chavez made his way toward him during a water break. He sighed and smiled. *It's not that I don't like Larry*, Bill thought. *It's just that I don't know what to say. Placing one's trust in Jesus is so important, but I don't know how to tell him what he needs to know. Boy, I feel like an idiot.*

"Hey, Bill!" Larry called. "Tell me more about Jesus! How did he come? Was he born, or did he just appear?"

"Larry, I'm not very good at this. There's probably someone a lot smarter than me that could help you with your questions," Bill responded.

"I don't really know anyone else, Bill, and you seem like a real guy to me," Larry confided. "Not everybody likes me, but you don't seem to mind me."

Bill laughed. "Larry, I like you just fine. All right, where do we start?"

And so Bill Cotton and others in the group began to share with Larry Chavez the story of Jesus Christ: His birth, His life, His death, and His resurrection. It made the morning pass quickly.

It was the last break before lunch, and Larry was still asking questions. "You said something about Jesus living inside you last night, Bill. What were you talking about?"

"When you accept who Jesus is and what he has done, the Holy Spirit comes to live inside you! The Spirit brings love, joy, peace, patience, kindness, goodness, and self-control—and a confidence that things will turn out all right."

"Bill, that may be all right for you, but if this Spirit lives in you, how can he be in me or anyone else?"

"Good question, Larry." Bill marveled at the thoughtful questions Chavez had asked. He had not thought of that. He drew a deep breath and a thought suddenly hit him.

"Have I got you stumped?" Larry grinned.

"Just about," Bill admitted. "Larry, do you breathe air?"

"Sure."

"Well, if air is inside you, how can it be inside me too?"

"Easy, there is enough for all of us."

"Exactly," Bill exclaimed. "The Holy Spirit is like air. You can't see it, but you can feel it moving in the world around you, and there is plenty of Jesus's Spirit for everyone to be filled."

A trumpet sounded, and they were on the march again. They covered a great distance before darkness forced them to stop for the night. They would restock provisions at Shepherd in the morning and add a thousand men to their number. Green Meadow was only one hard day's march away ... and then what?

Songs filled the camp that night, dispelling the tension everyone felt. Small wonder those who dwelt in this region lived in fear. A pall of dread clung to the land. Even so, when the trumpet sounded and silence filled the air, peace permeated the camp, and men slept soundly.

They were on the march before sunrise and soon found Shepherd's restock station and a thousand men to add to the muster. To everyone's surprise and joy, five hundred men from Northglen arrived just before they set out again. Starting from a full day's march behind, these men had caught up by marching double-time over countless miles.

The next break was longer as officers repositioned troops, moving Bill's unit forward, second to the front. Bob Walton's unit was leading the way. *At least there will be less dust this far forward*, Bill thought to himself.

Thus positioned, they marched out of Shepherd into a near vacuum of sound. There were no birds singing, and even the tramp of men's feet on the earth seemed dull and distant. Scouts rode ahead to find some reason for the discomfort everyone was feeling.

This was strange, new country for those who had spent their lives near the sea. Wide, rolling grasslands vanished as trees crept down steep mountain slopes. The Guardian Range disappeared behind towering trees, and the river now roared over its stony course below them. The path rose steeply west of Shepherd, and men felt quite isolated and alone, even though they marched in very close proximity.

Shepherd was the western terminal for shipping on the Crescent River, and warehouses lined the river. Shipping companies such as Devia Freight stored goods and produce here to ship down the river as needed, or westward over land.

A terrible friction had developed between Devia and Shepherd's producers—so great, in fact, that several men had organized their own marketing group. However, their warehouse had been broken into and ransacked, and several men had been hurt. Many suspected Devia of hiring the vandals, but no one had any proof. The business had stayed open, but few traded there for fear of retaliation from Devia.

Now Shepherd was deserted and silent except for those who remained to join Amity's growing army. Most had fled to Zaraphath, seeking refuge among a greater company of people, leaving a stark reminder of fear and foreboding.

The stop in Shepherd was brief, and its boarded windows and silent streets left a somber reminder of why they were here. Though the countryside was beautiful, with rugged hills climbing steeply from the cascading Crescent River and a narrow winding path that rose and fell among the trees, men began to wonder what peril might exist beyond the next turn.

The march became a climb, and few spoke as the miles passed. Larry didn't ask any questions, and Bill's mind was miles away, thinking about Mary and wondering why he had ever chosen to leave her side. It was not the last time he would ask himself that question.

The morning wore away, and the countryside moderated somewhat. The path was wider and the hills more gentle, but the trees were thicker. They stopped for a brief meal and then marched on in silence. Only the tramp of their feet and an occasional cough could be heard.

They had marched only an hour or so since their break when the harsh bray of a trumpet brought excitement to their step and dread to their hearts. Around a bend in the trees, a lone scout raced into view, spurring his horse toward the men of Amity.

Trumpets sounded along the entire column of men. Standing ten abreast, the men of Amity were trapped between the trees and the river. Commanders began shouting orders, and though there was little room for maneuverability, men hurried to their positions. Bob Walton's company had led the march all day, so Bob and others among his company's pikemen raced forward and planted the ends of their spear handles into the earth and held them at a forward angle. Then they crouched behind their shields, making a low wall, or parapet, lined with spears as the first line of defense.

Others from Bob's unit raced into the trees to find vantage points from which the archers could shoot. The swordsmen from Bill's unit moved forward to form a second line behind the pikemen. Any who passed the spears would contend with the drawn blades of this second line of defense. The remainder of Bill's unit raced into the noisy water of the Crescent River to block any enemy escape in that direction and to utilize their archery skills in the open terrain.

The best archers in Amity were behind Bill, making the third line of defense, but problems were immediately obvious. Amity's defense was miserably narrow, making it nearly impossible to move troops forward to replace fallen comrades. Too, Amity's cavalry was stuck behind thousands of soldiers on the road leaving them unable to respond. Despite the problems, Amity's training had been effective. It only took seconds for the men nearest the front to move into battle positions.

Bill found himself directly behind Bob Walton, and though he had spent weeks training in this very position, his mind went blank as the crimson-clad riders of Endor came galloping into view.

Bob glanced quickly over his shoulder and saw Bill standing upright, sword and shield drooping nearly to the ground. "Bill, get down!" he screamed.

Above the clatter of horse's hooves on the rocky soil, and amid shouts from men on both sides, Bill heard Bob's warning and dropped to one knee just as the first volley of arrows hissed angrily past him from the archers behind.

The dark horses of Endor were within twenty paces. Bill's heart stood still. The world around him seemed unreal. This couldn't be happening! Suddenly Bill was afraid. It was not a passive phobia but a maddening, mind-boggling fear. He desperately wanted to run away, but there was no escape.

Several horses fell with the first volley fired from Amity's archers, but Bill watched in horror as those behind plunged forward, coming directly at him. The angry blare of a nearby trumpet cleared his mind. The archers behind him lowered their bows, and Bill's row came to its feet. The men behind Bill drew their swords and waited in silence.

With a quick glance left and right, Bill saw the radiant, almost joyous face of Larry Chavez. This man who had grown up fighting was in his element, and this was his hour.

Bill gulped and looked straight ahead. Several horsemen bore down upon the position he and Bob Walton shared. Though Bob's spear never wavered, Bill shifted positions and tried to brace himself. Suddenly he heard a horse scream, and in the same instant he saw a dark shape hurtling through the air right at him. There was a terrible blow, and Bill's world went dark.

Far behind Bill, another battle was being fought. It did not involve enemy troops, and no officer could have guessed the impact that losing this battle would cause. A certain young man riding with the cavalry from Highland was losing his battle with fear.

Archer Williams was large for his age and was good with a horse. He'd had no problem convincing Vanderwick to let him come on this mission. However, when the youngster heard horses scream somewhere ahead of him, he became frightened.

With each sound of battle or scream of a horse, Williams cowered farther to the rear. He and his companions could not see anything but the backs of Amity's infantry, for the winding road and dense forest blocked all view of the battle ahead, but the afternoon air was full of the sounds of battle.

"What do you suppose is happening?" one man near Williams asked.

"I don't know," said another, "but I'd sure like a piece of the action."

Talk like that only served to frighten poor Williams even more. He wanted no part of anything that sounded so dreadful. While the others were pushing their way forward, Archer moved so slowly that before long he found himself at the very end of the line.

When the shouts of battle had grown to a deafening roar, Archer Williams could take no more. The battle raged unseen within a quarter of a mile from where he sat, but he could not, would not, go any closer. Glancing back, Archer realized that if he slipped around the last bend in the road, the others could not see him. Surely they would never miss him. He had to try! Quietly Archer turned his horse around. With every eye looking forward to see how the battle fared, no one noticed.

At first Williams barely moved, trying not to draw anyone's attention, and though the day was cool, sweat trickled down his brow. Hardly daring to breathe, he reached the first bend with no shout of discovery. Williams looked back to discover that the men of Amity had disappeared behind the trees. Pausing for a moment to collect his thoughts, he suddenly spurred his mount into a dead run. Archer Williams was going home.

The miles flew beneath his steed, and by late afternoon he was nearing the city of Zaraphath. He barely noticed the sentry stationed on the outskirts of town.

"Hey, kid!" a burly man shouted as he stepped into Williams's path.

Archer slowed his mount and came to a stop. It suddenly occurred to him how strange it would be to see one of Highland's horsemen riding back alone late in the afternoon.

"Yes, sir." Archer tried to make his voice sound calm, but it squeaked instead.

"Don't get excited, young man," the sentry said, grabbing the bridle of Williams's heaving mount. "You've been running this horse long and hard this afternoon."

Archer couldn't deny it, and he felt sorry for the chestnut gelding, but all he could say was, "Yes, sir!"

"What's your hurry, son?"

What was Archer to say? Should he tell them he had deserted the cavalry of Highland at the first sounds of battle? Never! Quick as a wink, he made up a story: "I'm being sent with a message to Master Philip, sir!"

"A likely lad and a likely task," the sentry said, nodding. "But what do you know of the army? Is all well?"

"I should say not!" Archer nearly shouted, letting down his guard after not being caught with his first lie.

Several other men joined the sentry, and one of them asked excitedly, "Not well? What do you mean? Quickly, tell us what you know!"

Realizing his folly, Archer grew more agitated. What should he say?

"Come," the sentry prodded. "If there is bad news, we'll hear it eventually. Tell us what happened."

Archer broke. "It was awful," he nearly bawled. "The battle was awful, with horses screaming and men dying."

"What happened?" the sentry demanded.

"Amity was attacked, and the soldiers fled before the armies of Jabin. Thousands are slain!"

The men questioning Archer grew pale. It was the sentry who recovered enough to ask, "What about Master Stafford, son? Is he all right?"

"That is the message I carry to Master Philip," Archer lied again. "John Stafford is dead!"

"What?" one man cried. "John Stafford is dead?" He turned and ran into town, scooping dust from the path and flinging it into the air. "Stafford is dead!" he shouted to everyone in the streets. "John Stafford is dead!"

Archer Williams was stunned by the man's reaction. He'd had no idea his story would cause such a scene. One thing he was grateful for: the sentry no longer seemed interested in detaining him.

"Sir," Archer asked timidly, "may I proceed?"

"Oh, certainly!" the big man said, releasing the horse and stepping from the path.

Archer lost no time in getting out of Zaraphath. Later that night, he found a ford that crossed the Crescent River, and he disappeared into Highland, never knowing the effect his words would have on the course of events in Amity.

Stars swam in a darkened sky, and somewhere bells were ringing. Bill couldn't imagine where he was or how he'd gotten here, but slowly he opened his eyes. A horse reared, screams fill the air, and hooves pulverized the sod inches from his face.

Frantically, Bill rolled away from the maddened charger. His sword was gone, and there was no time to look for it. At the back of his weapons belt was a sharp, two-edged hatchet. Instinctively his hand wrapped around its handle. It felt good in his hand. It was balanced, easy to swing, and razor sharp. Where a sword felt foreign in his hands, this hatchet reminded him of home and felling trees for his cabin.

Struggling to one knee, Bill viewed the chaos all about him. Men surged back and forth; horses without riders milled about, trampling anything in their path; and screams filled the air. The clash of metal on metal added dread to the scene.

To his left, Bill saw the black-and-gold standard of Amity. Clustered about it, a small band of men fought bravely. They were surrounded by the enemy on all sides. Bill turned that way. If die he must, that was where he would do it.

From nowhere, a lance struck Bill's shield and knocked him to the ground. Hooves churned about his head and body. Quickly he scrambled to his feet and raced for the standard of Amity. Swinging his weapon with great strokes, Bill cleared a path and found himself beside a gray-bearded man. Though the man appeared quite old, he fought tirelessly, and standing shoulder to shoulder, the two fought with the enemy, blow for blow.

During a sudden lull in the fighting, Bill realized that Amity was not retreating. They were in fact advancing into the enemy lines. Arrows filled the sky as the marksmen of Amity found their targets. Bill was suddenly aware that he was now surrounded by men in black and gold. Bill felt a human press pushing him faster and faster toward the bend in the road.

In sore distress, those opposing Amity suddenly broke ranks and fled. Bows sang and arrows hissed. The enemy fell. The attacked became the attackers. A great shout arose from the ranks of Amity.

Bill was among the first to reach the bend in the road. He watched in disbelief as the enemy tossed burning torches into the standing fields of ripening grain. Multiple fires sprang to life and spread with incredible speed, hiding the headlong retreat of Jabin's forces.

Through the smoke of a thousand fires, the men of Amity gave chase. Pockets of resistance formed and fled as the vanguard of Amity poured into the valley. Bill gave chase to a group of Jabin's men fleeing along the Crescent River. He sprinted on legs and feet that never seemed to tire. Whenever a man turned to fight, Bill cut him down until finally only one remained. Suddenly the man tripped and fell, and Bill was on him in an instant. When Bill rolled his enemy over, he was horrified to see that the "man" was no more than a boy and carried no weapon. "Oh, no!" Bill gasped. "What have I done?" Falling to his knees, Bill bowed his head in his hands and wept.

Time passed, but Bill could not move. A twig snapped behind him, but he could not turn away from the youth he had slain.

"Soldier!" The voice behind him was stern but gentle. Bill turned to see the gray-bearded man he'd fought beside on the road. It was John Stafford.

"Come, soldier!"

Bill remained on the ground. "I can go no farther!"

"Are you hurt?"

"I am undone," Bill said quietly. "I murdered a lad who carried no weapon!"

John studied the situation for a moment. The youth was clearly dressed in the garb of Jabin. "Come," he said, holding out his hand. "There is nothing we can do for the lad now."

Bill grasped Stafford's hand and rose to his feet. The two men stood for a long moment and then turned away.

The sun sank low in the western sky, and John was called away. Bill wandered slowly back to the site of the original attack. He struggled to catch his balance. What was that? A hat? No … a head! Blood made the road slick. He dropped to his knees and wretched.

Bill wiped his mouth and sat with his head in his hands. Suddenly he froze. He thought he'd heard someone call for help. Slowly he pushed himself to his knees and then to his feet. He began to search the bodies closest to him. Rolling a dark-haired man over, he heard a faint voice whisper, "Help me. My arm …"

Bill gasped. It was Larry Chavez. His eyes were glazed, and his face was pale. Bill could see that Larry's arm was badly broken, but that shouldn't have been the cause of his paleness. Glancing over Larry's body, Bill's heart nearly stopped beating. Where there should have been two legs, there was only one. Bill turned and gagged again.

"Help me," Larry whimpered.

Getting a grip on himself, Bill began to look for something to wrap Larry's stump. Having lost his own backpack, he spied another nearby. In the bottom of the pack was a large roll of cloth.

"Thanks," Bill said to the body lying under the pack. Suddenly he stopped and rolled the body over—and gasped again. It was Darren Ogilbe! The tall youth would never return to help his family pick fruit from the orchards north of Capri.

Returning to Chavez, Bill wrapped the bandage tightly around his stump. After some moments, he paused to examine his work. Larry's leg had finally stopped bleeding.

"My arm," Larry whispered.

Bill examined Larry's arm. It was broken above the elbow. Clipping the straps that held Larry's shield to his arm, Bill hacked a spear beam into shorter rods. Pulling Larry's arm straight, Bill laid the strips of wood around the break and bound the arm tightly. "That ought to do it," he said, satisfied after examining his labor.

Whether it was Bill's voice or the pain ripping through his clouded senses, Larry seemed to recognize Bill. "Am I … pretty bad?" he faltered.

"Some are worse!"

"Am I going to die?"

"No, you've made it longer than you should have already. You're a tough guy, Larry." Bill's reply brought a faint smile to Larry's lips, and he drifted back into oblivion.

Bill returned to Ogilbe. There was nothing he could do for that young man, but he pulled the cape and blanket from Darren's knapsack. "Sorry, friend," he said, "but it's going to a good cause."

Stepping to the side of the road, Bill spread the blanket under a tall pine. Returning to Larry, he carefully carried him to the pallet. Larry opened his eyes.

"You're going to be all right," Bill whispered.

There was a flicker of a smile, and Larry closed his weary eyes.

Bill returned to the road. Judging from where he had found Chavez and Ogilbe, Bob Walton should have been nearby. Bob had been directly in front of Bill when the attack had come. His mind replayed the scene. Bob's warning had saved his life.

Bill began to move fallen soldiers to the edge of the road. Those from Amity he laid on the north side of the road, those of Endor he laid nearest the river. Other men began to trickle back to the scene. Together they toiled to free those who were still pinned beneath bodies and wreckage.

They had nearly cleared the road, and Bill's hopes were growing, when he spied the one face he did not want to see. Bob Walton lay twisted and quiet upon the earth.

"Oh, no!" Bill groaned. It was the first that anyone had spoken in a long time. Others watched as Bill cradled the fallen man in his arms. "No, Bob, not you!"

To his surprise, Bob's eyes fluttered and opened. He opened his mouth and tried to speak.

"Save your strength, Bob," Bill said, gently laying a finger on Bob's lips.

Ever so slightly, Bob shook his head. With a great effort he whispered, "Tell Ella ... I love her!"

Bill nodded, not trusting his voice. Tears welled up in his eyes and his throat tightened. He thought of Ella: lively, gentle, laughing, always bursting with life and joy. Bill closed his eyes and bowed his head in grief.

Bob swallowed hard and whispered, "I'm about to go."

"Please don't!" Bill said, trying to hold back his tears.

"It's all right," Bob breathed. "I'm just … going home." A strange radiance filled his features. He had no fear of death.

Bill looked in wonder upon his friend. Bob's shallow breathing faltered. There was one final gasp, and all was silent. Bill sagged against Bob's broken body, and hot tears flowed from his weary eyes.

Finally Bill lifted his head and glanced around. Weary men stood silent, helms in hand. They had witnessed the severing of a close friendship, and they didn't know how to respond. Wiping his face, Bill thought he should say something, but his mind was blank. He had no words of comfort for himself, let alone for anyone else. Drawing his helm low over his face, he avoided their eyes and slowly carried his friend to the side of the road.

CHAPTER 12

No Place to Hide

The Crescent River churned in its bed, foaming and racing along as if a deadly battle had not been fought along its stony bank. Dark clouds promised a blustery night. Shadows crept among the thickets as darkness stalked the land.

"Hey!" a voice yelled. Bill and the others looked up to see an arrogant young officer on horseback trotting down the Greenway. "They are having formation in the meadow. Get over there double-quick!"

Straightening their backs from their labors, one man whispered softly, "I'll bet his mother never taught him to say please."

Someone laughed, and another man spoke softly enough that the officer could not hear him. "Formation? What about bedtime? Somehow, I bet we'll miss that detail tonight."

Bill and the others trudged to the meadow where a massive gathering was in process. Each unit was forming before its respective commander, and a head count was in progress. Everyone absent was noted and would later be detailed as either missing, wounded, or dead. Identification of casualties would require time and daylight.

Bill located some members of his unit, but he couldn't see his commander. Barker was there, but Daniel Pierce had been in charge of Bill's unit. Bill asked one of the men in his group, "Where's Pierce?"

"I don't know. We thought you might have found him back there in the road."

"What? Among the dead?" Bill asked.

"Officers die too," the man grunted.

Bill tried to absorb that thought. He'd always held officers in awe, almost as immortal. Putting his thoughts aside, he said, "I didn't see him, but others might have. Who takes his place?"

"I think that's what this is all about," the man said, nodding to where a group of officers milled about.

The decision was not long in coming. Bob and Bill's units were combined into one. Sixty-five men were dead or missing from the two units. By combining them, thirty-five men were left. Ten of these men would serve as John Stafford's bodyguard; the remainder would be doled out among the other units to fill their ranks.

Bill was among the thirty-five men standing before John Stafford, awaiting selection. He was exhausted, and the pungent smell of sweat that mixed with the acrid smell of smoke was heavy in the air. When Stafford saw Bill, there was a note of recognition between the two men.

"I'll take this man," Stafford said, pointing at Bill.

Bill stepped forward, but he couldn't believe his ears. *I can't serve the master*, he thought. *I'm guilty of murder, and he knows it!*

As if answering his thoughts, John spoke. His voice was low, for he addressed only the men he had chosen. "I have chosen you today, for I see in you something you probably do not see in yourselves. I believe each of you would give your life for me! I trust you will not let me down! Go, now. Eat and rest. We march yet tonight."

Bill considered Stafford's words. A huge trust had been laid on his shoulders, and he didn't even want the job. Looking about, he realized that the others had moved to the river and were washing their bodies or repacking their knapsacks. He followed suit and was soon splashing icy water from the Crescent over his face, neck, and hands. Finding a backpack without an owner wasn't too hard, and taking a morsel of bread from its contents, Bill sat to eat.

It seemed only moments before a trumpet called him to attention. Scrambling to his feet, he felt disoriented and confused. It was much darker than when he'd sat down to eat. He barely recognized the other members of the bodyguard, though he did know a few of them by name.

Two units were placed in charge of clearing the battlefield and identifying all casualties. Everyone else was to march.

The night promised rain, so cloaks were pulled from the packs and slipped on. The long black garments concealed the men in the darkness, and moving like a shadows, they crossed the river and passed westward into the night.

Bill took his place beside John Stafford as they marched toward Headwater. Though he was at the front of the line, it was still difficult to breathe! Smoldering homes and fields belched acrid smoke into the night air.

As they approached the large estate of Andre Barleyman on the edge of Headwater, John stopped and sent an order back through the officers. "The men are to look straight ahead! They are not to look right or left!"

Though Barleyman's estate was surrounded by a high wall, it had been overrun and set on fire. Flames still flickered from the ruined buildings, casting eerie shadows all about the area. A thin pole with a round object on top stood before the gate. Bill could not identify the object in the darkness but felt a strange sense of dread.

Bill watched as John Stafford rode forward and dismounted at the gate of the Barleyman estate. He held a torch aloft and witnessed a grisly specter. Andre Barleyman's head sat atop an enemy spear. John lifted Barleyman's head from the spear and set it respectfully to one side. He then hewed the spear into several pieces. "Is this how your friends treat you?" he asked no one in particular. He returned to the group, grateful the night was dark. Thin poles lined the road all the way through Headwater, and they bore the heads of men, women, and children. This was a sight John did not want his men to see.

All through the long night, John thought of Master Devia and the cold, sightless eyes of Andre Barleyman. They had presented Jabin as such a nice guy at the council. How could they have been so deceived?

The night was long, but the road to Green Meadow was worn and easy to follow. The forces of Amity passed swiftly through the dark shadows, and Bill was glad for the march. It took his mind off the afternoon's battle and the young man who had died at his hand in the forest. Still, guilt pressed hard upon him. He was alive, and Bob was not. The question of why enveloped his mind.

Slowly his thoughts turned to Mary. He wondered how she and the baby were doing. The horror of the day faded as Bill thought of the long winter nights when he and Mary had cuddled under their heavy quilts.

Stumbling in a hole, Bill was brought sharply back to reality. He wasn't home! His loving wife could not soothe away his worries.

The miles stretched on. Somewhere during the night, he realized that the forest had disappeared. The land lay in great open folds before them.

They had finally climbed to the pass, otherwise known as Green Meadow. For several miles the land rolled in a grassy glade between the Guardian Range to the north and the Independence Mountains to the south.

Bill noticed fires dotting the countryside. He did not know if they were homesteads, trees, or fields yet aflame. Regardless, he wondered if Amity was already lost.

Miles passed under their feet, yet they tramped resolutely forward. There was a red glow on the western horizon, and dread crept into every heart. Green Meadow was on fire.

Their pace quickened. The red glow in the night sky cast an eerie spell, drawing all men to its light. But another light garnered men's attention as well. Dark clouds had gathered, and now they began a relentless assault upon the Guardian Range. Bolts of lightning stabbed at the granite peaks as peals of thunder rolled down into the grasslands below. Each rumble of thunder was amplified as it bounced off the Independence Mountains and echoed back across the valley.

Bill's cloak had seemed cumbersome all night, but now he was glad for its warmth. Great drops of rain began to fall, but Bill remained dry beneath the heavy cloak.

The lights of countless fires disappeared as a drenching rain suddenly raced across the meadow. Even the red glow in the western sky dimmed and went out in the deluge.

The dusty road turned into a quagmire. Men slipped and fell in the greasy mud. Moving to the grass along the side, they fared much better, but that soon lost any resemblance to sod. Those in the back fared the worst, for thousands of footfalls churned the sod into a gummy slime that threatened to halt their progress altogether.

Everyone was weary and discouraged by the time they finally stopped. The night was nearly spent, as it was only one hour until dawn.

A message filtered from John Stafford back through the officers to the men: "It seems darkest, and the power of the enemy greatest, just before dawn. We have seen the work of our enemy, but take courage; joy comes in the morning. The Lord will march before us as our shield and protector. Eat and rest. Battle will be joined at dawn."

The rain eased, and men dropped in the mud, searching wearily for food and drink among their supplies. Bill ate quickly and settled himself upon the wet grass. He pulled his cloak tight around his shoulders and closed his eyes.

"Hey, wake up," someone whispered as a hand roughly shook him.

Bill yawned and shook sleep from his head. All about him, the earth was black and damp. Across the valley he could see stone chimneys standing like lone sentinels where cabins had been.

Bill shook his head in disbelief. The loss was immeasurable. Looking up the narrowing mountain pass, he studied the terrain, looking for Green Meadow. He had never seen the city, but he had marched a long way to rescue it. Had the march been in vain?

While officers plotted strategy, Bill packed his gear and prepared for battle. A quiet tension grew among the men. Not everyone had experienced the initial shock of battle, but all had seen its effects. Each man struggled with the thought of facing people who wished to kill them.

Archers nervously fingered the arrows in their quivers; swordsmen grasped and released the hilts of their swords, and spears waved about in the long lines of assembled men.

"Why don't we get started?" Bill heard one man ask.

"We'll be fighting soon enough," said another.

"I know, but this waiting makes me edgy!"

"Me too."

After what seemed an interminable wait, officers began to gallop back to their units. Men began to spread across the rolling countryside. John Stafford and the men with him stayed in position, but those behind him were fanning to the left and right. Those at the back were nearly running to reach their positions.

Minutes passed, and then suddenly a command was issued: "Move out, double-time!"

Bill was nearly jogging to keep pace. John Stafford rode in front, the standard bearer of Amity at his side. Bill and the rest of John's bodyguard were close behind. A large V-shaped formation moved forward, much like a flock of geese flying over during migration.

Bill glanced over his shoulder only once. A line ten men deep and nearly a mile wide raced up and over the rolling hills. He quickly let the sight settle in his memory, for it took all of his concentration to keep his footing and his pace. Moving ever more swiftly, they turned from the path and made directly toward Green Meadow.

The earth flew under their feet. Topping the last hill, Bill gasped at the wonder that met his eyes. Stretching as far as the eye could see were banners and tents. The forces of Jabin truly were as innumerable as the sand on the seashore.

Bill glanced up at John Stafford and was amazed to see him smiling. Their approach had not been detected. The enemy was totally unprepared. The men of Amity heard the braying of horns and terrified cries as Jabin's forces rose from sleep. John signaled, and the men secured their shields and lowered their spears for the attack.

A trumpet sounded, and there was no time to think. Bill ran to catch the galloping horse of his master as John raced into battle. He heard the clash of weapons and the screams of men swell about him. His only thought was to stay with John Stafford. Men and weapons swirled around him, but suddenly he realized that these men were not from Amity.

Jabin's camp was in chaos. Drunken men emerged from their tents, only to take up arms against their own men. Bill noted that Stafford was on foot and forging his way toward the standard of Jabin's household, a red flag with a silver crescent moon.

Valiant soldiers gathered about Jabin's banner in opposition to John. Swords clashed and men shouted as Bill raced to his master's side. The fighting was intense, and it seemed that every enemy stroke was aimed at John.

Bill swung his hatchet madly at all who opposed him, but a blow struck his shield so hard that he went down. One deft movement from John Stafford's sword gave Bill time to regain his feet, and he came up swinging. After that, Bill let nothing come between himself and John Stafford. His moves seemed guided, and his strength never wavered. Doggedly, John, Bill, and others of the guard moved closer to Jabin's tent. The fighting was intense but brief. Suddenly, the men of Endor turned and ran. They had given Jabin time to escape, and now they fled in full retreat.

John sent the men of Amity in hot pursuit, not wanting to give Jabin time to regroup. He, however, turned toward his bodyguards with two questions. "Where are my sons? And where is the garrison?"

Bill nearly ran to keep pace with John's long strides. As they hurried amid the debris, he noted many stone cottages gutted by fire. The pass had been heavily populated, but now all was in ruins.

Still, not all had been destroyed, Bill realized as they made their way toward the center of town. He had never seen a fortress before, and this was a wonder. Towering up from the earth was a great stone structure of carefully cut granite. Tiny windows appeared forty feet above the ground, and much farther up, a jagged parapet capped the wall. Guard towers loomed at each corner, and a beautiful tower rose in majesty from the very center of the fortress, raising its cylindrical head far into the heavens.

Bill's eyes followed the tower up to the tiny room at its summit. "The view from there must be amazing," he murmured.

"He must be able to see for miles from that vantage point." The voice startled Bill. John Stafford was staring at the tower with the same awe in his eyes that Bill felt in his heart. "This has changed a great deal," John continued. "There was just a little church here years ago when Devia's father was the minister. This is incredible!"

They had begun to circle the fortress in search of the gate when they were intercepted by a horseman. Bill and the rest of John's bodyguard drew their swords and lowered their spears for battle. Heedless of his peril, the horseman galloped straight for John Stafford. At the last possible moment, he reined, dismounted, and fell at John's feet.

John recognized the rider as James's messenger who had ridden out with Seagood only a few nights before. "Up, lad," John said quickly. "Have you a message?"

"You must come!" the lad exclaimed. "Your son is at death's door!"

"Where is he?" John demanded. "Take me to him!"

The lad jumped up. "Take my horse, sir. I'll ride behind you!"

John took the reins, but one of the bodyguards grabbed his sleeve and said, "Sir, it might be a trap."

John glanced at his men. "Follow as quickly as you can."

After mounting quickly and pulling the lad up behind him, John turned and was off. Bill looked at the others and then began to run in pursuit, hoping not to lose sight of the retreating pair. The horse bearing his master disappeared over an embankment, and Bill pounded on. His legs began to feel like jelly, and his breath was coming in ragged gasps.

Upon reaching the summit, he saw a meadow stretching out below him with a rocky butte protruding from its rolling slopes. Tents were pitched about the butte's stony crown, and that was where John Stafford was headed. Gasping for breath, Bill plunged over the edge, determined to stay near the one he was called to serve.

Green Meadow was a high mountain meadow located between the Guardian Range and the Independence Mountains. This narrow strip of grassland served as the only access to Amity from the western slopes. It was about three miles wide at the narrowest point and contained several deep valleys and many rocky buttes.

James Stafford had been assigned to guard this mountain pass, and in so doing he had divided his men into four command centers. These centers were strategically located to thwart Jabin's movement, and the plan had been largely successful. However, a fair number of Jabin's men had managed to slip past Amity's archers and form a dangerous army behind James's defenses.

This fraction of Jabin's army had pillaged and burned everything of value east of Green Meadow. Unchecked, they had turned toward Headwater. Though they met organized resistance at Headwater, it did not take long to dispatch the city's defenses. After killing every man, woman, and child in Headwater, they turned their attention farther east.

When they met John Stafford on the road above Shepherd, they feigned retreat only to regroup in smaller bands, spreading their terror far and wide throughout all of Amity.

"Mother!" Mary gasped as she rushed into the store. "Mother, I've heard the most terrible news!"

"Good gracious, child!" Dolly scolded. "Think of the baby! Mary, you mustn't run like that, and you mustn't get so excited. Calm yourself, and then tell me your news." Dolly never stopped dusting the knickknacks on the shelf.

Mary's voice caught as she tried to speak. "Oh, Mother, John Stafford is dead! The army was routed, and thousands have been killed!"

Dolly stopped dusting, and her face turned pale. "Where did you hear this nonsense?" she demanded sharply. "It's a lie, I tell you!"

Dolly's confidence settled Mary somewhat, but the thought of Bill lying dead somewhere was devastating. "But Mother, I heard the news from Gary Longbottom, and he lives near the barracks. It was the talk all over town."

"Well, if that's the talk of the town," Dolly bristled, "people had better be quiet! Now, for you, young lady, you get yourself upstairs and lie down to rest. I won't tolerate any more of this foolishness!"

A sense of calm poured through Mary as she climbed the stairs. It was good to have someone take charge when the world was turning upside down. Dolly helped Mary slip from her dress and poured water in a basin so she could bathe.

The cool water helped calm her nerves, and Mary felt much better after slipping into her nightgown. The sun was still up but hung low on the horizon. She wanted to stay up and talk, but Dolly would have nothing of it.

"You get into that bed and rest!" Dolly said, tucking in the covers and soothing the worried wrinkles from her daughter's brow. "You've heard fear talking in the streets, child, and fear says the most outrageous things."

Mary marveled at her mother. She wavered between loving and hating the woman. Times like these couldn't shake Dolly, and tonight Mary was glad.

Watching the shadows lengthen in the room, Mary thought about the last few days. It had been fun to learn more about her mother. This was the first time they had exchanged more than simple courtesy. They had actually shared their dreams and desires. Much had centered on the coming baby. Would it be a boy or a girl, and what would they name it? Mary rubbed her swollen tummy and whispered, "Everything is going to be all right, William." She couldn't say why she knew it would be a boy, but she did. "Your grandmother is right. Everything will be all right."

With these words swirling through her mind, Mary drifted off to sleep.

Downstairs in the kitchen, Dolly poured a large cup of black coffee. Leaning over the table, she sipped the hot brew and tried to sort things out in her mind. What if the report were true? What if John Stafford was dead and the army defeated? What of young Philip in Stonewall? Many said he was too young and inexperienced to be a good leader. What then? Where should she go? She even wondered if maybe, just maybe, she should have taken the advice so many had offered and moved to Waterfront.

"Well, it's too late for that now." She sighed. "We'll just have to put a brave face on it and try to ride out the storm."

The light burned late in the shop as Dolly checked and then rechecked the locks on the doors. She felt a strange uneasiness. Stepping out briefly, she thought she smelled smoke in the air. That was not unusual in fall, winter, or springtime, but this was the middle of summer. "Something's afoot," she muttered, and a chill ran up her spine. Turning, she stepped inside and bolted the door.

"Mary, wake up!" Dolly's whisper was demanding, but it fit so well into Mary's dream that she merely rolled over. Insistent fingers poked her ribs, and again Dolly's voice whispered, "Mary, come to the window and look outside."

Finally she opened her eyes. The room was dark, but she could see her mother step past the window. It was a moonless night out, or else clouds had covered the moon, for it was very dark.

Suddenly Mary was wide awake. "What is it?" she hissed, pulling the covers up to her chin in defense against the darkness.

"Come and see," Dolly whispered.

Slipping from the protection of her blankets, Mary tiptoed across the room to the window where her mother was standing.

"Something is coming down the street." Dolly pointed north along Orchard Creek Avenue.

Mary peered into the darkness, thinking her mother must be seeing things, but suddenly she too saw movement. She saw one, then another object move on the dark street below. Her voice caught as she spoke. "I see, but what is it?"

Glancing at her mother, Mary realized that Dolly was fully dressed. "Mother, haven't you gone to bed?" she whispered.

"Hush and get dressed," Dolly snapped. Mary was turning to obey when her mother suddenly grabbed her arm. "Look!" she hissed.

Passing directly below their window were five darkly clad figures on horseback. They rode quietly, but the faint clatter of hooves could be heard on the cobblestone pavement.

Mary felt her throat constrict, and fear wrapped its bony fingers around her heart. Her dream was coming true! Outside her window, the agents of evil stalked her very soul. She had to escape, but where?

Dolly sensed the growing terror in her daughter's posture. She turned to shush her, but too late. Mary's fear had reached a mighty crescendo, and it poured out in a loud, airy scream.

Shocked, Dolly clamped a firm hand over Mary's mouth and hissed, "When will you ever learn to control yourself? Should we invite them in for tea?"

Mary clung to her mother, but her eyes frantically searched the room for an escape. Glancing out the window, the street seemed clear. Maybe the men hadn't noticed!

Suddenly Mary noticed a shadow moving near the wall directly below them. She gasped. Both women heard the faint, almost imperceptible tinkle of glass breaking downstairs.

They stood still, not daring to breathe or make a sound. Holding each other tight, they waited. They didn't hear the latch lift, but when the front door swung open, the maiden merrily played her tune.

There was complete silence for a few moments, and then coarse whispers drifted up the stairs. Mary tried to check the rising tide of fear she felt. She concentrated on her mother's strong arms wrapped around her. *I will not scream again,* she told herself firmly. *I will control myself. I will come out of this alive!*

Suddenly Mary felt a stab of pain in her lower back. She needed to move, to shift her body's weight to ease the cramp that threatened to engulf her entire body, but she dared not move. The pain grew and spread in intensity, and she stifled the agony she felt.

Dolly must have felt the muscles tighten in her daughter's swollen tummy, for she breathed a nearly silent prayer. "Lord, deliver us!" Slowly the pressure subsided, and both women sighed with relief.

The intruders were chatting downstairs. They had opened a music box, and a melody filled the air. Both women relaxed—maybe too much, for the pain that hit Mary with her second contraction was so intense and unexpected that she cried out without thinking.

Dolly's face twisted with rage, and her hand swung in reflex action. The slap landed on Mary's face, echoing across the room.

Mary's eyes filled with tears. She hadn't meant to cry out! Her pleading eyes were met with scorn. Suddenly both women froze as they heard the heavy scrape of a boot on the bottom stair.

Bedtime Ends Grandpa Bill's Story

"Ahem!" Mary cleared her throat.

Bill glanced in her direction. The light was dim in the room, but he could see stern lines upon his wife's brow. The wind moaned outside, and snow pecked against the glass window panes. Every child sat breathless, waiting for Grandpa to continue.

"That's all for tonight!" Bill said decisively.

"But, Grandpa, you can't stop there!" wailed a chorus of young voices.

Once again, Bill glanced at his lovely bride, her eyes now sparkling with approval. "I'm sorry, everyone, but it is bedtime. Maybe I can finish the story tomorrow."

Destry grimaced but said nothing. She desperately hoped the wind would abate so they could begin their journey home in the morning. She hurried to gather her son from Bill's lap. "Come, Robbie," she almost scolded. "It is way past your bedtime."

"Yes, Mother," he responded quietly.

Gradually the room emptied amid the grumpy protests of weary children.

BOOK TWO

Facing the Defiler: Enduring the Flames

CHAPTER 13

Christmas Morning at the Cottons'

The wind did not abate. In fact, it moaned around the house all night and into the morning. Huge drifts surrounded the buildings, and still the wind raged on.

Destry was grateful to be inside. She'd caught a glimpse of the snow as the men returned from feeding the livestock. The house was warm and filled with food and good company, at least from the ladies.

She glanced at her mother-in-law. Mary's snow-white hair bobbed as she moved about the kitchen, as lithe and spry as a child, yet the woman was seasoned with years of experience and love. *How can she love that brute of a man she married?* Destry wondered.

Peeking into the parlor, she witnessed eight small children helping Grandpa stoke the fireplace. Chagrined, Destry wondered why everyone seemed to love the scary old man with only one hand, especially her own Robbie.

But her chagrin turned to fear and then outright rage when Bill suddenly caught Robbie around the waist and tossed him nearly to the ceiling, catching him deftly as he came down. Robbie's squeals of delight kept her lips sealed, but her heart was pounding, and her face was flushed with fury.

Along with Robbie's peals of laughter was a chorus of voices calling, "Grandpa, finish the story. You promised."

"Shouldn't we wait for the ladies?"

"No!" came the immediate response.

"Where should we begin?"

"Right where we stopped last night!"

"How about we back up and bring some other people into our story?" Bill asked.

"But why, Grandpa?"

"There was a lot happening in the world, and the Creator of all mankind was not just working in the lives of your grandmother and me.

He brought many people together to show us His power and mercy. If we leave out the stories of others, we might miss some of the majesty of our Lord."

"Oh, all right," the children reluctantly agreed. "But let's start right now!"

"Well, I doubt the ladies would mind too much," Bill said with a smile. "Now, long before I ever saw Green Meadow ..."

In his command center on a rocky bluff outside Green Meadow, James massaged his temples to ease the throbbing in his head. Things were so different from one year ago. He'd been a hero then. Thomas, Seagood, and many others had joined Gaff at the Battle of Great Bend and beaten back a marauding band of thieves that threatened to invade the land of Emancipation. After that battle, people cheered whenever the army rode through town. People who had been fearful were no longer afraid. It was a wonderful feeling.

However, nine months had passed since James and Thomas had volunteered to serve with a garrison stationed at Green Meadow. The purpose for the garrison was primarily to secure the border and bring security to the people of Amity, but if trouble came on the western slopes, as it had during the battle of Great Bend, troops from Amity would be able to respond much more quickly. When the garrison had arrived at Green Meadow, they'd been met with open arms. Everyone, except Devia, had been thrilled to have them there. The people donated food, and even Devia had felt a certain obligation to assist.

During the winter months, while Devia's warehouses stood nearly empty, he housed the garrison within their walls. However, as winter began to pass, Devia encouraged a shift in the public's attitude. He had hoped to win the loyalty of James Stafford during his stay, but since that had failed, changes were in store.

Under the pretense of making room in his warehouses for spring commodities, he booted the garrison out, and he privately encouraged people to stop selling their products to the soldiers. Many complied with Devia.

James had struggled to relocate his troops and purchase supplies for his men. In the process, he had relied on Devia more than was expedient, thus incurring the wrath of Devia's competitors. James no longer felt like a hero. He felt unwanted in town and disliked by his own men. He could not buy enough food to keep the camp's larders stocked, and everyone was hungry. Morale was very low among his men.

In a deep ravine not far from the command center and less than a mile from Green Meadow, Thomas watched as his archers hit nine out of ten bull's-eyes. A young lad who sat watching laughed and said, "I'll bet Samoth would like to see this!"

Thomas smiled ruefully. "He never comes close enough to the camp!"

"Sure he does!" the boy countered. "I saw him headed for Captain Stafford's tent before I came down here."

Thomas spun and caught the boy's shoulders in his broad hands. "How long ago was this?" he implored. Thomas spoke with such intensity that the boy cowered a little, wondering if he had said something wrong.

Thomas relaxed. "I'm sorry! I didn't mean to startle you. I just had a few things I wanted to ask Samoth if I had known he was here."

The boy gulped. "Maybe an hour ago. I didn't know you wanted to see Samoth."

Thomas laughed. "And it's a good thing too. I wouldn't want my thoughts to be an open book to everyone." With a gentle hand, he ruffled the lad's curly hair. "Thanks for telling me now."

Thomas turned and called one of the other men. "Diedrich, you are in charge. Have each man shoot one hundred arrows more. By the time you finish, it will be time for lunch."

The young officer received his orders, grimacing at the long practice schedule. "How infernal ready can one get?" he muttered. Turning back to the men, he knew what their response would be. Their fingers were already tender.

As Thomas turned to leave, he called over his shoulder, "Diedrich, make it a contest! Highest score gets a double portion of tonight's meal."

"All right," Diedrich said with a smile. "That's more like it!"

Thomas strode quickly to James's command center. Guards saluted smartly as he ducked through the tent flaps that were popping in the wind. He paused to let his eyes adjust to the dim light.

The tent was large and contained several cots for the guards when they were off duty. A second opening led to the commander's quarters. Stepping to this opening, Thomas paused and gathered his thoughts. He could feel his heart beating fast and wondered if he would always be nervous around his elder brother.

"Sir," Thomas said as he pulled the flap to one side.

"Who is it?" called an upbeat voice from inside.

"Thomas," he said, stepping into James's barren quarters. "May I see you for a moment?"

A single candle flickered from its perch on the rickety old crate serving as James's desk. It illuminated a neatly made cot on one side of the room, with weapons carefully placed alongside. On the desk were several papers, neatly arranged, one of which seemed to be under consideration by the man behind the desk.

Pushing back the crate upon which he sat, James rose. "Thomas, come in!"

The brothers were much alike: tall, muscular, and about the same height. Both had thick brown hair curling about their temples. James shaved his rugged jaw, while Thomas allowed his beard to grow.

Motioning to another crate, James sat down and asked, "What brings you here?"

"Has Samoth been here?" Thomas asked bluntly.

James's face clouded slightly. "Yes," he said flatly. "Did you need to see him?"

Thomas bristled but kept his voice under control. "You know I wanted to talk to him the next time he was here."

James looked blankly at the desktop. "Sorry. I forgot. You were rather busy with archery practice, were you not?"

"Rather."

Silence grew until James cleared his throat. "Look, what did you need to know? Maybe I can answer your questions."

"All right," Thomas said. "To begin with, where has Samoth been all this time? He left over two weeks ago with a special weapons shipment to Gaff. Gaff is stationed this side of Great Bend. The round trip could not possibly take more than four days."

James smiled. "Thomas, you are too suspicious of Samoth. He didn't take just Gaff's shipment with him; he took others. He was gone longer than he told us he would be, but you have to admit, we have curtailed his shipments lately."

"Look, I don't trust Samoth. I think …" Thomas paused. "I think he has been lying to us about what he's hauling for freight and where he is taking it. I'd like to inspect some of his loads and just see what is really in those boxes."

"We can't start meddling in civilian business transactions!"

"All right, maybe we can't inspect his freight, but can we stop his use of slaves?"

"Are you referring to the crews that are cutting granite for the fortress?"

"Yes. I think they are slaves."

"Do you have any proof, or are you simply making an accusation?"

"I've known for some time that the men working for Samoth were foreigners. I've tried to talk to some of them, and they can't understand me."

"Have you been bothering Samoth's men again? Aren't you busy enough here?"

"The other day I rode alongside that caravan headed back to town carrying the granite stone—and James, some of the men were bleeding."

"A fall perhaps." James waved him off. "Thomas, what are you trying to make of this?"

"If it had been just one man, you might be right, but I rode the entire length of that caravan, and it was the rule, not the exception. I think those men have been beaten."

"Stone quarries are dangerous places to work. I don't find it inconceivable that a number of men could be hurt working there. Besides, it isn't any of my business."

"James, the men are so tired they sleep while driving their wagons. I think they cut stone all day, drive home and unload it, and then lay that stone all night—only to turn around and do it all again. The work proceeds at a furious rate."

James pounded his desk in frustration. "What is your point, Thomas? What do you want me to do?"

"Shouldn't Samoth be confronted about using slave labor?"

"Number one, we don't know he is using slave labor; and number two, it isn't any of my business."

"It's wrong to benefit from the unwilling sweat of another man's labor," Thomas countered.

"We don't know it is unwilling labor!" James shouted. "Those men may be working night and day for a very handsome price. They may be wealthy men when this project is complete. Truthfully, Thomas, aren't you just angry that Devia kicked us out of his warehouse so he could turn it into a fortress? You know he has every right to do whatever he wants with his own property."

"Of course he can build a fortress," Thomas snapped. "Yes, sometimes I am angry about being evicted. Not only has it made life harder for the men but it seems to have been designed to create bad feelings between us and the community more than to open up space for incoming goods. Look, I really don't care what Samoth does with his property, but he shouldn't misuse people."

"What do you want me to do?" James growled. "Stick my nose in everyone's business? Am I to set standards for everyone else to live up to?"

Thomas thought about that for a moment. "No, it isn't right to set standards for others, but neither can we ignore the standards of common decency. I'm going to get to know those men if I can, and help them if at all possible."

James swept a weary hand over his forehead. "Thomas, don't you have enough to do?" He spoke with exasperation, not anger, for he knew Thomas had made up his mind.

Thomas smiled. "I still want to see Samoth about this."

"Watch yourself, Thomas. Samoth can be pure poison if you get him upset."

"Thank you," Thomas smiled. He realized James had just given his permission to proceed with Samoth, because he had not received an order to refrain. He saluted smartly and turned to leave.

"Thomas," James called, "be careful."

Thomas grinned. "I will."

The flickering light from several bonfires cast ominous shadows upon the work. Jaroth straightened and groaned. His fingers were cracked and bleeding. Every muscle in his body ached. He was so weary he didn't know if he could lift another stone into place.

"You! Get back to work, you scurvy dog!" the guard shouted.

Jaroth heard the guard's words, but decided to ignore them a moment longer. He had cut stone blocks in the quarry all day and had hauled them to the top of the fortress wall all night. With only a brief interlude for stale bread and sour beer about midnight, Jaroth didn't really care what that foreman did to him.

A whip snapped viciously behind his shoulders. "I'm talking to you, swine. Get back to work, or I'll assign you to the quarry again today."

Jaroth bent over his pile of stone. He might endure a beating, but not another day in the quarry without sleep. He breathed a sigh of relief when the slave driver moved on down the line. Much as he feared the foreman, it was Samoth that sent chills down his spine.

"Did you visit with James Stafford today?" Master Devia asked.

"Yes."

"What did he want?"

"To order supplies," Samoth responded.

"Was that all?"

"Mostly."

"What else?"

"He voiced an interest in our labor crew."

"What did you tell him?" asked the old man.

"That it was none of his business."

"Good! How is the project proceeding?" Devia asked.

"The catwalks, battlements, and corner towers are complete, Father."

"What about my tower?"

"I have too few men."

"Why didn't you take more?" Master Devia demanded.

"I've had no time to go back for more."

"Let this be a lesson to you! When you reach out to grasp a thing, take all you can get, for the opportunity may never again present itself to you."

"Yes, Father."

"Things are happening quickly," Devia said. "The Lord of Endor moves. He calculates that the time is ripe. We must be ready, or we shall be swallowed up like the rest."

"Our defenses are ready. It is only your tower that remains."

"My tower of vision." The old man smiled warmly. "Samoth, you are a fool. You should have built the tower first. Protection from the Power on High surpasses that of walls and barred gates."

"Make up your mind! Do you want to keep armies out or get in touch with some unseen power? I, for one, fear the sword of James Stafford more than any unseen God."

"Silence!" the old man roared. "You talk like a madman. There is unspeakable power in Endor. Watch that it does not consume you!"

"Ha! All that awaits me in Endor is a soft bed and a warm body. I do not fear the unseen powers you bow and scrape the floor to please."

"I will pray that the powers on high forgive me for raising a fool. Get back to work! My tower must be completed this week. Amity awaits my wisdom. This is my hour. I pray your incompetence does not block my way!"

Samoth turned without a word and stormed from the room, slamming the door behind him. He stomped out of the palace and made two complete circuits around the temple he was supposed to complete. As he finished his second lap, he noticed several things they could do to speed the building process. Feeling a little better about the deadline, he went to tell the foreman that no one could stop working.

Samoth's foreman was not a popular man, but when he told everyone they had to go back to the quarry without a rest, there was nearly a riot. Things settled down quickly when the guards began cracking their whips, but one man stood his ground.

"I'm not going back until I get some rest!" Jaroth demanded.

The foreman ordered six guards to take the big black man down, and it might have been a fair fight if they had all been empty-handed like Jaroth. The guards had clubs, whips, and ropes, and it wasn't long before they had their troublemaker trussed up tight and tied to a post in the middle of the compound.

The foreman wasn't going to lay a finger on Jaroth; he'd give Samoth that pleasure. He found Samoth in his office and held out the whip in his hand. "We have a man that needs a little persuasion, boss."

"Who is it?"

"The big black one."

"I've been waiting for him," Samoth said as he removed his jacket and took the whip from his foreman. "Just let me at him."

There was not a sound in the compound except the dull thump of leather striking flesh. Jaroth would not satisfy Samoth with a single cry of pain. Time and again the leather thongs ripped into his flesh and cut bloody trails across his abdomen, but Jaroth remained silent.

Samoth had long wanted to subdue this man, to make him cringe and cower, but the black man refused to give him any satisfaction.

Finally exhausted, Samoth laid the whip aside. "Untie him and get him in his wagon," Samoth told the guards. "He will go to the quarry, and he will load stone!" Jaroth never said a word, but his eyes were filled with defiance as he was led away.

Samoth's anger flashed, but he was too tired to respond. He just wanted to be alone. Panting, he staggered toward the one place he was sure to find solitude: the fortress towers. He found the stairs and began a slow climb to the observation deck. At the top, Samoth was chagrined to find the sneering face of his foreman. "I need some air," he snapped. "I'll take your post for an hour."

Without a word, the foreman turned and disappeared down the staircase.

I don't like that man, Samoth thought. *He knows too much.* Samoth stepped to the railing and watched the foreman shuffle across the courtyard below. *He'll get some beer and bread*, he thought. *Oh well. Let him!*

Samoth began to pace back and forth, growing angrier with each step. He'd beaten that slave until he should not have been able to move, but the man had still been defiant when he walked away.

Striking his fist into his palm, Samoth seethed. "How dare one man slow down the work! I won't let this slave, or Stafford—or even God in heaven—stand in my way. Anyone who does is going to pay dearly."

Thomas quietly sat astride his mount at the bottom of a deep ravine. The morning light was dim, but he could hear the creaking wheels of a caravan upon the stony trail. *If only I could get someone to talk to me*, he thought.

Wagons slowly crept down the slope, out of Devia's sight. This was where Thomas liked to meet them. He watched their descent, wondering which drover he should try to speak to today. He spied one man slumped forward on his seat. Riding forward to investigate, he saw a large red stain upon the man's shirt and breeches. Drawing alongside the wagon, he called, "Are you hurt?"

A dark face turned toward him. The man's eyes were clouded with pain, and he winced when his wagon wheel dropped into a hole and jarred the entire wagon.

"Hold up!" Thomas shouted, but the caravan never altered its pace. Thomas swung from his saddle to the dirty, rock-gouged floor of the wagon bed. Finding a hole in the sideboard, he tied off his horse and scrambled onto the seat. Half expecting the man to resist him, he was surprised when the man handed him the reins. Even as he hesitated over what to do next, he received another shock.

The man turned to Thomas and asked weakly, "Whisky?"

Stunned that the man spoke his language, Thomas stammered, "N-no! Why do you need whiskey?"

"Kill ... pain," the man whispered.

Thomas tied the team's reins to the wagon's hand brake. It was apparent that the caravan was not going to stop, nor were the nags pulling this wagon going to stray. They merely plodded along, following the wagon in front of them.

With his hands free, Thomas helped the man clamber over the seat into the wagon bed where he could lie flat. Stripping off the man's cloak, Thomas folded it into a pillow for him to rest his head upon.

Trying to find comfort, the man drew his knees toward his chest, wincing every time the wagon hit another bump.

Thomas quickly searched through his saddlebag and withdrew a small flask of ointment. Then he carefully opened the man's shirt. The sight made him sick. The man's abdomen was ripped and bloody, and muscles twitched in the open air.

Thomas struggled to keep from gagging as he opened his flask and daubed ointment on the wounds. A pungent aroma drifted away upon the breeze. Drooping heads perked up on the wagons nearby, and the injured man opened his eyes in surprise. Recognizing Thomas, he whispered, "Go!"

"I want to help." Thomas gestured with the flask.

"No!" came the reply, and the man feebly pulled his shirt back over his wounds. The wagon suddenly lurched and threw the man into the sideboard. He rolled back on the floor with a groan.

"Just take it easy," Thomas said softly. "Let me help you."

Reluctantly Jaroth allowed Thomas to reopen his shirt. Thomas spread a small amount of ointment upon the raw wounds. Almost immediately he could sense the man relaxing as his eyes closed and he breathed deeply.

"Thank you," Jaroth managed to croak, forcing a weak smile.

Thomas returned the smile and then noticed that the wagon had stopped. Several faces peered at him over the sideboard. The ointment's aroma had finally caught the attention of the entire caravan.

There was an angry shout from the head drover. He was making his way back along the wagons, shouting in his foreign tongue and shaking his fists. The men cowered and ran for their wagons.

"What is he saying?" Thomas asked.

"Just go!" Jaroth whispered fiercely. "If we are late to the quarry, there will be more beatings!"

Thomas nodded and helped the man to his feet.

Jaroth studied Thomas for a moment and then smiled. "Thank you!"

Thomas untied his mount and leaped into his saddle, raising his hand in salute. As the caravan slowly creaked down the path, Thomas thought, *I still don't know if these men are slaves, but they are being abused. This has to stop!*

The air was heavy inside the command center as the brothers eyed each other. "Look, James," Thomas shouted, "we have to make Samoth stop abusing his own people!"

"Thomas, it isn't my place to tell Samoth how to run his business!"

"We have to do something," Thomas countered. "That man was in terrible shape!"

"Don't we have enough suffering among our own men? Why must we worry about his?"

"Of course we have suffering in our camp, but not because you or I have beaten any of the men!"

James sighed heavily and sat down on his crate. He ran his fingers through his thick mop of hair. "I wish I could just be a commander of a military unit and not worry about the morality of my neighbors. I know you are right, brother. I spoke to Samoth yesterday of your concern, and now you report this incident. It seems to me our concern may actually be making their situation worse. And now you want me to confront Samoth again?"

Thomas bowed his head. He knew the burden of the camp was heavy enough for any man. The coolness of the community had not made life any easier. "I'm sorry. I didn't know you had spoken to anyone about this."

"Of course you didn't," James blurted. "I was in town getting supplies yesterday and saw Samoth, so I mentioned your concerns. He became defensive and told me to mind my own business. I meant to tell you when I got back, but other things crowded it out of my mind."

Thomas knew that James dealt with much more than just camp matters. Civilians and soldiers alike came to James for a decision or favor. Some came with complaints, just as he was doing right now. "I'm sorry, brother. I have only made your burdens heavier. Let me talk to Samoth myself about this matter, and you need no longer worry about it."

"No!" James spoke with alarm. "No, I don't think you should do that, Thomas. You don't get along well with Samoth. You never have!"

"We've had our differences, but I'll be polite. I'm sure things will go all right between us."

James frowned. "You have duties here, Thomas. The spearmen need practice on frontline defense again. I rely heavily upon you to work with the men. You have a better way with them than I do." James lowered his head. "Sometimes I think you would be a better commander than I."

Thomas knew that pride drove James to excellence. Of the two of them, James was the better swordsman, scholar, marksman, and fighter. He had always felt the need to prove himself to others. Under the current stress, pride was taking its toll. The cracks of humanity were beginning to show.

"James, I don't want your responsibilities," Thomas said quietly. "I'll go work with the men. If you don't want me to pursue this with Samoth, I won't."

"Good!" James said, relaxing. "I will address this. Just, please, stay away from Samoth."

"Yes, sir!" Thomas saluted smartly.

James's shoulders drooped. "Thomas, I don't like it when we squabble. I'll take care of this, I promise."

"All right," Thomas said, turning to go.

"Thomas," James said, "thank you for bringing this to my attention."

Thomas nodded and stepped through the tent flap.

James marveled at the tapestries that lined the hallway leading to Samoth's office, but when the chamberlain opened the office door, he caught his breath. Light spilled into the room from the cathedral windows lining one wall, while tapestries lined the others. Samoth sat behind a large, ornately carved mahogany desk with two large captain's chairs facing him. A huge circular rug covered the stone floor beneath the desk and chairs. Samoth rose, displaying an impeccable suit, clean-shaven, handsome face, and outstretched hand. There was a slight tightening of Samoth's jaw.

"James, to what do I owe the honor of your presence this day?" Samoth's words were smooth and graceful, and one could imagine that he meant them if not for the stiffening of his elegant features and the narrowing of his clear blue eyes.

James refused to be intimidated. He knew he too was an imposing figure. He was impeccably clean and neat, if not elegant, and his simple uniform enhanced his broad, powerful frame. When he wore the black helm of Amity, it sat upon his head as regally as any crown, and a sword rode in its sheath at his side. His dark eyes showed no emotion.

"Samoth, we need to talk," he said civilly.

Samoth stiffened visibly as he sat back down in his high-back chair, but he said amiably, "Of course, James. You know I am always at your service."

A wry smile crossed James's lips. "To be sure," he said, putting aside the polite lie. "I have men getting supplies downstairs."

"Good!" Samoth relaxed and gestured toward a cabinet stocked with the finest wines. "Something to drink?"

"Not this time, thanks."

"Well, at least have a chair."

James could tell that Samoth was on edge, and tensions might ease if he complied. Carefully he lowered himself onto one of the waiting chairs. "I've heard a report that some of your men were injured this morning. Do you know what happened or whether they need medical attention?"

Samoth bristled. "What business is it of yours? Do I ask about the welfare of your men?"

"Not unless they have caused a disturbance in Green Meadow," James countered. He smiled, thinking of the times when Samoth had brought news of one of his men's misdeeds.

"I have already taken care of this matter," Samoth said flatly.

"I thought I could offer medical services if you need them," James responded.

"We have our own medicine," Samoth said sullenly. Then he brightened, "Who did you say brought you news of the event?"

"A scout," James replied.

"When and where did he see these men?"

"This morning he crossed paths with a caravan of your hired men."

"Hired men?" Samoth looked puzzled. "Oh, yes! The hired men worked late last night, and this morning there was a scuffle. You know how tempers can flair when men get tired. I guess someone pulled a knife. We asked the man not to go out today, but you know how tough these men are. He wanted to go. Said he had to make some more money. He doesn't get paid to lie around."

James looked doubtful but said nothing.

"Believe me, James, everything is under control. Thank you for your concern," Samoth said coolly. They both rose from their chairs.

"Thank you for your time," James said without emotion. Without another word, he turned and strode quickly from the room.

As the door closed behind him, James knew that Samoth had been lying about the men being hired. So, Thomas was right. Samoth was using slave labor. *Well,* he thought, *how do I deal with this?*

For the next several days, James sought to keep Thomas and Samoth apart. He feared that someone would get hurt if they ever got together, but not everything was going badly for him. Green Meadow's coolness toward the garrison was beginning to thaw. Devia had enraged many of his competitors by implying that they would have to fend for themselves if trouble ever came to Green Meadow. Many had come to court James's favor as the threat of war loomed on the horizon.

James had hoped to find a compromise that satisfied nearly everyone—until Irene Stanley brought a delegation to his command center.

James had met Helberg and Irene Stanley before, and he knew they farmed on the western slope. The western slope was an area not really claimed by Emancipation or Amity or anyone else, so life there was a bit wild and unrestrained. Helberg and Irene were pioneers who were not afraid to settle new territory or live with some unsavory conditions. They didn't have a lot of neighbors on the western slopes, but they were very close to the ones they had. James knew these things about Helberg and Irene Stanley. What he didn't know was why Irene and several of her friends were in his command center.

"Mrs. Stanley," James said as he ushered Irene and her friends into his office. "What can I do for you?"

Irene was not a woman to waste words. She explained how several of the neighbors had been losing livestock and farm tools ever since the winter snow had melted. Things had become so bad that twenty men from the surrounding farms had gathered and gone in search of the thieves. "And the men have not come back!" Irene exclaimed.

Irene Stanley stood unflinching in front of James. She and her neighbors had come directly to him with their troubles, bypassing Master Devia altogether. Now, here she stood, expecting some kind of a response.

James shifted his weight uncomfortably. He wasn't sure what to do. "Ladies," he began, "I am not authorized to travel beyond the borders of Amity. You could speak to Master Devia. He is—"

"Devia." Irene stamped her foot impatiently on the canvas floor. "I wouldn't go to him if my life depended on it. I imagine he is behind all this."

"My husband doesn't trust Samoth or his father," said a pretty young woman in the group. "I came to Irene, and she came to you. We were hoping you might send some men out to look for our husbands."

Just then, George Greenwold stepped into the tent, saw the gathering, and turned to leave.

"George!" James cried. "Come in! I need your help."

George had to hear the story again, and one fact that stayed consistent, regardless of who told the tale, was that none of the women wanted to return to their homes. They were tired, hungry, and footsore. Though provisions were not plentiful in camp, James ordered a meal for the ladies from the larder, and in a short time their first grievance was amended. Housing was more difficult. They could not stay in the camp. After much discussion, James assigned George Greenwold the responsibility of finding housing for the women in Green Meadow.

Though the women had been fed and were about to find housing, James had not yet promised any specific action. The women continued to plead their case to James, until Irene Stanley stood and faced them. "The commander needs time to plan his strategy," she said. "We must allow him to do what he thinks is best." She turned and looked directly into James Stafford's eyes and said, "Thank you, Mister Stafford, for your cooperation." Turning, she led the women quietly from the commander's tent.

James sat alone, turning the news over in his mind. "Oh, Lord," he prayed, "what am I to do?"

CHAPTER 14

The Plot Thickens

Thomas sat alone in the narrow canyon, awaiting the caravan of wagons that carried stone to Green Meadow. Many questions raced through his mind. *Have I missed the caravan today? Is Samoth done hauling stone? Does he know I helped that injured man? Is the man going to be all right?*

Thomas came back to the present when his horse snorted and stamped the ground. There was a familiar sound of hooves on stone and wheels descending the steep path into the ravine.

Straining to see through the predawn darkness, Thomas watched as one wagon after another passed his position. He should have spotted the man he had assisted by now.

Thomas raised his hand and shouted, "Good morning, friends!"

"It's a trap!" someone yelled.

Thomas turned toward the voice and heard the angry hiss of a passing arrow.

"Run!" someone yelled.

Thomas obeyed without question. He plunged blindly into the trees and down the ravine. He finally stopped to listen for pursuit and could hear none.

His immediate danger past, Thomas began to think about what had just happened. *I've met this caravan multiple times,* Thomas thought, *but the black man I assisted is the only man to ever speak to me in my language. I wonder if he shouted the warning. If he did, he saved my life. If Samoth wanted me dead, what will he do to the man who just saved me?*

The more Thomas thought about his close encounter, the more convinced he was that the man who had shouted a warning to him was in terrible danger.

James watched as Thomas ran the men through their drills. He noticed that Thomas walked more slowly and had little enthusiasm for the activities. It seemed he was merely going through the motions. Even though Thomas acted lethargic, the men rallied around him as they practiced mock drills against invisible foes.

James signaled a bugler, whose clarion call brought the drills to a halt. "Take a breather, men," he called. "I need to speak with your commander." James beckoned to Thomas.

Thomas joined him, and the two men walked some distance before speaking. James broke the silence. "Thomas, what is bothering you?"

"Why do you ask?" Thomas queried, avoiding James's eyes.

"I know you too well, little brother. Something is eating you. Your mind is miles away. You might as well tell me what it is and get it out of your system."

Thomas hung his head. "I've disobeyed your orders," he said meekly.

"What are you talking about?" James demanded.

"I met the caravan again this morning," Thomas began.

"All right," James said. "What happened?"

"It was a trap, James. Someone tried to kill me. Someone in that caravan shouted a warning as an arrow shot past my head. I'm not certain, but I think the man who warned me was the same man I helped the other day. I ran away, James. I left that man alone. If he foiled someone's attempt on my life, what do you think that person will do to him?"

James's heart was beating fast. He rubbed the back of his neck to relieve the stress he felt. "That was too close, Thomas. Promise me you will never again meet that caravan alone!"

Thomas studied the ground and said meekly, "All right."

"It appears that this morning I came very close to losing the best commander I have. I cannot afford to lose you!"

Silence ensued, and finally Thomas asked, "Do you think Samoth is behind this?"

James was hurrying from the command center when he saw George Greenwold. "Greenwold!" he called. "Come with me. Our scouts have sighted enemy troops on the Western Slope. I want to check it out for myself."

Greenwold's face grew hard, but he said nothing. Both men slid to the bottom of the hill where their horses were tethered. Mounting quickly, they turned and rode west. Crossing a ravine, they climbed to the meadow. Devia's fortress stood dark and menacing against the horizon.

As they approached the citadel, James asked, "Were you able to find all the women a place to stay?"

"Aye, but that was a morbid task, and I wouldn't have done it for anyone but you."

James smiled. "You talk rough, but your heart is as tender as my brother's."

Greenwold ignored the comment, choosing rather to study Devia's fortress. "Devia's up to no good."

"Why do you say that, George?"

"This castle, in part. You know he'd like to be rid of your father and be the king of Amity himself."

"My father is not the king of Amity. He's more of a guardian than a king."

"You're blind, James. The Stafford name holds tremendous sway in Amity. Samoth and Devia both know it and hate you because of it. They'd love to rule Amity and see you hang, if they could."

"George, you are beginning to sound like my brother."

They were rounding the corner of Devia's fortress when they pulled up short. James saw the bodies of two men: naked, bloody, bloated, and hanging by the neck above the northern gates of the fortress. James and George stared in disbelief

"Whew!" whistled Greenwold. "What do you make of that?"

"It might have been disciplinary action," James said stiffly.

"Discipline?" George said quietly. "Looks more like a public execution to me."

"Me too," James said, nodding.

George sensed James's darkening mood and decided to pry no further. He must know something he wasn't sharing. Changing the subject, he asked, "How'd you hear about enemy troops over here?"

"I sent a few scouts out to look for Stanley and his neighbors. When they spotted troops, they returned to tell me."

"When was that?"

"This morning!"

George raised his eyebrows.

James continued, "The scouts didn't get far before spotting them. To stay out of sight, they circled wide to the south. There were troops everywhere; they estimated about two thousand men."

Greenwold whistled again. "That's a lot of men to move overnight!"

"I hope the scouts were guessing high."

"Were they Jabin's troops?"

"Our scouts didn't see the familiar red banners of Jabin's elite corps, but he has such a coalition that they may be his, even though they don't look like it."

Riding easily, they topped a small hill and stopped short. Rows of tents stretched away before them.

"Hiyah!" a voice yelled in the distance. Dark-clad soldiers emerged from their tents and leaped upon waiting mounts. In moments a fair-sized cavalry was racing toward the very hill where James and George sat.

The men turned their horses and fled.

James was near Devia's fortress before he slowed to look back. There was no visible sign of pursuit. In his mind he could see the foreign soldiers returning to their tents, laughing. His heart pounded, and his face turned red. He wondered if the men in Devia's fortress had seen their retreat. Were they laughing too?

They circled wide around the fortress walls, avoiding the grisly scene at the gates. Neither man spoke until they reached the command center and went inside.

"George, I need you to go to Stonewall. I'm calling for a council."

Greenwold said nothing, but his eyebrows arched high on his forehead.

James noticed and growled. "I've got to have direction! You are a forceful man, George. Convince every village master to meet at Stonewall as soon as possible."

"And what shall I tell your father?"

"Tell him everything. Don't hide anything from him!"

George nodded.

James suddenly grabbed George's arm. "Wait! Thomas thought something was amiss with that weapons shipment to Gaff, but I didn't take him seriously. I wish I had!"

"What's that?" George asked.

"Oh, it's probably nothing," James snapped. He grabbed some paper and opened a bottle of ink. Setting quill to paper, he scribbled a few words and handed the paper to Greenwold. "There," he said, "this is a summons to council. Show that to every village master. If they don't recognize my signature, they may recognize my horse."

"You're going to send me on the black mare of Stafford House?" George asked with incredulity. "None but a Stafford has ever sat astride that horse."

"Well, you will!" James said, returning Greenwold's gaze. "You have to convince everyone of our urgent need."

"Aye." George turned to leave.

"George," James called him back. "This could be a matter of life and death."

George frowned, but he could feel a chill run down his spine as he turned to go.

"Thomas, there are some things I want you to do for me," James said without looking up from the map stretched out before him.

"Yes, sir."

"I've sent Greenwold to Stonewall. He is instructed to call every village master to council. I hope he will help swing the council in our favor."

There was a pause, so Thomas asked, "Why are you calling Amity to council, James?"

"Sit down," James said, motioning. He then told Thomas of his morning's activities and how the scouts he'd sent to search for Stanley had spotted troops west of Green Meadow. Upon their return, he had taken Greenwold with him to check it out. "George and I were chased by several hundred men, but they stopped chasing us by the time we reached Devia's fortress. I've sent scouts out several times each hour to keep track of their numbers and movement."

Thomas grew sober. "Where and how many?"

"Come and look at the map," James suggested. "Each time a set of scouts comes in, they update up me on the enemy's numbers and position. Each X indicates approximately one hundred men and where they were last seen."

Already the map had an alarming number of Xs covering the Western Slope. Thomas eyed the map, and then his brother.

"We are closer to Gaff and his men than to Father," James said quietly. "But unfortunately Jabin's men are between Gaff and us. Our only hope is that Father will raise an army quickly and come to our rescue!"

The brothers looked at each other, and James said what he knew Thomas must be thinking. "I know! I should have moved sooner. It takes too long to muster an army and move it here from Stonewall. We'll have to delay everything as long as we can, play for time. Meanwhile, we have a community at risk."

"What do you want me to do?" Thomas asked.

"The troops must be on full alert tonight. Triple the guards. And there must be no campfires or torches."

"Yes, sir!"

"Thomas, I want you to explain to the men why we're increasing security, but keep it low-key. We don't need a panic."

"I understand. Is there anything else?"

"I'm issuing an order for the evacuation of all women and children from Green Meadow."

Thomas's eyebrows shot up. "Have you spoken to Devia?"

"No! When war is imminent, this is standard procedure. Devia should not have a problem with that."

"All right, whatever you say."

James looked at Thomas. "Prep the men, and get the camp in order. Remember—no campfires!"

"Right!"

"When you have the camp settled, go to Green Meadow and urge people to leave. Don't force them to go, but let them know that evacuation has been ordered."

"I'll do my best, sir," Thomas said and turned to leave.

"And Thomas," James called.

Thomas turned. "Yes?"

"Stay away from Devia's fortress."

"Why?"

"I gave you an order. Do you understand?"

"I understand the order, but I don't understand why."

"Maybe I can explain it someday. Maybe by then I'll understand it myself. Now, go! I want all campfires out before dark."

Loaded carts jostled over the rutted Greenway by morning's light. Many families were fleeing. Among them were Irene Stanley and her friends.

From a farmhouse near the road, a man watched the stream of humanity pass by, until he spied a familiar face. "Hey, Sam!" the man called. "What are you doing?"

"Leaving!"

"Why?"

"Commander Stafford ordered an evacuation last night. Jabin has an army camped just west of town."

"What right has Stafford to order us around? He's not the master of Green Meadow. He can order his troops around, but not me! Besides, there's a fortress if war does come."

"You mean Devia's dungeon?"

"Why do you call it that?"

"Did you see the men he hanged there yesterday?"

"What about it?"

"I'm thinking they disagreed with Devia on some small matter, so he hanged them. I don't want to be locked in the same cage with that madman."

"You don't say? Well, I reckon they had it coming."

"Suit yourself. I'm getting my wife and children out! If James thinks there is going to be a war, I don't want any part of it."

"There is no protection at Headwater except a flask of beer."

"I'm going farther. Thomas says there will be help at Zaraphath."

"Zaraphath! That's a long way. I'll take my chances right here with Devia and his fortress. He has the right idea. You know, it's uncanny, almost like he could see into the future. He started that structure this winter, and it looks like he's finished just in time."

"Looks planned to me."

"You don't like him, do you?"

"I don't trust him, and I'm leaving."

"You just watch! Devia will come out of this one better than anyone else, and I wouldn't be surprised if those who side with him won't benefit too."

CHAPTER 15

Breaking Point

James could hear Samoth coming long before he stormed into the command center. "What is the meaning of this, James? My town is in chaos!"

"Didn't anyone teach you that it's nice to be announced?" James snapped, coming to his feet.

"You ordered an evacuation. Do you think you own this place?"

"For your information, war is imminent. I have jurisdiction over the civilian population in time of war. I also must protect them. That, Samoth, is why I issued evacuation orders. I can't and won't try to enforce the order, but it's out there, and if people are wise, they will leave."

"Well, we'll just see about that!" Samoth shouted, turning to leave.

James grabbed Samoth's arm and spun him around. Poking a finger in Samoth's face, he shouted, "Now, you listen! You'll not interfere with anyone who wishes to leave! I'll provide a military escort, if that's what it takes."

Jerking his arm free, Samoth stomped out of the tent without another word.

It was only a matter of minutes before James sent a messenger asking Thomas to come to the command center. When Thomas arrived, James lost no time in spelling out what he wanted. "Thomas, I want you to make sure the road stays open from here to Headwater."

"Why, James? It shouldn't be blocked east, should it?"

"I'm not sure. Samoth was furious about the evacuation. He may try to prevent the civilians from escaping."

"Why would he care? He never seemed to care about the people before."

"I'm beginning to see that, Thomas. I'm afraid you've been right all along. I've played the fool! Do you forgive me for not taking you more seriously?"

"Of course. I might not be right, either."

"Well, we need to work together—now more than ever. Before you go, Thomas …"

"Yes?"

"What do you know about that boy from town who hangs around you all the time?"

"Not much, really. What do you want to know?"

"Do you trust him?"

"I guess so."

"Would you trust him with your life?"

"Yes, I think I would. Why?"

"I want to send him to Father. We can't wait a week for help. It takes too long to go through the council."

Thomas eyed James for a long moment. "How bad is it?"

"Look at the map." James beckoned him over. The Western Slope was a mass of black Xs. "Reports indicate that nearly ten thousand men have moved into the forest on the Western Slope!"

The color drained from Thomas's face. "We're outnumbered, ten to one."

"It may well be twenty to one before we're through," James said grimly.

Thomas was silent.

James continued. "Thomas, do you think the lad could reach Father and impress upon him our need for reinforcements?"

"I'm sure he could," Thomas responded.

"Good! Bring him in. I'll get a horse for him."

Thomas turned and strode out into the morning sunshine.

Thomas and five other men formed an escort for a large number of men and women fleeing from Green Meadow. These refugees had been mocked and ridiculed for leaving town, but with James's warning, they had packed their belongings and fled. Now, as they neared Headwater, they could see lots of other refugees camped along the road.

It didn't take long to see why these people had stopped where they had. Near Headwater, fences lined the Greenway, separating the road from the showy homes and fields of the local farmers. At this location some rogues had overturned several wagons and blocked the road.

Thomas and his companions rode forward to confront the thugs blocking the road. "Clear the road!" Thomas ordered. His men advanced toward the overturned carts. There were twenty men visible, and more were hidden behind the carts. Some were armed with clubs, and a few even had swords.

"Are you going to make us?" shouted a surly man who acted as a spokesman for the rabble.

"I have orders to see that these people are free to pass," Thomas said evenly.

"We have orders to see they stay!"

"Who issued your orders?" Thomas asked.

"It makes no difference. Now, don't come any closer," the surly man warned.

Thomas rode forward with confidence. The men beside him were relaxed but ready. At a single flick of his wrist, the horses bolted. Few could describe what had happened. One moment there were two groups of men—the next, only one.

The fight was over almost before it started. Six men lay dead upon the ground, the surly spokesman among them. The rest of the rabble readily dropped their weapons in submission.

The wagons were moved, the road was cleared, and the people were allowed to pass. The ruffians who survived were given shovels and ordered to bury the dead.

When Thomas and his guard finally parted company with the refugees, it was a subdued group that passed. Those who had fled their homes had witnessed the fearful efficiency of military training, yet tears filled many eyes. With the growing threat of war, people knew that they might never see these six gallant horsemen again.

When Thomas and his men returned to camp, James asked to see him. "We've been summoned to a parley," James said as Thomas entered the command center.

"Who called for a parley?" Thomas asked.

"I'm not sure if it was Devia or Jabin."

"You're not going, are you?"

"Why not?"

"It's a trap, James! If they can lure you into their web, they will have you. It would cost a thousand men their lives if you were captured on the battlefield, and they know it."

"You rate me pretty high, little brother, but I see your point. I thought it sounded like a good idea."

"You couldn't possibly reason with those men."

"No, and I could never make any deals with them. I'm not authorized by the council to do so. But talking also takes time, and I want to buy all the time I can. Maybe reinforcements will come soon."

"Well, don't buy any time with your life," Thomas demanded unhappily.

"All right, all right!"

James watched as Thomas settled onto the crate opposite his desk. "Are you all right?" he asked.

"I think so," Thomas responded. "It bothers me that we killed six men today."

"I'm sorry too, but I gave you an order, and you carried it out. If there's any complaint, I'll deal with it."

"So, tell me about this parley," Thomas queried. "When and where is it supposed to take place?"

"Tomorrow morning at Devia's fortress," James answered.

"Who set the location?"

"I did."

"You? Why at the fortress?"

"It's the most visible location, and I wanted all parties to be there. Look, I know you are unhappy about this, but talking does take time, and maybe help will come."

"What kind of help can Father send on such short notice?"

"I hope he sends Seagood and the mounted guard."

Thomas was silent for a moment and then asked, "Did you ask for Seagood?"

"No."

"What if Father doesn't send him?"

"Then I've misjudged Father, and we are going to be alone."

Sentries were constantly monitoring the western meadow. Thomas rode with three other men. Though he was off duty for a few hours to get some rest, Thomas was too keyed up to sleep. Instead he'd spelled a man who had been on duty for thirty-six hours and needed some sleep. This group of four sentries would ride a circuit that took them by Devia's fortress and then west into the meadow. The foursome would split, two headed north and two south. They would monitor enemy forces and then circle back and meet again at camp.

They were near Devia's fortress when Thomas remembered James's warning to avoid it. Turning to his partner, he asked, "Scrubby, what is at the fortress?"

"What do you mean, captain?"

"I had orders from Commander Stafford not to go near the fortress. Is there something dreadful there that he is trying to spare me from seeing?"

"Yes, sir," Scrubby responded. "Two chaps were hanged from the gateposts several days ago, and they ain't been cut down. They are starting to rot, and maggots are falling out of them onto the ground."

A chill ran down Thomas's spine. He could feel his pulse hammer in his veins. "Did you know them?"

"No, sir."

"Was there anything special about either of them?"

Scrubby pondered a moment and then said, "Well, one chap was real dark. I hadn't seen any like him around here."

Thomas shook his head in disbelief. The man he had helped in the caravan had been of dark complexion.

Scrubby stared at Thomas and asked, "Is something wrong, sir?"

Thomas didn't answer directly. "Are they still there?" he asked.

"I reckon. They were the last time I rode circuit. I think they're going to leave them there. You can see for yourself in a moment. We're almost there."

They turned the corner and headed down the north side of the fortress. The night was dark, but Thomas didn't have to see the bodies to know they were there. The odor was unbearable. The others hurried by, but Thomas lingered. "So, that's the way you want to play, is it?" he muttered to himself.

"It's pretty bad, captain. I'd come away from there if I was you." Scrubby tried not to gag as he spoke.

Thomas was grim when he joined the others, and all he would say was, "I've got an appointment with Samoth first thing in the morning."

After his return to camp, Thomas could not shake the memory of the men hanging from Devia's fortress. As he still had an hour free before briefing, he turned his horse back toward Green Meadow. He rode slowly through the morning's growing light. *What can I do?* he wondered.

Rounding the corner of Devia's fortress, Thomas could see more clearly the scene that had been hidden in the dark. The men's sunbaked bodies were bloated and barely recognizable, and the smell was worse. *I should have stayed and tried to rescue the man who warned me,* Thomas thought. *Instead I ran, and these men died.*

As Thomas stared at the bodies, he felt certain that he was being watched from the towers above. "All right!" he said aloud, startled by the sound of his own voice. "I can at least bury my friends."

The bodies were high off the ground. Circling beneath them, Thomas steadied his mount and crawled slowly to his knees. Then, ever so slowly, he came to his feet in the saddle.

"Steady boy," he said softly to his horse. With his sword, he could just nick the rope above the dark man's head. "Steady," he said soothingly to his horse. With a sudden flick of his wrist, the rope snapped, and the dark body plunged to the ground.

Startled by the sudden motion, the horse bolted, and Thomas fell, head over heels. Dusting himself off, Thomas caught his frightened mount and began calming it with soft words until it regained its composure.

"Maybe I should bury one at a time," he said, ruefully eyeing the second body swaying in the air.

Thomas found a rock large enough to tie his horse's reins to so it would not bolt again. Then with one deep breath, he stooped and lifted what remained of his friend to the saddle. Turning his back to the fortress, he walked away, knowing he made a perfect target for anyone on the wall. "Kill me if you want," he muttered, "but I have to do this for my friend."

The ground was rocky, but Thomas managed to chip out a shallow grave and ease the dead man into the hollow. He felt so responsible for this man's death. Remorse filled Thomas's mind as he began to toss dirt over the body, and perspiration trickled down his brow.

"You did a nice job, Thomas."

Startled, Thomas looked up into the leering face of Samoth. Even as he reached for his sword, Thomas heard a boot scrape on the rocks behind him, and all went dark.

CHAPTER 16

Realization

All officers were required to meet at the command center each morning for the daily briefing. When Thomas failed to appear, James asked, "Has anyone seen Thomas?"

An aide quickly answered, "No, sir."

"He's always here for briefing."

"I can check his quarters, sir."

"He's not there!" James growled. "I already checked. I really need him!"

"Maybe he's still on circuit, sir."

"He's not scheduled for circuit," James said.

"I know that, sir, but he rode circuit during the night."

"He what?" James roared.

"VanWickle had been on for thirty-six, sir, and Captain said he could take a breather. So, Captain rode in his place."

"Did he ride past the fortress?" James asked.

"That's their route, sir."

"Never mind about Thomas, then. I know where he is."

"Where will I find him, sir?"

"I doubt we will," James responded grimly.

"Sir?"

James appeared to shrivel and age before the startled attendant's eyes. "Are you all right, sir?" the young man asked.

"No!" James snapped. "I am not all right. Nothing is all right!" He turned on his heel and strode away.

Ten riders galloped toward the gates of Devia's fortress. They did not know what they would find, but all were armed and prepared for trouble. Rounding the last bend, James checked his gait. It was time for the parley, but no one else was there.

James noticed that there was only one body hanging near the gate. "It's gone!" he said aloud.

"What's gone, sir?"

"The dark body that was hanging here," James said.

"I wish the other was gone too. Whew, what a smell!"

"But why would it be gone?" James asked.

"I guess someone wanted to give it a proper burial."

"A proper burial," James murmured. "That sounds like Thomas."

Leaping from his saddle, James strode to the gate and pounded as loudly as he could. "Samoth!" he shouted. "Come out here! If this is a parley, where is everyone?"

Silence met their ears.

"Samoth!" James roared. "What happened to the other body?"

James's men grew uneasy. Dozens of archers might be waiting with fingers upon taught strings, yet they stayed by their commander. They had no idea why the missing body troubled him so.

James grew frantic. Screaming at the top of his lungs, he pummeled the heavy doors of the fortress with his fists. Several of his men leaped from their mounts and pulled him away. "Don't break your bones on these heavy doors, sir. It won't make Samoth come out if he's not willing."

Leaping forward, James tore from their clutches and raced back to the heavy gates. Drawing his dagger, he screamed, "Traitor!" And with a madman's strength, he plunged his knife into the silent wood, burying the blade clear to the hilt.

The men of the garrison had marched to a position west of Green Meadow during the night and had taken possession of a hill overlooking the main road into Green Meadow from the west. That road bisected the town into north and south and ran along the northern side of Devia's fortress. After fortifying their positions, they stood fidgeting in the predawn darkness. Everyone knew by now that yesterday's parley had been nothing more than a ruse. Thomas was missing, and James was depressed and angry. Every moment the forces of Jabin grew larger, and help had not come.

When James turned to face his men, he looked haggard and worn, but his voice rang sharp and clear. "Gentlemen!" he called, and every ear grew attentive.

"You have left home, family, and friends. The hordes of Jabin are poised to destroy all that you know, and you are the only barrier between those you love and the destruction Jabin will bring."

His clipped words fell like frost on a cold winter's morning.

"Yet we are not alone." James's voice warmed, and so did his men's hearts. "There is comfort and strength for those who are in Christ Jesus! If you seek His refuge, He will be your shield, whether in life or death. Take a moment to speak with the Lord. Be sure you are secure in Him."

A low murmur spread through the lines of men. Some men addressed the Almighty for the first time in their lives, asking for His strength and comfort. Others spent their time renewing a lifelong friendship.

Moments passed before James spoke again. "Gentlemen," he said, and the formation grew silent. "You have not always received praise from home or family. You have not always been accepted well in this community."

There was a slight stir among the men.

"But you are the best soldiers in the world! With less, I would be afraid to go into battle, but I am not afraid! I know who stands beside me, and you will not let me down!"

Every man squared his shoulders and stood a little taller.

"Help is on the way," James called, "but now duty calls! We must hold the enemy at bay, and we shall!"

The meadow shook when the garrison, as if one mighty man, shouted their response.

James had placed his men strategically so the enemy would pay a heavy price to enter Amity. Still, as water flows around rocks in a river, Jabin's masses, outnumbering James's more than ten to one, managed to flow around the pockets of resistance the garrison had formed. James knew the fight was futile, but he knew they had to try.

James could not have known that anyone would wander into Green Meadow on the morning of battle. That a young woman who had been away tending her ailing grandmother would return today was inconceivable.

It was early morning when Jennifer came to Green Meadow. She went straight to her parents' home, only to find it empty, looted, and burned. She walked down abandoned streets and wondered where everyone had gone. She had no way of knowing that many of her friends had fled to Zaraphath some days earlier, or that the other civilians in town had fled into Devia's fortress during the night and were now locked away, safe and sound.

She was unsure where to go, when she heard a loud shout from the meadow west of town. Hurrying toward the sound, she came to the last row of houses before the grasslands of the Western Slope appeared. Creeping into someone's ruined garden, she peered over the fence and saw the banner of Amity fluttering in the wind on a small hill just west of town. Line after line of dark-clad men rushed up the hill, only to fall in a hail of arrows. Further down the hill a small band of men battled with the dark hordes. She could hear the clash of steel and the screams of men and horses.

Not knowing where to go, Jennifer remained hidden behind the garden fence and watched as men fought, hour after hour. When the sun passed midday, Jennifer realized that something had changed. The men on the hill were moving. They continued to fight the enemy, but they were making an orderly retreat and coming her way. Since the town had been looted during the night, and little of any value remained, Green Meadow had not been the scene of much action during the day. A few soldiers from both sides had ridden through town from time to time, but she had remained out of sight. Now, with the fiercest fighting moving her way, she wondered, *Where can I go? Where will I be safe?*

As the sounds of war grew ever closer, she began to see the battle in much greater detail. She could hear the cries of men and the gurgle of throats gasping for air. She heard the rip of flesh as swords slashed through human bodies. The fighting was close—so close that she wondered when they would smash the fence behind which she was hiding.

Suddenly Jennifer heard a cry and turned to see two strange men pointing at her. She leaped from her hiding spot and raced quickly through another yard and out into a street. That street had been empty this morning, but it was empty no longer. Nearly fifty men in strange dark garb were at the south end of the street. Jennifer turned north and ran with all the speed she could toward Devia's fortress. She heard horses galloping on the street behind her, and she darted between some buildings. Flattening herself against a wall, she watched as several horsemen galloped past. She turned and darted from behind the buildings, turning her steps once again toward the fortress.

Fighting was growing heavy in Green Meadow. The men of Amity were retreating back toward the command center east of town, but they gave ground slowly. Fighting from house to house, street to street, and yard to yard, they made Jabin pay for every inch of ground he acquired. Jennifer managed to stay a few blocks ahead of the worst fighting until she finally reached Devia's fortress. She thought it strange that none of the dark, swarthy men she had been evading were anywhere near the fortress. She also thought it strange that no arrows flew from the fortress high above.

There were no gates in the solid southern or eastern walls of the fortress, but finally Jennifer found a gate in the northern wall. Pounding frantically on the heavy wooden doors, she begged and pleaded to be let in, but there was no response from within. In despair, she fell against the door, curled into a tight little ball, and wept.

James and several of his men had taken refuge behind a stone wall for a much-needed breather. Glancing around, he realized that this wall had recently been someone's home. Taking a sip of water from his pouch, James thought about his losses today and wondered if they would have been less had Thomas been here. *Oh, Thomas,* he thought, *where did you go? What could have become of you?* At that moment he spied his messenger dashing toward the battle on his pony. James stepped into view and waved the man over. "What are you doing here? This is no place for you or your pony!"

"I've good news, sir!" the envoy panted. "Seagood and the mounted guard have been spotted and are only moments away!"

"Great news!" James whooped, pounding his messenger on the back.

"I did see something strange, sir," the envoy continued.

"Be quick, man!" James ordered.

"As I rounded the fortress a moment ago, a young lady was trying to get inside, and they wouldn't open for her."

"What?" James roared. With blinding revelation, James finally understood why Thomas had been so determined to help the helpless and protect the downtrodden. A thought flashed through his mind: *I'll do right by you, brother!*

"Give me your horse," James demanded.

"What?" the startled envoy asked.

"I'll take the girl to the command center."

"But, sir …" The envoy's words were lost in bedlam as Jabin's men suddenly overran their position. After striking down several of the enemy, James leaped onto his messenger's pony and raced through the fighting.

Thundering toward Devia's fortress, he spied the girl huddled against the door. He spurred the pony faster.

Jennifer looked up to see a rider bearing down on her, and she assumed the worst. Gathering up her skirts, she turned and ran along the fortress walls. She doubted she could escape, but she dared not wait to face this rider unarmed.

The rider closed in quickly on the fleeing girl and then checked his gait to match her pace. Gripping the saddle tightly, he leaned far to one side, scooped Jennifer off her feet, and heaved her over the saddle. Turning back onto the road, he made a straight path toward the command center.

Not to be taken so easily, Jennifer fought, squirmed, scratched, and bit until the rider nearly lost his grip on her. "Take it easy!" he shouted. "I'm on your side!"

When she heard the familiar speech of Amity, Jennifer ceased to struggle. Craning her neck to look upon her captor, she recognized the handsome captain of the garrison whom so many of the girls in Green Meadow had secretly longed to meet these last months. He was dirty, and heavy stubble covered his jaw, but there was no doubt: this was James Stafford.

Jennifer smiled to herself and relaxed for the first time since she had returned from her grandmother's house. If the other girls only knew that she was being rescued by the handsome and daring Prince Charming! Her pleasant reverie lasted only a moment, for she heard the hiss of an arrow and felt James stiffen. Then she heard another, and another.

James's face turned pale, and his strong grip on Jennifer began to weaken. Without being driven, the pony slowed to a trot and finally to a walk. By this time, Jennifer's feet were nearly touching the ground.

Slipping from James's grasp, Jennifer touched the earth, turned, and gasped. Four arrows protruded from James's back.

"I've been hit," he whispered. His eyes were wide, and his skin had grown pale. Slowly he slid from the saddle. "Ride ... for ... help." He gestured weakly toward a canvas tent on a rocky bluff some distance away.

"But—" she stammered.

"Go." He sighed and dropped to his knees.

With sudden determination, Jennifer grabbed the pony's reins and swung into the saddle. Maybe she could get help.

Picking her way down a stone-covered slope, she spied a band of dusty horsemen galloping up the ravine. Not sure whether they were friend or foe, she hesitated, but only for a moment. James needed help. Slapping her heels into the startled pony's ribs, she made straight for the riders.

Seagood and his men had seen the command center some distance back and were rapidly making their way toward it. Then they spied a girl charging toward them as if in full attack, though she wore no armor and carried no gear.

"Whoa, missy!" Rudy called as he grabbed the bridle of her heaving pony.

"Please, please!" the girl sobbed. "Commander Stafford has been shot! He's on the hill!" She pointed vaguely behind her.

"Wart, take this girl to the command center. The rest of you, with me!" Rudy's voice thundered.

In a blur of dust and sweat-soaked horseflesh, they were off.

Jennifer covered her face, wondering if she had done the right thing. Suddenly she realized that everything was quiet.

Looking up, she saw a thin boy holding the reins of her tired pony. He gently soothed her mount into quiet submission. "Rudy says I need to take you to that tent up there."

Jennifer allowed her eyes to follow his gesture to where a canvas tent stood on a rocky bluff. Weary beyond belief, she nodded and quietly slid from the pony's saddle.

Wart offered his hand and seemed relieved when she modestly refused. Together they walked up the slope past sentries who looked too tired to challenge them.

Everyone in camp knew that James was dying. Jabin's forces had overrun nearly every position that James had protected, except one. James's command center still controlled the main road into Amity, and if this last bastion fell, Jabin would sweep into Amity like a flood, bringing destruction to an unsuspecting land.

When James had been carried back to the command center, many men would have thrown in the towel, but not these men. They had fought to keep Amity safe, and with the coming of Seagood, they persevered. The battle raged for days, with Rudy shouting orders and men fighting a battle they were sure to lose. Still, they would not quit. Some prayed that help would come on the morrow; others hoped their end would be swift and painless.

Men watched in dismay as Jabin's forces set fire to more houses, fields, and forest.

"Looks like a storm is brewing," a sentry commented as a scout passed his position.

"Good! Rain might put out some of Jabin's fires. There won't be much left if this keeps on."

"Not much left now! Say, what do you hear about Commander Stafford?"

"He's still hanging on!"

"That is one tough man," the sentry said. "I hope when my time comes, I don't have to linger like that. I guess though, if he can do it, maybe I can too."

The bellow of horns woke those of the garrison who remained. Grabbing their weapons, they scrambled to battle positions. Across the ravine, long columns of unfamiliar men stormed the sleeping hordes of Jabin. James's men shook their heads. Were they dreaming? Who was this strange new ally? Some thought they were seeing angels.

There was a hoarse cry when someone spotted the banner of Amity snapping in the wind. Those who had prayed for help knelt to thank the Lord, while others merely wept tears of joy. It seemed their tribulation was over. Help had arrived!

CHAPTER 17

One Final Mission

John Stafford did not notice the war-ravaged countryside or the tight grip of his wiry guide around his waist. James was dying, and no other thought could enter his troubled mind.

The lad, nicknamed Wart, suddenly slipped from behind the saddle and, motioning to John, started to scramble up a steep slope that led to a large canvas tent at the top of the hill. John dismounted and followed as fast as his legs would carry him.

Two sentries jumped to attention when John entered the tent. It was dark inside, and John paused for a moment to let his eyes adjust. As features began to take shape, he recognized one of the sentries. "How bad is he, Mark?" John asked.

"He's bad, sir. I'm glad you're here!"

John clapped his hand on Mark's shoulder, took a deep breath, and lifted the panel leading to the inner room.

Oil lamps dimly illumined the inner quarters. Men stood quietly clustered here and there. John recognized Seagood at once and made his way toward him. A young man he didn't recognize lay writhing under Seagood's care. *Is that my son?* he wondered.

The young man thrashed violently while Seagood tried to restrain him. At John's approach, Seagood yielded, placing James's clenched fist between his father's thick, warm fingers.

Kneeling, John studied the young man before him. His son's teeth were clenched, his eyes shut tight. *Yes,* John thought. *James fought with life. It would be like him to fight with death as well.*

"I'm here, Son," John said aloud.

For a brief moment, James opened his eyes, and John witnessed the terror of a haunted soul. The grim reaper was stalking his son, and he was powerless to protect him. "James!" John called. "I am your father!"

James turned, recognition in his eyes. His body relaxed, and he tried to speak.

John laid a finger across his lips. "Save your strength, Son," he whispered.

Anger flashed across James's dark eyes. "Thomas …" he managed to gasp.

John leaned closer, and Seagood edged nearer the cot, keen interest sparkling in his eyes.

"Yes," John said. "What about Thomas?"

James's lips moved, and John leaned even closer. "What?" he asked.

James grimaced as pain sent a tremor through his entire body. With visible effort to gather his strength, James managed to whisper, "Kidnapped!" Then he fell back on the cot, exhausted.

John was mute with shock. He looked at Seagood for an explanation but found nothing. "Kidnapped?" he heard himself ask. "What do you mean? Kidnapped by whom, and why?"

He looked back at James, but all was silent. The young man was relaxed and quiet: content, as if he had fulfilled some great mission. Pain no longer furrowed his brow, and his hand relaxed between John's fingers. He'd found peace.

"James, what do you mean kidnapped?" John asked once more, but there was no reply.

Jennifer sat behind a tree, watching and listening to every sound that emitted from the command center. Above the rhythm of her pounding heart, she could hear voices. Wiping her tears away, she watched as a young man scrambled up the rocky slope.

"Master Stafford!" the man cried as he hurried for the tent.

A huge guard stepped into the courier's path. "What is it, man? Lord Stafford's son has just died! Must you barge in on his grief?"

"I'm sorry, sir!" the messenger panted, "but Gaff has come! The enemy is in disarray!"

"Gaff!" the sentry shouted. "That is good news!" Quickly he pulled the envoy into the tent.

Seconds later, men poured from the tent, scrambling down the hill to mount their horses. Within moments they were thundering toward the distant clash of battle.

In their wake, everything grew strangely quiet. Jennifer watched the exhausted sentries settle back into their positions. Everything seemed deserted.

Angry thoughts raced through her head. *How can John Stafford leave his departed son so quickly?* But grief replaced her anger. *James Stafford is dead, and it's my fault. If I'd never come back to Green Meadow, James would still be alive.* She buried her head in her arms and wept.

Gradually her tears subsided. Looking around, she realized that the sound of battle had grown dim. Over the past days she'd grown immune to the clash of weapons, for her ears had been tuned to the moans and cries from inside James's tent. That man was her reality, and he was dead because of her.

She stole a glance at the tent and tried to stifle the secret longing in her heart. She wanted to see James one last time, but she supposed the sentries would prevent her.

She sat still for a bit longer, until finally desire overcame her better judgment. She silently stood and looked around. The sentries stationed at the bottom of the hill had not noticed her movement. Slowly she made her way to the door of the tent.

Holding her breath, she listened. She could hear nothing from within. Timidly, she raised the flap and slipped inside.

The sudden darkness startled her, and she stood motionless until her eyes adjusted to the dim light. She was in a lounge lined with bunks. Cautiously, she glanced at each bunk, half expecting to see a soldier asleep, or worse yet, awake and watchful. The room was empty.

Quietly she crossed the floor to the next flap. Pulling the flap back ever so slightly, she peeked inside. Several oil lamps still burned, illuminating the room with a dim light. She expected someone to be standing guard, but she saw no one.

Breathing deeply, she tried to calm the pounding of her heart. *What will they do to me if I'm caught?* she wondered. She swallowed hard and stepped into the room. She'd come this far, and she wasn't going to turn back now. After all, she only wanted one last look.

Her boldness faded as fast as it had come. This room was so foreign to her. It was stark and masculine. There were no adornments on the walls, no light from outside, and no curtains—only two crate chairs, a crate desk, and one cot.

Her eyes remained fixed upon the cot, and her feet were drawn irresistibly toward the sheet-covered body that lay there. Hardly daring to breathe lest she awaken someone in the camp, she knelt beside the cot.

Slowly, fearfully, she drew back the sheet. She closed her eyes, dreading to see death, yet curiosity drove her on. Opening her eyes, she breathed a sigh of relief. James's face was not drawn or twisted in agony or pain. It was peaceful, as if he were only sleeping.

Jennifer marveled. James was not defeated. Much the opposite! He merely appeared to be resting after winning a great battle.

The remorse of her own soul began to diminish as she looked upon his sweet repose. Gently her finger strayed to his face. It was cool but not cold or clammy. The rough bristles grown during days of unending pain lay thick upon his solid jaw. She felt an ache in her heart to do something for this man who had given himself for her.

Suddenly motivated, she stood. Looking around the room, she spied a wash basin and pitcher. Gathering them, she found a few clean bandages. "These will do," she said aloud, and her voice startled her. But she had purpose now, and she lent herself to the task at hand.

The grime that covered James was soon washed away, along with days of sweat and dust from the battlefield. She remembered the gallant young commander, clean-shaven and handsome. She was at a loss for only a few moments and soon was rummaging about the room as if she were in charge of the entire grounds. In a small box beneath the rickety desk, she found a small leather pouch in which were a razor and several personal items.

Razor in hand, she set to work. She had done this for her father many times since he'd lost his arm in the battle at Great Bend last summer. Soon she was wiping the last bit of suds from James's face.

Carefully she sponged her cloth over James's hair and smoothed it into position. Lovingly she washed his hands and gently laid them upon his chest. She was so involved with her task that she had no idea how long she had been in the tent or what was happening in the world outside.

She left the sheet rolled down, exposing her handiwork. Stepping back, she viewed the results and was pleasantly surprised. James appeared to be sleeping peacefully upon his cot, hands folded upon his breast, without a care or fear in the world.

Her heart suddenly skipped a beat. "Voices," she whispered. Trembling, she glanced about the room. There were no cubbyholes, no closets, not a single place to hide. She stepped to the door, hoping to slip out unnoticed, but to her dismay, at that very moment, the outer tent flap was pulled aside, and several men entered the outer room.

Dropping the flap, Jennifer stood frozen in place.

"Let's make plans here," she heard a tired but resonant voice say.

There was the growing sound of more and more voices outside. Obviously, a fairly large group of men had come back to the tent. *Why didn't I hear them coming?* she wondered.

"I wish we'd caught Jabin!" spoke an unfamiliar voice.

"Me too, but his party is greatly diminished," said another.

"More's the pity," said the first. "The slain were probably good men who had fallen under bad leadership."

"I suppose that's true."

"Excuse me, sir!" A different voice spoke softly. "Is this where James …?"

"Son, don't trouble John with that just now."

"It's all right, Gaff. Frankly, James is closer to my heart just now than deciding what to do about Jabin."

"We must be swift, John. We can't let that weasel go far, or we'll all pay dearly."

"I know the wisdom of what you say, but grief speaks loudest to my heart just now. Come, Mathias. I'll take you to him."

The flap to the inner room began to open. Jennifer stepped quickly to one side, and a sentry stepped through, holding the flap open for John to enter. As John stepped into the room, the sentry stepped back and brushed against Jennifer.

"What the—" he sputtered, dropping the flap and drawing his blade.

Swords cleared their sheaths, and Jennifer fell to her knees, crying, "Mercy! I meant no harm!"

"What are you doing here?" the sentry snapped, dragging the poor girl to her feet.

"Mark, be gentle!" John demanded. "Who are you, young lady?"

Rudy stepped forward. "She's the girl who told us James had been wounded!"

John's countenance softened. "Please, everyone, leave us alone. I'd like to talk with this girl in private for a moment." He motioned the others to leave.

People reluctantly obeyed, but there arose such a cacophony of voices in the outer lobby that Jennifer could barely hear herself think.

John moved to the door and addressed the group. "Gentlemen, would you please go outside?"

There was a good deal of grumbling, but eventually the confusion subsided. Jennifer trembled, as John now turned his full attention upon her.

"Don't worry, lass," he said softly. "No one is going to harm you."

"I'm so sorry!" she stammered as tears sprang afresh in her eyes.

"Don't cry," John said softly. "Can you tell me what you know of my son's death?"

The man was so kind and gentle. Jennifer wiped her eyes, but she could not look into his face. She felt his hands on her shoulders and finally began to speak. "Your son learned his kindness from you," she began. She looked up to see a rueful smile cross John's lips, warming his expression.

"Thank you. My son did not show kindness to everyone, but I'm glad he did to you."

Jennifer bowed her head, afraid to trust her voice. She knew it was kindness that had brought James to her rescue at the fortress gates. He had saved her life, only to lose his own.

During her silence, John turned toward James's cot. "What?" he whispered.

Jennifer followed his gaze. James was clean, shaven, and appeared to be sleeping.

"What happened?" John asked, incredulous at the transformation.

"I—" Jennifer stammered. "I wanted to see him one last time, and I wanted to do something for him." Her mouth felt dry. She felt that her words formed a feeble excuse.

John strode quickly to the cot and knelt beside his son. Jennifer watched from a distance, feeling awkward and very much alone.

John knelt silently for what seemed to Jennifer a very long time, but when he finally turned to her, tears were streaming down his cheeks. His voice broke, and it seemed all he could do to whisper, "Thank you!"

She blushed and dropped her eyes.

"You must have loved him very much?" John asked.

Her eyes glistened as she looked into the eyes of the man before her. "Yes, but only from afar."

John rose and wrapped an understanding arm about her shoulders. "That is how everyone loved him," he said softly. "He never allowed anyone close enough to really know him."

Jennifer could sense a father's regret.

"What happened?" John asked gently.

Slowly and carefully, Jennifer described her mission away from home, her return, the frightening battle, her fear, her rejection at the fortress, her deliverance, James's wounds, and her brief stay in the camp.

John's eyes clouded as she spoke, and when she finished, he pulled her into his arms and held her tight against his chest. She could hear the steady beating of his heart. Imperceptibly at first, but with growing emphasis, she could feel great spasms shake his body. Hot tears splashed into her hair from above, and she felt her own tears run unchecked down her cheeks. Together they poured out their grief and loss.

After tears had drained their anguish, they pulled apart, and neither felt embarrassed. "Dear child," John said. "You have done a lovely thing for my son. You have also done a lovely thing for me. Thank you for sharing my pain and my loss."

CHAPTER 18

Last Rites

After Jennifer left the tent, John knelt beside James's body and prayed. "Lord, I came into this world with nothing, and I shall leave the same way. All that I have is from You. Take my firstborn son and cradle him in Your arms. Keep him safe until one day I shall see him again in the glory of Your kingdom. Amen."

John rose and stepped from the tent. Down the hill from the command center, he could hear a boisterous conversation taking place. "We should go after Jabin now!" one voice demanded. "He'll do more damage if we leave him alone!"

"He'll be back! We beat him badly last year at Great Bend, but he's already back this spring."

"I agree," chimed in another. "He'll cause grief wherever he is. If he's not disturbing us, he will be destroying someone else. We can't allow him to continue unchecked."

After scrambling down the hill, the gathering encouraged John to join the conversation. "I dare not say too much," John said flatly. "My words could be construed as wanting vengeance for James's death."

"John, be reasonable," Gaff growled. "From what we've heard about when and where James was attacked, this tragedy could more aptly be laid at Devia's feet."

"As could the kidnapping of Thomas," another said hotly.

"We don't know where to lay the blame for that," John said coolly. "In fact, we don't know if James knew something, or if he was guessing. He died before he could tell us more."

"Just the same, we must pursue and, if possible, eliminate Jabin. The man is a terror to mankind, and he has to be stopped!"

"If we remove him from the scene, another just as bad will arise to take his place," Stafford said. "The human heart is wicked beyond all measure."

"John, I know that," Gaff grumbled. "But we have to move while we can, before Jabin rebuilds and strikes again."

"Very well," John said. "I will abide by the decision of this council, with one condition."

"Good," Gaff said. "What is the condition?"

"I will go with you, but my men must choose for themselves whether they will go or stay."

"What?" Gaff exploded. "You can't be serious! We are going to need every available man to chase that villain out of the mountains."

"I know," John said quietly. "But my men signed up for the protection of Amity, not for world adventures."

"John, you give your people too much freedom and too many choices."

"I don't want an unwilling soldier behind or beside me in the thick of battle. I only want those who are committed to the cause. I can't afford to have dissenters among my men!"

Gaff shook his head. "All right! I just hope we don't pay too dearly for your folly."

"Gaff, you will see. More can be accomplished with a few who are committed than with multitudes who don't care about the cause."

Inquiry was made throughout the garrison about Thomas's disappearance, and finally two men came forward who had ridden with him the last night he was seen.

"Yes, sir, we rode a circuit with Thomas that night," one man responded to John's questions.

"Did he seem distraught or agitated about anything?"

"Yes, sir. He was real interested in the men Devia had hanged outside the fortress. He stayed near their rotting bodies longer than I could stand to. I think he was trying to identify them."

"I thought he must have known them," the other man said, "because when he rejoined us on the circuit, he sure was upset."

Suddenly the first man came to life. "That's right," he said. "I remember Thomas saying that he was going to see Samoth first thing in the morning."

"Samoth Devia?" John asked.

"Yes, sir!" both men chorused.

"Were there any of Jabin's men near the area that night?"

"No, sir. They hadn't made their move yet. They were located about two miles west, all along the edge of the forest. Our orders were to report any movement toward Green Meadow or our positions. There was no movement that night, sir."

"Tell me more about why Thomas said he was meeting Samoth," John said.

"I didn't know what he was talking about, sir. He might have meant the parley."

"The parley?" John echoed.

"I rode with James and a small group of men to the fortress the next morning for a parley with Jabin. Devia was supposed to be the intermediary. That was when we discovered the missing body. Commander James went crazy. He started screaming and calling curses down on Devia! We tried to restrain him, sir, but he broke free and smote the gates with his knife. He drove that blade in, clean up to the hilt. He wasn't the same after that, sir. I think he aged ten years that morning. O' course, that was when everything else started, and Jabin's troops began to move in the meadow. We had our hands full the next few days until you and your men showed up. We'd just about given up hope."

John sat silent for a moment. The information he'd heard was fragmented and gave him little insight into the problem. He studied the men before him. They were dirty, exhausted, and as thin as razor blades, yet they seemed honest men, soldiers to the core.

"Do you know anything else about Thomas?" he finally asked.

"No, sir," both men chorused.

"I thank you both for this information. Gaff has a larder under his jurisdiction. See Captain Wilmont outside, and he will see that you get something to eat. Then I want you to take the rest of the day off from your duties and get some rest."

There was an unexpected pause as the men turned to go. "If you please, sir," one man ventured, "I wouldn't mind getting a bite to eat, but I've a brother I'm still searching for."

John felt smitten. He was not the only one to lose a family member. This man had taken time to tell him about James and Thomas, all the while wondering about the fate of his own brother. John understood the man's helplessness. He would be unable to rest until his brother's fate was known.

"Permission granted, soldier. I pray the Lord will help you find your brother alive and well."

Both men thanked him with their eyes and turned to leave.

Jennifer carefully washed her face. A slight smile tugged at her lips. After days without care or attention, she wondered if she would ever be clean again. Running a comb though her tangled hair, she winced as it caught in a mat of knots. *I must hurry!* she chided herself.

John had ordered James's body removed from the command center for final viewing, and then he had turned James's living quarters over to Jennifer. Having sectioned off one small corner of the inner room, Jennifer made her preparations in semi-privacy, for the entire command center had become a makeshift hospital. Men who had sustained injuries filled nearly every corner of the tent and the surrounding area.

Jennifer tried to hurry, but the comb snagged in yet another set of tangles. She'd spent the afternoon cleaning wounds and cooling fevered brows, not cleaning her own face or combing her hair. It was nearly sundown, and John Stafford would be calling for her any minute.

Can I really do this? Jennifer wondered, a sudden pang of remorse wrenching her heart. *James is gone. I will never see him again.* She was to accompany John Stafford to James's bier, leading the entire procession of soldiers past his grave.

"Miss Jennifer!" A voice broke into her confused thoughts, bringing her back to reality. "Master Stafford is waiting."

Oh my! she thought. Her hands began to tremble. "I'm just about ready," she called, brushing tousled hair back from her face.

Slipping around the curtain, she stepped quickly toward the door. A hand brushed her skirt as she passed one of the many cots. "Miss Jennifer," a badly wounded soldier whispered. "Don't leave me."

Jennifer knelt beside the suffering man and swept her fingers gently over his moist brow. "I must step out for a moment, but I'll be back." The man's skin felt damp and clammy, and she feared he was in shock. Jennifer bowed her head. "Dear Lord, please let him live," she whispered.

She heard her name from countless cots as she passed. Without a doubt, this was where she belonged. Her heart ached for these mauled and maimed men.

Stepping from the darkness of the tent, fresh air and a golden sunset dazzled her senses. John Stafford was waiting. He smiled and offered his arm.

His clothes were fresh and clean, and he wore no armor. His head was bare, save for a shock of unruly, windblown hair. She marveled at his appearance. He was no warrior tonight, merely an aging father about to bury his son. Her heart ached for the graying man.

She stepped quickly to receive his arm. Together they descended the stony path to the valley below.

What a sight they made: an old man and a young lady, arm in arm, carefully picking their way down the hill in the last rays of a dying day. Many men would remember that sight long after they'd forgotten James's bier or the bitter battles they had fought.

Torches lit the procession as thousands paid their last respects. Out of sight, but not out of mind, the gates of Devia remained closed and silent.

Kneeling beside the open grave, Jennifer tossed the first handful of dirt upon the body. James looked so peaceful; she found it hard to feel sorry for him.

Her mind drifted to the men lining the floors of the command center. This would not be a peaceful night of tranquility for them. Those with less grievous wounds were bunked outside. She could hear their cries as pain ate holes into their courage and pride.

"Are you ready to go?"

She heard the familiar voice beside her. She knew men were all about her, but she was aware of only one. She took John's hand and rose to her feet. "Yes, I need to return. I've already been away too long."

Even in the torchlight, she could see concern written upon John's face. "Are you sure you will be all right?" he asked. "The lads tell me the tent is full!"

"I have plenty of room for myself, and my heart would be at peace in no other location. I only hope to share some comfort with these poor men."

John smiled at her. "You are a brave young woman, but you must allow time for your own rest. Tomorrow will require strength to pass its tests as well."

She nodded and took his arm. Together they ascended the steep hill to the tent.

"I would like to speak with you tomorrow," John said. "We cannot leave you or those who are injured here indefinitely."

She nodded and started to turn away.

John's big hands caught her shoulders and turned her once again to face him. Looking deeply into her eyes, his voice faltered. "Thank you for helping me through this evening."

Impulsively, she threw her arms around his neck and planted a soft kiss on his cheek. Turning, she slipped through the tent's flap.

John could hear a cacophony of voices rise to meet her entrance. "Miss Jennifer, help me!"

CHAPTER 19

A Quest Begins

A new command center was established across the ravine from Jennifer's hospital. There Gaff, Stafford, and various officers interviewed those who'd had contact with Thomas in the days before his disappearance. Outside, thousands of soldiers searched through the dead on the battlefield. Thomas's body was not found. Hope grew that he was indeed alive somewhere. Jabin's stronghold in Endor was mentioned time and time again.

"Why would anyone take Thomas to Endor?" John asked.

"Where would you take the kidnapped prince of Amity?" Gaff asked.

There was a long pause. "You know, we're not sure he was kidnapped," John said.

"Jabin has no use for another dead body. If Thomas had been slain, they would have let him lie. I say he has been kidnapped and is probably at Endor. If he's not there, then where is he?"

"What about Devia's fortress?" someone asked.

"Too close," another voice responded. "Someone inside would get word to us."

"Maybe." John's tone was reluctant. "But why do you keep tying Samoth to this affair?"

"Thomas and Samoth have never been on good terms, sir," Rudy said quickly.

John smiled. "How do you know so much about my son's relationships?"

Rudy began again. "Sir, it has never been a secret that Samoth and his father long to exert the power and authority over people that you and your sons are able to do. They could have the throne and be the lords of Amity—if your family were out of the way. Samoth is the same age as Thomas, but he has always walked in his shadow, and his resentment runs high."

"And I'll vouch that Samoth is in league with Jabin," Gaff added. "Endor seems likely to me."

Rudy glanced at Seagood before speaking and then added, "Excuse me, sir, but Seagood and I volunteer to go to Endor to find Thomas."

"I want to go as well," Mathias demanded. "The family of Gaff should be represented."

John smiled at their willingness but shook his head. "No, I can't let you go. It would cost you your lives."

Gaff surprised John. "I disagree with you, John. I think the boys should go. If they travel light, they might be able to catch Samoth before he reaches the safety of Endor. If we march with an army, we will be opposed all the way, giving him too much time. Speed is essential."

"But you can't send your son!"

"Why not?" Gaff asked. "Mathias is of age. But three is not enough. I would recommend six. They can travel quickly, yet they will have plenty of fighting power in a pinch. However"—and he looked directly at his son—"you must not use confrontation but stealth as your weapon."

John looked about the determined faces within the group. "All right," he said. "It seems to be settled. Seagood," he said, turning to the grave young man, "pick three more men to accompany you, and set out tonight under the cover of darkness."

Seagood stepped along the rows of volunteers.

Darren Yeoman had grown up in the house of Stafford. He had been a constant companion to James and Thomas from the earliest days. Last summer he had fought by their side in the battle of Great Bend. He, among all the men assembled, probably knew the mind and thoughts of Thomas better than most. Seagood chose him.

Clyde Fost stood out as well. Bodyguard and companion of Thomas, he was among those most devastated by his master's disappearance. He felt personally responsible. He would travel with the six.

The group needed one more man. Seagood stepped down the line, examining each man. A boy inched forward as Seagood approached.

"No! Not you, Wart!" Rudy called from behind Seagood. "You don't realize the danger. We need warriors, not boys!"

Undaunted, the lad continued to look Seagood straight in the eyes. Then he spoke. "I know some of the languages and customs of the men of the north. I may not be a warrior, but I'm not afraid."

Smiling, Seagood leaned back and studied the lad before him.

"Wart, how do you know the languages?" Rudy asked. He knew the lad had been very fond of Thomas and would do anything for him. He hoped Wart wasn't making up a story just to be chosen.

"My father was a boatman on the Great River above the Fords," the boy said proudly, and then his eyes dropped. "That is, until he disappeared."

"Can you speak the language of Endor?" Rudy asked.

"Understand it better than speak it, sir. But I would do my best."

Seagood seemed satisfied. Giving a nod, the group was complete. They would leave yet tonight.

"Wart, how is it you know all about this country?" Rudy asked.

"I don't know all about it. I've been on the river several times with my father, but he didn't let me go often. There were too many pirates, and my presence would have made his travels too dangerous." Wart went silent and bit his tongue. He felt sure there were some in this group who resented his presence. They thought he was too young and would hinder their progress.

"Where did you stay while your father was gone?"

"We had a cabin on the west side of the river."

The stillness was broken only by their conversation. Mathias and Seagood led the procession, followed by Clyde and Darren. Rudy and Wart brought up the rear. They followed the main road west from Green Meadow. Gaff's men held the road secure, and the group was forced to stop at many check stations. Mathias was readily recognized by his fellow countrymen, and that helped speed them on their journey.

Their route was a constant descent coming off the mountain pass at Green Meadow, and they were making good time. There was a long silence before Wart asked, "Rudy, do you know what route we are taking?"

"No."

The silence lingered. They passed another checkpoint.

"This saddle sure is getting hard," Wart complained some time later.

"I told you it wasn't going to be easy." Rudy laughed. "Now you'll just have to hang in there. We have barely started."

To Wart it felt like they had ridden all night when they came to yet another check station. Rudy had shaken him from a half sleep as they'd neared the circle of light around a campfire. Wart heard Mathias ask the sentry, "Do we still hold the road to the Fords?"

"There is no guarantee, sir. Our scouts report nothing, but we have had no forces west of this point for days."

Rudy pushed forward to join the conversation, and Mathias turned to address the group. "Where do we go from here? The most secure road leads southwest to Great Bend. We could take the river from there."

"And add several days to our journey," Clyde said quietly.

"Yes," Mathias said rather stiffly. "Or we could take the road west. It is unsure, but it angles over the mountains until it reaches the Fords on the Great River."

Rudy studied Seagood's impassive face for a while and then said, "I cast my vote for the road to the Fords. It will shorten our time on the river."

Seagood nodded, and everyone remounted, turning their horses toward the northwest.

Now, an army checkpoint is not a homey place, but any time out of a saddle can be restful. A small fire crackled near the road and brought with it a sense of civilization and friends. Leaving the fire behind brought a deep sense of loneliness upon the travelers. The clopping of horses' hooves was the only sound to disturb the night.

It was very late when a crescent moon rose in the eastern sky. Veiled behind thin clouds, it cast eerie shadows across their path. The twisted limbs of scrub oaks looked like giant trolls reaching out to devour the little group.

An owl hooted overhead, and Wart shivered, glad to be in the company of others. The path rose steeply at the foot of each mountain and dropped sharply into the valley beyond. Dense forest growth in the valleys turned the path black as ink, and the air was so cold it seemed to chill one's very soul. Wart thought morning would never come.

Finally the sky began to soften from black to gray, and colors began to greet the land through which they rode. Not one homestead, campfire, or traveler had greeted them since the last check point.

The tiny group huddled behind a huge boulder at the top of an especially high mountain pass. The crisp, cold air stung their faces and numbed their fingers. The high, thin clouds were turning shades of red and orange, illuminating an undulating pattern of hills that separated them from the Great River and Fords.

Rudy finally spoke. "We'd better make camp. There is no use in us being seen and announcing our mission to the entire world."

They quickly descended the mountain and found a spot some distance from the path in the valley below. Watering their horses at a small stream, they unsaddled, rubbed, and tethered their stock. Then, without the pleasure of a campfire or warm food, they bunked down.

Wart was asleep before his head hit the sod.

"Get up, sleepyhead!" A boot gently raked Wart's ribs. Wart opened his eyes and marveled. It wasn't fully light yet.

"Hey, can't a guy get any rest?"

There were a couple of snickers from the group. "Get any rest?" Rudy mocked. "We let you sleep all day. Don't tell me you want to sleep all night too!"

Bewildered, the lad sat up. The light was just about as dim as when he had fallen asleep. Trying to get his bearings, Wart remembered seeing his shadow before hitting the sod; now it lay on the opposite side of his body.

"All day!" he said, stretching.

"Come on, sleeping beauty," Rudy said cheerfully. "We may even make the Fords before dawn if we can get everyone up and moving."

In truth, Wart had slept all day. Others had taken turns standing guard through the eventless day. No one had passed on the road, and even birds sang little to break the silence.

Jumping up, Wart began to roll his blanket. His stomach growled, and he remembered how hungry he had been before falling asleep.

"Take time to eat," Rudy said, laughing. "We don't want your stomach waking the countryside tonight."

Wart sniffed the air. Something was cooking. Mathias, Clyde, and Darren were seated around a small, smokeless campfire. Several small quail were simmering over the glow of the coals.

It was dusk when they departed. Wart was still licking his fingers. He turned to Rudy and asked, "Who got the birds?"

"Seagood was scouting when he came across the covey."

"Boy, I'm glad he found them. I was about to starve!"

"So I noticed. Doesn't the food in the pack excite you anymore?"

Wart wrinkled his nose. "Excite? No. But it will do in a pinch, I guess."

Rudy smiled. "You might just make it yet, boy!"

They rode silently through the night, topping each mountain only to follow the twisting path into the valley beyond. Wart didn't know how many hours they had ridden, and he didn't care after the first several.

Mathias rode beside him this night. He didn't have much to say, and Wart wondered if the man didn't like him. *Maybe he thinks I was too forward at the selection process*, Wart thought. *Maybe he thinks Seagood could have made a better choice.*

Wart remained silent a long time, his thoughts constantly accusing him. *Maybe Seagood could have chosen better*, he thought, wincing at his own admission.

It was very late when Seagood brought the group to a halt. Silently they sat in the darkness, listening. With a quick movement, Seagood reined his horse into the bushes along the path. The others followed suit, and in moments they were huddled in dark shadows a short distance from the path.

Wart was dying to ask what was going on, for he had not seen or heard a thing, but the tension he sensed in the others kept him silent. After some moments, he slowly began to hear a faint sound. Imperceptible at first, it grew more distinct. It was the clatter of horses' hooves.

A few moments later, a large company of horsemen came galloping up the road. Mathias grabbed for his sword, but Seagood held his arm.

The riders passed recklessly into the night. They were disorganized and heedless of their surroundings. Minutes passed. Gradually the noise of their passing subsided. Still, Seagood made no move, waiting, tense and silent.

"We should have waylaid them!" Mathias whispered. "They will probably attack the supply line to Green Meadow."

"The six of us were no match for them," Clyde whispered.

"We could have made them pay for their carelessness," Mathias retorted.

"That isn't our mission," Rudy said quietly. "We are to find and rescue Thomas. No doubt, routing that company would have been about as easy."

"Well, which way do we go now?" Darren asked, changing the subject. "This road may be crawling with soldiers."

A lengthy discussion ensued. Some thought going back to the road was too risky. Others argued that it was the only way to the Fords. They were about to take a vote when a small voice broke in. "I think I know another way."

Stunned to silence, the group turned to look at Wart. He had been studying the dark terrain while they discussed their plight. Leading his horse into their midst, he spoke quietly. "The Fords are a common exchange point for river traffic. Barges from north and south meet wagons from east and west. Goods are bartered or exchanged, and then everyone goes back home."

The group shifted restlessly. They knew this information already.

"If we go back to the road, we don't know who we might meet," Wart said.

Someone stirred, and someone else cleared his throat. As they began to consider this, they realized they might meet a caravan of merchants. Traveling in the western wild was dangerous, and to lessen the risk, many traders hired bands of ruffians or renegade soldiers to escort them over the roads. They had no idea what they might find at the Fords.

Wart continued. "On one of my father's runs, we cached our goods to avoid bandits. We later packed those goods through these mountains following deer trails. I'm sure we could go straight north through these mountains and hit the river unobserved."

There was a long moment of silence, and then Rudy asked, "How far is it?"

"Are these paths known by others?" Darren asked.

"I don't know how far it is," Wart stammered. "We traveled in daylight, and it didn't take all day, but we could see where we were going. I don't know how many people use those paths, but I doubt very many."

"How long ago was this?" Rudy persisted.

"I don't remember exactly," Wart said, "but it was several years."

"Could you find this path in the dark?"

"I don't know," Wart said honestly. "Path or no path, I know the river is straight north over several hills."

Seagood stirred and studied the boy intently. Wart could actually feel the inspection more than see it, but undaunted, he held his ground and returned Seagood's gaze.

Rudy watched the exchange between the two, and after a long moment he said, "Well, gentlemen, it appears we are going to follow the Wart."

Wart began to tremble. *I don't want to lead these men! Why did I ever open my mouth?*

Scrambling over rocky terrain, Rudy tried to keep pace with the wiry boy. Like shadowy phantoms, he could just see the others ahead, leading their horses through the darkness. He had lost ground going up the very first slope and had continued to fall farther behind. The path was nearly impossible to see.

"Maybe if I cut through I can catch up with the others," he muttered. Stepping off the path, he immediately encountered brambles with long thorns. They clung to his face, arms, and clothing. "Ouch! Hey! Slow down up there!"

The others stopped at the sound of his voice. Darren and Clyde returned to find Rudy still struggling to free himself.

"What kind of goose chase is that boy taking us on?" Rudy fumed when Darren was close enough to hear him.

"It's a rough path, mate, but we are going north, and we should hit the river soon."

Rudy sputtered. "If I could get my hands on that boy right now ..."

"Easy, mate. Let me help you." Strong hands grappled with the resilient thorns.

"I don't think he knows where he's going!" Rudy growled as they finally freed his ponderous bulk from the briars.

"Well, he found this path," Darren said.

Rudy considered this. They had fought their way through thick underbrush until they had finally fallen into a stream. Tired, chilled, and soaked to the bone, they had followed the stream until Wart had whispered, "I think this is it."

At that point the group had been grateful just to get out of the water. They had hoped the path would prove easier passage than the stream, but in this they were all sorely disappointed. Rough, twisting, and covered with loose stones, the path tried everyone's patience. It did, however, reach the summit of a mountain ridge, whereupon it plummeted again into the dense foliage on the other side.

Rudy was still muttering murderous threats under his breath.

"The path is getting better, mate," Darren encouraged. "Come on." He nudged the heavy man and whispered, "You don't think Seagood could be misguided by a youth, now, do you?" Together they scrambled to join the others.

The stars were beginning to dim and the sky to grow light when at last they stood on a hill overlooking the Great River. Exhausted, they stared in silence at the dark, turbulent ribbon of water churning its way to the sea.

"Good show, mate!" Darren was the first to fully comprehend the significance of their night's journey. "You saved us a lot of time, lad!"

Everyone began to see the truth of Darren's words. One after another, they slapped Wart on the back, congratulating him for a good night's labor.

Even Rudy felt a stirring of gratitude in his heart. Laying his big hand on Wart's shoulder, his voice boomed. "Wart, I owe you an apology. I said some rum things about you tonight. But here we are! Do you forgive me for not trusting you earlier?"

"Sure, Rudy," said Wart's small, wavering voice. "But you might be too early with your apology. I'm not sure where we are!"

CHAPTER 20

Perilous Choices

Long after Seagood and his men had left to find Thomas, John sat alone beside James's grave. The agony of his loss consumed his strength and courage. With immense effort, he tore his thoughts away from James and Thomas and considered the men and women of Amity. *I must move on*, he thought. *Others need me, though I feel I have little to offer.* "Lord," he whispered, "I need your strength, for I have none of my own!"

John Stafford finally arose and walked slowly to the new command center where his cot was waiting. Making a pillow of his cloak, he lay down and fell asleep instantly.

Suddenly someone was shaking him awake. "Gaff to see you, sir!"

John stretched and slowly sat up, running fingers through his tousled hair and wiping sleep from his eyes.

A large man strode rapidly toward him. "John, what are we going to do with the casualties?"

"I say, Gaff. You have an abrupt way of starting a man's day."

Gaff studied John's face and eyes and then softened his approach. "I'm sorry, John. Didn't you sleep well?"

"Yes and no. I have found some comfort in the Lord."

"Good. I'm glad for you."

"Gaff, I need to ask you a question before we discuss our plans. Is that all right?"

"Certainly, John. Fire away."

"Why did you let Mathias leave with the others for Endor? We don't even know Thomas is there. Do you realize you may never see your son again?"

Gaff became quiet, and the two fathers studied each other. "John, of a truth, I wouldn't have let him go. But to Mathias, life without Thomas would be no life at all. I never knew anyone so devoted to another. He wanted to go because he loved your son. I think that is true of all who set their feet upon that path."

John struggled to control his emotions. "But you may lose your son."

"I may," Gaff said gravely. "But I would not restrain the path of love. Mathias was driven to go, he could do nothing else."

"But it's so painful to lose a son."

Gaff offered John a hand and pulled him to his feet. Leaning heavily upon each other, the two men embraced for a long time.

Gaff, Stafford, and other high-level commanders decided that the wounded could not remain so close to Devia's fortress. While it seemed that they should have received more help close to Green Meadow, the fortress had not yet opened or offered any assistance to the men of Amity or Emancipation.

John Stafford walked slowly from the command center toward the infirmary to inform Jennifer of their decision to move the wounded. After climbing the steep hill, John asked the sentry if Miss Jennifer was available and turned to wait.

Scanning the countryside, John realized Devia's fortress dominated the scenery. The structure seemed to exude Devia's presence far and wide. *I wonder what your next move will be*, he thought.

Jennifer emerged from the tent, rumpled and weary, to find John Stafford waiting.

"Are you all right, young lady?" he asked.

She smiled a tired smile and nodded. "It was a long night, and several of my patients did not survive."

"I'm sorry," John said, laying a comforting hand on her shoulder. "You must not feel you have failed in your labors. The Lord is the author and sustainer of life. He will eventually draw all men unto Himself, whether to judgment or blessing. But it is the Lord who draws them. So take heart. Life and death are in His hands, not yours."

Hearing those words, Jennifer felt a great burden lift from her shoulders. During the night, there had been times she'd thought she could endure no more suffering. She had watched strong men pass with little more than a whimper. She had done all she could for the men, but still she couldn't bear to let them go. However, John's words seemed to shift her burden to the broad shoulders of a loving Lord who could bear such trials. As peace settled her soul, she smiled at John and said, "Thank you for those words."

John merely nodded. "But now the reason I am here. You will need to leave this place."

"What?" Jennifer faltered. "Why?"

"I've set aside a number of men to see you safely to your grandmother's farm."

Jennifer gestured feebly toward the tent. "What about these men?" Despair filled her heart. "What about my family?" She glanced back at Devia's fortress.

She tried to turn away, but John grabbed her shoulders and held her firmly. "The men," he said softly, "will go with you."

Alarmed, Jennifer responded, "But, sir, some are so weak, the move may kill them."

"Gaff has provided wagons for the journey. Still, some may not survive."

"Then why move?" Jennifer pleaded. "Shouldn't we stay near the fortress for protection and provision?"

"May I remind you how much help you received from them in your time of need?"

Her countenance fell, but still she struggled. "I understand, but what about my family?"

"How many are they?"

"I left my father, mother, and a younger sister here. I also have an older brother who has been away for some time."

"So, if your family is inside the fortress, your father has your mother and sister to care for?"

"Yes."

"What if things are not good inside Devia's fortress? Would your father want you there under his care or in the distant abode of your grandmother?"

Jennifer shifted uneasily. She remembered her father's words: *Child, if anything should happen to us here at Green Meadow, flee to your grandmother's or seek help from the garrison. They are honest men. They will help you.*

John spoke before Jennifer could respond. "Child, I won't force you to go. I simply ask that you trust me to do what I think is best for you. I will, however, let you choose."

Jennifer felt humble before this powerful man. She knew men would forfeit their lives at his command, yet she was free to accept or reject his will. How could she refuse? Struggling to find her voice, she said, "I'll go."

"Someone needs to care for these wounded. Will you do that for me?" John asked.

"Yes."

"Even if it means you leave your family?"

"Yes," she whispered. Suddenly, joy filled her soul as she relinquished her will for that of the master. She looked into John Stafford's eyes and was startled to see tears.

"Thank you," he said, wiping his eyes.

She was astonished that her simple obedience could move the master to tears. Leaping into his open arms, she was astonished at the emotions that flooded her soul.

He held her tight and then withdrew to study her face. "Are you very sure?"

"With all my heart."

Men carried the wounded to wagons, and Jennifer packed every supply she could find around them. The morning was filled with activity, but shortly before noon, everything was packed.

Jennifer settled upon a wagon seat, and they were off. Her heart soared. She had so much to think about and so much to do. There would be shelters to build, water to carry, and a hospital to set up. She was grateful for the extra men and wagons that had been donated to the cause.

Wart stood near the bank of the Great River. The breeze was cool, and he felt chilled to the bone. "I can hear the rapids upstream," he said, "but there should have been a sandbar here."

"Rivers are always changing, Wart," Rudy said cheerfully. "Don't worry. Seagood has seen something the rest of us have not. He'll find a way to ford this river!"

The others voiced their confidence, but Wart hung back. The fast-flowing water seemed deep and foreboding. *I'd better man up*, he thought, *or the others will know they should have chosen someone else.*

Wart watched while Seagood poked a long branch into the river in various places. Finally Seagood seemed satisfied, and he had all the men tie themselves together with strong rope before they waded into the water.

Seagood led the way, followed by Rudy. When Rudy was about knee deep in water, he turned and shouted to Wart, "Watch for washouts. They could be deep!"

Wart used his feet to feel the river bed before him. Darren, Clyde, and Mathias followed suit. The current was stronger than it appeared, and Wart could feel the rope tighten about his waist as the river's flow tried to set him adrift. He could barely set one foot in front of the other.

Twice Seagood disappeared from sight, but Rudy, with his great strength, was able to pull him back to the surface. Without hesitation, Seagood would strike out again in a slightly different direction and lead on.

They were little more than halfway across when they heard a cry from the back. Clyde and his mount had strayed only slightly from Seagood's path, but both had found deep water. When Darren turned to assist his comrade, his own horse floundered into a hole.

Everything happened so fast. Clyde's horse reappeared, thrashing water to foam, and the cries of the men were drowned out by the screams of the floundering animals.

"Wart, hold my horse!" Rudy shouted as he surged back toward the commotion, but Rudy's change of course pulled Seagood backward and under the water.

Darren pulled hard on the rope that tethered Clyde to him. "Watch the horses!" Mathias screamed. Just then, Darren's horse found solid footing, and he lurched from the hole into which he had fallen. His movement knocked Darren off balance, and he fell into the churning current. His body was sucked beneath the surface immediately.

Mathias grabbed for Darren's leg, but the rope connecting them grew taut and snapped. Darren was adrift, but the rope holding him to Clyde pulled him beneath the surface.

"The rope broke!" Mathias shouted. He was frantically trying to calm Darren's horse and keep his own from bolting.

Wart tried to hold three horses while Clyde's mount drifted further down the stream.

A man's head broke the surface of the water some ways downstream. Mathis yelled, "It's Darren!" Rudy flung a rope his direction, but Darren offered no response. Seagood slashed the rope tethering him to Rudy and swam after the body. Seagood finally grabbed Darren and began pulling him to the opposite shore.

Rudy, taking his cue from Seagood, turned, took charge of two horses from Wart and began to wade across the river.

"What about Clyde?" Wart shouted.

Rudy acted as though he was deaf and kept walking.

Following in Rudy's wake, Wart felt the water rise to his neck and sweep him off his feet. He clung tightly to his horse, and the rope about his waist grew taut as Rudy and Mathias held his drift in check.

Finally there was solid sand beneath his feet. The shore was near. They all waded into the brush along the shore and stood gasping for breath.

Tying the horses to a low branch, Rudy turned to Wart and said, "Watch these!" Then he and Mathias slashed the rope tying them to Wart and rushed downstream to where Seagood was nearing the shore with Darren in tow.

The two men pulled the body ashore while Seagood struck out into the water again, swimming upstream to where Clyde had fallen from sight. While Mathias and Rudy tried to restore Darren's breathing, Seagood dived beneath the surface of the river over and over.

Wart felt so helpless watching Seagood dive and Rudy and Mathias labor over Darren. All he could do was talk softly to the frightened horses and watch. When Seagood had stayed under the surface far too long one time, Wart yelled downstream, "Rudy, Seagood isn't coming up!"

Rudy leaped into the water and swam upstream. Seagood's haggard face appeared just as Rudy was about to dive beneath the surface to look for him. Grasping his master, Rudy pulled the empty-handed Seagood back to shore.

Everyone sat wrapped in cloaks as their clothes dried near a smokeless fire. Silence loomed ominously between them. They shivered with more than the cold.

Wart glanced first at Seagood and then at Rudy. He felt responsible for both Clyde's and Darren's deaths. If he'd just kept his mouth shut, maybe all six members of the group would still be alive. No one spoke to him about his role in the men's deaths, but he knew he was guilty. He felt so alone. Were they avoiding him on purpose?

Seagood stared blankly at the fire while Mathias sat apart. Rudy watched his master intently, and Wart shivered, feeling miserable.

Suddenly, Seagood began to move his hands.

"Is that what happened?" Rudy asked.

When Seagood nodded, Rudy held up his hand and turned away. Wart watched as tears rolled down the big man's cheeks.

This is no time to ask questions, Wart thought. *They don't want to talk to me anyway.* With that, he curled up near the fire and tried to still the convulsions shaking his body.

Wart woke to see Rudy sitting quietly by the fire. Mathias and Seagood were nowhere to be seen. "Rudy?" he asked hesitantly.

The big man stirred and looked at Wart. "Oh! Hey, did you have a good sleep?" He tried to sound cheerful.

"I guess," Wart said, rubbing his eyes. "I didn't realize I had gone to sleep. Where are the others?"

Rudy grew sober. "They are digging a grave, Wart."

There was a long, awkward silence before Wart blurted, "Listen, Rudy. I'm sorry I suggested this route. I didn't know this would happen!"

Rudy looked startled, and then his eyes narrowed. "Don't tell me you think you had something to do with their deaths?"

It was Wart's turn to be surprised. "I thought you guys were angry with me."

In an instant, Rudy was at his side. "No. Where did you get such an idea?"

Wart did not answer.

"We all knew the river would be dangerous," Rudy said, "and many men have drowned trying to cross it. Though we hadn't yet come to it, there is a road on the east side of the river that leads to Endor, but it leads through territory under Jabin's control. We wanted to cross the river to travel unnoticed over here. That decision cost two men their lives, not you."

Wart remembered watching Rudy and Mathias struggle to revive Darren, and Seagood's unsuccessful attempts to retrieve Clyde from his watery grave. Slowly he began to realize that the others felt equally responsible for their comrades' deaths.

In an unusual display of affection, Wart gave Rudy a big hug. "Thanks, Rudy. I thought you guys didn't like me. No one would talk to me."

The big man returned Wart's hug. "I'm sorry, Wart. I'm afraid we were too caught up in our own grief to worry about yours."

In a sudden change of subject, Wart blurted, "Rudy, what did Seagood tell you?"

Rudy stiffened, a painful expression twisting his face. "Clyde died a bad death, boy. Real bad."

"What happened?"

"I've said all I'm going to say."

That was all Wart would ever know of Clyde's death. Afraid to ask more about the incident, he changed the subject to a more practical matter. "Is there anything to eat?"

"Leave it to a growing boy." Rudy smiled. He was more than happy to change the subject.

Wart was dressed, and a young rabbit was roasting over the fire when Seagood and Mathias returned. Everyone seemed more relaxed.

They were still eating when Rudy rubbed the back of his neck. "Is someone watching us?" he asked uncomfortably.

Seagood rose and disappeared into the bushes. Wart stared around the clearing. *Nothing has changed*, he thought. *Or has it?* Wart noticed that Rudy and Mathias had drawn their swords and were searching the brush near the camp. When Seagood returned, he was scowling.

"Did you find anyone?" Rudy asked.

Seagood shook his head, but everyone knew they had unwanted company.

CHAPTER 21

Into the Unknown

Safe inside their grandpa's parlor, surrounded by family, and near the comfort of a roaring fire, eight grandchildren watched their grandfather breathlessly. They could hear the wind howling outside, and the constant pecking of snow against the windows intensified the tension of Grandpa's story.

Robbie, seated once again on his grandfather's lap, turned with huge eyes and looked into his grandfather's face. "How did you lose your hand, Grandpa?"

Destry bit her lip and felt her body aflame with embarrassment.

"I'm about to come to that part, Grandson," Bill said quietly. "Those of us with John Stafford were busy following the battle at Green Meadow. We had collected many of those fallen in battle before gathering to march after Jabin."

Out of bowshot from Devia's fortress, Gaff and Stafford watched as the men of Amity and Emancipation settled into formation. Gaff's troops were separated from Amity's by a narrow gap in the press of humanity. John listened as Gaff spoke with great animation. "John, be reasonable! If you leave troops here, they may just assist Devia with whatever scheme he attempts. You won a battle on his doorstep, and he hasn't even acknowledged your presence!"

"Gaff, we've discussed this before. My men signed up to protect Amity. They have been faithful thus far, and I expect them to remain so. I shall be grateful for all who go on with us, and I expect those who remain to be faithful here."

"But we need their swords!"

"Not if we don't have their hearts!" John countered.

"John, this is foolish! If you grant your men freedom, they won't march off to war. Who would?"

"Some will leave me," John conceded. "But I believe most will come with me."

"I'll have to see it to believe it," Gaff growled.

John just smiled. A young officer rode up and saluted. "All men are present and accounted for, sir."

Gaff scowled at John. "I will not let my men witness your mass desertion." Wheeling his mount, he shouted orders, and the men of Emancipation spun on their heels and turned their backs on John Stafford and his people.

Gaff threaded his way between his own companies and then turned to face his men. "Men of Emancipation!" His voice carried across the meadow. "We are about to embark on a long, dangerous mission. Jabin is our target, and we will not stop until he is captured or destroyed. A battle won or lost will not deter us. We must and we will defeat this enemy!"

Raising his hand toward heaven, Gaff shouted, "I commend you into the peace and presence of our Lord and Creator! We go with God!"

John sat and listened. When Gaff had concluded, John turned to his own men. Marshaled before him were nearly fifteen thousand men. Located at the far end of the formation were those who remained from the garrison. Not three full companies had survived. Battle had decimated their numbers but not their spirits.

John dismounted and strolled along the columns of men. All eyes focused on him. "Men of Amity, you have answered the call to arms. You have left those you love and the comforts of home to face battle and death."

He paused and then continued. "Today you have fulfilled your commitment. You have defended Amity and her borders."

He stopped and looked directly at his men, and in a voice loud enough for all to hear, he said, "I release you from your obligations."

A ripple of surprise and excitement flowed through the men.

John continued. "I will go with Gaff. If you wish, you may join me. There is no shame for those who stay, and no guarantees for those who go."

John's stroll had left him standing before the remnants of James's garrison. Addressing the men before him, he said, "Men of the garrison, you have borne this burden the longest. You have been separated from family and have endured local indifference. You were attacked viciously, and yet you never gave way. When outnumbered by overwhelming odds, you did not flee. When your comrades fell at your right or your left, you did not give up. You stood your ground and held the enemy at bay. You, more than anyone, should be free from the agony of this war."

"The choice is before you. Step forward if you will follow me into battle. If not, remain where you are."

Without a moment's hesitation, every man from James's garrison stepped forward.

Bill watched with the rest of John's bodyguard as company after company stepped forward to join Stafford and his mission. Very few men chose to stay. Bill was glad, for he did not want to chase Jabin and his forces alone.

John eventually rejoined his bodyguard. "Well, lads," he said, "are you ready for a long march?"

"Right behind you, sir," one man called.

There was a snicker, and another man laughed. "We're some bodyguards," he said. "Our master rides off, and we stand around waiting for him to return."

John joined the laughter. "Seriously, lads, you may have chosen the easier route. Those who stay behind will bury the dead. That task alone will take a month."

"What will Devia think of you leaving soldiers on his doorstep, Captain?" asked a stout little fellow nicknamed Stubby.

John studied his little group. "I don't know," he said. "I do hope Jan DeKlerk is tough enough not to buckle under Devia's clever tongue."

Far up the line, an order was given, and the men fell into step. Bill was glad to be on the move. If they were just going to sit around, he wanted to be sitting with Mary at home.

They had not marched far when Stubby leaned close to Bill and said, "What the master said sure makes me uncomfortable."

"What does, Stubby?" Bill asked.

"You heard Stafford say that Jan DeKlerk is heading up those who stayed behind."

"Yes, why does that make you uncomfortable? Do you know him?"

"Know him? We grew up together. We were playmates, neighbors, friends for a long time."

"What's the problem? Aren't you glad for him?"

"I would have been five years ago, but he's changed."

"How?"

"I can't really say. It's more of an attitude than anything else. Back then, I'd have said he was the nicest man I knew, but not now. He got into business for himself and became a river rat. There's nothing wrong with boatmen, and I've plenty of friends who work barge traffic on the river, but Jan got in and wanted it all. There's no way a beginner can get all the business. You start with one raft and one pole and go to work. If you can find good help, you get a second pole, and it makes the travel faster and safer. If people like your work, in a year or two you buy a second raft and hire more men, but not Jan. First year, he had five rafts and some very unsavory chaps helping him. Oh, he makes a lot of money, but those bums working for him are the terror of the river."

"What do you mean?" Bill asked.

"According to my friends, they don't think twice about stealing loads. Some lad has a load consigned at a fair price, and DeKlerk's men show up and undercut his bid. They threaten to rough up the seller unless he agrees. I guess in a few cases they actually have."

"Where did DeKlerk get these characters?"

"I don't know. Some say they're wayward boys who grew up without proper guidance, and Jan doesn't know how to handle them. Others say they are actually some of Devia's hired thugs. I tend to think they are Devia's men. Where did Jan get all the money to buy five rafts when just getting started? I know his family isn't rich, and it takes some backing to get going in the river trade."

"So what are you saying? Is Jan DeKlerk actually working for Master Devia?"

"Maybe."

Wart could feel tension in the camp. Seagood had planned to start after lunch, but knowing they were being watched had unnerved them all. It was decided that they would begin their journey after dark and make their way the best they could.

When Wart was alone with Rudy in the clearing, he complained, "I wish you hadn't insisted I tell you all I know about this area."

"Why?" Rudy asked.

"The last time I made a suggestion, two men died. Besides, it's been a long time since I was here. It may have changed. It may no longer be safe. I don't want anyone else to get killed on account of my suggestions."

"Hey, take it easy," Rudy warned. "No one died because of your suggestions or because you shared what knowledge you had with us. You simply shared what you knew; we made a decision and acted upon it. Things didn't turn out the way we wanted, but you are taking too much responsibility for Clyde and Darren. All you told us was that there was another path to the river. We took it from there."

"Yes," Wart said, "and now we are only four instead of six."

"And you think if we'd ridden to the Fords and come upriver, everything would have been fine?"

"I guess so."

"We might have met another group of Jabin's forces. There's a good chance none of us would have made it this far. Do you know what Darren was afraid of? Well, I'll tell you. He thought that band of riders that passed us in the dark were Jabin's cavalry. He was sure there would be infantry somewhere behind them. He thought the Fords might literally be crawling with enemy troops. He was overjoyed at the thought of cutting across the mountains and hitting the river above the Fords."

Rudy paused for breath. "I think Mathias thought the same thing, though he was afraid Jabin would march on Emancipation's weak point, and he wanted to aid his own people."

Just then, Mathias came into the clearing. "Rudy, are you sharing military secrets?"

"No, Mat. I was just trying to explain to Wart that Clyde and Darren's deaths were not his fault. And now because he's told us what he knows about this side of the river, he thinks something bad will happen to us again."

"The river claimed Clyde and Darren, not your information," Mathias agreed. "And as for this path—Seagood and I had seen it earlier. We didn't know what to make of it. It was good to know it was a portage trail around the rapids. That doesn't mean it is safe, but it does give us a reason for its existence."

Mathias ruffled Wart's hair. "Let me tell you something else. Seagood and I have scouted enough to know that a lot of horses and men have passed down this trail recently." Wart's eyes grew large as saucers.

"It appears Jabin is preparing a rear attack. He floated an entire army and cavalry down the river sometime yesterday. If we had chosen the route to the Fords, we likely would have met Jabin's army there and perished. If we had been one day sooner on this path, we might have met our end right here."

Wart's eyes grew even larger. "How did we miss Jabin's army?" he asked.

"And how did Seagood get us off the road in time to miss the cavalry?" Mathias asked. "No one else had a clue it was even around."

"The Lord was with us," Rudy said softly. Wart had not heard Rudy talk much about God, but he was beginning to sense that there was something much deeper about these men.

The sun sank low, and shadows grew long. By the time Seagood returned, the horses were saddled and waiting.

"Is the coast clear?" Rudy asked.

Seagood nodded and led the group south to the site of Darren's grave. They stood in silence, looking first at the fresh mound of earth, and then out over the cold, churning water. Rudy spoke softly. "Lord, watch over our friends until we meet again."

Meet again? Wart was puzzled. *What does that mean?* He decided this was not the best time to ask a lot of questions. Quietly mounting his horse, he followed the others into the gloom.

Everyone dismounted at the portage, and even Wart could see that the ground had been trampled by the feet of men and horses.

Rudy, Mathias, and Wart stood quietly, holding their horses while Seagood scouted the area.

"So, what do you know about the Gray Lands, Wart?" Rudy asked.

"On this side of the river, a path runs nearly parallel to the river through a fairly thick forest. The Gray Lands are west of here and are inhabited by quiet, retiring people. That is all I really know."

"Did you ever meet anyone from the Gray Lands?" Rudy asked. "Are they friendly?"

"No, I don't think I've ever met anyone from there," Wart responded.

"I've heard that the Gray Lands are full of witches," Mathias said, "and I half believe it. I still have the feeling we are being watched."

They heard movement in the bushes, and Seagood appeared. He gestured for them to follow, and for nearly a mile they led their horses around bushes, briars, and plum thickets. Finally they came to a path no wider than a deer trail in a forest. Mounting, they began a slow journey north. They heard the hoot of an owl nearby, only to have it answered from deeper in the shadows.

"This place gives me the creeps," Rudy whispered. "I'm sure someone is out there, but I can't see anyone." They were about to move on when Wart saw a flash of silver.

"Seagood," he whispered excitedly. Seagood's eyes followed the boy's pointing finger. The next instant, Seagood was on the ground and racing through the underbrush.

"Down," Rudy hissed, but Mathias was already on the ground, sword drawn and ready for battle. Wart slid from his mount, and with an unsteady hand, he drew his dagger.

"Hold the horses, boy," Rudy commanded.

Mathias crept forward and disappeared into the dark shrubbery.

"Rats!" Rudy fumed. "Now we're split up. Stay with me, Wart! It won't be good if we all get separated. What was that?"

They heard a scuffle in the bushes, but they couldn't see a thing.

"Rudy," Wart whispered.

"What is it, boy?"

"I'm scared!"

"Hang on to your courage, boy! Nothing has fallen from the trees yet."

That thought hadn't occurred to Wart, and he peered anxiously into the trees above him.

"Sorry," Rudy said with a smile. He surveyed the limbs overhead and then turned his attention to the dark shrubbery where they had heard the scuffle. "Sure wish those two hadn't been so quick to rush out there."

Wart peered anxiously around Rudy's broad shoulders. A twig snapped behind him, and a large hand clamped over his mouth.

CHAPTER 22

Captivity

Consciousness brought Thomas no relief. Samoth had bound, gagged, and stuffed him into a box among the rest of the cargo. A hired man rode with Samoth as their wagon bounced along a rutted trail heading north. Thomas kicked at the box and only succeeded in cutting his wrists, as his feet and hands were tied together.

"I guess you didn't kill him after all," a muffled voice spoke.

"Shut up! Of course I didn't kill him. We have to make one more checkpoint, and then the coast is clear."

The creak of leather and the squawk of wheels on worn axles slowed and came to a stop.

"Who goes there?" a voice called.

"Samoth Devia."

"What brings you out so early in the morning?" the sentry asked pleasantly.

"I have to work for a living."

Choosing to ignore Samoth's comment, the sentry stepped near the wagon and held his torch aloft. "Captain didn't tell us you were coming. What are you carrying?"

Samoth bristled. He hated these checkpoints. "Emergency supplies," he lied.

"Headed north? We could use them better than Jabin."

"They aren't for Jabin," Samoth said slowly. "They are for a refugee camp some miles north."

"You'll never deliver them." The sentry swept his hand across the western horizon where campfires glowed as far as the eye could see. "Jabin's men will stop you and take your supplies, sure as anything."

"You are wasting my time," Samoth said, his voice becoming shrill. "I have no quarrel with Jabin. He lets me travel and trade anywhere I want." Samoth studied the sentry with a knowing smile. "What quarrel do *you* have with Jabin? Wouldn't you rather be at home with your family than out here patrolling a border you never saw before a year ago?"

The man hesitated, and Samoth knew he had struck a nerve. Continuing, he asked, "Tell me why you are opposed to Jabin. He is no threat to you."

As if waking from a dream, the man shook himself. "I have never suffered personally, but Jabin's works are well known. Lies and terror follow his every move. I am opposed to that!"

"You're a fool. You could have all this world has to offer if you would just try to get along with both sides. Why should we even choose sides?"

The sentry rubbed his chin. "Well, the Good Book says you can't serve two masters. Either you will love one and hate the other, or you will be obedient to one and despise the other."

"Will you let me pass?" Samoth asked, trying to change the subject.

"What are you carrying?"

"Supplies!"

"I know that. What kind of supplies?"

"Flour, hardtack, biscuits ... you know, things for the larder."

"No weapons?"

"No, I don't have any weapons!" Samoth said.

"What's in the long box?" the sentry asked, holding his torch above the wagon to illuminate its contents.

"Those are wrapped cheeses," Samoth said smoothly.

"Can I take a look?"

"I don't want to break the seal," Samoth said. "The cheese will spoil more quickly if we do."

"All right," the sentry said, turning away. "I suppose you will only feed the enemy another day. You may pass."

Inside the long box, Thomas tried to shout, but the rag stuffed in his mouth muffled his voice. He tried kicking again, but each movement made the ropes cut more deeply into his flesh.

His heart sank as the wagon lurched into motion. Where was he headed?

Above the creak of the wagon, he heard Samoth mutter, "The road is free and clear from here on. James should train his sentries better."

Thomas drifted in and out of consciousness. Voices spoke, but as if from another world. He did hear Samoth's hired man ask, "Think we ought to let him out?"

"Why?"

"I need to stretch, and I thought maybe he did too. That is a mighty small box."

"Are you getting soft on me?" Samoth asked with a snarl.

"Just asking," the voice mumbled.

Thomas could hear nothing but the squeak of leather and the groan of wagon wheels on a rutted road. One bone-jarring bump melted into another. His aching body sought relief. Eventually he passed out, and oblivion brought the only comfort he could find.

Thomas awoke as the wagon rolled to a stop. Boots scraped on the wagon bed. The squawk of nails being ripped from lumber penetrated Thomas's darkened mind.

When the lid was pried from Thomas's confines, sunlight and fresh air flooded around him, giving him new hope. Blinded and dazed, Thomas heard a voice demand, "Get out!"

Rough hands jerked Thomas from his prison, slashed the rope that bound his hands to his feet, and stood him on the ground. His head felt light, and the world swirled before his eyes. Still bound and gagged, Thomas collapsed on the sod, helpless before his captors.

"He's about done in," someone said. Thomas tried to locate the man speaking.

"He'll get worse if he doesn't cater to the Lady," Samoth said savagely. "I'll see to it personally."

"I thought you said you might need protection," the man said. "Look at him. He's too weak to stand up. I've wasted the trip."

"We're not inside Endor yet," Samoth replied. "I don't want him to escape. Once we get him to Endor, there will be no escape."

"Why didn't you just kill him?"

"I'll take him to Maria. She likes to dominate the souls of men, and a corpse can do nothing to satisfy her. Besides, I would rather have Thomas suffer a haunting memory of his loss than obtain the instant forgetfulness of death. Someday he will see me on his father's throne."

The hired man stepped to where Thomas lay, drew his dagger, and with a deft movement cut the cords binding Thomas's feet. "How about his hands?" he asked Samoth.

"Leave them tied."

The man removed Thomas's gag and then held a flask filled with dark liquid to Thomas's lips. The liquid smelled putrid, and Thomas tried to pull away. Prying Thomas's jaws apart, the man poured some liquid into Thomas's mouth. At first it was cool, but quickly it began to burn. Liquid fire trickled down Thomas's throat.

Thomas jerked violently, escaping his captor as he rolled across the grass.

"Ha!" the man laughed. "I didn't think he had that much life left in him."

Thomas turned, wild-eyed, to view his captors. A sour-faced man of huge stature accompanied Samoth. Both were laughing hard.

"Good!" Samoth roared. "See why I didn't want his hands free? With that stuff in him, he might have fought us both." He sat down on the cart, still laughing. "He'll do all right now. We can get him into the city on his own feet."

The hired man stooped to help Thomas to his feet, but Thomas went limp.

Samoth's laughter died on his lips. "Is that the way you want to play?" he shouted. With one swift kick, his boot found its mark, and Thomas's world went dark.

Stumbling forward, half-carried by Samoth and his companion, Thomas vaguely remembered the frowning entrance of Endor. He could hear laughter and jeers.

"What did you bring us today, Samoth? A comedian? He can't even walk!"

"Good old Samoth," someone shouted. "You never leave us without some entertainment."

Not everyone mocked as Thomas staggered across Endor's courtyard. There were those who eyed the newcomer with pity. He was one more soul entering their world of despair.

Thomas was taken to a massive building and dragged through many winding passages. When they came to a staircase, he was shoved down into the darkness. In the pale light of a flickering torch, Thomas watched a man unlock a door and swing it wide. A ghastly stench swept into the hall.

Thomas was pushed inside and hurled against the wall. Exhausted, he slumped to the floor. His bonds were cut, and his arms fell free. He heard a crack as if wood were striking bone. There was a flash of pain, and once again his world went dark.

Thomas awoke to the low moan of human misery. He did not know if he had uttered the sound or if others were near. Opening his eyes, he could see nothing. *Have I gone blind?* he wondered. In desperation he tried to rub his eyes, but his wrists were held to the wall by shackles.

Afraid and confused, he cried out, "Is anybody there?"

All sound ceased. Thomas was entombed in silence.

Slowly regaining his composure, Thomas became aware of a dull throbbing in his head. Leaning toward his right hand, he touched a large lump above his right ear. Gingerly his fingers explored the wound. Large as a goose egg, the top of the lump was open and oozed fluid.

"Keep quiet!" said a voice in the darkness.

Thomas jumped at the sound and asked, "Where are you?"

"Not so loud," the man hissed. "Do you want the guard to come back?"

Thomas asked no more questions. If guards had put that lump on his head, he surely didn't want to incur any more abuse from their hands. He sat silent in the darkness, slowly becoming aware of his surroundings. He could hear the ragged breathing of people and the soft scurry of mice along the floor.

Suddenly, every sound in the room ceased when a key scraped in the lock.

"I tried to warn you," a voice whispered nearby.

The door squealed on rusty hinges, and torchlight flooded the cavern. Nearly naked men were chained to the walls on every side. Thomas shuddered.

"Which one does she want?"

"That one," a man said, pointing toward Thomas.

"Why this one?" the first man asked, jabbing his staff savagely into Thomas's stomach.

"Hey, no need for that!" the other man said sharply.

"What does it matter?"

"Watch what you say. Such a comment could put you on the rack."

"Yeah, yeah. I'm real worried."

"Besides, she prefers them alive, not dead."

"They're all as good as dead in this stinking hole."

The chains fell from Thomas's wrists, and he doubled over in pain. The same staff came down hard on his back, "Get up, scum!"

Thomas staggered to his feet, wobbled on feeble legs, and tottered toward the door.

Somewhere behind him, he heard a voice jeer, "Lucky dog!"

A tower soared above the dungeon where Thomas was kept, and in this tower resided the beautiful princess of Endor, daughter of Jabin. She bore a title unlike any in the kingdom. She was known as the Goddess of the Moon. Each month at full moon, Maria led her people in worshipping the gods of fertility and love. She was surrounded by guards and loving admirers, like Samoth, who would do anything at her bidding. Today was no different.

Alone with Samoth, Maria twirled before him and brushed her fingers along his jaw. "My prophet," she cooed. "Did you bring me a knight in shining armor?" Her voice was soft and sensuous.

"Just another toy, my lady," Samoth said nonchalantly. He tossed his shirt over the dresser and began splashing water on his face from the wash basin.

Though the light was dim, he peered for some time into the brass mirror that hung by the basin. He didn't hear her movement, but suddenly he felt her cool fingers touch his naked ribs. Her hands encircled his firm torso and combed the thick hair on his chest.

"You've been away a long time," she said.

He felt the warmth of her body against his back. "Absence makes the body fonder," he said, turning to meet her moist, parted lips.

The two embraced, searching for the one thing they had never found: true love.

Morning found Maria alone. Samoth had departed before she awoke, and now she sat at her mirror, watching as a maiden combed her long dark hair. "Why doesn't he stay?" she fussed.

The maiden did not answer but continued to comb and braid the Ravenna's hair.

Maria stared glumly into the polished brass. "He loves me, you know."

The brush caught in her long dark hair, and Maria was instantly defensive. "I know he loves me. Why else would he bring me servants? And he doesn't just bring servants; he makes the servants love me. They *want* to serve me. They relish coming into my presence." She tried to sound confident, but her voice was a little too shrill.

The maiden pulled the brush through the knots in Maria's hair but did not reply.

Maria thought of the worship service and the clamoring congregation, everyone reaching out to touch her. It was so thrilling! She wished it wasn't limited to each full moon.

"At least today is special," she said. "Samoth brought another group of men for my royal guard." She smiled to herself. She knew the only thing they guarded her from were lonely nights while Samoth was away. That happened nearly all the time nowadays.

Her guards were flirtatious, fun, and oh so loyal—just like so many slobbering dogs. They were no challenge at all.

"What I want," Maria said boldly, "is someone who will resist me just to make it fun. I'm bored with these men who simply pant when they escort me anywhere." Maria glanced in the mirror and caught the shocked expression on her maiden's face. A haughty smile crossed her lips as she spoke. "I'm sure you don't understand."

The maiden said nothing. Blushing deeply, she busied her fingers with combs and pins, quickly shaping the Ravenna's thick hair.

Thomas and nine other men stood in a waiting room high in the Temple of the Moon. Colorful tapestries hung on the walls, and large windows flooded the room with light. This group was awaiting the Ravenna's inspection. Thomas's situation had improved dramatically since he'd been removed from the dungeons below. He'd been fed and bathed, his hair clipped and his face shaved, and today he wore the scarlet breeches and white shirt of the court gentry. The wound above his right ear had been carefully treated, and he was nearly healed.

He'd understood little that had been said during the last few days, for the language of Endor was foreign to his ears. However, it seemed that several men from this very group could be chosen to serve as guards in the realm of the Goddess. He wasn't enthused by the thought of serving a woman who thought she was divine.

Thomas glanced out the window to the courtyard far below. *I wonder if anyone from home has a clue where I am,* he pondered as he surveyed the unfamiliar surroundings. His thoughts were interrupted by a knock on the door.

Maria walked swiftly down the corridor amidst a flourish of petticoats and the soft whisper of satin. Four men escorted her, two carrying torches to light the hallway, and the others holding her arms for support. Behind Maria, a maiden carried her train.

They reached a doorway where Melzar, the chief jailer, stood bedecked in the stunning crimson and gold of Endor's stewards. Bowing low, he asked, "Are you ready, my lady?"

"How many are there?" she asked.

"Ten, my lady."

"Why so few?" she asked.

"There has been little time since your last choosing," Melzar responded.

"Silence," Maria demanded. *Will I find anyone to resist me among so few?* she wondered. Breathing deeply, she composed her thoughts and said, "I'm ready."

A trumpet sounded, and Maria swished into a room where ten men stood awaiting her inspection. She was taken aback. These were some of the most handsome men she had ever seen, and her cheeks grew warm.

She could feel every eye in the room admiring her. A giddy sense of power coursed through her veins. She could choose one or all of these handsome men to accompany her, guard her, or protect her. And they all wanted to.

But wait! she thought. A flicker of doubt crossed her mind. Not all eyes were on her. One man stared straight ahead as if she hadn't entered the room. Her heart beat faster: a conquest. "The gods have not let me down," she whispered.

With cool deliberation, she walked along the line of men, admiring each one in turn. The longing in each man's eyes gave her a sense of satisfaction. She knew they had never witnessed such grace and beauty before, and they longed to be a part of her court.

She finally came to the man who had garnered her attention. Breathing deeply, Maria studied him. Thomas stared at the wall as if he were made of stone. She stepped directly into his line of vision and studied his eyes. They were not glassy but clear and cool. Not haughty but calm and unmoved. In fact, he seemed to look right through her.

A flood of emotions poured through Maria. She'd forgotten the deep emotions of a conquest. Seductively, she moved closer to the nameless man. Her fingertips brushed lightly upon his cheek. She peered into his expressionless face. Bruises were healing under his skin.

With a wry smile, she spoke to the chamberlain. "Where did this one come from?"

"Some say he is a prince of Amity," Melzar answered.

Maria caught her breath. Thoughts raced through her mind. *My father hates Amity with a passion and has decreed that all from there should die, but I know there are many in the prison, and he does not seem to care. What would happen if I took a prince from that country into my guard, or maybe even to my own bosom?*

She could feel color rush to her face. It was so forbidden, so wrong, yet so tempting. Trying to cover her emotions, she turned angrily to the chamberlain. "Melzar!" she stormed. "Why have you presented this man with bruises? You know I can have nothing defiled!"

"Time was short, my lady, and he came to me bruised and beaten. I've done the best I could with him in the short time I was given."

Maria dismissed the entire proceeding with a wave of her hand. "Take this one back! I will interview him when he is fully healed. The rest of these men I will take into my service. Show them their quarters and instruct them in their new duties. That is all!"

Maria whirled to make her exit, brushing lightly against Thomas. She watched to see if he showed the slightest reaction. There was none.

With a great flourish, Maria's petticoats rustled as she hurried from the room.

After the Ravenna's inspection, Melzar led Thomas down to his own quarters in the prison and lectured him on the folly of spurning the Lady of Endor. For some strange reason he felt drawn to this young prince of Amity, and in the days that followed, he began to tutor Thomas in the language, customs, and worship of Endor. The young man proved such a willing student that Melzar began to share more and more of his time and knowledge with Thomas.

One day as Thomas walked the halls of the tower with Melzar, he asked, "Are there dungeons below us in this building?"

"Yes," Melzar answered.

Thomas liked the old jailer. He had begun to think of him as a surrogate father figure. "May I ask you a question?"

"Speak your mind," Melzar responded.

"Would you let me share your duties and lighten your burdens?"

Caution shaded Melzar's countenance. "You wouldn't try to trick me? Any attempt to escape will forfeit my life."

Thomas frowned. "I hoped I had won your trust. A shared burden is lighter for both."

Melzar narrowed his eyes, and Thomas sensed the man's doubts.

On a hunch, Thomas suddenly asked, "Are you afraid of me or for me?"

"You are a very perceptive young man," Melzar said. "If you must know, I am afraid for you. I was instructed to send you back to the Goddess when you were healed, but I am reluctant to do so. I'm hoping in time she will forget you are here. Now I must decide whether to let you help me."

Thomas watched as Melzar struggled to reach a decision. "All right, let's give this a try," the old man finally replied. "Come with me."

Melzar collected bread from the kitchen, and Thomas carried a pail of water as they descended from the prison into the dungeon beneath. The stench was awful! The smell of decay permeated the air.

The first cell they entered, Thomas feared he would gag while holding a torch and Melzar's basket of bread. Melzar began distributing crusts of bread to each man in chains. They came to a man who hung motionless against the wall, and Melzar began to pass him by.

"Sir, shouldn't we awaken him for his morsel?"

"There is no need, my son."

Thomas bent, touched the man, and withdrew his hand in revulsion. "He's dead!"

"What did you expect?"

"Shouldn't we remove him?"

"I don't have time," Melzar answered.

Thomas was shocked. His mind raced. These were men, not animals chained to the wall. They had hopes, dreams, desires, and emotions that no other creature on earth could experience. To leave the dead among the living would dehumanize the prisoners into something akin to trash. Thomas could not imagine allowing that to continue.

Thomas spoke earnestly. "Melzar, if you don't have time, let me remove the dead from among the living."

"I cannot allow that." Melzar's face grew stern. "You would need to leave the temple, and I would forfeit my life."

"Is there not a room within the temple we could devote strictly to the dead?"

Melzar considered in silence as they continued passing out their morsels of bread. Again and again they passed hands that no longer reached for the crusts of life. They finished their labor and fled to the fresher air of the hallway.

Melzar hesitated. "There is a room ..." he began, his face pale and his eyes darting nervously about the hallway. "I will show you the way."

Thomas followed his keeper down many flights of stairs into the very bowels of the earth. Here the stench of rotting flesh was almost unbearable. Melzar stopped his descent and turned to Thomas. "I cannot do what you ask. I fear for myself, and I fear for you. This is the realm of the forgotten."

Thomas fought to control his churning stomach, and he held his nose. "Lead on, my friend. Our heavenly Father will give us strength."

Melzar frowned but turned and slowly descended two more flights of stairs. The air was ripe, and the stench of decay burned their eyes and noses. Even the torchlight dimmed in the pall of this terrible place.

An iron door stood at the bottom of the stairs. With a trembling hand, Melzar searched through his keys and selected one. Holding the key up for Thomas's inspection, he said, "This is the key to the oubliette, the land of the forgotten." With that he slipped the key in the lock and opened the door.

Melzar had given Thomas permission to remove the dead from the dungeon as long as he brought them to the oubliette. This room at the very deepest level of the dungeon was never visited by the prison guards, and once people passed through the door, they were never seen again.

It was appalling work, but Thomas was given broad freedoms and a wide assortment of keys to access many areas of the dungeon he otherwise would never have had. Each day he would open a new cell, remove the dead from the walls, and carry them to the oubliette. When he closed and locked the door at night, he sealed the living from the dead.

"Don't let any part of your body cross the threshold," Melzar warned Thomas, "for no one knows exactly what is on the other side. No one who has crossed that threshold has ever returned."

Torches flickered and barely lit the steps leading down to the iron door. One by one Thomas carried dead bodies to the door, laid them on the threshold, and used a long pole to push them into the darkness on the other side.

There must be a ledge about three feet inside the door, Thomas reasoned, but he could see nothing beyond the threshold. He wondered if some dark magic kept light from penetrating the darkness. Even a burning torch would disappear from view in the inky darkness of the oubliette. *Though I can't see what's inside,* Thomas considered, *there must be a deep abyss. I have to push the bodies some distance before they slip over the edge, but I never hear them hit the bottom.*

He once again turned to climb the stairs. Several cells had been cleansed, he thought with some satisfaction. Did he dare start another? He suddenly noticed a door in the dungeon that he had not noticed before. A human skull hung upon a peg beside the door.

Is this where men are brought to die? he mused. *What are their crimes? Did they oppose the Goddess or refuse her service?*

On impulse, he withdrew the ring of keys Melzar had loaned him. Trying key after key, one finally slid into the lock upon the door. Turning the key and lifting the latch, the door swung wide. The reek of decay assailed his nostrils.

Skeletons hung in chains from the walls. A few gaunt men raised sunken eyes to view the intruder. Thomas cried out in horror. "Haven't you been fed?" These men were not facing execution by gallows, sword, or fire. They were being starved!

"Master," a hoarse whisper met his ears. He searched for the owner of the voice and found a shell of a man, wasted to skin and bone.

The man stirred, and Thomas leaned near, hoping to catch any word he might utter, but the poor man's throat was so dry he could not rasp another word.

"I'll get you water," Thomas said, rising quickly. There was a fountain near the guard station. Washing his hands in the basin, Thomas looked for a cup. Not seeing one, and not wishing to attract attention, he cupped his hands, filled them with water and hurried back to the cell.

The old man's tightly drawn features did not move, and Thomas feared he was too late. "I have water for you," he said softly.

The old man's eyes flickered, and Thomas poured water into his parted lips a little at a time. Weakened as he was, the old man tried to stand. "Save your strength, my good man," Thomas encouraged.

"Master, Thomas," the man croaked hoarsely.

Thomas was shocked. "You know me?" he managed to whisper.

"I always believed I would be rescued, but I never dreamed it would be the son of my lord who would come to this dreadful place. I am Helberg Stanley, a loyal servant to your father."

Thomas stared in disbelief. Stanley was not a ruler, but on the Western Slope, many men looked to him for guidance and leadership.

"How is it you came here, my lord?" Thomas asked.

"It's a long story," Stanley whispered. "But don't speak so openly. The walls have ears. Even one's thoughts become public knowledge here."

"Why should I be afraid of revealing my heart to you?"

"We are not alone. Amity is hated here—and much more so its prince."

"I can't leave you here. You've not eaten, and I've given you only a drop of water."

"Show me no favors, for I am not liked here."

"Why? What have you done to deserve this?"

"Hush. Get water for all," the old man whispered.

Thomas rose to obey and surveyed the room. How was he to get water to those yet alive in this dreadful place? Then he remembered. Other cells had a bucket and ladle. In short order, he returned and began to offer each man the water of life.

The men in this cell responded differently from those in the other cells. In most cells, Thomas was viewed as an attendant doing an unpleasant task. But the men in this cell were supposed to die, and they were not given food or water. Some saw Thomas as an angel of mercy, others viewed him with suspicion.

One man asked, "What have you to do with us?" His speech was broken and heavy with accent, but he spoke the common tongue well enough for Thomas to understand.

"I came to remove the dead from among you," Thomas said simply.

"We are all dead men! Do you give water and hope only to prolong our suffering? Leave me alone and let me die."

The man had willingly taken the water offered moments before, so Thomas was gentle in his response. "I'll not force anything upon you. You are free to choose life or death."

Thomas's work continued in the days that followed as one body after another disappeared through the door at the bottom of the stairs. He had cleansed the cell where he'd found Helberg Stanley as well as many others. But the labor was beginning to take its toll. He grew weary as he climbed the stairs again, and stumbling, he lay prone on the steps. One by one, the torches in the stairwells began to flicker and go out. Darkness enshrouded him, and a terror slowly spread up the dungeon stairs. With growing menace, it numbed his heart and quelled his spirit.

"I need to close that door," he whispered. His mind had grown dull, but he could imagine spirits of the dead creeping up the staircase toward the place where he lay. Thomas knew he was being irrational, but still the thought preyed on his mind.

Then he heard the soft scurry of padded feet. His heart pounded in his chest, and he struggled to choke back his fear. Something furry brushed his leg. Sweat beaded on his brow.

Jumping up, he raced up the stairs and grabbed another torch. Its flame burned low and sputtered in his hand. With bated breath he descended into the darkness.

His eye caught a movement. "Rats." He sighed. "I should have known."

Though his fear abated with the knowledge, an unearthly presence still lingered in the air. At the bottom of the stairs, he found only the gaping doorway and darkness—nothing else. Giving the door a shove, he heard the satisfying click of the lock as it banged shut.

Maria's knuckles were white as she yanked a brush viciously through her hair. Nothing was going right! Samoth had been there last night, but there had been no pleasure in his embrace. She hoped he hadn't noticed her preoccupation.

"That bungling Melzar!" she stormed.

All Melzar had said when she'd questioned him about the prisoner was, "He isn't healing as fast as he should. Each day he becomes covered with a deathlike smell, and each night his clothes have to be burned with fire."

Her brow furrowed. *I should have that old man executed!* she thought vengefully. She managed a few more swipes at her hair. She was in such a foul mood that she had refused help in preparing for bed.

"The prisoner did not appear about to die!" she raged. "What is Melzar doing? Making him ill?" Suddenly she paused. "I'll simply order the prisoner to be brought after he is properly cleaned tomorrow. That will put an end to this delay."

She stopped and looked in the mirror. "But I can't be defiled! Full moon is only two nights from now."

Normally the thought of worship under the moon made her giddy with anticipation. Tonight it made her realize that she would have to wait several more days to see the one of her dreams.

"Well, I can wait. I don't want to anger the gods." She took a deep breath. "Besides, it gives me extra time to prepare."

With that settled, she walked to her gown room. "Now, what should I wear?" Her eyes fell upon one of her most revealing garments. A slow smile spread across her lips. "Shame on you," she whispered.

Melzar had managed to keep Thomas away from the Goddess of the Moon for several weeks. During that time, Thomas had cleansed much of the dungeon, and life had become easier for Melzar. Most cells were clean and tidy, and everything was in order. The smell in the dungeon had improved dramatically.

Thomas had recruited help from several cells and had persuaded Melzar to release these men into his care. Stanley was the first among the men Melzar approved to work about the prison with Thomas. Just this morning, Melzar had seen several men carrying pails of water to scrub a holding cell. True, the guards weren't too happy about so many people roaming the halls, but even they had to admit that the odor was better, and nothing had happened yet. Just the same, they remained wary.

Days quickly ran together. One day as Thomas was making his rounds delivering bread and water to the prisoners, he noticed a man holding his thumb across his forefinger in the sign of a cross. It was the secret sign from the old stories. Stanley had remembered the sign and started its use after Thomas had gotten him released to a work crew. That sign let Thomas know who was safe to talk to and who wasn't.

Thomas's eyes met those of the prisoner making the sign, and he nodded. Carefully he dipped his ladle in the bucket and held the water near the man's lips. Hidden by Thomas's body and the ladle, the man whispered softly, "Beware the third man down, my lord. I think he suspects who you are."

"Why would he want to harm someone who brings him food and water, cleans his cell, and eases his discomfort?" Thomas asked.

"He is devoted to 'the Lady' and loves her greatly. Word has reached us that she sent for you and you refused. There are those who think people who deny the Lady should be put to death."

"Do they know Melzar is the reason for the delay?"

"It is suspected. Everyone knows his workload is less and conditions are better. If you remain here, it may go hard on him as well."

Their conversation was interrupted when the prisoner in question began to yell, "Hey, what's going on there? Don't give him all the water."

Thomas nodded his thanks, offered the water, and moved on down the line.

Thomas finished his duties in the cells and returned to Melzar's quarters. He found Melzar reclining on his cot. "May I have a word, Melzar?"

"Certainly." Melzar sat up and waved for Thomas to enter. "Is there something you need?"

"I need you to send me to the Ravenna," Thomas said.

Melzar turned very pale. Glancing nervously around, he motioned Thomas closer. "My son," he said, "if you reject the service of the Lady again, she will order your execution. You have become very special to me, and I cannot bear the thought of losing you."

Thomas nodded. "You've told me that before, but there is talk in the cells that you are refusing to send me to her. If that becomes well known, your life will be forfeit. You must let me go to her before you are in danger."

"A woman spurned is a fearful thing," Melzar warned.

"You have not said exactly what it is she expects of me, yet you have said enough to make me wary."

"I am frightened for you, my son. Have I not told you that all who cross her die a horrible death?"

"You have warned me," Thomas replied.

"Yet you consider opposing her?"

"I must live with my conscience."

"Then you are determined to go?" Melzar asked.

"Yes," Thomas answered.

"Then you must be presentable," Melzar said. "You must take a bath, and I will pick out the clothes you must wear."

An hour later, the two men stepped into a corridor, and Melzar remained silent as he led Thomas past the guard station. Once they had traversed a long hall, his steps slowed as if he was reluctant to leave his charge. His eyes darted about, searching for listening ears. "The Lady desires men as a spider hungers for flies. She will devour you and reduce you to nothing. Look at the guards. They are mindless slaves, obeying her every command, lusting for her favors. At random, she gives them just enough to keep them wanting more."

Thomas smiled at the man he'd come to love. "Melzar, I want to thank you for this warning."

The old man began to tremble. "I shall be slain if the walls should repeat my words."

"I would have learned the truth eventually, from others if not from you. Our heavenly Father reveals the truth to every man's heart."

Melzar frowned as they proceeded slowly down the long corridor. "Your words frighten me, my son. Who is this god who reveals secrets to men's hearts?"

"He is the Lord Almighty," Thomas said, "the creator of heaven and earth."

"What kind of god is he?"

"Our Lord is gracious and merciful, giving freely and expecting nothing in return. He knows man is but dust."

"How do you worship a god who expects nothing of you?"

"Religion tries to make man right with God. It offers penance and punishment, hoping to appease God. However, the Lord will not accept such human payment, for our righteousness is as dirty rags to Him, and our offerings are unholy. But the Lord sent His Son as a holy sacrifice, that whoever believes in Him should never perish but have everlasting life."

"Tell me more!" Melzar demanded, excitement growing in his eyes.

"The Lord became flesh and dwelt among us. Completely divine, yet all man."

"Like the Goddess of the Moon?" Melzar interrupted excitedly.

"No!" Thomas said firmly. "She is trying to build an empire on this earth by feigning deity, but Jesus left the wonders of heaven to become a servant. He took our sin upon Himself and suffered in our place. He came not to lord it over us but to give us life!"

Melzar stood quietly, trying to digest this information. "But I ask you again, how do you worship a god like that?"

"Our Lord became a servant, and we follow his example. When we humble ourselves to serve one another, we experience freedom from our selfishness. This is the highest praise and worship we can offer."

"So, service is your sacrifice? That is what is required of you?"

"We serve not to purchase our salvation; rather we serve out of gratitude for the salvation Jesus has already given."

"My heart is troubled!" Melzar said frankly. "The words you speak move me, but I do not know how to respond."

"Yield to the conviction of the Holy Spirit. Accept what Jesus has already done. Cling to Jesus's death and resurrection. Our heavenly Father will accept all who come to Jesus in faith. Salvation is a free gift to all who believe. Simply take the Lord at His word."

The fear in Melzar's eyes was replaced with wonder and amazement. "You mean I can be right with God, without the rituals of the Goddess?"

"Yes!" Thomas responded. "The rituals of religion only glorify and gratify the flesh. You cannot please our heavenly Father by participating in their practice."

"Were you worshipping your God by cleaning the prison cells?"

"Yes, in part. You see, I believe the Lord has sent me here. I know you think Samoth brought me, and he did, but the Lord allowed it to happen. I have been able to share the Divine One's love with many people here, but my time may be nearly over."

Wonder grew in the old man's eyes. "Can I have this same calmness of spirit that you possess?"

"Yes," Thomas said. "Place your trust in Jesus Christ, and He will give you peace."

They had reached the top floor of the temple. The next flight of stairs led to the roof. Melzar touched Thomas's arm. "We have spoken openly, but we can do so no longer. The Lady's chamber is just down the hall, with guards about the door. Your time of testing is at hand. I will now bid you farewell, for I cannot do so at the door."

They faced each other with eyes of admiration and deep respect. Melzar trembled as he spoke. "I hope your God is with you." The men grasped each other's shoulders.

Suddenly Thomas took Melzar's hand in his own. He quickly formed a cross with Melzar's thumb and forefinger. "This is a sign among believers here. If you flash this signal upon greeting someone and it is returned, you will have found a brother in Christ. They will support you in the coming days. I may not return, but there are others here who serve the Lord of heaven and earth. They will show you the way of truth and mercy. I pray the Lord will be gracious to you."

Melzar studied the sign in his hand for a moment and then nodded. Stepping from the shadows, they continued down the hallway.

CHAPTER 23

The Interview

Maria had received word: she would finally get to interview the man who had tortured her thoughts for so many weeks. She'd sent her maidens to their rooms, and now she stared at her reflection in the mirror. She tucked a stray hair firmly back in place. *Is everything perfect?* she thought nervously and then stopped. "Why am I behaving like this? I am divine. He is nothing but a slave."

She chided her folly but continued to fuss over her appearance. She must win him, but how?

Her fingers traced the lace fringe of her gown's plunging neckline. A smile crossed her lips. "How can any man resist this?" she cooed, admiring the view. Hadn't her maidens said the same? She was stunning, and she knew it.

Dabbing light-blue powder about her eyes, she whispered viciously, "Melzar, you'd better not deny me today, or I'll have your head!"

There were sounds at the outer door, and a guard called, "Your Majesty! The chamberlain has come with his charge."

Maria studied herself in the mirror. Everything was perfect. "Melzar may enter," she called.

She was dazzling! Her deep-blue gown clung tellingly to her shapely torso, its broad skirt trailing gently to the floor. Her face was as white as a midsummer moon and her hair as black as a midnight sky. The crown she wore sparkled like a myriad of stars.

When Melzar entered, Maria could see from his stunned expression he had never seen her so dangerously beautiful. "M-my lady!" he stammered, bowing low. "Your servant," he said, presenting Thomas, bedecked in crimson pants and a white satin shirt.

Maria felt triumphant. She had never seen Melzar so moved by her appearance. She sternly tried to control her voice, for she felt as giddy as a schoolchild. She dared not look at the man she longed to possess. "Thank you, Melzar," she said somewhat forcefully. "You are free to go!"

The old man lingered for a moment and then turned away. Thomas saw the terror in his eye, and he flashed Melzar "their" signal.

The guard showed no sign of leaving. With some irritation, Maria turned to him and said, "I will no longer need your services!" The guard reluctantly stepped outside and closed the door.

Finally, she had the man of her dreams alone. Maria slowly turned to view her conquest. Her heart was racing. *Will he be looking at me?* she wondered. A tremor ran through her body. There was a breathless moment before her eyes met his.

Her heart skipped a beat, but not from the joy she was anticipating. The young man was indeed looking at her, but he did not seem dazzled by her beauty. He did not seem to be impressed with what he saw. She searched his eyes for emotion but found only pity. Had something gone wrong with her outfit?

Blushing, she drew her revealing neckline together and took a few steps toward the mirror. With a quick check of her attire, she casually asked, "Are your injuries quite healed?"

Thomas bowed slightly and smiled. "Your chamberlain has taken good care of me."

"You speak the language of Endor," she said approvingly.

"Only a little," Thomas admitted. "The language of Endor is only one of the many things Melzar has taught me during my stay."

His smile encouraged her to step forward, but she stopped when she felt his disapproval. "Won't you let me examine your wounds?" she asked reproachfully.

"They are quite healed!"

There was an awkward silence, and Maria felt frustration growing. She was supposed to be in control, yet this slave was setting the pace and agenda. That wasn't what she wanted. She thought about her gown and all her hours of preparation and grew irritated. This man should be groveling at her feet. Still, she had wanted a challenge, and the gods had certainly given her one.

"Do you know why I have sent for you?" she asked, the old authority returning to her voice.

"Not exactly," Thomas answered carefully. His very countenance exuded authority, and none would question that he was of noble birth. The manner in which he took control threw Maria into complete disarray.

But, Maria thought, *he's in my court now. He is nothing but a slave here! I will set the agenda and move forward.*

"Do you like my gown?" she asked, making a seductive turn that revealed her bare back and shapely figure. She moved within his grasp, and their eyes met again.

"I doubt you brought me here to critique your wardrobe."

"Oh!" She pouted. "Don't treat me harshly when I've been so lonely," she said, reaching up and lightly brushing her fingertips over the rugged lines of his jaw. "Won't you come and give me a little company?" She turned toward her private quarters.

"No."

She whirled, anger flashing in her eyes, but she quickly softened and changed her approach. "Where do you come from?"

"Amity," he answered.

"Are you of noble lineage?" she asked, admiring the composure with which he held himself.

"I am of the house and lineage of Stafford," Thomas said quietly.

She already knew this, but hearing it from the man's own lips sent a shiver down her spine. If her father were here, this man would be dead, and she would be considered a traitor. Yet here she was alone with the Prince of Amity. A thrill pulsed through her veins. She would defy her father. She would keep this man for herself.

A plan began to form in Maria's mind. *I'll marry him,* she thought. *We will unite our kingdoms! I will forget Samoth, for he has nothing. Instead I will make this man my own.*

"Come." Maria gently steered Thomas toward a small table in the apartment. The table was in full view of the maids' quarters, so he followed. "I'll have the maid bring wine while we sit and talk." Thomas held her chair, and when she was seated, he crossed and sat on the opposite side of the table.

"You are different from any man I have ever met," Maria said as she brushed a hair from her face.

"Is that good or bad?" Thomas asked.

"It's different and rather exciting. I'm a little unsure of myself. I usually take the lead, and most fall in line, but not you."

Thomas made no comment while the maid produced two crystal goblets and a bottle of wine. She poured the wine and turned questioning eyes upon her mistress.

"That will be all," Maria said as she waved the girl away. Turning to Thomas, she picked up her glass and held it aloft. "Will you offer a toast?"

"Under different circumstances, I would gladly offer a toast to your health, but I cannot wish you to remain as you are," Thomas said calmly.

Maria studied him closely. Was he mocking her? "In what circumstances would you toast my health?" she asked.

"I would toast your health if you were truly free," Thomas responded.

A cloud passed over Maria's face. "Truly free? Whatever do you mean?"

"Dear lady," Thomas began, "you are a prisoner here, just like me."

"I beg your pardon," she protested. "I am the Ravenna, Goddess of the Moon. I am not a prisoner."

Thomas leaned back in his chair. "Yes, you are those things, and I'm sure your position gives you these pleasant rooms and many servants. But when are you free to walk the meadows, smell the flowers, or feel the grass beneath your feet? When can you look at the full moon and simply thank God for His creation and not feel you must perform some ritual to please the gods?"

"I have all I need," Maria said defensively.

"No, my lady," Thomas said softly. "You lack one very important thing."

"And what is that?" Maria asked.

"You don't have Jesus. You can never experience true freedom until you accept Him into your life."

Maria sat quietly for a moment. "Who is this Jesus?" she asked.

"He is the savior of mankind," Thomas answered quietly.

This is not how it's supposed to be going, Maria thought. *I wanted to talk of marriage and uniting our kingdoms, and he wants to talk religion. Well, I can play along. I can be sweet and listen.*

"How can I receive this thing you think I lack?" she asked, her voice remaining smooth.

"Leave this charade and join those who believe," Thomas said evenly.

Maria stiffened. "Charade?" she asked, her voice becoming cool. "Who do you think I am? I am divine! I control the ebb and flow of life. Mankind lives or dies at my bidding. Do you think I am playing a game?"

Thomas watched her carefully.

"Besides," Maria continued, "I cannot leave. There are only two ways out of the palace: through the front gate, or death."

Thomas did not answer.

Maria suddenly felt helpless. This man was right. She was a prisoner here. Anger suddenly welled up inside her. Trying to regain her authority, she snapped, "Do you realize the power I have over your life? I can offer life and love, or I can have you executed."

"The Lord gives all things," Thomas said quietly. "You would have no power over me if it had not been given you from above."

Maria felt the expression on her face change. "I know my own power," she spat. "I thought I would make you my own. What a fool I've been. You have rebuffed me at every turn, throttling the mercy I meant for you. You even mock my authority! Is this god you believe in able to save you from my hand, or will he let you die?"

"He is able to save," Thomas said quietly, "but He may allow me to die. He has asked others to endure such sacrifice. He asked it of His own Son."

"You are a greater fool than I thought!" Maria shouted. "Loyalty should bring rewards, not death. No one in his right mind would serve a God who would ask such sacrifice."

Unflinching, Thomas remained calm throughout her tirade.

Maria decided to soften her approach. "Come," she said. "Let us reason together. You should not die. I will harbor you and keep you from my father. He has decreed that all from Amity must die. Become loyal to me, and I will reward you and make you great in my kingdom. You will have power and authority over many because of me. Don't be a fool. Don't follow a god who asks you to die for him."

Thomas just smiled and gently shook his head.

Anger flashed in Maria's eyes. "Can't you see the paths of life and death? Why won't you choose life?"

"I have chosen eternal life in Jesus Christ," Thomas said quietly. "He has set me free. I may rot in your prison or die at your command, but I shall remain forever free in Jesus."

Maria's countenance became cold and hard. "You will regret this!" she said between clenched teeth. Turning toward her outer door, she called, "Guards!"

Several men burst into her room with swords drawn.

"Take this man away," she ordered. "Make him honor me, but spare his life. I want to hear him recant with my own ears."

Savage smiles passed around the group. "We've been waiting for this one," someone sneered as rough hands dragged Thomas from the room.

Maria put her hands over her ears. She could hear each shriek that echoed in the hallway. What had she done? The face of the handsome slave grew in her mind. The memory of his eyes pierced her soul. A dark cloud covered her heart. "If he thinks his god has set him free, he is mistaken. He is mine! He can never escape."

A mournful howl dwindled to a pathetic whimper.

Maria's heart melted. "Enough!" she cried out to no one. "Bring him to me. I will heal his wounds. I will set him free."

Another scream tore at her heart.

"Stop it!" she screamed into her empty room.

Suddenly Maria heard the latch to her room click softly. She leaped to her feet, wondering who would intrude upon her sorrow. Peeking from her bedroom, she saw Samoth slip quietly into the outer room and reclose the door.

She panicked. *What should I do? I can't let Samoth see me like this.*

Samoth stole across the richly covered floor, clearly reveling that he alone could enter her chambers unannounced.

Maria plopped down before her mirror, yanked a brush through her tangled hair, and tried to dry her tears.

"My lady," Samoth called coaxingly as he entered her private quarters.

"My prophet," she responded without feeling.

Samoth studied her from the doorway. Maria was quiet and pensive, withdrawn into a world of her own. "Is something wrong?" he asked.

"Just leave me alone," she said heatedly.

Samoth studied her for a long moment. "I thought I heard screams from your room, and I was worried about your safety. Are you sure everything is all right?"

She knew he was lying. Samoth only came to her when he needed entertainment. Suddenly she was angry with him and with herself. She felt used and dirty.

Samoth moved closer, and his hand stroked her exposed back. Maria had quite forgotten that she was still wearing the gown she had chosen for the interview.

"Don't, Samoth!" she heard herself say. She had always yielded to his touch before, so her words surprised them both.

Samoth withdrew his hand, but it was his turn to be angry. "Something is wrong!" he declared. "Hadn't you better tell me? Is it the man being tortured downstairs? I thought you had more stomach than that. A little screaming shouldn't harm romance, should it?" He reached for her bare shoulders.

She pulled away. "I'm upset, that's all," she retorted. She had to think of something fast. Turning toward Samoth, she asked, "Do you love me?"

"Of course I do. You know that!"

"Will you marry me and take me away from here?"

"Whoa," Samoth said, backing away. "Who has been planting those ideas in your pretty little head?"

There was a knock at the outer door, and the maid discreetly slipped out to answer. In a moment she returned to her mistress and announced, "My lady, they have brought him back."

CHAPTER 24

Condemned

Guards held Thomas upright in the doorway. Samoth glanced at the broken man but did not appear to recognize Thomas at all.

Maria was shocked. This man did not even resemble the man she had longed for! She dared not look into his eyes. Struggling to control her emotions, she asked the guards, "Has he recanted?"

"No, my lady!"

Anger suddenly filled Maria's heart. Boldly turning to Thomas, she asked, "Don't you see the power I have over you?"

Thomas raised his head, and from his battered face, his eyes met hers. In a voice barely above a whisper, he said, "Dear lady, you would have no power if my Lord had not given it to you."

Maria's eyes turned cold, and deep furrows deformed the lovely lines of her face.

There was no defiance or anger as Thomas whispered, "Please, do not turn your back on the heavenly Father's love. Yield to Him and find peace for your soul."

The room grew silent. No one had ever addressed the princess so boldly.

Maria felt the color drain from her cheeks, and a deep pain settled in her chest. She wanted this man so badly she could not remain angry, but what of those watching? They were shocked by Thomas's boldness. She dared not lose face before the guards or Samoth. She was, after all, divine.

Turning to Samoth, she suddenly realized that he was the answer to her problem. Looking back at Thomas, she asked, "So, you still want me to give up my throne and come with you to Amity?" She watched for Samoth's reaction. She was sure he had not yet recognized her prisoner.

"Samoth," she said, looking full into his face. "This Prince of Amity claims he is free while I am held prisoner."

"Prince of Amity," one guard whispered. "If I had known …"

Maria held out her hand for silence. "Let it be known that the Queen of Heaven is supreme. I shall continue to reign when this man is forgotten. Send him and his freedom to the oubliette!"

Shock registered around the room. The oubliette! Few had ever seen its dreaded door, but all had heard the stories.

Though others stood in dread silence, Samoth came to life. Recognition and hatred suddenly showed on his face and seemed to stir him into action. "I will toss this imposter through the door myself," he whispered savagely.

Maria nodded her assent. "Thank you, my prophet!" She was glad the task was out of her hands.

Thomas caught Maria's eye and spoke to her softly. "You may forget me, but the Lord Almighty will never forget you!"

Maria felt the color drain from her face, and Samoth snarled, "Get this scum out of here!"

The guards dragged Thomas into the hall, and Samoth shouted, "Hold him!" Jerking Thomas around to face him, he snapped, "Trying to steal my woman?" And with that his fist slammed into Thomas's stomach.

Other fists flew. Men trained to hate Amity vented their wrath upon its prince. He must die, for he had rejected and humiliated their queen.

Finally Samoth fell away, exhausted. "Enough," he panted. "Let him live to feel the terror of the dark door."

Though the beating had come to a halt, the guards still hurled insults at their victim as they dragged Thomas down the hall.

The chamberlain's quarters were near the guard station, and Melzar was startled by heavy pounding on his door. "Melzar, open up!" demanded a loud voice.

The old man, attired in the impeccable garb of the high court, opened the door to reveal Samoth and a group of guards supporting a limp and bloodied man.

Samoth stepped forward and shouted, "Jabin has appointed you keeper of the keys, and by command of the Queen of Heaven, this man is condemned to the land of the forgotten!" Even as Samoth spoke, the men around him withdrew in fear.

Melzar felt a bit dizzy as he turned to examine the prisoner. *Who is this?* he wondered. Suddenly Thomas raised his head, and his swollen eyes met those of his friend.

Melzar gasped. "What has this man done to deserve such a fate?"

"Why does it matter to you, old man?" Samoth said with a sneer.

"I do not readily hand out the keys to the darkened door," Melzar said steadily. "It must be a very serious charge indeed."

"He asked the Lady to leave her throne," Samoth said. "We will put an end to such insolence. Quick, give us the key."

Melzar scowled and fumbled through the many keys on his ring. Finally he withdrew a long black key, which he touched with loathing. Presenting it to Samoth, he said, "I cannot come with you. I have many pressing concerns. You may open the door yourself."

Samoth seemed to recoil. "Give the key to him," he said, pointing to the burly man who was holding Thomas. The big man scowled but took the key in trembling fingers.

Melzar turned troubled eyes upon Thomas. How could he lose such a friend? But wait! What was that? What was Thomas doing with his hand?

To Melzar's surprise and great joy, he noticed that Thomas had crossed his forefinger and thumb to form a cross. The old man looked again into the face of his friend and saw a faint smile.

A strange boldness enveloped the old man, and with only a glance at Samoth, he crossed his own thumb and forefinger. Thomas and Melzar's eyes met one last time, and Melzar's heart leaped for joy.

The guards grew more pensive with each descending step, but strangely, Thomas gained new strength. He was familiar with these steps, and the stench did not render him afraid. Had he not traversed these steps countless times in his attempt to cleanse the prison?

The group moved more slowly with each descending flight, and those at the rear fled when they were out of Samoth's sight. Only a very few reached the final flight of steps to the heavy iron door. Samoth's torch flickered in the stagnant air. He stopped at the landing and held his torch aloft. "Take him down and unlock the door," he commanded.

The men holding Thomas stood as if riveted to the floor. They felt a tug as Thomas began to lead the way. Step by step, they descended until they stood before the frightful door. The guard with the key could not move.

Thomas turned to him. "Let me," he said, reaching for the key. A few moments passed as he fumbled with the lock, but everyone heard a loud click, and darkness swirled into the stairwell as the dark door swung open. A putrid odor poured onto the landing and began to climb the stairs.

The guards threw their weapons down and raced up the stairs toward Samoth's light.

In the growing darkness, Thomas turned to face Samoth. "I pray you find forgiveness in the Lord Jesus!" Raising his hand in farewell, he turned and stepped into the darkness.

"Shut that door!" Samoth screamed. Two men rushed down the stairs and slammed the door. The earth shuddered, and thunder boomed up the staircase. The darkness began to dissipate, and Samoth's torch once again shone bright.

"Give me that key," Samoth demanded. The guards raced back up the steps and placed the key in his outstretched palm. Samoth glanced at the key and realized for the first time that his hands were stained with Thomas's blood. Turning, he nearly ran up the stairs, hoping to find a wash basin to remove the last vestige of Thomas from his hands and his mind.

Maria tossed and turned beneath her covers. The night was young, but Samoth was already gone. His touch had left her cold and dissatisfied.

Tossing her covers aside, she leaped from the bed. At once she began to pace the room, feeling caged like some animal. She needed space, and when she spied the stairs leading to the roof, she instantly began to climb. She knew these stairs were only used on Holy Nights, but right now she didn't care. She climbed rapidly and only paused for a moment at the door that led to the roof. Should she go on? Why not? Who could stop her?

Lifting the latch, she shoved the heavy door aside and slipped quietly out onto the roof. Everything was quiet. Tonight, eerie shadows greeted her with mock severity. Tomorrow night things would be so different. She would be met with bonfires, people, praise, and adulation. She would be the center of her kingdom's attention.

She stepped quickly to the altar centered on the flagstone rooftop and rehearsed the ritual in her mind. Usually she felt exhilaration, but tonight everything seemed dull and absurd.

Trying to catch the thrill of former services, Maria climbed the altar's rough stone steps and knelt to stroke an imaginary sacrifice. Virgin maidens would dance and keep time in a circle below. Suddenly Maria stopped, disgust filling her soul. "I can't do this!" she cried.

Desperation filled her heart. She felt dirty and alone. Samoth was using her! Even this worship service reduced her to nothing more than a courtesan. Maria recoiled. Was she a deity or a laughingstock?

Bitter tears rolled down her cheeks. Falling prostrate upon the altar, Maria thought she heard a mournful wail far away. Her heart stood still. Had she only imagined it?

Visions of a handsome slave filled her mind. Could it have been …? Her mind reeled. Dreadful memories of Thomas's battered face focused in her mind. She shuddered at the thought of his dark tomb.

Turning her eyes to the brilliant moon above, she cried out, "What have I done?" Sobbing, Maria laid her head on the rough stones of the altar. The moon kept silent vigil as she wept.

Finally, her tears spent, Maria raised her head and studied her surroundings. Nothing had changed. She was still alone. "I have nowhere to turn," she said. "If I want power, I shall have to use my own. If I want counsel, I shall give my own. If I want comfort, I shall have to make my own!"

Resolve grew within her heart. Whether Samoth used her or not, whether she felt the thrill of worship or not, she would go on! She would persevere. "Tomorrow is a new day," she said with growing conviction. "Tomorrow is *my* day." Rising to her feet, Maria raised her fist to the moon. "I'll show you! I don't need you or anyone else. I can make it on my own!"

Far beneath Maria, in the depths of the earth, Thomas was fighting a battle of his own. He had been so bold when he could still see the light in Samoth's hand, but when the door crashed shut, his world disappeared in darkness. He heard the key scrape in the lock and reeled at the finality of his sentence. Terror gripped him as he groped for the wall. What lay beyond him? He had never been able to see beyond the door, but he was quite sure a narrow ledge was all that separated him from a very deep chasm. What would happen if he stepped one way or another? Would he disappear into the caverns below as had all those he had brought here?

What of Melzar? Would he come to the rescue? Would Samoth even return the key? All questions faded as Thomas realized he could not stand in the darkness forever. Carefully he dropped to one knee and settled to the ground, all the while touching the door with one hand. He did not want to lose that door! Placing his back against the cold iron aperture, Thomas settled back to see what would happen.

In what might have been minutes or hours—time was impossible to determine—there grew the sounds of small, padded feet scurrying all around him. Miniature voices called to each other in a language of their own.

Thomas shifted his weight more firmly against the door. When he dropped his hand to the floor, it bumped a furry creature, which let out a frightened squeal. Thomas jerked his hand away.

Thousands of tiny voices took up the frightened cry, and Thomas joined the clamor. "Oh, Lord," he shouted in desperation, "calm my fears!"

The cries of his unseen companions slowly subsided, and some sense of calm returned to Thomas. *Maybe it's nothing dreadful*, he thought as he brushed his hand slowly around at his side. His fingers connected with a large furry object, and the creature darted swiftly away.

Rats, Thomas thought with disgust. He moved his feet gingerly, but nothing seemed to contend for the space about them. *Rats must not like the edge of this cavern either*, he thought to himself.

Thomas began to realize that he could not move without disturbing a growing number of rats that, like him, were clinging to the wall. Easing himself forward, he heard tiny feet rush past him in their haste to some predetermined destination. All was good until Thomas suddenly realized he had lost the door. Which way should he move? Not daring to make a mistake, he wrapped his arms about his knees and sat perfectly still.

He sat for what seemed like years, pondering his next move. The wounds inflicted upon his body hurt so badly, and here in the darkness there was no distraction to take his mind from the pain. Thomas thought of Melzar occasionally, but as time lapsed, so did his hope of rescue.

An endless stream of unseen visitors passed close to Thomas. When some stopped to investigate, Thomas swung his arms to rebuff them, but eventually he grew too weary for even that limited activity.

Drifting into an eerie slumber, Thomas dreamed of rats feasting on an endless procession of corpses. He could hear the rats' laughter as they called to one another in their foreign tongue. Helplessly, Thomas watched lifeless men march down an endless stairway, plunging headlong into the abyss of the rat kingdom.

Suddenly Thomas saw his own face among those marching in the long procession. "No!" he tried to shout, but the line of men continued descending toward the abyss. "No!" he screamed again, but still they moved forward. The edge of the abyss loomed into sight, and unable to stop his own march, Thomas felt his stomach pitch as he fell headlong over the side. He imagined huge rats with forks and knives in their unwashed hands, and napkins about their necks, awaiting a signal from their king.

"No!" Thomas screamed as their sharp knives cut into his flesh.

Thomas awoke with a start to find that he was indeed surrounded by furry creatures. There was a sharp sting as another rat bit his leg. Thomas flailed wildly, and rats scattered. Kicking again, Thomas's legs suddenly sailed into nothingness.

Grasping madly for something to hold, Thomas's hands came up empty. His feet flailed as his body slid over the edge. A scream rent the darkness.

Silence settled upon the cavern, until once again the soft pad of tiny feet could be heard moving toward a feast already in progress.

CHAPTER 25

Detour

Rudy and Wart stood surrounded by tall trees and thick brush. The forest was dark, and little light filtered through the treetops. When Seagood and Mathias had darted into the surrounding brush, searching for the elusive watchers, Wart had not noticed movement in the shadows. Suddenly a hand reached from the underbrush, clamped over his mouth and jerked him backward off his feet. Twist as he might, he could not free himself from his captor.

With his back to Wart, Rudy hissed, "Quiet! I think I hear something."

Wart tried to shout, but all that escaped was a muffled, "Mmph!"

Rudy turned to discover two men on top of the squirming lad. Instantly, his sword cleared its sheath.

Six swords met his own, but what stopped Rudy was not fear for himself; it was the terror in Wart's eyes. A sword lay at Wart's throat. Reluctantly, Rudy tossed his own sword to the ground. "If this isn't a fine kettle of fish," the big man said with a groan. They were completely surrounded, and it was clear that more men were in the shadows. "Don't struggle, Wart. It won't make things easier."

Wart and Rudy tried to relax, but their captors didn't. No one moved.

"We lost him, Ru—" Mathias began as he and Seagood appeared from nowhere. They were instantly surrounded by drawn swords.

"Welcome home," Rudy called. "Wart and I thought we would throw a little party for you two. Don't look now, but there are more in the shadows."

"What is the meaning of this?" Mathias demanded.

Rudy shrugged and turned to his captors. "Our leader has returned," his voice boomed. "Summon your master and present your charge. We have done you no harm! Why are we being held in this manner?"

A cloaked man stepped from the shadows, his hood drawn low over his face. Seagood brushed past several blades to meet him.

"Are you the leader of this rabble?" Rudy asked. "What is our crime, and why have you taken us captive?"

The cloaked man studied Seagood and then turned to Rudy. "Why doesn't your master speak for himself?"

Rudy glanced at Seagood in surprise. Their captor clearly spoke in the common tongue of Amity.

"Who are you?" Rudy asked. "And why have you detained us?"

"I am Benhada Rooleen, Captain of the Southern Watch." The cloaked stranger threw the hood from his face.

"Dad!" Wart shouted in surprise.

The man held his hand up for silence, never taking his eyes off Seagood. "My lord," he said, bowing slightly. "I have presented myself. Now, will you be so good as to explain why you have disturbed us by entering the Gray Lands?"

Rudy studied Seagood for a moment and then spoke tentatively. "We tend to urgent business and did not realize we were trespassing. No harm was intended."

"You carefully guard your words. Will you tell me plainly where you are from and where you are going?" Benhada asked.

Rudy made no response, and Wart grew uneasy.

"You refuse to speak?" the man asked.

Silence met his question.

"I cannot let you pass!" Benhada said with finality.

"But Dad—" Wart exclaimed.

Again the man held up his hand for silence. "This I will do! If you promise to cooperate, I will escort you to Gray Haven. There the master and lady will decide your fate. The woods are full of my men. Should you try to escape, you will not go far."

Seagood weighed his options and nodded his assent.

"Release them," Benhada Rooleen called. His soldiers released their prisoners but kept a wary eye upon them.

Wart struggled from his captor's arms and rushed to his father. "Dad!" he cried and threw his arms around him.

"Who are these men with you, Son?" Captain Rooleen asked.

"Friends of James Stafford," Wart began, but he stopped at a glance from both Seagood and Rudy.

"James Stafford!" Benhada exclaimed. "Well, you have chosen noble companions. I am very pleased."

Everyone seemed to relax. Seagood and his party returned to their horses. Wart's father spoke to his men hidden in the underbrush. "Walk your mounts until we reach the road."

Upon reaching a narrow trail, everyone mounted, and Wart rode beside Rudy, who twisted and turned in his saddle. "What's the matter, Rudy? We are making good time!"

"We are going the wrong way, lad," Rudy whispered.

"I wonder where my dad is taking us."

"Is he really your father?" Rudy asked, his voice filled with suspicion.

"Sure," Wart said in surprise. "Don't you think I'd know my own dad?"

"Things are not always what they seem," Rudy whispered. "Don't tell him too much! We don't know if people in this country will be friendly with our purpose or not!"

"Why shouldn't they be?" Wart asked.

"I don't know. Nonetheless, beware!"

"Beware of what?" a voice cut in. Benhada had dropped back to ride beside his son.

"Aw, nothing, Dad," Wart answered easily. "Say, I've got a lot of catching up to do. Let's start with where you went. Why are you here, and where are you taking us?"

Benhada leaned back and laughed aloud. "You haven't changed a bit. You are still full of questions. I could always count on you to keep my trips down the river busy with questions." He settled into the easy gait of the road. "I suppose I should go back to the last run we made down the river together. Do you remember it?"

"Remember?" Wart said. "I've thought of nothing so much since we parted!"

"Remember how I feared bandits on the river?" Benhada asked.

"Yes."

"I left you at your aunt's because I thought the river was too dangerous. I did not intend to leave you there forever. I meant to return for you, but I never made it."

"I know. What happened?"

"I was attacked by bandits the very next day," Benhada explained.

"How did you escape?"

"I didn't, really," Benhada explained. "I was nearing the rapids and had camped for the night, not wanting to hit rough water in the dark. Bandits attacked my camp and beat me. I'm sure they thought I was dead, but I'll tell you more in a moment. Just now, we are about to enter the actual boundary of the Gray Lands."

The group topped a large hill and dropped into a sweeping valley beyond. The moon shone on a desolate land, void of grass or trees.

"Is this the Gray Lands?" Wart asked. "It doesn't look too great at night. Does it look any better in the daylight?"

"Not much," his father conceded.

"Dad, if this is the beginning of the Gray Lands, why are you stationed near the river?" Wart asked.

"The river separates the Gray Lands from Endor, and the area we have just ridden through forms a buffer zone between Endor and the Gray Lands. As times have grown more dangerous, the lord and lady of the Gray Lands have positioned more soldiers along the river to watch for enemies and to limit pirate activity. The land on this side of the river helps keep the Gray Lands safe," Benhada said.

"More soldiers?" Wart asked. "Did the Gray Lands have soldiers along the river when we lived here?"

"Yes," Benhada answered.

"You knew of them?" Wart asked in surprise.

"I knew of some," Benhada said. "I'm sure there were more than I realized."

"How did you come to be one of them?" Wart asked.

"The answer to that takes me back to the night I was robbed. As I said, I think the thieves were sure they had killed me, but when I finally awoke, I found myself in a strange camp. My goods and boat were gone, but I was alive."

Just then, the group came to a steep cliff blocking their path. "There is a path that climbs the face of this cliff. There is no other passage for many miles. We must proceed in single file."

Wart had to hold his questions until everyone had reached the top. When all had turned northwest again, others joined the father and son.

No one cared to stray from the group as the barrenness of the countryside loomed before them.

"What happened after you recovered?" Wart asked his father.

"I met a pleasant fellow among my rescuers," Benhada said simply. "Not that they weren't all pleasant enough," he hurried on to say, "but I learned that very few of them were able to speak. However, this older gentleman could talk, and talk he did. He seemed to know all about me. He told me of my rescue, and since I was able to speak, he offered me a position with the very men who had rescued me. Since I no longer had a boat, and river traffic was so dangerous, I decided to accept his offer. I have been employed by the Gray Lands since."

"That's why I never saw you again."

"I am sorry about that," Benhada said. "You were nowhere to be found when I heard your aunt was gone and discovered her place abandoned. I didn't know where to look for you."

"After Auntie died," Wart said, "I wandered downriver looking for you. I worked here and there until I came to Green Meadow." Wart stopped at a sharp glance from Rudy. His father noted the exchange but said nothing.

They rode in silence for some time before Wart spoke again. "Dad, if you thought we were enemies, why did you capture us instead of killing us outright?"

Benhada smiled. "I recognized you. Besides, it's not only for enemies we watch but for kings as well."

"Kings? What does that mean?" Wart asked.

Benhada leaned back in his saddle. "Many years ago, when the kingdoms east of the river were at war with each other, a gracious man ruled the Gray Lands. He allowed many refugees to enter his realm and come under his protection.

"Among those refugees was an incredibly beautiful woman. In time she captured the king's eye, if not his heart. It was only after they were married that he learned her true temperament. She was shrewd and conniving. She cared nothing for her husband or his people, and she tried to introduce strange, new religious ideas. The poor king's life would have been utter misery if a son and daughter had not entered their troubled marriage.

"Shortly after the birth of their daughter, the king was summoned to a distant country. Placing his brother in control of the Gray Lands, the king sailed away. He took his son with him, but he was unable to care for his infant daughter, so she remained with her mother."

"What happened to the king?" Wart asked.

"He never returned. Rumors spread through the country that his ship had wrecked and that he'd been lost at sea, but no one knew."

"What happened then?" Wart wanted to know.

"The queen tried to claim the throne, but many people were afraid of her, and they asked the king's brother to remain as guardian of the kingdom. Because the Lord Guardian could not bring himself to believe that the king had perished, he refused to leave his appointed position.

"Rumors spread throughout the kingdom that the queen had faked the summons that had drawn the king away from the Gray Lands. No one could prove the rumors wrong, and the Lord Guardian sent far and wide for information about his brother's whereabouts. He also placed soldiers along the river to watch for the king's return. Because of the nature of what we do, many people call us Watchers."

"So who was actually in charge of the kingdom?" Wart asked.

"Well, the Lord Guardian had been appointed by the king to rule before he left," Benhada explained, "but the queen claimed that the king had given her a tiny silver key on the day of their wedding. She said this was the key to the kingdom and gave her the authority to rule. When officials in the kingdom asked her to produce the key, she refused."

"What happened?" Rudy asked, having been drawn into the story.

"Tensions mounted between those who supported the king's brother and those who supported the queen, and it was feared that civil war might break out among the people. The Lord Guardian persuaded Astarte, the king's wife, to let the people decide who would rule. People from all over the kingdom gathered at Gray Haven on a specified day. When the king's brother stood, the crowd began to shout and cheer and nearly refused to stop. When Levi was finally able to speak, he offered the people comfort and counsel. However, when it was Astarte's turn to address the crowd, not one voice was raised in her support.

"Furious, Astarte shouted at the crowd. 'You mock me with your silence! If it is silence you want, it is silence you shall have. By the power of Beelzebub, may you never speak again!' She took something from beneath her cloak and hurled it into the sky. A terrible explosion rocked the gathering, and thick black smoke filled the air. When the smoke cleared, the queen was gone, and in her place was a tiny silver key with the letters *FAITH* raised upon the handle.

"The Lord Guardian snatched up the key and shouted to the crowd: 'The key to the kingdom!' but when the crowd tried to cheer, most found that they could not utter a sound."

Wart stared at his father.

"I know!" Benhada nodded. "It is an incredible story, but I heard it from the Lord Guardian himself. How the queen could inflict silence upon so many people was a mystery. Some wondered if it was by the power of her foreign religion, but no one could ask her, for she was gone!"

"Where did she go?" Wart asked.

"No one knows for sure, but some say that she and her supporters fled across the river where she met Jabin, and together they built the kingdom of Endor!"

Wart gasped, and Rudy's face grew dark with suspicion. The company rode on in silence for a long while before Wart turned to his father and asked, "But if the king is dead, why do people still watch for him?"

"After the queen's disappearance, the crowd dispersed and went to their homes. It was soon discovered that very few in the kingdom were able to speak. At first people thought this inability to speak would be temporary, but when it continued for weeks, they began to panic. The Lord Guardian began to fear that his people would flee the country, hoping to escape the curse. Going to his advisors, he shared his fears.

"One seer rose to his feet and proclaimed, 'We know that God is the healer of every infirmity, and He can overcome every power of darkness, but right now these people need hope. Let everyone know that a kingly man will one day come, and when he does, God will bring deliverance to the people. You must inform the Watchers on our border, and every citizen, to watch and wait with expectation, for no one knows the day or the hour of our visitation. We must be patient and persevere through this trial, for when the king appears, all will be made right.'

"The Lord Guardian made a proclamation that day and sent envoys throughout the kingdom, calling people to watch and wait. Copies of the seer's message were posted in every village and at every crossroads throughout the Gray Lands. The message gave people hope, and they have long endured their inability to speak while waiting patiently for the return of their king."

Benhada went on. "This all happened before you were born, Son. I was not aware of the Gray Land's trials, and the watchers along the river were so discreet that few were aware of their presence, let alone their limitations. The Lord Guardian has raised the king's daughter, and presently they rule the land together. But the people still watch and wait for this kingly man who will bring about their deliverance."

The company rode on in silence and covered many miles of rolling prairie. As the moon settled in the west and dawn spread its rosy colors across the eastern sky, they could see mesas protruding like ragged teeth upon the horizon.

"We'll take a short break," Benhada said, pulling his horse from the road into a grassy hollow. "Water your horses and stretch your legs."

They took their respite in a permanent campsite. Wood was neatly stacked under a rock ledge, and a spring bubbled with life-giving water at the bottom of the hill.

Wart stayed with his father while the others led their horses to the spring for water and grass. "Dad, how will people recognize their king?" he asked.

"I don't know," Benhada said, watching Seagood and the others return from the spring. "Your master commands much respect, doesn't he?"

"I think I would follow him anywhere," Wart responded.

When Seagood's company returned, Rudy asked bluntly, "When do we reach our destination?"

"I will announce you to the Lord and Lady of Gray Haven as soon as we reach the city." Benhada waved his hand, and all eyes turned to see the morning sun break upon the walls of Gray Haven, which was situated on the brow of the nearest mesa. In the distance they heard the sound of a trumpet announcing the dawn of a new day.

Helsa fingered the tiny key that hung around her neck. She had been summoned to the throne room to join her uncle Levi, the Lord Regent. She had not waited long before the doorman announced the arrival of Benhada Rooleen.

Levi rose to meet his friend. "Ben! What brings you so far from the river?"

"I need your guidance, my lord," Benhada said, bowing as he entered the room. "We detained a small party near the river, and they won't tell us their mission. I believe Endor may be their goal, and I thought it best to bring them to you."

"What kind of men are they, and where do they come from, Ben?" Levi asked.

"Most appear to be soldiers from Amity," Benhada replied. "However …"

Levi studied the Captain of the Watchers closely. "Are you holding something from me, Ben?"

"Well …" Benhada stalled. "My son rides with them."

"Your son!" Levi laughed. "Why did you bring them to me? You surely trust your son?"

"I do," Benhada agreed, "but the leader of their group is unable to speak, and he resembles the Lady Helsa in many respects. I just felt you should meet him."

Helsa felt her heart skip a beat, but glancing at her uncle, she could see that Levi was not pleased.

"Ben," Levi chided. "I'm not sure this is the right time or place for such a meeting."

Helsa reached for Levi's arm. Her heart was aflutter.

Levi turned to study his niece, his eyes full of love, as Helsa's heart swelled with anticipation and hope. "Very well," he sighed. He turned to Benhada. "Disarm your party and bring them here."

Benhada departed, and Helsa sprang to her feet. "Don't get your hopes up, dearest," Levi said. "There are many who cannot speak, nobleman and bum alike."

Helsa smiled and wrapped her arms about the doting old man's neck. Suddenly she stooped and kissed his cheek.

Levi laughed. "Nay, child! I love you too! But come, compose yourself. We are about to have company."

The door was closed, but Levi and Helsa could hear raised voices outside.

"Leave your weapons here," Benhada was saying firmly.

"I'll be glad to, Dad, but please don't make the others."

"All must disarm!" Benhada was adamant.

"Dad, we didn't cause trouble when we came with you. We will keep faith."

Intrigued by the conversation, Helsa broke protocol and slipped from her uncle's side. Hurrying to the door, she lifted the latch and witnessed three travel-weary men and one boy, their clothes rumpled and dirty from days in the saddle.

Wart dropped to his knees in astonishment.

"My lady!" Rudy said as he bowed beside Wart.

Mathias slowly bent his knee, clearly begrudging every delay their adventure had taken.

Two men remained standing: Benhada Rooleen and Seagood.

Seagood closed his eyes as memories flickered like phantoms through his mind. He could picture his father guiding him onto a boat and waving to a crowd where his mother had stood holding her new baby daughter. When Seagood opened his eyes, he saw his mother—or a likeness of her—standing before him.

Seagood gasped at the woman before him. Her nose and eyes mirrored his own. *Who is she?* he wondered.

"My lady!" Benhada exclaimed, bowing low.

"Helsa," her uncle chided as he finally reached her side and stepped between his niece and the lone man yet standing.

Benhada rose and turned to face Seagood. "You will bow before the Lady of the Gray Lands!"

Seagood stood motionless, staring as if in shock.

Benhada drew his sword and placed it at Seagood's neck. "Bow before the queen!" he shouted angrily.

Helsa slipped quickly around her uncle and laid a hand upon Benhada's shoulder.

Benhada yielded to her touch and, lowering his blade, stepped aside.

Everyone watched in amazement as Helsa did the unthinkable. Holding the folds of her robes, she curtsied low before Seagood.

"Helsa!" her uncle gasped.

"My lady!" Benhada exclaimed.

"Don't stare, Wart," Rudy hissed.

Helsa felt a gentle touch on her cheek. Looking up, she saw that the strange man was smiling. There was a light of recognition in his eyes, and she knew he understood. Flying into his arms, they held each other tight. Her brother had finally come home.

Levi, Helsa, and the travelers spent the day talking quietly around a fireplace. Levi told of things that had happened in the Gray Lands since the king had disappeared, and Rudy spoke guardedly of their current mission. Helsa clung to her brother as if he might disappear, and Levi struggled with the realization that his brother was truly gone.

It was a sad yet joyful occasion to let one dream go and to begin plans for another.

Wart's arms swung freely as he and his father walked quickly down the hallway. "Dad, how did you know?" he asked when they were an appropriate distance from the reunited family.

"Know what, Son?"

"That Seagood and the princess were brother and sister?"

"I didn't."

"But you brought us here just so the two could meet, didn't you? You had the authority to let us pass, but you came here instead."

Benhada stopped and looked at his son. "You are becoming very observant. You can glean a great deal of information even without asking questions. Strength will carry you far, but a man of understanding will go even further. I'm very proud of you, Son."

"But you haven't answered my question."

"About what?"

"How did you know?"

"I didn't. I thought I told you that."

"Then why didn't you let us go? Master Levi even said you had the authority to do so."

"You are persistent," Benhada said, chuckling. "Very well. I found it most intriguing that your master could not speak, and neither do most of the people in this land. I wondered if he was from here. And too, you were being very secretive about your mission. I felt certain Master Levi should know of your activity."

"Then you really didn't know Seagood and the Lady were brother and sister?"

"No! I thought I already told you that," Benhada said, laughing. "Now, no more questions. There is much that has to be done before you leave tomorrow."

Torches dimly lit the street where Benhada and Seagood's men had gathered. Wart sat shivering between Rudy and his father. Their horses stomped and snorted impatiently. Rudy held two extra mounts. One was for Seagood, and the other was for Master Thomas, if they should indeed be fortunate enough to find and rescue him.

"I wish he'd hurry," Wart whispered. "I'm freezing."

"He'll come," Rudy said. "Remember, Wart, that he hasn't seen his sister in many years. It would be hard to leave so soon."

"If it were me," Mathias added, "I'm not sure I would leave."

"You don't think he'll change his mind and stay, do you?" Wart asked with alarm.

"No," Rudy said emphatically. "Ah, here they are now, and isn't his sister beautiful?"

The group watched Seagood and Helsa descend a long staircase, hand in hand. As they neared the bottom, Helsa slowed her pace to counter that of her brother. At the bottom, Seagood turned and lifted his sister's hand to his lips. He knew the coming days would be very hard for those he left behind in the Gray Lands.

Seagood started to turn, but Helsa restrained him. Throwing her arms about his neck, she pulled him close and wept upon his broad shoulder. Ever so gently, Seagood pulled from her embrace, nodded, and turned to go.

Leaping into his saddle, Seagood turned to salute his sister one last time. She pulled her cloak tightly about her slender frame and raised her hand in farewell. Seagood wheeled his horse about and cantered away into the darkness.

Wart peered over his shoulder as they headed toward the city's gate. He saw the Lady Helsa still waving farewell to the party and felt a lump settle in his throat that threatened to remain there for a long time.

Seagood and his group reached the open prairie by full daylight and made only occasional stops during the day to water the horses. As evening drew near, they rode into less desolate country where an occasional tree and some green grass could be seen.

Wart singled out his father. "Are you coming all the way to Endor with us?" he asked.

"Hush, Son," his father chided. "This country has many ears, and you do not want your plans to go before you. However, in answer to your question, I will only go as far as the river. I must return to my post."

Wart could not hide his disappointment. He understood Lady Helsa's reluctance to release Seagood this morning. He had been separated from his father for only about a year, but he longed to stay by his side.

Benhada seemed to understand. "Son, you've grown into quite a young man. I wish we could stay together, but your friends are counting on you. You are part of their company now, and you have a job to do. I do not know how you will accomplish your mission, but if you each do your part and stay together, you may succeed."

They rode late into the evening. They would reach the river late tomorrow. There was little talk around a scant meal. A sentry was posted, and everyone else turned in. Though the sentry was relieved sometime during the night, Wart knew nothing until daylight began to soften the morning sky.

The smell of coffee woke the lad. Rolling out, he saw Rudy struggling over the embers of a smokeless fire. "What's to eat?" Wart asked.

Rudy laughed and sliced a few more strips of salt port into a skillet. He glanced at Wart. "We reach our crossing today."

Wart's face clouded. "I know. Dad told me last night."

"Are you going on with us, or staying with your father?"

Wart stared at Rudy in disbelief. "There isn't any choice, is there?"

"Sure, there is. Seagood knows how you feel. He feels it too. If you want to stay, he'll relieve you of your commitment."

"Are you trying to get rid of me?" The anger in Wart's voice surprised Rudy.

"No," Rudy responded. "Why do you say that?"

"I volunteered to find Master Thomas, not my dad. That has been a bonus. I know I've been a lot of trouble to you guys, but I want to see this through."

Rudy smiled and turned his back on the angry lad. "Now, now," he soothed. "No need for a tempest in a teapot. Nobody said anything about not wanting you, though rations may run mighty low before we get back."

"I can go without food as well as anybody!" Wart said hotly.

"I just thought you might like to think about it today and decide when we reach the crossing."

"I've made my choice. I don't have to think about it," Wart said.

Rudy turned back around, still smiling. "Good! I was hoping you felt that way. Guess I just needed to know. I'm glad you're on board, mate." His big hand clapped firmly over Wart's thin shoulder.

The anger melted from Wart's heart, and he felt fear creep in to take its place. "Rudy, I'm already scared. You won't leave me, will you?"

Rudy's jaw suddenly began to tremble, and tears threatened to spill from his eyes. Pulling Wart close, he whispered, "I'm going to stay with you as long as I can, boy. As long as I can."

Seagood and his party cleared another outpost of Watchers. It was growing dark, but they could hear the river churning in the distance.

Wart leaned close to his father. "There sure are a lot of Watchers in this area."

"You are near the very heart of our enemy's realm," Benhada replied. "We try to keep track of all their movements, but sometimes we fail. Jabin is crafty, slipping in and out without our knowledge."

"What about Endor?" Wart asked. "How do we get inside?"

"I have told your master all I know, and that is limited. We post a few men on the other side of the river, but that is very dangerous. Few venture near the castle."

They began their descent to the river. Even though Wart had plied his father with questions all day and knew much about Endor, he felt he was walking into a trap. No one seemed to have a plan for rescuing Thomas.

Twisting among the trees, they finally came to the water's edge.

Memories of their first crossing and the loss of both Clyde and Darren haunted the small party. All was somber and quiet.

Benhada was the first to speak. "Are you ready, my lord?" he asked Seagood. When Seagood nodded, Benhada set a special arrow to his bow. Attached to the arrow was a thin cord, which whistled as it sped across the water. Unseen hands removed the arrow from its mark and began to pull the cord across the river.

Benhada, Rudy, and Mathias uncovered a small raft hidden along the bank of the river. Heavy ropes snaked into the water behind the thin cord and began to cross the river. Strong hands across the river would pull the raft and its cargo safely to the other side.

Wart hugged his father before stepping onto the raft. "Will I see you again?" he asked.

"I hope so, Son," Benhada said, glad that the darkness hid the tears forming in his eyes.

The raft suddenly lurched and moved into the muddy water. Wart felt his heart sink. Across the river lay an adventure from which there seemed no return.

CHAPTER 26

Enemy Territory

Bill leaned heavily against a tree. His body ached, and he was ready to drop from exhaustion. *Just a moment longer*, he thought. *Then I must return to my post.*

Campfires dotted the valley below Bill. The sky turned crimson as dusk settled across the land. He often dreamed of Mary. Thoughts of her carried him down each winding path and filled each mountain hollow. This evening she was especially close as he gazed at the serene beauty of the evening sky.

I wonder how she is tonight, Bill pondered. *Has she had the baby? Is it a boy or a girl? What did she name it?*

Fading hues of color tinted the western sky. Campfires became beacons in the darkness. Bill stirred. He and Mary had loved this time of day when they could lay their daily routines aside and enjoy each other and the dying day. Now, each setting sun took them farther apart.

A twig snapped in the darkness, and Bill realized his folly: he'd abandoned his post. He started to turn, and then something slammed into his shoulder. It burned like a hot poker. His left arm dropped to his side, and his shield fell to the ground.

Tears of pain and frustration rendered him useless as men crept into the clearing. Gasping, he stumbled and bumped his shoulder on a tree. New shards of pain wakened him to the growing danger. Drawing his blade, he mustered enough strength to shout one word of warning to those in the valley below. "Attack!" His sword sliced the darkness, rending a hole in the onslaught.

John felt tension in the air. Danger seemed to lurk in every nook and corner. They had made camp early today, for tomorrow they crossed into Jeshemon. A bony ridge of rock was all that separated the once proud kingdoms.

Jeshemon and Geba were only two of the many kingdom states that had fallen to the fierce and assertive aggression of Jabin and his confederation. Now they were all one, and they were at war with Amity.

John withdrew from the campfire. He had no desire to chat or tell stories tonight. Still, it was comforting to hear his men joke and tell tall tales back and forth.

Resting in the shadows, John thought of the long march from Green Meadow and the fierce battle at Watershed. For days Jabin had hurled his forces against those of Gaff and Stafford—to little or no avail.

But one morning the armies of Amity and Emancipation had awakened to find no enemy camped against them. Their initial euphoria had given way when it was discovered that about half the enemy had withdrawn to the east, and the other half north. The army had to divide to pursue both factions. Gaff had gone east and John north.

The days since had been dreadful. Every tree or bush seemed to hold enemy fighters. Often they would strike unseen and then disappear into the hills. These hit-and-run tactics were exhausting, far more so than the outright venom of a frontal assault. Every step was dogged with fear.

Then they came to Deorn, a city built squarely across their path. Its high armored wall blocked the road upon which they traveled. It had cost many lives and days of bone-breaking labor to conquer the stronghold.

While laboring at Deorn, news came that Gaff had taken Hesron and Lashish, and his campaign had turned north.

When Deorn finally fell, everyone was dismayed to find that so few had denied progress to the army of Amity. The cost had been large in lives, time, and morale.

Drought had come to the Mountains of Despair. The forest and meadows had become a tinderbox. John warily eyed the campfires all around him. Extreme caution had to be taken to keep the fires from spreading. A fire among the troops could be far more devastating than an enemy assault.

Suddenly John sat upright. He heard a scuffle in the rocks above him. "Douse the fire," he hissed, and an unseen boot kicked dirt over the feeble flames.

"Attack!" It was Bill's unmistakable voice directly above him. John looked left and right. Men were already scrambling up the rugged slope.

John surveyed the hill. The rocks were sharp and the incline steep, but he grabbed a protruding bush and pulled. Scraping his knees, cutting his hands, and bruising himself all over, John finally attained the summit. In the darkness, John heard rather than saw Bill fighting for his life. He could hear the angry hiss of Bill's blade, slashing left and right, plunging forward, only to recoil and strike again. Drawing his own blade, John heard a cry and saw shadows turn to flee. Swords in hand, the men of Amity took up the chase.

Bill staggered. One moment he was fighting for his life, and the next, his enemies were fleeing. He was confused until he saw the familiar helms of Amity dart past him. Help had come.

Trying to catch his breath, Bill suddenly felt nauseous and weak. He closed his eyes in an effort to stop his world from spinning. Opening them again, he saw a shadow move in the darkness, and he caught the faint glitter of steel. A burning pain seared his left arm. Bill raised his blade and lunged at the shadow. He felt the blade twist in his hand as he fell, and he remembered no more.

Archers lined the rim of Jeshemon Valley. Arrows fell thick upon fleeing shadows as they melted into the brush and trees below. With a great shout, John and his men leaped down the rocky crag in a fierce counterattack.

Amity's brutal assault caused Jabin's men to flee in confusion. Deeper into the forest the battle raged. From tree to tree, men cut down the enemy in the dark hollows of the forest.

A broad meadow opened before the onslaught. Archers took positions behind trees along the edge of the glade and cut down those who fled before them. An eerie light twinkled in the darkness, not in one location, but all across the meadow. By some unspoken word, light sprang from a myriad of torches.

"Fire," John breathed. "I can't believe they would use fire!" Yellow flames licked hungrily at the tall, dry grass. John watched in horror as hundreds of tiny lights suddenly roared into a wall of flame.

A breeze gathered at his back as the fire drew a tremendous breath and then rushed toward Stafford and his men with alarming speed.

"Retreat!" John shouted over the roar of the flames. It was agonizing to realize his folly. He was trapped! The enemy had feigned retreat only to box John's entire army between a rocky cliff and a raging furnace.

"Retreat!" John yelled again. He could hear fiendish laughter beyond the flames. The eerie light cast dancing shadows between the trees.

"Spare us, heavenly Father," John prayed as he raced into the forest. A strange moan caught his attention, and he slowed for a moment to understand its significance. "Wind!" He was horrified. He had seen fire race through treetops faster than any deer could run. "We are doomed!" he wept. Tears of frustration mingled with his sweat.

Suddenly John stopped. The breeze was cool and was growing in strength, but more importantly, it was in his face. Cold and tempestuous, a sudden gale unleashed itself upon the earth.

John forgot about the fire as the ground shook and trees bowed before something far greater. A large branch snapped from a tree nearby and narrowly missed John's head as it sailed by. He crawled behind a tree trunk and pulled his cloak tight around his head. He struggled to breathe as sand, twigs, and leaves filled the air.

"Oh, Lord, be merciful," John prayed as the wind ripped viciously through the trees. "Be with my men," he cried. "They have left home and family. They have faced the terror of foreign armies, but who can stand in Your presence?"

A deafening roar filled the air as his shelter shook and swayed. He wondered if anyone would survive. Suddenly, all was quiet. John didn't move. His ears told him it was over, but his heart was unsure.

"Somebody help me!" a pitiful cry cut through John's clouded mind. He clambered to his hands and knees, noting that all his limbs seemed to work. "Call again," he shouted. "I'm on my way."

Voices were raised all around John as men forgot about war, enemy attacks, or fire. All over the forest, men crawled from locations of refuge to assist those who could not.

Glancing over his shoulder, John saw an eerie light as fire danced upon the distant slopes of Jeshemon. The fire, intended to destroy him, had been turned upon the enemies of Amity. Racing unchecked, it consumed everything in its path.

Silently John bowed before his Creator and gave thanks for the wind's change of direction. He knew how close he and his men had come to being destroyed. Morning's light would tell the full story, but that would have to wait. Right now, there were those who needed his help.

CHAPTER 27

Regrouping

As dawn softened the eastern sky, John stood alone on the ridge of Jeshemon and surveyed the carnage below. What had once been a beautiful forest now lay shattered: a ruinous tangle of limbs and debris.

"It's a miracle," John said with a sigh. Weary as he was, he still marveled that they were missing only one man.

John's joy was mixed with sorrow, though, for the man they were missing was Bill Cotton. Bill was the lone survivor of the bodyguard John had formed after their first skirmish in Amity. Bill had been at John's side through thick and thin. Never once had he allowed a foe to come between them. Now he, like all the rest, was gone, and a replacement would have to be chosen.

John felt his loss acutely. He could not bear to leave without saying goodbye to his friend. But where was Bill? He had searched the ridge where he'd last seen Bill fighting the enemy, but to no avail. Men had been dispatched to gather Jabin's dead. They might find Bill, but John could not wait past noon.

John turned to gaze past the broken forest. The valley beyond was black and promised to hold grim tales. Already scouts were returning with tales of their fallen foe. The change of wind had taken Jabin's army by surprise. Thousands had fled the scorching flames. Most had not escaped.

Far away, smoke poured into a hazy sky. Fire still consumed the countryside with abandon.

John sighed and turned from the sight. Endor seemed so far away! Glancing one last time at the broken wood, a thought struck him. "If Bill is down there, how are we ever going to find him?" And his spirits sank even lower.

Two men found Bill at the bottom of the Jeshemon Ridge. An arrow was protruding from his shoulder, and his hand had been severed from his left arm. He was alive, but barely. Men were summoned, and a team carried Bill to a medic, who stretched the skin from Bill's arm to cover the protruding bones. It took quite a few stitches to close the wound and cover the bones, but when the medic was finished, he turned his attention to the arrow. It took considerably more time to open Bill's shoulder and remove the arrow, but once the wound was clean, that too was stitched shut.

John had joined several men who were praying for Bill while the medic did his work. When the surgeon was through, John rose from his knees and drew a small flask of oil from his knapsack. When he opened the flask, a strong, sweet odor permeated the air. He rubbed the oil over Bill's stump and shoulder.

"Bill," John called, holding the ointment under Bill's nose. "Come and join the living, Bill. Your mission in this world is not yet finished."

Slowly Bill opened his eyes, and recognition registered. "Master," he managed to croak.

There was not a dry eye among the men in their little group.

John Stafford assigned several men to care for Bill and to transport him back to Deorn to recuperate. It was a slow process, and they thought they'd lost Bill more than once before they got the big man back to the fortress. Once there, it took some time, but eventually Bill began to mend.

CHAPTER 28

Into the Jaws

Wart was growing uneasy the farther Seagood and his companions rode into Endor. "Rudy," he whispered, "how are we going to find Master Thomas?" At the sound of his whisper, everything in the forest grew deadly still.

Rudy held up a silencing finger, and the group waited several long minutes before proceeding again.

Wart gasped at a weed that looked like a man crouching in the shadows.

The group paused again, and this time Seagood got off to look around. The early part of their journey on this side of the river had been easy. Without a word, the Watchers had led them around countless bends in the brush and trees until they'd come to a road. Now Seagood and his party were alone.

The Watchers had still been with them when they'd spied the distant lights of Endor, but now the dreaded castle was very near. The chance of being discovered and captured grew with every movement.

They remained under the canopy of the forest about five furlongs from the walls of the cliff upon which Endor stood. The meadow between the castle and forest appeared tilled and tended as if it were a massive garden.

Seagood motioned, and the party followed him toward the river where brush and weeds would hide their passage. The longer they avoided discovery, the better.

The roar of the river drowned any noise they might make as they scurried over rocks and slipped on moss-covered stones. Progress was slow, but after a long while, they stopped at a point almost directly below a lookout tower. They were sheltered from view by four large trees that had been spared from the ax.

Wart could stand the suspense no longer. "What are we going to do now?" he whispered.

The goal had been to rescue Thomas, but now that they were here, they seemed no closer to fulfilling their mission than they had been at

Green Meadow. If the others had a plan, they hadn't shared it with him, and he was suspicious that they didn't know either. He was about to ask again when Rudy held up a warning finger.

Over the sound of the rushing water, they could distinctly hear the clop-clop of horses' hooves on stone pavement nearby.

They waited breathlessly, each man trying to quiet his horse from a sudden nicker that might betray them. They watched in silence as a patrol of twenty riders passed no more than thirty feet from their hiding place. The last rider in the party slowed his pace and dropped behind the others. He crossed the narrow strip of grass between the path and the cluster of trees. He was about to dismount when a sharp call from the squad leader caused him to wheel about and gallop back to the others.

The four men looked at each other and silently acknowledged how close they had come to discovery. Breathing deeply for a few moments, Seagood and Mathias handed their horses' reins to Wart and disappeared over the stones toward the river.

Rudy, in turn, handed his reins to Wart and turned to follow the others.

"Where are you going, and what am I supposed to do?" Wart whispered anxiously.

"We spotted a current in the river," Rudy said with significance.

"So?" Wart's voice demanded an explanation.

Turning back, Rudy decided it was time to do a little explaining. "Some of these old castles have a waterway beneath them," he stated. "The folks would build their castle near a river and dig an underground passage for water to flow under the castle." He paused to see if Wart understood. Wart didn't, so Rudy continued. "When we saw a current in the river, we wondered if it was the waterway under the castle. The inlet being upstream, we thought this might be the outlet."

"What if it is?" Wart asked dubiously.

"Don't be so dull, Wart! If we find the outlet to their water supply, we are halfway inside."

Wart stood still, trying to comprehend the meaning of all this. "You mean—" he started to ask.

"Precisely!" Rudy interrupted. "We go up the downspout, and we are inside. We find Thomas, come down with the water, mount up, and ride away."

Wart didn't feel very enthused.

Rudy saw the lad's disenchantment. "Well, what do you propose? Shall we just sit here on the doorstep and wait for Thomas to come to us?"

Wart felt sick. It was true: they didn't have a plan. His shoulders drooped.

Rudy sensed the boy's discouragement. "Buck up, lad! The Lord has brought us safe this far. He is able to finish our mission!"

Wart was silent. He thought of all they had encountered, including the recent near miss with the patrol.

"Don't lose faith, Wart!" Rudy said. "I know it doesn't sound like a very good plan, but if we do the best we can and trust in divine providence, He will either make our plan work, or He will open other doors. You've got to believe that. The Lord is faithful. He will never leave us or forsake us."

"What about Clyde and Darren?" Wart asked.

"The Lord removed them from this mission, Wart, but He never left them. They are with Him this very minute." He paused. "You know, I wouldn't be surprised if they were here with us right now."

Wart peered anxiously about, half expecting to see a ghost.

Rudy chuckled. "No, not where you can see them, Wart. And maybe I am superstitious. But see it as you will, the Lord sent an angel just now to protect us, and Clyde or Darren would make first-class angels for a mission like this."

A shiver ran down Wart's spine. He'd never thought about things like this before. But he'd never been around people who walked in faith so openly.

"Rudy," he began.

The big man had turned away and started for the river, but he stopped, turned to Wart, and asked, "What?"

"What if you can't swim all the way in without drowning?"

"We'll cross that problem when we get to it," Rudy said.

"But it's going to be light soon. How can you search the river in daylight?" Wart asked.

"We can't, but I'll never get there to help if you keep asking questions!"

"Rudy?"

"What!"

"Where should I take the horses?"

Rudy was growing impatient. "You have eyes. Look around!" And with that he was gone.

Wart felt very alone. Five horses gave him company but not much comfort. Gently rubbing several soft muzzles, he wondered where he could keep five horses out of sight—and what would he feed them. They might be here a very long time.

Wart studied their location. With daylight, they would be exposed. Wart tied the horses and scrambled over the rocks. Slipping from bush to bush, he neared the cliff. There had to be a better place to hide.

Upon his return, daylight was stronger, but so was his sense of confidence. Grasping two horses' halters, he began moving them to a location at the very foot of the cliff.

A narrow strip of jumbled rock separated the cliff from the river. Wart led the horses to a narrow overhang in the face of the cliff. It was nearly forty feet long, though only a few feet deep. A few wisps of tough grass survived among the rocks. Wart hobbled the horses and returned for the others. It wasn't a good hiding place, he knew, but it was hidden from the tower and the road. If Seagood wanted better, he'd have to look for it himself.

He had no sooner hobbled the last of the horses when Rudy came scrambling over the rocks, soaked and out of breath. "What on earth are you doing here?" he panted.

"Trying to get out of sight," Wart said defensively.

"From whom? Anyone on the river can see us, plain as day!"

"Do you have a better idea? You try to hide five horses. We can't be seen from the tower or the road!"

Rudy studied the surroundings. Shaking his head, he admitted, "I guess this is as good as it gets. We'll just hope that no one favorable to Jabin comes down the river."

Seagood and Mathias crawled up from the river under the cover of the prickly river brush. Seagood nodded his approval and stripped off his wet clothing. The others followed suit, stretching their garments over stones to dry, while Wart prepared a makeshift meal.

They conversed quietly, though no one could have heard them over the roar of the river. It seemed they had indeed found an outlet or underground stream feeding the river, but none had been able to penetrate the swift current rushing from the underground cave.

Exhausted from their night ride and their early morning labors, the others wrapped themselves in their cloaks and fell quickly into a deep sleep. Wart cleaned up and then got busy moving stones to make a more comfortable bed. Finally satisfied, he crept over to a narrow crevice in the wall and placed his back against a rather large stone, resolved to watch while the others slept. He had shifted his weight several times to get more comfortable when he felt something move.

Supposing his britches had slid upon the ground, Wart repositioned himself and leaned back. With a yell, both he and the stone at his back tumbled into the bowels of the earth.

Seagood was on his feet instantly. He saw Wart's feet disappear through a gaping hole in the side of the cliff.

The others woke and stared in disbelief at Seagood leaning far into the cavernous hole. Rudy grabbed a torch, and Mathias brought a coil of rope. Rudy lit the torch, and Seagood grabbed it, thrusting it deep inside the dark cavity. Wart lay some fifteen feet down on a narrow ledge of stone. Beyond him, the earth seemed to open into impenetrable darkness.

Rudy peeked into the cavern and yelled, "Wart, can you hear me?"

The lad stirred, and everyone rejoiced, but still they called encouragement. "Come on, Wart. You can do it! We'll get you out of there."

When Wart finally came to his senses, he jumped to his feet and shouted, "Hey, get me out of here!"

Mathias dropped his rope, and before they could secure it properly, Wart had shinnied up and out of the dark cavern. He was bumped, bruised, and scared, but otherwise not hurt too badly.

Wart gasped. "Something is dead down there. It smells awful."

Rudy laughed. "Boy, you just got the scare of a lifetime, and the first thing you do is complain about the smell." Then Rudy sniffed, and his expression changed. "Pugh! You smell terrible."

Rudy lost no time in rushing the boy to the river where he made him peel off his clothes and take a bath.

Meanwhile, Seagood and Mathias studied the dark cavern from their position topside.

Wart was dressed in clean attire, bathed and feeling much better, when Seagood motioned for a conference. Rudy studied the master's face and began to ask questions. Wart and Mathias observed the conversation with interest.

"What do you think this is?" Rudy asked.

Seagood shrugged.

"Does it run under the city?"

A nod!

"Is this our best route into the city?"

It was clear that Seagood didn't know.

"Do you think this is our best route to Thomas?"

Seagood shrugged, but there was a strange light in his eyes.

"Do we search the hole?" Rudy asked.

Seagood gave a slight nod.

"How many of us?" Rudy asked.

Seagood studied the group. Wart refused to look Seagood in the eye. He'd been down there already, and he didn't want to go back. He was ashamed of his fear, but he could not overcome it.

Mathias would not beg, but he would not be left behind. He had come to rescue Thomas. If this was the best route, nothing was going to stop him.

Rudy did not speak. He was loyal to Seagood, and though he might quiver with fear, he would stay with his master.

Seagood held up three fingers. Wart felt relief, but also a pang of fear. That meant he would be left alone to guard five horses and keep them ready for the hoped return of his companions.

Preparations were few. Armed only with swords, torches, and several long coils of rope, Seagood was the first to descend into the cavern's darkness, followed closely by Mathias.

Rudy double-checked the anchor knot before he descended. His eyes met Wart's. "It's going to be all right, boy." He smiled. "Have some faith!"

Wart nodded. He had lots of questions he wanted to ask, but he refrained. He knew Rudy's answer would be much like his father's: "You have eyes and a brain. Do what you can."

Rudy backed through the hole, cast Wart a grin, and disappeared from view. *Whew, this place does stink!* Rudy thought as he slid down the rope. *Something is dead down here!*

Seagood led the way with the torch. The narrow ledge that had caught Wart dissolved into a deep crevasse that split the earth. Seagood's torch could reveal no bottom. They anchored a rope and began another decent.

The walls of the fissure touched Rudy's broad shoulders. He had never felt so claustrophobic. He glanced up at the glimmer of daylight that shone far above. For a brief moment he wished he had stayed with Wart.

Grasping the rope, he let himself down, not wanting to be too far behind the others. He came to the end of the rope, and still his feet dangled in the air. Wedging his body between the rock walls, he peered about for his friends. Panic began to gnaw at him. *Where are they?* he wondered.

Suddenly a dim light from Seagood's torch flickered a few yards away. The others had worked their way down the walls and were standing on a stone floor.

Feeling the rocks bite into his shoulders, Rudy moved toward the light. As he brushed though a thousand cobwebs, Rudy tried to calm his fears. Only a few spiders were known to be poisonous, but who knew what lived down here.

The silence around Rudy was complete. Even the footfalls of his companions made no audible sound. He tried to think pleasant thoughts, but they too became dark whispers in his mind.

Reaching a solid shelf of stone, Rudy grabbed for an outcropping of rock to steady himself. Something smooth and cool slithered under his hand, and he recoiled. He could not see what it was, but his dark imagination could guess.

Stumbling forward, he tried to catch the others. Blackness covered the floor between them, and before he could think what it was, he stepped into nothing. A cry of terror rose to his lips, but hurling his strong arms against the jagged walls, he stopped his descent. Slowly he inched his way across the opening by wedging his frame and feet between the walls. A stone suddenly tore loose and fell. He listened a long time but never heard it strike the bottom.

Trembling, he reached the other side. Sinking to his knees, he crawled forward. The light was not far away, but it revealed very little around him.

Seagood and Mathias rounded a corner, and all went black. "Hey!" Rudy shouted. "Come back!" He crawled faster. His hand fell upon something that gave way beneath his tremendous weight. A low sigh escaped into the gloom. Unable to imagine what it was, he jumped up and ran blindly through the darkness. A shadow caught his foot and cast him headlong. Striking his head, Rudy knew no more.

Seagood examined Rudy while Mathias held the torch. Rudy's face, hands, and clothing had been torn, but his wounds did not look too severe. Pulling a small flask from his knapsack, Seagood dabbed some of the oil on Rudy's cuts, and soon the big man opened his eyes. Seeing Seagood, Rudy rolled away, turning his face to the wall.

Mathias punched Rudy's arm and rolled him back to face them. Seagood was grinning as he held out his hand to help him up.

Rudy groaned as he got to his feet. He stood for a bit, regaining his balance. Seagood again took the lead with Rudy in tow, while Mathias brought up the rear.

They watched for a passage that might lead up into the castle, but found only paths descending deeper into the earth. Seagood marked the walls with a piece of rock, hoping to retrace their steps later. Even so, everyone was becoming confused and disoriented.

They descended three landings from where Rudy had taken his fall and then paused for a conference. Seagood's eyes asked the question: Do we go on?

Mathias and Rudy looked at each other, and Mathias spoke. "We have to be under the castle at this moment. Who knows? These cracks might lead directly to the dungeon."

Rudy dreaded to think what they might find on the next level down, but they had come this far, so they might as well go on. Seagood nodded. Turning, he began to worm his way down another ragged crevice in the floor. The odor of rotting flesh intensified with each descent.

Suddenly all three could hear the rustle and squeak of vermin. Seagood signaled for another torch to be lit, and in the dim light of two flames, they saw countless rats below them.

They had come to a different type of room. The bottom of the crevasse didn't narrow to a level floor; rather, it opened into the roof of a larger room. It was forty feet to the bottom, and the floor was covered with thousands of rats of all sizes and colors.

Seagood began to look for a place to anchor his rope for his descent into the room below, but Rudy grabbed his arm and shook his head. "There are too many rats!" he shouted.

Seagood just smiled and began to loop the rope around Rudy's massive waist.

"Hey, just a minute," Rudy said. "I don't want to go down there."

Mathias grinned. "I think he just wants you to anchor the rope while he and I go down to look around."

"Oh," Rudy said sheepishly. He braced himself to hold Seagood's weight, and Seagood began to descend. As Seagood neared the floor below, Mathias prepared to follow him down.

"You won't be down there long, will you?" Rudy asked.

"I don't know. Why?" Mathias answered.

"I don't think I can handle the dark alone," Rudy answered truthfully. "May I keep one torch? It might help you mark your way back to the passage."

"That sounds reasonable," Mathias said. "Take mine."

The torch light fluttered about the crevasse as Mathias wiggled his way through the hole and into the room below.

Rudy watched in amazement as the vermin scattered from Seagood's torch. A few rats held their ground as the men began their search of the room but fled in terror when Seagood placed the torch near their fur.

They had nearly given up hope of finding anything in the cavernous room when Mathias noticed a small hole in the far end of the vault. Together the men studied the opening, and Seagood was first to squeeze his frame through the tiny portal. Rudy's heart sank as his friends disappeared from view.

Descending another narrow crevasse, the two men entered yet another vaulted chamber. Rats fled from their light. They had taken only a few steps when their light revealed a sight that chilled their souls. A man's skeleton lay across their path.

When Thomas fell from the ledge inside the oubliette's door, he landed in a pile of rotting human bodies, the very bodies he had discarded only days before. They softened his fall, but their decay and odor made him nauseous, and he was too weak to free himself from the muck and bones. In despair, he gave himself up for dead and drifted into an uneasy sleep.

In his dream, Thomas opened his eyes to a dim red light that filled his senses. It was warm, uncomfortably so, and the air was filled with acrid smoke. When Thomas moved his arms and legs, everything seemed to work.

He was thirsty and wanted to find water, but when he tried to stand, he found he could not. He did not know if he had sustained an injury or if he was merely weary or bound by some unseen tether. So he lay and studied his surroundings. The room was dark, save for the red light that escaped the glowing fissures scattered along the walls. He wondered if he had discovered some great furnace in the depths of the earth. Time passed, and the heat became unbearable.

"Is there no relief?" he asked aloud, and the sound of his voice frightened him. It was weak, and his throat was parched. "Can someone help me?" he demanded, but his words fell unheeded to the floor.

Frustrated, Thomas closed his eyes, and his mind began to drift. Where was he? How long had he been here? Where was his sense of time? Suddenly a dreadful thought entered his mind. *Have I died? Am I in hell?*

Minutes turned to hours, and hours stretched into ever-increasing misery. His throat burned as the heat around him intensified. His mind drifted to an old story he had heard of three men who had refused to obey a tyrant king. They had been thrown into a furnace, but they had fallen unharmed into the flames. When the king looked into that furnace, he saw four men walking about in the flames, and the fourth man looked divine.

As Thomas considered that ancient story, either his mind began to clear, or a light dawned upon his misery. Whichever it was, a pure, clear light began to fill the vault in which he lay.

He could see no figure, for the light was as bright as the sun: powerful, but not dreadful. He felt drawn to the light like a moth to a flame. Reaching out, Thomas sought to touch the light, and someone gripped his outstretched hand. He felt a warm strength flow through his body. The light pushed all darkness aside, in the vault and within Thomas as well.

For the first time, Thomas saw countless men and women chained to the walls of what could only be described as a huge dungeon. The prisoners writhed in their bonds, taking no notice of Thomas or the light.

He saw too what appeared to be a jailer garbed in hideous attire. This "monster" looked like a serpent, yet he walked like a man. Thomas watched as the jailer released a man from his fetters. Sensing his freedom, the man bolted with such agility that he had covered nearly thirty paces before the jailer's tail whipped out like a coiled rope and grabbed the man's feet, making him fall.

Thomas was surprised when he heard the jailer speak. Not only had the light given him eyes to see but ears to hear as well.

"Ha!" laughed the jailer. "You thought you could escape? Where would you go?"

Thomas grew impatient, but he had no strength to move. He turned again to the light, but it was gone! He felt a reassuring warmth flow through his fingers, and he could still see through the darkness. Examining his fist, he felt a strange excitement, for it glowed—not from without, like a candle, but from within. Opening his fingers, he found a tiny silver key with raised letters on its handle spelling the word *FAITH*. Turning the key over, he found that the letters had imprinted themselves in his palm. The imprint did not hurt, but it would not rub off.

Thomas watched the hideous jailer drag one prisoner after another from their bonds to a distant door. Behind that portal raged a fiery furnace from which heat poured into the dungeon.

"Wait," Thomas called, but his voice was feeble, and the jailer took no notice.

Looking once again at the tiny key in his hand, Thomas asked aloud, "I wonder what this key is for?"

"I'll take it for you," a voice said, startling Thomas. Looking up, he saw a kindly old gentleman standing before him. The man was garbed in white, complete with tunic, turban, and sandals.

The old man's voice was gentle and comforting. "I've been waiting for you."

Thomas was stunned. "You've been waiting for me?" he asked.

"Yes," the man answered. "I knew you would receive my key. It was taken from me long ago, and now, if you please, I would very much like to have it back."

Thomas closed his fingers tightly around the tiny key. "What key?" he asked.

"Don't tire me, boy," the old man said, clearly trying to remain calm. "I want the key. I saw him place that key in your hand."

"You saw whom? I didn't see anyone," Thomas responded truthfully. "Besides, what business is it of yours what another may bequeath?"

The old man's features twisted with rage. "It's my key, I tell you! Give it to me at once!" He raised his hand to strike Thomas, but suddenly he wavered and backed away.

Thomas discovered a sword at his side. Feeling a sudden inner strength, he drew the blade and rose to his feet, facing the old man. The key still glowed in his left hand while his right held the sword. "A light has come into the darkness, and the darkness has not overcome it," Thomas shouted.

The old man turned to flee, but he shouted over his shoulder, "The key is mine! I'll get it yet!"

Sheathing his blade, Thomas turned his attention to the key. A single silver chain ran through its handle. Looping the chain over his head, the key fell warm against his chest, filling his whole body with power and courage. What the key meant, why it had been entrusted to him, or why the old man laid claim to it, he did not know.

His thoughts were interrupted by a scream. Looking about, he saw a woman in the clutches of the serpent jailer. Though she fought and struggled, the jailer continued to drag her toward the flaming door.

"Halt!" Thomas's voice boomed, and the prison wall shook. This time the serpent turned to eye him closely.

"Who troubles my labor?" the creature asked.

"Vile creature, what are you doing with the girl?" Thomas asked. "She has no desire to go where you are taking her."

"This is not your business," the creature said, and he turned to go.

"Stay," Thomas commanded as he drew his blade. The serpent heeded the command but showed no fear of the sword. "The lady has no desire for the flames. Why should she go there?"

"You are in a realm that is not yours to command," the serpent growled. "Those who have fallen into darkness will weep and gnash their teeth. Do you not hear the sound of their cries?"

Thomas stilled his thoughts and listened intently. Indeed, the whole cavity was filled with the soft sounds of men and women weeping. They gnawed their tongues, grieving over past sins and shortcomings, so wrapped up in their own remorse that they could not perceive one another.

"Yonder," the serpent hissed, "are those who torment the unforgiving."

"Then hold yet a minute," Thomas said. Turning to the weeping woman, he spoke softly. "Daughter," he said. It took some moments, but her weeping subsided. "Do you believe in Jesus?"

First the woman looked at her jailer, who stood resolute and unmoving. He still held her firmly in his strong hands. Then she looked at Thomas. There was fear in her eyes, but she nodded dumbly.

"Why do you fear answering, my lady?" Thomas asked gently.

The woman took courage and found her voice. "I think I believed once, but life has treated me cruelly. I cannot forgive those who ..." Her voice trailed away.

Thomas tried to reach for her, but the serpent barred his way. "Our heavenly Father knows and understands," Thomas said to the woman. "He has felt every wound and sorrow that has come your way."

A look of wonder crossed the woman's face. "But I have no forgiveness in my heart, and when I could not forgive, I found myself in this dreadful place. I do not know how to escape."

Thomas asked, "Do you believe Jesus died for your sins?"

"Yes," she answered.

"Do you believe He loves you?"

The woman hesitated. "I used to think so. But I have been so wicked; I don't see how He could love me now. Daily I'm reminded of my sins. It is written on the food. It is whispered in the air until I think I may scream. But I cannot speak to the Lord. Jesus is pure; He could not listen to a sinner like me."

"Jesus is pure," Thomas said. "But this is love: not that we loved Him, but that He first loved us and gave His life for us!"

A great surge of power flowed through the girl, shocking her captor and causing him to release his grip.

Thomas continued. "Jesus is faithful, even when we are not. If we confess our sins, He is faithful and just and will forgive us our sins and purify us. He does not wait until we are holy to listen to our cry. The only acceptable sacrifice to God is a broken and contrite heart. Release your bitterness and let Jesus's love flow through you. You need not remain in this dungeon."

At these words, the jailer turned and fled. The woman stood alone before Thomas. Her hair was disheveled and her clothes were torn, but still he smiled upon her. She appeared shy, but she was the first to speak. "I know what you say is true, for it is written in the Book, but I do not know how to reach out and take it for myself."

Thomas remembered the key around his neck. He withdrew the tiny key, and its radiance filled the vault with shimmering light.

She gasped at its splendor. "What is it?" she asked.

"A token of the faith our Father has given you! Stretch forth your hand and touch the gift of God, for by faith you have been set free."

With trembling fingers, she reached toward the shining object in Thomas's hand. "Are you sure it is all right?" she asked.

"It is freely given to all who believe," Thomas said.

The instant her fingers touched the tiny key, several things happened at once. The woman disappeared, and bells began to clamor in the darkness. Voices were shouting, "There has been an escape. Bar the exits! Check the halls!"

Stunned by the woman's disappearance and the blur of activity, Thomas dropped the key back under his shirt collar and began his own search for the young maiden. He could not imagine where she had gone.

The jailer raced to Thomas. "Where is she?" he demanded. His eyes were full of venom. "You will tell me what you have done with her!"

"I don't know where she is," Thomas responded, "but if I did, I wouldn't tell you."

The great viper began a slow, hypnotic dance, wrapping his snakelike tail in large coils around the room. His head swayed left and right. "You have a key, don't you?" The serpent's voice was low and menacing.

"I'm not sure what you mean," Thomas said. He had a growing suspicion that the jailer was stalling for time. Why did he need time? Was he setting a trap? Thomas felt the danger before it happened.

With a sudden sweep of his arm, Thomas drew his sword and leaped across the serpent's coils. At the same moment, the serpent flung himself headlong into the exact position where Thomas had stood only a moment before. The move was so swift that he bowled down several grim creatures that had slipped up silently behind Thomas.

The blade in Thomas's hand swept a deadly arc, rending the serpent asunder. With a vile scream, the great serpent lashed out at Thomas. Plowing into the earth at Thomas's feet, he sent dirt flying in every direction.

Seizing the opportunity, Thomas ran to the nearest wall and found he could smash the chains of the bewildered prisoners. As the fetters fell from their limbs, something like scales fell from their eyes, and they perceived that their freedom was at hand.

A clamor of voices began calling, "Is there a way out? Show us the way."

Thomas shouted, "Jesus is the way, the truth, and the life. No one comes to the Father except through Him!"

The earth began to tremble, and the vault rippled like a wave upon the sea. All the powers of hell were shaken. With a roar, the entire structure began to collapse. In the bedlam, every captive was set free. A light broke through the darkness, revealing a stairway.

Thomas shouted over the confusion, "Walk in the light, for He is the light! Follow me!" Leaping up the stairs two at a time, he led a host of captives toward freedom. At the top of the stairs across a broad landing, a heavy iron door barred their escape. Thomas retrieved his key and found that it fit the lock perfectly.

The door swung open, and Thomas shouted, "Even the gates of hell shall not stand against faith in the Lord Jesus! Let us go onward and upward."

A beautiful woman stepped near the door, crying most piteously. "Oh, please help me, my lord," she said.

"What is it, lass?" Thomas asked, bending near her.

"I have lost something very precious to me. I think I have left it behind. Could you go back and look for it?" Her eyes were deeply beseeching, and her voice broke with emotion.

Bending still closer, Thomas spoke softly. "There is nothing of lasting value down there. Come away, and what you have lost will be replaced with something of far greater value."

He was caught off guard. She grabbed for the key in his hand. "It's mine!" The voice hardened, and her hand became thick and covered with scales.

Reeling in horror, Thomas beheld a terrible dragon where the woman had been. Its scales were plates of armor, and its breath was hot and foul. Spreading its massive body across the doorway, it roared, "The key is mine!" in a voice that rumbled like thunder.

"Believe in the Lord Jesus, and you will be saved!" Thomas shouted, drawing his sword. The dragon's armor plates could not withstand the sword of truth. For the Word of God is living and active, sharper than a two-edged sword, piercing to the division of soul and spirit, of joints and marrow, and discerning the thoughts and intentions of the heart.

Thomas and the beast battled back and forth. In a burst of will, Thomas drove the demon to the very edge of a great precipice. With a final lunge, he drove this blade deep into the heart of his enemy, shouting, "Return to your master, the father of all lies!"

A terrifying screech filled the ruined chamber as the great beast tumbled over the edge and plummeted toward his destruction. The dragon's massive tail unfurled, opening the exit but catching Thomas's legs and hurling him into space.

"Save yourselves!" Thomas screamed as he fell past those on the stairs. Obeying his command, they raced up the stairs and plunged through the door into freedom.

After falling for what seemed an age, Thomas awoke to a world of decay. There was no light. His key was missing, and he could not move. He had no concept of how long he lay there until a strange glimmer of light flickered around him. As the light grew, two shadowy creatures came toward him, and when each had taken an arm, they lifted him from the mire.

Mathias gasped. They had entered a chamber so corrupt that even Seagood turned away. Rats swarmed over a massive pile of decaying human bodies.

Before Seagood could leave, Mathias caught his arm. "No!" he said. "We have to look! We can't turn back now!"

Reluctantly the two men turned to the putrid pile of flesh. Scattering rats with their torch, they climbed into the pile. As they sank into the ooze, both men gagged.

Again Seagood turned to go, but Mathias called, "Wait! I saw something!"

In the faint torchlight, Seagood saw two eyes peering at him. Plowing through the bodies as if they were not there, he clambered to the top of the pile, Mathias right behind him.

Tears poured down their cheeks, and looking to heaven, they both gave thanks. Miracle of miracles, they had found Thomas.

CHAPTER 29

Escape

Wart peered into the dark hole long after his friends had passed from view. "What am I expecting anyway?" he chided himself. "Who knows how long this might take?"

He withdrew from the mouth of the cave and began to rub the horses. They ignored him and pulled greedily at the few coarse tufts of grass available. Their smooth coats felt good under his fingers, but he could see little point in rubbing them all day.

Leaving the horses, Wart decided to make a small pallet and get some sleep. Lying down, he twisted and turned, but sleep would not come.

Am I hungry? he wondered. *Not really. What should I do?*

Suddenly Wart heard laughter. Freezing in his tracks, he listened until he was satisfied that the voices were coming no closer, and then he decided he should check it out. Creeping toward the edge of their hidden camp, he was careful not to make a sound.

Peering cautiously over a large rock, he listened intently. Laughter came from the grove of trees where he and his friends had hidden upon their arrival. He couldn't see anyone, but every so often, he heard snatches of conversation. He was surprised to understand most of the words. Indeed, the more he listened, the more he understood. *Why,* he thought, *their language is only a variation of the one I grew up with.*

Then another thought entered his mind. Were these people from Endor, or were they his own people? Should he reveal himself to them and hope they were friendly? No! Seagood would never approve. He decided he should stay and listen. He might learn something useful.

The longer Wart listened, the more he was convinced that the voices belonged to one man and one woman. A deep masculine voice would say something, and a soft feminine voice would giggle. Her words were often lost in the roar of the river.

Wart caught one phrase that sounded like, "Let's warm up ... celebration tonight." followed by a giggle. The male voice said, "Hold still," which was followed by another giggle. "Ouch!" was followed by more laughter.

Wart sighed. "I guess I'm not going to learn anything." He pondered a bit and then brightened. "Wait! What's this about a celebration? Maybe the guards won't be so observant if there is a big party in town." Encouraged, he returned his attention to the couple.

All was silent. *Have I missed them?* he wondered. *Did they leave while I wasn't watching?* The sun crept higher in the sky. Suddenly Wart heard a man's voice. "Hey! We'd better get going! The work crews will be coming soon!"

Wart wondered what he meant by "work crews." He watched and listened. A tall man emerged from the trees, looked about, and beckoned. A young girl with disheveled hair and rumpled dress stepped out to join him. Their faces were quite rosy, and they bore very sheepish expressions. They slipped from the trees, scrambled to the top of the riverbank, and quickly climbed the pathway toward the city. They passed within twenty paces of Wart.

He did not have to wait long before he heard horses on the pavement. Four men abreast rode into view. They were clad in brilliant crimson, and they carried the armor of soldiers. Behind them marched a long procession of men, shackled together with chains. The prisoners carried hoes and spades and looked half starved. They were covered with only a few filthy rags for clothing, and the sores on their legs were bloody from iron bands biting into their flesh. Every man hobbled, trying to step in time with his neighbor so the chains binding their feet would not cause them to fall. Wart had never seen animals treated so cruelly. He was horrified by the inhumanity on display, but what devastated Wart most was the way the prisoners held their heads. They lived only to prevent the lash of a whip or the slash of a sword.

Careful to remain hidden, Wart watched as the long rows of men shuffled past. They were followed by a relatively large group of women, also equipped to work in the fields. The women were filthy and clad in rags, but they were not chained together. Though their circumstances were slightly less grim, their dehumanization impressed Wart just as deeply. Immediately following the women were four more crimson riders, and then all grew quiet.

Relieved not to have been discovered, Wart sat back and considered what he had seen. *If only I had some way to set those poor people free*, he thought.

As the sun passed midday, Wart began to fret about their camp's exposure to the river. If he had but known, there was little river traffic above Endor, for the current was too swift. The dock was downriver around a bend where the water slowed and formed a natural harbor. The road was paved from Endor's front gates to the river port.

Turning his attention to the river, Wart noted that it dropped steeply here, rushing over stones and boulders, churning the water to foam and making enough noise to drown all but the very loudest of sounds. "Really," Wart observed, "we can't be much safer than we are."

Wart checked the horses once more, rubbed each one carefully, and glanced into the dark hole. Then he slipped quietly to his pad on the ground and fell into an exhausted sleep.

Mathias and Seagood managed to lift Thomas from the pile of rotting flesh. In the light of their single torch, they wiped the worst of the slime from Thomas's face and arms using strips of cloth ripped from their own clothing.

Their initial euphoria at finding Thomas alive began to give way to the enormity of getting him out. He was more dead than alive and could not help in the least. They did not hold that against him, but it would make their climb to the river much more difficult.

Now they wished they had Rudy and his tremendous strength to assist them. Deciding they could wait no longer, they each chose an end— Seagood bearing Thomas's shoulders while Mathias took his feet—and carried Thomas to the first fissure in the earth.

Seagood studied the situation and then removed his last coil of rope. He began to loop the rope around Thomas's body, knotting the loops so they would not draw tight against him. He handed one end to Mathias and took the other himself. He had made a type of crude sling to carry Thomas in.

Seagood crawled into the fissure and turned to pull Thomas in after him. It would be slow and hard, not only for Seagood and Mathias but for Thomas as well. Each little move would bump and scrape all three men.

Even with all its failures, the sling appeared to work, and all three men cleared the first fissure.

In the wake of their first success, Seagood's torch began to sputter. Fearing they would be left in the dark, Mathias began to rue having left his torch with Rudy. They scrambled up another crevasse and were overjoyed to see the faint glow of Rudy's torch in the distance.

Seagood and Mathias crossed the vaulted room and finally got Rudy to understand that they had found Thomas. Rudy was so overjoyed that it took some time for him to understand that they needed his help as well. When Rudy finally understood that Mathias needed to climb the rope, he braced himself, and Mathias shinnied up the rope.

"We have Thomas tied to the end of your rope, and we need to pull him up," Mathias said.

Wrinkling his nose at Mathias's odor, Rudy pulled with a will. Mathias helped ease Thomas through the tiny hole in the vaulted room's ceiling. They had no sooner untied the sling from the rope when they sensed that something was amiss below.

Seagood's torch had gone out completely, and vermin had begun to squeal in delight or rage. Rudy lowered his torch into the darkened vault and was horrified to see a black shadow oozing into the large room.

Rudy flung his rope toward Seagood and yelled, "Watch out!"

Seagood stood transfixed. In the dim light of Rudy's torch, he could see nothing but thick folds of darkness wrapping about him. It had no shape or form, yet it moved with intentional malice.

"Seagood!" Rudy screamed. "Come on!"

Rudy felt movement at his side. Mathias held a stone in his hand.

"Good idea," Rudy said, "I'll get some more. Maybe we can drive that thing back."

"No, Rudy," Mathias said as he aimed a stone directly at Seagood. It barely missed striking him on the head.

"Are you crazy," Rudy yelled, but Mathias's stone had the desired effect of breaking the trance that held Seagood in place. Seeing the rope, Seagood grabbed it and climbed with a will.

His friends heaved him over the edge, and all three peered into the darkness below. The torch did not light the vault well, but what they saw caused all to gasp. Darkness was filling the cavern and rising directly toward them.

Seagood sought for something large enough to stop the hole. There was nothing.

"Let's run for it!" shouted Mathias.

Mathias grabbed the torch and took the lead. Rudy scooped Thomas off the floor, cradling him like an infant, and ran. Seagood drew his sword and brought up the rear, peering over his shoulder from time to time.

At each turn or junction, Mathias anxiously studied the walls to find Seagood's mark. They had successfully ascended several flights upward when Mathias could no longer find any markings.

"Help, Seagood!" Mathias yelled. "I cannot see your mark! Have I lost the way?"

Seagood squeezed past Rudy to assist Mathias in the front. He ran his hands over the rocky walls and then pulled away. His fingers were covered in a thick, black slime. All three men stared in disbelief. Seagood began to claw his way along the wall. Waving wildly, he pointed to his mark under some slime. They were not lost, but they could not imagine where the slime had come from.

Rudy let out a whimper. He could feel rather than see a growing menace approaching him from behind. Seagood now set the course, for he could remember more clearly their downward passage. Mathias slipped to the rear and drew his blade.

When Mathias took his new position, he noticed darkness creeping into the fissure they had just climbed. Mathias had never experienced anything like this. The darkness climbed silently upward, but the ageless whisper of despair flowed before it.

"Let's get out of here!" Mathias screamed.

Seagood turned and charged up the narrow hallway, Rudy hot on his heels. Rudy now carried Thomas over his shoulder like a large sack of potatoes. Mathias, sword drawn and ever glancing over his shoulder, hurried behind.

They had to stop several times to find their mark, but once they'd found it, they would race on and upward.

Suddenly they came to the large opening in the floor. Rudy remembered it all too well. He had nearly fallen into this dreadful hole on their way down. Strangely, this hole now brought them hope. They could not be far from the top.

Seagood wedged his arms against the walls and inched his way across the chasm. Rudy tossed the rope to him, and together they ported Thomas across the opening. Then Rudy began his journey across, followed closely by Mathias.

Regrouping, the company prepared for another climb. They were surprised when Seagood's mark showed clearly on the wall. They all wondered what had happened but decided not to stay and find out.

Resuming their burden, they fled up the well-marked hallway, coming to the last great stair. Seagood took the rope and led the way. Little by little, they inched themselves and their burden up the narrow crack in the earth.

Reaching the top, they expected to see daylight streaming into the hole Wart had fallen through, but all was dark.

The cliff under which Wart hid cast its shadow over the camp, making the darkness of night ever deeper. Wart sat in the darkness, shivering, thinking back on his day. It was cold now, but it had been very hot this afternoon when the sun had found their hiding spot. Though Wart had checked the dark hole in the mountainside many times that day, his friends had never appeared. Several times during the afternoon, he had heard voices on the road, and each time he had crept to the edge of the camp to listen. Time grew long, with little to do but wait. Finally he decided to pray.

Wart wasn't familiar with prayer, but he tried to mimic Rudy, who spoke to God as if he was talking to a friend. "God?" Wart faltered. "I don't really know how to talk to You … but Rudy, you know Rudy … he says everything will work out. He says I need faith, but I don't really know what that is. Could You give me faith? See, I'm afraid. I'm afraid I'll be discovered. I'm afraid my friends won't come back. I'm afraid things won't work out. Things didn't work out for Clyde and Darren. They died, and I'm afraid of dying." Wart tried to hold back a sob. He'd tried to be brave all day, but fear had eaten away at his resolve. Tears trickled down his cheeks.

Looking toward heaven, Wart tried again. "God, Rudy talks like You can actually be with people on this earth. I don't understand how, but if You can, will You go down in that dreadful hole and find my friends?"

The sun had fallen low on the horizon when Wart's prayer was interrupted by the sound of horses on the pathway above. Creeping to the edge of the camp, he listened with great intensity.

The armor-clad men of Endor were leading the prisoners back from the fields. However, two riders plodded their steeds up the cobblestone path behind the procession. They were talking back and forth, and Wart understood most of what they said.

"I suppose you're stuck with guard duty tonight," one said.

"Yeah, but you don't think I'll miss the show, do you?" the other responded.

"What show?" asked the first.

"Where have you been, man? This is full moon; it's party time tonight! I wouldn't miss that for the world."

Both men laughed, and turning the corner, they began the steep climb to the gates. Wart sat mulling over the new information. Did that mean the guard towers might be unmanned this evening? Somehow he suddenly felt certain they would. Looking toward heaven, he whispered, "Thank you!"

Dusk had turned to darkness, and there was still no sign of his friends. Wart wondered if they had found their way into the castle. If so, had they been captured? Would they ever find Thomas?

He was beginning to feel a deep sense of melancholy when he remembered Rudy's words: "Don't lose faith, Wart! I know it doesn't sound like much of a plan, but if we are faithful to do our best, our heavenly Father will either make it work or will open another door. You've got to believe that, Wart. The Lord is faithful. He will never leave us."

In the darkness, Wart slipped out and pulled several armloads of grass for the horses. The tough blades cut his fingers and arms, and he wished heartily that he had turned the horses loose to fend for themselves.

"I hope you like it," he said, watching the horses munch their meal. He rubbed his tender hands together and wished again that his friends would appear.

The moon shone brightly, casting their hideout in deep shadow. Wart tossed and turned many times before drifting into a fitful sleep where even his dreams were dark and foreboding. Suddenly Wart felt something cold and slimy slide across his leg. He sat bolt upright, his breath rapid and shallow.

He crept toward the dark hole in the side of the cliff. His mind must be playing tricks on him. He thought he heard voices. Inching toward the hole, he was amazed to see a light flickering within.

"Where on earth is that boy?" a familiar voice was saying.

It was Rudy's voice. Wart nearly squealed in delight. "Rudy!" he called.

"Wart!" Rudy shouted. "Toss down the rope. We've got to get out of here."

Wart had drawn up the rope during the day, fearing that something evil would use it to crawl up out of the dark cavern. Quickly he found the coil, checked its anchor, and tossed it to the men below.

"Is the rope anchored?" Mathias called.

"Yes," Wart answered.

"I'm coming up." In a moment, Mathias's head popped through the opening. "We've got Thomas," he panted.

"You do?" Wart was incredulous. He stepped back as Mathias turned to haul up his load.

"Give me a hand, Wart," Mathias called. The two eased Thomas over the edge and into the outer world. They untied Thomas's sling and tossed the rope back to the others.

Rudy, fully testing the rope's strength, was the next to labor into the world outside. Seagood was right behind him. Dousing their torch, the men quickly gathered stones from the river bank and began to stack them over the hole's entrance.

"What's happening?" Wart asked as he too gathered stones to assist them.

"There's something bad down there, Wart," Rudy said, but he would say no more.

They moved a small mountain of stones to cover the hole, and then they covered it with another layer.

With the hole securely covered, Wart realized the moon was about to illuminate their refuge. He also noticed a dreadful odor accompanying the men, though they didn't seem to notice. Their concern was for Thomas. Moving him near the river, they quickly stripped off his rags, washed and dried his body, and wrapped him in a blanket.

"We've got to get him out of here," Rudy said, straightening from his labors.

Wart busied himself with the horses while they worked on Thomas, and now the party was ready to move. "Rudy, how is Master Thomas going to ride?" he asked. "He can't sit up."

"We'll make a stretcher and sling it between two horses," Rudy said. The group looked to Seagood, who nodded while stripping off his own foul clothing.

"Wart," Rudy commanded, "find two strong sticks, fairly green and even in length."

Wart nodded, found his hatchet, and disappeared into the darkness. The others had finished cleaning up when he returned with two small ash trees in tow. They quickly trimmed the limbs and shaped the poles to fit their need. Wrapping the tree limbs with a blanket, they eased Thomas onto the makeshift stretcher and passed a rope around him to keep him in place.

They had spoken little while they worked, but now they needed to form a plan. "Do we follow the river like we came in?" Rudy asked.

Seagood nodded.

"That's going to be a lot harder," Mathias cautioned. "We'll have to keep Thomas fairly level over that rough ground."

Wart tried to stay out of plan making. He remembered all too well the river crossing, but now he spoke reluctantly. "I think it might be safe to use the road. I overheard some men today. One was scheduled for guard duty tonight, but he was going to some sort of celebration instead. The road would be a lot faster and easier."

Seagood eyed the boy, studied the riverbank, and then nodded his assent.

They packed Thomas between two horses and stepped from their hideout. Scrambling up the steep slope, they quickly made the road. Keeping their horses off the paving stones, they mounted and moved at an easy pace, trying not to attract any attention in the tower far overhead.

They covered the open ground between Endor and the forest quickly and decided to stay on the road. It cut through the forest fairly straight, and so they made good time. They stopped several times to adjust the stretcher, secure the ropes, and offer Thomas tiny sips of water. On one such occasion, Rudy felt Thomas's face and exclaimed, "This man is burning up!"

Mathias took the lead, and Seagood followed on one of the horses carrying Thomas. Wart and Rudy brought up the rear. They had just topped a small incline when a hand reached from the shadows and pulled the empty horse under Thomas into the thicket.

Mathias leaped from his horse and tackled the man. The two struggled until Rudy placed his sword on the newcomer's throat. "Explain your actions, or forfeit your life," he demanded harshly.

Seagood laid his hand on Rudy's shoulder and stooped to examine the man on the ground. Suddenly he stood and signaled to let the man go. Mathias and Rudy stepped back, and the man leaped to his feet, pointing wildly down the road. Everyone turned and saw an array of torches rounding a bend in the road. It was part of Jabin's mounted guard making its way to Endor.

The stranger rushed into a tangled web of forest and beckoned them to follow. Without hesitation, they followed the man onto a narrow path that wound through thick, thorny river brush. No one knew if Jabin's guard had seen them or not.

Wart brought up the rear, and he kept glancing over his shoulder. He could see Jabin's men passing along the road. Suddenly an arrow struck the tree slightly to his right. "Rudy," he hissed, "they've seen us."

The big man stepped to one side. "Go ahead, boy," he said, and Wart slipped past him. Another arrow struck the tree close to Rudy. "And hurry."

A cry rang out behind them. "Halt! Halt in the name of Endor!" Wart understood the words, but the others understood their meaning.

Jabin's guard plunged into the thicket after them, but they had not seen the path, and thorns ripped at their clothing and flesh in the dark.

A fiendish laugh filled the air. Shivering, Wart looked back and saw several men sweep torches into the brush. The dry plants caught fire instantly, and before anyone could react, the forest was ablaze.

Suddenly, Watchers appeared everywhere. One grabbed Wart's mount while another pushed Wart, Seagood, and the others toward the river. Several rafts floated near the banks.

"This way," someone said as strong hands propelled Wart onto the waiting raft. When Wart turned, he saw it was his father. "Dad!" he cried.

"There's not time now, Son," Benhada said. "Just stay low on the raft. Don't become a target for their archers."

"But will you get away?" Wart cried.

"Probably! Now go!" his father replied.

Rudy was the last to board, and his weight tipped the raft dangerously in the water. However, strong hands across the river pulled the raft quickly and quietly to safety. There were many hands to unload the party and their cargo, and soon the four companions were mounted again and riding west.

The Watchers returned to the river to rescue their comrades across the water.

The company rode in silence until they cleared the forest and passed into open country. Rough hills rose barren and bleak all around them. Wart loved this reckless country where forest and desert lay side by side. He wasn't sure in the dark, but he thought they couldn't be far from his childhood home.

They stopped to check the stretcher, and Rudy fussed again. "We got to stop dragging Thomas all over the country. He's burning up."

"There's not a house in sight," Mathias said. "I don't think anyone lives here."

Seagood leaned over from his horse to stroke Thomas's face as if totally unaware of their predicament. Rudy could not understand his lack of leadership. Ever since they had departed the caverns, he had become a follower instead of a leader.

"Sure, people live here," Wart said.

"Where?" Mathias demanded. "I don't see any signs of life."

"Shepherds live up in those hills," Wart explained, pointing to lonely canyons etched in the rugged hills. "There are caves back in there that they've turned into homes."

Rudy studied Wart with growing wonder. What would they do without him? He was a living book of knowledge. "Do you think you could find one of those homes?" he asked.

"I think so," Wart said.

"We really need to stop and care for Thomas. He can't travel much farther," Rudy said.

"I don't think I've ever been here," Wart said, "but let's take this ravine. We shouldn't have to go too far."

Everyone turned to follow the lad while Seagood sat quietly lost in thought beside Thomas. They had not traveled far when Wart stopped. "Here's a residence."

Rudy looked all about and wondered if the lad had gone daft. There was little to be seen in the moonlight, but there was nothing to suggest a residence. "Where?" he demanded.

Wart swung off his mount and stepped into dark shadows along a wall of stone. Disappearing from view, Rudy could hear him knocking at a door.

"Well, I'm blessed," Rudy whispered to Mathias. "I thought the lad was pulling our leg."

"He may be," Mathias said. "No one is answering the door."

"Maybe we could use the house if it's empty," Rudy said.

Wart returned to the group. "I'm sorry. They must be asleep for the night."

"There is no light," Mathias observed.

"That doesn't mean much," Wart said. "They might think we are robbers—or worse, Jabin's men. I wish there was some way to let them know."

Suddenly Seagood stirred and dismounted as if awakening from a dream. Striding into the shadows, he found the door and rapped a distinct code: three staccato raps, a pause, two raps and then a single rap. There was a long pause, and the series was repeated. Seagood repeated this process three times and then stopped and waited quietly.

Rudy leaned close to Mathias. "I'm afraid the strain has been too much for him."

Mathias didn't answer, but to everyone's amazement, the door creaked slightly and swung open.

CHAPTER 30

Deliverance

Inside the cave, an oil lamp flickered on the table, illuminating a tiny room. The old shepherd and his wife had gladly surrendered their only bed to the grievously wounded man. Though Mandra bowed to Seagood, it was Wart who chatted with the old couple.

Rudy, Mathias, and Seagood labored over Thomas, bathing his wounds and applying liberally the healing balm of Amity. Its bittersweet aroma filled the tiny house and brought encouragement to those in the outer room. The house was a cave, and the bedroom was separated from the main room by only a single woolen blanket.

"So you see," Wart was explaining, "the silent man is Lord Hesketh, prince of the Gray Lands."

The couple sat in astonishment. "I had given up hope," Mandra said. "I feared the king would not return in our day."

"It's like a dream," Mandra's wife whispered.

"The man my friends are trying to save is Master Thomas, Prince of Amity," Wart announced proudly, bringing further astonishment to the old couple.

"Two kings in our humble house." Mandra shook his head.

Just then, Rudy came from behind the curtain. His huge frame eased into a chair near the table. His eyes were dark and troubled. Weariness washed his features. "I'm afraid we're going to lose him, Wart," the big man said, his head sinking to his hands.

Mandra's wife rubbed the big man's shoulders and said to her husband, "Too bad the Lady of Healing is not here."

"What's this about a lady of healing?" Wart asked excitedly.

"The Ravenna," the woman said, nodding. "It is said that she has healing power within her fingers."

"Are you talking about the Ravenna of the Gray Lands?" Wart grew more excited. "Do you mean the Lady Helsa?"

The old couple cowered. "Do not speak her name so freely, young man," Mandra said. "She is held in very high esteem here. Many are the tales of the Ravenna's healing power. We do not know if they are true, but the stories are abundant among the shepherds we know."

"Rudy." Wart shook his friend's shoulder. Rudy raised his head, tears in his eyes. He couldn't understand how Wart communicated with this couple. He could hear the couple speaking, but their words meant nothing to him.

"Rudy!" Wart said excitedly. "These people believe there is a lady with healing in her fingers."

"Oh, Wart," Rudy interrupted. "Everyone believes some fool story."

"No, Rudy," Wart insisted. "They believe it is the Lady Helsa who has healing power."

Rudy sat up straighter. "What?" he asked.

"That's what they believe," Wart insisted. "They wish she were here to help Master Thomas."

Rudy leaped from the chair, nearly knocking the table over in his haste, and rushed behind the curtain. There was a muffled conversation in the bedroom.

Moments later, Seagood emerged from the room with Rudy in tow. Mandra and his wife bowed at Seagood's appearance, but the men paid no heed. They rushed outside as Rudy shouted over his shoulder, "We are going to get the Lady Helsa."

Wart looked at the bewildered couple kneeling on the floor. "Really, you do not need to bow to Seagood," Wart said. "He doesn't think of himself as royal."

They heard the clatter of hooves outside, so they were surprised when Rudy came back through the door.

"What's wrong?" Wart cried, for Rudy's face was pale and distraught.

"He went alone," Rudy managed to say. "He didn't want me along. He's never left me behind before."

Mandra's wife laid a gentle hand on Rudy's arm. "You are too tired," she said in her native tongue. The couple made a pallet near the fire, and soon Rudy was fast asleep.

Daylight rimmed the edge of the world in pastel blue as Seagood rode out of the ravine. He noted all the landmarks for his return and turned his mount west. He kept the pace easy as he collected his thoughts.

He remembered the crowds waving for both Helsa and himself, but there had been no cheering. The populace had remained silent, as had he and his sister. Wasn't the true king supposed to free his people from their curse of silence? Seagood wondered. If he was the king, why hadn't the curse disappeared?

I guess I'm just a soldier, Seagood thought. *Even though I grew up in Stonewall under John Stafford of Amity, I have not been trained to rule a nation. I can lead men into battle, but I have never tried to guide them into a safer, more prosperous way of life. Levi and Helsa are doing quite well leading the Gray Lands. They do not need me.*

Seagood had been away from his homeland too long. True, he had been raised by the ruler of Amity, but James, Thomas, and Philip had all been groomed to lead, while Seagood had chosen to withdraw from those lessons. He had not wanted to impose himself upon Amity, but now he was wishing he had sat in on some of those sessions. He might be feeling more confident now if he had.

What would happen if Thomas did recover—if, when he returned to the Gray Lands, he won the crowds over with his ability to speak, his wisdom, and his sophisticated manners? What if Helsa were to fall in love with Thomas? She was already considered the queen, and if she and Thomas married, that would make him the king.

Seagood shook himself. He didn't like this feeling of jealously that had come worming its way into his heart. He loved Thomas and wanted what was best for him, and he also wanted to rule the Gray Lands himself.

Seagood was troubled by his thoughts. He forced himself to remember the distant details of his childhood: the terrifying days adrift at sea and the lonely days after his rescue. He'd lost his ability to speak while on ship with his father. Even after his rescue, he could not communicate with people. He'd felt wretched and alone. Many days he'd hoped his father or someone he knew would come to his rescue, but no one came. He'd tried to act tough, but he remembered how scared he really was. That was how it had been on the day John Stafford came to his room.

John Stafford had stood in his doorway and watched him for quite some time. He'd seemed friendly enough, but Seagood had remained indifferent. Finally, the big man had walked over and asked, "I say, lad, are you hoping someone will rescue their shipmate?"

Seagood had been startled to think that this man could read his thoughts. He had merely stared at John Stafford while two boys peeked around their father's legs.

"Do you see that tower over there?" John had asked, pointing to a tower on the nearby fortress of Stonewall.

Seagood had nodded.

"That is a much better place from which to watch the sea. That's where we live, so I should know. Why don't you come home to live with us?" John had asked. "From there you can watch the sea as much as you like."

Thomas had stepped from behind his father, offered his hand, and said, "I'd like another brother."

James had stepped out and countered, "Yeah, Thomas wants another brother because he can't whip me, and I'll bet you can't either."

Seagood smiled. He had gone home with the Stafford's and had grown to manhood in their home. The gracious Helen had raised him as one of her own.

But Amity would never be his. It belonged to Thomas or Philip. This wild, barren land was his home, and these were his people, his kingdom. But an ugly fear arose in his mind again. Would his people choose Thomas as their ruler?

Seagood felt wretched. Turning his thoughts toward heaven, he silently prayed, *Heavenly Father, You have guided me all these years. You kept me safe upon the sea and brought me to Stafford House. By the strangest of events, You brought me to my own home and my sister once again. You have given me a kingdom. But now, would You have me yield my kingdom to Thomas? I want to be willing to do so! Restore the love I once had for my brother!*

Tender memories flooded Seagood's mind. During their rough-and-tumble play as children, Seagood could not remember James ever saying "I'm sorry," but Thomas had always been offering his hand and asking, "Are you all right?"

Now Thomas was at death's door, and Seagood wavered in the balance. His eyes burned with tears of shame. Turning west upon a dusty trail, he slapped the reigns of his mount and raced toward his home.

Helsa stood by her eastern window, studying the long shadows cast by the setting sun.

"Helsa." The voice startled her. She had heard no one enter the room. Seeing her uncle Levi, her anxiety subsided.

"Do you expect your brother so soon?" the old gentleman asked.

Helsa looked away from his searching eyes.

"Nay, lass!" the old man said seriously. "Your brother embarked on a dangerous mission. His only hope is if the Almighty One opens a path for him."

Helsa turned to her uncle with wide, frightened eyes.

Levi held up his hand. "Slow down, child. I said the Lord would have to open a door, and I believe He will." Helsa relaxed a little, and he continued. "Besides, it is only the third day since they left, and they would barely have had time to ride to Endor and back, let alone look for their companion."

Helsa breathed a deep sigh and looked out the window again.

"Will you sup with me?" her uncle asked.

Reluctantly, Helsa followed the old man from the room.

"Will there be anything else, dearie?" Helsa's maid asked as she turned the bedding down and laid Helsa's night things in order. She bustled about the room, straightening little things here and there to give purpose to her presence.

Helsa shook her head, but the maid appeared to have no intention of leaving.

"It's no good!" the maid grumbled. "No good at all!"

Helsa stopped brushing her hair and turned to the old woman.

"I mean," the woman continued, "your brother skipping off into the unknown." She looked at Helsa and wagged her finger vigorously. "Bewitched, that was what he was. He should have stayed right here. Why, the king himself couldn't have had a better welcome! But did he stay? Not for a minute!"

It had been this way for the last two nights. Helsa knew her elderly maid could go on for hours if she didn't put a stop to it. She slipped over and embraced the old woman's shoulders.

"Oh, dearie," the old woman sobbed. "He shouldn't have left you."

Helsa gently steered the woman toward the door.

"But you waited and hoped so long, and I see your disappointment!"

They reached the doorway, and Helsa stooped to kiss the wrinkled cheek.

"I love you so much," the old woman choked.

Helsa wrapped her arms about her maid, and they embraced for a long moment. Both women's cheeks were damp when they finally parted.

"My lady!" a voice called urgently from the corridor.

Helsa stirred. It seemed only moments since her head had touched the pillow.

"Lady Helsa," the voice persisted.

She wanted to shout "Go away," but of course she couldn't. Reluctantly she left the warmth of her bed and shivered when her feet hit the cold floor. The room was dark, save for one lamp burning very low upon the shelf.

"Lady Helsa," the voice called again.

It sounded like her uncle's messenger boy, but why would he come in the middle of the night? Fear shot though Helsa. Something must be terribly wrong!

Lifting the latch, she peered into the hallway. The messenger boy quickly turned his head and looked away. Helsa realized she had forgotten to slip into her robe. Clutching her gown about her, she touched the boy's arm.

"My lady," the boy announced into the hall, "the Lord Guardian asks you to come to the throne room at once. A guest awaits you!" He glanced discreetly at Helsa to see if she understood. She nodded, and he fled down the hallway.

Who can the guest be? she wondered. *They close the gates at sundown and do not open them until morning's light. Why would they open them at this late hour?*

Anxiety mingled with expectation as she slipped into her dress and footwear. Her legs felt shaky as she stepped into the ancient corridor. There was no one about, so she nearly flew down the hallway. Outside the throne room, she stopped to calm herself and catch her breath.

Her fingers touched the latch as she looked up and down the hallway. She saw nothing out of place, no one stirring. The palace seemed to be asleep for the night, but her heart told her something very alive was on the other side of the door.

She lifted the latch and pushed the door aside. The room was far brighter than the hallway, and it took a moment for her eyes to adjust. She could see two guards beside her uncle, and the old man wore an expression of deep concern upon his face.

Another figure moved at her arrival. She caught his movement out of the corner of her eye. Turning, she stopped short. Her brother had returned!

Rushing to him and holding him tight, she thought of the strange men who had accompanied him. Though their language had sounded somewhat different, she had understood every word they'd said. She did not know why they referred to her brother as Seagood when his given name was Hesketh, but none of that mattered while she held her brother in her arms.

"Children, children," the old man pleaded after a long moment.

Dutifully, Helsa turned to face her uncle Levi, but she still clung to her brother, hardly daring to believe that he was really there. She looked first at her uncle and then back to her brother. She knew her uncle was speaking, but her heart was so full that she only caught snatches of what he said.

"Helsa ..." Her eyes drifted toward her uncle. "Brother ..." She glanced back to her brother. "He wants to ride back ..." A shadow quenched the sunshine she felt in her soul. " ... go with him! What will you do?"

Fearful of losing her brother again so soon, she wrapped her arms tightly about Hesketh's broad chest and clung to him in desperation. She would not lose him again.

"Child," the old man said sternly but with no trace of anger. "I don't think you heard a single word I said."

His gentle rebuke stung her, and though she continued to cling to her brother, she tried to concentrate on her uncle's words.

"Helsa, your brother's mission has been successful, but now he needs your help. A man is dying, and an old woman has suggested that you, the Lady of Gray Haven, might have healing in your fingertips. Your brother's mission is so urgent that he wants you to return with him yet tonight. What will you do?" Levi asked.

Helsa's mind was a blur. *Healing in my fingertips? What does that mean?*

I've never healed anyone! Yet Hesketh wants me to ride with him to help a dying man? Bewildered, she looked at her brother.

The urgency written across his face spoke volumes to her heart. His eyes said, "Trust me. Time is short! Please come."

She knew her brother could read the answer in her eyes.

She released her brother and fell before her uncle. Looking up, she nodded.

"Helsa!" the old man exclaimed. "Do you know what you are doing?"

She didn't care. Her brother had asked her to go, and she would go.

"Your absence will leave the Gray Lands without a lord or a lady," Levi complained. "People may lose heart. They look to you for hope, you know."

Helsa lifted the tiny chain holding the key to the kingdom from around her neck. It had become the symbol of all her hopes and dreams. Gently prying open her uncle's thick fingers, she carefully placed the tiny key in his palm.

"Helsa, you can't!" he bellowed, but she was already on the move. Quickly she embraced her uncle and then her brother. Her eyes and countenance spoke clearly: *Wait right here until I return*. And with that, she fled from the room.

"Trickery and bedevilment," Helsa's maid stormed. "Why would your brother waltz in and steal you away?" Helsa paid little attention to her maid's endless chatter as she frantically packed the things she thought she might need. She would be riding horseback tonight, no carriage. She would need to wear her riding habit.

"I won't stand for it," the old maid fumed. "Someone should lock him up or something."

Healing, Helsa thought. *I do have some medicines*. Quickly she gathered several small items and packed them neatly into a satchel.

"Someone's got to stop this nonsense," the old woman wailed. "Hesketh has ridden all day. If you both must go, at least get some rest and ride at daylight."

Rain, Helsa thought, grabbing her heavy riding cloak. It would serve as a night robe if she had any need of that. A smile crossed her lips at the thought of wearing that heavy old cloak over her silk nightie. She blushed.

Reaching into the satchel, she removed her neatly folded silk nightgown. *I'll just stay dressed for the duration*, she thought.

"Oh, my dearest child," the old woman sobbed. "It is so late tonight. Must you really go?"

Helsa glanced in the mirror. She saw a riding habit, thick sweater, scarf, riding hat, and boots. *Hat and boots*, she thought. She crossed the room, opened a drawer, and snatched a light cloak and some sensible shoes.

She strode to the door. She didn't look very feminine, but for the first time in a long time, she felt very alive.

Helsa stepped unannounced into the throne room. She was surprised to see a large group of men milling about in full armor.

Hesketh raised his hand, and all activity stopped. He alone had watched the side door for his sister's return.

She blushed as all eyes turned to her. Gracefully she strode across the room. She nearly resembled one of the men, ready to ride, but without the armor.

"Lady Helsa," her uncle began, a little flustered to see her in such attire. "You will not be riding alone. This portion of the guard will ride with you and Lord Hesketh to your destination. That is the only way I will allow you to leave tonight. You must promise to return as soon as this poor fellow can be moved. Is that understood?"

Helsa nodded, though her eyes never left her brother's face. Hesketh looked himself again. Some of the weariness seemed to have fallen from his shoulders. His eyes approved her garb, so she felt more comfortable than she'd imagined she could.

The group turned to go.

"Lord Hesketh and Lady Helsa," Levi called.

They turned at his summons.

"Do not fail to return to me," Levi warned. "The kingdom rests upon your shoulders."

They both bowed low and stepped from the room.

Though Mathias worked without ceasing, the fever inside Thomas refused to abate. Wart and the old couple carried water and helped all they could, as did Rudy when he finally woke from his restless sleep.

While Thomas tossed upon the bed in Mandra's home, his spirit began a journey into a world of fear, darkness, and captivity. Thomas found himself in a very dark room. *There is no need to fear the darkness*, Thomas thought. *I have survived darkness before, and this time I have the key. Wait! Where is my key?*

Frantically he reached for the chain about his neck. The key was still there, resting warm against his chest. Lifting the key from around his neck, he gripped it firmly in his fist, and a sense of peace flooded his soul.

He was not sure if his eyes were adjusting to the dark or if the key was once again illuminating the room. How could such a small key unlock such strange, dark mysteries?

Struggling to rise, Thomas peered into the darkness. The floor all about him was covered with something that resembled shattered glass, though it was much more personal. It was as if he were in a place where human hopes and dreams lay shattered on the ground.

Holding his fist high above his head, the key shone with brilliance, revealing a path stretching out before him in the darkness. Without really knowing why, he began to walk slowly down the path. When he had traveled several paces, he noticed the sparkle of a thousand tiny lights reflecting about the room. Stopping to investigate, he saw the most beautiful jewel lying just beneath the broken glass.

He began to reach for the jewel, but something stayed his hand. The jagged glass would surely cut him to ribbons if he tried to take this jewel for his own. It was difficult to leave such a treasure, but something urged him forward.

Seek ye first the kingdom of God, a voice sounded in his mind.

Thomas pondered the words. What did they mean? Surely the path to heaven did not pass through such a place as this. If this were indeed the path to heaven, which way should he go? The path extended before him and behind.

He who puts his hand to the plow and looks back is not worthy of the kingdom of God. The familiar words again passed through his mind. All right, he resolved, he would not turn back. He would proceed forward, trusting that this was an adventure the Lord had set before him.

Thomas moved carefully, but still the jagged glass near the path occasionally caught and cut his legs. Shadows danced, and fear crept into his heart, but still Thomas moved forward.

The darkness suddenly came to life as wings brushed past him in a flurry of activity. "Bats," Thomas breathed, trying to calm his nerves. "It was only bats."

The path was long, and Thomas traveled slowly. Growing quite thirsty, he immediately heard the sound of water trickling into a pool somewhere ahead. Peering into the darkness, a happy thought filled his mind. *If anyone thirsts, let him come to Me and drink.*

Sure enough, just ahead he spied water dripping into a dark pool. *Surely the Lord has provided for me even in this dark place*, Thomas reasoned. But just as Thomas reached toward the dark liquid, he spied something white lying to one side. Upon examination, he saw that it was a bone—not just one bone, but an entire skeleton lay near the pool of gathering fluid.

Thomas stepped back quickly. *Is this water poisoned?* he wondered. Though his thirst still raged, he turned back to the path.

He had not traveled far when he suddenly felt very hungry. To his surprise, around the next bend he saw a table set for two, with food upon the plates.

I am the bread of life, a voice spoke in his mind, but Thomas now wondered if this was the Lord's provision or another snare. He lingered near the table. The food looked so tempting, but hadn't Satan tempted Jesus to turn stones to bread when He had been hungry? Thomas remembered Jesus's response: "Man shall not live by bread alone, but by every word that proceeds from the mouth of God."

Thomas thought about the skeleton he had seen by the pool of water, and he leaned closer to examine the food. Suddenly he stepped away. This food was crawling with maggots. Turning, he hurried farther down the path.

When he rounded the next bend, he found that the path ended at a heavy wooden door. Had his journey come to an end? He seemed to be barred from moving forward. The words "knock, and the door will be open unto you" entered his mind.

Timidly he rapped on the door. Nothing happened, so he knocked louder. Still nothing happened, so he beat upon the door with all his strength.

When nothing happened, he turned and was surprised to see an old man dressed in white standing there. "What do you seek, my son?" the old gentleman asked.

Thomas struggled to find his voice and finally said, "I wish to pass through the door, sir."

"I will gladly open the door, if you will do one small thing for me," the old man said.

"And what is that, sir?" Thomas asked.

"Kneel and kiss my hand."

Thomas stood still. The man was dressed all in white, and light reflected all about him. Was he the Master? Slowly Thomas eased to one knee. He was confused. This was like—and yet unlike—his expectations of the Master. But hadn't the Lord said, "I am the way, the truth, and the life; no man comes to the Father except through me"?

Thomas had been searching for the kingdom. He had trusted the Lord to lead him through this dark world. Why should he now be unsure? This man had offered to let him enter, so he must be the Lord.

"Master," Thomas said, taking the offered hand. It felt hot to his touch. Thomas's lips drew near the man's fingers.

They will look upon him whom they have pierced and mourn, said a voice inside his head. Jesus had been hanged on a cross. Nails had been driven through his hands and feet, and a spear had been shoved into his side. Thomas searched the hand he held. There was no such wound.

"Imposter!" he cried, leaping to his feet. "You are none other than the devil, clothed as an angel of light. Be gone, Satan, for it is written, 'You shall worship the Lord, and Him alone shall you serve!'"

In a flash of crimson, the man disappeared in a cloud of thick smoke.

Thomas shivered. The door still barred his path, and he was shaken by his near encounter. Hunger and thirst were nearly driving him crazy. How could he pass through the door?

Suddenly he remembered the key. Would it unlock the door?

Searching the door carefully with his hands, he located a small hole near the center of the massive wooden structure. Inserting the key, he found that it fit perfectly. Slowly Thomas turned the key, heard a satisfying click, and felt the door move on its hinges.

With an easy push, the door swung open before him, and Thomas stepped into the room beyond. All was silent. He could feel an ancient bondage filling the darkest recesses of the huge vault.

The floor was rough, but a path wound down a steep slope. Several times Thomas scraped his feet along the path, but no sound met his ears. The silence became oppressive.

Rounding a bend, Thomas was surprised to see a strange light. He stood many long moments, trying to decide what it was he saw. A silvery-gray surface, flat and smooth, shimmered in the darkness. Cautiously he crept closer, for the light seemed to have a definite edge.

Carefully Thomas bent to examine the surface from which light poured into the cavern—and a haggard face peered back at him. Leaping back, Thomas cried aloud, but he heard no sound. He tried to yell, and he felt air pass through his throat, but he heard nothing.

Terror crept over him. *Am I deaf?* he wondered. *Is there a strange spell over this place that no sound can penetrate?*

Slowly, Thomas recovered his senses. He stepped to the light again and realized that he was looking into water. *It is an underground lake*, he mused. The water was reflecting the light that shone from the key in his hand.

He looked once again into the water and saw the same haggard face. This time he nearly laughed at his reflection. *I look terrible*, he thought.

Thomas knelt and was about to dip his fingers into the water when a motion caught his eye from deep beneath the water's surface. He leaned back, careful not to disturb the water, as ripples could blur his vision.

Thomas watched an entire company riding on horseback. He knew he must be seeing things, for the riders were under the water and made no sound whatsoever. They were small and distant, yet even as he watched, they moved ever closer.

When they had come within bowshot of where Thomas knelt, they reigned in. He could see them quite clearly. A man and a woman dressed in scarlet and purple were surrounded by many fully armed warriors. The entire party seemed to be a royal couple and their entourage. The woman's dark hair fell gracefully around the pale, delicate features of her face. Though wearing robes of royalty, she sat astride her mount like the warriors with whom she rode. She wore a thin band of silver on her head, and though her hands were delicate and small, they held the reigns of her horse with authority. *Alas*, Thomas mused to himself. *A woman has caught my eye, but she belongs to another.* Thomas noted the grim expression of the man by the woman's side.

The men who rode with the couple were much like their king: grim, hard-faced, and somehow familiar. The party seemed to be having a conversation, but there were no words. They spoke with their hands and their eyes. Thomas was sure he had witnessed that type of speech before, but where?

Thomas held his key higher to get a better view and then noticed something truly dreadful. A great winged creature hovered near the party, not really flying but rather hanging in the air. It was covered with dark hair, like feathers, on huge, outstretched wings, and its eyes shone like embers in its vile head.

When the lovely lady turned to speak, the vile creature wrapped its talons around her throat. Thomas leaped to his feet to shout a warning but to no avail. The horrid creature held the woman's throat, but she seemed to take no notice. She merely closed her mouth and shook her head.

Thomas drew his sword, seething in rage. If only he could reach the party, he would make the vile creature pay for touching that beautiful woman. But he could not, for they were nothing more than characters in a dream. He dared not step into the water, lest ripples should break the spell and end the vision.

The king tried to speak, and the creature grabbed his throat. Thomas marveled that the man did not draw his blade and smite the beast asunder, for he was a worthy warrior; but he seemed to take no notice. Among the guard, no one saw the creature or perceived their master's peril.

Thomas again tried to shout a warning, but no sound came from his mouth. Silently Thomas prayed, "Oh, Lord, I am powerless to change this situation. I cannot warn these people of their danger, nor can I effect their deliverance. Come to their aid, I beg You, in Jesus's name."

Even as he spoke, a distant light sped toward him. The glow from the key in his hand grew stronger, and the vision became clearer. One lone rider bore down upon the unsuspecting group. Thomas was aware of the rider's dazzling appearance. His horse was as white as snow, and the crown upon his brow shone like the morning sun. The lake shimmered in the glow. This holy one's eyes shone like beryl, and a sharp, two-edged sword issued from his mouth. Thomas knelt at the water's edge.

The party on horseback rested for only a moment and then started again on their journey, taking no notice of the vile creature or the heavenly apparition that approached them.

"Stop!" Thomas yelled. "Your deliverance draws near!" But neither Thomas nor the group heard his warning.

The sinister creature did, however, notice the new arrival, and it turned to fight. A terrible battle took place. The creature fought with all its craft and zeal, striking with its deadly talons, only to be rebuffed at every turn. The two engaged their full strength, but suddenly the beast was hurled toward the surface of the water.

A terrifying shriek filled the cavern as the surface of the water exploded into a boiling cauldron. Steam smote Thomas on the shore, and for a brief instant, he witnessed the beast and rider strike blows on the lake's surface. In a blinding flash, the white rider was gone, and the cavern became dark and foreboding.

All was silent, and then Thomas thought he heard the soft hiss of a serpent gliding across the water. A tremor ran through his body. "What are you doing in my realm?" whispered a voice filled with hatred.

Thomas spoke, and now his voice echoed across the water. "What is your name?" he asked.

"Silence," the beast answered. "It was you who called for the white rider. You will pay for your interference." Lightning flashed in the darkness, and Thomas dived behind a stone. Thunder roared, shattering the silence into a thousand splinters. Thomas cowered behind the rock, shivering with fright.

"Come out and fight," the beast roared.

A strange strength stirred within Thomas. He crept from behind the rock and faced the beast. "You come with fear and bondage, but I come in the name of Jesus Christ!" Thomas shouted.

A horrible scream rent the darkness, echoing from corner to corner of the cavern, and the lake foamed in violent frenzy. Scalding water boiled upon the shore, but Thomas held his ground. The light in Thomas's hand grew and illuminated the beast as it raced across the water to engage him in battle.

With a sure grip on his sword, Thomas held the key before him like a shield. A bolt of fire came hurtling toward him. He staggered when the fire struck, and when he regained his balance, the beast was upon him.

The attack was more sudden and ferocious than anything Thomas had ever known. In one swift blow, the beast hurled Thomas to the ground. He rolled quickly to one side as a fiery dart smote the earth where he had been. Flapping its enormous wings, the beast filled the cavern with blinding dust from the ancient floor.

Thomas closed his eyes for an instant, and in that moment the beast struck with its deadly talons. Thomas felt them rip across his body. "Help me, Lord," he cried.

The monster leaped into the air, determined to crush his adversary with one final blow.

With strength beyond his own, Thomas held the blade aloft in his hand. Gloating in its victory, the creature did not notice Thomas's blade, and he came crashing down upon its razor-sharp point.

Thomas lay beneath the vanquished monster. He could not move. "Help me!" he whispered, but his voice was lost in the silent cavern. Hope faltered, and his life lingered in the balance.

Suddenly he heard someone whisper "My lord," and the sound was as sweet and pure as a mountain stream awakening from a long winter's sleep.

Seagood, Helsa, and the party had ridden almost nonstop, and it was growing dark as they entered Mandra's courtyard. They had stopped only for brief intervals along the way. Helsa was good in the saddle, but today she had ridden with men accustomed to that lifestyle. When she slid from her horse, her bones ached, and she felt exhausted, yet she entered the shepherd's cave with anticipation and bated breath.

"Seagood!" Rudy shouted, rushing from the curtained bedroom at the sound of their arrival. Mandra and his wife bowed low to the Lord and the Lady.

Weary as they were from the ride, Seagood studied Rudy and asked with his eyes the question that had haunted him throughout his long journey. *Is Thomas alive?*

"Barely," Rudy said. "Mathias has not left his side. Thomas is delirious. He babbles nonsense and will take no water. His fever rages, and we cannot keep him cool."

Seagood dampened a cloth in the water basin and slipped behind the curtain that separated Thomas from the main room. Unsure what else to do, Helsa followed.

Thomas was pallid and still, and Helsa gasped when she saw him. She thought they had come too late. She sank to the floor, and tears filled her eyes. Before she realized what she was doing, she whispered, "My lord!"

The room grew silent. Seagood stared around the room. He knew that neither he nor his sister could speak. In fact, since the curse, very few in the Gray Lands could speak, but he'd just heard someone whisper, and he was sure it hadn't been Rudy or Mathias. Turning to his sister, he whispered, "Helsa!" A look of incredulity spread across his face. "You ... you can talk! I can talk!" he said more boldly. "Dear heavenly Father!" Seagood sank to his knees and raised his hands in prayer. "I thank You, Lord! You have lifted the curse from my people!" He turned to where Thomas lay. "This must be the man foretold by the prophets."

Slowly Seagood rose from his knees and addressed everyone in the room. "The prophets foretold that the curse would be lifted with the coming of the king. That did not happen when I came to the Gray Lands, but now that Thomas is here ..." He studied every face in the room. Pointing to where Thomas lay, he said, "I tell you, the king has come!"

Suddenly there was shouting outside, and Seagood, Rudy, and Mathias rushed out to investigate. Wart and the old couple went as far as the door, leaving Helsa alone with Thomas.

Helsa laid her cheek upon Thomas's fevered hand. Her tears washed through his fingers. "Oh, my king," she sobbed. "You have removed my reproach. Do not leave me now."

Thomas's fever broke suddenly, and he struggled to move. His breath came in great, ragged gasps. Fearing that Thomas had entered the throes of death, Helsa withdrew. Thomas opened his eyes and stared in disbelief, for before him stood the beautiful Lady of the Lake.

CHAPTER 31

Healing

During Thomas's convalescence, messengers traveled back a forth between Mandra's cave and Gray Haven. The entire kingdom had been set free. The morning after Helsa met Thomas, people awakened from their slumber to open their mouths, and for the first time in years, words spilled out.

The nation was giddy with excitement. Everyone knew the king had surely returned, for the prophecy had been fulfilled and the curse of silence lifted. Extensive plans were being made at Gray Haven for the king's arrival.

Things were calmer back at Mandra's cave. One morning, Wart and Rudy sat outside Mandra's house with their backs against the wall, soaking up sunshine. They knew these days of leisure would come to an end, so they were taking advantage of the ones they had. "Rudy," Wart asked, "what's it like to fall in love?"

"Ah-hah," the big man laughed. "Who is the lucky girl? I didn't know you had your eye on anyone."

"Not me, silly," Wart said, leaning forward and peering inside Mandra's house. Putting his finger across his lips, he motioned for Rudy to look inside.

The door was ajar, letting fresh air into the kitchen. The cot had been moved to the outer room, and Thomas lay quietly with his head resting on Helsa's lap. She ran her fingers gently through his hair, massaging his scalp and temples. Dreamy contentment covered Thomas's sleeping features.

Rudy cleared his throat and motioned Wart away from the door. Glancing about, he saw several of Seagood's company still in the courtyard. "There's not much danger for Thomas here," he announced far louder than was necessary. "Ahem!" he cleared his throat again and glanced into the house. "It doesn't look like we're needed around here, Wart!"

The "sleeping" Thomas grinned and weakly waved the vocal intruder away, never opening his eyes for fear the spell would be broken and his "therapy" would end.

Rudy grinned and waved to Helsa, who blushed and lowered her eyes. "Wart," Rudy bellowed to no one in particular, "I think you and I need to go fishing."

Thomas healed quickly. His attitude was good, and his strength was returning. He would carry permanent scars from his ordeal, and sometimes his companions worried about him, for he would ask the strangest questions, such as "Did you see the size of that monster?" or "I've lost the key! Have you seen my key?"

Seagood had already turned the kingdom over to Thomas in his mind. Thomas's coming had fulfilled the prophecies by lifting the curse of silence, so surely he was the promised king.

Strangely, his heart was not burdened at the thought of losing the kingdom. He rejoiced to see strength and vigor return to his master. He noticed too that Helsa was a changed person. He didn't resent her attraction to Thomas, but he did feel some regret when he remembered how desperately she had clung to him before.

He watched as Thomas and Helsa bade farewell to Mandra and his wife, thanking them over and over for their labors and for the use of their home during Thomas's recovery. They walked hand in hand across the courtyard to where Rudy waited to assist them into their saddles.

I lose my kingdom and my sister, yet I rejoice, Seagood thought. He raised his eyes to heaven and whispered, "Thank you."

The blare of trumpets split the morning air. The riders rode three abreast: Thomas in the center, Hesketh to his right, and Helsa to his left. Cheering crowds lined the roads as almost an entire nation poured out to see the lords and lady.

Some questioned whether the man riding in the center was really their king. They had expected the king of old to return, or some powerful warlord to come in great strength. This man appeared tired and feeble from his ordeal. Was he really the deliverer?

Even if Thomas was not all that people might have expected, that did not stop them from celebrating. The many long years of silence were over, and deliverance had come. It was time to rejoice!

The sound of feasting and merriment echoed through the halls. Minstrels played their instruments and composed songs about mighty deeds. Hesketh, Thomas, and Mathias spoke little and withdrew early, as did the Lady Helsa and her uncle. But stories were abundant as Rudy and Wart told of their own adventures.

In a quiet room far from the noise and merriment, Hesketh revealed his plan for the coronation of Thomas. "We shall do it soon—the day after tomorrow, if you like."

Thomas stood and turned to those who were gathered in the room. "The Gray Lands belong to you and your lovely sister, Lord Hesketh. Levi and Helsa have walked with your people through the darkness of a dreadful time in your history. You, Hesketh, the rightful ruler, have returned to your people. My life is richer for having known you throughout my childhood, and I owe you my life because you came to my rescue. But I cannot accept the kingship. It is yours. My home is in Amity by the sea. I shall remain here only until I can return to my father."

Thomas turned to Seagood and bowed low. "Hesketh, Lord of the Gray Lands, I humbly ask for peace between your kingdom and mine. I shall ever count you as my brother and my friend."

Thomas's words shocked the small cluster of people. Seagood's mouth moved, but he could find no words to say.

Helsa stood and took Thomas's arm. "But you have just arrived." Her eyes sought his. "What will we tell the people if you should leave? You have set our people free."

Thomas shook his head. "I have not set you free, dear lady," he said gently. "It was Jesus Christ who drove the demon from you. I fought my own battle with Silence, and he nearly bested me, but you came to my rescue." He gently patted her hand.

"He's slipping again," someone whispered to Levi, who was seated in the chair of honor.

"Slipping?" the old man asked aloud. "What do you mean?"

"He starts babbling about some key he thinks he's lost."

"Key!" Levi exclaimed, slapping his knee and rising from his chair. "That reminds me." With as much pomp and dignity as he could muster on the spot, Levi rose, crossed the room, and knelt before Lady Helsa. "On the night of your departure, dear child, you entrusted me with the emblem of your authority." He removed the key from about his neck where it lay hidden amidst the thick hair upon his chest, and he handed the key carefully to Helsa. "I now return this key to its rightful owner."

Helsa stood awkwardly, turning her eyes from her uncle to Thomas and then to her brother. "The kingdom is not mine," she said. "I relinquish it to whomever it rightfully belongs!"

"My key!" Thomas murmured. "Where did you find my key?"

The color drained from Helsa's face. She looked to her uncle and then her brother.

"My good man," Levi said a bit testily, "this key has always been in Lady Helsa's keeping. How can you now claim it?"

"Does it not have raised letters spelling the word *FAITH* upon its handle?" Thomas asked.

Seagood snatched the key from his sister's trembling hand and examined it carefully. His eyes rounded with wonder. "But how could you have known?"

A penetrating light shone in Thomas's eyes as he spoke. "It was given to me in my darkest hours," he said quietly, looking past everyone in the room. It seemed he was looking at a place no one else could see. "It shed light upon my path and gave me comfort in my moments of greatest need. Though it has marked me forever, it is more precious to me than life itself, for it is indeed the key to the kingdom. Not your kingdom or mine, but the kingdom of heaven. All who believe and cling to faith are heirs of our heavenly Father. Come, place the key in my hand, and see if it does not match my scar."

Everyone drew near. Seagood reluctantly placed the key in Thomas's outstretched hand. There, burned into his flesh, were scars now healed. Plain to all were the letters *FAITH* and the shape of a key. The two were identical.

CHAPTER 32

Evil Spreads

"Mandra, we must go. We can stay no longer." His wife's voice was pleading and persistent.

"Dearest, it seems foolish to leave our home because of a dream," Mandra protested.

"Not just once have I dreamed this dream," his wife responded. "I have dreamed these things often, but last night it became urgent."

Mandra sighed and scratched his grizzly chin. It would mean a lot of work, but if they could save the flock ... "All right," he agreed. "You get the supplies we'll need for several days. We can hide in the wilderness."

His wife shook her head. "Not just a few days. We must go for a long time."

"All right," he sighed. "Just remember, we have to carry everything we take."

They had been careful, but their supplies were nearly gone. Mandra finally convinced his wife he could return to their home, get supplies, and come back.

The moon was a thin crescent on the horizon when he slipped over the last ridge separating him from his home. He stopped short. In the pale light he could see a large company of mounted riders in his courtyard. His home was being invaded.

So, her dream came true, Mandra thought. He should have turned and fled, but he wondered who the villains were. Slipping closer, he peered over the ridge into his courtyard below. He could hear the distinct speech of Endor. These were Jabin's men. He watched as they broke his corrals to kindling and set them on fire. The door to his house had been ripped from its hinges and hurled onto the fire. Everything he and his wife valued was being destroyed by these senseless vandals.

"Curses," he whispered. Silently he backed away from the ledge. He'd seen all he could stand. Turning, he bumped into something solid, and strong hands seized him. He could not see his captors clearly in the dim light, but their crimson cloaks told the story. He was in Jabin's hands now.

A disheveled woman raced through the gates of Gray Haven when they opened at dawn, and guards had been forced to restrain her. Her clothes were tattered, and she spoke rapidly in a strange foreign language. Not knowing what to do with the woman, the guards brought her to the throne room where Thomas, Hesketh, Helsa, and Levi had gathered. The woman fell before the lords and lady, speaking nonstop, but no one could understand her.

Seagood stepped forward. "Who are you, good woman, and how may we help you?"

The woman rose to her knees and pleaded with the group, but still they could not understand what she said. "Will someone bring Wart in here?" Seagood asked.

When Wart joined the group, he recognized the old woman immediately and greeted her in her own language. "Hello! Where is your husband?"

The old woman turned to Wart and began to speak very rapidly. Wart nodded and then began to scowl. Turing to Seagood and the others, he said, "This is Mandra's wife, and she says Mandra has not returned."

Thomas, Seagood, and Helsa all leaped from their seats and rushed to the old woman. It was indeed her, but grief had so altered her features that they had not recognized her.

"Not returned?" Seagood questioned. "Find out more, Wart."

The old woman babbled on for some time before Wart again turned to the others. "It seems Mandra has disappeared. He was taken by Jabin's riders. At least, that is what his wife believes."

"Jabin's riders." Seagood's hand gripped the hilt of his sword.

The old woman nodded furiously and said, "Evil crosses river."

They might not have understood her words, but they grasped her meaning, and their faces grew pale.

In the safety of Gray Haven's throne room, multiple plans had been tossed about to rescue Mandra, Stanley, and the other believers held in Jabin's prisons. "This is madness!" Levi stormed. "If you had ten thousand men, you could not throw down Endor's gates. Yet you want twelve people to free Mandra from Jabin's grasp."

"It is not by might or by power, but by God's Spirit that men and women will be set free," Thomas stated quietly. "Endor will fall without shooting one arrow over its walls."

"Look," Hesketh said sharply, "either let me take an army, or let me go alone. Mandra came to my aid, and I will come to his."

"I have even greater reason to be in his debt," Thomas countered.

"May I go too?" The voice startled the men, and they saw that Helsa had returned from settling Mandra's wife into her new quarters. "I too stayed in their home."

"Sister," Hesketh began, "you cannot go. This trip will be far too dangerous. It could turn into war."

"It is not yet time for war," Thomas insisted. "If we wage war openly, all the slaves of Endor might be slain or hurled unwillingly against us in battle. There is another way."

CHAPTER 33

The Doors of Endor Open

From the highest tower in Endor, Maria watched as new slaves were marched across the courtyard. Most slaves were sullen or listless, their heads drooping nearly to their chests, but not these. These men marched across the square, heads held high, almost in defiance of the chains they wore.

She would have to speak with Samoth about such behavior. She liked to see spirit, but she would not tolerate defiance.

Turning from the window, she passed into her sewing room. Her new gown was still in progress: a daring, full-length dress made of nothing but lace. Open as low in the front as it was in the back, it would be stunning, for it enhanced all her graceful curves. *Maybe,* she thought, *I'll interview the new slaves in this gown when it's ready.*

The thought of those proud men growing weak at the sight of her made her tremble all over.

Conditions had changed dramatically in the dungeon since Thomas had first come to Endor. With Stanley acting as chief advisor to Melzar, prisoners were now interviewed and assessed upon their arrival. Then, depending on their abilities and attitudes, they were assigned either to supervised duties or confinement. Melzar was concluding one such interview with a prisoner who had recently been brought to Endor.

"Then you were a friend of his?" the prisoner asked.

"Yes," Melzar said. "The young prince of Amity brought life and hope to this dreary place. I still grieve his passing."

The Lord is everywhere, Mandra thought to himself. *Thomas was right. Even here, the jailer of Endor is one of God's own.* Mandra crossed his thumb and forefinger in the shape of a cross, just as Stanley had shown him. If he could get Melzar's attention, maybe they could speak as brothers, and Melzar could learn that Thomas was alive and well!

The old jailer was too distressed in his memories of Thomas to notice anything for some time, but when he finally noticed the secret sign, his jaw fell open. Glancing about, though no one else was present, he silently crossed his thumb over his forefinger.

The interview went much longer than expected. When Mandra explained that Thomas was alive and well in Gray Haven, Melzar had to learn every detail of his escape and rescue. Mandra shared everything he knew, and Melzar was beside himself with joy.

"You are sure?" Melzar asked again. "Young Thomas is really alive?"

"Yes." Mandra smiled. "While he recuperated in my home, he told me of your kindness to him and said that you had become a brother. I can see God's hand working great things in your life and in this place."

Melzar grew quiet. "I needed to hear that. I'm so glad you've come."

"I'm glad I'm here too," Mandra said, hugging the wizened old man tightly.

Certain aspects of life were predictable in Endor. Soon after Maria saw the new prisoners enter the compound, she wanted to interview them. Today it was even sooner than usual. "Bring them one at a time," she ordered. She had not slept well last night, as she kept thinking about the arrogant slaves. Odd that she should do that.

Samoth had not come to her when he'd brought the slaves, and Maria wondered why she didn't feel neglected.

"Your highness," Melzar said as he brought the first prisoner.

"Bow before me!" Maria demanded.

Though the prisoner did bow, Melzar remained standing as straight and tall as his aging body would allow. "Would you like me to stay?" he asked.

"No!" Maria considered Melzar. He no longer cringed before her, and she thought she liked his boldness, but she wasn't sure.

Melzar stepped quietly outside where the others stood waiting their turns to meet the princess. All were clean-shaven, bathed, and dressed in the garb of the temple. Melzar was usually given more time for preparation, but the Lady seemed unusually anxious to meet this group. He'd had less than twenty-four hours to get everyone groomed and somewhat ready for this interview. He was glad the prisoners were few in number and cooperative.

The last in line was Mandra. Melzar had arranged him thus, hoping to have a few private words with him before his interview. But the interviews progressed rather quickly and without event. Finally, only two prisoners were left in the outer room.

Mandra poked the aging man in front of him. "Take your time, Jonadab," he said. "I need to have a few words with our brother." Mandra nodded at Melzar.

Jonadab's eyebrows arched, but when the old jailer flashed him the secret signal, he smiled. "It is good," he said. He knew he had been treated well, something he had not expected in this place, but now he knew why.

A small bell rang, and Melzar left to attend to his duties. When he returned, he whispered to Jonadab, "I do not think it has been going well with the Ravenna today. Be careful what you say."

Jonadab smiled broadly, revealing several missing teeth. Melzar wondered if this tough old man was truly a shepherd as he claimed, or if he had really been a soldier all his life. He had all the markings of a man who knew how to fight.

"Beware," Melzar said again.

The old man nodded, and the two parted company.

Returning to Mandra, Melzar asked, "Do you remember what I told you about Thomas and how I warned him not to spurn the Lady?"

"I remember, and I am glad he did not give in," Mandra said.

"Then you will not give in?" Melzar asked.

"The Lord will help me," Mandra said. "He will give me the strength and courage to say no."

Melzar shook his head. He was amazed at how these simple believers found such courage. "I pray the Lord will grant you mercy," he whispered.

Jonadab apparently had little to say, for the interview had come to an end. The bell rang, and Melzar left Mandra alone.

Silently Mandra bowed his head. "Lord, give me wisdom," he prayed. It was his turn.

Maria was frustrated. She had yet to interview someone really interesting, and no one had even looked at her. She had not evoked one masculine response to her new lace gown, daring and risqué as it was. Was she losing her touch?

"This is the last, Your Highness," Melzar said from the door.

"Bring him in," Maria said.

Mandra walked boldly into her presence, planted his feet, and looked directly into her eyes.

"Will there be anything else?" Melzar asked from the door.

"No," Maria answered, a little annoyed that Melzar was still there. She shot him a warning glance when he lingered a moment longer.

Maria then began to study the man before her. He appeared more open than the others, and he reminded her of someone, but she could not think of whom. His face was clean-shaven and his hair clipped short. Though he was older, Maria thought he looked very handsome in his white shirt and crimson breeches. There was an appeal here that had not been in the others. Melzar did know his business, the old goat! He had saved the best for last.

"Where do you come from?" the Ravenna asked.

"The wilderness," Mandra answered.

His answer amused her. The others had said they came from the Gray Lands. She was sure he was from the same place, but she liked the change. "The wilderness?" she asked. "I suppose that could mean almost anywhere, for every country has a wilderness." She smiled. "Now, tell me where you come from."

"Across the river where the hand of Endor should not have reached," Mandra said with passion.

His answer stunned her. She was not in the habit of being rebuked by anyone, let alone a prisoner. Something about his manner intrigued her, though, so she continued. "What is your occupation?"

"I am a shepherd, as is my Master. I care for my sheep as He cares for His," Mandra stated.

Maria frowned. "You have a master? Who is he, and are you his slave?"

"Nay, lass," Mandra said. "I speak of the creator of heaven and earth. He is the great shepherd of all mankind."

Maria grew quiet. She had heard this before. This man reminded her of someone, but whom?

"Dear lady," Mandra continued, "I would not care to be in your shoes just now."

His words startled her: not so much what he'd said but that he had spoken unbidden before her. "Why?" she managed to ask.

"The ancient curse has been broken, and your kingdom is about to crumble," Mandra replied.

"What curse?" Maria asked. "What are you talking about?"

"Surely you have heard of the silence that lay upon the Gray Land?" Mandra asked.

She had. Her own mother had pronounced that curse upon those people.

"The curse has been broken," Mandra announced. "The king has come, and people speak freely in the Gray Lands."

"No!" Maria gasped. "You're lying."

"It's true," Mandra said. "And the old prophecy is about to be fulfilled."

"What prophecy?" Maria asked.

Mandra closed his eyes and began to quote some rhyme from memory. In a singsong chant, he began: "When darkness reaches beyond its grasp, evil will come to an end at last." Mandra spoke quietly now. "The river was your boundary, and crossing it spells your doom. Surly you knew this, my lady?"

There was silence for a moment before Mandra continued. "The overthrow of your empire will be swift and decisive." Mandra looked Maria in the eye. "It was spoken by the seers long ago. Your time draws to an end."

The color drained from Maria's face. "You mock me," she said, but her features belied her bold words. Terror threatened to overcome her. Once, long ago, her mother had spoken from her deathbed. "Never return to the Gray Lands," she had said. "On the day you do, you will lose all."

Maria had not understood those words that day, nor did she understand them today. How could she lose all? She regained her composure and asked, "What have I done to incur this judgment and doom?"

"You have raised your hand against the king's elect," Mandra said.

"Speak on," Maria commanded.

"You spurned the very one who sought to bring you out of bondage. He was beaten at your command and sent to the land of the lost. Now you seek to destroy those who have accepted his deliverance." Mandra spoke as one who knew what had happened.

Maria's mind was whirling. Who was this man? Of whom did he

speak? Narrowing her eyes to mere slits, she studied the prisoner intently. Finally she broke the silence. "Who is this man of whom you speak?"

"Thomas Stafford, Prince of Amity," Mandra said boldly.

Thomas! Maria's mind raced. Things had not been the same since that fateful day. He'd asked her to leave her kingdom, and she had refused. Everything had gone wrong since then. Oh, why had she ever met that man? That man! She suddenly realized that *this* man reminded her of Thomas. They both spoke with the same boldness about their Lord, and they spoke to her as if she were merely a person, not a princess or deity. *Is it even possible to control people like this?* she wondered.

Anger began to build within her. Who did this man think he was? "You are a fool!" she shouted. "Thomas of Amity is no more. He was beaten and cast into the land of the lost, from whence there is no return. You speak of one who is alive, but if Thomas has come to the Gray Lands, he comes as a spirit and not a man."

"More spirit than man when he came," Mandra said, "for he stood at death's door. But he trampled death's corridors and wrought a great deliverance. No, my lady, Thomas is not dead but very much alive. He is alive in body and alive in the hearts of his people."

"You lie!" Maria shouted. "He is dead, and his memory will be forgotten!"

"Nay, lady. His kingdom will surely grow, but your kingdom will come to an end!" Mandra said.

Her face grew livid with rage. "Guards!" she shrieked. Armed men leaped through a side door and grabbed Mandra roughly.

"Beat this liar," Maria stormed. "Throw him in the darkest cell where there will be weeping and gnashing of teeth. Maybe he will learn that there is only one worthy of worship, and that is me!"

Maria flung her robe across the bed. "Why did you cross the river to get those men?" she stormed.

"Whoa," Samoth soothed. "I brought those people for your pleasure. What does it matter where they came from?"

"Couldn't you have brought people from *this* side of the river?" Maria spat.

"Well," Samoth considered, "quite frankly, no. The war has taken every available man and boy on this side of the river." He hadn't expected a temper tantrum. Maria usually rewarded him royally when he brought her new slaves. He hadn't looked her up last night, and now he supposed she was angry about that. "Look," he stated flatly. "I'm sorry I didn't come in last night."

"I don't care if you ever come again, you fool!" Maria's dark hair tossed angrily to match the fire in her eyes.

"Now, wait just a minute …" Samoth began.

"No, you wait. The old prophecy might be coming to pass because you had to cross the river."

"What are you talking about?" Samoth asked.

"My mother told me on her deathbed that I should never reach across the river!" Maria shouted. "On the day I do, I will lose everything! I don't want to lose everything." She began to sob.

Samoth had never seen Maria like this. She looked so fragile, so human. He crossed the room and wrapped her in his arms. "Something had to be done, my love. You might have lost the kingdom to the Gray Landers if we had done nothing."

"What? Why?" Maria looked up.

"Several weeks ago there was a skirmish some miles downriver. The Gray Landers stole something, though we don't know what it was. They fought like wildcats when your father's men spotted them, and even though we burned the forest to the ground, the devils got away. We never caught a single one. Your father ordered raids into the borderlands to show those people they had better stay on their side of the river—or else!" Samoth felt very pleased to be the one to inform Maria of the past events.

"*Father* ordered the raids?" Maria asked, brightening. "If it was my father who reached across the river, and not me, maybe my mother's warning will not come to pass."

"I suppose," Samoth said with a shrug, "but I went along, thinking you might like a few more toys."

"They aren't much fun," she pouted. "I couldn't get a single one to look at me."

"Poor girl," Samoth crooned in her ear. His fingers began to trace the delicate seams of her gown. "A whip and a cell can change their attitudes. I'll work with them tomorrow."

"Oh, Samoth." Maria began to wilt in his arms. "You are so good to me. Not only do you bring me new subjects but you know how to make them love me."

"Yes, I do." His lips touched her long, graceful neck. "Forget the old prophecies. Let me be your prophet. I predict we will enjoy each other tonight and begin a long and sustained reign together tomorrow."

Maria melted, wrapping her body tightly against his. "Oh, Samoth," she whispered, "maybe I'm not a deity at all. You make me feel so weak."

"You're a goddess to me, and I worship you with all my heart."

Samoth woke to dim light filtering into the room. "Married?" he asked, wiping sleep from his eyes. "Who said anything about getting married?"

"You did," Maria said, brushing the wild tangles from her hair.

Samoth stretched and rubbed his eyes again. It had been a wild night. Between the wine and the woman, he wasn't sure what he might have said. "Well," he said, hesitating, "what exactly did I say?"

"Samoth," she crooned seductively. "You haven't forgotten, have you?" Maria turned toward him, her robe open nearly to the waist. She swayed seductively toward the bed.

Samoth began to fantasize.

"Remember," she whispered. "You said we would begin a long reign together, starting today."

"Oh." Had he really said that? "Well ... sure!" he began. "But do we really need to change things?"

"Don't you think you ought to ask my father?" Maria sighed.

"Ask him what?" Samoth ventured.

"For my hand in marriage, silly." Maria's anger had begun to flare. Clearly she was tired of this game. "Enough is enough. You weren't just toying with me, were you?"

Samoth could see that she had cooled a great deal toward him. "I would never toy with you, dear lady. Come, let's rekindle the fire."

"Not until you ask my father," she said, whirling away and storming from the room.

"Women," Samoth said, sitting up and scratching his head.

It was midmorning, and Jabin was bleary-eyed from another night of heavy drinking. He was in a dark humor and did not want to be bothered. The throne room seemed a safe place to escape interruptions. Suddenly the door opened and a messenger announced, "The young man, Samoth, is here to see you, sir."

"Bring the sneaky rascal in," Jabin ordered.

Their difference in age clashed horribly. Samoth was young and handsome; Jabin was neither. In his youth, Jabin had been a dashing young man, full of ambition, drive, and energy. Though his ambition was no less now than it had been, war, hatred, and cruelty had taken their toll upon his appearance.

Jabin sat on his throne, looking as large, old, and unbending as an oak tree. His features were carved in granite and distorted by bitterness. Heavy stubble covered his face, adding fierceness to his countenance, which wasn't necessary to intimidate the stoutest of souls.

"What do you want," he snarled when Samoth entered the room.

"Sir," said Samoth, bowing low. He was dressed in his finest, was clean-shaven, and appeared to be on his way to a formal dinner. "I've come to ask about future plans, sir."

"Future plans?" Jabin roared. "If the war doesn't turn around, we will all be hanging at the end of a rope."

"Is the war going badly?" Samoth asked from politeness. He didn't really care about the war, but he could see that it was heavy on Jabin's mind.

"Rotten!" Jabin snapped. "Two months ago we were camped on the doorstep of the richest plum in the world. Amity was virtually unprotected, with only one tiny garrison standing in my way. Now our troops flee on every side." He pounded his fist in his palm. "I've just come from heavy action with Gaff at Easterndown, and Stafford marches almost unopposed up the river road."

Samoth paled at the news. "I guess I haven't kept track of what is going on," he said feebly. "Have we any resistance for Stafford?"

"That's why I'm here!" Jabin shouted. "No one does anything around here but me. Then you prance in and ask about the war, without a care in the world."

"I'm sorry, sir," Samoth began. "I've been rather busy." He *had* been busy, directing raids almost every night into the Gray Lands. There had been heavy fighting as the Watchers repulsed almost every invasion. Many nights, Samoth had returned empty-handed.

"Oh, yes," Jabin jeered. "You have been busy with your pitiful raids, which net us nothing."

Now it was Samoth's turn to be angry. "Nothing?" he shouted. "How many men have I brought for your army? How many slaves have I brought for your gardens and labor camps? How many places have I spread your propaganda, turning people's hearts to you? I have worked long and hard for your cause! I'm not going to stand here while you ridicule all the work I have done for you and you alone." The two men glared at each other.

"Then why was I driven from Amity?" Jabin asked. "You and your father were to prepare the people for my coming. I was to be their salvation. The garrison was to be gone. Never in my life have I seen such a small force hold me back. Where were your troops when we fought at Green Meadow?" Jabin was growing angrier by the second. "I'll tell you where! They were holed up in your filthy little fortress. And who built that fortress while he should have been opening the road for me? You did!"

"I only did what my father told me to do!" Samoth retorted. "And James did not keep all the troops out of Amity. Violence surged as far east as Headwater. We even won some hearts at Stonewall! We pushed pacifism hard and won much sympathy for your cause!"

"Little good it's done me," Jabin shouted. "You've failed! Your father has his own designs. He wants Amity for himself! That fortress proves it! Neither of you even spoke with me when I was encamped at Green Meadow. You just lay low in that oversized house of yours."

"What did you expect? If we had come out and looked chummy with you, we would have looked suspicious to all the citizens of Amity," Samoth countered.

"You could have come by night and offered a show of force for the war," Jabin growled. "As it was, you did nothing to aid us in our time of need."

"Nothing?" Samoth said angrily. "You think getting rid of both James and Thomas Stafford is nothing? All your thousands of troops weren't able to do that!"

Jabin's eyes opened wide in surprise. "You got rid of both?"

Samoth began to swell with pride. "James was shot several times in the back from our walls."

"How did you lure him so close?" Jabin asked.

"He was a fool." Samoth laughed. "He rescued a girl who was shut outside our gates."

"Well, maybe your little stone house has done some good," Jabin snorted. "That should make Stafford squirm. Good job! You eliminated the eldest son. And what was that you said about Thomas?"

Samoth was fairly bursting with pride now. "I kidnapped him myself and brought him here to Endor."

"Here?" Jabin nearly shouted. "Do you mean I have Stafford's son here in Endor? I have a bargaining chip: Gaff and Stafford's surrender for Thomas's life." Jabin jumped up and hugged Samoth tight. "I take back what I said about you and your … no, I don't take back what I said about your father. He still is out for himself. But my boy, you truly are on my side." He beamed at Samoth.

Samoth suddenly felt sick. Where would this conversation lead? Jabin's praise would be short-lived when he realized that Thomas was no longer available. "Very good, sir," Samoth said, turning to leave.

"No, wait!" Jabin held up his hand.

Samoth reluctantly turned to face Jabin.

"When I came in here this morning, I could think of nowhere to turn, but you've given me an out," Jabin said. "What can I do for you?"

This was an unexpected ray of hope for Samoth. "How about your daughter's hand in marriage?" he asked.

Jabin's eyes narrowed. "Why do you want to marry her?"

"Well …" Samoth needed to think of an answer quickly. He had everything he wanted from Maria already, and he really didn't want to marry her, but how could he explain that? "I would like to enhance my position with you and your kingdom, sir," he lied.

Jabin stroked the rough stubble on his jaw as he considered. "I guess you have a way with people, and you definitely are a smooth talker. Some people might even think you are handsome. Maybe you would be an asset to my team. But if I find treachery in your words or actions, it will be your death!"

Samoth felt very vulnerable. The color drained from his face, but he stood nose to nose with the old tyrant, and his voice never faltered. "You can count on me."

CHAPTER 34

Making Plans

All the members of Seagood's team had assembled in the throne room along with Lady Helsa and Levi. "We ride at dawn," Seagood stated.

"Who is going?" Rudy asked.

"All present, barring the Lady and my uncle," Seagood said. "I cannot permit them to face such peril."

Wart glanced at Lady Helsa. Her head was bowed in submission, but he thought he saw dampness on her cheeks. *She wants to go, and I want to stay*, he thought to himself, but aloud he said, "May I help?"

All eyes turned to Wart, and Seagood smiled when he noticed the lad. "Well," he said, "we were hoping you would be our spokesman, Wart. None of us understands or speaks the language of Endor better than you. And you know the intentions of this court as well as we do. Are you willing to do that for us?"

"I can try," Wart said bravely, but his heart sank. It sounded like an important job, and he wasn't sure he was up to it.

Maria heard a door slam and footsteps race across her outer rooms. The door to her bedroom swung open, and Samoth panted breathlessly, "We've got to get out of here!"

"What are you talking about?" she asked coolly.

"Your father thinks we still have Thomas. He wants to use him as a bargaining chip with Gaff and Stafford. When he finds out you sent him to the oubliette, heads are going to roll."

Maria turned pale. She knew her father better than most, and she feared his violent temper. "Where can we go?" she heard herself asking.

Samoth was thinking out loud. "Stafford is marching on the city, and your father has pulled every available man to form a resistance. The countryside is nearly empty. If we could get outside these walls, we might have a chance. But we have to get moving. Your father is sure to check with Melzar. Is there a back stairway?"

Suddenly everything Maria loved, and all her lavish toys, seemed insignificant. Lose it all? She would lose nothing of real value if she fled this very moment with her lover. She would still have all that brought value to her life. "Maybe," she said, grabbing his sleeve. "Follow me!"

Dawn was beginning to soften the night sky in Gray Haven as the intrepid little group gathered at the palace steps. Hesketh dismounted, as did the others. He and Thomas climbed the steps to where Levi and Helsa stood waiting.

Hesketh took his sister's hand and said, "I'm sorry, sister. I cannot let you go."

"I know," she said. Her face was flushed, and her voice trembled as she spoke. Her eyes were puffy and betrayed a night of tears.

Hesketh turned away. He hated to see her in such distress, but he could not allow her to ride to the very gates of Endor.

Thomas waited until Hesketh had said his goodbye, and then he took Helsa's hand. "Dear lady," he said, his voice soft and low.

Her eyes glistened as he spoke.

"I love you," he whispered.

"Then why must you leave?" she asked.

"Helsa," Thomas said quietly but firmly, "the Lord has a plan to deliver those held captive by the power of Endor. God has spared me once, and He will do so again!"

Helsa knew she should be confident, but her heart wasn't sure. She did not answer.

"Helsa," Thomas said, "when this is over, I will go and prepare a place for you. Will you wait until I send for you?"

Helsa's eyes glistened, and she could feel her heart pounding in her chest. She knew in her heart that she had been his from the moment their eyes had met. "You mean—" She faltered.

"Yes, my love," he whispered. "When the time is right, I shall call for you. Will you come to Amity and marry me?"

Tears washed over her cheeks. She threw herself into his arms, and they held each other tight. "Yes," she whispered. "I'll come when you call." Finally, when she knew she could hold him no longer, she withdrew.

Thomas pulled the chain with the silver key from around his neck.

"I will call for you," he said. Handing her the chain, he said, "Keep this as a reminder of my promise." He turned, ran lightly down the steps, and mounted with the others.

Helsa clutched the key tight and watched the party ride away. It was long after they were out of sight that she opened her hand to inspect his gift. It was just what she expected. On the tiny silver key were the raised letters: *FAITH*.

Maria stopped where several hallways intersected. "We must go see Melzar," she said, panting. She pulled her skirts above her knees and started to run.

Samoth caught her arm and spun her around. "Are you crazy?" he hissed. "That is the first place your father will look."

"Maybe not," she fired back. "Besides, Melzar knows this temple like the back of his hand. He's been around forever. If there is a way out, he will know it."

They moved swiftly until they reached Melzar's room. Samoth paused at the heavy wooden door and listened intently. He heard low voices from within and whispered, "Someone is inside. Let's get out of here."

"It can't be Daddy," Maria said. "Whoever is in there is talking softly, almost as if they want to remain secret. Daddy yells. Come on. Let's go in."

Samoth suddenly grabbed her arm. "Hey, what is this? Are you going to betray me to your father? Wait a minute. I can see it now. You want to earn some favor by pointing all the blame at me!"

"That's not true!" Shock and anger shook Maria's voice. "I want to get out of here without being seen. Do you know how to do that?"

Samoth shook his head and softened his grip on her arm.

"I don't either," she shot at him. "Melzar is our only hope."

"But what if he is talking to some guard that will tell your father?" Samoth asked.

"We have to take that chance," Maria said. Without knocking, she lifted the latch and walked into the room. Sitting in a circle on the floor were six men, all clothed in the crimson garb of the temple guard. Maria had seen them all before, but the face that surprised her most was that of Mandra, the man she had interviewed only yesterday.

She was about to question Melzar about this when Samoth began to speak. "Melzar, do you know a good way out of here?"

Melzar moved his startled gaze from the Lady to Samoth. He spoke almost woodenly. "Past the guard station, take a left, and follow the hallway to the staircase. Then down and—"

"No, no, no," Samoth fumed. "I mean a back way. Something secret! Jabin must not see us."

Everyone turned to stare at Samoth.

Melzar's eyes narrowed. Turning to the Lady, he asked directly, "Are you in danger?"

Maria knew that Melzar had never loved her, but he had been in charge of this temple when her mother had reigned. Maria had grown up under his eye, if not under his care or teaching. There was an unspoken bond between them.

"Melzar," she pleaded. She looked into his eyes to see if he felt any sympathy. "When Daddy finds out what we've done, I'm afraid he'll be very angry. We want to escape, unseen if possible. I knew if anyone knew a way, it would be you." She sensed the old man softening. "Please help us, Melzar."

Glancing about the room, Melzar stroked his chin wearily.

Maria could see that Melzar was torn. She was seeking his protection, but Jabin was his master and had placed him here, and Jabin could easily remove him. And what about these men seated on the floor? Would they betray the lot of them?

"I can't hide you here," Melzar mumbled under his breath.

Maria knew he had taken their side and was taking his life in his hands to help them. "Thank you," she cried, hugging the old man's shoulders.

"You are not safe yet," the old man scolded. "Save your thanks until it is deserved. Will your father come looking for you soon?"

"He will come looking for *you*," Samoth interjected.

"Why?" Melzar asked.

"He thinks you are holding Thomas of Amity," Maria said. "Armies are marching upon Endor, and Daddy wants to use Thomas as a bargaining tool. But we … I threw him away." She bowed her head.

The men on the floor stirred restlessly and looked at each other. Melzar held up his hand, and his thumb and forefinger were crossed. He addressed them as men under his command. "You men need to get back to your duties!" He gave them a knowing glace, and at once they leaped to their feet and fled the room.

"Will they tell Jabin?" Samoth fretted.

"No," Melzar said. "They fear the wrath of Jabin as much as you. Quickly now, we must be moving. We will take the back stairs to the kitchen."

They descended two flights of stairs and rounded a bend where Melzar, who was in the lead, nearly bumped into a plump, elderly woman carrying a tray laden with fresh loaves of bread. Samoth and Maria halted out of sight around the corner.

"Quick, woman, I need your clothes," Melzar demanded of the startled woman.

"My lord—" she stammered. "Here? I—"

"For heaven's sake! Not the clothes you have on!" Melzar groaned. It wasn't as if he had asked for clothing from the woman's personal wardrobe. She was in charge of all the slave women's apparel. "I need an extra dress or so—make it two. And fetch two cloaks for me as well."

The large woman carefully placed her tray of steaming bread on a bench and fled to her quarters.

Melzar scooped several of the hot rolls from the tray and handed them around the corner to Samoth and Maria. "Eat these," he said. "Lord knows when you will get a chance to eat again."

"What are you doing with us?" Samoth asked between mouthfuls. His fear seemed to have subsided as his appetite returned.

"There is a labor force of women who go out to the gardens every day," Melzar explained. "I'm hoping to pass you off as female slaves. Once you are outside the city gates, you might make your escape complete."

"Why must we dress as women?" Samoth asked. "Wouldn't it be easier to pass Maria off as a man than me as a woman?"

"It would," Melzar said. "However, the women slaves are free to move about outside, while the men are shackled together before they leave the fortress. As men it would be impossible to escape."

"But—" Maria began. The reality of becoming a slave, escaping the city, and living as a fugitive began to weigh heavily upon her.

"Shh," Melzar shushed her. "I hear someone coming." He stepped around the corner and positioned himself near the hot rolls. The woman was bustling down the hallway, carrying several items in her arms.

"There, Lord Melzar," she puffed as she drew near. "You had me so flustered I forgot to ask what sizes you needed."

Melzar hadn't thought of that either. "I'm sorry I caught you by surprise, good lady. I do hope you have brought at least one large dress."

"I did!" The woman beamed. "I don't know why. Just the first one I came to, I guess."

He took the items from her hand and said, "I took liberty with a loaf or two from your tray. They are very good! Where are they going?"

She frowned and wagged a finger at him. "They were going to the master's chambers. There were plenty for you in the kitchen, mind you."

"They were for the master?" Melzar asked uneasily. "Can you restock the tray before you go?"

"I most certainly can and will," the woman responded.

"Are you taking it to his rooms or elsewhere?" Melzar asked, trying to sound causal.

"His rooms," she laughed. "More like a pigsty, it is. He and his officers have been drinking again. They got wind of some great plan this morning, and they've been having a party ever since. I don't know why I worry about how many loaves are on the tray. They won't even know there's a tray of bread. But as sure as I take a tray one loaf short, it'll be my demise."

Melzar feared this tirade could go on all day if he didn't cut it short, but it was comforting to know Jabin's whereabouts. It might give them time to work his plan. "Excuse me," he interrupted the woman, "but the master may want his bread, dear lady."

"Dear me, you are right!" She snatched the tray from the bench and bustled into the kitchen.

Melzar waited until she was out of sight, and then he ducked around the corner. "Here, get these on," he said, tossing Samoth and Maria the ragged dresses and heavy cloaks.

"You mean here?" Maria began to protest.

"Yes, here," Melzar snapped. "I'll watch the hallway. Just hurry."

Samoth looked at Maria and grinned. Even in the dark shadows, Maria felt very conspicuous as she unbuttoned her collar.

"What do we do with these?" Samoth asked, holding out his shirt and breeches to Melzar.

"I'll take everything and roll it up inside your shirt," Melzar said. "How does the dress fit?"

"Lousy!" Samoth grumbled.

Maria stifled a giggle. She had never seen Samoth so—she couldn't find a word for it. He seemed so human. She wanted to throw her arms around his neck and give him a hug, but Melzar seemed in such a hurry.

"Are you ready, my Lady?" Melzar asked, his back still discreetly turned to her activities.

"Yes," she said, tying the belt around her waist.

Melzar turned to inspect the disguises and nearly laughed. Maria resembled a princess in a tattered work frock, and Samoth looked utterly ridiculous in a ragged dress that barely covered his knees.

"The boots and shoes will have to go!" Melzar announced as he began wadding their clothing inside Samoth's shirt.

"Oh," Maria gasped, looking at her rolled-up dress. "You'll wrinkle it."

Melzar looked up. "Dear lady," he said, "you will never see this dress again. Does it matter if it has some wrinkles?"

The stark reality of leaving her things struck home. Turning away, Maria fought to hold back her tears.

"Now, off with those boots and shoes," Melzar demanded. "Slaves don't have such a luxury."

Like compliant children, they sat and removed their shoes, tossing them into the growing pile on the floor.

"Now for some dirt," Melzar said, wiping his hands in the built-up grime along the floor. Starting with Samoth, Melzar began blackening his face, hands, and arms.

Maria laughed at Samoth's faces, but when Melzar turned to her, her eyes widened. "You wouldn't dare," she said, horrified.

"Not if you'll do it yourself," Melzar said without emotion. He turned his attention back to Samoth. "Put on this cloak, and pull the hood over your head. Your hair is too much like a man's."

"That's because I am a man," Samoth growled.

"Oh, Highness," Melzar said to Maria. "You will need to remove your hair ribbons and tangle your hair." He glanced over his shoulder and smiled as Maria gingerly dabbed dust from the floor upon her cheeks.

CHAPTER 35

The Road to Freedom

Seagood and those in his company had ridden hard all day. The shadows were long when they dropped into the green valley surrounding the river.

Wart was excited. He hoped to see his father during the crossing. He'd been afraid to ask whether everyone had survived the fire and the fight with Jabin's men the night they'd brought Thomas out of Endor.

Few people in the Gray Lands seemed to know about the Watchers or their quiet deeds of heroism. They did not know about the battles fought or the people who placed their lives on the line daily for their country.

"That would be just like Dad," Wart said without realizing he'd spoken aloud.

"What?" Rudy's voice startled Wart. "Wart, are you all right?"

Blinking, Wart shook his head, "I'm fine, Rudy. I've just been thinking."

"Out loud?" Rudy laughed.

"Why?" Wart wondered. "Did I say something?"

"You've been babbling on and off all day," Rudy teased.

Wart could feel his ears growing hot, but he didn't know whether to believe his friend or not. Sometimes Rudy could stretch the truth. Wart just grinned. "Did I give any secrets away?"

"Yes, you did!" Rudy said matter-of-factly. "It seems you don't think the Watchers get enough credit in all of this."

Wart turned bright-red. He had been speaking his mind.

"Well, I agree with you," Rudy continued. "They protect everyone, but people act like they don't even exist. But you must remember, Wart, the Watchers serve the king, and their reward is from him. They are not searching for accolades among the people. They serve the master, not the minstrels."

Wart knew Rudy was right. He knew his father did not want his exploits mentioned in song. It bothered Wart that his own activities had been put to music, especially when his own deeds were nothing compared to those of his father.

Wart's thoughts were interrupted when a lone rider crossed the party's path and signaled them to stop. "Who are you?" the sentry called. "State your business."

Seagood rode forward with Thomas to identify themselves to the sentinel. The man quickly dismounted and bowed deeply. "Forgive me, my lords."

"You were just doing your job," Seagood stated. "You were right to stop us."

"My lord," the man said, "have you told the entire nation your plans?"

"No," Seagood said. "Why?"

"Today many people have come to the river seeking passage to the other side. They want to witness the fall of Endor. We expected you to come with an army, but all I see is this small group."

"What have you done with those who have come?" Thomas asked.

"We ferried them across the river," the young man said. "We didn't know if they were part of your battle plan or not."

"Are they equipped for battle?" Seagood asked.

"No, sir. Most carry staffs. I think they are shepherds," the sentinel said.

"Good!" Thomas responded. "They may well be of use to us. We will join them."

"Are you crazy?" Seagood exploded. "If we're going to war, why didn't you let me bring an army?"

"The battle we fight will not be with sword or bow," Thomas said. "We are going to catch the hearts and dreams of the prisoners within Endor and play with Jabin's mind enough to make him unsure of his next move. The Lord will deliver Endor into our hands without our firing a shot."

Seagood ground his teeth in frustration but shouted to those behind him, "We will pass and join the others."

Wart was among the last to cross the river. He had searched every nook and hollow for his father but all in vain. He was afraid to ask anyone about his father, for fear he would learn of his father's death. He could not bear that! It seemed better to hope that his father was alive than to know he was dead.

The raft dipped dangerously in the water when he and his mount stepped onto its rough surface. Quietly he rubbed the horse's muzzle and whispered soft words in its ears. He saw strong men in the shadows of the eastern shore laboring to pull the raft across the river.

They stepped ashore, and Wart led his horse toward a large gathering of people. Campfires flickered, and shadows danced among the trees and brush. Suddenly something grabbed him from the shadows. He whirled on his heels, fists up, ready for a fight.

"Well met, my son," a voice spoke.

Wart did not lower his guard until the man stepped into the light. Benhada smiled and held out his arms. Wart nearly collapsed from relief. "Dad," he whispered, "you're alive."

"Alive?" the older man questioned. "Did someone say I was not?"

"No one said anything," Wart blurted. "The last time I saw you, you were fighting with Jabin's men, the forest was on fire, and your backs were to the river. I didn't see how you could survive."

Benhada grew quiet. "It was touch and go for a while that night," he admitted. "We were driven into the water, but rafts downstream managed to pluck everyone from the river."

"What do you mean, 'that night'?" Wart asked. "Have you had more battles?"

"For a while raiders came across the river almost every night," Benhada said. "We have fought some terrible battles and have lost some good men."

"But how can we camp on the east side of the river if there are attacks on the west?" Wart asked.

"I don't know what is happening," Benhada admitted, "but some great change has taken place. The forays onto our side of the river have stopped. Troops have been moving south, and nothing lies between here and the city of Endor."

"I don't understand," Wart said.

"I don't either, Son," Benhada said. "Either the Lord is opening a path to Endor, or Jabin is setting a trap. Only time will tell."

Stanley glanced both ways down the hall before lifting the latch to Melzar's door. "Melzar," he called as he entered the chief warden's apartment. "There is rumor in the cells of a rebellion in the making."

Melzar studied "Old Stanley," who had become one of his closest advisors. Thomas had rescued Stanley from starvation in the dungeon and had brought him to Melzar as an aide and fellow believer. Stanley and others Melzar now knew as "brothers" had become a great comfort to him. Not only did they feed and care for the other prisoners but they listened to everything that was said. No spoken word in the dungeon escaped Melzar's ears.

"Rebellion?" Melzar asked. "What kind of rebellion?"

"Rumor of Maria's flight has spread. There is anger in both the guardhouse and the cells at her deposition. You know that many view her as divine, even though they may be beaten or killed at her bidding."

Melzar knew all too well the loyalty given the Lady of the Temple. "What exactly is being said?" he asked Stanley.

"That Jabin should be executed and the Lady placed on the throne," the old man said.

"That is dangerous and foolish talk," Melzar huffed. "The entire temple guard could not withstand one hour of an attack from the palace. This kind of talk will endanger the Lady's life even more."

There was a sudden rapping at the door, and someone whispered, "Melzar."

"Come in," Melzar answered.

Mandra slipped quietly through the door and closed it behind him. "He's coming," he whispered.

"Who?" asked Melzar.

"Jabin and a group of very drunken men," said Mandra.

Melzar took a deep breath and studied the men before him. "All right," he said. "Both of you go to the lower levels. Prepare the others for what might happen. If things get ugly, release the prisoners."

"But—" Stanley began.

"If Jabin begins a killing spree, he will not stop for a cell door. I will not have those under my care butchered while chained to a wall. Release them and allow them to flee or fight as they choose," Melzar said.

"What about you?" Stanley asked.

"I am in no great danger," Melzar lied. "Jabin will come here when he cannot find his daughter."

"But you can't face him alone," Stanley argued. "Let me stay with you."

"You will not!" Melzar said firmly. "You are more important to me down below with the prisoners."

"But how will we know if we should release the prisoners?" Mandra asked.

"Watch and listen," Melzar said. "If the killing begins, you will know. Now, hurry out the back door, both of you."

"This place stinks," Samoth hissed.

"Hush," Maria whispered. "You will wake everyone."

"I'm still hungry, and I don't like pretending to be a woman. Why didn't Melzar dress you up as a man?" Samoth grumbled.

"Melzar told us the men are shackled when they leave the castle, but the women are not," Maria whispered.

"Well, let's just hope they don't decide to keep us inside the city tomorrow," Samoth said.

Maria swallowed hard. What would happen if they could not escape? Trying to remain calm, she whispered, "Yes, let's hope that doesn't happen."

They were cramped in a dark, narrow corridor where the smell of unwashed bodies filled the air. There was no privacy, as the cots were jammed tightly together.

A voice spoke from somewhere in the room. "Quiet, you two! Do you want the guards to come in here?"

Maria and Samoth remained quiet for what seemed like ages, but finally Samoth asked, "How am I going to shave?"

Maria was startled. She had not thought of this, and she guessed Melzar hadn't either. "I don't know," she whispered. "Why are you asking me? I don't have the answers."

A voice in the room broke in. "Hey, since you two want to talk all night, here's the latest news. Word has it that if Jabin starts to kill prisoners, the guards will set us free."

Frightening thoughts formed in Maria's mind. "But why would Fa—" She caught herself. "But why would Jabin want to kill his own people?"

"The rebellion," the voice said. "Where have you kids been? The Lady and Samoth have gone into hiding. The guards want to kill Jabin and put the Lady on the throne. I'm all for it. She's got to be better than that old tyrant."

Maria remained silent, but not Samoth. In his most feminine whisper, he asked, "Hey, lady, where are you getting your information?"

"Through the network," the voice answered.

"What network?" Samoth asked.

"We have people on the outside too," the woman said. "Hey, where have you two been?"

"Ah …" Samoth began.

"We've been confined to the upper quarters," Maria broke in. "We've heard nothing of the network."

The ensuing silence made Maria wonder if the woman believed her story. However, she finally said, "You probably don't hear much news up there. You're probably all right, but I wouldn't put it past Jabin to plant spies in here."

"So, who's behind the order to free the prisoners?" Samoth persisted.

"Melzar, of course."

CHAPTER 36

Plans Unravel

"Melzzzzar," Jabin bellowed as he staggered down the hall.

Melzar swung the door to his apartment wide and bowed low before the Master of Endor. "My Lord Jabin," he said politely. "Please, come in."

Only five of the many men with Jabin entered the jailer's tiny apartment. Two men held Jabin upright, for he was terribly drunk. "Whearsh my dauster?" he slurred.

"I imagine she is in her quarters, sir," Melzar said crisply.

"No shesh snot," Jabin roared, wagging a finger in Melzar's face. "Snot all day. Dat fool boy wash her lash visitor. Now, whash do you knowsh, Melzzzar?"

"Oh my!" Melzar feigned concern. "What should we do?"

"Melzar," Jabin seemed to sober quickly, and his voice became angry. "I haven't kept you here for nothing! You hear everything. Nothing escapes your ears, old man, but you can tell me later. I'm here after a more important pigeon than my daughter. I've been told you have Stafford's son—Thomas, I think he was called. I want him."

"He was in my custody, sir, but he is no longer," Melzar said quietly.

"What?" Jabin swore. "Where is he?"

"He lost the Lady's favor," Melzar said.

"So?"

"He was sent to the oubliette, sir," Melzar said.

The color drained from the faces of the men with Jabin, and several backed from the room.

"Ha!" cried Jabin, a jolly tone returning to his voice. "She sent him there, did she? Good lass! How long ago was this, Melzar? It doesn't matter. He's still there. I still have my bargaining chip. I just won't mention whether he's dead or alive. Ha ha!"

Jabin's mirth did not spread to his men, and Melzar stood speechless. This wasn't the reaction he had expected.

"I'm sure," Jabin continued, "that it is a small matter for my chief jailer to find this prisoner, isn't it, Melzar?" His yellow teeth showed beneath his dark features.

"Sir?" Melzar asked.

"You heard me. I want you to retrieve his body from the pit!" Jabin scowled.

"But, sir ..." Melzar began.

"You see," Jabin said, turning to his companions, "my chief jailer understands me completely." He laughed. His companions withdrew, hoping none of them would be chosen to accompany the unlucky Melzar.

"Now," said Jabin, "we need to hurry. You'll need a long rope and a torch. Come, Melzar!"

After collecting a few necessary items, Melzar and a small group of men began their long march to the bottom of the dungeon. The knot in Melzar's stomach grew tighter with each descending step. He tried to remember the stories Mandra had told of Thomas going this same route. Thomas had survived his ordeal, or at least that was the story. Would he be so fortunate? Melzar thought of Stanley, Mandra, and the others. What would become of them? Would they come looking for him? "Lord," he prayed, "watch over Your servant."

"Hurry up!" Jabin shouted from above.

He's afraid too, thought Melzar. *Will I have the courage to let myself into the pit like Thomas did?* Melzar quailed at the thought.

According to Mandra, Thomas said there is a landing just inside the door, he thought. *If I can stay there long enough, maybe someone will rescue me.*

Hope grew as he neared the final flight of stairs. The men pushing him along slowed their pace. Melzar descended the final flight and stood alone before the door. He withdrew a large ring of keys and began to fumble for the right one. "Stand back," he announced, but he had no need. There was no one beside him.

"Hurry up," Jabin yelled from the landing above. "Get on with it!"

Time seemed to stand still. Melzar found the key and held it aloft. Inserting it in the lock, he twisted his wrist. There was an audible click, and the door swung open. A putrid smell poured into the staircase. Melzar coughed, and two of his captors wretched upon the stairs.

Melzar began tying the rope around his waist and then to the door. "I won't be long," he announced. "I might need some help when I find the body. Will anyone join me?"

Melzar did not expect an answer. His external calmness had unnerved everyone, and even Jabin made no response.

"Very well," Melzar said with a flourish. "Here I go!" He grabbed the torch from the man nearest him and stepped into the darkness.

"Shut the door!" Jabin screamed. Two men grabbed the door and swung it shut with a resounding boom. Melzar was sealed in the land of the forgotten.

Fiendish laughter resounded in the stairwell, the echoes of a madman.

With no opposition, Seagood's party was making good time walking their mounts up the river road. Eventually, Wart was called forward to converse with the lords. "You know what to say?" Thomas asked.

"I think so, sir," Wart responded. "You want me to ask that Mandra and everyone from Amity or the Gray Lands be released to you."

"That's right," Thomas agreed.

"But, sir, why would Jabin listen to us? Won't he just ignore twelve men standing on his doorstep asking for the release of certain prisoners? We are no threat to him inside his fortress, and even if he does release the prisoners we ask for, what happens to everyone else? You should have seen those poor men marching off to the gardens. Do we just leave them here?"

Seagood looked at Thomas. "My question exactly!" He and Thomas had had this same discussion many times in the last few hours.

"Wart," Thomas began, "it's only fair that we ask Jabin to release the prisoners he has unlawfully taken from our kingdoms so we can return them to their families. We need to give God the opportunity to work on Jabin's heart, and maybe he will do the right thing. If he refuses, then God will make the next move. Something is going to happen inside Endor that we cannot see, but something will move Jabin's hand. As for the other prisoners, it's not that we don't want to free them, but we have no idea where to send them. We have no jurisdiction over them, and we have no authority to demand their release."

"But shouldn't all who are held against their will be set free?" Wart asked.

"It seems Jabin is as likely to free everyone as he is to free just Mandra or Stanley," Seagood responded.

Thomas was reminded of his conversations with James and how idealistic he had been. Decisions became much harder when you had to consider the practical consequences of your actions. It was easy to want to help the downtrodden, but only God knew how people would react to your efforts. Within moments, Thomas was lost in thought. *How can I only ask for Mandra or Stanley? Are there others from the Gray Lands or Amity inside that I don't know to ask for? But on the other hand, how can I ask for everyone? Most of the prisoners are from countries other than Amity or the Gray Lands. Jabin has conquered many countries that Seagood and I have no right to rule. What should I do?*

Wart mistook Thomas's silence as a dismissal, and he fell back to join Rudy and Mathias. They were flanked by a sizable number of Watchers, of which his father was a part. Behind them followed countless numbers of barefoot people winding their way silently through the forest of Endor.

Somewhere among the trees, a thrush warbled its throaty song, followed by the soft hoot of an owl nearby.

"Imagine putting those birds in a cage," Seagood said, gently shaking Thomas's shoulder.

Thomas stirred from his thoughts. "What?" he asked.

"Think how any creature born free must feel when placed in a cage," Seagood repeated.

"You really think we should proclaim freedom for everyone under Jabin's rule, don't you?" Thomas asked.

"Why should we stop with those from our own realms?" Seagood asked. "All men seek to be free."

"But to whom will they belong?" Thomas asked. "Who will govern them?"

"Maybe you, maybe me, or maybe someone else," Seagood said. "Give them their freedom and let them choose."

"I wish I had your confidence. I'm afraid that once they have their freedom they could become as bad as Jabin himself."

"They might," Seagood said soberly. "Let's open their cage and find out."

"Wart," Thomas called, and the lad rode forward. "Between you and Seagood, I've changed my mind. Proclaim freedom to everyone."

"Are you serious?" Thomas could hear the enthusiasm in Wart's voice.

"Yes!" Thomas said.

"What a terrible night," Samoth groaned as he rolled over one last time.

"Get up!" a guard yelled from the other side of a locked door.

"Stuff it, buster," Samoth growled under his breath.

"Shh." Maria poked him. "I want to get out of here. This may be our chance."

An old woman waddling by cackled, "Quit yer talking, dearies. There's cold biscuits and water fer breakfast. Eat now, or wait til sundown. There's nothing to eat while we're outside."

Samoth and Maria nodded at each other with a knowing glance, and Maria nearly gasped. A deep shadow darkened Samoth's elegant jawline. Normally she thought his beard at this stage looked manly, but this morning it frightened her.

"Let's get some grub," Samoth grunted as he rolled off the cot.

"You can't go like that!" she whispered. "Your beard is showing!"

Samoth rubbed his chin and looked at her. "What shall I do?"

"Stay here," she ordered. "I'll get you something to eat. Now, cover your face."

"With what?" he asked.

"Your cloak, silly." She turned and strode to the table. A mixture of crumbs and cloudy water met her eyes. Her stomach churned at the sight of women wolfing down food that looked so unappealing.

"What about yer friend?" an old woman asked, jerking a finger toward Samoth.

"She's not feeling well this morning," Maria said. She would let Samoth have her portion; she certainly could never eat such fare.

"Maybe I ought to take a look," the old woman offered.

"No," Maria said quickly. "I mean, she'll be all right after she gets some food."

"Well, suite yerself," the old lady said. "I'm able to help a few."

I doubt it, Maria thought as she raked a few crumbs into her hand and filled a dirty cup with even dirtier looking water.

"Sorry," she said as she handed Samoth the cup and dumped the crumbs into his outstretched hand. "That's all they had."

"Better than nothing," he said with a shrug, wolfing the crumbs down in a single bite. She marveled at his attitude. Maybe he was tougher than she thought.

"Let's move it!" a guard shouted from outside.

Maria carefully wrapped Samoth's cloak further around him, and the two fell in line.

It was nearly dawn when Thomas and his company entered the clearing below Endor. Doubts surged as they gathered at the edge of the forest. It seemed absurd for a mere handful of men to approach the impregnable walls of the fortress.

As the vanguard prepared to ride to the very gates of Endor, Seagood opened a package he had been carrying and distributed twelve gray cloaks. "Our number is determined," he said. "This is a gift from the Lady of Gray Haven."

Wart received his cloak gladly. It was light to the touch, but it felt warm and comfortable when he slipped it over his shoulders. He felt a surge of courage when he thought of the gracious woman who had bestowed such a gift upon him, insignificant as he was.

"Our mission will be dangerous," Seagood was saying. "We will be within bowshot of the walls."

Thomas pulled Wart aside. "The people inside those walls must hear the proclamation of freedom. Are you up to the task, Wart?"

"I think so," Wart said, though he felt little confidence. He was no hero, and he did not like danger, but he was glad to be on this mission if it meant those poor people inside this castle would never wear a leg chain again. He was haunted by man's inhumanity toward man.

Finally the group was ready. Eleven men and one boy mounted their horses and followed the pavement toward Endor. When they reached the steep incline leading to the gates, Thomas turned and spoke to the group. "This is the Lord's mission. Trust and watch his hand at work."

Jabin was awakened by the sound of voices in the hallway. Yesterday's drinking spree had left his head full of cobwebs.

Someone was pounding on his door and shouting, "Wake up, sir! We have visitors."

"Who?" Jabin asked, his head clearing a little.

"They have no banner or device, sir, but they all are wearing gray cloaks," the messenger said.

"Gray?" Jabin stroked his chin. "Where are they?"

"On the flat, sir," the messenger said. "We've kept the work crews inside."

Jabin leaped from his bed, all traces of yesterday's binge gone. "Well, let's see what they have to say."

Long columns of slaves stood restlessly inside the fortress walls. Maria grew disgusted listening to the constant whispers of these wretched people. Impatiently, she tapped an old woman in front of her and asked, "Why aren't we going out?"

"The gates are still barred," the old woman said.

"Why?" Maria asked, casting a furtive glance at Samoth.

"They say there is a company of soldiers in the flat," the old woman responded.

"Soldiers?" Maria asked. "To whom do they belong?"

"No one knows," the old woman said, "but they are all dressed in gray. I hereby dub them the Gray Company. May they keep us out of the fields forever." The old woman cackled, proud of her originality.

Gray? Maria's face turned ashen. Echoing in her mind were her mother's words: *Disturb not the Gray Lands. In the day you do, you will lose all!* Another thought disturbed her. Only two days earlier, a slave had stood before her and boldly proclaimed that Thomas of Amity was not dead but was alive and well in the Gray Lands.

The group of slaves where she stood was near a lattice screening them from the immediate view of the catwalks high above. Maria peered through the lattice to the outer walls. They seemed so high from down here. She didn't think she had ever seen them from this level. Suddenly her heart stood still. There, nearly one hundred feet above her, stood her father. One minute he was staring over the wall, and the next, he turned and looked directly at her.

Seagood's riders met no resistance as they crossed the clearing and climbed the ramp to Endor's gates, but they were sure their presence was known.

"Sound carries well here," Seagood whispered to Wart. "Be sure to speak loudly, and everyone inside is sure to hear you."

The monstrous towers on either side of the gate frowned menacingly upon the visitors, making them feel most unwelcome. Seagood produced a white cloth from somewhere inside his cloak and waved the sign of parley. The party halted thirty paces from the gate.

"All right, Wart," Thomas said. "Speak up."

Wart urged his horse forward several paces and stood in the stirrups, shouting to the men on the wall in the language of Endor. "Listen, you servants of Jabin and all who are held captive against your will. The reign of Jabin is over! His power is broken! His day has come to an end!"

Thomas looked at Seagood with a puzzled expression. He knew some of the language of Endor, and this was not the speech he'd expected Wart to give.

Wart continued. "The God of heaven bought freedom for all mankind with His Son's death and resurrection. He grants freedom for the captive, rest for the weary, food for the hungry, and heavenly water for all who thirst!" Wart's voice grew in intensity. "Today is the day of your salvation. In the names of Jesus Christ and Thomas of Amity, we demand you open these gates and let our people go!"

"Get back where we can see you!" Cracking his whip, a guard inside Endor's walls shouted at the slaves milling about in the courtyard.

Samoth pulled Maria into the crowd and asked, "What's the matter? You're trembling!"

"It's Daddy!" she whispered.

"Where?" Samoth asked, looking about.

"Up there." Maria pointed toward the catwalks.

"Did he see you?" Samoth asked.

"I don't know," she said. "It felt like he looked right at me, but I was behind the lattice, and there are lots of people. I hope he didn't recognize me."

They fell silent, for a youthful voice was echoing across the plaza. It spoke of freedom and salvation. For a moment, hope kindled in every heart.

"It's too good to be true," someone whispered.

"The true king will bring freedom to the downtrodden," another said.

"The king has returned!" someone shouted.

Maria could not believe her ears. She had heard that Thomas was alive and was king of the Gray Lands, but this was not possible. He had passed into the land of the lost, never to return.

Several women began to laugh and sing.

"Stop that!" a guard shouted, cracking his whip above their heads.

Other women mocked the guard and jeered. One scooped up a handful of dust and hurled it into the air, shouting, "Long live the king!"

A guard drew his sword, and several women rushed him.

"There's going to be a riot," Maria whispered, trying to distance herself from the fray.

"There may be freedom yet," Samoth said, fierce defiance written on his brow. "If Melzar will just throw open the prisons, we stand a chance of deposing your father and placing you on the throne."

"No!" Maria screamed, but it was too late. In one swift movement, Samoth bowled over a nearby guard and grabbed his sword. "Rally to me!" he cried, felling another guard. "Up with the Lady! Down with the tyrant!"

Shouts resounded across the square. Shackled men attacked their guards, found the keys, unlocked their chains, and poured into the square, spoiling for a fight. High above from a temple window, two men watched in horror. Mandra turned to Stanley and said, "It's happening, just as Melzar feared."

"Shall we release the prisoners?" Stanley asked.

"Yes!"

Jabin grew angrier with every word. Who was this youth to proclaim the end of his reign and freedom to the slaves? He glanced over his shoulder at the empire beneath him. All was orderly and peaceful. He had nothing to fear. But wait! Who was that? He thought he recognized someone in the crowds—but that couldn't be. These were common slaves. He had nothing to do with them.

Turning back to the youth outside, he wondered if he had missed something. He heard the name Thomas of Amity. Outside? Never! He was in the oubliette!

He heard the clash of steel beneath him. Turning, he could not believe his eyes. The peaceful scene of a moment before was now total chaos. Slaves overwhelmed their captors with little more than dust and rocks.

Jabin turned to the sentinel beside him. "Silence that squeaking little rat outside. I have a riot to quell." He ran across the catwalks, gathering reinforcements.

No one saw the sentinel fit an arrow to his string or his muscles tense as he drew the bow. No one heard the twang as his fingers released the cord, for shouts of freedom raged in the courtyard below.

Seagood grew uneasy as Wart continued to speak. He could see no danger, but he sensed a growing disaster. A slight movement overhead caught his eye. He leaped forward to grab Wart from danger, but the boy was gone. One moment Wart was standing in the stirrups of his saddle proclaiming freedom to the oppressed; the next he lay in a pool of his own blood on the ground.

Seagood dropped the flag of parley he had been holding and leaped to the pavement. Within seconds, eleven men had gathered around Wart's fallen body. An arrow had found Wart's heart and ended his life immediately. He had not seen his doom or felt his fall.

Not a word was spoken as Rudy, Mathias, Thomas, and Seagood shouldered their young companion and began their retreat from Endor's gates. Others gathered the horses, but the white flag of parley lay abandoned, its fibers turning crimson where it touched the dark pool on the ground.

Maria watched in disbelief as Samoth cut a swath across the courtyard. His skill with a sword appeared great, but few armed men opposed him. "Rally to me!" his voice thundered across the square. "Fight for the Lady! Fight for your queen!"

To her dismay, the prison doors suddenly flew open, and half-starved prisoners poured into the courtyard. Behind them stepped the crimson-and-white-clad guard of the temple. These were her hand-chosen men, fully armed and prepared to place her on the throne. She should have been exultant, but she felt empty.

"No," she whispered. "It's not supposed to happen this way."

"Come on, missy," a voice cackled behind her. "Arm yourself or find a place to hide. Jabin ain't going to take this lying down."

Maria turned to see an old woman carrying a large stick hobble into the square.

"No," Maria whispered to her. "You'll be killed." But her words were lost in the clamor and confusion.

Jabin's guard, dressed in black, feigned retreat before Samoth and the temple guard. It even appeared for a brief moment that some of Jabin's troops would join the insurrection.

Suddenly a trumpet sounded from one tower and was answered on every side. Men in black poured from every quarter into the square. The short-lived freedom of the oppressed ended abruptly. Before most had voiced their joy, they began to howl with fear. Hemmed in between long spears and sharp swords, they found no escape.

Only the temple guard gave battle. The remaining population ran in fear and confusion. Panic turned to bedlam as people jammed into a great human vise, crushing life and breath from those trapped in the middle or unlucky enough to fall beneath their feet.

Maria felt herself pulled into the frantic human tangle, unable to flee and unwilling to stay.

Wart was carried to the edge of the forest east of Endor. Rudy sat in silent vigil as mourners passed their fallen companion. Thomas, unable to bear his remorse, sat alone beneath a tree with his back to the scene. He was not aware that a man had drawn near.

"Sir," a voice spoke, startling Thomas from his reverie.

"What?" Thomas managed to ask.

A tall man stepped before Thomas. He was clad as one of the Watchers, and though Thomas did not recognize him, he rose to greet him. "What can I do for you?" he asked.

"My lord," the man began, "I am the lad's father."

The color drained from Thomas face. He stepped forward, unsure how to proceed. "I ... I'm so dreadfully sorry. I should never—"

"Peace, my lord," the man said, holding up his hand. "My son knew the danger. We spoke briefly as we journeyed from the river. He really wanted to proclaim freedom to the slaves. Thank you for giving him that opportunity." The man shuffled his feet and looked away. "I understood my son's motivation," the man said. "But he said something else I did not understand. That is why I have come to you."

"What did he say?" Thomas asked.

"He said he was no longer afraid to die," the man said. "My son was always afraid of death, but today he talked about living forever. Do you understand this riddle? I do not, and it troubles me that my son found some magic I do not possess."

"Your words comfort me more than you know," Thomas said quietly. "It was not magic that your son possessed. It was God's grace. Let us sit, and I'll explain it to you."

CHAPTER 37

Quelling the Rebellion

The rebellion's tide of fortune turned quickly, yet there remained a few pockets of resistance. Samoth and the temple guard fought bravely, but their numbers and strength could not match the overwhelming power of Jabin's men. One by one they fell.

Maria heard the crack of whips as men began to herd the group she was in toward the palace. "Move along," a soldier shouted, cracking a whip above her head. She ducked behind several women to avoid the lash.

Just like cattle jostling about in a tightly fenced corral, their group moved awkwardly but steadily toward Jabin's palace.

There was a shout, and Maria became aware of a battle raging only yards away. Glancing through the populace, she saw that Samoth was alone, fighting for his life. Their eyes met for a brief instant, and in that moment he let down his guard. He grimaced as a sword pierced his side. Shielding her eyes from the scene, Maria saw no more.

Jabin sat in the balcony and watched as those captured in the riot were herded into the room below and, one by one, beheaded. A boisterous crowd shouted, "Kill them! Kill them! Long live Jabin!"

Jabin had enjoyed the spectacle for a while, but he was beginning to tire of the sport. Taking a long gulp from a bottle, he turned to an aide and said, "Continue here while I stretch my legs."

"Next!" the aide shouted as Jabin stepped from the room.

Jabin walked down several dark corridors. *I wonder*, he mused, *would I know any of these people if I saw them closer?*

Opening a door, he stepped onto a balcony overlooking a large ballroom. Many prisoners had been herded into this room to await their execution. He leaned against the railing and studied the faces below. Most he had never seen.

Samoth and Maria had run Endor ever since the war had begun. That had been a mistake, Jabin thought. But Samoth would never trouble him again. Soldiers had begun to pile the dead in the courtyard, and Samoth had been identified among the slain—wearing a dress, no less. Jabin smiled at that.

Jabin thought about Maria. She was probably the real threat. Those who had joined the rebellion wanted to place her on the throne. She might prove to be far more dangerous than a dozen men like Samoth.

Jabin felt a strange sensation, as if someone were watching him. He searched the milling crowd. It was nothing, he decided and turned to leave. That was when he saw her.

"Guards!" he shouted. "Seize that woman!" His voice filled the entire ballroom, startling guards and prisoners alike.

"Which one, Master?" someone shouted from below.

Maria ducked behind an old gentleman.

"There!" Jabin shouted, pointing his finger. "She's behind that old man."

There were many old men in the crowd, and the guards were at a loss. But following Jabin's directions, they finally caught up with Maria and grabbed her wrist.

Turning to face Jabin, they shouted, "Is this the one?"

"Yes!" He smiled. "Bring her to me."

"You little witch!" Jabin roared, backhanding Maria hard across her face.

Maria staggered, and tears sprang to her eyes, but she would not allow herself to cry. Her hands were bound tightly behind her back, so she could not sooth the sting on her cheek.

"You are just like your mother!" Jabin shouted. "She always sought more power. I gave you the temple and all the slaves you wanted, but that wasn't enough. You wanted the entire kingdom."

"But it wasn't my idea—" Maria began.

"Liar!" Jabin roared, striking Maria so savagely she fell to the floor. "Do you want to be a queen?" he asked, his voice becoming low and menacing. "I'll make you a queen! Get up!" He jerked her to her feet.

Jabin hurried Maria back to the temple and half led, half dragged the girl to her dressing room. "You will be a queen, and you will put on a show for your subjects!" he shouted. He opened her wardrobe, grabbed a dark-blue gown, and tossed it at her. "Get dressed like a queen," he spat.

"My hands," Maria said meekly.

His dagger flashed, and she wondered if it would cut her bonds or her flesh, but the cords fell from her wrists. She felt rather than saw her father turn away. "Make it fast!" she heard him growl. "We don't want to keep your subjects waiting!" With that, he stomped from her room and slammed the door.

Her hands instinctively moved to where her father's blows had fallen. Glancing in the mirror, she saw that her cheeks were swollen and red, but there was little she could do for them now. Slipping out of her rags, she paused only briefly to wash the dirt from her body before slipping into the gown. Her fingers traced the lace edging down her exquisite torso. She turned to examine herself in the mirror.

Maria could not believe her eyes. Staring from the glass was a man garbed in brilliant light. His face was gentle, his countenance mild. He held out his hands to her, and she could see that he had scars in his palms. Suddenly she noticed another man beside the first. The second seemed plain, almost common beside the first, but she recognized the second man and spoke the name that came to her mind: "Thomas."

The plain man looked at her and smiled. "My lady," he said, bowing slightly. "Meet my Master, the King of Kings and Lord of Lords."

She turned her gaze upon the man beside Thomas. Never had she beheld such grace, beauty, or holiness. She curtsied low, bowing both her body and soul before him.

Again he smiled and held out his hands. "Come!" he said softly. "And I will give you rest."

Nodding, she reached for the nail scarred hands, and warmth flooded her soul.

Suddenly the latch to her door clicked, and Maria heard boots strike the floor. "Come!" a harsh voice demanded.

Maria nearly had to run to keep pace with her father's angry stride. They crossed the square where bodies still lay in the afternoon sun. Jabin's hand bit like iron into her wrist.

They entered the palace from a side door and climbed the stairs two at a time. She raced along, holding her long skirt in one hand while trying desperately not to trip and fall. They strode down a long corridor and came to a small door with guards on either side.

Jabin spun Maria around to face him. "You are going to see your subjects one last time," he jeered. "And you are going to behave like a queen."

"Bind her!" he barked to one of the guards.

She felt cords pull her wrists tight together behind her back, and she tried not to cry when they bit angrily into her flesh.

"Not just her hands," Jabin growled. "Bind her elbows."

The cords about her wrists did not loosen, but Maria felt another chord slip around her elbows.

"Make them touch," Jabin commanded.

She gasped when, with a sudden jerk, both her shoulders were wrenched from their sockets. She writhed in agony and could scarcely breathe.

"Now, act like a queen," Jabin sneered, grabbing her arm and jerking her through the door. He led her onto a balcony overlooking a large ballroom. "Behold your queen!" he bellowed. Every eye turned toward the balcony. Jabin forced Maria to the railing. Through tear-filled eyes, she could see horror written on faces below. She stood silent before her subjects.

Suddenly Jabin grabbed her hair and jerked her head back to expose her long, graceful neck. He stepped behind her, and she saw a flash of steel. Unable to move, she stood straight and tall. She heard voices below her moaning, "No, not her!" But the voices grew distant as she saw a great light growing in her mind.

Focusing her thoughts upon the light, Maria saw the King of Kings standing before her with his arms outstretched. A smile touched her lips, even as Jabin swung his blade. An explosion filled the room, and Jabin's sword shattered in his hand, hurling him across the balcony. Blinding light and a deafening roar filled the ballroom. Jabin covered his head and tried to hide.

Maria felt she had awakened from a bad dream. All her pains and fetters were gone, and she felt freer than she had ever known. The world around her was filled with light, and in the midst of that light stood the King of Kings. Maria fell to her knees before the Master. She felt a warm hand on her cheek and heard someone say her name. Looking up, she saw Jesus reaching for her. He helped her to her feet and said, "Welcome home, dear child! Come. I have prepared a place for you."

CHAPTER 38

Dispelling the Darkness

Jabin groaned and rolled over in his bed. "Master!" He heard a voice calling, but it seemed thin and far away. He reached for another bottle, but nothing could erase the memory of the blinding light or the blow that had physically thrown him across the balcony. When he had finally crawled to his feet, he could not even see his daughter, for she was bathed in a dazzling light that forced him to shield his eyes and dart for the door. Staggering down the hall, he kept asking himself, *What happened?* It did not matter how much he drank. He could not escape the memory of his daughter or the light.

"Master!" the voice called again.

"Yes," he mumbled.

"Guards have spotted movement on the plain," the messenger said from the hallway. "They want you to take a look."

"Very well." Jabin tried to clear his mind. *A walk in the fresh air would do me good*, he thought. He poured a glass of brandy and gulped down its contents. It burned in his stomach but did little to warm him. "I'll be right there," he shouted, setting down the glass and lifting the bottle to his lips.

The night was cold and clear upon the battlements. Jabin shivered as he watched a curious movement of lights below on the plain. Two sets of lights marched down the forest road. One set turned right and the other left as they entered the plain where slaves had labored to feed the kingdom of Endor for a generation. The night was dark, and none could determine the nature of their visitors, for all were clad in dark cloaks.

"What do you make of it, sir?" the sentinel asked Jabin.

Jabin said nothing but continued to study the movement of the lights. When the western arc of lights came to the river, it did not stop but crossed the river and moved along the opposite bank.

"It appears to be a ring of fire," the sentry said, a bit disconcerted by his master's silence.

"A ring of fire," Jabin mumbled, and then he straightened. "That's it," he said. Stafford had broken through Jabin's lines and was trying to hem him in. The fool! He was using torches, telegraphing his every move. Jabin would have used darkness and surprise if the tables had been turned.

Jabin turned to an aide. "Assemble the officers in the galley. We will ride in ten minutes. The north road still appears to be open."

"That's right, ma'am," Benhada said. "Hold the torches as far from your body as you can. It will appear that two men are marching side by side."

"Will we be attacked?" the woman asked.

"I don't think so, ma'am," Benhada replied, hoping he was right.

"Will we need to cross the river?" she asked.

"No," the captain said. "We have Watchers on the other side."

"How long will the torches burn?" she asked.

"Long enough," Benhada said, hoping to heaven that he was right.

Thomas, Seagood, Mathias, and Rudy were hidden near the ramp leading to Endor's gates. Their horses tugged at the reins, nervous and ready for action.

"I hope this works," Rudy whispered.

"If it doesn't," Thomas said, "I will have blundered again."

"I don't know what they are thinking inside, but if I saw these torches, I would assume a great army had arrived and was about to set siege to the castle."

"I hope that's what they are thinking," Thomas said. "If Jabin is scared, he may make a run for it."

"We may lose him," Seagood warned. "He should pay for his crimes against humanity, to say nothing of our young friend, Wart."

All four men grew silent at the thought of their fallen comrade.

After some moments, Thomas spoke. "Our young friend wanted to free the slaves from this place. We may indeed lose Jabin tonight, but if he leaves, I feel certain that those left behind will surrender. Then we can set the captives free."

Seagood shook his head. "If we achieve that, Wart will not have died in vain," he said with a sigh.

"Hush," Mathias whispered. "I hear someone coming."

Iron hinges groaned as the dark doors of Endor began to swing open, followed closely by the clatter of hooves as thirty or more horses quietly descended from the gates above. When they hit the level, they turned north toward the only road that yet appeared to be open.

Rudy was glad Jabin's men were turning to flee. He did not like the thought of four men fighting against thirty in the daylight, but such odds in the dark were unthinkable.

"Gentlemen," Thomas said aloud, making Rudy jump in his saddle. "Shall we escort our guests to the border?"

The question *why* came to Rudy's mind, but Seagood said, "I'll even make the introductions." In one swift movement, he raised a bow, placed an arrow to the string, and fired. The arrow whined through the air and sent a chill down Rudy's spine.

"Ho ho!" Thomas laughed aloud and nudged his mount onto the road.

Jabin's men heard the voices and the arrow and spurred their horses into flight.

Rudy shrugged his shoulders to ease a pain in his back. He suddenly felt disoriented and shaky. Maybe he was just tired. They had ridden all day and marched all night, only to lose Wart at this very gate. It seemed foolish to be making this midnight ride.

He watched the others disappear. How could they keep going? He slid from his saddle and began to walk, his head spinning. He rubbed his eyes. It seemed so dark! Disoriented, he suddenly felt afraid. "Where am I?" he asked aloud.

"Shh!" someone whispered nearby. "Not so loud."

"Who are you?" Rudy demanded. He tried to find the speaker. "Where are you?"

"Rudy," the voice called, "you've got to warn our friends!"

"Who are you?" Rudy asked again.

"More riders have left the castle," the voice said. "Our friends will be caught between the two groups. If you run, you will catch them where the road turns east. Now go!"

Rudy had never been quick on his feet, but now as he began to run, he could not believe his speed. He leaped over rocks and boulders in the dark as if they were not there. He scrambled up inclines and raced through fields of beans and potatoes. Suddenly he could see the riders of Jabin away to his right, and not far behind followed Seagood, Thomas, and Mathias.

Charging forward, he came to a place where the road turned east and found himself between Jabin and his friends. As they rounded the bend, he began to shout and wave. "Get off the road," he yelled. "You are being followed."

The three men reigned in sharply. "Rudy," Seagood demanded. "How did you get here, and where is your horse?"

"There is no time," Rudy panted. "There are riders behind you. Now follow me." He leaped off the path and led the others deep into the brush along the road.

The three men hurried into a shallow valley and stopped to listen. Above them on the road thundered the hooves of a hundred or more horses.

When Jabin's cavalry had passed, Seagood turned to ask, "Rudy, how did you know?" But the three men were alone.

CHAPTER 39

Change of Regime

They found Rudy the following morning near the gates of Endor. He lay facedown on the ground with a black arrow protruding from his back.

Thomas spoke quietly to the small group gathered around the two fresh mounds of earth beside the road to Endor. "Our friends Rudy and Wart became brothers in this life, and they were not long parted. God used them to touch people's lives on this earth, and I believe He will continue to use them as they walk the corridors of heaven. Their service to mankind will never be forgotten."

A man slipped quietly from the shadows and touched Benhada's arm. "Cap'n," the Watcher whispered. "Three men have been seen leaving the city."

Benhada touched Seagood's arm, and the small gathering moved quickly from the somber scene. They gathered at the forest's edge and watched three men ride across the clearing bearing a white flag of parley. "The scum," Mathias spat. "I'd like to give them a taste of my steel."

"Peace, Mathias," Thomas said. "If there is treachery here, let it be from their side, not ours."

They held their weapons and watched as the party drew near. Suddenly Thomas sheathed his sword and ran forward with a shout of joy. "Stanley!" he cried. "You're alive!"

The old farmer slid from his horse, and the two men embraced. Thomas stepped back and looked in the older man's eyes. "What is going on in the city?"

The old man looked weary as he spoke. "My lord, the city, or what's left of it, is yours."

Thomas, Seagood, and their party rode through the gates of Endor. They were astonished by what they saw. Jabin and his men had left a mess. Dead bodies lay unheeded throughout the courtyard and in every building. They had never witnessed such wanton disregard for human life.

Thomas turned to his men. "Seagood, have your Watchers secure the grounds. Mathias, gather as many as you can to clear the dead. Stanley, take me to the dungeons to release the prisoners and set them free."

Everyone was conscripted for the labor.

Two days passed before Maria was discovered in a ballroom balcony. She was buried with dignity in a grave of her own, but no special ceremonies were held in her honor.

Finding Maria's remains reminded Thomas of another person he had failed to see: Melzar. Where was the old jailer? Thomas began to ask everyone what had happened to Melzar, but no one seemed to know.

On the beginning of the fourth day of their occupation, Thomas finally met someone who knew the events of that fateful day. Grabbing Mathias and Seagood, Thomas searched Melzar's room until he found the key to the bottomless pit. They bounded down the stairs, taking several at a stride, until they neared the bottom. Thomas began to move more slowly, and Seagood and Mathias caught up with him.

"I see why they call this the land of the forgotten," Mathias said. "We've taken so many turns and descended so far, I hope you know your way out," he said to Thomas.

"Somehow this seems more frightening than coming to the cavern from below as we did," Seagood whispered.

"What if he's not here?" Thomas asked. "Do we go after him as you came after me?"

The men stared at each other in silence, dreading even the thought.

"Dear heavenly Father," Thomas prayed, "prepare our hearts."

Together they descended the last flight of stairs and stood before the door. With a trembling hand, Thomas inserted the key in the lock. He swallowed hard and twisted his wrist. They heard a click.

"Give me a hand," he whispered. The three men pulled on the heavy door. A deep darkness and putrid stench poured into the stairwell as the door swung on its hinges. There, lashed securely to the door, was a very old and very frail man. He slowly turned his hollow eyes toward their torchlight and moved his mouth.

"Melzar!" Thomas cried. They quickly released the old man from his bonds, and as the others carried Melzar up the stairs, Thomas studied the key in his hand. *What if there are others we need to find down here?*

Reluctantly he closed and locked the door, putting the key into his pocket. *I pray I never need to open that door again.*

He heard voices above anxiously calling, and he shouted, "I'm coming." Then he turned and raced up the stairs, two by two.

The cleanup continued, but Thomas spent as much time as he could by Melzar's side. The old man's nightmare would never be fully known, as he seemed to waver between coherent thought and random raving.

One day, during one of Melzar's more lucid moments, Thomas asked him, "Do you remember Maria?"

Recognition flickered in the old man's eyes. "Yes," he whispered. "Very lovely. Very dangerous."

"Do you know what happened to her?" Thomas asked.

"Tried to escape," Melzar said. "I tried to help her."

Thomas could scarcely believe his ears. Melzar had not been this coherent since his rescue. Hardly daring to breathe lest he break the spell, Thomas waited.

Melzar spoke slowly. "I saw her again."

"Where?" Thomas asked.

"She was in the light," Melzar whispered. He was growing very weak.

"What light?" Thomas asked. "Where was the light?"

"With Jesus," Melzar sighed, and he breathed no more.

"All right!" Kelsey put down her mending and stood up. "That is enough! If Grandpa hasn't scared you children yet, he should have. You probably won't sleep a wink!"

Destry was startled by her sister-in-law's outburst, but she had to agree. She felt shivers run up and down her spine. The fire had burned low, and maybe the house was just cold, but she couldn't stop shivering. She wasn't sure she could ever get the images of that old man out of her mind.

"But, Grandpa, what happened to Melzar?" Joshua asked.

"He died, Joshua. He joined his Lord in heaven. Both he and Maria came to the light, and the light set them free."

"No more questions," Kelsey said firmly, giving her father-in-law a withering glance. Bill shrugged and grinned. "It's late!" Kelsey said. "I want every last one of you in the loft," she said, pointing. "And no talking once you get there!"

There was a general grumbling as seven little bodies began to stir. Robbie sat up and looked hopefully at his mother, but Destry shook her head and held out her hands. He dutifully plodded to her embrace. "You need to stay with us tonight," she said.

Destry watched her sister-in-law herd seven children into the hallway and toward the stairs. She admired the woman's boldness and wished she could be as forthcoming. Holding Robbie tight, she wondered when Philip would finally let her leave.

"Grandpa?" Robbie asked from his mother's arms. "How did you and Grandma get back together?"

Destry was chagrined at her son's question, and seven children struggled to come back into the room.

"Dad!" Kelsey exclaimed in exasperation.

Bill held up his hand. "Your aunt is right, Robbie. No more questions tonight. It's bedtime for us all. Maybe I can tell you that story tomorrow."

"Dad!" Philip shouted. "That's a bit unfair. You know we're leaving tomorrow."

"Oh, that's right." Bill frowned.

"Don't start!" Philip warned.

Bill simply held up his hand in surrender and shrugged.

"Sorry, Dad," Philip said. "I didn't mean to make a scene."

"It's getting very late," Mary scolded. "Everyone needs to be in bed."

Ned stirred in his chair and said sleepily, "Say, it's getting late. We need to hit the hay." There was movement from all corners of the room, and soon everyone was telling everyone else good night.

"Merry Christmas," Bill and Mary called as the last of their children slipped off to bed. They stood alone before the fire. "It's really hard for her, isn't it?" Bill asked, thinking of Destry.

"She's a lovely girl, Bill," Mary said.

"I know," Bill said. "I wish she would let us get to know her and Robbie. Part of me wishes Philip had never joined the army. He might have met a local girl and lived around here."

"You know better than any of us that we can't undo the past," Mary said, patting her husband's arm. "Just enjoy them while they're here, all right?"

"Sure," Bill said, grinning. "Say, how come you're so smart?"

"I'm not!" she countered. "I'm just fortunate to have married you."

They held each other tight and turned toward their room. The embers of a dying fire crackled softly in the hearth, and the wind moaned through the trees outside, driving flecks of snow against the side of the house.

BOOK THREE

Restoration: Beyond the Fire

CHAPTER 40

Nighttime at the Cottons

"Mother."

Destry stirred at the sound of her son's voice but snuggled deeper into her blankets.

"Mother, can I watch Grandpa stoke the fire?"

Destry pulled the covers from her head and felt the cold bite her nose and ears. "Robbie," she whispered, "why are you awake?"

"I was asleep," he said, "but I heard Grandpa stoking the fire and thought it would be fun to watch him."

Destry listened intently and heard the reassuring shuffle of feet and the bump of logs, as someone was indeed refueling the fireplace. She started to say no because it was too cold to be running around the house at night, but she stopped. Robbie seemed to adore his grandpa. She shuddered, partly from the cold and partly from the thought of Bill Cotton. His maimed arm gave her the creeps.

"Well, all right," she said, "but hurry back to bed. It's a very cold night."

She heard the bump of Robbie's cast as he slipped from the cot where he had been sleeping. She shivered at the thought of his tiny feet on the cold, hard floor. She was about to change her mind when she realized he was already out the door. *Oh well*, she thought, *we'll be leaving in the morning, anyway.*

Robbie slipped quietly to the parlor, expecting to see the huge shoulders of his grandpa stooped in front of the fireplace, but he stopped when he realized it was someone else. "Uncle Ned," Robbie said timidly.

The big man turned and smiled at the intruder. "Morning to ya, Master Robbie. Up a bit early, aren't ya?"

Ned was still dressed in the same rumpled clothes he had been wearing last night. Robbie had a suspicion he had never gone to bed but rather had slept in his chair all night.

"Come to light the fire with me, did ya?" Ned was big, but not like Grandpa. Ned's bigness seemed soft and friendly, not strong and ferocious. Robbie could imagine Grandpa with his one arm and deep lines in his face, marching into battle. But Ned didn't look like a warrior. His smile was contagious, and his open arms were inviting.

A small yellow flame crept around the side of a log in the fireplace and cast eerie shadows all around the room. Robbie shivered. He was cold and more than a little frightened.

"Let's move Grandpa's chair a little closer to the fire," Ned suggested.

Robbie watched as Uncle Ned easily lifted the huge chair and set it softly down near the fireplace. *Maybe*, he thought, *Uncle Ned could be a warrior.*

Ned settled into the chair, stretching his feet out near the crackling flames. Robbie said nothing but stared with wide eyes at the activity. It didn't seem to bother Ned. "Ah!" he sighed, wiggling deeper into the chair. "Now it's all ready," he said. "Come and warm yourself with me, Master Robbie."

The little boy crept toward the chair. Ned's huge hands wrapped about Robbie's tiny chest, and he swept Robbie into his warm and waiting lap. Uncle Ned was softer than Grandpa. He was softer than Robbie's dad or mother.

"Ya got cold standing in the shadows!" Uncle Ned chided softly. Thick arms wrapped about the boy, protecting him from the cold or any harm that might be near. Though Robbie had only met the man several days ago, he felt safe in his lap.

"Uncle Ned?" Robbie asked, looking up at the big man's face, "did you hear Grandpa's story?"

"Most of it," Ned yawned.

"But I thought you were asleep," Robbie said.

"I ..." Ned hesitated. "I listen better with my eyes closed," he said lamely.

"Do you think it was an angel that gave Thomas his key?" Robbie asked thoughtfully.

Ned pondered that. "Maybe I missed that part of the story," he said. "I'm not sure. What do you think, Robbie?"

"I think it must have been angels," Robbie said with conviction. "But Uncle Ned, are angels real, or are they just for stories?"

"Well," the big man said. "I haven't thought too much about it, but angels are a lot like God. They don't change much with the passing of time. I imagine they are still around. But tell me now, why are ya so interested in angels, Master Robbie?"

"Will you fall asleep if I tell you a story?" Robbie asked.

Ned squirmed uncomfortably under the lad's perceptive question. "Tell ya the truth, lad: stories do tend to make me sleepy. I promise I'll try to listen to yours because it must be mighty important."

Robbie snuggled tighter into Ned's lap. He liked the honesty of this big man. He didn't actually think Ned would hear much of his story, but he wanted to tell someone. "Do you know how I broke my leg?" he asked.

"I gather you fell from the barn loft," Ned said, yawning dangerously.

"That's what my mother thinks," Robbie said quietly. "Do you want to know what really happened?"

"Suppose ya tell me," Ned yawned again.

Mindful his audience was getting pretty comfortable, Robbie launched into the story he had been afraid to tell his parents for weeks.

Destry awoke with a start. Half sitting up in bed, she spotted Robbie's empty cot. "Robbie," she whispered. "Robbie!"

Philip stirred as she slipped out of bed. *Brrr!* She shivered, pulling a heavy robe about her shoulders. *I should never have let Robbie go out to watch Grandpa stoke the fire*, she thought. *What are people going to think? They'll think I'm not a good mother. They'll think I let my child wander around a freezing house while I sleep.* She chided herself with every step as she slipped from the room into the hallway.

As she tiptoed down the hall, she noticed that everyone else had left their doors open so heat from the fireplace would dispel some of the cold in their rooms. All seemed quiet in the dim light of early dawn. Her bare feet padded softly on the smooth hardwood floor. This was a pleasant house.

Her eyes strayed as she passed the last bedroom before the parlor. Bill's bare shoulder and stump were draped over a lump of blankets on the bed. Even in the dim light, she could see the carvings of men and swords on the headboard. She shivered. *What strange people*, she thought.

Suddenly she stopped. If Grandpa was here in bed, where was Robbie? She had expected to find Robbie with his grandpa.

Her pace quickened, as did her pulse. *Where is that boy?* She glanced in the kitchen, and seeing no one, she turned back to the parlor. Bill's huge chair was pulled near the fire. Was Robbie alone in that chair, without a cover and getting cold?

Padding quickly across the room, she stopped in her tracks. There was her son, wrapped tightly in the arms of his uncle Ned. Both were sound asleep with a look of contentment on their faces.

Destry had not met Ned until several days ago, but the scene that met her eyes made her smile. Ned was such a big man, and Robbie was so small. The child was covered and cradled in the most loving manner. She was quite sure Robbie was safe and sound.

Afraid of breaking the spell, Destry turned and tiptoed back to their room. *Maybe,* she thought as she climbed back under the covers. *Maybe this isn't such a bad gathering after all.* Philip stirred and pulled her cold body next to his. Dreamy contentment filled her mind as sleep wrapped enchantment around her heart.

"Breakfast anyone!" Bill called from the kitchen. Mary bustled about the stove, and the clink of utensils resounded down the hall.

Ned and Robbie were the first people Destry saw as she padded into the kitchen. Philip's arm was about her waist, giving her confidence, but the sight of those two grinning at her from across the table sent shock waves through her soul. What had they been telling the others?

"Morning, Mom," Robbie called cheerfully. "Can we stay today and let Grandpa finish his story?"

Philip glanced at his father. "Dad?" he asked with a question in his voice.

Bill shrugged. "I haven't said a word. The wind went down last night, and we can probably have the sled dug out by midmorning."

Mary smiled at her man. The tension in the room thawed several degrees. Philip nodded, seated Destry, and then settled beside her. Destry noticed that most of the family was there, save some children, but then she realized that Maria, Bill and Mary's daughter, was missing. She always sat beside her massive husband, Ned.

Destry leaned close to her husband and whispered, "Philip, where is your sister?" She and Philip had spoken often in the last two days of their doubts about the man Maria had chosen. Ned seemed quite laid back and possibly a bit lazy.

Not taking time to think it through, Philip turned and asked casually, "Hey, Ned, where is Sis?"

Ned turned his well-fed face to Philip and said, "She should be the one to tell ya, but mornings aren't her best time of day."

The room grew very quiet, and every eye turned toward Ned.

Ned looked around the room, and his face grew red. "I ... well ... we ..." He stumbled over the words. "She and I ... blast it all, we're going to have a baby."

Eyes grew wide around the room. Ned and Maria had been married quite a few years, and it had appeared to everyone that they were not going to have children. Some even wondered if they should.

Something inside Destry warmed at the thought of this big man holding a tiny baby. The vision of her own son wrapped in his huge arms had melted her heart. "Oh, Ned!" she blurted without thinking. "I'm so glad for you!"

She rarely spoke in the presence of the whole family, and the warmth with which she addressed Ned surprised everyone, including her. She blushed deeply as the whole family stopped staring at Ned and turned their eyes on her.

"Well," Philip stammered, "congratulations, Ned!"

Ned turned an even deeper shade of red. "Thanks, but could ya all act surprised when she tells ya? I didn't mean to spoil it for her."

Mary patted Ned's broad shoulder and stooped to kiss his cheek. "Believe me, we are all thrilled, and we won't spoil Maria's announcement."

Indeed, the others were glad they had a little time to digest the news so their joy for Maria could be genuine.

"The sled's out," Philip called from the door. "Are you ready to go?" he asked as Destry stepped to the entrance to greet him.

She pulled her snow-covered man into the house and closed the door behind him. "You're letting in a lot of cold," she chided. "Philip?" She stood on tiptoes to reach his ear. "Can we stay another day? Robbie really wants Grandpa to finish his story."

Philip's eyebrows rose in surprise. "What about celebrating a late Christmas with your parents?"

"They'll understand," she said. "It might be quite some time before we get back here again."

"Oh, boy," Philip said with a grimace. "The boys are going to trounce me good when they find out they did all that work for nothing!" Destry loved him for understanding.

The family had eaten an early dinner after the "boys" had come in from moving snow. The women were finished cleaning in the kitchen, and everyone was gathering in the parlor. Bill grinned as Robbie climbed into his lap. He looked at Destry and mouthed the words, "Thank you!" She blushed and turned to the embroidery in her lap.

Bill surveyed the room. Thomas was stretched out near the fireplace, his three boys curled up near him. Kelsey sat on a straight-backed chair at the edge of the circle, her fingers busy with darning. James and his wife Doreen sat in the circle near Philip and Destry. Ned was in his usual easy chair with Maria curled up on his lap. Her face was still aglow from the praise the family had bestowed on her good news. Bill had a grandson on each knee, and his only granddaughter was perched on his lap as well. The two oldest grandsons lay on the rugs near Grandpa's feet.

"The Lord has blessed me richly," he said, looking at Mary and then his family. "I am so thankful for each one of you."

Ned yawned and shifted in his chair. "Ned," Maria began to scold. "Daddy's going to finish his story."

"Don't bother him, Sis," Philip said from across the room. "He moved more snow this morning than the rest of us put together."

"That's right," Thomas added, "and I'm shot."

Maria smiled and nestled tighter against her man. She was glad he was gaining her family's acceptance.

"None of you would be here if the Lord had not reunited your grandmother and me," Bill said. Mary glanced up and saw Bill smiling at her. She smiled and returned to her knitting. After all, now she had someone new to knit for.

"But how did that happen, Grandpa?" a little voice asked.

"Should I start with Grandma's story, or should I pick up where I left off with Thomas Stafford?" Bill asked.

Answers swirled around the room, but in the end, Mary herself suggested they finish Thomas Stafford's story.

"All right," Bill said doubtfully, "but it's a long story."

CHAPTER 41

Reunion

Melzar was buried quietly beside Maria. Few mourned his passing, but to Thomas, Stanley, and Mandra he had become a brother and almost a father figure. Stories of the rebellion continued to filter in, and it seemed that Melzar had grown quite strong in his faith and bold enough to face his own demise with great courage.

Thomas and some of his companions were standing near Melzar's grave when a messenger rode into the city with great haste. He inquired where Thomas was, and upon hearing, he rode to the cemetery.

"My lord," he called, sliding from his mount. "The army of Amity is marching on Endor. The enemy is in disarray! Watchers are taking prisoners beyond count, and many of the enemy have thrown down their weapons and are fleeing into the mountains!"

The small company was stunned by the good news. Thomas immediately dropped to his knees and prayed, "Thank You, Lord! May this war soon be over and may Your peace settle over Bashan forever!"

"Amen," echoed his friends.

The men under John Stafford had been on the offensive for weeks, but after the battle at Jeshemon, they no longer simply went through the motions. This war had become a fight they intended to win. Every time they encountered Jabin's forces, the men of Amity attacked with a ferocity that even began to worry John.

The enemy noticed the change as well. The soldiers of Amity were gentlemen no longer. But Jabin's forces remained tough, until one day everything changed. The men of Amity awoke to find less resistance than they had the day before. Jabin's men seemed to have lost their will to fight. Some threw down their weapons and surrendered; others disappeared into the mountains.

John was encouraged but not overconfident. He had been tricked by the enemy before. Was this another ruse?

The very next day their scouts saw men of a strange garb attacking the enemy flanks. No one knew who the newcomers were or why they were attacking Jabin's forces, but Stafford and his army were thankful. As darkness fell that night, several thousand of Jabin's men still stood between the army of Amity and their unknown allies.

That night John could not sleep. Hundreds of questions nagged him for answers. Even if he beat Jabin's forces in pitched battle, how would he gain entrance to Endor? The fortress was impregnable. And even if he should gain entrance, how would he find Thomas? Was Thomas even alive? Even if John won this war, what would he have gained?

The camp was dark and quiet. No fires dotted the countryside. John quietly rolled his blanket and stuffed it into his backpack. One of his new bodyguards stirred.

"Did you need something, sir?" he whispered.

John waved off his new man. "Catch a few more winks," he replied. Seeking a place to be alone, John almost laughed. Did he need something? Yes, he needed something. He needed to lay down his sword and pick up a plow. He needed to see every spear turned into a pruning hook. John sighed. Yes, he needed a great deal, but no man on earth could give him what he needed. He looked to heaven and whispered, "In Your time, Lord. You make all things beautiful in Your time."

The camp began to stir before the first rays of dawn colored the sky, and when birds should have voiced their morning songs, trumpets called men to arms. Company by company, the army of Amity assembled to face the foe, but the foe was nearly gone. Instead of the thousands they had expected to meet in battle, there were only a few hundred, and they were not armed. Each one held a white rag in the air.

The men of Amity did not raise a shout of victory, though, for behind what remained of Jabin's army were gray riders, unrecognizable in their gear, riding toward Jabin's surrendering troops.

John summoned his commanders, and they rode forward for parley. The gray riders continued to bear down on Jabin's men. Finally both parties halted some distance from the surrendering men.

One gray rider stood in his stirrups and shouted to the men of Amity. "Is John Stafford still the master of Amity?"

John looked at his commanders. *Is this some kind of trick?* he wondered.

"He is!" John shouted back. "Who wants to know?"

"The Master of Endor!" was the reply.

John groaned inwardly. "Who speaks for Jabin?" he called.

"I speak for myself!" the gray rider said, moving into Jabin's men. He was flanked closely by two fell soldiers, also garbed in gray.

"It might be a trap," one of John's commanders whispered. "Go no farther!"

"Identify yourself!" John demanded.

"I am he who was lost but now am found, thought dead but am now alive! I lay claim to the throne of Amity and to your heart as well," the hooded warrior said.

A dread fear fell over Jabin's men. They fell prostrate in the road, nearly forgotten.

John began to bristle. "Don't use riddles with me," he shouted. "State your claim, and be quick about it."

"The master of Amity used to have a quick wit and a deep love for riddles," the man said. "Is he a changed man from when I last met him?"

John was troubled. The gray rider's voice was familiar, and if he were still home, that voice would belong to Thomas. But he was nowhere near home, and no one knew where Thomas was, or even if he was alive. He looked to his officers for help, but they too were perplexed. Something about this confrontation excited yet terrified John. "When have we met, sir, and how can you claim the throne of Amity or my heart?"

"You loved me once. Do you still?" The gray rider suddenly tossed his gray hood aside.

Thomas sat smiling less than ten paces from his father. John was speechless, and the world seemed to stop turning. Seagood and Mathias also threw back their gray hoods and grinned. The very men John had feared to be dead were right there in front of him.

"Thomas?" John's voice cracked with emotion. "Is it really you?"

"I've changed, Father," Thomas said, laughing, "but I'm not a ghost. You, on the other hand, are as pale as a sheet."

John's heart was pounding, and he felt dizzy. Awkwardly he slipped from his saddle and stumbled forward to greet his son. In the midst of Jabin's surrendering men, Thomas leaped from his saddle and raced to hug his father.

CHAPTER 42

Unsettling News

The days that followed were filled with complex and tedious matters concerning an even distribution of food and supplies, equipping refugees to travel home, and the repatriation of land. Leaders great and small came to bring organization during the aftermath of war. Endor became a vast refugee camp and information center. People from many nations and tongues sought to find loved ones within its walls.

Men and women were interviewed, families were reunited, and old property lines restored. Thousands of people began the difficult process of starting their lives over again.

John and Thomas remained busy at Endor, but as days turned into weeks, they grew restless and longed for home.

Gaff had recently come, and thousands of additional soldiers camped in the plains below the city.

As they often did on clear nights when stars filled the sky and campfires dotted the valley below, John and Thomas climbed the battlements of Endor to find solitude and to quietly fellowship together.

Tonight they listened to men singing in the camp. "I'm glad to hear our men singing again," John confessed. "I was afraid they had become too hard to enjoy life."

"The music makes me homesick," Thomas replied.

Thomas and his father failed to see a solitary courier emerge from the southern forest. He was stopped by sentries but was allowed to pass on his way to find Gaff.

"Thomas, tell me about Lady Helsa," John said, leaning against the balustrade and studying his son.

"She is the most gentle and loving person I have ever met, Father. You already know she is Seagood's little sister, so that tells you a great deal about her character."

John laughed out loud. He could remember many things about Seagood that were precocious if not obnoxious. He wondered if little sister might have some of the same nature. Before he could pursue this thought with Thomas, they heard footsteps on the catwalks. In another moment, they saw Gaff scrambling up the ladder to their tower.

"Some watchmen you two make," he puffed as he crawled through the opening. "We could be under attack, and you two would never know it."

"We finally found one quiet place in the city, and you have to disturb us," John said, smiling. But he knew something was wrong, or Gaff would never have bothered them.

"We just received a messenger," Gaff said seriously.

"Who sent this messenger?" John asked.

"He was one of my men, John," Gaff said. "Amity is at war!"

An army in the field can be mobilized very quickly, and the next morning, camps were being broken and supplies loaded for the long march home. Most of the army of Amity, and a large portion of Gaff's men from Emancipation, would begin the march by midday. Seagood would remain at Endor, presiding over refugees and the aftermath of Jabin's tyranny. Several thousand men would remain in Endor to assist him in his labors.

Shortly after noon, the combined armies of Amity and Emancipation began their long march south. Fire had devoured much of the country through which they passed, but these soldiers had become familiar with short rations and hard treks. They hoped to reach Deorn within two days, and after Deorn there still remained several days of hard travel before reaching Amity. Thomas rode between Gaff and his father, hoping to catch any new information that might trickle in from home.

It seemed that Devia had proclaimed himself king and controlled most of Amity, while Philip Stafford still held sway over Stonewall, Waterfront, and Sebring. Master Devia had marshaled a sizable army, while many men under Philip's command were either too old or too frightened to be of much value. No one knew if Philip could survive until they returned.

It seemed impossible, but in the months they had been away, Master Devia had built a wall sealing Amity from the rest of the world, and they were on the outside.

Bill had spent weeks in Deorn, recovering from his injuries. He grew restless as he healed, but when he heard that John Stafford and the army were headed home, he could barely contain his excitement. Most of his companions at Deorn were soldiers from Amity, and every conversation centered on their desire to finally get home.

The thought of seeing John Stafford again nearly drove Bill crazy. He paced from the entrance to Deorn, through the courtyard, and back to the entrance, over and over—only to be told by a returning sentry that Stafford and the army would not arrive until the following day.

Bill slept well that night and was up early, but the day passed slowly. Every few minutes, he paced through the gates and out into the countryside. As the afternoon wore on, his journeys grew longer, and he ranged farther outside the fortress, so anxious was he to see John Stafford and the men of Amity again.

As the sun sank low on the horizon, there came a cry from the tower. "Watch the wall, mates! There's an army on the move!"

Bill hurried down the road where he could see a cloud of dust swirling above long columns of men as they marched toward Deorn. His heart leaped at the sight but then sank just as quickly. He suddenly realized how foolish he must look. He was several furlongs from the city and all alone, like a faithful dog waiting for his master's return. The men of Amity were too close now for him to run and hide. He tried to stand a little straighter, but a burning sense of humiliation coursed through his veins.

Bill could see five horsemen leading the dusty columns of men. He recognized the standards of Amity and Emancipation, but the riders were too far away to recognize. Suddenly two riders broke formation and headed his way. Supposing them to be guards sent to check him out, Bill stood at attention and waited patiently. He was alone and unarmed, but he was unafraid. These were his comrades-in-arms.

Bill was surprised when a familiar voice shouted, "Bill! Bill Cotton! It's good to see you." John reigned in his horse, dismounted, and covered the few steps between himself and Bill in a heartbeat. Wrapping strong arms around Bill, John gave him a powerful hug.

Flustered, Bill tried to speak. "Sir!"

"Forget the formalities, Bill!" John roared. "I want you to meet my son Thomas."

Thomas laughed and jumped down from his mount to shake Bill's hand vigorously. "It is good to meet the man who saved my father's life time after time."

"What?" Bill began to ask, but Thomas interrupted again.

"Dad has told of your adventures together. In fact, you are nearly all he has spoken of on our march."

"The stories were mostly true," John laughed. "But seriously, Bill, you were one of my closest friends on our march together. I was devastated when I thought I had lost you on the Jeshemon Ridge. You cannot believe how good it is to see you up and well."

Bill nodded, not sure he could trust his voice.

"Come," John motioned. "Let us walk to the fortress. It's not far."

Walking seemed to stabilize Bill's emotions, and soon he trusted his voice enough to address Thomas. "I feel I should know you, sir. Your father spoke of little besides you on our march north. I'm so glad to see you alive and well."

"God answered many prayers, though some good friends lost their lives to bring about my deliverance," Thomas said soberly. "But I am glad to be here."

The three men slowly made their way toward the fortress of Deorn.

Later that evening, Gaff called a meeting that John could not avoid, so Thomas decided to stay with Bill. The two men chatted as if they had known each other all their lives. Thomas told of his adventures, and Bill spoke of Mary and home. After an hour of chitchat, Bill finally managed to ask what he had wanted to ask since meeting Thomas on the road.

"Sir," Bill began, "may I be so bold as to ask you something?"

"Of course, Bill! Ask away."

"I'm not sure what I see in your eyes, sir."

"My eyes?" Thomas laughed. "Do I have something in them?"

"I'm sorry," Bill stammered. "I shouldn't have asked."

"No, it is fine to ask, but what do you see?" Thomas laughed.

"I see life and death, pain and suffering, and still I see joy," Bill responded. "I do not understand what I see."

Thomas grew very quiet. "Well said, Bill Cotton! You do indeed see all those things, for I have seen a great wonder." Thomas was silent for a moment, and then he continued. "I've seen Him, Bill! I've seen Jesus!"

Gaff's meeting had informed John and the officers of the latest information he'd received about the status of Amity. "We must be ready to march at dawn," Gaff concluded.

John waited until the others had left the room. "I'm going to take Bill Cotton with me tomorrow," he said.

"John!" Gaff exploded. "You can't be serious! We have several hard days' march, and the men must be ready to fight when they reach the wall Devia has built. If you take wounded men with us, they will only slow us down!"

"Gaff, Bill Cotton was not just my bodyguard; he is my friend. We'll find a horse for him to ride, but I won't leave him behind."

"Very well," Gaff grumped. "Do things your own way." Gaff scowled and shook his head. Stafford rarely did things the way Gaff thought they ought to be done, but he had to admit, things usually turned out pretty good for him anyway.

It was midmorning three days later when the army of Amity emerged from the wooded mountain slopes into the clearing west of Green Meadow. Gaff and John rode ahead, flanked by their standard bearers. Thomas and Bill followed closely in their wake. All was quiet except for an occasional snort from a horse or the snap of banners in the cool mountain breeze. Though they had been warned of what was ahead, a chill swept over the gathering. Running the entire breadth of the pass, a dark wall loomed ominously across the charred earth of what once had been Green Meadow.

CHAPTER 43

Amity

One small event can change the course of history. Months earlier in Amity, a young man on the edge of battle had lost his nerve. It was not unthinkable that he would turn and flee, for the fear of battle can unnerve the bravest of hearts. But when he lied and said that John Stafford had been killed in battle, he had set in motion a chain of events that had rocked Amity to its core.

Beginning in Zaraphath and spreading far and wide, it was rumored that John Stafford was dead. It did not matter that the story was untrue, for John Stafford was not around to prove he was still alive. Fear can make reasonable people do irrational things. Regional leaders who had depended on John Stafford for guidance were suddenly at a loss. Philip Stafford was young and inexperienced, and no other leaders stood out to take control. Into this vacuum of leadership created by one lie had stepped Master Devia.

Devia had long sought a leadership role in Amity. He had become the master of Green Meadow by becoming the wealthiest and most powerful man west of Zaraphath, but the leadership of Green Meadow was not enough to satisfy his lust for power. He wanted to rule all of Amity. He envied John Stafford and his sons for the respect they received throughout Amity. He longed to bark orders and make all people jump to do his bidding.

Devia had become quite adept at giving orders by building the largest overland freight company in Amity, and having made a fortune there, he had financed Samoth's bid to take over the river business as well. The Crescent River ran almost the length of Amity and cut it nearly in half, dividing it into north and south. How best could he influence an entire nation but to control its main artery of commerce?

Though Devia did not control all business on the Crescent River, his influence there was growing. He had recruited most of Samoth's barge men, and a good many louts up and down the river, with a promise of free Barleyman beer for their services. These men simply had to go into local grog shops and bad-mouth Stafford's leadership while speaking well of Devia. Devia soon had a large following, especially on the river. When the rumor hit that John Stafford had been killed in battle, it was a logical step for these same men to insist that Devia be made king of Amity.

With fear and uncertainty controlling the majority of people, those who followed Philip Stafford were easily intimidated. Vocal opponents to Master Devia soon found themselves shipped to Green Meadow where they began the back-breaking labor of building a stone wall across the mountain pass to isolate Amity further from the rest of the world.

Into this mix of events, many in Amity's population had been displaced. Well-meaning leaders had sent many of their people east, thinking they would be more secure if Amity were invaded, but this placed a huge strain on the food supply and housing in Amity's easternmost cities. Refugees were growing impatient with the shortages inflicted by too many people and too little food. Riots were beginning to break out in Sebring and Waterfront, and people were afraid Philip Stafford was too young and inexperienced to resolve the issues.

Only one week into his leadership role in Amity, the streets of Waterfront were jammed with thousands of people shouting, "We want food! We want food!" The rowdier ones among the crowd swung sticks and threatened to break shop windows to steal the goods inside. Those who supported Philip were shoved around or beaten by those who supported Devia, and most of the older folks just watched in disbelief. Everyone was frustrated by the shortage of supplies and space. Rooms were full, pantries were empty, and most of the laborers had marched away to war.

Philip and his envoy pushed their way into the press of people, but their shouts of "Make way!" were drowned by the roar of the crowd. The rumors of John Stafford's death had caused an unrest that the official communiqué of victory at Green Meadow had failed to dispel.

No one was satisfied. It appeared that a bountiful harvest waited in the fields, but there was no one to bring it in. What good was a victory at Green Meadow if everyone here was about to starve?

Philip shouted and waved in vain. "There's a wagon!" he shouted to his aide. "Let's see if we can get to it."

The two men pushed and shoved their way toward a wagon caught in the mass of people. As they neared, Philip shouted to the driver, "May we use your wagon?"

The old man grinned a toothless grin. "Sure, son. But in this crowd, you won't go far. I been setting here all morning, and old Betsy ain't moved an inch."

"I want to talk to the crowd," Philip said, crawling into the seat beside the old man.

"This crowd ain't much interested in talking, young man," the old fellow said. "They want to see someone get hurt."

"I hope you're wrong," Philip said, climbing over the seat into the wagon box. For the first time, he could see the vast extent of the crowd. "Men and women of Amity!" he shouted.

"We want food! We want food!"

Philip watched as the crowd pushed and shoved each other rudely, and it was getting worse by the minute. He pulled a small silver trumpet from his cloak and placed it to his lips.

A clarion call echoed from the storefronts and buildings all around the square. The chanting stopped, and a wary silence ensued.

Taking quick advantage of the lull, Philip shouted, "Men and women of Amity, I have heard your call for food, and I have a plan."

Few in this crowd actually knew Philip. Even those living in Waterfront or Sebring seldom saw him. He was a very private individual, keeping to his books, his friends, and himself. The crowd, unsure who was addressing them, remained silent long enough to hear more.

"Local farmers need labor," Philip explained, "and you need food! The farmers have agreed to let anyone who helps them harvest keep one third of all they gather. We can solve two problems at once. The abundant crop will be harvested, and you will be fed."

There was an uneasy silence as people began to digest the offer. Suddenly a woman in the crowd spoke. "You mean, I'll have to go to the field and work like a man?" The lady was dressed in very stylish attire and looked unaccustomed to manual labor.

Several in the crowd laughed, but most remained silent.

"Yes," Philip answered. "I'm afraid we all must do things we have never done before, but our heavenly Father has provided enough food for everyone, if we are willing to work for it."

"That's easy for you to say," someone shouted. "You sit in your castle while people serve you, Philip Stafford!"

Philip wanted to see his accuser. The voice sounded familiar, but the crowd was too large to identify one voice.

"You want to put us to work, do you?" someone else shouted. "Go to work yourself. We want food!"

"I'll work beside you in the fields!" Philip shouted, but the people had taken up the chant for food, and his voice was lost. Suddenly rough hands grabbed Philip and dragged him out of the wagon. Several boisterous fellows had decided to let the crowd make sport of Philip Stafford.

Philip's aide was on the opposite side of the wagon and could not get to the men, but the old fellow in the wagon came to life. Swinging his staff with a quickness that surprised everyone, he whacked one thug soundly on the arm. The crowd could hear the crack above the chant. The injured man dropped Philip, but the other fellow turned to the old man, ready for trouble. At that moment, Philip's aide freed his spear from the press of people, and its sharp tip pressed into the bully's flesh.

The chanting stopped with the sudden flurry of activity. "Stop this!" Philip shouted as he freed himself and climbed back into the wagon. "There is no need for violence. We are all in this together! Over five hundred men and women are inside the fortress, and soon they will be hungry too." Philip drew his breath, and this time the crowd let him continue. "It is written in God's Word that if a man will not work, he shall not eat. In our present situation, I think we must apply those words to women and children as well."

"But I don't know how to reap grain," one woman called.

"I will work beside you," Philip said. "We will learn together. The farmers will teach us!"

A calmness began to settle over the crowd when a familiar voice again shouted, "Look, Stafford, I already have two families with me. What more do you want?"

The crowd stirred uneasily. Philip wished he could see his antagonist.

Suddenly the old man in the wagon stood to his full height and raised his staff high above the crowd. Some thought he was about to strike Philip, but instead he dropped to his knees and offered his staff to Philip. Many felt sorry for the old fellow.

Philip was embarrassed, and he wished he could pull the man to his feet. "Don't do that!" he insisted.

"Master Stafford!" the old man said. "I did not realize who you were. Forgive me and take me into your service."

Many an old heart was moved by the scene. Loyalty to the Stafford family ran deep in Waterfront, especially among the older generation. There were grandmas and grandpas all over the square who suddenly felt quite young again. They began to surge forward, shouting, "Take me into your service as well, my lord!"

Philip raised his hands and shouted. "People, you may serve Amity and yourselves by dispersing this crowd today and preparing yourselves for work tomorrow. Meet me in the fields outside town, and we will serve Amity together."

Beginning with the eldest, the crowd began to disperse, each man and woman to their home. Philip's words made sense. They could serve both Amity and themselves. There were lots of people in the crowd that day who hoped their neighbors hadn't seen them. Tomorrow this gathering would be judged as a huge mistake.

Across the square, shielding himself from view, a tall man watched as the crowd trickled out of the market, leaving Philip and his aide alone with the old man in the wagon. The quiet observer pressed his lips together in a hard line. "I'll get you next time, Philip Stafford," he said.

A fortress of gray stone surrounded a tower of grace and beauty in Green Meadow. The fortress was for Master Devia's protection, and the tower was for his inspiration and comfort. Originally built as a sanctuary for those seeking religious guidance, the tower had become a palace of sorts, where Master Devia held court over his growing dominion. A grand throne sat upon the dais in his sanctuary, and there Devia reclined upon thick cushions, with elegant carpets at his feet. A silver platter filled with pastries sat near his throne. He motioned with his fingers to four men standing in chains before him. "Captain, who are these men?" he asked.

"They are laggards, sir," the captain of the bodyguard replied.

"What were they doing?" Devia asked.

"They were burying their dead, Your Majesty," the captain answered.

Devia pointed to one man in the group and said, "You look able to speak for the others. How do you answer the charge?"

The man stepped forward timidly. "Master Devia—"

The captain of the bodyguard struck the man savagely and shouted, "You will address our Lord as Your Majesty!"

The man cringed and began again. "Your Majesty, we were only trying to bury our dead! I lost a son." He indicated another man. "And my friend lost his wife. These other two"—he pointed to the other men—"were just helping us bury our dead."

"Times are tragic," Devia moaned. "You have seen for yourself the horror of war: dead bodies everywhere. To search for and bury each person individually would require a vast amount of time and manpower."

"But, sir," the man began, "Master Stafford left many men for this very purpose."

Devia bristled. "Is John Stafford the master of Green Meadow? Is John Stafford even here? Does he even care about your dead? No! All he cares about is waging war and bringing destruction to others. You and I are the only ones who are here to deal with reality!"

The men did not answer.

"It takes far too much time to bury your dead," Devia said. "Do you not realize that we could be attacked again? Where will you hide if an enemy invades?"

Several thought of saying that they might hide in Devia's fortress, but none dared say anything.

"We have no protection," Devia proclaimed. "There is nothing to prevent countless armies from marching into Amity! The wall is of paramount importance. It must become the top priority in every heart! Every able-bodied man must put his back into the labor!"

"But the dead—" one man began.

"The dead will not defend you," Devia shouted. "The wall will!"

"We can't leave our dead exposed!" one of the four implored.

"Pile them and burn them," Devia snapped. "That is an order!"

"But, sir ..." The men began to plead.

"Guards!" Devia shouted. "Give each of these men forty stripes. Maybe they will learn to obey my orders without question. Get them out of here!"

"Please, sir," the leader of the group cried. "Have mercy on us!"

Devia smiled as several guards dragged the men from the room.

Following the battle of Green Meadow, work on the wall had progressed at a furious rate. Every horse, wagon, shovel, and pick was conscripted for the job. All the men Stafford had left behind joined the men and women of Green Meadow. They threw themselves into the work. At first they were afraid of another attack, and later they became even more terrified of Master Devia's strong-arm tactics. No one wanted to see his wife or child flogged, so everyone fell in line. Within one week, the wall's foundation was laid.

As the wall began to grow, so did frustration among the workers.

"There will be no break for lunch today," the foreman told a group of workers.

Men stationed near the wall began to grumble. "Hard labor makes for huge appetites."

"And a saucy tongue calls for a whipping block," the foreman shouted.

"I'm not your slave!" another man shouted.

"You are not your own either," the foreman said. "If it were not for Master Devia's kindness, you would have been killed during the battle."

The men were silent.

"Are there any more complaints?" the foreman asked.

No one stirred. Despair began to prevail. People felt trapped. How could anyone break Devia's control?

"Then get back to work!" the foreman shouted.

The streets of Green Meadow were busy. Everywhere, homes ruined during the battle were being dismantled. Men tossed blackened stones into waiting wagons.

"You would have men tear down their own homes?" a newcomer asked the foreman.

"The quarries are too slow. Work on the wall will progress much quicker if we use the dressed stone we find here," the foreman answered.

"Shouldn't these people be rebuilding their homes? Where will they live?" the man asked.

"There is room in the fortress for them," said the foreman.

"That may be fine during a time of war, but they can't live there forever!" the man said.

"Who said anything about forever? First we have to build the wall and prepare for winter. There will be plenty of time to build homes next spring," said the foreman.

"You expect people to live in cramped squalor for nearly a year?" the man asked.

"They have no choice!"

"Women and children must go to the fields. Now, move it!" The officer shouting orders was clad in crimson and white. No one knew where he had come from, but he seemed to have the authority of Devia behind him.

"Wait!" one man shouted. "My wife is expecting a baby. You can't ask her to plant beans and potatoes!"

The officer wheeled about to face the man. With one swift movement, his sword rested at the man's neck. A wicked sneer crossed the commander's lips. "Do you want this community to starve?"

The workman was angry, but he did not answer. His wife clung to his arm and whispered, "I'll go! Don't anger him! What would I do if he were to kill you?"

"You've got a smart woman there, mister," the officer snarled. "Don't anger me! You know food is short already. If crops aren't planted, there will be no harvest before winter, and then we'd all be hungry, right? Master Devia is looking out for all our best interests."

"May I go in her place?" the man asked.

"Men work the wall; women and children, the fields," the officer said, looking around the compound. "Now, let's have no more delay. Move out!"

As the officer turned and walked away, the man muttered, "Just one time, I'd like to find that guy without his weapons."

"I'll be fine," the woman said to her husband. "Don't anger them again. Remember Martha's husband? I couldn't bear being a widow." Her brown eyes met his.

"All right," the man whispered, "but they'd better not hurt you."

"I'll be fine." She smiled. "Now, hurry before he comes back."

One by one, the men went back to work on the wall, but everyone wondered who the redcoats were that were replacing the commanders of Amity.

Katherine had persuaded the cook to leave the kitchen door ajar to allow her entrance. She stole quickly through the darkened halls of Stonewall to the balcony door. Looking around to see if anyone was watching, she lifted the latch and stepped quietly into the night air.

She was hoping to surprise Philip after his hard day in the harvest field, but when she turned, she jumped with fright. An old man stood staring at her.

She gasped. "Lord Rhoop! I'm sorry! I didn't know you were here." She wheeled around, searching frantically for the door latch.

"Katherine Gammel," the old man said. "I would like a word with you before Philip arrives."

Hearing her name, Katherine leaned heavily against the wall and tried to slow the hammering of her heart. She turned to face Lord Rhoop.

"Do you come here often?" Rhoop asked. His voice was neither accusing nor demanding. "It is a lovely place."

Katherine wanted to answer, but she didn't trust her voice.

The kindly old man seemed to understand. He beckoned to an old wooden bench among the ivy and ferns.

Katherine stepped slowly to the old bench and seated herself. Rhoop did not speak, so Katherine finally broke the silence. "I used to come here with Philip," she said, feeling suddenly very shy.

Rhoop smiled under thinning whiskers.

Silence fell between the two, and Katherine felt terribly awkward. "I really must be going," she said, starting to her feet. "I'm sorry I bothered you." She wished now that cook had not left the kitchen door open for her.

"Katherine," the old man said, "I wouldn't be here except that Philip likes to come here after the day's work. It is one of the last quiet places left to meet."

"I know," Katherine said, "and I really am sorry I bothered you."

"As I was about to say," Rhoop broke in, "I think you should stay. Philip might need some special comfort this evening."

Katherine blushed deeply and was glad the darkness hid her face.

"Please stay," Rhoop continued. "The news I have for Philip should be heard by you as well."

Katherine looked at Rhoop in surprise, but before she could ask any questions, they both heard a jolly voice booming down the hall. "Ho ho, my good Rhoop! What tales of woe and disaster can you tell me tonight?" Katherine wished she could disappear.

The door opened with a flourish, and Philip understood the scene at a glance. "Company tonight!" he sang, swooping down on the bench and wrapping his arm around Katherine's shoulder. "A good night for viewing the stars, don't you think, Rhoop?" He laughed.

The old man could not conceal his mirth. "Ideal," he commented.

Katherine blushed. She wondered if these men had formed a conspiracy, they were so alike. She sighed and rested her head on Philip's shoulder. She liked the earthy odors of sun, dust, and hard labor. Still, she had no business here, and she began to rise. "You men have business to discuss," she said.

Philip caught Katherine's slender waist and gently pulled her back. Turning to Rhoop, he said, "We have nothing to discuss that Katherine can't hear, do we?"

The old man shook his head, and Philip turned back to Katherine. "See? I would like to watch the stars come out again with you by my side."

A distant lamp in the city caught the twinkle in Philip's eye, and Katherine thought it the loveliest sight she had ever seen. "Very well," she said with a sigh, "if you are quite sure I won't be a bother."

"Quite," Rhoop said quickly.

Katherine relaxed and snuggled under Philip's strong arm. The evening air was taking on a chill.

"How does the harvest proceed?" Rhoop asked.

"It's going well," Philip responded. "The wheat is coming in, and the farmers are happy. It has made a huge difference with the refugees as well. Their food is bought at the price of some blisters and hard feelings, but your plan is working out very nicely. Barley is nearing harvest, and that should keep people busy most of the summer."

"Good," Rhoop said. "But don't make harvest your only concern."

"Has something happened?" Philip asked with sudden concern.

"There have been more reports of unrest in the west. Master Devia is building a wall."

Philip grew very still. "What do you mean, building a wall?" he demanded.

"He is building a fortification that stretches all across the pass, from the Independence Mountains to the Guardian Range," Rhoop explained.

"But that is over three miles," Philip exclaimed. "Where on earth is he finding the labor?"

"He is using the men who did not follow your father north," Rhoop said. "He is also using the citizens of Green Meadow."

"Civilians?" Philip asked in disbelief. "I can understand using soldiers, but why civilians? Who made this report, Rhoop?"

"A river merchant by the name of Ralph Crider," Rhoop answered.

"Can he be trusted?" Philip asked.

"He has worked the river a long time, Philip. But on his last journey upriver, he was not met at the docks in Shepherd. He could not find a wagon for hire, but he did get a cart to deliver his goods directly to Green Meadow. When he neared the city, he saw women and children being herded into communal gardens at the ends of whips, while men and boys worked on the wall. He came to inform you as soon as he returned."

Philip stood and began to pace the floor. "Amity has civilians in slavery!" He pounded a fist into his palm. "Although I suppose there are those who think I am doing the same thing here."

"They might if you were driving people to the field with whips," Rhoop said.

"What about the wall?" Philip asked, changing the subject. "Isn't that a project for the council? Of course, it could be argued that there wasn't time for council deliberation."

"Philip," Rhoop said, "there is more news, if you can bear it."

"What else, Rhoop?"

"As the wall grows, so does Devia's arrogance. He has proclaimed himself king of Amity, and any who oppose his authority are taken to Green Meadow and forced to work on the wall."

Philip sat down on the bench next to Katherine, and she slipped her hand into his.

"Shall I continue?" Rhoop asked.

Philip nodded his head.

"Ralph Crider found that many have already pledged their loyalty to Devia. Zaraphath, Deep Delving, and those left around Headwater all support him. The people of Shepherd have gone into hiding. Highland,

Capri, and Southglen are wavering in Devia's favor. At this moment, you have only Waterfront and Northglen on your side, for Sebring is not entirely with you."

"Why?" Philip asked, looking up. "Has something happened in Sebring?"

"Crider stopped at a grog shop after returning home," Rhoop said. "Inside were some unsavory chaps who spoke openly that the country would be better off under Devia. There was a brave young man who raised his glass and offered a toast to the House of Stafford. Before the crowd could join him, the thugs hustled the young man outside, and no one has seen him since. When the ruffians returned to the grog shop, nothing more was said about the House of Stafford."

Rhoop suddenly exclaimed, "Philip Stafford has no right to rule!" Then he studied Philip's reaction. "That is what most men were saying before Crider left the grog shop."

"They are right," Philip said, looking up at Rhoop. "I would not be here if Father hadn't pushed the council to appoint me."

"There is yet more," Rhoop said quietly.

"More?" Philip asked, shaking his head.

"There is a reward of five hundred gold shekels for your life, Philip. Someone wants you dead!"

Katherine gasped.

"You should not go to the harvest fields tomorrow," Rhoop said. "You would be far too exposed. Five hundred shekels is enough money to tempt even your most loyal subjects!"

Philip sat for a long while. When he finally spoke, his voice was so soft that Rhoop and Katherine could hardly hear him. "This morning I was the ruler of Amity. Tonight I am a fugitive." He turned to Rhoop. "Someone is trying to frighten me out of doing my duty, Rhoop, but it will take more than this. If I'm killed going to the fields, so be it, but people are going to know I am here to help them, no matter what."

"Good for you!" Rhoop smiled. "I was hoping you would say that."

Katherine gripped Philip's hand and then released it. Standing, she stepped to the railing. Far below she could see the Crescent River churning between its muddy banks. Across the river, light shone from nearly every house in Waterfront. The walls of Stafford House blocked her view of

Sebring, but in her mind she could see her cousin Mercinor Gammel. He would be willing to pay such a sum, though it wouldn't be with his own money. The money would come from much father west, and she could think of someone who hated Philip enough to spend that kind of money.

Mercinor Gammel walked the docks of Sebring, keeping to the shadows. Candlelight from nearby taverns left the docks largely in darkness. He did not know who he was meeting or where, but he had received a summons to meet on the docks. It had been this way since he had first been asked to help with Stafford's overthrow. Gammel leaned against a boat moored to a piling and stretched his legs. *I wish they would quit meeting me like this,* he thought. *I know they don't want to reveal themselves until the proper time, but this is ridiculous!*

Gammel watched a man stagger unsteadily from a nearby tavern, followed closely by two burly thugs. The bullies grabbed the drunk, removed his money pouch and a knife, and then struck him savagely and pushed him into the water. Gammel heard a splash and watched the men return to the tavern. *Where is that fool I am supposed to meet?* Gammel wondered. Suddenly he heard the scrape of a blade clearing its sheath. A shiver ran down his spine. "Who's there?" he whispered.

A voice spoke from the darkness. "Where have you been, Gammel? I've been waiting all night."

"I wasn't told where to find you. The message said to meet you on the docks," Gammel complained. "I've been waking these docks since dark. I was about to give up."

"Why haven't you removed Philip from power?" the voice asked.

"Look, I've tried everything," Gammel said in exasperation. "Philip doesn't intimidate easily. He still goes into the harvest fields, even though there is a price on his head."

"He has to have some weakness," the voice demanded.

Gammel considered Philip: the man didn't drink, smoke, carouse, or party. He did study the Holy Scriptures a great deal, but even Mercinor didn't think that was a weakness.

"Does he have any close friends?" the voice asked.

"Sure," Gammel responded. "I can think of two immediately: Rhoop and Gandrel."

"Get them!" the voice demanded.

"What do you mean?" Gammel asked.

"Win them for the Master," the voice said.

"That's impossible," Mercinor said. "Rhoop is Philip's advisor, and Gandrel is just a gardener in Waterfront who doesn't care who is in power as long as he can tend his garden. Besides, he is very loyal to Philip."

"If they won't come willingly, take them by force," the voice said.

"Kidnapping?" Mercinor was incredulous. What was he getting into?

"Call it what you want," the voice said. "It might get results, and the Master wants results. Is there anyone else, a woman by chance?"

"Katherine." Mercinor chided himself. Why hadn't he thought of her before? She would be an easier target than either Rhoop or Gandrel.

"All right," he said aloud. "I'll do it."

"You'd better," the voice warned. "The Master wants this taken care of immediately. Do you understand?"

"Yes," Mercinor said, and he was about to add that they need not be so pushy, when he heard several other blades being drawn in the dark. He wisely kept his mouth shut.

A menacing whisper cut the air. "Don't fail us, Mercinor Gammel!"

Master Devia did not have a large audience as he sat upon his throne at Green Meadow and issued his decree. "I want control of every city, village, house, and farm! Secure people's cooperation by flattery or intimidation, whichever is needed. Do you understand?"

"Yes, sir!" Jan DeKlerk answered.

"Move quickly! You shouldn't meet much resistance until you near Stonewall and Waterfront. We have men in Sebring, which should weaken Philip's position considerably."

"What about Capri?"

"That is a good question, but I think they will fall in line."

"What do we do with dissidents?"

"Send them here! They can work on the wall!"

"When do we leave, sir?"

"Tomorrow morning. Conscript troops from every town you enter, and gather enough foodstuffs for your men. Keep law and order. I want no looting! If you need extra supplies, requisition them. I'll see that you get what you need."

"Very good, sir!"

"Captain, things are going well, but I don't want any snags in my plan. Capture Stonewall and send for me. I want the throne!"

"Yes, sir! Is that all, sir?"

"There is one more thing, DeKlerk: God's speed."

Jan DeKlerk clicked his heels and saluted smartly. Turning, he thought to himself, *You old cheat! What would you know about God's speed? Besides, do you think I'll conquer this country just to give it to you? Not by a long shot!*

Jan DeKlerk followed Master Devia's orders to the letter. Taking nearly one thousand men with him from the soldiers that John Stafford had left behind and from the men of Green Meadow, he hoped to build his numbers to over eight thousand by the time he gathered men from other towns and villages throughout Amity. It was a heady experience to lead such a large force of men.

Starting early, they set a steady pace and had reached the ruins of Headwater by midmorning. Soon after passing Headwater, a young man clad in crimson and white rode forward and called out, "Captain DeKlerk!"

Jan studied the brash young man and asked, "What do you need, Braten?"

"There is a makeshift hospital some miles south of here, sir. Should I ride over and see if any of the men are able to march with us?" Braten asked.

Jan DeKlerk rode in silence for a few moments. He wanted able-bodied men who wouldn't slow him down. "No," he answered. But as an afterthought he asked, "Do they have any supplies we could use?"

"They probably don't have much," Braten responded. "Devia cut off their supplies some time ago."

"How do you know all this?" DeKlerk asked.

"I've been keeping my eye on that place, boss," Braten sneered. "There's a good-looking gal running things there. How about I take a few of the boys over and grab everything that's useful and destroy the rest?"

Captain DeKlerk studied Braten for a few minutes. The man was treacherous, but he knew his trade. What did it matter to DeKlerk if one small group of maimed soldiers lived or died? If it meant that Braten was out of DeKlerk's hair for a while, it was well worth the mission. "All right. Go steal what you want, and kill the men. But bring me the girl."

Braten grinned. "Sure thing, cap'n!" Pulling out of formation, he began to call companions by name. Jan glanced back as Braten and nearly twenty men headed south. They were all clad in crimson and white.

I should have known, DeKlerk thought to himself. *Those men are all Jabin's. I doubt they need that many, but I wish they'd get what they deserve.*

CHAPTER 44

Jennifer's Hospital

While political intrigue rocked the major cities of Amity, casting everyone into a state of confusion and fear, some remote regions of the country seemed to be forgotten. John Stafford had sent a young woman by the name of Jennifer away from Green Meadow along with several wagons filled with wounded men. Because she wanted to help these men, she was to take the wounded to her grandmother's farm and care for them far from the ravages of war. The plan had worked quite nicely as long as shipments of supplies came every week, but when John Stafford and the army of Amity had marched north to chase Jabin, the supplies had begun to dwindle in volume and regularity.

Jennifer had rationed their supplies carefully, but things were looking desperate. "I could use some help with the dishes," she called. A groan arose from those seated around the barn, but several men struggled to their feet.

Larry Chavez was among the first. Jennifer had helped him so much, it was the least he could do. He remembered all too well the dark days after he'd lost his leg. At that time he'd wanted to die, but then Jennifer had come into this life.

Holding his bowl in one hand, he gripped a homemade crutch in the other. Balancing on one leg, he tried to walk. "Aye, lassie!" he called. "I'll give ye a hand!" he said, trying to imitate the brogue her father had used in Green Meadow.

Jennifer giggled. "That sounds funny coming from you," she said.

He grinned. "How am I doing?"

"Lovely," she said, beaming. Stepping near, she planted a light kiss on his cheek and then dashed off to collect more wooden bowls.

Larry used his forearm to mop the sweat from his brow. "It's tough work just to get up," he mused. "Can I take your bowl, Carter?" he asked. James Carter was a wiry chap who had lost both his legs in the battle of Green Meadow.

"Thanks, Larry!" Carter said, handing over his empty bowl.

Larry balanced both bowls in one hand and hobbled outside. Jennifer was already at the washtub, elbow-deep in suds, washing the dinner dishes. Larry had almost reached her when Carter's bowl slipped from his fingers, hit the ground, and rolled under a nearby tree.

Jennifer could see his plight, but rather than dash after the bowl, she merely asked, "Did you lose something, Larry?"

"Yes, dear," Larry responded sarcastically.

Jennifer wasn't cruel. She knew it was important that these men learn to laugh at themselves and become self-reliant again. Her own father had lost an arm in the Battle of Great Bend, and it had taken months for her family to learn that life goes on.

Larry dropped his remaining bowl into the wash water and studied the slender girl before him. "How do you do it?" he asked. "You work all day, take care of everyone, and yet never seem to grow weary?"

Jennifer turned and gave him a mischievous smile, but for the first time, Larry noted lines about her eyes that shouldn't have been there. Turning away quickly, he hobbled to the tree and retrieved the fallen bowl. He was more than a little angry with himself and everyone else. They all placed too many demands on this poor girl!

When Larry returned with the bowl, Jennifer noted his dark mood. "Thank you, Larry," she said, taking the bowl. "Is something wrong?"

"No," he growled and quickly changed the subject. "Is there anything else I can do to help?"

"Well ..." Jennifer paused. "The chores will have to be finished before I can read this afternoon."

"All right," Larry said decisively. "I'll get started."

Jennifer touched his arm. "Larry, are you sure you're all right?"

Larry looked her straight in the eyes. "No," he said. "I'm worried about you."

Jennifer tipped back her head and laughed from her heart. "Larry, you had me worried. I thought something was wrong. I'm all right. Now, you get some of the others to help you, and I'll be ready in no time."

Larry turned to the weathered old barn that served as their makeshift hospital. "Hey, guys," he shouted, "Miss Jennifer will read to us as soon as we get the chores done!"

"I'll roll bandages," someone shouted.

"I'll sweep the floor," called another.

The chores were completed in record time, and the men gathered in a large circle around Miss Jennifer. Larry couldn't believe how everyone waited with such eagerness for Miss Jennifer to read the scriptures. At first he hadn't been too interested, but after a few sessions, he too was hooked.

Jennifer opened her Bible and looked around the room, a deep sense of satisfaction and gratitude filling her heart. "Let's begin with a word of prayer," she said.

Every head bowed.

"Dear Lord," she began, "You have blessed us richly, having given us life and breath today. You have given us this special hour to spend with You. Open our hearts, Lord, and let Your Word come to life within us. We ask this in Jesus's name, amen."

"Amen," echoed a chorus of voices around the barn. Larry remained silent. He wasn't sure how to deal with this part of reading time, but if it helped Miss Jennifer, it was all right with him.

"Today," Jennifer said, "we will read a parable, or story, that Jesus told many years ago."

As Larry listened to Jennifer's melodious voice, tender thoughts flowed through his mind. Suddenly he snapped out of his daydream, for Jennifer was reading.

"A man planted a vineyard, let it out to tenants, and then moved away. When harvest time came, the master sent a servant to collect his share of the crop. The tenants beat the master's servant and sent him away empty-handed. The master then sent another servant, but the tenants mistreated him as well. The owner of the vineyard sent yet a third servant, but he too was rejected. Finally the owner of the vineyard said, 'I will send my own son. They will respect him.'

"But when the tenants saw the son, they said to themselves, 'This is the heir. Let us kill him, and the inheritance will be ours!' And they cast the owner's son out of the vineyard and killed him."

Chavez shivered. Though Miss Jennifer read on, he thought about what he had heard. The owner of the vineyard was undoubtedly supposed to represent God, and His Son was Jesus. Larry knew Jesus had come into the world and that the world had rejected and killed Him, just like the tenants had done in the story.

Larry suddenly felt sick. Was he guilty of murdering Jesus? Had he done just what the evil tenants in the story had done? He quietly struggled to his feet. He needed some fresh air.

Once outside, Larry felt much better. He hobbled into the trees, found a pleasant spot, and sank to the ground. He had to think.

The story troubled him. The landowner had built an entire vineyard and had given it to the men in the story. All the landowner wanted from them was a share of the fruit. That didn't seem unreasonable. And then a thought hit Larry. Maybe the Creator of heaven had given each person on the face of the earth a vineyard! That vineyard could be the air one breathed or the food one ate. Everything came from the Master's hand, didn't it?

I have air to breathe and food to eat, Larry thought. *If God has given me those things as a vineyard, what can I give Him in return?*

Closing his eyes, Larry reveled in the quiet afternoon. Birds sang merrily among the trees, and a squirrel chattered down by the creek. The scent of wild roses wafted upon the air, and a deep sense of gratitude filled Larry's heart.

Suddenly Larry knew what he could give the Master. He could give thanks. He really didn't know how to pray, but imitating Miss Jennifer, he bowed his head and began. "Lord, I'm way behind giving You any fruit from my vineyard, but if You'll accept it, I want to give You my thanks."

Minutes became hours, and Larry had no idea how long he sat by the tree. But the longer he thanked the Lord for his blessings, the closer he felt to the Almighty One.

"Lord," he said, weeping, "I owe You everything. My life is a wreck! I have lived as if You didn't even exist. I'm just like the wicked tenants in the story. I've rejected You over and over. I'm so sorry! Please forgive me."

Shadows were growing long when Larry felt a gentle hand on his shoulder.

"Oh!" He jumped, awakening to his surroundings.

Jennifer knelt beside him, concern etched into her features. "Larry, are you all right?" she asked.

Larry tried his voice, but it sounded shaky. "Yes," he managed. "I think I'm all right."

"Are you sure?" she asked.

"I—" Larry stalled. "I hope I'm a different man than you once knew."

Jennifer's eyes grew wide. "What are you saying, Larry?"

"I—I gave my life to Jesus," he stammered.

"Oh, Larry," Jennifer gasped, throwing her arms around his neck and hugging him furiously. "You don't know how I've been praying for you."

Larry looked into the excited girl's eyes. "Thank you, Miss Jennifer," he managed to whisper. "You helped me see my need."

"Oh, Larry." Her lips trembled, and her eyes filled with tears. She buried her head in his shoulder, and they wept together in the joy of the moment.

The very next morning, Carter complained, "Hey, what's going on? Can't a guy get a decent meal around here?"

"Knock it off," Larry snapped. "You're getting as much as everyone else."

"Hey, don't get sore, Larry," Carter apologized. "I didn't mean anything by it. What happened to all the food, anyway?"

"I don't know," Larry growled, "but we haven't had a shipment for several weeks, and things are getting pretty tight."

"Look, I'm sorry!" Carter apologized again. "I didn't mean to complain."

"I know," Larry said, "and I shouldn't be angry. It's just that Miss Jennifer is doing all she can, and, well … ah, just forget it!"

Carter studied Larry Chavez. He knew what Larry was thinking because everyone in camp felt the same way. They all loved Jennifer and wanted to protect her and keep her safe. "I understand, Larry. Really, I do."

"Maybe someone thinks we've lived on charity long enough," someone else said.

"I don't know what anyone thinks, but we're going to have to do something quick, or we're going to starve," Larry said.

"Are there nuts and berries in the woods?" someone asked.

"If we had some seeds, we could plant a garden," another suggested.

"Are you going to plant it with your sword?"

"What will we eat until things grow?"

"Look," Carter said, "why don't some of you carry me down to the creek, and I'll try to shoot a deer."

"Hey, that's a good idea," several voices chorused.

"If you lie down on your cot, Carter," Larry suggested, "maybe several of us can grab an edge of the cot and carry you to the stream."

"Great!" Carter exclaimed, easing himself onto his back. Someone handed him his bow and arrows, and he held them tightly in his hands.

Jennifer was folding bandages outside when she heard the commotion. Looking up from her labors, she witnessed the strangest sight. Eight men, some missing an arm or a leg, hobbled out of the barn with a cot on their shoulders. Over the edge of the cot she could see James Carter's beady black eyes.

The whole scene reminded Jennifer of a giant spider staggering about after ingesting something very disagreeable. "Ahem!" She cleared her throat, trying hard not to laugh. "Just where do you gentlemen think you are going?"

"Hunting," said a man who was missing one hand but had a firm grip on the cot with his other.

"Well, you look formidable enough!" she said placidly. "Really, what are you doing?"

"We're taking Carter to the stream. He thinks he might bag a deer or something for us to eat," Larry said.

Jennifer bit her lip. She knew better than any of them just how short their food supply was, but to watch "her" men attempt to solve the problem themselves nearly broke her heart. "Are you sure it's safe?" she asked.

"It's better than starving," Carter suggested.

"Miss Jennifer wasn't concerned about you, Carter," someone said. "She was worried about the animals!"

"Oh, I think the animals are safe enough," someone else said. Someone snickered. Someone else guffawed. In a moment, Carter's cot was rocking dangerously. Everyone was laughing, even Carter.

"Hey, stop it, you guys!" Carter shouted between bursts of laughter. "You're going to scare all the deer out of the country."

Jennifer shook her head and watched with growing respect as her strange "family" hobbled their way toward the creek.

"You guys are going to thank me yet!" she heard Cater say as the pack of men moved slowly out of sight. Jennifer smiled and returned to her labor. There were so many others who needed her care; she couldn't spend too much time worrying about those crazy guys.

It was hours later when Jennifer came into the barn to check on the men. "Has anybody checked on James?" she asked. Everyone was exceptionally quiet. She hoped it was simply exhaustion from the morning's labors.

"Miss Jennifer," one man said, "Carter told us not to come too often or we'd scare the wildlife away."

Jennifer nodded, but Carter was due to have his bandages changed. Looking from man to man around the room, she asked, "How will we know if he's all right?"

Everyone fidgeted. They could tell Miss Jennifer was getting worried. A man by the name of Benya Hefington, the only officer in the group, spoke up. "If it will make you feel better, ma'am, I'll go check on him."

Ben was better on his feet than most, for he had two legs. He was missing an arm, but he was healing nicely, and Jennifer was glad for his offer. "Would you please, Benya?"

"Hey, Ben," someone called. "Don't forget to signal him when you get there. Knowing Carter, he might shoot anything that moves." He tossed the officer a strangely whittled piece of wood.

Benya Hefington placed the little whistle to his lips and blew. The shrill blast startled everyone in camp.

"Gracious," Jennifer exclaimed. "I guess you *will* scare all the wildlife out of the forest."

Benya smiled, bowed to Jennifer, and left the barn. Moments later a faint whistle drifted on the breeze.

All conversation stopped as they strained their ears to listen. "Was that Ben?" somebody asked.

"Ben couldn't have gone that far yet," someone else commented.

Jennifer looked around the room. "What exactly was your signal, gentlemen?"

"Well," Larry said carefully, "we didn't really set up a signal with Carter. We just gave him a whistle and told him not to shoot if he heard one blowing near him."

Jennifer wrung her hands. Anxiety had finally taken its toll. "Why did I ever let you move James?" she asked. "Something has gone wrong. I just know it!"

Every man hung his head. No one had wanted this. To bring distress to their beloved Miss Jennifer had been the last thing on their minds.

"Hey, look!" someone shouted. "Ben's coming on the run."

Every head came up, and all eyes peered out the open barn door. Benya Hefington was racing up the trail like a scared rabbit. He crossed the open space between the cottage and barn in an instant.

"Get your weapons and scatter, men!" he shouted.

"Benya, your shoulder is bleeding," Jennifer said, trying to grab him as he rushed into the barn.

"What is it, Ben?" men were shouting as they grabbed for the few weapons they had.

"Jabin's troops!" he panted.

"Jabin?" someone asked. "We whipped him at Green Meadow."

"I don't care," Benya shouted. "There are about twenty redcoats riding up the road. It has to be a raiding party. Those who can walk, help those who can't. Get everyone into the trees. We won't be sitting targets for anyone!"

Jennifer quickly grabbed what supplies she could carry, not wanting to lose a single precious item. She suddenly dropped everything and cried, "Grandmother!" In an instant, she was racing across the yard toward the cottage.

Men ran, limped, hobbled, or were carried to the edge of the clearing. There they fanned out, hiding the most incapacitated men carefully under bushes and behind trees.

"Did you see them, Ben?" Larry asked the young officer.

"Yes," Ben answered. "Did you hear Carter whistle?"

"We heard a whistle anyway," Larry responded.

"Well, that was Carter. I crashed through the bushes toward his whistle and saw them out on the road. Every last one of them was wearing those red coats we fought at Green Meadow."

"Get down!" Larry whispered. "They're here!"

The men could hear the thunder of hooves as horsemen surged around the corner and galloped into the yard. Their leader swung from the saddle and surveyed the surroundings. Everything looked deserted. He motioned for some men to search the barn while he headed for the house.

"Oh, no!" Larry whispered. "Jennifer is in there!"

"She is?" Benya whispered in horror.

They watched several crimson-clad men amble toward the cottage. "Open up!" Braten yelled. When they tried the door, they found it locked.

"Good!" Larry whispered, barely daring to breathe. He was angry with himself for forgetting the women.

Braten tried the door again but to no avail. He put his shoulder to the door and shoved. A small cluster of men began to gather about the door. Several tried to force the door open with their weight.

"I'm not messing around with this!" said one of the crimson-clad riders, and he walked to a window. Picking up a piece of firewood, he hurled it through the window and began to crawl in. When he was about halfway through, he suddenly slumped and went limp.

"What's going on?" Braten yelled.

The man did not move.

"Good girl!" Benya whispered savagely.

They heard another glass break and saw men stationing themselves at every window. Another man tried to gain entrance, but he too fell limp. Others tried, and finally someone succeeded at getting inside. Several tense moments passed, and a terrible scream rent the air. The cottage door flew open, and Braten marched inside.

Minutes passed before Benya Hefington grabbed Larry's arm and whispered, "Look!"

Two men carried a large bundle out of the house. It was a rolled blanket, tied at either end. In a moment the bundle was slung over the back of a packhorse.

Benya swore. "Those swine! I'll bet they're trying to take Miss Jennifer!" He leaped to his feet and raced across the clearing, brandishing his sword. One of Braten's men turned and saw Benya's charge, but Benya cut him down before he could draw his own blade.

Another redcoat shouted, "Attack!" and Braten bounded from the cottage. He raced for the horse bearing the bundle.

In seconds, Benya Hefington was surrounded by redcoats and was fighting for his life. He felled another man, but before he could strike the

BEYOND THE FIRE

third, men began to fall around him. Arrows filled the clearing as the men of Amity fought back.

A savage cry welled from Benya's lips. "For Jennifer!" he shouted.

Around the edge of the clearing, men shouted, "For Jennifer!"

Braten leaped into a saddle, grabbed the reins of the packhorse, and turned to flee.

With savage fury, Benya swung his blade at Braten, but another redcoat stepped into its path and intercepted the blow.

Devia's men were scrambling for their horses, but only seven were still on their feet. More arrows streaked across the clearing.

Larry struggled to get up. "Botheration!" he fumed. Braten and his cargo had raced out of the clearing before Larry could reach the road. He met the next rider, though. With no weapon but his crutch, Larry balanced on one leg and swung his crutch at the knees of the horseman's mount. The frightened beast reared, dumping his rider onto Larry, and both men went tumbling.

Another horseman plowed into the fray. With another volley of arrows, everything suddenly grew quiet.

The yard began to stir as men hobbled from their hiding places, swords and bows in hand.

"Aaah!" A scream rent the air, and all eyes turned toward the cottage. Benya stepped from the doorway and fell prostrate on the sod. Larry struggled to get up. He could only watch as others raced to Benya's side.

"Ben," someone asked, "are you hurt?"

"No!" Ben sobbed. "They've taken Jennifer! She's not here!"

Across the clearing, Larry heard, and he wanted to curse. He'd been too late! It had been Jennifer inside that blanket on the packhorse. That was what Ben had meant!

As the truth sank in, a sickening silence covered the camp.

"What about Grandma?" someone asked.

"Dead!" Benya said dully. No one was surprised.

Larry hobbled slowly across the clearing. He noticed that Ben's shoulder was bleeding badly. "Come on, Ben," he said. "We have to get you bandaged. Is anyone else hurt?"

"Does it matter?" Benya cried angrily. "We let them take Miss Jennifer! We all deserve to die!"

"Wait a minute," someone said. "What's that sound?"

Everyone grew silent and strained their ears. A shrill whistle wafted on the afternoon breeze.

"It's Carter," someone blurted.

"Quick, back into the trees," someone shouted. "It may be another raid."

Everyone hobbled toward the trees, but even as they moved, the whistle kept blowing.

Larry motioned for everyone to stop. "Look, Carter's either hurt or in trouble. There is no other reason he would keep blowing that whistle."

"It may be a trap," someone said.

"Trap or no, I've got to find out!" Larry said.

"Me too!"

When it looked as though everyone was going to make the trek to the creek, Benya Hefington took charge. "We need someone to guard the camp. The best archers and the least mobile will stay here. The rest of you, come with me."

Larry couldn't walk very well, but he had been among those who had carried Carter to the creek this morning, and he wasn't going to be left behind. Benya led his little group through the thickets to where they had left James Carter, but Carter wasn't there.

"Carter!" Benya yelled.

"Carter!" everyone began to shout.

Someone had the sense to shush them long enough to listen for a response from their friend. They heard a faint whistle farther downstream.

"How did Carter get down there?" Larry puffed, trying hard to keep up with the group.

"Someone had to have carried him," said Tyrel Tucker, a square-jawed fellow who had fought beside Carter in the Battle of Green Meadow. "They must have taken him by surprise, though, because he was the best archer James Stafford had."

They rounded a bend in the stream and surveyed the countryside. The forest opened into a broad meadow where the road dipped to cross the stream.

It took a moment to comprehend what they were seeing. A large bundle lay low in the water, with Carter nearly drowning beneath it! There was a man dressed in crimson nearby, facedown in the water, an arrow protruding from his side. On the far side of the creek, two horses pulled contentedly at the tall grass.

The group rushed forward, and several men relieved Carter of his burden while others lifted him from the stream.

Carter coughed water from his nose and mouth. "Whew!" he puffed. "I didn't think you guys were ever going to come!"

Questions flowed faster than the brook. "What happened? How did you get down here? Are you all right?"

"Don't mind me, guys. There's somebody in that blanket. I heard a cry when it hit the water."

Benya slashed the cords that held the blanket shut. "It's Jennifer!" he cried. Her skin was pale, and blood trickled from a cut on her forehead.

"Is she breathing?" Carter puffed. "I thought it might be her." His breath was short, and he was exhausted from his labor.

"No," someone said. Several men laid Miss Jennifer with her face to the bank and began to press on her back.

"What happened, Carter?" Benya asked tersely.

"I saw Jabin's men coming and tried to warn you," James said. "I didn't know if you could hear me all the way up there."

"We heard you, all right," Ben said. "Thanks to you, we're alive."

"Two men broke from the party and came in search of my signal," James told the group. "They never got close. You'll find them out there in the trees, but they'll never hurt anyone again."

"What about this one?" Ben asked, pointing at the man lying nearby.

"I heard you guys fighting up on the hill," Carter wheezed. He was pale and weak, and it was getting hard for him to talk. "I knew they would come back this way, and I wanted to cut them off if I could. Using my hands as feet, I partly swam and partly floated downstream. I got to that bend when I saw this guy. I didn't know what was in the bundle, but I figured he was trying to get away with something important."

Everyone looked back to the bend Carter had indicated. It was several hundred feet away.

"Don't tell me you hit a moving target from that distance?" someone asked.

Carter was growing very tired. "Okay, I won't tell you, but there he is."

Tucker elbowed Larry in the ribs. "I told you he was the best."

One of the men huddled over Jennifer called out, "She still ain't breathing, Ben!"

"What happened to her, Carter?" Ben demanded.

Larry noted that Carter was growing very pale.

"She fell!" Carter rasped, his breath growing shallow.

"Give him a break, Ben," Larry said tersely. "He's in no shape to be talking." Larry studied Carter's wounds. His skin had been scraped and torn on the rocky creek bed, and his stumps looked nasty.

"I heard someone cry when the bundle hit the water," Carter gasped. "I hurried to get there, but when I tried to lift the bundle out of the water, I couldn't."

"Save your strength, Carter," Larry demanded. He was ripping his own shirt into strips. "Help me wrap him up, fellows."

Benya waded into the stream and looked back at the bank. Men were working over both Miss Jennifer and Carter. Somehow he felt guilty that either of them had been hurt. "Oh, Lord," he whispered, "save them."

Suddenly he heard a cough. He whirled to see Miss Jennifer spewing water from her nose and mouth. "Atta girl," he whispered to himself. "Keep it up." He waded toward the bank.

"She's coming around!" someone shouted, and nearly everyone gathered around her. Ben nearly bowled them over in his zeal to get to her.

"Help her up!" he shouted. At that moment, Jennifer coughed, blowing more water out of her nose and mouth. She opened her eyes and tried to speak but coughed instead.

Men eased her to a sitting position. Feebly she shook her head to free her face from the long damp strands of hair that clung to it. Jennifer gazed into a sea of familiar faces. Trying to smile, color crept into her cheeks. "Thank you," she whispered.

The group fell silent, grateful to hear Miss Jennifer's voice. Suddenly Carter broke the silence. "I told you guys you were going to thank me."

They set Miss Jennifer on one of the horses that had remained nearby, and several men escorted her back to the camp. They would tell the others what had happened and prepare a place for Carter.

Benya, Larry, and the others quickly cut two saplings and used the wet blanket to make a pallet. Gently they laid James Carter on the pallet and lifted him to their shoulders. Slowly they carried him back to camp.

Carter received a hero's welcome when he arrived, but he was too weak to join in the merriment. As evening fell, so did everyone's hope that the young man would survive.

Though Jennifer was exhausted, she stayed by Carter's side throughout the night, and now she prayed, "Dear Lord, please grant James victory. He gave all he had to save me. Please, please, save him." She'd done all she knew to do, and still James Carter thrashed in agony. Jennifer wept for him.

As sunlight spilled into the farmyard, Carter suddenly grew calm. Jennifer watched in amazement as the fever that had ravaged his body broke, and the lines of pain on his face eased. As others woke from their slumber, James Wesley Carter eased into a deep and healing sleep. God had answered Jennifer's prayers. Carter was going to make it.

The days that followed were a mixture of joy and sorrow. The horses killed in battle were butchered, and the meat was hung out to dry. The dead were buried, and the campsite was scoured. The cottage was cleansed, but weeks passed before Miss Jennifer could enter her grandmother's cottage alone. She never spoke of her ordeal, and laughter graced her features less frequently, but Jennifer was determined life would remain fun.

Time passed, and battle scars turned to blisters. Together, Miss Jennifer's little family tilled the earth with makeshift tools and planted a garden. Though isolated and forgotten by the rest of world, the men with Miss Jennifer had no idea how fortunate they really were.

CHAPTER 45

The Cotton Household

"Grandpa," a little voice sounded in the room. "What happened to Grandma? We haven't heard about her in long time."

"Well, Grandson, I haven't talked about your grandmother much because she went through a very hard time, and sometimes this story makes her sad."

There was a sudden hush in the room, and everyone felt quite subdued.

"Mary," Bill began, "shall I tell the children your story?"

Mary looked up from her knitting. She smiled and then turned back to her labors. "I suppose," she said. "It might be helpful to someone else."

Bill remained silent as his lovely bride worked her needles. Mary stopped her labors and glanced around the room. Her eyes finally met Bill's, and though not a word was spoken, she returned to her knitting with a smile on her lips.

"Well, children!" Bill said. "Your grandmother and great-grandmother were in a terrible predicament. Strange men had broken into their shop and …"

In the darkness of their room, Mary clung to her mother. They could hear the staircase groan under the weight of their intruder. Dolly scanned the room. "Quick!" she hissed. "Slide the bed against the door."

Though Mary had been paralyzed by fear, her mother's sure movements gave her a sense of direction. She stepped to the foot of the bed and pushed. Nothing happened.

Dolly had better fortune. She had positioned herself at the heavy headboard. Throwing her considerable weight into the project, Mary not only heard but felt the heavy bed begin to move.

The footsteps on the stairway stopped and then began to race up the stairs.

"Push, Mary!" Dolly hissed.

Frantically, Mary did push. With a lurch, the bed slid noisily across the floor and bumped into the door. At that moment the latch on the door lifted, and the door opened, but only an inch or two.

"Scream!" Dolly cried. "Scream for all you are worth! If there's a man left in this town that is worth his salt, you'll get his attention." She grabbed the heavy brass pitcher from the wash stand. "If it's a fight they want, it's a fight they are going to get," she said, setting her jaw.

Mary trembled as she slid open the bedroom window. "Help!" she cried into the empty street below.

"Scream!" Dolly shouted as she clambered up onto the bed, the brass pitcher firmly in her hand. "Again!" she yelled.

The thick door began to splinter under the intruder's heavy blows. With a sudden crash, the upper half of the door gave way. A dark shadow filled the doorway. Mary's nightmare had come to life. Terror swept over the poor girl, and she screamed. Mary's scream so shocked the intruder, Dolly, and Mary that all three stood stock-still—but only for a moment.

The intruder broke the spell and began to push through the splintered door, widening his path. Mary screamed again and again. Dolly raised the brass pitcher over her head. When the intruder's head cleared the doorway, Dolly swung the pitcher down as hard as she could. There was the sound of a loud crack, and the man collapsed at her feet.

Between Mary's screams, Dolly could hear men shouting from the street below. "It's the Trumbell place!"

Dolly stood over her victim and shouted, "Mary, help me get his sword!" She tugged desperately at the blade that was pinned beneath the man's body.

Dolly could hear the clash of steel in the rooms below as the garrison finally confronted Dolly's midnight marauders. Dolly continued her struggle until finally she freed the intruder's blade, and there she stood on Mary's bed, brandishing the sword and daring anyone to enter the room.

The sights and sounds were too much for Mary. Her screaming suddenly stopped, and she slumped to the floor.

"It's a sweet little boy, Mary," Dolly said gently.

Mary lay still as tears ran freely down her cheeks. "Mama," she said, breathing deeply, "may I see him?"

Dolly held up a tiny bundle. A squirming red body was lovingly wrapped in the corner of a quilt. Suddenly a little leg popped out, and a tiny voice began to howl.

Mary's heart melted. "Oh!" she cried. "May I hold him?" Her arms reached instinctively for the bundle.

"Yes, darling." Dolly sighed, easing the babe to his mother's breast. "That's what he's wanting," she said.

Within moments, wailing was replaced by sighs.

"Oh, Mama, he's perfect!" Mary breathed. The tiny babe opened his eyes and stared at his mother. "Oh, you are a darling," she whispered.

Dolly sat on the edge of the bed. Tightness pulled at her chest, and pain shot down her left leg. Her arms ached, and she felt nauseous. "The night's been too long," she thought to herself.

The pain in her chest eased, and she watched Mary cluck and coo to the bundle in her arms. Dolly had never seen her daughter so content. "He is perfect," she said. "Do you have a name for him?"

"William Trumbell Cotton," Mary said without looking up.

Dolly caught her breath and grimaced as another "spell" struck and then passed, but she said nothing. She didn't want to spoil this precious moment for her daughter.

After several days, Dolly was still exhausted. She couldn't seem to catch her breath, but Mary didn't appear to notice. She was completely absorbed with young Master William.

No! Dolly told herself. *I won't mention my troubles. Young William's fever is enough for Mary to worry about.* Dolly lifted a pail of cool water and tiptoed into the room, hoping not to disturb the baby.

Mary looked up. "Mother, I wish Dr. Ganton hadn't left with the army. I don't think William is getting any better."

Mary failed to see the lines etched on Dolly's face. Suddenly the older woman gasped and grabbed for a chair. Water spilled as the pail hit the floor.

"Mother!" Mary cried, leaping to her mother's side. "What's wrong?"

"I can't ... get ... my breath!" Dolly panted. Her face was drawn and gray. "I can't ..." And then all was silent.

"Mother!"

Some days later, a young man by the name of Walley heard screams from the abandoned side of town, and he went to investigate. Under one of the huge cottonwood trees that lined Orchard Creek Avenue, he noticed a woman lying facedown in the dirt. He watched for quite some time as she pounded the ground with her fists and screamed in anger at God. Finally the young woman's hysteria slowed to deep, retching convulsions. "Ma'am," the lad whispered, stepping closer. "Ma'am!"

Mary lifted her head. Her face was puffy from crying, and dark circles surrounded her eyes. She saw the boy but turned away, trying to ignore him.

"Ma'am!" the boy tried again, a little frightened. "Can I get someone to help you?" he asked.

"No one can help me!" Mary screamed.

Walley stepped back quickly. "Is something wrong?" he asked, not knowing what to say.

"I can't go home," Mary cried, vaguely waving her hand in the air.

"Why?" Walley asked.

"Everyone is dead!" Mary wailed. She had finally admitted it. Her mother had died carrying water to her room, and fever had taken the life from her baby boy. Mary had covered her mother where she'd fallen on the floor, and baby William was carefully wrapped in a blanket lying on her bed. She turned on Walley as if it was his fault and screamed, "Go away! Leave me alone!"

The boy backed away slowly, and the woman took no more notice of him. Reaching an intersection of streets in town, Walley stood indecisively for a few moments. Suddenly he said, "I know. I'll get Captain Armonson." With that, he turned and raced toward the garrison.

Captain Armonson of the Capri garrison did come and help Mary back to her home. In the hours that followed, men came to remove the bodies of her mother and her son, carrying them to the cemetery where they were given a proper burial.

The third day after Mary met Captain Armonson, she was beginning to adjust to her new life. That evening when Armonson came to call again, he asked her, "Are you sure you will be all right?"

Mary was in her own kitchen. She felt more composed than she had in days. "I'm sure," she said, but her heart quelled at the thought of being alone. She watched Captain Armonson from behind the dark veil she wore. He was so much like Bill. "Captain," she said, "you have been so kind. Thank you so much for all you have done."

"You have suffered a great tragedy, Mrs. Cotton," Armonson said. "Should I send a man around once in a while to see how you are doing?"

Mary glanced at the boy beside Captain Armonson. She had begun to enjoy the lad who had found her wallowing in pity some days before. "No, Captain," she said. "Just send Walley when you can."

The young boy's eyes sparkled, and he grinned from ear to ear. "I can carry water or dig potatoes or whatever, Mrs. Cotton," he said, bubbling with excitement.

Mary nodded at Captain Armonson. "We'll manage nicely," she said, rising from her chair. "You have more important duties than to tend a troublesome woman like me."

Captain Armonson smiled. "No trouble, ma'am. I'll send Walley by every morning to check on you."

With that, both Walley and Captain Armonson left the house, and Mary was alone.

Just two days later, Mary was scraping the last of the flour from her crock and sifting it into a mixing bowl. Walley would be here soon, and she didn't want to be late.

Mary had grown quite fond of Walley. Each morning he arrived with a large pail of water and something else besides. Sometimes it was an armload of potatoes from a neighbor's garden, or maybe a load of wood from a deserted back porch. Though he was looting her neighbors' deserted gardens, Mary didn't know how she would have survived without him. His visits broke the lonely ritual she observed each day.

She poured thin batter on a hot griddle. "Pancakes for us both," she mused. As she waited to flip the first cakes, she searched her larder for the last pat of butter. "We'll have a party today, for I don't know what we'll eat tomorrow—unless Walley steals more potatoes." Inwardly she hoped the lad would find something. She had come to depend on him so much.

Suddenly she heard someone calling, "Mrs. Cotton!" The voice was coming from her front door, so Mary hurried through the house.

Opening the door, she discovered Walley, laden with not only a large pail of water but many fine potatoes as well.

"Walley!" she exclaimed. "Where did you find such nice potatoes?"

"They are from the garrison larder, ma'am," he said.

"Walley!" she gasped. "How could you?"

"Captain Armonson sent them," Walley explained. "Rations are low everywhere, and he thought you might need them."

Mary relaxed. "Thank heavens," she sighed. "You must thank him for me."

Walley grinned, and then he produced something else. "I found this too," he said, pulling a large black book from under his shirt.

"A book?" Mary asked. "Where did you find this?"

Walley squirmed a bit uncomfortably. "In the church."

"Walley!" Mary exclaimed. "You wouldn't steal from a church, would you?"

"I didn't steal it," Walley countered. "I only borrowed it so you could read to me. I'll take it back, I promise."

Mary felt a deep revulsion. She wanted nothing to do with God. God had allowed her husband to leave with the army. He had let her mother die, and He'd taken their precious baby away from her. She certainly didn't want to read about God, but the prospect of another lonely day loomed large before her.

"All right," she said reluctantly. "Only, let's celebrate with hotcakes just now. Who knows what tomorrow will bring?"

After cleaning the breakfast dishes, and since it promised to be a lovely day, Mary and Walley settled on the front steps of the shop to read. Mary marveled at the lad beside her. Though it was obvious that he couldn't read, Walley understood every word. Frequently he would ask her to reread certain passages, for he didn't want to miss a single thought.

I just wish Walley could read this for himself, Mary thought.

As the days slid by, Mary began to discover that reading to Walley not only filled many lonely hours but it brought healing to her own heart as well.

Armed with Walley's careful mental notes, Mary began to enjoy the Bible's unfolding drama. She discovered the patriarchs and Psalmist felt many of the same fears and frustrations she did. But while they found their strength in God, she began to realize that she didn't even know Him.

But Mary was content. Walley provided everything she needed. Each morning he arrived with food, water, and other supplies. She had no idea where things came from, and she soon stopped asking. Walley's companionship gave her ample reason to get up and face each new day.

One day, Mary paused while reading. Tears filled her eyes, but she didn't want to cry because she knew Walley would ask questions.

The Bible lay open on her lap, but her heart was in turmoil. She had just finished reading of the crucifixion of Jesus Christ. She could not imagine people being so cruel. *Why would anyone kill a man so blameless and good?* she wondered.

Walley's voice shattered her thoughts. "You must understand this better than anyone."

Bewildered, Mary shook her head. "Why would you say that, Walley?"

"God's only Son died, just like yours," Walley said seriously.

The truth of Walley's words struck home. God had lost His only Son, and so had she. There were differences, of course. Jesus had been brutally murdered by the very people he had come to save. Her son, on the other hand, had died of a fever. If only she had known what to do or where to take her baby, he might still be with her. Mary felt so guilty. *I loved William so much,* she thought. *When I lost him, I thought it was God's fault.*

Tears rolled down Mary's cheeks. *Would I have killed Jesus?* She hated to admit it, but she had been so angry at God when baby William had died that she probably would have driven the nails in Jesus's hands if she could have.

"You know," Walley said quietly, "Jesus is kind of like my dad."

"How?" Mary asked meekly. This child was teaching her, whether he knew it or not.

"Dad loved Amity so much that he was willing to lay down his life for her," he said.

"Walley," Mary said, puzzled, "I don't see how that fits in with this story."

"Jesus loved you and me so much that He was willing to die for us!" Walley stated.

Mary was troubled. She felt silly asking a child questions, but she needed to know. "Walley," she said, "I know the Bible says that Jesus died to take man's sin away, but if He did remove sin, why is evil still in the world, and why do we have to suffer?"

Walley looked at her with keen, clear eyes. "Miss Mary," he began, "the crucible is for silver and the furnace for gold, but trials come to test our hearts."

Mary frowned, and Walley continued, "We know ore is thrown into a furnace to melt the gold trapped within. Once melted, the gold runs into a pan and is given to the goldsmith to make beautiful things, like a crown or a setting for a jewel. The stone from which the gold came is worth nothing and is discarded.

"Trials come into our lives to prove what kind of people we are. Just as a lump of ore is thrown into the fire, so a sinful world hurls difficulties and hardship our way. Those trials will bring out the good that is inside while exposing the bad for what it is and eventually throwing it away. Trials reveal that some people have really good hearts, while others are cold as stone."

"But how does one know whether a heart is good or bad?" Mary asked.

"God always knows the good from the bad," Walley said, "but there are things that are obvious to everyone. A good heart is kind, generous, and open to sharing God's love. And as a special blessing, the Lord grants His peace to all who trust in Him."

"And they won't have any more problems?" Mary asked.

"I didn't say that!" Walley countered. "And neither did Jesus. Remember, He said, 'In this world you will have tribulation, but be of good cheer, for I have overcome the world.'"

Mary could remember reading those words, but she hadn't understood them then, nor did she now.

Walley went on. "Jesus wants everyone to experience a place of peace, a refuge, like Stonewall—a safe place to go, regardless of what is happening in your life."

"Where is this refuge, Walley?" Mary asked. Her heart longed for such a place, but she had no knowledge of such a retreat nearby.

"Peace is found in the person of Jesus Christ, Miss Mary." Walley's voice was confident.

Mary wanted to believe, but how could she? "Walley, how can Jesus give me this peace? Didn't He die for our sins?"

"He died, yes, but He was raised to life on the third day, and now He sits at the right hand of God the Father," Walley said. "He wants you to abide in Him that He might live through you. That is where you find true peace: not in the absence of trouble but in the presence of the Lord!"

Mary felt desperate. "Walley, I don't know Him. I don't know how to reach Him."

"Believe in the Lord Jesus, and you will be saved," Walley quoted. "Miss Mary," he said, searching her eyes, "do you believe Jesus is the Son of God?"

"I have no reason not to," Mary said. "It says so in this book." Her fingers reverently touched the book in her lap.

"Do you believe you are a sinner in need of a savior?" Walley asked.

"Walley!" Mary blushed, color rising in her cheeks. She could not look him in the eyes. "I …" She paused. "I guess I'm not perfect."

Walley smiled, but his eyes fell. "Miss Mary, do you realize you can't reach the Father or that blessed place of peace without help from a stronger guiding hand?"

Pride suddenly welled up in Mary's soul. How dare this young boy tell her what she could and could not do! Though she did not speak, her face stiffened with determination, and when her eyes met his, they were cold and hard.

Walley's enthusiasm faded. "Miss Mary," he whispered, "we choose where we live."

"What do you mean?" Mary's voice was brittle, and it sounded harsh within the confines of the room. She was sorry. She didn't mean to be angry.

"Every day we choose whether we will live inside or outside the Lord's peace and protection. I chose to stay in Capri rather than follow Aunt Hilda to Waterfront," Walley said.

Mary remained silent, but her mind was busy. Life hadn't given her a choice. Or had it? She thought of all the people who had offered to take her east. She had stubbornly refused every offer. At the time, she had thought she knew what was best, but now she was alone. She had no husband, no mother, and no baby. Her dreams had vanished. All she had was a skinny kid who was rapidly turning into a preacher!

Mary's voice broke the silence. "Walley, I'm stuck here. There is no other place I can go."

"Do you mean here in Capri?" Walley asked, his head tipped to one side.

Mary nodded.

"We're not stuck!" Walley grinned. "The road is still open. We can flee to Stonewall tonight. I'll go with you."

Mary felt her heart skip a beat. Who was this child, anyway? "But Walley," she protested, "what will I do with my things?"

"Leave them!" he said. "Pack a few clothes, and let's go!"

A daring urge swept over Mary. Should she try it? "Maybe," she said aloud, but even as she spoke, common sense began to wash over her. "Walley, I can't just leave all my things. Besides, I don't know anyone at Stonewall."

"I'll bet there are a lot of people you know who are already there," Walley stated.

The gentle Ella Walton came to Mary's mind. How she longed to see Ella again.

Walley sensed her indecision. "The longer we wait, the harder the journey may become. Master Devia may close the road before long. His influence grows stronger within the barracks and what is left of the city."

Mary shivered. "But Master Devia is from Amity! He would not bring trouble upon his own people as Jabin would have done."

"I don't know," Walley said uncomfortably. "The things I hear don't sound too good. I really don't want to find myself in his camp."

"Walley," Mary said. "You don't sound like yourself!" She had heard reports of men on the march, bringing peace to Amity. If the last report she had heard was true, they were near Capri. Besides, Captain Armonson knew of their approach. He had hoped they would bring more food to what was left of Capri.

Mary began to dream. If there was a large army coming, wasn't it likely that Bill would be among them? That thought filled her with the deepest longing. "No, Walley," she said firmly. "I cannot leave Capri tonight."

Though his face fell, Walley put on a brave smile as he rose to leave. "Very well," he said, "but you must remember that no matter what happens, you can choose to live in the peace and presence of the Lord. The key is faith. Reach out to Him in faith, and the Lord will grant you His peace and rest."

Mary could sense Walley's disappointment, and she hated that she had caused it. She rose and followed the boy to the front door. "Thank you, Walley." She felt as if something very important was slipping away from her. "Walley?" she called after him. "Will you be by in the morning?"

"I will if I can," he answered.

Mary was troubled by Walley's parting words. After locking the door, she turned weary steps toward the stairs and climbed to her bedroom, knowing she would long consider the words spoken this day.

CHAPTER 46

Dark Days in Capri

Mary awoke to a gloomy world. She wondered if it was early. Glancing out the window, she fussed, "Clouds!" She hated dreary days; they seemed so much longer.

The water in her basin was cold, and it brought her sharply to her senses. She glanced at the clock on her wall. It was late. Walley should have been there already. Quickly she slipped into her dress. *I wonder if he knocked at my door trying to wake me*, she thought.

She stepped to her bedroom door and inspected the heavy wooden panels. Walley had helped her move this door from her father's workroom downstairs to replace the door that had been shattered the night intruders had entered the store and her life had been changed. She shuddered at the memory.

Touching this door's latch, she could smell the faint odor of lacquer and paint. Fond memories of her father passed through her mind.

Quietly she stepped from the room and glided down the stairs—and then froze. Someone was standing by her back door. No one had ever been there before. *Is it Walley?* she wondered. Taking several deep breaths, she walked very quietly across the kitchen to the back door.

She quickly slid the bolt and lifted the latch. The door swung open, and a man nearly fell at her feet. She recognized him instantly. "Ed Turner!" she gasped. "What on earth are you doing lurking at my door?"

The man regained his balance and turned to face Mary. She understood the look of shock on his face when he was off balance, but anger clouded his features when he heard her use the word *lurking*.

"I ain't lurking, Ms. Cotton," the man said. "I've got orders!"

"Who gave you orders to stand at my back door?" she demanded.

"Captain!" Turner leered at her, showing off his missing teeth.

Mary felt shock and surprise. "Captain Armonson?" she asked. "But why? And where is Walley?"

Ed Turner puffed out his chest. "Captain Armonson is no longer in command at Capri. Captain DeKlerk arrived last night, and there have been some changes. I've been promoted to sergeant!" Turner's excessive pride threatened the buttons on his new red coat.

Mary suddenly shivered. "Where is Captain Armonson?" she persisted. "And why didn't Walley come this morning?"

"We put the runt to work in the kitchen. There are lots more men to feed, and there's a lot more food to cook." Ed Turner rubbed his ample belly and belched.

Mary felt utter revulsion, but she asked once again, "What about Captain Armonson?"

"He needed a little ... training." Turner grinned. "He was sent west for a little reeducation."

Mary recalled Walley's words last night. It was becoming painfully obvious that he'd known more than he'd let on.

"Well," she said with determination, "if Walley can't bring my water, I'll have to go myself." She stooped to pick up the bucket that sat by the back door.

"Sorry, ma'am." Turner's missing teeth mocked her. "You are not to leave this house."

"Why?" Mary asked, her anger beginning to replace her fear. "I'll get water if I want to." She started to brush past Ed Turner, but he grabbed her arm and shoved her roughly back into the house.

"You're not going anywhere, missy," he barked. "I've got my orders!"

Mary was flustered and angry now. "Who gave these ridiculous orders?" she snapped. "I'd like to give them a piece of my mind."

"Captain Jan DeKlerk is his name, and you'll get to see him, but you won't have to leave the house to do it." Ed Turner's smile was none too pleasant.

Mary shrank back, a horrible thought crossing her mind. "Why?" she asked softly.

"He'll be along sometime today," Turner sneered.

"How does he know where I live?" she asked.

"We've been watching that kid come over here. Say, what do you do with a kid all day?" Turner asked, slowly inching his way through the door. "Now, I could understand you and me spending all day together."

With one swift movement, Mary shoved Turner outside and slammed the door. She slid the bolt and raced to the front door. Another man wearing a red coat blocked her escape there. Tears of frustration filled her eyes. Creeping back through the house and up to her bedroom, Mary fell upon her bed and sobbed herself to sleep.

Mary awoke with a start. Someone was pounding at her door. She listened, and suddenly a voice shouted angrily, "Open up, or we'll break the door down!" Mary recognized the voice of Ed Turner.

A second voice interrupted Turner. "This is Captain DeKlerk of occupational forces! May I come in?"

Mary crept down the stairs. If it was the new commander, maybe she could impress on him her need of food and water.

Mary inched toward the door. "I'll not open for the likes of you, Ed Turner!"

The second voice grew hard. "Did you harm her, Turner?"

"Didn't do a thing, Captain," Turner said. "I just followed your orders."

"She sounds frightened," DeKlerk said. "You are dismissed, Turner! Don't come around here again!"

"But Captain," Ed argued.

"You are dismissed," DeKlerk ordered.

"Yes, sir," came the sullen reply.

Mary heard a shuffling of boots outside, followed by the second voice saying, "Ma'am, Sergeant Turner will no longer trouble you. I am Captain DeKlerk of occupational forces. I would be pleased to discuss our new regulations with you and clear up any misunderstandings you might have."

Cautiously, Mary slid the bolt and lifted the latch.

A tall, handsome man stood outside. He had a disarming smile. Tipping his hat, he bowed low and asked, "May I have the pleasure?"

Mary felt rather self-conscious. "Pleased," she said, giving a slight half curtsy.

"Is there a place we might talk?" DeKlerk asked.

Mary turned and led him to the kitchen. He slid the bolt on the door and followed. Silently she gestured to a chair. She couldn't offer him tea or anything to drink, for she was out of water.

Taking the situation in at a glance, DeKlerk settled easily into a chair and motioned that she should do the same. "Ma'am," he said easily, "I'm glad you locked your door. That is a good habit to get into."

There was a long pause, for Mary said nothing.

Captain DeKlerk tried again. "Did Sergeant Turner trouble you?"

Color rushed to Mary's cheeks, but she still said nothing.

"I see!" DeKlerk said with finality. "I assure you, he will not trouble you again!"

"Thank you," Mary said a little stiffly. "Captain," she suddenly blurted, "why am I being held a prisoner?"

"A prisoner?" DeKlerk's eyebrows arched. "You are not being held prisoner, Miss ..." He paused, clearly waiting for her to give him her name, but she said nothing. "I placed guards here to protect you, my dear lady." His voice was smooth.

"Protect me!" said Mary. "From what?"

"Men like Turner!" DeKlerk said flatly. "I have a rather unruly bunch of men. They have been deprived the pleasures of home for a long time, if you know what I mean." He looked knowingly into Mary's eyes.

She could feel her cheeks burn, and she quickly turned away.

"I want everyone to remain safe during our stay," DeKlerk said. "Do you have any needs?"

Mary met the captain's eyes. "Yes," she said boldly. "I will need water each day, and my larder is nearly empty. Captain Armonson always sent a few potatoes each day with a lad named Walley, but you apparently have a different use for the food and for Walley's services."

Jan DeKlerk rubbed his chin thoughtfully. "I don't know a lad by that name. Someone must have prevented his coming, but food and water I can supply."

Mary's eyes brightened. Maybe this man wasn't so bad after all. "Thank you, Captain," she said.

"Why don't you call me Jan?" he said. "All my friends do."

Mary blushed, but a smile crept to the corners of her mouth. "Very well, Jan. Thank you!"

Jan DeKlerk kept his word. Every morning a man arrived with two large pails of water and a basket of produce. Mary could scarcely believe her eyes.

Captain DeKlerk came to call nearly every day, and though his visits were brief and formal, they always left Mary feeling uncomfortable.

One evening she heard a knock at the door. "Ms. Cotton!" She recognized the captain's voice. "May I come in?"

"Just a moment," she called, wiping her hands. She untied her apron before slipping to the back door. Sliding the bolt, she lifted the latch.

"Evening, ma'am!" Jan DeKlerk looked so very tall and handsome with his hat in his hand and a smile upon his clean-shaven face.

"Good evening, captain," Mary said politely. "Would you like to come in?" She felt a nervous tension growing within her.

"Thank you." DeKlerk stepped past her and strolled toward the kitchen.

Nodding at the guard outside, Mary latched and bolted the door.

Jan inhaled deeply, enjoying the aroma of freshly baked bread and boiling corn on the cob. "Ah, I've come at a bad time! You haven't eaten!"

"Would you care to join me?" Mary asked, feeling a blend of emotions as she did so. She would enjoy the company, but her preparations were rather short for two people.

"Do you have enough?" Jan asked pleasantly.

"Yes," Mary lied. "I fixed too much for myself!" She carefully removed and broke the ear of corn in pieces and sliced several thin slices from her small loaf of bread. Glancing around, she spied Captain DeKlerk's hat hanging casually on the hall tree. That was not a problem, but she felt her stomach tighten.

"I haven't any meat," she said. "Do you mind?"

"Not at all," Jan said, leaning back in his chair. "Whatever you have prepared will be fine."

Mary quickly laid plates and silver on the table. Setting out the food, she said, "Now we are ready."

They spoke little as they ate, and Mary cleared the table soon after they finished their meager meal. She was nearly finished with the dishes when she felt movement in the room. Turning, she saw Jan rising from his chair, lines of concern etched on his face.

"Miss Mary," he said softly.

Mary was stunned. No one had called her that since Walley's last visit.

Jan noticed her reaction, and he reached out to hold her shoulders. "Do you remember asking about your husband's status?"

Mary nodded. Captain DeKlerk looked so grave that a cloud passed over her heart.

"I am sorry to inform you," Jan said. "Your husband was killed in heavy fighting some miles north of Green Meadow."

Mary felt the room spin. She closed her eyes and clung tightly to the man before her. When the full impact of his words struck her, she gasped, "Oh, no!" Suddenly her knees buckled, and she fell heavily into Jan's strong arms.

The bedroom was still quite dark as Mary watched Jan button his shirt with swift, sure fingers. He sat on the edge of her bed and pulled on his boots.

"Nobody around here can handle the smallest problem," he grumbled. The gray hues of dawn cast strange shadows about the room. "Lock the door behind me," he said as he stomped out the door.

Mary listened to him clomp down the stairs and out the back door. She lay quiet for several minutes, anger building within her. Silently she slipped from the bed, stepped to the wash basin, and began scouring her skin roughly. She wiped a tear from her eye.

Why do I feel so dirty? she wondered. *Bill is dead! What does it matter?*

The night she had learned of Bill's death, she'd felt so alone. Jan's strong arms had given her the comfort she thought she needed. It had been easy to let him stay. But now she angrily splashed water in her face. "It isn't right," she fumed. "He should at least say he loves me!"

Mary grabbed the wash basin, marched to her window, and hurled the contents outside. Marching back, she finished dressing.

Below in the street, a man wearing a red coat had taken a sudden and unexpected bath. Swearing softly, Ed Turner looked up at Mary's window and smiled a terrible smile.

It was late morning, and Mary was consoling herself with a cup of hot coffee. Maybe it wasn't wrong to let Jan in each evening. He had been kind to her. She glanced at the ample supply of bread and produce on her counter.

She heard sounds at the back door. *Why do they always use the back door?* she thought to herself. Suddenly she remembered that she had failed to follow Jan down this morning and bolt the door behind him.

Mary's guard had discovered her unlocked door, retrieved her empty pail, fetched water from the town well, and returned. He'd left the pail just inside and had discreetly closed the door.

There's nothing to worry about, Mary thought. *The guard is still at the door.* Still, something troubled her. She rose from her chair and slipped into the hallway.

Mary froze. She could hear the unmistakable voice of Ed Turner saying, "Get away from that door, or I'll cut you in half."

"Turner, get out of here!" Mary didn't know her guard's name, but he had a pleasant, boyish voice. "Captain DeKlerk will have you thrown in the brig if you cross this threshold."

"Captain DeKlerk!" Scorn filled Turner's voice. "He can't keep her all to himself!"

"Put your blade away, Turner. The rest of you, get out of here." A note of fear made the young man's voice tremble slightly.

Mary stood frozen with horror. She heard the rasp of metal and then a thump against her door.

She flew to throw the bolt, but it was too late. The door came crashing open, nearly knocking her down. A grisly scene met her eyes. Her young guard lay across the step in a growing crimson pool.

"Well," Ed Turner mocked, holding his stained sword aloft, "if it isn't Captain DeKlerk's woman!"

"Ed Turner," Mary stormed, "you get out of here!" She tried to slam the door, but he was too quick for her. Stepping over the fallen guard, he grabbed Mary's arm and pushed her into the kitchen. "Come on, fellows," he called. "I smell coffee."

Once in the kitchen, Mary twisted free of Ed's grasp and turned to face her tormentors. Ten rough-looking men stood facing her. "What do you want, Ed Turner?" she shouted.

"Now, that's not very neighborly," Ed said, trying to caress her cheek.

Mary jerked away and fled to the other side of the room. There was a chuckle from one of the men.

"We've been doing some hard riding for Captain DeKlerk," Ed Turner drawled. "And since we just got into town this morning, we thought a cup of coffee for the men would be a gracious thing for you to offer."

"There's coffee in the pot," she said, pointing to the stove. "Help yourself." Silently she prayed that Jan would appear and throw these no-goods out of her house.

"That's not what I had in mind," Ed said, pointing with his darkly stained blade. "Why don't you get some cups and serve us?"

Mary shivered. Maybe she could get the guard's attention at the front door, but Ed read her mind. "No, missy," he said. "We finished him off before we came to the back door. One of my men is stationed there right now, so everything looks nice and cozy."

"What do you want?" Mary asked again, glaring at Turner.

"Coffee," he said pointing his sword at the stove.

Mary grabbed a potholder and lifted the heavy pot. She spun quickly, but the flat of Turner's blade struck her arm, and the pot splashed noisily to the floor. Scalding coffee spattered around the room.

"That wasn't a bit nice, Mary," Turner chided. "You soaked me once this morning, and now you've tried again. I guess I'm going to have to teach you a lesson. Upstairs!" he demanded.

"No!" Mary retorted, rubbing her arm gingerly.

The tip of Turner's blade touched her throat. He motioned the men behind him to step aside. "You threw water from your window this morning and soaked me. Now, I think you are going to pay for your insolence."

"You're a swine, Ed Turner," Mary seethed.

Turner only smiled, yellow teeth protruding from his grizzled lips. "Maybe I am," he said, "but I've been called worse. Now, I need something only you can provide, missy."

"Men," Turner ordered. "Block the doors! We don't want the little lady to bolt on us, do we?" Turner lowered his blade to the top button on Mary's dress and severed the thread. The button fell to the floor and rolled under the table. "Now, get upstairs," he ordered. The motion of his blade was so subtle that Mary didn't realize he had pricked her skin. Something warm ran down her neck.

Near tears, Mary brushed past Ed Turner and walked to the staircase. She could hear coarse laughter behind her. Reaching her bedroom door, her fingers touched the latch. Memories of her loving father crossed her mind. "Oh, Daddy!" she sobbed.

She could hear boots lumbering up the stairs. "Oh, no!" Alarm filled her mind. "They wouldn't really go through with this!"

She slipped through the door and quickly swung it shut. The latch clicked, and she desperately wished she had a bolt on this door as well. Her eyes frantically searched the room for something to block the door. She took one step toward the dresser, and a terrible crash resounded as the door flew open and knocked her to the floor.

Mary closed her eyes, but she could not block out the sound of laughter or the scrape of boots as men shuffled into the room.

"I hate you," she breathed through clenched teeth. She turned to see Ed Turner's eyes flaming with lust. His sword pinned her to the floor. "No more tricks!" he roared.

"I hate you, Ed Turner!" She hurled the words at him.

Turner suddenly laughed and turned to the men filing into the room. "Well, isn't it nice she appreciates the finer things in—"

He never finished his sentence. In his moment of inattention, Mary saw her chance and made her move.

Brushing his sword to one side, she leaped up with all the fury of a wildcat. Screaming, clawing, kicking, and biting, she tore not only the sword from his hand but the sight from his eyes.

Time passed slowly, and rough hands finally shook Mary awake. "Why didn't you lock the door behind me this morning?" a voice was asking.

The room was dark, but through the one eye that was not swollen shut, Mary could see Jan towering over her.

"I warned you about my men!" Jan shouted. "Why didn't you lock the door? Now look at you! You're a mess! You're of no use to me now."

Mary began to sob as she awakened to the pain that filled her body. "I'm hurting, Jan. Please help me!"

"I'll get a pail of water, but you'll have to do the rest. I don't have time to play nursemaid to people who don't follow orders."

Jan stomped from the room and slammed the door. Mary heard him tramp down the stairs. She tried to shut out reality. At first she did not think about Ed Turner or the men with him, but the longer she lay there, the more she remembered. Hatred filled her heart when she thought of her abusers.

Her hair was matted to her face and neck, and she shook from the cold, but she was far too weak to seek warmth beneath a quilt. A clock ticked somewhere in the room, and the sound seemed to swirl around her.

Remembering the button Ed Turner had cut from her dress, her fingers painfully sought the other buttons. Her cheeks began to burn. Her collar was gone, and her dress had nearly been ripped from her body.

She tried to move but nearly fainted from the pain that overwhelmed her. She wondered if Jan would return, but quickly decided he would not.

Sometime later she heard the scrape of boots on the stairs, and presently Jan appeared with a bucket of water. He stood towering above her, pail in hand. "You lazy wench," he spat. "You haven't moved an inch since I left. I ought to …"

Mary heard the water slosh as he set the pail down, and then she heard the scrape of steel as he drew his sword.

"Go ahead," Mary whispered. "Surely a big strong man like you can kill a defenseless woman." Though she had enough spunk to taunt Jan, something inside her died. Jan didn't care what happened to her. No one cared.

Self-pity washed over Mary. She wished she could die. Jan had begun her mockery, and it was only fitting that he should finish it. Her affair with Jan was probably known all over town. She would be an outcast from anyone who cared about anything. Let Jan kill her. Her life was over anyway.

She was so absorbed in her own thoughts that she didn't hear Jan shouting until she caught the end of his words: "And may your saucy tongue perish with you!" She watched Jan turn his back and shout, "Goodbye and good riddance!"

Startled into reality, Mary wondered what Jan might have said, but she doubted it would have made her feel any better. She was alone now, really alone.

As the evening brought darkness, visions of terror crept through Mary's mind. Shadowy ghouls and monsters filled her room. Slowly the monsters melted into one great demon. His eyes captured the last rays of sunlight, and he laughed hauntingly into her soul.

One day drifted into another. Mary had little strength and no will to move. Jan had never returned. *I wish I could die*, she thought. *If only Jan had run his sword through me, my suffering would have ended, but even if I were to rise from this bed now, where would I go? Who would accept me after what*

I have done? No one! Well, Jan failed to end my suffering, but I won't! I'll refuse to move, eat, or drink. I'll die right where I am. People will find me and realize they could have saved me, and they'll blame themselves for my death.

But as Mary grew weaker, she began to fret. *What if people only find a skeleton? Will anyone ever know how badly I have been treated?* If they didn't know, it would ruin her fantasy.

Mary had been hurt badly. Worse, she was now dehydrated and half starved. A fever caused her to sweat profusely one moment and shake with chills the next. For the first time in days, she realized that the clock on the wall no longer ticked. *It's all over*, she reasoned. *Time has run out for me.*

She closed her eyes in resignation, and from somewhere in her mind, she thought she heard Walley's voice. Mary drew the quilts around her. She couldn't let Walley see her in this condition.

Once again she thought she heard Walley speaking, but she couldn't make out what he was saying. *Talk to me, Walley*, Mary silently pleaded. *I really need someone!*

Am I losing my mind? Mary wondered. But when she listened a third time, she thought she heard Walley say, *You can have peace in Jesus. Faith is the key.*

The moment passed, but Mary continued to wrestle with what she'd heard. How could she ever find peace and rest now?

As the sun sank in the western sky, shadow monsters reappeared in her room. She tried to ignore them, but they grew and multiplied in her muddled mind. A whisper slid through the room. "There is no peace for you," it hissed.

"Who's there?" Mary demanded.

Nothing moved but the shadows on her wall. They grew larger each moment, devouring every last ember of light until they turned on Mary. "All have sinned and fallen short of the glory of God," they whispered as they closed in to devour her.

"There are none righteous, no not one," the voice said, growing louder. "The wages of sin is death!" Even in the darkness, Mary could see the outline of a strange monster wagging a finger in her face. It opened its mouth, and red flame poured forth as it laughed. "And you are a sinner!"

Unable to resist their accusations, Mary felt herself being swept into another world.

Dreadful visions of terror passed through Mary's mind. They seemed so real she could not decide if she was dreaming or if she had indeed fallen into a world of misery and torment. Amid the taunts and jeers of her accusers, she heard the unmistakable wail of human agony.

Searching the dark caverns of her soul, Mary spied a hideous creature. She wanted to flee but could not, for chains held her to the wall.

Mary cowered as the creature approached, and though not a word was spoken, the chains fell from her wrists. She tried to run.

"Come," the creature said, gripping her tightly.

"No!" she pleaded. "Where are you taking me?"

The creature did not speak but pulled her toward a door. Through its open portal she could hear cries of terror and feel scorching heat blast her face.

"No!" she screamed. She fought to free herself from the hideous creature but to no avail.

A brilliant light suddenly flooded the darkness surrounding her. The light was pure and holy. She realized she was no longer held captive, but still she was unable to move. She shaded her eyes from the light, and that was when she saw him.

An angel stood between her and the dreadful door where the monster had been taking her. The light shone from the angel's hand, and without knowing why, Mary fell prostrate at his feet.

She felt a warm hand take her own, and she rose to her feet. The terrible creature was gone, and a man stood before her, smiling. "Come," he said. "You can find peace through faith in Jesus Christ." The man held a tiny silver key in his hand with the letters *FAITH* raised upon its handle. Light poured from that key and filled the depths of Mary's dark mind with hope. She could almost hear Walley saying, "Faith is the key." With great fear and trembling, she reached out and touched the key.

Ella Walton tucked her little Bonny into bed. "Lord," she prayed, wrapping a blanket about the child, "surround my Bonny with Your love, and guard her sleep." Kissing the tiny forehead, she whispered, "Good night, my love."

"When will Daddy come home?" the little girl asked.

"He'll come as soon as he can, sweetheart," Ella said softly.

"But what if Daddy's dead?" the child persisted.

Ella was silent for a moment. The idea troubled her deeply. "Bonny, we don't know where or how Daddy is tonight, but Jesus does. He is watching over Daddy right now."

"But Mommy," the little girl asked. "If Jesus is watching Daddy right now, how can he watch over me?"

Ella laughed. "Jesus is big enough to watch over everyone," she said.

"Wow!" Bonny whispered.

"Now, you need to go to sleep, dear," Ella said, tucking the little girl under her quilt.

"Momma?" the little girl quizzed.

"What is it, dear?" Ella asked.

"I wish Daddy could tuck me in."

"I do too, sweetheart," Ella said, trying to swallow the lump that had formed in her throat. "Good night, and sleep tight." She rose and stepped from the room where other children also lay bundled in their cots.

Ella stopped at her own cot and sank to her knees. She was nearly too tired to pray, but prayer seemed to be her only source of strength some days.

She was about to begin when she heard another voice. "Ella, are you all right?" She looked up to see Leone, the newest addition to their already crowded home.

"Hi, Leone," Ella said. "Yes, I'm fine. I was just getting ready to pray."

Leone dropped to her own cot and began pulling worn shoes from her feet. "If you pray as hard as you work, I should think God would have to listen to you."

Ella smiled. "You know that's not why the Lord listens to people."

"No?" Leone studied Ella for a moment. "Why does He listen, then?"

"The Lord listens because He loves us and cares for us," Ella explained. "Our smallest need is His concern."

"You don't believe that, do you?" Leone asked.

"I certainly do," Ella said, laughing.

"Didn't your old man get shipped out just like mine?" Leone asked.

"Bob volunteered," Ella corrected. "And yes, he left with the others."

"Well, look at you," Leone said. "You slave all day, pray all night, and take care of everyone's kids the rest of the time. I don't understand. If God loves you like you say, why does He make you endure so much?"

"The work I don't mind," Ella said. "And the children I love. But it's when I pray that I find peace and comfort for myself."

"That's beyond me," Leone said with a sigh. She slipped from her dress and pulled the covers over her aching body.

"Leone," Ella said softly. "Would you like me to pray for your husband?"

There was a long pause. "Sure, I guess so," Leone said. "It can't hurt."

"Do you miss him?" Ella asked.

"He's a drunken bum," Leone said. "But," she added a bit wistfully, "I do miss him."

"Well, tonight I'll start praying for Evert," Ella said.

Leone rocked up on one elbow and smiled. "Thank you, Ella," she said. "I'd like that."

It was dark all over Waterfront, but Ella remained on her knees. Something was troubling her. "Who is it, Lord?" she asked. "Who am I to pray for? Who have I missed?" She rocked back and forth, and sweat trickled down her brow.

Prayer was difficult tonight. Something was wrong, or someone was in deep distress, but who?

Mentally, Ella reviewed her list. The children, Bob, Leone, Evert, Linda, Ronald, Betty, Bill … Bill! "That's it!" she whispered. "Not Betty's Bill, but another." Her mind raced back to Capri and her neighbors, Bill and Mary Cotton. How could she have forgotten them?

"Lord, thank You for Bill Cotton," she prayed. "I am so glad he gave his heart to You. I am so thankful Bob has a good friend to pray and share his journey with. Watch over them both."

Ella thought of Mary. "Lord, be with Mary just now. I know she has rejected Your love in the past, but do not turn her away. Protect her and bring her into Your special place of peace."

A great burden rolled from Ella's heart. She felt peace for the first time all evening. "Thank You, Lord," she whispered. "I pray all these things in Jesus's name, amen."

Silently Ella crawled onto her cot. Pulling the covers over her shoulders, she fell instantly asleep.

CHAPTER 47

A New Beginning

Mary awoke with a start and lay breathless. Her heart was pounding for joy. *Who was that wonderful man who offered me the light of life?* she wondered. *Where was he, and where have I been?*

The sun filled her room with brilliant light. Joyfully she stretched forth her hand—and then suddenly stopped. *Where is the key? I thought I had the key!* Her spirits sank when she realized it might have been a dream. She was still in her own bed, and she was still dehydrated, weak, and ill, but she thought, *If that was a dream, it was the most remarkable dream I have ever had.*

She lay still and considered her experience. What was hell like? Had she just experienced it? She shuddered. Would she still be in torment if that stranger had not shared the light of faith with her?

Faith! The word resounded in her mind. *Was it faith that transported me from that horrible dark world back to this one? Was it faith that set me free?*

Mary breathed deeply, rapture flooding her soul. It was good to be alive! Just as daylight banished shadow demons from this world, so faith had driven the darkness from her soul.

"It's true," Mary sighed. "I can find peace in Jesus. He does love me!" She felt like dancing.

Mary finally began to observe the world around her. Her room was a mess. She slowly turned her head and realized that she too was a mess. Her body still hurt, but she could see out of both eyes, and she was on the mend. She shivered and pulled the quilt over her emaciated frame.

I must look a fright, she thought in horror, and then she laughed. It was a genuine laugh that broke the silence. She laughed when she thought of someone finding her as a living skeleton. She could imagine the shock in their eyes.

Mary was chagrined: ladies should not think of such things. But even her reproof made her laugh.

Reality finally brought her down with a bump. She was weak, thirsty, hungry, and terribly unkempt. Another laugh welled up from within her and bubbled into the room.

"Isn't it wonderful?" She laughed. "I want to be presentable! I do care whether I live or die!"

Summoning all her strength, Mary crawled to the edge of the bed in search of water. "Thank you!" she cried when she spied a bucket only two feet from the bed.

It was harder than she imagined, getting a drink. She could not reach the bucket, nor did she have a dipper in hand. Finally she eased her body to the floor and hung her head over the bucket, lapping water as a kitten might drink milk from a saucer.

Mary leaned against the bed and tried to get her bearings. "Good," she said. The mirror was broken. She wouldn't have to see what she looked like. Though she was famished, she knew that would have to wait. She was much too weak to navigate the steps downstairs, and she couldn't risk anyone coming to the store and seeing her nearly naked. *I hope they didn't destroy what few clothes I brought with me*, she thought.

She carefully dipped the corner of a quilt in the pail of water and began to wash her body. The more she washed, the more she remembered. Several men had carried Ed Turner out after she had attacked him, but others had pounced on her, beaten her, ripped her clothing, and raped her repeatedly.

Anger and shame boiled in her heart. *That was days ago*, she thought. *I must put all that behind me, or I will lose the joy I had when I awoke this morning. Just because terrible things happened, they do not change the fact that Jesus loves me.*

A quick wash and an attitude adjustment made her feel like a new person. "Now to get dressed," she said. She noticed that her wardrobe had been scattered around the room. She was a bit upset to think that strangers had handled her "private things," but that was in the past. "Let's go on from here!" she sang out.

She was growing stronger by the minute, but she still did not trust her strength to stand on her feet. Crawling across the floor, she examined her dresses and chose a long blue frock with a white lace collar. Soon she was struggling with the difficult task of getting dressed without standing.

By midmorning, the room had changed considerably. Mary's clothing was stacked neatly, and her personal belongings were stashed out of sight.

Returning to the pail for refreshment, Mary discovered that the water was quite foul from her constant usage. She was anxious to find fresh water, but she wasn't ready to walk to the public well, nor did she want to be seen by anyone in town. She wondered if people in town knew what had happened and if they would spurn her because of it.

She knew she shouldn't care what people thought, but she did. Her heavenly Father had given her a new start. She was forgiven, so she should move forward.

The afternoon was growing hot when Mary decided to navigate the stairs. Her strength was returning, and the thought of food downstairs nearly drove her mad. She was able to walk across the room by grasping one piece of furniture and then another.

Stopping at her bedroom door, she caressed the wooden panels lovingly. Mary could still smell the lacquer and paint from her father's workshop, and she whispered, "I'm sorry, Daddy! I didn't mean to tarnish your good name."

It was either remembering her father or the walk across the floor that suddenly drained her energy. She struggled to lift the latch and slip into the hallway. She was so exhausted by the time she reached the stairs that she had to sit down and scoot down the staircase one step at a time.

Fumbling into the kitchen, she found to her extreme joy a pail of clean water. It wasn't fresh, but it was clear and wholesome in appearance. Her bread had molded, but by carefully tearing the green away, she found the rest quite palatable.

Mary set the table with what food and drink she could manage to prepare and collapsed in a chair. Bowing her head, she genuinely thanked her heavenly Father for His providence.

The afternoon gave way to evening, and then daylight faded entirely. Still Mary sat alone in the gloomy kitchen, planning her next move. Food and water had strengthened her, but she was reluctant to make the arduous climb to her bedroom.

She would not light a lamp or a fire. There was no reason to call attention to the house. Though she had thanked her heavenly Father for Jan several times through the day, she was not ready to encounter him tonight.

Anger flared deep within her as she thought of Jan's use and abuse of her, but she did not want to go down the dark road of hatred again. Suddenly she froze. She heard the latch on the front door click and the hinges squeak as it opened.

She held her breath. Was it Jan? Suddenly a more terrifying thought came to her: was it Ed Turner's friends again? Mary truly wanted to forgive those men, but the thought of seeing them tonight turned her resolve to putty.

A floorboard creaked. Mary hardly dared to breathe. *Heavenly Father,* she prayed silently, *protect me!*

"Miss Mary," a voice whispered in the hallway.

Walley had called her that, but so had Jan. *Oh, please, please let this be Walley,* she prayed.

"Miss Mary," the voice called again.

Mary grew more confident. "Is that you, Walley?" she called.

Movement in the hallway stopped.

Mary mustered all her courage and called, "Walley, I'm in the kitchen." Even as she spoke, she wondered if she had made a mistake.

The floor creaked again, and Mary jumped when a small silhouette appeared in the doorway. "Walley," she whispered, "is that you?"

"Miss Mary," the lad cried, his voice nearly squeaking for joy. "You're alive!"

Mary struggled from her chair, and Walley was at her side, hugging her with all his strength. "They said you were dead, and the sign on the door warned of plague," Walley whispered.

Dead? Plague? A sign on the door? What is that all about? Mary wondered. Suddenly she recalled Jan's parting words. He had threatened her with something, but she'd missed what it was. Had Jan tried to isolate her from help or from danger?

In her weakened condition, she sat back down. "Walley," she confided, "I'm not dead, but I surely would have been before morning—but for the grace of our heavenly Father."

Walley held her hand. His keen eyes searched hers, confusion written on his face.

Mary looked directly into the lad's eyes. "I've given my heart to Jesus, Walley!"

CHAPTER 48

A Daring Escape

They laughed and cried together. Mary had never seen anyone so excited.

"I've prayed for you every day!" Walley exclaimed. "I wanted you to know how much Jesus loves you!"

"Your prayers have been answered, Walley," Mary said. "The Lord has given me a new start. But I don't know where to begin." She confided in the child as if he were her brother.

Walley suddenly jumped to his feet. "We have to get out of here!"

"Why?" Mary asked in surprise.

"Captain DeKlerk's men will be looking everywhere for me, and those phony quarantine signs on your door won't stop them. Everyone knows we spent a lot of time together. This house will be one of the first places they'll search. You are no longer safe here!"

"Where will we go?" Mary heard herself ask.

"Do you know the back road that leads to Waterfront through the forest?" Walley asked.

Mary nodded. She had played on that road as a child, but she had never followed it all the way to Waterfront. "But it was a long time ago," she said.

"But you know where it starts on the edge of town?" Walley asked.

"Yes."

"Good," Walley said. "We'll try to get to that road tonight and travel as far as we can. If something should happen to me, you must follow that road until you come to Waterfront."

Mary's eyes widened. "Are you in some kind of trouble? Twice you have alluded to the fact that someone is or will be looking for you. Why?"

"I've been confined to the kitchen," Walley said, "but tonight I was asked to run an errand for an officer. I took a note to Commander Powell. He was detained, so I waited. When Commander Powell finally came, I handed him the message and ran."

"Why did you run, Walley?" Mary asked.

"I—" Walley hung his head. "I opened the note and read the message."

"Walley!" Mary exclaimed. She didn't know if she was more put out about him reading the officer's note or that he had tricked her into reading from the Bible.

"Master Devia is bringing more troops from the west. In a few days, a huge army will march on Waterfront. Someone has to warn Philip as soon as possible."

Mary turned pale. "Did you run straight here?" she asked.

"No." Walley grinned. "I made sure several men saw me near the river. I hid along the docks and used back alleys until I came to your house. I couldn't leave town without knowing …"

Mary pulled the ragged boy close. "Thank you, Walley," she said, "but you have stayed too long. They could come at any moment. You must leave at once!"

"Me?" Walley asked. "You're coming too, aren't you?"

"I'm afraid I'm too weak, Walley," Mary said. "I could never endure such a walk."

"But I can't leave without you!" Walley stated.

"Walley, I just got out of bed this morning for the first time in days. I can't walk all the way to Waterfront."

"Can you walk around the room?" Walley asked.

"I suppose," Mary said. "But what does that have to do with it?"

"Everything," Walley said. "We can't possibly get to Waterfront tonight anyway. If you can walk around the room, that's a start. Once you've started, the Holy Spirit will give you the strength to continue. But we have to start."

"Very well," Mary said, "but I'm afraid I will only slow you down."

"Let's worry about that later," Walley said. "We need to get a good drink before we leave. Will you need anything else?" He turned apprehensive eyes on her. They both remembered his last invitation to leave Capri. She had not been able to leave her "things" then.

Touching Walley's arm, Mary whispered, "I won't need anything else."

Mary's dress blended with the night. Walley had persuaded her to remove her white lace collar. Now she was glad she had. A pigeon, startled by their passage, fluttered into the night sky, its white wings shining brightly. "Mary," she scolded herself, "you are just going to have to learn to trust and obey. Stop trying to insert your own will into everything."

Holding Walley's hand, she was amazed that her feet stayed beneath her. She seemed to grow stronger as she walked. She knew weariness would set in soon, but so far, so good.

The alley behind her house opened into a residential square where all the homes were surrounded by very tall fences. Together they passed unseen through the shadows.

"We'll have to cross the street here," Walley whispered. "Can you run?"

"I'll try," Mary said, lifting her skirt to her knees. She waited for Walley's signal and then darted across the street and into some trees.

She was winded but able to catch her breath as they slipped from tree to tree. Another sprint brought them near the eastern edge of town.

Walley stopped suddenly in front of her.

"Whatever—" she began. But Walley shushed her so fast she held her tongue. They leaned against a ruin of a shed, and suddenly Mary stopped breathing. She could hear footsteps coming down the street. Walley motioned her to get down, and her knees had barely touched the earth when two men passed within twenty feet of them.

The two glanced at each other and breathed deeply. Walley crept to the corner of the shed and examined the street.

"It looks clear," he whispered. "The next alley opens onto the road to Waterfront."

Mary searched her memory, but she was quite sure the lad was correct.

"Remember," Walley said, "if anything happens to me, you keep going. Find someone loyal to Philip Stafford, and warn him of attack."

"Why are you telling me this, Walley?" Mary quizzed.

"Because Philip must be warned, and my task is nearly over," Walley said.

"What are you talking about?" Mary demanded.

"I only have one more race to run!" Walley grinned. "The street looks clear. Are you ready to run?"

Mary was upset and confused, but there was no more time for questions. She nodded.

Together they stepped from the shadows and into the street. They did not run but walked briskly. Mary thought they had made it, but then she heard a shout behind her.

"Halt! Who goes there?"

Walley pushed her into the shadows. "Run!" he whispered. "I'll draw them off."

"Walley!" she gasped, but he was gone.

"I'm here, slowpokes!" Walley shouted to the guards.

Mary could not believe her ears or eyes. Walley stood in the middle of the street, shouting at the guards. He never once looked back at her but dashed farther into the street.

She knew she should run, but she stood transfixed. How could she leave Walley now?

Two men rushed past her hiding spot as they pursued Walley. "Halt!" one cried. "Halt or I'll shoot!"

"Run, Walley," Mary whispered. She could see the lad racing for the stone fence that surrounded Master Johnson's estate. The fence was much higher than Walley's head, and Mary began to fret. *He'll never be able to clear that wall*, she thought. *He'll be trapped!*

Walley reached the wall and jumped. His hands caught the upper layer of stone, and he scrambled quickly over the top.

Mary drew a deep breath, gathered her skirt to her knees, and fled into the night.

CHAPTER 49

Stonewall

Gandrel had been found dead at his home, and he had not died of old age. Multiple stab wounds covered his body, and his knuckles were skinned and bloody as if he had put up a good fight before going down.

"I want a full investigation," Philip demanded. "Gandrel's death must not go unpunished!"

Clarence Tiel was young and had no experience with murder. Indeed, he had only worked in the constable's office a little over three weeks. "But, sir," he said, "we don't know anything."

"Talk to his neighbors! Ask everyone he did business with! I want to know who killed my friend!" Philip shouted angrily.

"Easy, Philip!" Rhoop interrupted. "The lad is young!"

"Look, Rhoop, someone is planning our demise," Philip exclaimed. "There's a bounty on my life, you've been threatened, and Gandrel is dead! Where will this end? We have to find the culprit!"

Rhoop didn't respond. He knew Philip would eventually get his emotions under control.

Katherine had been with Philip when he'd received the news of Gandrel's death. She couldn't help wondering if her cousin Mercinor Gammel had had anything to do with it, but murder?

She listened to more questions and fewer answers before rising to leave.

"Where are you going?" Philip asked.

"Home," she said. "I'm not accomplishing anything here."

"Katherine, you can't go out tonight." Philip was gentle but firm.

"Well, I can't stay here," she argued.

"I'm afraid I agree with Philip, Lady Katherine," Rhoop inserted. "It seems much too dangerous to send you out after dark."

"Katherine, you are in danger because of me," Philip said sadly. "All my closest friends are in danger."

Katherine turned away. *Is a close friend all I am to you?* she wondered.

"It wouldn't be right to stay," she said quietly.

Rhoop eyed the girl closely. "If propriety is your problem, you may stay in the barracks with the refugee children. I'm sure they could use a helping hand."

Katherine's eyes began to sparkle. "Could I?"

Both men nodded.

"Could you send someone to my father's house to let them know where I am?" she asked.

"With pleasure."

"Where is the old man?" the voice asked.

"Dead!" Mercinor snapped. "He wouldn't come peaceably." Gammel wondered how he'd ever gotten mixed up in this. He was sick of these clandestine meetings in the dark, never seeing a human face, only hearing a voice.

"Can't you do anything right?" the voice asked.

Mercinor bristled, but he held his tongue in check.

"Get the girl!" the voice demanded.

"What girl?" Mercinor asked, stalling.

"Don't be stupid. Philip Stafford's girlfriend! We might be able to control him if we have her," the voice said.

Mercinor tarried. He didn't like Katherine, but turning her over to this voice in the dark was unthinkable.

"Do we have the wrong man for the job?" the voice asked.

"What do you mean?" Mercinor snapped. "I'll do it!"

"Prove it! Bring Katherine here tomorrow night, no excuses. And she'd better be alive!" The dark figure turned and disappeared into the night.

"Pushy old buzzard!" Mercinor grumbled. Being near the Tapestry Inn, he decided a little Barleyman brew might calm his nerves. Turning, he disappeared inside.

Philip and Katherine rode their horses slowly through the streets of Waterfront. Wheat harvest was complete, and people were readying themselves for the barley harvest. The atmosphere was much calmer than it had been during the riotous days after rumors of John Stafford's death had washed across the nation like a destroying cancer.

This was Philip's first day away from harvest, and he was taking advantage of the opportunity to see how things were going elsewhere among the people. However, Katherine was determined that the day should not be all work. When they reached the outskirts of town, she slapped her mount with the reins and shouted, "Race you to the top of the hill!"

Philip wasn't ready for her challenge, but when Katherine raced by, his gelding responded. Philip's horse, Shadow, was the fastest horse in Northglen, and he would never settle for second place in any race.

The earth flashed beneath Philip, and in a few moments Shadow had passed Katherine, leaving her far behind.

Though Philip pulled on the reins, Shadow ran undaunted toward the towering hills north and west of Waterfront. From far behind, they heard Katherine whistle, and Shadow began to slow his pace. Philip drew rein and was about to stop when Katherine thundered past, shouting, "What's the matter, slowpokes?"

Philip grinned and followed the saucy girl. Once again, Shadow took up the challenge. Soon they were neck and neck with Katherine's horse.

They slowed when they came to a small meadow, and there they walked their horses for a few minutes before dismounting. "You should pay more attention to your horse, Philip," Katherine teased.

"He slowed for your whistle," Philip said. "I didn't know he would do that."

"He won't for everyone," Katherine said, smiling. "Only for me."

"Really!" Philip cried in mock dismay. "Have you been teaching my horse bad manners?" he asked.

Katherine gently stroked Shadow's flaring nostrils. "He can run like the wind, Philip." Her eyes shone with admiration.

"Yes," Philip admitted. "It felt like I was flying."

"You darling," Katherine murmured, laying her head on the gelding's neck. Shadow playfully nipped at her shoulder. She straightened and shook her finger. "Now, behave yourself, Shadow."

Philip smiled. Katherine loved horses as much as life itself. Suddenly he wanted to hold her. Philip had always enjoyed Katherine's friendship, her laughter and frolics, but today he wanted more. He wanted to capture her joy, her life, her heart.

Katherine sensed that something was different. Tossing her braids, she met his eyes and then quickly turned away.

"I—I'm sorry, Katherine," Philip stammered.

"Sorry for what?" she asked, never taking her eyes from Philip's gelding.

"I'm not sure," Philip said. "I guess I was afraid."

"Afraid of what?"

"Afraid of my thoughts," Philip finished.

"Philip, you don't have a bad thought in your body."

Philip stepped close, and Katherine turned to meet him. The wind tossed stray hairs across her face, and her eyes sparkled like stars in a midnight sky.

"Katherine, I … " Philip began.

Katherine closed her eyes. It seemed her dreams would come true.

Suddenly the breeze carried the distant bray of a trumpet to their ears. Katherine jumped as Philip moved toward the horses. "There's trouble in town."

Philip and Katherine traded horses before racing back to town, and Katherine felt right at home on Shadow's back. She did think it strange to see Philip riding her little gray mare. They hurried out of the hills, and once they hit the flats, they raced toward the outskirts of town.

The sun was low in the western sky when Philip slowed Katherine's mare to a trot and swung to the ground. "Katherine," he called, "go straight to Stonewall. Tell Rhoop to send Peter with half the garrison!"

Katherine nodded, watching as Philip strapped on his armor. The young man turned to her. "Shadow bears you well."

"He's wonderful to ride, Philip. Thank you for the opportunity." Katherine started to dismount, but Philip stopped her.

"Don't get down, Katherine. Shadow is yours," he said.

"What?"

"Shadow can outrun almost anything on four legs, and I'm hoping he can keep you out of danger," Philip said.

"But you can't give him away," Katherine protested. "He's your horse!"

"He's not mine," Philip said with a smile. "No one owns that horse. He is his own master, Katherine, and I think he's chosen you."

Katherine tried to blink back the tears that threatened to spill from her eyes. Stroking Shadow's powerful neck, she watched Philip lift his shield from the saddle and strap it to his arm. She thought he looked a little silly.

He was a farmer, not a warrior. Weapons looked out of place on his solid but gentle body.

Finding her voice, she asked, "Won't you need Shadow worse than I do?" Silently she wished the great horse would carry Philip far away from danger.

"I won't need a horse, Katherine. I'll be on foot."

"Why?"

"Because everyone else will be on foot," Philip responded. He wrapped his huge hands around hers. "Katherine, will you do something for me?"

"Of course, I will, Philip," she said. "I'll ride into battle at your side, if you wish." She actually considered herself a better candidate for battle than Philip.

"No." Philip smiled. "What I'm going to ask of you is harder than that."

Katherine frowned. "What is it, Philip?" She could not imagine what horrible task he was about to ask of her.

"I want you to pray," Philip answered. "Ask the Lord to protect Amity and bring dismay to our enemies."

"Pray?" Katherine asked, a bit crestfallen.

Philip noted her disappointment. "It's a harder task than you might think."

Katherine squeezed his hand. "Of course I'll pray for you, Philip."

"Katherine, I don't think you realize what a difficult task I'm giving you. I may do battle on the field, but so will you. Unseen forces will keep you so busy you may forget to pray. They will discourage you until you feel everything is lost. The devil will try to sidetrack you in as many ways as he can. But you can overcome him! You must do battle to be victorious in prayer."

Katherine bit her lip. She was thoroughly taken aback. Apparently the role of a prayer warrior was harder than she realized. Maybe she didn't fully understand prayer or the power of the devil to hinder her.

Philip noted the change in her attitude. "Thank you, Katherine." His lips touched her fingers, and he turned away.

Katherine bit her lip. Was she to be dismissed so easily?

Suddenly Philip turned back. "Katherine."

In an instant she was off Shadow's back and into Philip's strong arms. "Oh, Philip!" she cried. "I'm so afraid for you. Please don't go!"

"I have to go, Katherine," Philip responded. "The people of Amity need me. But don't worry. The Lord will keep us safe."

Katherine wanted to believe that, but her faith seemed so small.

"Can you pray with me?" Philip asked.

Obediently Katherine bowed her head, but her mind drifted back to those brief moments far out in the country when Philip had held her in his arms. Suddenly her mind came back to the present, and she heard Philip pray, "Not our will, but Your will be done."

Suddenly a terrible thought struck her. *What if it was the Lord's plan that Philip should die? How could she accept that?* Opening her eyes, she studied the man before her. In minutes he might be fighting for his life.

She hugged Philip tighter. She could sense his impatience, but still she clung to him. When she finally released him, her cheeks were damp with tears.

Philip gently brushed her cheek. "You will pray, won't you?" he asked.

Katherine nodded without speaking. Fumbling for Shadow's stirrups, she swung into the saddle. Philip reached for her. Their fingers touched, and their eyes met. And then he was off, running toward town. A horn was blowing, and Katherine could imagine the clash of weapons and the sounds of war.

In the shadow of some trees not far from the river, Mercinor Gammel lowered his spyglass and frowned. "It's working," he said. Even as he spoke, his conscience smote him. *How can I betray my own cousin?* he wondered. *Still, she asked for it by siding with Philip. He's out of power now, and I can't help it if something bad happens to her.*

"Great." His companion grinned.

"You keep Philip busy," Mercinor said. "Break windows, burn houses, whatever it takes. There is no real need for violence. There will be enough of that when Jan DeKlerk gets here. But if you get a clear shot at Philip, take it. The reward money stands until tomorrow."

"What are you going to do?" his companion asked.

"I'll get Katherine."

Katherine rode Shadow and led her mare through the darkened streets of Waterfront. She thought about how large the town seemed tonight. Stonewall was only a distant tower in the darkening sky.

Suddenly a door opened on a nearby cottage. Candle light filtered into the dark street, and she saw an old man step from the house. He turned and spoke to a girl inside. "Calm the little ones, and do not open this door to anyone! Do you understand?"

"Yes, Papa," the girl said. "Must you go?"

"Amity is in need," the old man said.

"But—" she began.

"I'll be fine," he said. "The bugle calls, and I must follow."

"Oh, Papa!" The girl began to cry. "It's just that … I love you!"

Katherine watched the old man hug his daughter. She felt awkward to be a witness to such a tender parting, but the street was narrow, and to pass would cause greater interruption.

"There, there," the old man whispered. "I shan't be gone long."

"Papa, I wish you would stay," the girl begged.

"You need not fear," the old man replied. "I can't go too far with this old body." The old man released his daughter and turned into the street.

Katherine was humbled by the old man's determination, but she was alarmed as well. The staff in his hand was the only weapon he carried. Philip was in trouble if this was his only aid.

Turning around, the old man was surprised to see Katherine. Suddenly aware of his attention, she began to pass. Awkwardly she said, "Thank you for supporting Philip."

The old man stepped back to let her pass and said, "It's my pleasure, ma'am."

Katherine made a mental note of the house and its surroundings. She was going to pay this family a visit when life settled down again.

Riding on, lost in thought, Katherine came to the Greenway. A movement along the river caught her attention, but she paid it little heed. It was probably a riverboatman tying down his load.

Everything seemed quiet and peaceful. Then suddenly someone shouted, "Halt! Who goes there?"

Without thinking, she responded, "Katherine Gammel. I'm seeking passage to—" Her voice broke off. Had she said too much already?

"Katherine?" a voice asked from the darkness.

She recognized the voice. "Mercinor, is that you?" she called, relief taking the edge from her voice.

A dark figure approached. "Katherine, why are you riding alone?" Mercinor asked.

"Mercinor!" Katherine exclaimed, seeing a fearful glint in the man's eyes. "Is something wrong?"

"I should say," Mercinor lied. "Haven't you heard? Some of Philip's men got into it with old Rhoop and deserted. They stormed out of Stonewall and burned the tug, and now they are terrorizing Waterfront."

"No!" Katherine exclaimed. "But Mercinor, I have to see Rhoop right away."

"Well, there's no crossing the river on this side. The tug is gone, and I wouldn't send my worst enemy down there right now."

"What can I do?" Katherine asked in growing desperation. She wondered if Rhoop was still in charge. Would he be able to send Philip any help?

"I have a raft on the river, Katherine," Mercinor said casually. "I could take you and your horses to Sebring. The tug is still intact on that side."

Katherine felt a great relief. She guessed that if men had had to break out of Stonewall, it must mean there were still men loyal to Philip inside. She could at least deliver Philip's message to Rhoop.

"All right," she agreed, and she slipped from Shadow's massive back.

Leaving the dusty road, they half walked and half slid down the grassy bank to the river. The smell of Barleyman wafted on the night air, and several unsavory chaps reached out to help Katherine and the horses onto a large raft.

"You didn't tell me you had a crew," Katherine said calmly, but she felt a sudden sense of alarm. Hadn't she always been suspicious of her cousin? Yet here she was, stepping onto his raft with a dozen or so of his thugs in the dark of night. *Katherine*, she chided herself, *you are a fool!*

"I've never learned to run a raft by myself," Mercinor said easily. "They're so big and unwieldy. The river always shifts them around."

That's the first thing a riverman learns, Katherine thought, but she kept her tongue in check. She didn't like where she was, but she didn't want to make her situation worse.

"Where are we taking her, boss?" one of Mercinor's men asked. The question was benign, but it frightened Katherine.

"The docks," Mercinor replied.

The docks! An alarm sounded in Katherine's mind. It was the one part of Sebring where she was afraid to travel after dark.

The raft was about midriver when Katherine began to devise a plan. Men were positioned evenly around the edges of the raft. Each pulled on a long rope or manned a long pole to maneuver the raft across the river. If she were to bolt on her own, they would be sure to grab her, but what if Shadow leaped off the raft, and she merely went with him?

Katherine had watched Philip train Shadow to leap forward when he clucked his tongue. She didn't know if Shadow would bolt for her or not, but she decided to give it a try. Reaching up and gripping Shadow's saddle firmly, she clicked her tongue.

Everything happened at once. Shadow leaped forward, taking Katherine and three men with him into the river. Though her plan had worked, she was mentally unprepared for their dive into the water. Shadow sank deep into the river, taking Katherine down with him, and she thought they would never feel air around them again.

However, once their heads broke the water's surface, she could feel the gelding swimming powerfully toward Waterfront's shore. She could also hear Mercinor shouting, "Don't shoot! We want her alive!"

Then she heard her cousin shout something that chilled her to the bone. "Hey, Slavich, head her off!" Peering about in the darkness, Katherine could see another raft upstream suddenly veer straight for her. *Help us, Lord,* she prayed. *We have to reach the shore!*

Shadow swam like a champion while Katherine trailed in his wake. Poles sloshed in the water as the raft drew near. "Come on, Shadow," Katherine whispered.

"There she is!" someone shouted. "Give me a rope!"

"Faster, Shadow!" Katherine begged. Suddenly they jolted to a stop. Katherine felt mud beneath her feet. Shadow flailed for footing and then, with a great surge, leaped from the water.

Dangling like a wet noodle beside the great horse, Katherine watched men leap ashore.

"Don't let her escape!" Mercinor shouted.

Still clinging to the saddle, Katherine shouted, "Run!" to the horse. She tried to swing into the saddle, but Shadow was heaving himself up the steep river bank and dragging Katherine through the thorns and brambles along the bank. With the saddle slamming into her face and arms, and thorns ripping at her soaked clothing, Katherine thought it a miracle when she reached the Greenway still gripping the saddle horn.

"Steady!" she whispered, setting her foot firmly in the stirrups. Bruised and bleeding, she swung herself into the saddle.

Checking her grip, Katherine shouted, "Now!" and Shadow plunged forward into the darkness.

She could hear Mercinor shout from the river, "Stop her!" and several dark shapes appeared on the road before her. Shadow never slowed his pace but plowed directly into the men on the path, sending them sprawling.

Someone swore.

Katherine smiled, but her satisfaction was brief. There were horsemen on the road ahead, blocking her path. Mercinor's men were behind. Without a moment's hesitation, she turned Shadow off the road and into the briars and thorns of Northglen Forest.

CHAPTER 50

New Faith

I've got to catch my breath, Mary thought, leaning heavily against a tree. She was exhausted but thrilled to have come so far. *Thank You for giving me such strength, Lord,* she prayed silently.

As she caught her breath, Mary considered her surroundings. She was deep in a forest known for its stories of ghosts and goblins. *And why am I here?* she thought. *I'm here because a ten-year-old boy talked me into leaving home.*

A few days ago, she would have cursed Walley's desertion of her, but not tonight. *Lord, be with Walley and keep him safe,* she thought. *Thank You for sending him into my life.*

Mary's change of attitude was remarkable. For the first time, she had begun to trust someone stronger than herself.

Where to now, Lord? she wondered. It still felt strange to talk to her heavenly Father this way, but He seemed to listen and answer.

Her thoughts were shattered by a commotion in the trees some distance away. Peering out from the tangled branches around her, she saw a huge beast crash through the thickets and stop on the path. It was much too dark to determine what kind of animal it was, but when it turned and began to move in her direction, she heard the distinct clop of hooves. Mary was sure it was a horse but unsure if it had a rider and, if it did, whether that rider was friend or foe.

Mary closed her eyes and silently prayed, *Dear Lord, You have brought me this far. Keep me safe.* To her dismay, the clopping of hooves stopped on the road opposite the tree behind which she was hiding.

Holding her breath, Mary opened her eyes and peeked around the tree. A huge horse stood several feet away, quietly watching her. Though the horse was saddled, she did not think it bore a rider. Silently Mary crept from her hiding place and stepped onto the road.

"Hello there," she whispered. She stopped and smiled. She must be losing her mind. She was talking to a horse. At this close range, the horse seemed huge, and it was black as coal. She watched as the creature suddenly swung his head around and nipped at his saddle.

"Does it hurt you?" she whispered, thinking the animal might be uncomfortable with the saddle. And then a crazy idea hit her. *Maybe the horse wants to take me somewhere!*

What should I do, Lord? Mary asked. *Do You want this horse to take me somewhere?*

The idea seemed ludicrous. Mary had never ridden a horse in her life. How could she start tonight, in the dark, on an unfamiliar road and on such a huge animal as this?

Suddenly the great animal swung his head around and nipped at his saddle again. Mary shook her head and reached for the great animal's flaring nostrils. They felt as soft as silk, and she suddenly had an incredible longing to ride this animal.

"All right, Lord," she whispered. "If he'll let me get on, I'll let You lead him." To her amazement, the horse stood perfectly still.

Mary now faced a dilemma. She had never been around horses, and she had no idea how to mount them. With trembling hands, she began to search the great animal and soon found what appeared to be the rung of a ladder suspended beneath the saddle, high in the air. She thought that might be the way up, but she could not raise her foot high enough. Turning, she spied a stump several feet away, and she stepped up on its rough surface. Now, to her dismay, the horse was too far away.

"Here, horsey," she whispered. To her amazement, the great animal snorted, stepped near the stump, and stood patiently, watching Mary.

Carefully Mary placed one foot in the stirrup and swung her free leg over the saddle. The top of the saddle had a handle, and she gripped that handle for dear life. She was no sooner seated when the horse turned and began to canter up the road.

He had not gone far before he turned off the road and into the thickets. Limbs raked Mary's arms and legs, and briars near the ground tore at her skirt. "What are you doing?" she cried.

She had barely finished speaking when the great animal stopped. Mary looked into the shrubbery and saw the crumpled form of a human. Slipping awkwardly from the saddle, she waded through the brush and stared in horror. It was a woman!

Suddenly the woman stirred, and Mary stepped back. "Are you all right?" she asked softly.

The woman opened her eyes and tried to sit up. She was rubbing her head. "Where am I?" she asked.

"I don't really know," Mary said. "We are somewhere in a forest, and apparently your horse brought me here to you."

"Shadow!" the woman exclaimed, beginning to stir. "Where is he?"

"He's here!" Mary assured her as the woman struggled to get to her feet.

"Please help me to Shadow," the woman begged.

"Are you able to ride?" Mary asked.

"I think so," the woman answered. "I must have hit my head on a tree limb. I don't think anything is broken, but I really don't feel very good."

"You have a nasty-looking cut on your forehead," Mary cautioned.

The woman put her fingers gingerly to her head and winced. "Ouch!" She groaned. "Maybe I should sit a bit longer," she said, slowly sinking to the ground. "By the way, my name is Katherine Gammel. Who are you?"

The ladies shared their stories for several minutes, but as Mary finished detailing why Walley had encouraged her to leave Capri, Katherine stood up. "We have to warn Philip," she said. "Can you ride?"

"Not very well," Mary admitted. "Your horse brought me here, so if the Lord is willing, He may take me farther."

"Good!" Katherine said. "We'll ride double. Do you want the front or the back?"

Mary was puzzled. *The front or back of what?* she wondered. "You choose," she said hopefully.

"Fine!" Katherine said. "I'll take the saddle, and you can ride behind me." Even though she was still a bit shaky, Katherine used the stirrup and stepped lightly into the saddle.

Mary was impressed and a bit chagrined. She still could not get her foot as high as the stirrup.

"How did you manage before?" Katherine asked.

"I stood on a stump, and your horse came to me," Mary said and smiled. "I really think the Lord wanted us to meet."

"I think you're right," Katherine mused. "Here, grab the saddle horn with your left hand and give me your right. I'll pull you up, and when your foot reaches the stirrup, get a hold and swing your right leg over."

It was awkward, but in the end Mary finally gained a berth behind Katherine on the massive back of Shadow. The saddle trappings cut into her emaciated thighs, but she refused to complain. She was, after all, now above the worst of the thorns. Neither woman spoke as Shadow stepped through the brambles.

When they reached the road, Mary asked, "Which way should we go?"

"If what Walley told you is true," Katherine said, "we must head east toward Waterfront. That was where I last saw Philip."

The women followed the path through Northglen forest for what seemed hours. Mary nearly fell asleep, and Katherine wasn't much better. Katherine had given Shadow the reins. She merely clung to the saddle, letting Shadow take them where he wanted. Mary gipped Katherine so tight that her ribs hurt, but neither woman complained.

"Where are we?" Mary's voice startled Katherine to wakefulness.

Katherine shook her head to clear her mind. Shadow had stopped his steady plod and was standing as still as stone. The ladies looked across a large meadow dotted with campfires.

"Are they friends or enemies?" Mary asked.

"I don't know."

"Why did the horse stop?" Mary asked. "Is he afraid?"

"I don't know that either!" Katherine whispered.

"If he's afraid, we should turn back," Mary whispered firmly.

"You place a lot of trust in this horse, don't you?" Katherine asked.

"I can't explain it," Mary said, "but I think the Lord is leading him. Walley sent me on a mission to warn Philip, and I don't want to make a mistake now."

"All right," Katherine agreed, gathering Shadow's reins in her hands.

"Don't move!" a voice from the darkness demanded. Both women froze. "You can't leave without speaking to the Master of Amity!"

Katherine felt Mary's fingers tighten on her ribs. Her own heart was beating fast. She looked around, half expecting to see Mercinor somewhere nearby.

An old man stepped from the shadows and grabbed the horse's bridle.

He stepped into the light and peered up at the women. "What are you doing here?" he exclaimed when he saw Katherine.

Katherine looked in astonishment at the weathered old man she had seen earlier this very evening in Waterfront.

"Who is it?" a voice behind the old man asked.

"Just a couple of girls!" the old man said.

"No matter," the voice said. "Philip must speak with anyone who disturbs the camp."

Katherine felt Mary's fingers ease their grip on her aching ribs, and they both sighed with relief. As the old man began his slow journey down the hill, Katherine gently reached up and patted the bobbing neck of her weary mount. Shadow had brought them safely home.

As they passed rows of tents, Katherine could hear voices saying, "It's Katherine Gammel!" She felt like she had been well introduced when they finally stopped, and strong hands lifted her and Mary from Shadow's back.

"Katherine!" Philip's familiar voice spoke. "Are you all right?"

The women were settled near a small fire, and Katherine realized for the first time how cold she was. She held her hands out to the flames, and her teeth began to chatter. "The fire feels really good," she managed to whisper.

Philip wrapped a blanket around her shoulders. "You must be freezing," he said.

Katherine glanced at her attire and blushed. Her skirt hung in ribbons around her legs, and her top barely covered her torso. "I'm sorry," she whispered. "I didn't know I looked such a fright."

"Hang the looks," Philip said. "Are you all right?"

"I think so." Katherine smiled.

"Where on earth have you been?" Philip asked again.

"We've ridden through part of Northglen Forest."

"Northglen?" Philip was incredulous. "Why?"

"I was trying to escape from Mercinor," Katherine said.

"Your cousin?" Philip was astonished. "What was he doing?"

"I'm not sure ... but I think he was kidnapping me!" Katherine said, suddenly confused.

"If you please, sir," Mary interjected. "You must move your troops at once. Master Devia has moved a large number of troops into Capri, and they could attack at any minute."

Philip looked at the woman who had ridden in with Katherine, and his jaw dropped. He glanced at Katherine for some explanation, but Katherine was speechless. The firelight clearly revealed the woman who had ridden with her through the forest. Her "friend" was nothing more than a skeleton covered with skin. Large masses of disheveled hair fell from her skull, and her eyes were sunken almost from view.

Her mission complete, Mary toppled with exhaustion.

Philip rushed to her side and cradled her emaciated body in his arms. He looked to Katherine for some explanation, but there was no answer. Katherine had fainted.

"Where is Katherine?" the voice whispered in the darkness.

"She got away," Mercinor said flatly. In truth, he was glad she had escaped. He was beginning to resent this whole arrangement.

"You idiot!" the voice hissed. Mercinor heard a blade clear its sheath, but he did not flinch. "Look, you imbecile, I'll give you one more chance. Meet with Philip and persuade him to surrender. If you succeed, both you and Philip will save your lives."

Mercinor thought of a stinging rebuttal but decided to hold his tongue. The man's sword disappeared, and he heard several other weapons sliding quietly back into hiding. He was glad he had kept quiet.

As his hooded contact disappeared into darkness, Mercinor turned his back to the docks. "The Two Maids Tavern and a mug of Barleyman should cure my ills," he thought. Stepping toward the dimly lit grog shop, he was grateful to put the shadows behind him, even if only for a while.

CHAPTER 51

Choices

Philip accompanied the men carrying Katherine and her friend until they reached the edge of Waterfront, and then he returned to the camp. *What did that strange woman mean about Devia's army being about to destroy us?* he wondered as he walked. He was nearly back to his quarters when he saw Shadow stomping restlessly near his tent. He stooped to examine the cuts on the great horse's legs and belly and then began the slow process of bathing each wound and rubbing balm into each cut. Several men assisted him. They were nearly finished when a youth hurried toward him and said, "Mercinor Gammel is waiting to speak with you, sir."

"Mercinor?" Philip asked. He was the last person Philip had expected to see. He did not understand Katherine's story, but if it were true, he would need to be wary of Mercinor.

"Give me a few minutes to finish here, and then bring him to my tent," Philip said.

"Yes, sir," the lad responded and walked quickly away.

Philip had just sent Shadow away with another lad when Mercinor Gammel appeared in the campfire light. "Good evening, Mercinor." Philip tried to sound genial. "What brings you out so late tonight?"

"I'm sorry for the intrusion, Philip," Mercinor said rapidly, "but I wanted to warn you."

"Warn me of what?" Philip asked casually.

"Your doom!" Mercinor said with flair. "You and your men will be slaughtered tomorrow morning."

Is Mercinor trying to frighten me into surrender? Philip wondered. If what Katherine's friend said was true, Mercinor might just be telling the truth. "I know," he said calmly.

"You—what?" Mercinor stammered. "But how?"

"A woman from Capri just informed me. You have merely confirmed her report," Philip said coolly.

Mercinor stood with his mouth agape.

Philip eyed Mercinor and then continued. "I don't suppose you know who else I've seen?"

"I have no idea," Mercinor grumbled. Philip noticed Mercinor's shoulders sag and his enthusiasm ebb. It looked as if Mercinor's pride had taken a blow to know that a woman had stolen his thunder.

"I've just been chatting with your cousin," Philip goaded.

Mercinor jerked to attention. "Who?" he asked.

"Katherine Gammel," Philip stated flatly. "She is your cousin, is she not?"

"Yes, but …" Mercinor began.

"I don't suppose you know where Katherine has been, do you?" Philip asked.

"No, I—" Mercinor stammered.

"I didn't think you would. I doubt you have seen Katherine for days, have you?"

"As a matter of fact—"

"She escaped from your raft by jumping into the river and fleeing into Northglen Forest!" Philip interrupted.

Even in the firelight, Philip could see the color drain from Mercinor's face.

"Why did you tell her the tug had been burned?" Philip demanded. "Where were you taking her, Mercinor? You nearly scared your cousin out of her mind!"

"No, Philip!" Mercinor shouted, waving his hands for Philip to stop. "You've got to believe me. I was only trying to protect her! She is in danger every minute she is near you. Philip, don't you realize Master Devia is out to get you? He'll destroy everyone who is close to you!"

Philip became quiet.

"Look at the threats against Rhoop!" Mercinor stated. "And look at old Gandrel; he's dead, isn't he? Everyone knows Katherine is sweet on you. I was afraid she would be the next target. Do you know where she is now?"

"Stonewall," Philip said, looking away. Maybe Katherine had been wrong about Mercinor. Maybe it was all a mistake.

"Well, at least she'll be safe for a while," Mercinor began. "But how long can your fortress stand against the world, Philip. Look around! Amity is changing. You and your men cannot stand against Master Devia's army."

"I know," Philip said quietly.

"Well?" Mercinor said. "What are you going to do about it?"

"Nothing!" Philip said.

"Nothing!" Mercinor shouted. "You can't be serious! They will kill you and your men, Philip! Why don't you surrender quietly, and maybe Devia will offer you clemency."

"Aren't you forgetting that my father committed Amity into my care? I can't just surrender," Philip argued.

"Philip," Mercinor pleaded. "Think of your men and the people of Waterfront and Sebring. Add to those people all the refugees who have come here for protection. If you resist Master Devia, there will be war, and thousands of innocent people could be killed. You don't want their deaths on your conscience, do you? You just need to be a little more tolerant—"

Philip cut him off. "More tolerant! Evil flourishes in the name of tolerance. It is high time someone took a stand for what is right. Right now I'm finished with tolerance!"

Mercinor was aghast. "Philip, this posturing will only get you killed. You have to think about the good of the nation. If you want to die, that is your choice, but you can't ask others to die with you!"

Philip remained silent.

"Look, Philip," Mercinor pleaded. "Come to terms with Master Devia. Everyone else has, and they aren't faring too badly. In fact, things are going quite well in Zaraphath and Deep Delving. The mines are busier than ever. River traffic has never been so good."

"Is commerce everything to you, Mercinor?" Philip asked coldly. "The woman who fled Capri tonight was terrified of Devia's rule!"

"I don't believe it!" Mercinor snapped. He sounded sure of himself, but his face showed a hint of doubt.

"The woman had been starved and abused and was in no shape to travel, but she fled rather than spend one more day under Devia's rule. How can you believe that everything will be all right once Devia takes over?" Philip leaned forward. "You've been listening to a lie, Mercinor! Someone promised you riches and power if the Stafford family was overthrown." He inched closer to Katherine's cousin.

"No!" Mercinor pleaded, backing away.

"You planned the attack on Katherine, didn't you? Did you kill Gandrel yourself, or was it one of your men?" Philip accused.

"Philip," Mercinor begged, "you have no proof. You can't establish—"

"I have proof enough!" Philip shouted. "Katherine's been right about you all along!"

"Philip, wait!" Mercinor fell to his knees, lifting his arms before him. "Katherine and I have never seen eye to eye. Don't listen to her!"

"I haven't listened to her enough!" Philip roared. "It was a wicked thing you did, chasing your own cousin into Northglen Forest. Katherine is fortunate to be alive!"

"Look, Philip," Mercinor began again. "I didn't mean—"

"Get out of here!" Philip shouted. "Go back to your master and find out how merciful and kind he is! I charge you with only one thing, Mercinor Gammel. Don't ever go near Katherine again!"

"Philip ..." Mercinor protested.

"Be gone!" Philip shouted.

Mercinor suddenly rose to his feet and stood tall, his face hardened with hatred. "You are going to regret this," he hissed. Turning away, his eyes flashed in the firelight.

"Shall we stop him?" an old man asked anxiously.

"No," Philip responded. "Leave him alone. He'll receive his reward."

It was still an hour to sunup, and Philip sat holding his head in his hands. Had Mercinor been right? Did he have any right to put innocent men and women into open conflict with Master Devia? He heard a sound and looked up to see Peter Sikes hurrying toward him. "Peter!" Philip called. "What do our scouts report?"

Sikes looked grim. "There is a large army stationed just east of Capri, sir."

"Did the scouts get an estimate of how many were there?" Philip asked.

"They estimated fifteen thousand, sir," Sikes responded.

"How many men do we have, Peter?" Philip asked, already knowing the answer.

"Three hundred, sir!" Peter responded.

"What about our volunteers?" Philip asked.

"The old men, sir?" Peter asked. "I'm not really sure. Quite a few of them went home after serving sentry duty."

Philip smiled. Peter was so by-the-book. A haphazard approach to war didn't sit well with him. Philip wasn't sure he could depend on the old men either, but they were nearly all he had, and the Creator of heaven and earth could use any willing heart. "What do you suggest, Peter?"

"I think we should retreat and defend Stonewall, sir," Peter said without hesitation.

Philip nodded. It was the answer he had expected. "What shall we do with the citizens of Waterfront and Sebring?" he asked.

The young officer suddenly looked at his feet as he answered. "We can prolong the battle if we leave them outside."

"Only prolong, not win?" Philip asked directly.

"Victory against such odds is very slim, sir," Peter responded. "However, we might be able to hold Stonewall until your father returns."

"All right," Philip said as he considered the possibilities.

Peter Sikes looked up expectantly. "Sir?" he questioned.

"It's settled," Philip stated. "I do not know when my father will return, and I refuse to sit like a caged animal inside Stonewall while Devia has his way with the people who have come under my care. Peter, you and I will take our stand against Devia in the open. If we fail, we fail!"

Though the order sealed his fate, Peter Sikes stood unflinching. "Yes, sir!"

"Send a message to Rhoop and tell him to begin evacuating everyone from Waterfront and Sebring into Stonewall immediately," Philip said.

"Yes, sir!"

CHAPTER 52

Taking a Stand

"Peter, divide the men into three companies. I want you on my right and Andrew on my left, with the volunteers gathered behind me. We can block the road to Waterfront unless they cross the river or enter the forest." Philip's orders were crisp and clear.

"Yes, sir!" Peter turned and began to shout orders.

They had marched hard all morning and had reached a place where Northglen forest nearly touched the river. With the field thus narrowed, Philip could block the Greenway and thus deprive Devia of his goal, if only for a while.

Across the small valley, Philip could see a vast army milling about on the distant hillside. While Peter positioned his men, Philip noticed among his company several hundred well-trained soldiers from Stonewall, although most had never seen battle. Behind those men was a gathering of old men clinging to sticks and clubs. Among the volunteers, Philip spied a child.

Beckoning to the boy, Philip asked, "What are you doing here, lad?"

"I came to help fight, sir," the lad said boldly.

Philip frowned. "It may not be a pretty sight."

"I ain't scared!" the boy said with determination.

Philip studied the lad for some moments and then nodded gravely. "All right, but you need to stay in the back. I need my best men back there. Will you do that for me?"

"Yes, sir," the lad said as he turned and marched boldly to the back of the gathering. There were smiles among the men.

"Gentlemen," Philip said, and all eyes turned to him. "We have the enemy right where we want them. It will cost them dearly to proceed beyond this point."

There was a slight murmur among the men as they considered what it would cost each one of them if the enemy moved beyond this point, but Philip continued to speak. "Remember your families. You are here because of them. We need not be afraid, for the Lord is our refuge and our fortress. He shall be our shield and buckler. We will not fear the terror of night or the arrow by day. Though a thousand shall fall at thy side, and ten thousand at thy right hand, yet no evil shall befall thee."

"Let us pray," Philip said, sinking to one knee. Every man took a knee and bowed his head. "Lord, You have promised to protect us if we trust in You. Become a bulwark against our enemies and cover us with Your grace and mercy. Help us stand against all that is wrong. We place our trust in You alone, amen."

There was a quiet murmuring of "amen" among the men, and slowly they arose to take their positions. Something had happened in those few moments on their knees. The men had changed. There was no longer a spirit of fear among them. They had given themselves to the Lord, and however this turned out, they would be with Him. It was with grim determination that they gripped their clubs, spears, and swords.

Philip noted the change and nodded his approval. Quietly he chose twelve men to form a central guard, a bulwark upon which the enemy would fall, and placing himself front and center of that bulwark, he turned to await the onslaught.

Across the valley, Devia's army continued to mill about in confusion. Peter left his position and strode to Philip's side. "What do you make of it, sir? Are they trying to intimidate us with their numbers?"

"I don't know," Philip responded. Then with sudden inspiration, he shouted. "That's it! We'll give them a chance to surrender."

"Sir?" Peter questioned.

Philip didn't answer but rapidly pulled the knapsack from his back and procured a scrap of paper and some ink. Quickly he jotted a note on the paper, folded it in half, and called for the lad near the back.

"Sir?" the lad asked as he approached.

"Would you deliver a message for me?" Philip asked.

"Yes, sir!" the boy said, eager to be of service.

"It will be dangerous," Philip said. "You will have to cross into enemy territory."

"I can do that, sir," the lad stated with confidence.

Philip handed the boy his note and a large white flag. "See the man on the black horse near that cabin?" he asked.

The boy studied the opposite hill for a few moments and then nodded.

"Take this note to that man, and wave the white flag as you go," Philip instructed.

The lad nodded and took off sprinting toward the enemy lines.

"That's Jan DeKlerk, isn't it?" Philip asked Peter.

"I think so," Peter answered. "But, sir, should you have sent a child?"

"He has a flag of parley," Philip answered. "He should be safe enough."

"I hope you're right," Peter responded. "From all I hear, Jan DeKlerk is a treacherous man."

The exuberance on Philip's features faded. "You're right," he muttered. "I've been a fool."

Jan DeKlerk stood in his stirrups. It had taken all morning to move less than one mile. Everything was going wrong.

He watched Philip positioning his men, and he turned to his leading officer. "Who does Stafford think he's fooling? That ragged gathering can never stop me!"

"You're right, sir." Christopher Heims grinned.

Jan glanced over his shoulder as another company of his own men shifted positions. "What the devil is going on?" He directed his question toward Heims.

"I'll check on it, sir," the officer responded.

Jan's henchman was gone only a few minutes before returning. "We have a small problem, sir," he said. "The men from Amity balk at fighting with Stafford's son."

Color crept into Jan's neck and rose to his temples. "We'll see about that!" He wheeled his horse around to face his troops. He felt a sudden thrill as he viewed the massive number of men under his command.

"Men of Amity!" DeKlerk shouted, raising his hand to garner attention. Company commanders shouted orders, and men began to settle. Finally, the vast army grew quiet. "You have heard that Philip Stafford holds Amity for his father. That is not true! John Stafford is dead!" The field had grown quite silent, and Jan DeKlerk continued. "Since your master is dead, why should you serve his son? You are free to choose your own master now!"

Men looked sheepishly at one another. "It would be nice to have a say in things," said one man.

"We already do," said another.

"Well," shouted Jan DeKlerk, "who will rule? Stafford or you?"

"We will!" was the reply, but it was mostly the men dressed in crimson and white who responded. "We will," they cried again, and a few more voices joined their ranks.

"Who?" Jan DeKlerk shouted.

"We will!" The response was stronger this time. "We will, we will, we will!"

"Who will rule Amity?" DeKlerk shouted, waving his sword in the air.

"*We will! We will!*" the men shouted, and their voices nearly shook the ground.

Heims tapped DeKlerk's shoulder. "Sir, they've sent a parley."

Jan whirled about to see a boy racing up the slope, waving a white flag as he ran. "Sir!" the lad shouted as he ran. "A message for the commander!"

Jan rode forward to meet him. "I'll take that," DeKlerk said, reaching for the note.

"Shall I wait for a reply?" the boy asked anxiously.

Jan nodded and opened the note. Slowly his face grew red. Philip was not surrendering. He was granting amnesty to all who threw down their weapons.

Standing in his stirrups, Jan screamed, "Death to you!" across the valley. He ripped the paper to shreds and tossed the pieces into the wind.

The lad turned pale and saw his chance of escape dwindling fast. Turning, he fled toward the stream and the relative safety of Philip's small band of soldiers.

"Kill that boy!" DeKlerk screamed. The men of Amity looked at one another in dismay. The boy had come under a white flag and was carrying no weapons, but two men dressed in crimson pulled arrows from their quivers, placed them on the string, and took aim.

The lad had nearly reached the stream when he caught his foot on a stone and fell headlong to the ground. Two arrows zipped over his head. In a flash the lad was on his feet and racing toward the men behind Philip Stafford.

Philip ran forward. "Come on, lad." Grabbing the boy, he steered the lad through the men to the rear. "Are you all right?" Philip asked.

The lad sank to his knees and began to weep. "I'm so ashamed!" he sobbed. "I shouldn't have run."

"You did the right thing," Philip said gravely. "I was wrong to send you. Jan DeKlerk is more treacherous than I realized. You can run like the wind. If we survive today, I will have much need of your speed and courage."

"Really?" The lad looked up in surprise.

"Absolutely!" Philip smiled and ruffled the lad's curly hair. "You are a good man!"

Their words were cut short as Peter Sikes shouted, "Here they come!"

Philip pushed his way to the front to witness several hundred crimson-clad horsemen forming ranks to begin their charge.

Peter Sikes ran toward his own company, shouting orders as he ran. "Archers, arrows to the string, and wait for my command!"

Philip heard a man near his right shoulder mutter, "I want the one carrying their flag!" He glanced over his shoulder to see an old man with a long sharpened stick in his hand. A fierce light shone in the man's eyes, and age seemed to have fallen from his shoulders.

"He's all yours!" Philip replied, and he braced himself for the onslaught.

The cavalry was dressed in red, and Philip was glad. He would not be fighting against men from Amity, at least for the moment.

Away to Philip's right, Sikes watched as the cavalry came within range. "Fire!" he shouted, and the sky turned dark with deadly projectiles.

One could prepare for life's trials, but until tested, he could never be sure he had learned the right lessons. Philip knew the art and theory of war, but this was the first real test of his skill. With one hand he gripped his sword, with the other his shield. Philip watched the ranks of horsemen thin, and then suddenly they were upon him. There was no time to think, only to react: step, slash, thrust; step, slash, thrust. There were deafening shrieks as horses plunged mindlessly into the fray, casting their burdens wherever they might fall. Men who were whole one moment, were limbless or lifeless the next.

All was chaos for a few moments, and then it was over. The cavalry withdrew to regroup. Philip surveyed his losses. "You!" he shouted. "Move the wounded to the rear." Old men surged forward, and willing hands reached for those in need.

Men were still moving the maimed to the rear when Peter Sikes shouted, "Here they come again!"

Disheartened, Philip returned to his position. He had so few troops. He could ill afford to lose any more.

Jan DeKlerk watched as Philip's men turned the cavalry once again. "It's impossible!" he raged.

Heims merely shook his head.

They were not the only ones watching. The men of Amity serving under Jan DeKlerk stared in disbelief as the cavalry's dwindling numbers gathered to charge again.

"It'll be our turn soon," one man said. "If the cavalry fails, they will call upon us!"

"If horsemen can't get through, how can we?" one man asked.

"Sheer numbers," said another. "Philip can't kill us all!"

Men grew somber. "Should we even fight Philip Stafford?" one man asked. "Does it really matter who rules Amity?"

"Quiet in the ranks!" a crimson-clad horseman shouted nearby. "Get in formation, or I'll put you on report!"

The horseman rode on down the line, and one man spat on the ground. "I'm so sick of that line. Do this or that! If you don't, I'll put you on report! I'm tempted to see if he would!"

"Don't do it!" another man warned. "They'll send you back to work on the wall."

"Boy, I wish I'd never joined DeKlerk!" another man said.

"Time's up!" a man hollered. "We're about to receive marching orders."

The men watched what was left of DeKlerk's cavalry retreat across the stream and climb the hill toward their commanders. Their numbers were few, and though they had made a valiant attempt, they had failed to route Philip.

Within minutes the orders came. There was a massive shift of companies. Men from Amity moved to the front while crimson-clad recruits fell in behind.

"I don't like the way this is shaping up," one man near the front commented. Others nodded, and then they were on the move.

Fifty men abreast, they marched down the hill with Jan DeKlerk and the cavalry in the lead. Their feet trampled the sod and sullied the stream. Scrambling through the muck, men surged up the hill.

Brothers Lance and Loren Newcastle found themselves on the front lines. Strangely, their pace slowed with each step. Ahead of them, the cavalry charged into Philip's lines yet again, and they heard the screams of battle.

Suddenly Lance grabbed his brother's arm. "Loren, there's Dad!"

"Where?" Loren asked.

"Right beside Master Philip," Lance responded.

Loren studied the scene before him and tried to see through the horses and men. "I don't ..." he began, and then he shouted, "You're right! I see him!"

Philip had taken the few minutes between battles to rearrange his men. He had losses, but not as many as he had feared. He was wondering how long they could hold out when he spied an old man with long white hair standing among his men. He did not recognize the man, but he could see that the man was armed only with a silver trumpet in his hand. Before he could ask any questions, he heard Peter Sikes yell, "Here they come again!"

Philip positioned himself for battle and heard Peter shout commands. Arrows flew, and horsemen once again thundered upon the intrepid gathering. Suddenly Philip heard the most beautiful sound: a clarion call, clear and shrill, resounding across the meadow. The enemy advance slowed, and Philip felt a new sense of purpose. He'd been called to take his stand, and he determined in his heart that no one would pass beyond this point.

Every man on the field of battle felt an expectancy in the air, as if something were about to happen, though no one knew just what it would be.

Lance and Loren Newcastle stared as if they had awakened from a dream. They looked at the weapons in their hands, and Lance, being the more outspoken, threw his to the ground. "I ain't fighting my dad, Loren! They can't make me!"

For thousands of men, there was a terrible moment of indecision. Loren watched his brother and suddenly knew what he had to do. He wasn't going to fight with his father either. There were men loyal to Jabin fighting alongside him on this hillside, and he knew it. He'd left Sebring months ago to keep these very men out of Amity, and now, though he had marched beside them for weeks, he would do so no longer.

With sword in hand, Loren turned and hurled himself at the nearest crimson-clad officer. Lance watched in horror—and then grabbed his own blade and followed his brother.

Within seconds, every man on the hillside was fighting for his life. As a reaper gathers wheat into a barn, so war gathers men into the winepress of judgment. On the gentle slopes of Amity, the grim reaper swung his scythe.

Jan DeKlerk stood in his stirrups. The braying trumpet grated on his nerves, and he knew something was wrong—dreadfully wrong.

There was a shout and the clash of steel behind him. Turning, he was dismayed to see his army fighting amongst themselves.

What should he do? He tried to think, but only one plan came to his mind: destroy Philip Stafford. He had lived it, breathed it, and planned it for so long that it was part of the fabric of his soul. His army could wait. Philip Stafford had to die!

"Heims!" he shouted above the clamor of battle. "Kill Philip!"

His henchman nodded and lowered his spear for the attack.

Philip heard a battle cry, but he had no time to consider what it might mean. Two horsemen bore down on him. He leaped to one side and stabbed at the first to pass. The horse reared, and its rider nimbly jumped to the ground, landing on his feet, sword and shield in hand. Philip rapidly scanned the field for the other man on horseback.

With one sweeping glance, Philip saw his men rushing down toward the stream into the teaming hordes of Jan DeKlerk's army. "Wait!" he called, but no one heard his call. Suddenly he was alone with one enemy he could see, and one he could not!

Darting to one side, Philip barely escaped a blow to his exposed legs.

Sidestepping another slash, Philip recognized the man with whom he fought. Christopher Heims was from Sebring. He was the only man to best James in a tournament years ago. They had used wooden sticks that day, but today it would be a fight to the finish.

Philip circled. Steel clashed as he caught Heims's blow with one of his own. Both men fell back, waiting. Heims was playing for time. Philip stepped over a body and struck at Heims's legs. The man leaped away and delivered a blow that sent Philip reeling.

A horse nickered nearby, and Philip turned to see Jan DeKlerk. Sunlight reflected from Jan's spear, and before Philip could move, its steel point slid between his ribs. Twisting away, Philip felt something warm soak his shirt.

Stepping back quickly to keep both Heims and DeKlerk in view, Philip tripped over a body and fell. Laughing aloud, Jan DeKlerk dropped his spear and swept his sword from its scabbard.

Philip rolled quickly to one side, just escaping a blow from Heims, and then scrambled to his feet. DeKlerk urged his mount into the fray and came between Heims and Philip, blocking his henchman from the action. Philip ducked DeKlerk's blow and in return stabbed upward at the man. His sword was yanked from his hand as DeKlerk's horse reared, throwing Philip backward to the ground. Heims came at Philip with blows left and right, and Philip maneuvered his shield up and down to ward off Heims's attack.

Philip was growing weak, but with a desperate kick, he caught Heims in the belly and sent him reeling. Rolling away, he pulled the shield over his body, waiting for the next blow to fall, but it never came.

Panting, Philip rose to one elbow and surveyed the carnage around him. Slowly he rose to his knees and then to his feet. Heims lay staring into heaven with a fixed gaze several feet away. He had tripped and fallen backward upon a broken spear shaft. The jagged handle had run through his body.

Turning, Philip searched for Jan DeKlerk. A movement caught his attention, and he stared in horror. Jan DeKlerk was struggling to rise to his feet, but the point of a sword was protruding from his back. Jan dropped to his knees, looked at Philip with wide eyes, and fell facedown on the sod. Stepping closer, Philip realized that the blade in DeKlerk's body was his own.

CHAPTER 53

A Different Battlefield

It was midmorning before Katherine awoke in a wing of Stonewall's barracks that had been converted to a hospital ward. She was bruised, sore, and covered with bandages from the many cuts she had received in Northglen Forest. Though her wounds were severe, she felt very fortunate upon seeing her newfound friend. Exposure and multiple lacerations on Mary's weakened body had sent her system into shock. Her breathing was shallow, and her heart was fluttering with a weak, rapid pulse. It was clear that Mary might not survive. Katherine immediately began to mop Mary's forehead with a damp cloth to cool the fever that raged within her body.

Hours passed as Katherine fretted and worked to cool Mary. Occasionally she thought of Philip and wondered what was going on in the outside world. If only she could get free long enough to find Master Rhoop and learn what Philip was facing! Another long hour passed before a hospital aide came to assist with Mary and give Katherine a few moments of much-needed rest.

Stepping outside the hospital, Katherine saw a very large number of people entering Stonewall from both the Waterfront ferry and the ferry from Sebring. *What is going on?* she wondered. She had to find Rhoop.

Hurrying across the courtyard to Stonewall's great house, she rushed through the crowded hallways, hoping to find Rhoop in his room. When she rapped softly at his door, there was no answer, but when she turned around, he was standing only inches from her. "Master Rhoop!" she cried.

The old man smiled. "Yes, Lady Katherine?" he asked.

"What is happening?" Katherine asked bluntly. "Why is Stonewall filling up with people from Waterfront and Sebring?"

The old man seemed aged beyond his years. "Katherine," he began, "I've had a message from Philip."

Rhoop handed Katherine a ragged piece of paper, which she grabbed and began to read. Overwhelmed by the words she read, she fell to her knees. The note ordered Rhoop to bring everyone who was willing inside the fortress for protection, while Philip would lead about three hundred men west to face Devia's army of fifteen thousand. "The odds are not good," Philip wrote, "but God used three hundred men with Gideon to route a far larger army of Midianites. If all goes well, people can leave the fortress very soon. If not, hold Stonewall as long as you can and pray Father comes to your rescue." Philip had signed his note, "In God's hands, Philip."

All this happened while I slept! Katherine thought. *Where is Philip now? Is he all right? Will soldiers be encamped against us tomorrow?*

In a daze, Katherine left Rhoop and returned to the hospital to find that Mary was better. Her fever had broken, and she was resting comfortably. Now Katherine sought a quiet place to gather her thoughts. Refugees filled the chapel and library. It seemed that every corner of the big house was full. Remembering the balcony, she rushed through the corridors, hoping to find solitude among the plants and ferns overlooking the river.

Reaching her destination, she carefully lifted the latch and opened the door. *Thank heavens!* she thought. *There's no one here!* Closing the door, she sank to her knees in relief.

Folding her arms atop a rough wooden bench, Katherine rested her head in her hands. *Not everything is going badly*, she thought. *Mary is better.* Suddenly, she stopped. "Oh, no!" she whispered. "I've forgotten to pray."

Chiding herself, Katherine recalled Philip's warning that the devil was a master at derailing prayer. She had become so caught up in her work that she'd forgotten to pray at all. Falling prostrate upon the floor, she cried out, "Oh, Lord, forgive me!"

A thousand images raced through her mind. Trying to pray for each one, she found that her mind strayed quickly back to Philip. "Oh, Lord!" she whispered. "Protect Philip!" Tears stung her eyes, and a lump formed in her throat. In her mind she could see swords glittering in the morning sun. Suddenly she saw dead bodies lying on the ground, and among them was the pale face of Philip Stafford.

"No!" she whispered. "Philip!" she cried. Suddenly she stirred. Opening her eyes, she noted that the shadows of evening had grown long. "Oh, no!" she groaned. "I've slept!"

CHAPTER 54

Mercy

Clutching his side, Philip stumbled toward the battlefront. His officers, Peter and Andrew, had gathered many among the opposition into their own ranks and were now driving a large number of Devia's army back up the opposite hill. Though Philip should have been elated by the sight, he was not. Bodies lay strewn across the hillside in alarming numbers. Somehow he had to stop the killing!

Resolve drove him forward, but he misjudged his step and fell headlong over the bodies of Lance and Loren Newcastle. He knew the brothers. They were good men, as was their father who had stood by him today. It was clear from the bodies surrounding them that they had turned on the redcoats in the end. Philip wanted to cry. How many others had been deceived until the very last moment?

"Master Philip?" a small voice sounded above him.

Philip looked up into the startled face of the lad who had delivered his message to DeKlerk.

"Are you hurt, sir?" the boy asked.

"Just a scratch," Philip responded, but his stained shirt, pale face, and trembling limbs belied his words.

"You need help," the lad stated. "I'll get someone."

Philip closed his eyes and felt a strange comfort. He thought of Katherine, and a smile touched his lips. When someone called his name, he wanted it to be Katherine, so he was a little disappointed to find Peter Sikes looking down at him.

Philip's mind returned to the battlefield. "Peter," he whispered, "call off the pursuit!"

Sikes was clearly annoyed. "But, sir!" he resisted. "Many have turned to us in this battle, and the others flee before us!"

"Too many have died!" Philip coughed. "Call off the pursuit, and let those who flee consider their plight tonight."

"But they have made their choice!" Peter persisted.

"Many who fight for us now were aligned with the enemy this morning," Philip said. "We must give them time to reconsider."

"Yes, sir," Peter said reluctantly. Turning to a fellow officer, he gave the order to call men from the pursuit.

A trumpet sounded and men slowly gave up the chase. Returning in small groups, some began to put out fires the enemy had set in its retreat. Others began to search for family or friends among the casualties.

Philip was eased onto a pile of cloaks, and Peter bathed his wound. Drawing a needle and thread from his pack, Peter began to close Philip's injury. Philip was a fortunate man. His wound was large but not deep. With a little care, he would heal.

When Peter was finished, Philip asked for a piece of paper. Quickly he wrote a note to Master Rhoop. "Where is my boy?" he asked.

The lad who had found him stepped forward, "Here, sir!"

"I have an errand for you, son," Philip said.

"I'll do anything, sir," the lad replied.

"I know," Philip said. "You've proved yourself more than once today already. Take this note to Master Rhoop at Stonewall. Tell the guards you have a message from Philip Stafford, and they will let you through."

"Yes, sir!" The lad grinned from ear to ear. He was about to leave when Philip spoke again.

"Just a moment, lad," Philip said. He tore a second piece of paper and began jotting another note. "Do you know Katherine Gammel?"

"I should hope so," the lad said. "I've seen her on the streets of Sebring many times."

"Good man!" Philip said, smiling. "You have two notes now. The first goes to Master Rhoop, and the second to Lady Katherine. You should find both inside Stonewall. Are you able to deliver these notes for me?"

"Yes, sir!" the lad said as he turned and raced toward Stonewall.

CHAPTER 55

New Revelations

Several days had passed, and Katherine watched through one of Stonewall's many windows as Mary made her way toward the cemetery. *I think I'll join her*, she thought as she hurried down a long hallway. She stepped outside into the sunshine and moved quietly behind Mary.

"It's good to see you out and about, Mary," Katherine said.

Startled, Mary spun around and blushed deeply. She noticed Katherine studying the cloak she wore with its hood pulled over her head. She flushed a deeper shade of red. "I ... couldn't go out in public ... without ..." she stammered.

Katherine touched her friend's arm. "Of course, you couldn't!" she cried. "I didn't mean to embarrass you."

"It's too warm to be wearing a cloak, isn't it?" Mary asked.

"It's all right." Katherine laughed.

"It's just that I have no ... hair."

"I know." Katherine patted Mary's arm. "It fell out after your fever. I would do the same thing."

"I was hoping no one would recognize me," Mary said, blushing again.

Katherine laughed outright and hugged Mary tight. "You are wonderful, Mary. I'm so glad to have you for a friend. But why are you here?"

The smile slipped from Mary's face. She turned away and leaned against the cemetery fence. "This is where I feel closest to everyone I knew."

"Mary!" Katherine exclaimed. "Why?"

When Mary looked up, her eyes were moist. "Lady Katherine," she said, "I've lost everyone I know. My father, mother, husband, and baby are all gone. You are my only friend. Soon I will be well, and I will have to leave you, but I don't know where I will go. I doubt anyone would receive me now."

Katherine grabbed Mary's hands. "Then stay with me," she pleaded. "Please don't go! More casualties come every day, and we are already overwhelmed. Stay and help me, please."

Mary's eyes widened. "But—"

Katherine placed a finger over Mary's lips to stop her protest. "I know how it feels to be alone," she said. "My mother died years ago, and my father is off to war. My cousin turned traitor, and Philip is ..."

Now it was Mary's turn to comfort. It was no secret that Katherine was in love with Philip. Mary also knew that Katherine had not heard from Philip in days. "Then you haven't heard from him since that first night?" Mary asked.

"No," Katherine said, pulling a well-worn scrap of paper from her pocket. "This is all I have of him," she said, handing the treasure to Mary.

Mary touched the paper reverently, and her eyes asked if she should read the inscription.

Katherine nodded. "Go ahead; read it."

Mary opened the note and read, "The Lord is faithful! Amity is His! Keep praying! Signed P." Mary's eyes grew wide, and she asked, "Is this all he wrote?"

Katherine bit her lower lip to stop it from quivering. She could not trust her voice, so she only nodded.

Mary slowly sank to the ground. How often had she longed for some word from Bill and never received it? She felt bad for her friend. Katherine settled on the ground beside her, and tears slid down both women's cheeks.

Some days later, Katherine returned to the room she shared with Mary. Opening the door, she spied her friend quietly brushing the white fluff appearing on her scalp. Mary caught sight of Katherine staring and said brightly, "Look! I have hair!"

Katherine smiled and thought of all the disappointments that had come into their lives. Mary seemed to be coping so well. *Now, if only Philip would write*, she thought. "Let's do something different today," she said impulsively.

Mary turned to her friend. "What about the hospital?"

"It's our day off from the wards," Katherine said brightly. She didn't really have anything in mind, but a plan was rapidly forming. "I want to visit a house in Waterfront. Would you like to come with me?"

The women giggled like schoolgirls as they made their way across the river and through the winding streets of Waterfront. It was a lovely day, and after the oppression of the hospital ward, the outing brought some much-needed relief.

"Do you know your way to this house?" Mary asked.

"I think so," Katherine responded.

"You're not sure?"

"It was dark when I was there."

"What if we go to the wrong place, and a handsome young prince answers the door?" Mary asked.

The girls giggled. "The only man I saw that night was handsome enough but a little too old!" Katherine laughed.

"Keeping him for yourself?" Mary teased.

The town was busy. People seemed oblivious to the fact that only a few miles away a war raged, threatening to tear Amity apart. There was no immediate danger here, so life went on.

The markets teemed with people bartering for tomatoes, potatoes, and fish. Goat's milk was ladled through open kitchen windows into waiting containers. Children played in the streets, tossing dust or chasing each other with sticks.

The girls were amazed that everything seemed so normal. They had just left the halls of Stonewall where wounded soldiers were a grim reminder of the travail that still gripped the nation.

But here in the streets of Waterfront, the war seemed distant. The carnival-like atmosphere charged the girls' senses and filled their hearts with expectancy.

Pushing on, the girls left the markets behind and slipped quietly into the residential outskirts of town. Katherine tried to retrace her steps but found she had forgotten much since that fateful night.

Finally they turned into a street she remembered. Several homes had been burned to the ground, but most remained functional. The girls became quiet as Katherine recounted her movements that night to Mary. This part of Waterfront seemed somber and quiet.

"Here it is!" Katherine exclaimed as they turned a corner into a narrow street. She grabbed Mary's hand and began to pull her toward the house.

Something was wrong. No children played in the street; no milkmen ladled their wares. All was quiet and pensive.

Mary slowed her pace. "Are you sure we should disturb these people?"

If Katherine heard Mary's question, she did not respond. She marched straight to the house in question and knocked on the door. When there was no immediate response, Mary repeated, "Maybe we shouldn't bother them."

Katherine looked through the window. She was reluctant to abandon their mission.

Mary clutched her arm. "Come along, Katherine. Let's leave this place."

"I think ... yes, someone is in there," Katherine said. "They either didn't hear me, or they didn't want to answer the door."

"Maybe they don't want to be bothered," Mary said. "Let's go!"

"Don't be a goose, Mary," Katherine responded. "I was curious before, but now I simply have to find out about these people. We've come too far to turn around now."

"Please!" Mary begged. "There's something wrong here, Katherine. I think we should leave."

"And miss an adventure?" Katherine laughed. "Besides, I think someone is coming. I saw movement in the hall."

"Don't spy on them," Mary pleaded.

Both girls were startled when the door suddenly swung open, and a gruff old woman appeared. "What do you want?" she asked suspiciously.

Katherine suddenly wavered. "I'm sorry," she began. "I was looking for a house where an old man lived with his daughter and grandchildren. I saw them on the night of the disturbance some weeks ago, and I was wondering ... how things were going?" Katherine suddenly realized how ridiculous she must appear to this woman, and she wished Mary had succeeded in making her leave.

"I don't know what you're talking about," the old woman said, and she was about to shut the door.

"Sister." A feeble voice drifted out of the house. "Let her in."

The old woman scowled, staring intently at the girls.

"Let her in!" the voice said again. "There was a young woman on a grand horse that night, and I should very much like to see her again."

The old woman stood her ground and whispered, "Have a care for the dying. You should have left us in peace."

"Dying?" Katherine found her voice and her courage. "We work in the hospital wards in Stonewall," she said, pointing to Mary. "Maybe we can help."

The old woman wavered, and Katherine pushed her way inside. "Where is he?" she asked.

Reluctantly the old woman turned and led the pair into the dark, musty little house. "He's in here," she said, pointing to a little room off the hall. The room was clearly a bedroom, but the curtains were drawn so tightly that little else could be seen of its contents or occupants.

Katherine glanced at Mary, and both women stepped into the room. After their eyes had adjusted to the light, they perceived a young woman sitting beside a bed that held an older man.

"Come in," the young woman said. "Father is anxious to meet you."

"Why?" Katherine managed to ask.

"Lass," the old man said softly. "I saw you the night of the riots. I joined Master Philip and saw you again when you rode into the camp. You probably don't remember me, but I remember that the horse you rode carried two women." The old man looked at Mary. "Were you the other woman?" he asked.

"Yes," Mary said quietly, "but I'm sure my appearance has changed since that night."

The old man whispered, "You were both in bad shape that night. I am glad to see you are healing." The old man sudden grasped Katherine's hand. "I wanted to thank you, young lady, for giving me purpose for my life."

"I don't understand," Katherine responded.

"I love my daughter and her children," the old man said feebly, "and I joined Philip to protect them." The old man looked lovingly at his daughter, who clutched his other hand between hers. "But when I saw you in the camp that night, torn and bruised, and I learned that Devia's men had done this to you, I was determined to stay with Philip and fight to protect not just my own family but also those I did not know."

Katherine sat on the edge of the old man's bed, holding his free hand in her own.

"I have wondered about your welfare," the old man said. "When you rode into camp, you were torn and bruised almost as bad as your horse. To see you alive and well makes me feel that my sacrifice was worth it." The old man leaned back and closed his eyes, and his daughter kissed his fingers gently.

"Is something wrong?" Katherine asked hesitantly.

"Good heavens, child!" the old woman exclaimed. "The darn fool went off to war and lost a leg!"

Mary and Katherine stared at each other in horror. "I'm so sorry," Katherine managed to say. "I didn't know!"

"Of course you didn't," the old lady scoffed. "How would you know?"

"How did it happen?" Katherine asked quietly.

The old man stirred and raised his head.

"Don't try to talk, Papa," the man's daughter pleaded. "Save your strength."

"Nonsense, Hilda," the old man said. "This girl knows Master Philip. She should be told."

Hilda bowed her head, and her father continued, "I stayed with Master Philip, even after many others left. I felt I had another mission to complete, though I didn't know what it was."

The old man took a deep breath. "My small effort will never be remembered, but I am satisfied I have done my job."

Katherine's curiosity overwhelmed her, and she asked, "What happened?"

"The morning after you came into our camp, we marched nearly to Capri. We took our stand with Master Philip, and I watched him fight one battle after another. I was able to help drag the most badly injured men to the rear, but suddenly I found the battle raging all around me. I had no weapon, so I darted back and forth, trying to avoid horses and men, but someone knocked me down, and horses trampled the earth all around me. I thought I was a goner, but suddenly everything grew quiet. I could see everyone had left except Master Philip and two men from Devia's army."

"Listen to him talk!" the old woman sneered.

"Then what happened?" Katherine asked breathlessly. Mary and Hilda leaned forward too, hanging on every word, while the old man's sister sulked near the door.

"Master Philip was fighting with a man not far from where I lay, and he was taking a beating. I inched closer, wondering what I could do to help him, but having no weapon, I felt rather helpless. Then I spied the broken handle of a spear nearby, and I grabbed it up. I hadn't moved more than a foot when a horseman charged past me and struck Master Philip down!"

Katherine gasped, but the old man continued. "Philip jumped up, but now he had two men with which to contend. I wondered what I could do. The horseman attacked Philip again, and I couldn't see what was happening, but when I next saw Philip, he was down. The man nearest me was attacking Philip left and right. I couldn't move fast enough to help, but suddenly Philip kicked him hard and sent him reeling my way. I aimed my stick at the falling man, and his full weight drove my broken spear through his body before he fell on me, forcing my leg down on the edge of a broken sword. The man never moved again, and I thought how silly I'd been not to notice the sword lying there. I thought my life would end right there, but someone discovered me, and though I lost a leg, I'm sure I helped spare Master Philip's life."

The old man closed his eyes. Telling his tale had given him much satisfaction, but it had drained him of any remaining energy.

Katherine felt her heart pounding. "You ... saved Philip's life!" she whispered.

The old man nodded. "Though no one knew."

Katherine wiped the tears from her eyes. "I know," she said. "And you will always have my undying gratitude. What else can I do to thank you?"

The old man's head sank onto his pillow. "Just look after Master Philip, and I'll be happy."

"You have my word," Katherine said.

"Thank you," the old man whispered.

Hilda clung to her father as both she and Katherine wept openly. Hilda was losing her father, and Katherine had nearly been robbed of Philip. Both women were feeling their loss acutely. Katherine rose and circled the bed to give Hilda a hug.

"Neither of you should weep for me," the old man whispered. "I have found my peace, and I give the Creator of heaven and earth my thanks and praise." The old man sighed, and the room grew silent.

"The curse of Hefington is complete," the old woman said. "Now you have seen your show, so be off with you!"

"Hefington?" Mary whispered. She had remained silent, but now she turned to the old woman. "Did you say the curse of Hefington?" she asked.

"Aye," said the old woman. "Every male by that name has disappeared from the face of the earth. My brother was the last, so be off with you!"

"But I knew a Hefington in Capri," Mary argued. "In fact, he helped me escape."

"I'm from Capri," Hilda said, "but I only knew one Hefington there. He was my brother Benya. He served in the garrison at Green Meadow, and we heard he was killed there. Do you remember this Hefington's name?" she asked Mary.

"His name was Walley," Mary said. "He said his father was a boatman, and he lived with his aunt. He was supposed to come to Waterfront with her, but he stayed on in Capri. Oh, he was such a comfort to me."

Hilda grew quite pale. "Was this Walley a grown man?" she asked.

"Oh, no!" Mary replied. "He was only about ten years old, though he acted much older. Did you know him?"

Hilda began to tremble. She shook her head vigorously as if to ward off some terrible specter. "No!" she gasped.

"What's wrong?" Katherine asked, suddenly concerned.

"My brother worked on the river," Hilda said, "and he had a son named Wallace that I used to care for!"

Mary was ecstatic. "Then you are Walley's aunt!"

"She *was* Wallace's aunt," the old woman interrupted.

"Was?"

"Wallace died nine years ago—before his first birthday," the old woman growled.

"Have I gone insane?" Mary asked, gripping Katherine's arm as they walked down the narrow street.

Katherine didn't answer. It was all too fantastic! The bright sunlight made the whole experience seem like a strange dream. She wanted to pinch herself to be sure she was still in the real world, yet Mary's grasp on her arm assured her that she was.

"Lady Katherine!" A shrill voice called and brought the girls to a halt. A lad ran down the street, and Katherine felt her heart skip a beat. It was the same lad who had carried a message from Philip before.

"Yes!" Katherine called. "Do you have a message for me?"

"Yes, ma'am," the boy said, struggling to free a note from the leather pouch at his side.

"Does all go well with Master Philip?" Katherine asked, studying the lad's features.

"Very well, ma'am," he said, waving a second note in the air. "This needs to go to Master Rhoop."

"Thank you," Katherine called as the boy raced away.

Mary watched as Katherine opened and devoured her note in silence. "Is it good news?" she asked tentatively.

Katherine looked up and nodded, tears streaming down her cheeks. She handed the note to Mary. With trembling fingers, Mary opened the letter and read:

Dearest Katherine,

Every day the Lord brings us one step closer to victory. Highland is ours! Outside Zaraphath the forests and fields lie in ashes. I ache for those who will find their homes destroyed.

Early this morning we routed a large company and nearly captured Master Devia. Had the Lord given him into our hands, this whole affair might have ended today. But the tide is turning. We face less opposition daily. Zaraphath and Deep Delving are the last two strongholds between us and Green Meadow.

As victory seems more certain, I ask that you would pray for wisdom. Every day we fight with men from Amity. I do not know how we will restore peace once this terrible affair is over. Amity will never be the same. Much has been lost, but even if all else is lost, I pray you will remember me with affection. Your love is a treasure I could not bear to lose.

I have found little time to write, but my heart has been with you since the day we parted. May the Holy One watch over you and keep you safe until we meet again.

Yours truly, Philip

"He does care!" Katherine cried. Tears splashed unheeded over her cheeks. Though she tried to control her emotions, she found it useless.

Mary hugged her friend. "Did you ever doubt it?" she asked.

"He never wrote," Katherine complained. "I know he was occupied, but he never wrote!"

Mary stared at her friend. "Katherine, Philip is carrying the entire burden of Amity on his shoulders."

"I know," Katherine sobbed. "I'm sorry. I shouldn't have said anything. I didn't mean to sound demanding. It's just so hard not to know."

Mary thought of all the times she had wished for a letter from Bill. Putting her arms around Katherine, the two women held each other tight.

CHAPTER 56

The Tide Turns

"Keep moving!" a voice demanded in the darkness. "There's no shirking on this trip!" Mercinor Gammel felt sure it was the same voice that had ordered him around on the docks of Sebring. *I wish I could see the owner of that voice*, he thought. *But Devia and his minions have to do everything at night. I am so sick of this!*

While Master Devia rode in a covered litter carried by six unfortunate men, Gammel sat astride a pony, watching the group struggle over the rough terrain. Seeing others stumble and sweat for Devia's comfort somehow made him feel better; however, when his own pony tripped, nearly pitching him off, the pleasure of seeing his companions suffer disappeared. Swearing softly, he wished he could have had at least one beer to cool his thirst, but no, the great Master Devia who had promised so much was nothing more than a petty tyrant. The very liquor that had won him such a following was now banned from all those nearest the throne. Mercinor silently cursed the day he had been introduced to Master Devia, yet he plodded on through the night, escorting Devia's wagon filled with the royal comforts of tent, throne, carpets, and tapestries.

Days passed, and what was left of Devia's army suffered one loss after another to Philip Stafford. Almost daily the "royal court" was forced to move to safer territory, and the conditions were not improving. Mercinor had been forced to give up his pony, and now he labored among a large group of men either pushing or pulling Devia's royal wagon up the winding path toward Green Meadow. The entire party trudged through a wasteland of ash and soot. *Why all this senseless destruction?* Mercinor wondered.

Pausing at the top of a ridge, Mercinor reeled when he saw Devia's stronghold for the first time. Dark granite towers pierced the horizon like menacing fangs. Green Meadow had once been a lovely place. Now it seemed cold and barren.

A whip cracked overhead. "Get moving!" the foreman shouted.

Obediently, Mercinor and those with him put their shoulders to the task and bounced the wagon over a deep rut in the road. By late afternoon, Mercinor and his companions had brought Master Devia's wagon into the stronghold.

"Get the gear inside," someone shouted, and Mercinor shouldered the lightest-looking bundle. His feet hurt, and he was exhausted. He wanted a drink and a long hot bath, but those pleasantries were reserved for Master Devia alone.

Inside the fortress walls, there was constant activity. Women and children carried heavy loads of mortar and stone. *Just like ants*, Mercinor thought. *Not really people at all.*

"What are you looking at?" a guard shouted, striking Mercinor with the butt of his spear.

Mercinor glared at the guard but said nothing. "We have to get this wagon unloaded," the guard said, "and it goes faster if everyone works."

Mercinor thought of a good many things he might say, but he chose to refrain. Hefting his load, he fell in line with his comrades marching into the huge warehouses beneath the bastille.

Though the halls and rooms were dark, Mercinor could still see mountains of wheat, wool, and dried fruits piled everywhere. He passed rooms containing silks and cottons. Other rooms were filled with wine, beer, and rum in such quantities that it made Mercinor's head swim. *If I could sell but one room of all this, I would be wealthy for the rest of my life*, he dreamed.

He was ushered into an empty storage room. "Royal bedroll," he muttered as he dropped his burden at a clerk's feet. Back in the hallway, Mercinor marveled at the tapestries hanging in storage. Even in the darkness, their rich colors and graceful shapes filled Mercinor with awe.

Following the others back into the light of day, Mercinor saw that the wagon was empty, and he breathed a sigh of relief. Now maybe he could get a drink and find a place to rest.

"Smith! Dixon! Gammel! Reed! Perry and Waterman! Report to the king at once!" The courier's voice shattered Mercinor's hopes.

Mercinor found the others, and together they followed the courier into Devia's palace. Stepping beneath graceful stone arches, he entered the palace's outer courtyard. Scattered about the lawn were statues of incredible beauty, but guarding the entrance of the palace was the most fearful sculpture he'd ever seen. A single dragon lay upon the southern steps. Its great mouth was open, revealing a forked tongue and dreadful teeth. Its massive body stretched the entire ascent of the stairway, and its huge tail formed the arch under which visitors had to pass to enter the hallway. The long expanse of its ragged tail formed the railing upon the north side of the staircase.

Mercinor shuddered. *What kind of man would require his guests to pass beneath such a monster?*

"What's the problem?" A guard punched Mercinor. "Afraid of the dragon?" He laughed. "You don't need to worry. He only eats those who have offended the king."

Mercinor did not laugh. He knew the dragon was made of stone, but the menace it placed on his heart was very real indeed.

Once inside, Mercinor marveled. Everything spoke of luxury. Tapestries lined the hallways, and each corner was graced with a beautiful piece of art. Some of the art depicted celestial creatures, lovely and noble, while other art depicted the underworld, terrifyingly fierce. It troubled Mercinor to see the frequent mixing of the best and worst of both worlds. *What kind of man is this?* he wondered.

A guard stood on either side of the arch leading into the lord's chamber. The bust of a goddess graced one side of the hall, her sightless ivory eyes surveying the room. Standing opposite her was a jade-eyed replica of Apollyon, the most feared demon of the underworld.

"Remove your weapons," the chamberlain demanded. "You will have no need of them."

Mercinor unbuckled his belt. It felt good to be rid of the heavy sword that hung around his waist, but he also felt somewhat naked without it. Mercinor was not, however, completely defenseless. Concealed beneath his shirt, he kept a short dagger. Though it was seldom used and few knew of its existence, it would go with him today. His fingers carefully avoided the familiar hilt. He did not want to alert anyone to its presence.

As the doors swung open, Mercinor glanced at his companions. *They don't seem nervous,* he thought. *Why am I? Maybe this is customary for those close to the master, but I have never done this before.*

"Enter!" a herald called from the inner court. Mercinor stepped through the doors with deepening dread. Master Devia sat upon a golden throne, his sour face peering from beneath a scraggly white beard. Mercinor glanced nervously at those beside him. Their faces shone expectantly, clear of doubt or worry, as if they were about to receive new orders from their master.

"Read the charges!" Devia said.

Charges? Mercinor felt the color drain from his face. *What charges?* Silently he faced the throne. Devia's eyes seemed devoid of life. *Is there any warmth in this man at all?* Mercinor wondered.

A voice began to read, "Perry: two counts murder and one count rebellion." It was not Perry's charges that caught Mercinor's attention. It was the voice reading the charges. Again he thought he should know the owner of that voice. Who was that man?

"Forgiven." The cold word slipped from between the thin lips of Master Devia.

"Waterman: three counts kidnapping and two counts murder," said the voice.

Mercinor looked around. A clean-shaven man dressed in priestly robes read Waterman's charges from a small black pamphlet. Mercinor searched his brain. *I've see that man before, but where?* he thought.

"Forgiven!" said Devia.

The accuser did not look up but continued to read. Mercinor began to wonder if the man had worked on the river. He seemed so familiar.

Mercinor relaxed a little. It seemed that murder and kidnapping to further Devia's kingdom were forgivable offenses. Mercinor thought of the things he'd done for Devia. At first it had bothered him to do such things, but since Devia was such a religious man, he would never ask a man to do something really wrong, would he? After all, Devia talked with God! If Devia told you to do something, then it must be God's will, right? Also, if Devia forgave you, you were certainly forgiven. Mercinor thought about how good forgiveness was going to feel.

"... insubordination!"

"Forgiven!" Devia said.

I missed it! Gammel thought. *I don't even know who was just forgiven.*

"Gammel!" the accuser read.

Mercinor breathed deeply, wondering what "crimes" they would say he'd committed. Was it larceny, theft, burglary, or drunkenness? He tried to relax as he waited for the verdict. The others had been forgiven, surely he would be too.

"One count treason!"

Treason? Treason against whom? Mercinor felt his heart hammering in his chest.

"Failure to secure Sebring and Waterfront for the king!" the accuser read.

Mercinor tried to find his voice. "Treason?" he croaked. "Failure, maybe, but I have always been loyal in your service."

"The gallows!" Devia hissed, turning his dark eyes upon Mercinor. "Because of your bungling, I have been driven away from that which I desired most." Master Devia pointed a bony finger in Mercinor's face, and his eyes shone with malice. "You will not fail me again!" he said.

Mercinor could not believe his ears. He looked upon Master Devia's face, and the eyes he saw reminded him of the statue of Apollyon or the great dragon outside the palace.

Strong hands grabbed Mercinor, but he was not a man to give up easily. His mind suddenly grew sharp. He had been wondering where he had met the accuser before, and now he knew. It was the same voice that had been giving him orders on the docks of Sebring for the last several months. It was the same voice that had threatened him every time one of Devia's plans failed. It was the voice that had goaded him into trying to kidnap his own cousin Katherine.

Anger cleared his mind. He would shut that voice up once and for all. He now knew who the accuser was: Mr. Milk Toast himself, Jiles McCormick. That simpering pansy didn't have the gumption to stand up to a mouse. How dare he accuse Mercinor of treason?

All the questions in his mind had been answered in the blink of an eye, and now he had only one plan of action. He'd make them pay, starting with Jiles McCormick. He moved with the strength of ten men. Grabbing the knife beneath his shirt, he yanked it into view.

There were shouts of dismay all around the room, and dozens of hands sought to subdue him, but Mercinor leaped forward. He was going to silence that hateful voice, but Devia's throne stood between him and the accuser. Devia could die too, Mercinor thought, but he was going to finish Jiles McCormick.

Mercinor shook free of multiple hands and charged toward Devia's throne. Plunging his dagger deep into Devia's body, he yanked it out and prepared to leap upon McCormick. Rough hands dragged him back onto Devia's lap.

The old man's eyes were wide with shock and surprise, but Mercinor's dagger was still free to move. Slashing wildly, he plunged the blade into Devia again and again.

"Stop him!" someone yelled, but the guards caught in the press of humanity near Devia had no room to pull their weapons. Finally a soldier from the back of the room approached, lowered his spear over the mob, and drove its point deep into Mercinor's side.

Mercinor was suddenly dizzy. He pulled his dagger from Devia's body and wobbled for a moment. The last face he saw before his eyes lost focus was that of Jiles McCormick. McCormick was laughing at him. Mercinor opened his mouth to curse the man, but no sound passed his lips.

As Mercinor Gammel sank lifeless to the floor, Jiles McCormick turned and slipped quietly from the room. Outside in the courtyard, people were certain they saw a tiny puff of smoke escape the guardian dragon's mouth.

CHAPTER 57

Darkness Covers Green Meadow

Jiles McCormick slipped quickly through a side door and glanced over his shoulder. "Good riddance to them both," he muttered. Closing the door softly, he hurried down the hallway. Guards would soon seal the room, and everyone would be questioned longer than was expedient.

"Halt!" a guard shouted, blocking McCormick's escape.

"Summon the guards!" McCormick shouted. "There's a rebellion!"

"What?" the guard grunted. "Where?"

"In the throne room," McCormick gasped, pointing in the direction from which he had come. "That Gammel fellow has gone crazy!"

In the dim light, McCormick saw the guard's face turn as red as the crimson jacket he wore. The sentry raced up the hallway, calling for reinforcements as he ran.

Jiles sighed. "At least I know which way not to go," he muttered. Stepping to the intersection of several hallways, he turned and fled in the opposite direction.

Jiles McCormick found the cellars to his liking. They were dark, quiet, and entirely without people. Here, in complete darkness, he carefully laid his plans. When all sounds of movement had ceased in the rooms above him, McCormick stirred. The room was as black as ink and silent as death. His hour had come, and he would make his move.

Moving stealthily, McCormick climbed the steps to the main floor and slipped into the hallway, passing unnoticed through Devia's palace. He carefully avoided every guard station on his way to the Tower of the Stars.

In his mind, Jiles McCormick reviewed his plan and thanked Mercinor Gammel again. This could not have happened so soon if Gammel hadn't killed Devia. The fool had saved McCormick from having to kill the old man himself. Now, all he had to do was climb to the top of the tower and draw strength from the night sky. In the morning light, he would sound the trumpet and descend to take the throne.

My reign will evoke both joy and terror for I shall be the priest of heaven for all men, McCormick thought grandly. He found the staircase and began to climb the steps one by one. "Master of Darkness," he whispered as he climbed, "you have brought me this far. Do not betray me now. Grant me the desires of my heart, for I have come to do your will."

Even as he spoke, Jiles McCormick marveled at the strength of the stones beneath his feet. They had been cut precisely and placed together in such a way that they had not even needed mortar to stay in place. McCormick thought Devia's palace was perfect. It seemed odd that the man would spend so much time and energy building this palace just for Jiles McCormick. He almost laughed at the futility of his mentor.

Each step carried McCormick higher, and an ever-increasing vista met his eyes. Lights burned in the watchtowers at the four corners of the fortress, but the Tower of the Stars stood in total darkness.

McCormick smiled. Darkness was his friend. It protected him and gave him power. It had been a useful servant.

The stairs wound around the outside of the tower, and the higher he climbed, the colder the night air became. Only once did McCormick glance into the courtyard below. He nearly swooned at the height, and he grabbed for the wall.

"Master of Darkness," he cried, "save me!" Slowly his head cleared, and his wobbling knees became firm. He began to climb once again.

"Yes!" Jiles murmured exultantly as the top came into view. "Always the darkness has been my friend. Tonight it shall become my slave!" A heady sense of power surged through his veins. "I shall plant my feet upon the high places and stand where mortal man cannot go!"

McCormick planted his feet firmly upon one step after another. He was only two steps from the top. "Tomorrow I shall claim the throne and the woman I desire." He pictured the lovely Katherine Gammel in his mind and cursed Mercinor for his bungling attempts to abduct her or eliminate Philip Stafford.

One thought clouded McCormick's otherwise perfect night. Why did Katherine only have eyes for Philip Stafford? She had never given Jiles a second glance.

That will change, McCormick thought forcefully. *Tomorrow Philip will hang, and Katherine will be mine.* Thick clouds hid the light of the stars and cast a shadow across McCormick's heart. "I tell you, I will have

Katherine if I have to bind her and place my boot upon her neck!" he shouted, shaking his fist in the darkness.

Engrossed in his fantasy, Jiles McCormick raised his boot and brought it crashing down upon Katherine Gammel's neck, but the next-to-the-last step was loose and gave way beneath his foot. For one brief instant, Jiles McCormick felt suspended in space, and then with a scream, he fell.

CHAPTER 58

A New Day

As dawn began to soften the eastern sky and many were trying to ward off the cold, Philip began to pray. "Lord, maker of heaven and earth," he said, "You raise the lowly and bring low the mighty."

Peter Sikes stood some distance away, irreverently eyeing Devia's castle. He glanced at Philip and shook his head. "It's going to take more than prayer to get in there," he muttered.

He jumped when a hand fell upon his shoulder. "Do you have any ideas?" Philip asked.

"We'll need siege works, battering rams, and more men than we can muster, sir," Peter responded. "Without them, I don't think we have a chance."

"Don't you believe the Lord can hand it over to us, Peter?" Philip asked.

Peter remained silent.

"Do you remember the story of Jericho and how Jehovah destroyed the city walls for the Israelites?" Philip asked.

"Yes, sir," Peter responded. "But we can't march around the city."

"It wasn't the marching of men or the blowing of trumpets that flattened the walls, Peter. It was the power of the Almighty One. All Joshua and the Israelites had to do was to be faithful and march forward in His strength, not their own. That is all the Lord wants of us. We must march forward, expecting great things from Him."

Peter wasn't sure how to respond, so he said, "Yes, sir."

"Don't worry, Peter." Philip slapped him on the shoulder. "Something good is going to happen. Have some men climb the wall. We need to be ready to open the gates when my father returns."

When Philip was gone, Peter took one last look at Devia's fortress. "It will take a miracle," he muttered to himself. "Nothing short of a miracle." Then he ordered men to climb Amity's wall and set a watch.

Guards stood at each of the towers in Devia's fortress. All night they had watched, wondering what the morning would bring.

The city was now quiet, but yesterday, when rumor had spread that Devia was dead, men and women of one accord had attacked the barracks of the hated redcoats. These outsiders had lived royally at the expense of everyone else. They had formed the backbone of Devia's strength by enforcing every unpopular decree.

At sundown, Green Meadow's militia held the upper hand, but no one really knew who controlled the city.

With redcoats inside and Philip's army outside the fortress walls, Commander Barret Blakely watched Philip's men climb to the balustrade on the border wall that Devia had pushed so hard to build. Sterns, his second in command, stood by his side and asked, "What will you do, sir?"

"I've received no orders," Blakely said.

Sterns was known for speaking his mind. "Sir, we have waited all night for someone to rise to power, but no one has. I think the city is waiting for you to take charge."

"Me?" Blakely questioned.

"Yes, sir!" Sterns responded. "Men know you to be capable. Most will trust any decision you make."

"I can't make decisions for others!" Blakely exclaimed.

"Then decide for yourself, and the rest of us will follow," Sterns said.

Just then a young soldier hurried across the catwalks. "Captain Blakely, sir!"

Blakely stirred. "Yes, soldier."

"Troops are climbing from the forest road on the western slopes. They carry the standards of Gaff and Stafford!" the man said.

Blakely nodded to Sterns. "Well, if people are willing to follow me, I'm ready for this war to be over. Prepare to open the gates!"

Miles of wall met John Stafford's eyes. The mountain pass at Green Meadow was completely blocked. What would they do if this wall was held against them?

Nearing the fortress, John slowed his pace when he heard the distant bray of a trumpet. Thomas, John, and Gaff exchanged glances and then rode forward to within fifty yards of the gate. As if obeying some unspoken command, the huge doors slowly swung open, and John stared through the gates to see old men and young boys dancing and cheering. Men high upon the wall began to shout greetings and thanks for deliverance.

Gaff laughed out loud. "John! These cannot be Devia's men. They're opening the gates and welcoming you home!"

Men began to swarm out of the gates, racing to John Stafford and shouting their joy as they ran.

Gaff, John, and Thomas slowly began to make their way through the crowd toward the gates. Across the sea of humanity, John continued to watch for Philip. *Where would he be?* John asked himself. *Most likely he would find a quiet spot away from the crowd.* Looking beyond the mobs, John finally saw three men standing alone, away from the crowds and celebration. John recognized his son immediately, and he knew the men with him were his commanders Peter and Andrew. *Heaven be praised!* John prayed silently. Then, pointing, he shouted to Gaff and Thomas. "Philip is over there!"

The old men surrounding John parted only enough to let them pass. Philip hobbled forward on tired legs while John and Thomas slid from their saddles. There was not a dry eye in the crowd as the Stafford family embraced.

Suddenly a trumpet sounded from the walls of Devia's fortress. The celebration died, and silence settled over the meadow. *Devia, you old rascal,* John thought, turning his eyes toward the fortress. *What are you going to do now?*

John, Philip, Thomas, Gaff, and Mathias moved toward the gates of Devia's fortress. They intended to be on the front lines if any attack came, but no well-trained army poured forth in battle array. Two lone men walked through the castle gates, and each carried a white flag.

In complete silence, the Stafford men fell to their knees, offering prayers of thanksgiving and lifting their hands in praise to the Lord. Slowly, Gaff joined them, as did his son, Mathias, and within moments nearly every man on the plain had bent his knee, including Peter Sikes. God had indeed preformed a miracle! When those on the walls of Devia's fortress witnessed the humbling of Amity, they too bowed their heads and hearts before the Lord. When John Stafford rose to his feet, cheers resounded from field and fortress alike. The war was over!

CHAPTER 59

New Challenges

Messengers raced across Amity with the news. Celebrations broke out in every district, but in Stonewall and Waterfront, people also began preparations to return to their homes. All too soon their elation would turn to tears as they realized the cost of their freedom.

Amity would never be the same. Homes and fields had disappeared in smoke and ash. Whole forests had been set ablaze. Much of the verdant valley along the Crescent River resembled a barren wasteland.

Deep scars marred the land, and nearly every family had suffered loss. Yet for a brief moment all was set aside. The war was over!

Stonewall had been stocked with provisions for a siege, but now Rhoop began distributing goods to those most in need. The courtyard teemed with people looking for a handout, and it was wild with celebration.

Amid the ruckus, Mary desperately sought to find Katherine. Catching a glimpse of auburn hair, she waded into the crowd, not sure it was Katherine but afraid not to try. Bumped and jostled about, she lost sight of her quarry as she neared the hospital. Turning from the madness of the courtyard, she found relative calm and quiet in the wards.

When her eyes adjusted to the darkness inside the building, she saw men sitting on their cots, calling out words of thanksgiving to one another. At the far end of the room, she spied Katherine, busily washing and bandaging wounds.

"Katherine!" she cried as she sped across the room. "What are you doing? The whole world is celebrating!"

"I know," Katherine said calmly. "But celebrations don't change these men's bandages."

Mary felt her face grow hot. She'd quite forgotten her duties in the joy of the moment. "Let me take your place."

"There's no need," Katherine said. "I've seen the courtyard."

"But you haven't seen the messenger from Philip," Mary said, her eyes twinkling.

Katherine gasped, her work entirely forgotten. "Does he have a letter for me?"

Mary gently pushed Katherine aside and took up her labor. "He's in Lord Rhoop's chambers," she volunteered.

In a flurry of motion, Katherine brushed a kiss upon Mary's cheek and fled the room.

Carefully unfolding the crisp paper, Katherine noted the bold handwriting. This letter had been written upon a table rather than a rock or someone's knee. Trying to steady her hand, Katherine read the inscription.

> Dearest Katherine,
>
> I'm sure by now you have heard that the war is over. The Lord Almighty has spared Amity and has brought both Father and Thomas home. I have so much to be thankful for.
>
> Father has aged terribly, and Thomas is different too. I think both suffered horribly during their time away, but enough about my family.
>
> I suppose you have heard that Jabin was dethroned. Guess who took his place. Seagood! That's right, our own Seagood.
>
> There is some sad news too. Mercinor is dead. You were right all along. He was in Devia's employ, but it may give you some consolation to know that Mercinor killed Master Devia in the end and thus brought this war to a close much sooner than we had hoped. For that, I am forever indebted to your cousin.
>
> You may remember Jiles McCormick. We found him outside Devia's palace. He was at the bottom of the tallest tower I have ever seen. Apparently he had fallen. I climbed that tower, and Katherine, you should see the view. It is breathtaking.
>
> We hope to start home soon. I wish it was today, but both Father and Thomas feel we should move slowly.

They want to spread encouragement and healing along the way. I know they are right, but I'm rather anxious to get home.

I spoke with your father yesterday, and that brings me to the point of this letter. Katherine, I cannot imagine living the rest of my life without you. Would you consider marrying me? Please don't answer at once, but bring it to the Lord in prayer.

I have other news, but my heart is so full I cannot think clearly! Until we meet, I shall wait with bated breath to know your answer!

With love,

Philip

Katherine clutched the note tight to her breast. Tears spilled over her cheeks and onto the paper. "Yes, Philip," she whispered, her heart overflowing. Turning, she raced for the hospital wards. "I've got to find Mary."

After a few weeks at Green Meadow, Gaff made preparations to go home. He had helped John map a strategy for restoration, and then, feeling the need to return to his own people, he had declined to ride all the way to Stonewall.

With a hearty farewell, Gaff and his men departed Amity, leaving only Mathias behind. Mathias could not bear the thought of leaving Thomas. Jokingly Mathias predicted that he would remain a bachelor until his dying day. Never were any words more unfounded.

After weeks of work and waiting, the day of the Staffords' departure finally arrived. Placing Commander Blakely in charge of Green Meadow for the interim, John Stafford's parting words granted pardon far and wide. Not a dry eye remained in all of Green Meadow as John set out. Healing had begun.

With his men well rested, John made good time until he reached Headwater. There he was reminded of the hospital that had been established after the battle of Green Meadow. Stories of Jennifer and her brave deeds became the conversation of the hour. Thomas, Mathias, and a small company decided to ride out and see what had become of Jennifer and "her men."

Evening was fast approaching as the men rode off, so they carried supplies to camp overnight, not knowing what they might find. They rode several miles up a winding valley until their path crossed a stream. During the entire ride they saw no signs of life or activity.

Climbing the hills into the forest, they suddenly entered a small clearing. Oil lamps illuminated a small cabin and the nearby barn. Men limped or hobbled about the barnyard, unaware of the visitors.

Thomas and his company had ridden quite some distance into the clearing before an alarm was raised. "Intruders! Man your weapons!"

The company halted, and Thomas called out, "Peace, friends. Do not be alarmed. The war is over!"

His words were met with stony silence. Disbelief was strong. The men in this camp had lived in isolation and fear for so long that hope had become a twisted mockery. They silently gripped their weapons, wary and aloof.

Thomas slowly rode toward a line of armed men. "Men of Amity, I am Thomas Stafford!"

"Don't come any closer!" shouted a large man striding forward. "We don't have anything you need."

"Benya?" Thomas asked. "Is that really you?"

There was a low murmur among the men, and the big man stopped in his tracks.

"Benya Hefington!" Thomas called. "I know you! Don't you remember me?"

The man stepped back a pace or two. Thomas was about to move forward again when a young woman appeared in the cabin doorway.

Jennifer stared, her eyes wide with wonder. In the dim light, she thought she beheld James Stafford with a beard. "My lord," she whispered, stepping forward. "I thought you were dead! I was with your father when we buried you!"

Thomas smiled. Was he always to walk in his brother's shadow? "Not so, my lady!" Thomas said. "I am not James. He is dead. I am his brother Thomas."

Jennifer fell to her knees and cried, "My lord!"

That single gesture ripped all doubt and fear from every man in the clearing. Men crept cautiously from the shadows. "Is the war really over?" someone called.

"Yes," Thomas responded.

"Praise the Lord!" someone shouted, and then bedlam broke loose. Men shouted and hugged each other for joy.

Mathias rushed forward to meet the brave and beautiful girl of so many stories. Never had he been so moved. When Jennifer looked up and their eyes met, Mathias lost his heart forever. He had seen all of Amity he needed to see. If this girl would have him, he silently vowed never to stray from her side.

Those from Jennifer's hospital who could march home joined John Stafford at Headwater. Those who couldn't were carried in wagons. When Bill Cotton was reunited with Larry Chavez, they became inseparable. Bill, with two good legs and one good arm, and Larry, with two good arms and one good leg, made a perfect match. Together they marched in the wake of Amity's returning heroes.

Crowds met them at Zaraphath, but beyond that city the countryside was stark and barren. Few folks met them on the Greenway, and fewer still greeted them as they entered the war-torn village of Capri.

Bill searched the few faces that lined the streets of Capri and suddenly stiffened. Ella Walton stood some distance from the road. She was searching among the marching men for the one face she dearly longed to see.

Bill's heart sank, and a flood of emotions washed over his soul. *How can I tell her about Bob?* he wondered. Nudging Larry, he pointed her out.

"Your woman?" Larry asked.

"Bob's widow," Bill answered.

Larry's smile faded. "Hey, man. You don't want me around!"

"Oh, yes, I do!" Bill gripped Larry's shoulder more tightly. "I just don't know how to tell her."

"Just be honest," Larry said.

Bill pulled Larry with him out of the column of marching men. He remembered Thomas's invitation: "Remember, Bill, Stonewall is always open to you." Part of Bill wished he could march straight to Stonewall today and miss this confrontation with Ella.

Bill knew that Ella did not recognize him as they made their way toward her. She continued to watch as men marched past her on their way home.

"Ella!" Bill called.

Ella Walton jumped at the sound of her name. It took her a few moments to place the voice, but once she did, she laughed. "Bill Cotton!"

Bill's hair had grown long, and a heavy beard covered his once clean-shaven face. Ella would never have recognized him if not for his voice, and she tried to act sociable while still watching for her husband.

"Ella, this is Larry Chavez," Bill said, nodding to the man at his shoulder. Larry flashed a grin and nodded.

"I'm very pleased to meet you, Mr. Chavez." Ella curtsied politely, and then she threw herself against Bill's chest, hugging him tightly. Bill wrapped his stump around her shoulders and held her. Finally she looked into his eyes and asked, "Is Bob ...?"

Bill's eyes had clouded, and his lower lip was quivering as he shook his head.

Ella's eyes grew large, and her face grew pale. Her body slumped against Bill, and she began to sob.

Bill held the trembling woman and remembered the day he had found Bob broken and dying in the road. His own tears spilled into Ella's hair. They held each other tight, oblivious to the world for a long while. Larry remained still and watched the last of Stafford's men march out of town.

Ella finally looked up and wiped her moist cheeks. "Are you sure, Bill?" she asked, her voice wavering.

Bill only nodded.

Ella took a deep breath and drew upon a deep inner strength. Wiping the muddy trails on Bill's cheek, she asked, "Were you with him?"

Again Bill nodded.

"I'm glad," she sighed. "At least he wasn't alone."

Bill struggled to find his voice. "He ... really ... loved you," he faltered.

Her resolve failed, and she fell heavily against Bill, weeping unrestrained tears. There they stood, broken souls amid the rubble of a war-torn city. Finally Ella pulled her emotions together and withdrew from Bill's embrace. Wiping her face with her hands, she looked at the men before her. "Well, if you two aren't a sight!" she said, placing her hands on her hips. "I imagine you are exhausted too. It's a long walk home, but I have a place you can rest, and we'll get you something to eat after you clean up."

Walking proved to be good therapy. Moving their limbs freed their tongues as well. Taking turns, Bill and Larry shared their versions of the battle of Green Meadow. Though their stories varied somewhat, Ella was able to picture the event quite well. Secretly she longed to see the place and to know exactly where Bob was buried.

They had passed nearly through Capri before Bill found the courage to ask about Mary. "Ella, have you seen Mary anywhere?" he asked during a lull in the conversation.

Ella stopped short, and her face turned very pale. "Bill, I'm so sorry! I'm afraid I haven't even thought of her since I returned from Waterfront. I know your cabin was destroyed. I'm so very sorry."

"Was it burned?" Bill asked.

"Mostly," Ella responded. "There may be a few things you can salvage."

"Do you know about Dolly Trumbell's place?" Bill inquired.

Ella's face brightened. "I don't know," she said. "I haven't been by there."

"Well, let's go by there now," Larry said, growing anxious for his friend.

They turned north and picked their way across the ruined city. Devia's forces had entered Capri with no intention of leaving. Wood and stone had been torn from buildings to make barricades and shelters. Trees had been felled, and trenches had been dug everywhere. When Devia had finally been driven from Capri, Jabin's trademark of torch-and-destroy had prevailed.

Bill felt growing despair as they reached Orchard Creek Avenue. The paving stones had been ripped up to make walls and barricades, and the ancient trees had been felled to block roads and streets. It was hard work just to blaze a trail down the street.

Looking up, Bill's heart leaped for joy. There were buildings on Dolly's block. The butcher shop was still standing, though its windows were boarded shut. Then Bill stopped. Dolly's building had taken the abuse for all on that block. The stone front of Tinker Trumbell's store was all that remained.

Bill forced himself to look through the gaping front door only to see the alley behind the store and the sky above. Nothing remained.

CHAPTER 60

Starting Over

Bill pushed his plate away. He couldn't eat. "Thank you, Ella," he said politely. "If you would excuse me, I think I'll go back into town to see if anyone knows about Mary."

Ella and Larry exchanged glances. They had watched Bill rummage through what was left of his cabin before he would consent to follow them here. He had salvaged a charred headboard, which was strange and grotesque, to be sure. They wondered at his excitement when he found it.

"Bill, don't you think you should rest?" Ella asked.

"I don't think I can rest without knowing about Mary," he stated. "She could be hurt or needing help."

Ella nodded and laid her hand on his shoulder. "I understand."

Bill looked into her gentle eyes. If anyone understood his anxiety, it would be Ella. "Thank you for all you have done," Bill said, taking her hand in his. "You have been so kind."

"You will come back?" Ella asked, watching Bill closely.

"I'm not sure," Bill said honestly. "I don't know where my search for Mary will take me."

"Why don't I go with you?" Larry suggested.

Bill shook his head. "Not this time, friend," Bill said. "I need to do this alone."

Larry and Ella watched Bill lumber his way to the door. His one hope for months had been to return to Mary and his baby, but now that hope was slipping away.

The door closed, and Ella turned to Larry. "He won't hurt himself, will he?" she asked.

"No," Larry answered thoughtfully. "At least, I don't think so. But if you are any good at praying, now would be a good time to start."

Several days passed, and Bill had not returned to Ella Walton's home. When Ella voiced her concern, Larry volunteered to find him. Hobbling on a crutch and a leg, Larry headed for Bill's old cabin. "He's right where I thought he would be," Larry grumbled under his breath, "sitting in the ashes of his burned-out cabin." Larry carefully crossed the stream at the bottom of the hill and struggled toward the cabin.

"Hey, Bill!" Larry shouted. "Where have you been?"

Leaning against what was left of his cabin, Bill barely noticed the additional voice. All around him he could hear the clash and clamor of battle. Fresh mounds of earth testified to the devastation that had prevailed in his little valley.

"Hey, Bill!" Larry called again. "What are you doing?"

Not even looking up, Bill replied, "She died here! I can feel it in my bones."

"Who died here?" Larry asked.

"Mary."

"How do you know?"

Bill motioned to the fresh mounds of earth. "She was caught in the battle and was buried with the others," he reasoned.

"You sound pretty sure of yourself," Larry said.

"No one in town knew anything," Bill responded.

"And you asked everyone?"

"Everyone I could. One man named Armonson even showed me the graves of Dolly and my son."

Larry shook his head sadly. He knew just how badly Bill had wanted a son. He had talked about Mary and his baby all the way to Capri. But rather than yield to sympathy, Larry continued to pepper Bill with questions. "How do you know Mary is dead?"

"Where else could she be?" Bill asked. "She never wanted to leave Capri."

Larry grabbed his friend's shoulder. "Look, where would she go after losing her mother and son? Do you think she would stay here? Amity is a big country. Don't you think she might try somewhere else, like Stonewall, Waterfront, or Sebring? All right, you know about your mother-in-law and your son, and I'm sorry for your loss, Bill, but you don't know about Mary. As long as there is doubt, there is hope. Now, come with me, and let's get some food and rest. Miss Ella is worried sick about you."

Larry's words had given Bill hope, but he still wrestled with self-pity. "Why should Ella care what happens to me?" he asked.

"I don't know!" Larry said defensively. "I don't know why she should care about me either. I'm a total stranger, but she does care about me!"

His words were met with silence, making him even angrier. "Listen, pal," Larry began. "Miss Ella was hit with some pretty hard news the other day. She dreamed of seeing Bob again, and now she never will, but she isn't wallowing in self-pity. She's working hard to make a life for herself and her kid. Now, I don't know why, but she's included both of us in her life, and you're too caught up in your own grief to even give her a hand. Is this how you're going to thank her, by staying here and starving? A lot of good you'll do anyone that way!"

Bill remained silent, but his eyes had lost their apathy. Larry knew he was treading on dangerous ground, but he continued. "Look at you: a big, strong man sitting here doing nothing while Miss Ella works her fingers to the bone. I'm not much good, but at least I try to help her!"

Bill stirred. "You're right, Larry," he said quietly. Looking at the fresh mounds of earth, he whispered, "If only I knew." Clambering to his feet, he took Larry's crutch and wrapped his arm around Larry's shoulder. Together the two men turned their steps toward Ella's home.

CHAPTER 61

Change

"Hurry up, Mary," Katherine called. "They'll be here any minute!" The girls darted between rows of soldiers marching across the courtyard.

"Where are we going?" Mary panted as they neared the wall.

"Up there!" Katherine said, pointing to the guard tower directly above them.

Mary slowed her pace. "Isn't that for the guards?" she asked, clutching Katherine's arm.

"Usually!" Katherine laughed. "Now, don't be a goose. Let's go!"

Mary planted her feet.

"Look," Katherine said impatiently, "Master Rhoop gave his permission. Now hurry up or we'll miss them!" She grabbed Mary's hand and began to drag her up the stairs. "Philip and I watched the army assemble and march away from here. I know it will be the best place to watch them return."

Mary said no more. It was useless trying to dissuade her headstrong friend. Besides, her own curiosity had been roused. She wanted to see John Stafford, and though she knew Bill was dead, there might be someone else she recognized.

They raced up several flights of steps to emerge upon a small parapet where a lone sentry stood on duty. Below them swept a vast array of banners stretching from Sebring to Waterfront. Barges and rafts had been lashed together across the river, making it look like one continuous city. Thousands of people lined the Greenway.

Though Master Rhoop had orchestrated a massive celebration for the return of John Stafford and his victorious men, the soldiers' mothers, fathers, wives, and children needed no encouragement to turn out today. Pressing close together, they all hoped to catch a glimpse of their loved ones marching home.

Mary thought about the way she and Bill had parted. She was sorry for the anger and resentment she had displayed. She felt her face grow warm with the memory. Here were thousands of people, all watching, waiting, and hoping to see their loved ones return. *If only I could do this over,* she thought. *I would have sent Bill off so differently. I wish I could see him one more time to let him know how sorry I am and how much I love him.*

Her thoughts were interrupted by the distant sound of singing. A dull white cloud billowed on the horizon, marking the arrival of Stafford's men.

Mary's heart leaped into her throat as the first riders came into view. A roar issued from the crowd, and cheers swelled as long columns of men marched into sight. Rose petals were tossed into the breeze and fluttered to the ground.

"Is that Lord Stafford and his sons?" she asked, grabbing for Katherine's arm but finding no one there.

"It is," a deep voice rumbled.

Mary jumped. She glanced at the sentry, and her face grew hot. "I—I'm sorry," she stammered. "I thought my friend was here."

"No, ma'am. She left as soon as you arrived." The sentry smiled.

Mary glanced at the door to the staircase.

"It's all right, ma'am," the guard reassured her. "I've received orders to let you stay."

Mary smiled and nodded her thanks. Katherine had left no stone unturned. She couldn't help but think how kind the young man seemed. He reminded her of Bill somehow, and that thought made tears spring to her eyes. *No!* she told herself firmly. *I just have to get through today. There will be time for crying later.*

Grateful, she stepped back to the railing. This was a wonderful location. She could see everything from its lofty height, yet she wondered where Katherine had gone.

The men had been marching quickly, and to Mary's surprise, the three leading horsemen were already near the tug.

Glancing down to the ramp leading to the river, Mary suddenly spied Katherine. *Of course,* she thought to herself. *That is exactly where she should be. I hope I would have done the same if I were in her shoes.*

"Company halt!" someone shouted.

Mary watched as thousands of men, moving as one, came to a halt and stood rigidly at attention. It was a breathtaking sight. The crowd grew quiet.

Thomas stood in his saddle's stirrups and began to address the crowd.

"It is good you are here today to join us as we thank the Lord of heaven and earth for His deliverance. Many of your loved ones are finally home. Some still serve Lord Hesketh of the Gray Lands, and others have paid for our freedom with their lives and will never return."

Men and women began to peer anxiously into the rows of soldiers, hoping to catch a glimpse of their own loved ones.

"The Lord has seen us through this peril," Thomas continued. "All things are in His hands: life, death, joy, sorrow, wholeness, and healing. We once again commit ourselves entirely into His care."

Thomas turned to his men. "You have served with honor and have fulfilled your obligations. You need to report to the armories tomorrow morning to check in your weapons, but for now, you are dismissed!"

A reaction started among the soldiers and spread to the surrounding crowd as hats flew into the air and cheers rocketed toward heaven. The war was finally over! Chaos reigned as men sought reunion with their families.

Three men turned away from the chaos. Silently and without fanfare, they boarded the tug. Slowly, strong ropes pulled the men toward Stonewall's side of the river. Mary watched Katherine leap over the last bit of water to be caught in Philip's strong arms. As happy as Mary was for her friend, she could not help wishing Bill had also been on that ferry. Oh how she longed to feel his arms around her again.

Philip had only been home a few days, and already Mary was decorating the old house for a wedding. Katherine hurried into the chapel and pulled Mary away from the cedar boughs she was twisting around a stone column. "Mary, you have to meet the family. I know everyone is just dying to meet you."

Mary was reluctant to meet these famous people, though at one time in her life she would have jumped at such an opportunity. *What should I say?* she thought. *How should I act?*

"Don't be a goose!" Katherine exclaimed. She had been pulling Mary the entire way, and both women were showing signs of fatigue before they reached the library.

"Are they in the library?" Mary asked.

"Yes, silly!" Katherine responded. "I think every other room in Stonewall is being prepared for our wedding tomorrow."

How well Mary knew. The last few days had been wild with preparations. She still did not understand the urgency, but whatever Katherine and Philip wanted was fine with her. However, she did wonder what she would do after they were married. Until now, she'd been able to avoid thinking about that, as both women had thrown themselves into decorating the old gray stone house.

Many rooms in Stonewall were still filled with refugees and recovering soldiers, but flowers graced the walls and hallways. The chapel was a sight to behold. Candles and greenery adorned every arched window. Vines were wound around the rough wooden benches lining either side of the center aisle. Mary's fingers were sore from rose thorns and cedar boughs.

Katherine gave Mary no chance to break away as she threw the library door open and shouted, "Here she is!"

"Katherine!" someone cried merrily. Mary instantly recognized Philip. He was not much taller than she was, but he was broad and solid. His face was clean-shaven, and blond hair swirled about his ears and neck.

Off to one side, an aging likeness of Philip rose from his chair. John Stafford's smile and youthful bow could not belie his failing health.

Beside John, Mary spotted Master Rhoop. The old man greeted her with a twinkle in his eye, and Mary smiled. She'd grown to love Rhoop as if he were her own father. Together they had planned much of Philip and Katherine's coming wedding.

Mary glanced about the room, searching for the now-famous Thomas. So much had been said of him: "He has changed. Looks right through you, he does. He gives me the creeps!" She wondered how one man could evoke such varied sentiment.

Thomas sat near the fireplace as if he were warming himself, though no wood crackled upon the grate. When their eyes met, Mary gasped. In her mind, she was transported back to a world filled with darkness and terror, but light had come into that darkness. Light, life, and hope had come into her heart through faith—and this man had held the key.

Mary looked deeply into Thomas's eyes and realized he also remembered. "It was you!" she whispered.

Thomas nodded. "I have often wondered where you went."

"Faith set me free, but you held the key," Mary responded. "Thank you!"

Everyone in the room watched the exchange with growing surprise.

"Mary!" Katherine exclaimed. "I thought you said you had never met Thomas!"

As Mary curtsied low before Thomas, she said, "I was wrong, Katherine. We simply had not been introduced."

Thomas smiled broadly and bowed low to Mary. "And now we have!"

The following morning, Rhoop led Philip and Katherine in their marriage vows. The chapel was filled with wounded soldiers and refugees, and thousands waited in the courtyard outside to wish them well.

Mary had feared that Katherine's marriage would leave her bereft and searching for a place to go, but Thomas needed someone to go to Gray Haven to bring his fiancée back to Stonewall. Philip, Katherine, and Mary were chosen, and they were to leave early the next morning.

Mary placed a neatly folded garment in a small traveling bag and looked around the room. A knock at her door caused her to jump, and she called out, "Who is it?"

"It's me!" Katherine called. "May I come in?"

Mary rushed to the door and curtsied as Katherine swept into the room. "My lady!" she teased.

Katherine scowled menacingly and then burst out laughing. "Oh, Mary," she said, "what would I have done without you these last few days? You've kept me from going insane!"

Mary returned her laugh and then grew serious. "Thank you for taking me. I didn't know what I would do after you and Philip were married."

"Mary, I could never leave you! You have become my very best friend—besides Philip, of course." Katherine spoke seriously. "Are you nearly ready?"

"I think so," Mary said.

"Good! Philip wants to leave tonight," Katherine warned.

"Tonight?" Mary asked. "Why so sudden?"

"I'm not sure," Katherine said, lowering her voice to a whisper. "But I know Thomas wants to keep our trip a secret. After all, we are going to meet his future bride. No one knows what might happen if Jabin should learn of our plans."

Mary suddenly shivered. She had not realized that they might be moving into Jabin's path.

Katherine grasped her hand. "Don't worry, Mary. We won't be alone. Thomas is traveling with us to Green Meadow, and Philip will stay with us until we reach the Gray Lands. We will be safe enough with Lady Helsa while Philip travels on to Endor."

"You mean Philip is going to leave us alone in a foreign land?" Mary was thunderstruck.

"We'll be fine, Mary!" Katherine exclaimed. "Just think of all the fun we'll have together. This is going to be such an adventure!"

"I hope so," Mary whispered.

Mary's heart pounded as Thomas led their cart onto the tug. She was no longer sure whether to be grateful or angry at having been chosen to embark on this adventure.

The lights of Waterfront calmed her fears, but all too soon the travelers were out of town, and Mary was startled by every shadow. She was indeed grateful not to be alone when they passed the lonely mounds at Battle Creek and her own half-burned cabin.

It was still an hour before dawn when they reached the outskirts of Capri, but even in the darkness, Mary was shocked by the destruction. Little of what she remembered had survived. She wondered about her mother's home and the graveyard where her infant son was buried.

On impulse, Mary whispered her desires to Katherine, who in turn spoke to the men. Both men nodded and turned the cart northward along Orchard Creek. Traversing the once paved street, Mary saw to her dismay that everything had changed. The trees were gone, and few houses remained.

Nearing the north edge of town, Mary stared in disbelief. In the block of homes where Dolly's store had been, the neighbor's house was standing, though flames had charred the north wall. Next door, the butcher shop seemed unscathed, its thatched roof looking exactly as Mary remembered it. Farther down the street, other homes remained intact, but her mother's store was gone, burned to the ground. Nothing remained except the stone front. She closed her eyes and recalled so many memories.

"Do you want me to go with you?" Philip asked.

"No," Mary said. "There is nothing here. Could we visit the cemetery?"

The paving stones had been torn from the street, and it required some effort to turn the cart around in the soft clay, but soon they were jolting on through the city. Philip stopped beside what once had been a lovely little cemetery. Broken trees lay strewn about, and grave markers were missing, but Mary slipped from the cart and made her way to a location permanently fixed in her mind. The others followed at a respectful distance.

Kneeling beside two mounds of earth, Mary reached inside her heavy cloak and produced two small roses. When she had plucked them from the gardens of Stonewall, she had never dreamed she'd be able to leave them here. Gently patting the moist black soil, she turned and rose to leave.

"I'm sorry," Thomas said as he helped her onto the cart.

Mary nodded, not trusting her voice. Eventually she whispered, "Thank you for stopping." She settled onto the seat and looked away. She couldn't cry now. There would be time enough for crying later.

It was nearly dawn as Bill strode down the road. He didn't really know where he was going, but he felt certain he needed to hurry. It had been hard to leave Larry and Ella, but the corrals were repaired and the house mended, and Larry had proven he could do the chores by himself.

Bill felt restless and needed a change. His mind had been so busy that he was surprised to find himself in front of Dolly Trumbell's burned-out shell of a house. *Why did I come here?* he wondered. *It hasn't changed since I was here last. I've already sifted through the ashes.*

Turning back to the street, he suddenly stopped. In the soft clay of the road, cart tracks had turned around right in front of Dolly's building. The tracks were clearly fresh, for traffic had not yet flattened them.

Why would anyone turn around right here? he wondered. *There are easier places to turn around.* From the signs in the road, he could see that the cart had been small, pulled by a donkey and led by two men. He decided to follow these tracks as far as he could, if for no other reason than to hone his tracking skills.

The tracks led him to a small cemetery. A depression in the rut signaled that the cart had stopped in one spot for a while. Dropping to one knee, he studied the impressions in the soft soil. There had been two women on the cart, and one of them had led the others across the cemetery.

Bill's heart beat faster. The footprints led directly to the graves of Dolly

Trumbell and his own infant son. He only knew this because Captain Armonson had pointed them out to him earlier.

Two red roses lay upon the earthen mounds. *Is Mary alive?* Bill shook his head. *Not likely, but who else would place flowers here?*

Quickly he raced back to where the cart had stopped. Could he follow its tracks through the city? Would he be able to catch up with the cart? Was this why he'd felt such an urgency to leave Ella's this morning?

Bill pressed his body against the one remaining wall of his cabin. It was little protection from the cold night air, but he was tired from his fruitless search. He had asked everyone he'd met, and he'd searched Capri high and low, but he had failed to find the cart for which he looked.

Now he began to consider his options. He could rebuild his cabin in this very location, but without Mary, that seemed pointless. This had been their spot. Thomas's invitation to Stonewall kept coming back to his mind, time and time again.

As morning light filled the eastern sky, Bill walked to the Greenway and looked back at the charred remains of what had once had been his home. Turning away, he began the long walk to Stonewall.

Bill stood, dejected, in Stonewall's ancient hallway. For two weeks he'd presented himself to the steward, only to hear, "Come back tomorrow. Master Thomas should be back any day now." Bill considered the last two weeks. The wait had not been horrible, for he had slept in the barracks with other refugees and had eaten their fare. But he felt the need to move on with his life.

Another day of waiting, Bill thought. *Maybe I should just go home, but where is that? I don't know where else to go.*

"Bill Cotton!" a familiar voice shouted. Bill turned to see Thomas Stafford hurrying down the hall to greet him. They hugged, and Thomas stepped back to examine his friend. "So, you've come?" Thomas asked, the joy in his eyes clouding. Bill nodded, and Thomas shook his head. "I'm sorry. It's like that all over Amity. But come. I have just returned, and I'm glad to see you!"

Bill tarried, and Thomas turned to look at him. "Is something wrong, Bill?"

"I don't want to burden you, sir," Bill ventured.

Thomas laughed out loud. "You, a burden? I should say not! In fact, I need a person I can trust to run some errands for me. First thing I need you to do is to meet with Master Johnson of Capri. There are several things we need to discuss with him." Thomas began to recite a never-ending list of jobs as he ushered Bill into Stonewall's great house.

Nights were growing long, and days were growing cold when Philip, Katherine, and Mary arrived at Gray Haven. The women bonded with Helsa immediately, and Levi was grateful for their company. Philip hurried to Endor to offer Seagood assistance, and the women began knitting mittens for the servants' children. It was not long before frozen talons of snow gripped the earth, and the north wind howled through the towers.

Sitting near the hearth one evening, Levi watched as the ladies chatted amiably. *This is how life was meant to be*, he mused. *I wish it could last forever.* Christmas was just around the corner, and Philip would bring his report about Hesketh and Endor.

Days passed, and Philip did arrive for Christmas. His presence cheered Katherine, but his report about Endor dampened everyone's spirits. Jabin had regrouped in the northlands and had returned with thousands of men. Endor was under siege. Philip doubted that war would spread to Gray Haven while winter remained, but with the coming of spring, no one knew whether the Watchers or Seagood's army could hold Jabin back.

When Philip returned to Endor, the castle at Gray Haven seemed much too cold and confining. Despite the fear of war, everyone longed for spring.

Warmer weather finally came to the Gray Lands, and one bright morning Helsa convinced her uncle to let the ladies out to search for flowers.

"I hope the crocuses are still blooming," she said brightly to her companions. "I was beginning to think Uncle Levi would never let us leave the castle!"

Mary bent to smell the wild roses along the path. "You know, it's the fear of Jabin that makes your uncle so careful."

"I know," Helsa chirped, "but the courtyard is much too small and stuffy on a beautiful day like this!"

Everyone agreed. The day was beautiful. Sprays of color dotted the normally barren hillsides, and the air was awash with the sensuous, almost pungent odor of moist earth warming in the sun. It was heavenly.

"Poor Robert!" Helsa addressed her bodyguard. "I doubt very much that you wanted to pick flowers today."

The big man turned quite red and cleared his throat. "This is fine, Lady Helsa," he said stiffly. Robert McCloskey was in charge of twenty men assigned to protect these ladies on their outing. He had not balked when receiving his orders this morning, but now he dared not let on.

"I doubt it was necessary for you to come," Helsa continued. "But Uncle Levi is so …"

"Protective of you," finished Katherine. "Helsa, you know Levi loves you like a daughter."

"I know." Helsa sighed. The bright sun and the intoxicating smell of the flowers soon drove grumpy thoughts far from everyone's mind. The girls lingered over one group of flowers and then another.

Though McCloskey had not hesitated to come this morning, something now made him uneasy. There had been no reports of enemy movements on this side of the river, but his unrest grew with each passing moment.

"Oh, look!" Helsa cried, peering over the rim of the mesa. "The best flowers are down here!" Like ducklings following their mother to water, Katherine and Mary followed Helsa over the edge of the mesa and disappeared from view. They found the steep hillside cluttered with rocks, scattered tufts of grass, and a vast assortment of wildflowers.

"Don't stray far!" McCloskey called. He could see most of the depression and the valley road beyond. Although everything looked all right, something felt wrong.

The ladies scattered from one flower to the next with little regard for time, distance, or each other. Clearly their minds were occupied elsewhere, drinking in the beauty of the day. Helsa strayed farthest.

McCloskey watched the girls and stifled the urge to call them back. There was no appearance of danger. In fact, everything was too quiet. Mentally he reviewed the scene and then stopped short. There was no wildlife. On a fine spring morning like this, he should have seen several ground squirrels or at least a rabbit. Something was wrong.

A movement among the rocks caught McCloskey's eye. Forgetting the need to take cover, he stepped forward to warn the girls, but his warning never came. His large body, outlined on the rim of the mesa, made a good target, and one arrow pierced his throat as three more struck his chest.

Just as Helsa bent to pick a daisy, she saw a swarthy little man leap from behind a rock. A large animal skin flew over her head, and she was instantly wrestled to the ground. Paralyzed with fear, she presented little challenge as several men bound her hands and feet. Mary fared little better. Only Katherine moved quickly enough to evade her attacker's assault. She turned on her assailants with the fury of a tiger, and her screams brought the remainder of the royal guard on the run.

Unable to see, and nearly suffocating beneath the animal skin, Mary knew she was being carried swiftly down the slope. When she heard Katherine's screams, she fought and twisted like an eel. Slipping from her captor's hands, Mary fell, her head striking something hard, and she knew no more.

"She's coming around." Mary heard the words but had no idea who had spoken or what they meant. Cautiously, she opened her eyes.

"Can you hear me?" Philip asked.

Mary tried to nod, but the movement sent shards of pain streaking through her body.

"Don't try to move," Philip warned.

Mary closed her eyes and tried to think where she was. Suddenly she gripped Philip's arm. "Helsa and Katherine!" she whispered. "Are they all right?"

"They'll be fine," Philip said, patting her hand reassuringly. "Katherine took a few knocks before we got to her, but she is young and strong, and she will recover quickly. Helsa wasn't hurt so badly, but she is frail, and the shock of the ordeal has dealt her a terrible blow."

A worried expression crossed Mary's face, and she struggled to get up. "Please take me to them," she whispered.

"Dearest Mary," Philip soothed, "we might let you see them tomorrow, but you need to rest today. Everyone is being well cared for in your absence."

Mary smiled and closed her eyes. Releasing Philip's arm, she sank beneath the covers and relaxed. It wasn't until late in the night that she awoke with a start and realized Philip had not been at Gray Haven for months. Why was he here now?

"Philip says we must leave soon," Katherine said quietly. "The roads may soon be held against us."

A chill ran up Mary's spine, and she glanced at Helsa. It seemed the gracious Lady of Gray Haven would never recover. Lady Helsa's innocence was gone. A man was dead because she had wanted to pick flowers. Her guilt had driven her into withdrawal. Mary glanced at Katherine and whispered, "What about Helsa?"

Katherine shrugged and turned to Helsa. "Has Philip spoken to you about our plans?"

Helsa nodded. "You know, I've waited for this day so long, but now that it's here, I feel so unsure. I still love Thomas, and I want to go to him, but these are my people. Uncle Levi has been so dear to me, and I don't even know how my brother fares in his battle with Jabin. Is it right that I should run when my people are facing war?"

Mary reached for Helsa's hand, but she had no words of comfort to offer. It was Katherine who spoke. "You will not be running from danger by leaving with Philip," she said. "The roads may be held against us."

"I suppose everyone who is near me will share the fate of poor Robert," Helsa bemoaned.

Mary and Katherine glanced at each other. They knew Helsa felt responsible for McCloskey's death.

"No one knows the future," Katherine said, "but we are not taking an army. Philip will take only one escort for each of us."

"Why so few?" Mary asked in alarm.

"We have more need of speed than protection," Katherine said.

"If haste will save lives," Helsa said firmly, "then let us go. Tell Philip I'll be ready when he calls."

Later that night, Helsa and her companions were escorted quietly to the gates of Gray Haven. Without fanfare or ceremony, six horses bore their riders into the darkness.

CHAPTER 62

Journey Home

Philip's party had taken a circuitous route to avoid armed resistance. The Great River was flooding from spring thaws, and they all had nearly drowned trying to cross it. Other than that, they had suffered only the normal aches, pains, and deprivations of time in the saddle. Still, Helsa had mixed feelings when they climbed out of the forest to the open meadow west of Devia's fortress and she saw the wall that sealed Amity from the rest of the world. Her aching limbs, the dark wall, and a chilly breeze combined to make her first view of Amity rather unappealing. *Is this really where I want to spend the rest of my life?* she wondered.

They rode slowly across the open fields toward the entrance to Amity. As the gates came into view, the ladies stayed back with their escorts, and Philip rode on ahead.

"Stay where you are!" a voice boomed from the wall above them. "Who are you, and why do you disturb the peace of Amity?"

The group watched as Philip tossed the cloak from his head and shoulders, allowing the helm and armor of Amity to shine in the morning sun. He stood in his stirrups and shouted, "I am Philip Stafford, and my party seeks audience with the master of Amity! Will you let us enter?"

Silence ensued, and Helsa held her breath. *Will they even let us in?* she wondered. *Will this place ever feel like home?*

She thought of her uncle Levi and the sense of security he had always provided her. Life here would be so different, so strange. Suddenly she longed for her dear old maid who had fussed nonstop every night before she would go to bed. Oh, how she hungered for the familiarity of home.

Then she remembered Hesketh and his ongoing battle with Jabin. Panic nearly overwhelmed her as she thought of her beloved homeland and her people in their struggle with evil. Would the Gray Lands fall as so many other kingdoms had? As dark thoughts festered in her mind, Helsa recalled a poem her uncle Levi used to recite about Jabin when she was very young. *Goodness,* she thought, *has Jabin been around that long? Will war and evil never end?*

Tears welled up in Helsa's eyes as she thought about Hesketh, her people, and the poem about Jabin.

> *Jabin, they say, is an angel of light,*
> *Offering hope to those in the midst of night.*
> *But he rules with fear and the crack of a whip*
> *Like a demon at the head of his ship.*
> *A king he thinks he'll always be,*
> *But God alone rules destiny.*

Mary touched Helsa's arm. "Is something wrong?"

Helsa merely shook her head. Her heart was too full for words.

"Look!" Mary whispered. "The gates are opening!"

Drying her eyes, Helsa watched as massive gates began to swing open. From high above came the sound of music. A score of men lined the walls, and that many more marched out the gates to greet them. In beautiful harmony, they raised their voices:

> Come weary traveler; do not fear,
> For peace and rest await you here.
> Find joy and comfort for your soul,
> Until your heart is safe and whole.
> This wall is not to block thee out
> But free thee from thy fear and doubt.
> The portal now will open wide.
> To you we say, come on inside.
> To us is given the curious fate
> To wait for you beside this gate.

Helsa would have laughed outright if her heart had not been so full, but suddenly she grew sober. Her own people had suffered for years from a curse that was not of their own making, but the men on this wall had just endured a devastating civil war; yet here they were, composing and singing a song just to welcome her to Amity. *What a strange and wonderful place this must be,* she marveled.

At Philip's signal, the group moved forward to join him, and when Helsa drew near, she could see a mischievous twinkle in Philip's eye. The party pushed their way forward into a mass of cheering soldiers.

Helsa felt a warm hand on her shoulder and turned to see Philip's boyish grin. "Welcome to Amity, Lady Helsa!" he said.

Inside the walls of Amity there was a huge gathering. People from near and far had flocked to the gates to enjoy this moment. Soldiers began to open a path for Philip's party to make their way to Devia's fortress. Helsa was bewildered. She could not imagine why there were so many people, and they all seemed to be cheering and waving and tossing flowers into the air. What was the celebration?

Making their way slowly up the hill, they witnessed another great flurry of activity around the entrance to Devia's fortress. Helsa wondered if a refugee camp had been established, for there were tents and shelters everywhere on the hillside. She was right about the refugee camp, but the weary, war-torn people living there were also celebrating some great event. *Are these people celebrating Philip's return to Amity?* she wondered, and so it would seem, for as Philip and his party passed, everyone stood to cheer.

"We knew you'd make it!" one man shouted, slapping Philip on the back.

"Right on time too!" another quipped.

"Hurry!" called another. "We can't get this party started until everyone is ready!"

Helsa looked at Mary in bewilderment, and Katherine laughed out loud. "Don't you know what is happening?"

Helsa shook her head.

"This is your homecoming party!" Katherine shouted over the clamor.

"What?" Helsa asked, blushing deeply.

Katherine laughed again. "You really didn't guess?" she asked. "This is only the beginning!"

Helsa's mouth dropped open, but there was no time for words as the crowd swept the princess into the citadel where the comforts of hearth and home were awaiting her arrival.

Helsa had never felt so pampered. Her every need was quickly met, and every desire freely granted. She would have been totally overwhelmed except that Katherine and Mary never left her side.

Hot baths, wholesome food, and soft beds washed away the injuries she'd suffered during their flight from the Gray Lands. However, after what seemed a very short time, Helsa was confronted with the inevitable need to leave Green Meadow and finish the journey.

The day of their departure dawned fair and beautiful. Helsa awoke fresh and ready to go. At breakfast she learned that Philip had planned one last stop before their departure.

Pulling Katherine aside, she asked, "What is Philip planning to do, drown us like he nearly did when we crossed the river?"

Katherine smiled, but her eyes were serious. "He wanted to see his brother's grave."

Helsa suddenly turned pale and grabbed Katherine's hand. "I'm so sorry! I didn't know!"

"Of course you didn't," Katherine soothed. "Philip rarely speaks of it."

"What happened?" Helsa asked.

"His brother was shot while trying to rescue a girl during the defense of Green Meadow," Katherine explained. "He died some days later."

Helsa thought of Robert McCloskey and said no more.

The wagon turned from the path and jolted down a rugged ravine. Helsa gritted her teeth as the wooden seat slammed into her back. The side rail whacked her legs, and Mary grabbed her to keep her from flying off the seat. Though the ride was terrible, Helsa felt sure no one could understand the wretchedness she felt in her soul.

At the foot of a stony bluff, Philip drew the wagon to a halt and climbed out.

Helsa bit her lip, and Mary gently patted her knee. "You did not plan Robert's death," she whispered.

Tears instantly filled Helsa's eyes. *How does Mary know? Is guilt written all over my face?* Helsa did feel responsible for Robert's death, but she didn't know how to undo the events of that day.

The small party watched as Philip knelt beside the simple cross that marked James's grave. No one spoke or even moved. They did not want to disturb these quiet moments of reflection. In the silence, Helsa began to understand she was not alone. They all, she supposed, felt bad about something in their lives they were unable to change. There really was only one path left open, and that was to move on. *Mary is right,* Helsa thought. *I didn't plan Robert's death. Yes, I wanted to get out of the castle, but I never meant for Robert to die. I need to let this go!*

Bowing her head, Helsa silently prayed. *Lord, forgive me. I cannot change the past. Help me to move on. I want to start my life over, please!*

Suddenly Helsa felt a great burden lifted from her shoulders. She could breathe deeply for the first time in weeks. Tears streamed down her cheeks, but they were not tears of guilt or shame. They were tears of joy.

When Philip arose, he saw Helsa weeping and rushed to her side. "My lady," he asked, "have I brought you pain by bringing you here?"

Helsa shook her head, and when their eyes met, she knew Philip understood.

There was little conversation as they passed through Headwater. The charred homes and massive burial sites rekindled Helsa's fear for her beloved homeland.

They spent their first night at Shepherd's Inn, a quaint little cottage that had miraculously been spared during Devia's retreat. The food was good, the beds were adequate, and Helsa was so exhausted that she slept soundly.

The next morning found them on the road again, but soon every town and village began to look the same to Helsa. No matter where they passed, people facing the enormous task of rebuilding their lives would stop their labors and line the road to cheer as the little party made its way eastward. Helsa wondered at this, but again she assumed people were cheering for Philip, as he had played a major role in Amity's deliverance.

Helsa grew anxious as one day rolled into another. Several times she tried to voice her concerns, but everyone seemed occupied with thoughts of their own.

Is Thomas the same gentle man I fell in love with? Helsa wondered. *Has he become unapproachable? Is he really as different as people seem to think?*

Helsa also wanted to know about Stonewall, but when she tried to ask Philip, he merely said, "It's adequate."

Being thus ignored, Helsa fell into the habit of daydreaming. At times when she thought of Thomas, she wanted to leap from the wagon and run on ahead. Other times she thought of the comforts of Green Meadow and wanted to turn around.

Among her thoughts were alarming visions of her brother defending the Gray Lands, fighting with evil and walking down dark roads of danger.

Philip seemed to sense her darker moods and tried to pass the time by describing the plant life they saw or relating some tidbit from Amity's history. Sometimes his tales involved desperate battles and valiant feats of men or women, but more often they involved the nurture and care of some rare species of plant.

Katherine, Mary, and even the mounted guard who rode beside the wagon regaled Helsa with far more information than she could ever remember, but of the things she really wanted to know about—Thomas and Stonewall—they said very little.

So, on the afternoon that Philip drove them into Waterfront, Helsa was so engrossed in her own thoughts that she failed to notice that the buildings in this town had not been destroyed by war.

They stopped at Manor House, and Philip turned to his passengers. "I think we'd better stop early today." He winked at Mary and his beloved Katherine, but the girls were already climbing down from the wagon, glad to be this close to home.

Helsa was ready for a bath and bed. She did not know what tomorrow would bring, but she would meet Thomas in her dreams tonight, and she wanted to waste no time in getting there.

Morning came early as a brisk sea breeze drove the lingering mists of night from the land.

"Wake up, sleepyhead!" Mary called to Helsa.

Night still lingered in the corners of the room, but birds sang merrily outside. Helsa rolled over, struggling to wake from her dreams. "Why so early?" she asked as Mary carried a lantern into her room.

"We have a big day today," Mary teased, "and we don't want to be late!"

"Late!" Helsa exclaimed. "Will we reach Stonewall today?"

"All in good time," Mary soothed. "Now, slip into these traveling clothes. Breakfast is ready!"

Helsa was greeted noisily when she entered the inn's long, narrow dining hall.

The smell of hot coffee mingled with barley cakes and butter. A wholesome breakfast enhanced by friendly conversation started the day in the most delicious manner.

With the meal out of the way, Katherine slipped to Helsa's side. "Now, shall we get dressed?"

"Aren't we dressed already?" Helsa asked, lifting a pleat in her firm cotton frock. "I'm ready to travel."

"We had something a little different planned for today," Katherine said with a giggle. Helsa planted her feet as Katherine tugged at her hand. "Come on!"

Their skirts swayed in the breeze as they waited outside the inn. "Why are we dressed so nice for another day in the wagon?" Helsa asked.

Katherine was about to give some answer when they heard the inn door open, and Philip stepped into the light. Gone was his military garb, and in its place was a flawless suit. Even Katherine had never seen him so handsome.

"Sorry, ladies," Philip said with a twinkle in his eyes, "but the wagon stays here today. We will have to walk."

Helsa glanced first at Katherine and then at Mary. Neither woman seemed surprised by the announcement. She looked at her own billowing gown and Philip's fine suit, and her face reddened slightly. "All right!" she said, squaring her shoulders. "What is going on here?"

With a disarming smile, Philip took her arm and led her to the Greenway. "*We* are going on, Lady Helsa." He turned her eastward, where a great mass of stone appeared to rise from the sea. The sun rose slowly over the ramparts and towers of Stonewall, etching this moment forever in Helsa's memory.

She had not known what to expect of Stonewall, but this was beyond her wildest imagination. Though large and unquestionably strong, this citadel by the sea did not intimidate her in any way. It seemed to beckon her, and a feeling of warmth and calm soothed her soul. *Is this really my new home?* she wondered.

Her eyes were moist when she glanced at Philip. "It's beautiful!" she whispered.

Philip pulled her close. "I'm sorry we teased you, but I can't believe you didn't see this when we arrived yesterday."

Helsa dabbed at her eyes. "I've been so caught up in my own thoughts, I couldn't see beyond the end of my nose."

Stepping farther into the road, Helsa viewed Stonewall a bit longer. "Is Thomas there?" she asked.

"He's waiting for you at the ferry," Philip smiled. "Shall we go?"

"Yes!" Helsa said, and taking Philip's arm, she felt as if she were stepping into a dream.

The morning sun caught the river's bobbing surface and transformed it into a vast display of shimmering jewels. As if on cue, people poured from buildings and bystreets to line the road. Cheers resounded from willing throats, and flower petals fell like rain.

Tears streamed down Helsa's cheeks. Turning to Mary, she asked, "Is this really happening, or am I dreaming?"

"You are not dreaming, my lady," Mary said through tears of her own. "This is your day."

With grace and dignity, Philip moved the party forward with deliberate steps. The mounted guard, immaculate for inspection, rode behind, and before them, the crowd parted to let them pass.

The constant cheers and applause from the adoring crowd numbed Helsa and dulled her senses. She suddenly came to life, though, when the crowd parted to reveal one lone man standing on the grassy slope near the river. Months of waiting were nearly over, and her heart raced wildly within her breast.

For a brief moment, Helsa felt unsure of what lay before her, but lowering her eyes, she followed Philip's lead until they came to a halt.

Slowly lifting her head, she gazed into Thomas's eyes, and in that instant, every fear fled as her heart melted with love. This man was not aloof; he was merely alone. She longed to reach out to him and hold him close.

Philip patted her hand, soldiers of Amity held the crowd at bay, and

Mary handed her the wedding bouquet. Katherine gave Helsa a gentle hug. The girls stepped aside as Philip presented the Lady Helsa to Thomas.

Helsa was surprised, for Thomas was no longer alone. An ancient man had suddenly appeared and was standing by Thomas's side. Clinging to Philip's arm, Helsa knew she was ready, so why did she feel this nagging reluctance to take the next step?

Sensing her uncertainty, Thomas stepped forward. A smile softened his face as he held out his hands. His eyes held her captive, but for one brief instant she glanced down at his hands. There, burned into the flesh of his palm, was the enduring emblem of his suffering and her salvation. All her reservations fled.

Having left everything she owned behind, Helsa wondered what she could give this man who meant so much to her. The clothes on her back, the shoes on her feet, and even the food she had eaten had come from this man. Releasing Philip's arm, Helsa reached for Thomas and offered him the only things that were hers to give: her heart, her mind, and her soul.

On the grassy slope beside the Crescent River, Master Rhoop led the couple in their vows before the Creator of heaven and earth, and the citizens of Amity. The Lady Helsa had finally come home.

CHAPTER 63

Stonewall

Less than one week after Thomas and Helsa's wedding, Katherine came to Mary's room and announced, "Thomas and Philip are going to war!"

Mary stiffened. Life had settled into a pleasant routine in Stonewall. Mary was serving Lady Helsa, but she met with Katherine as often as she could. Her quarters were small but adequate, and she was never expected to do any hard or demeaning labor. Life was almost perfect, if only Katherine could refrain from such gloomy talk.

"Philip says the call to arms has already gone out," Katherine stated. "And Thomas sent a man to Emancipation to enlist Gaff's help."

"But the marriage feast is barely over!" Mary complained. "Surely Thomas won't leave his bride so soon!"

"He has to go!" Katherine insisted. "It's Helsa's brother he's trying to rescue!"

"Lord Hesketh?" Mary gasped.

"They say he has been driven from Endor and is about to lose Gray Haven," Katherine said. "Seagood—I mean, Lord Hesketh—sent a plea for help that arrived the very evening of Thomas and Helsa's wedding. Plans were being made during the wedding feast!"

Mary sighed. She had seen and felt the devastation of war too often. She could not imagine Gray Haven under attack or destroyed. Poor Helsa: she would be devastated by the news. "Have you told Helsa?" Mary asked.

"She knows," Katherine said. "The men told her the night they heard it themselves."

"How is she handling it?" Mary asked.

"Let's go see!"

Bill marveled at the crowds gathering in Waterfront. Much had happened since he had left for Emancipation. On a crowded street corner, two men were hacking at a pile of hay with wooden swords while the crowd cheered them on. He wondered if they would feel so brave if the hay were fighting back.

Looking across rows of expectant young faces, Bill thought of the gallant and noble dreams he'd held only one year ago. Would these young men be so anxious to leave their families and friends if they knew the horror that lay before them?

Bill wondered about that himself. Would he have left Mary one year ago if he'd known then what he knew now? Would he have been willing to leave everything for the Master? "Yes!" he said aloud.

His traveling companion turned to look at him curiously. "Hey, partner, have you been out in the sun too long?" he asked.

"No." Bill grinned sheepishly. "You just caught me thinking out loud."

They came to the ferry and crossed the river, unnoticed among the throng. Bill left his horse with his friend and headed for the great house.

He met a pleasant young man on the path, who asked, "Are you looking for Master Thomas?"

"Yes, I am," Bill stated.

"You'll have to wait," the young man answered. "He's been tied up in meetings all morning. They say he's talking strategy."

"I wouldn't be surprised," Bill responded and turned again for the house.

"They won't let you in," the young man said, "but I wouldn't blame you for trying. There are three good-looking ladies in there, and only two of them are married. Look for the one with snow-white hair. She's as pretty as a picture."

"This is no time to be thinking about women," Bill grumped.

"Maybe," the young man agreed, "but a good memory can carry a man a long way."

Bill considered the man's words as he turned back toward the house. He knew both Thomas and Philip had recently married, so he supposed that accounted for two of the women. But who was the third? He couldn't help but think about Mary and wonder what had happened to her.

The old man watching the door knew Bill and only nodded as he passed. Once inside the great house, it felt like a vacuum compared to the hustle and bustle in the courtyard. A steward stepped quickly down the corridor to meet Bill. "Do you have business with the Master?" the steward asked.

"I do," Bill answered. The man was new, and Bill didn't recognize him.

"Would you state your name and business, please?" the steward said politely. "I will report to the Master as soon as he is available, and then I will assign you a time to return."

"My name is William Cotton, and I have just returned from Emancipation with important news for Master Thomas about the war," Bill said, trying to remain calm.

"I'm sure you feel your business is urgent," the steward said primly. "Everyone does. However, you will just have to wait your turn."

Bill felt his patience growing thin. "Just tell Thomas I'm here, and let him decide if he will see me or not."

"I'm sorry," the steward said. "I cannot do that. Master Thomas is in conference just now, and I—"

"Then I'll announce myself!" Bill said, brushing past the steward.

"But you can't!" the steward wailed. "Guards, stop that man!"

Two burly fellows blocked the door to the conference room. "Hold it right there," said the more articulate of the two, pointing his spear directly at Bill's chest.

Irritation had been steeping inside Bill until suddenly it was fully brewed. In a flash of movement, Bill used his stump to brush the spear aside as he reached for the door. A fist landed squarely on his jawbone.

Bill's temper flared, and his fingers coiled into a fist. Sidestepping a second blow aimed at his jaw, he came back swinging. His fist connected, and one guard hit the floor. Again Bill reached for the door, but the second guard wrapped strong arms around Bill's neck. Bill pivoted quickly and slammed the guard into the door. It crashed open, and both men spilled into the conference room, thrashing and punching each other on the floor.

Rhoop and John Stafford were in the middle of a heated conversation with Philip and Thomas. Katherine, Helsa, and Mary had just brought refreshments into the room when Bill and the guard crashed through the doors. Everyone stood spellbound as the two men grappled viciously.

With a sudden movement, Bill rolled to the top and twisted the guard's arm behind his back. With a shout of triumph, Bill whipped his stump into the air. Victory was his!

The women shrank back, but Philip came running. "Good move!" he exclaimed. "You'll have to teach me that one." An accomplished wrestler himself, Philip was quickly at Bill's side, untangling the two men. "Who are you, my good fellow?" Philip asked Bill.

"William Cotton," was the answer, but the voice was not Bill's. Thomas came striding across the room. "You've come from Gaff! Will he join our campaign?"

"Bill!" Philip was incredulous. "I didn't recognize you without your beard!"

All talk was interrupted by a scream. Looking about, they saw that Lady Helsa was pale and staring at the floor. At her feet lay the limp form of a woman with snow-white hair.

CHAPTER 64

Bill Cotton's House

Amidst boisterous complaint from the grandchildren, Bill stopped telling his story long enough for the family to eat supper. The world was dark outside when the family returned to the parlor, but once everyone was settled around the fire, he continued.

"Words cannot describe what I felt as I gathered your grandmother into my arms." Bill ruffled Robbie's hair. "Just think: after all those months of searching, your grandmother was right there in the Master's house."

"What did you do, Grandpa?" Robbie asked with wide eyes.

"I told Thomas my news from Gaff, and then I whisked your grandmother away to the library where we could talk. I started talking that day, and I guess I've never been able to stop."

Bill glanced at Mary across the room. She looked up from her needles and smiled.

"But, Grandpa," Joshua said, "what about the final battle with Jabin?"

"Well, I felt different about going to war, knowing that your grandmother was alive," Bill said. "But I had made a vow to follow Thomas, and I intended to keep it."

"I'm sorry, Mary," Bill said, shaking his head. "I don't want to leave you again, but I promised."

"I know," Mary soothed, pressing her finger to Bill's lips. "You have to go, but I'll pray for you every moment you are away."

Bill hugged Mary so hard she thought her bones might break, but she didn't want him to stop. She was determined her husband would carry a different memory with him this time when he went away.

"You'll be late," she whispered, pushing Bill ever so gently away. She turned to lift his shield. She'd worked very hard to design a harness that would hold Bill's shield in place even without a hand. She began to strap the shield to Bill's arm.

"Mary," Bill teased, "I'll be the only man to eat with his shield, sleep with his shield, and take a bath with his shield."

"Well, you'd better not take it off or mess with the bindings, Bill Cotton, or you'll have me to contend with when you return!"

Bill pulled her close. "You'd better believe I'll contend with you when I get back, young lady!"

Mary smiled, brushed her husband aside, and returned to her work. When the shield was securely in place, she stepped back to examine her handiwork. Looking up at Bill, she scowled and said, "Remember what I told you."

The two suddenly laughed, and Mary gave Bill a hug and kiss that would carry him for weeks on end.

Bill looked around the parlor at his family. "It was early morning when we rode through the massive gates at Green Meadow," he said. "Scouts had informed us Jabin was with a vanguard of elite troops somewhere across the meadow, hidden in the darkness." Bill spoke quietly as he gently caressed Robbie's small mop of curly hair.

"Lord Hesketh had driven Jabin's troops away from the gates of Gray Haven, but they were regrouping in the wilderness of the Gray Lands. Gaff was unable to come to our aide, for he was under attack near Great Bend. We had to face Jabin alone.

"I glanced around at those who were assembling on the meadow, and it seemed we all had one thing in common: not one man in the leading vanguard was entirely whole. Every man I saw was scarred in some fashion. For some, the scars were emotional and didn't show, but for others, the wounds were obvious. Larry Chavez was there. Though he was missing a leg, he refused to stay home, and he was as mobile as anyone when mounted on a horse. He caught my eye when he rode through the gate and waved. He may have been the only man to act as though he was going on a picnic.

"I watched as the strength of Amity poured onto the field. Captains arranged their men, and I took my place beside Philip.

"Finally, Thomas drew his sword and raised it to the sky. The darkness had given way to an overcast dawn. One single ray of sunshine broke through the clouds and struck Thomas's upturned blade. A shiver ran down my spine, and I wondered if God had given His blessing.

"But time for contemplation was over, for with a loud cry, Thomas surged forward. Philip and I were hot on his heels. I could hear the thunder of horses racing behind me as we charged down the hill. Far overhead I heard an eagle cry, but I felt no fear. After all, this was the Lord's battle!"

"Ahem!" Mary cleared her throat. "Don't you think we should let the children get some sleep tonight?" she asked.

"Oh, Grandma!" a chorus of voices complained around the room. "Can't Grandpa tell us more about the final battle?"

Bill glanced at Mary and grinned. "Well, I will tell you this much: we won! Jabin fled before us. His armies were routed, and we drove them all the way to Promontory Point."

"What about Lord Hesketh?" Joshua asked.

"He had driven Jabin's army from the Gray Lands by the time we could assist him, and Gaff had routed his enemies in Emancipation. You know," Bill said, "many people from the Gray Lands and Emancipation have come to Amity to live, and many from Amity have gone into the wider world. The mixing of our peoples has been a good thing."

Mary smiled her approval. She was quite sure their talk the night before had given Bill those words.

Bill winked and grinned. "Now, I think your grandmother is right. It's high time we all went to bed."

There were grumbles from the children and a general commotion as people began to stir from their places. Suddenly everyone heard Robbie ask, "Grandpa, do you believe in angels?"

"Why, yes, I do!" Bill answered immediately, though a little surprised at the sudden change of subject. "Why do you ask, Robbie?"

"Can they really protect people?" Robbie asked.

"Well, yes," Bill said. "I'm sure they can and do keep people safe."

"I mean, wasn't that an angel that helped Grandma escape Capri?" Robbie continued.

The room grew suddenly quiet as everyone began to focus on this unexpected conversation. Destry looked uneasy. "Really, Robbie," she protested, "do you have to ask such questions?"

To everyone's surprise, it was Ned who came to Robbie's defense.

"Robbie has a story I think everyone ought to hear." The entire family turned their gaze upon Ned, and his face grew quite red. He didn't like the attention, but he continued. "It's all right, Robbie. Go ahead and tell the story you told me this morning."

All eyes turned to Robbie, and Ned sighed with relief.

"Robbie, were you bothering Uncle Ned?" Destry asked.

"He's the only one who would listen," Robbie said, his voice wavering. He glanced at his uncle, glad to have one ally in the room but a little unsure of his uncle's support. "You believe my story, don't you, Uncle Ned?"

Once again Ned found himself the center of attention. He rubbed his forehead nervously. "Just tell your story, Robbie. We're all listening."

"Well," Robbie said, "this broken leg didn't happen the way everyone thinks it did."

"What?" Destry began, but Bill raised his hand for silence.

"I wanted to tell you, Mother," Robbie said, "but the man told me you wouldn't understand."

"Who told you I wouldn't understand?" Destry fumed. "What are you talking about?"

Robbie was still on his grandpa's lap, but he squirmed nervously. Bill leaned close to his ear and said, "Why don't you tell us your story, Robbie?"

"Well," Robbie began again, "the day I broke my leg, Mother told me not to play too far from the house. I went to play in the barn, but I started to pretend I was Thomas of Amity, and soon I forgot where I was. I started chasing bad guys around the barn and out into the woods. I ran and ran until suddenly I was at the top of Promontory Point."

"Robbie!" Destry exclaimed. "That's nearly two miles from home. What on earth were you thinking?"

"Please," Bill said, holding up his hand. "Let's hear what Robbie has to say."

Robbie was glad to have another advocate in the room, and when it was quiet, he began yet again. "Bad guys were all around me, but I was safe because Bosco, our dog, was with me. I drew my knife and slashed back and forth, driving Jabin's men right to the cliff. I must have gotten too close to the edge, because Bosco began to bark. When I turned to see why he was barking, I slipped and fell."

"Robbie Cotton!" Destry shouted, leaping to her feet. "You're scaring me to death!"

"I'm sorry, but the angel said I wasn't supposed to tell you that until Christmas," Robbie whimpered.

There was a rustle of surprise around the room, but when Destry spoke again, the anger in her voice was unmistakable. "Robbie Cotton, this has gone on long enough." She was about to take her son out of the room when Bill again motioned for calm.

Robbie looked rather pathetic. "I really met them, Mother."

"You met whom?" Destry snapped.

"The angels!" Robbie answered. "Well, I only saw one, but I know there was another."

"Robbie!" Philip said, rising from his chair. "I think you've been listening to Grandpa too long, and now you're making up stories of your own. We need to have a talk."

"But the angels are real, Father," Robbie protested.

Bill opened his mouth to intervene, but Ned spoke first. "Listen, everyone. I think ya need to hear Robbie's story. Please let him tell it!"

Robbie watched as his parents slowly settled back into their chairs. When he glanced at his mother, he read a clear message in her eyes: "You'd better not embarrass your father or me any further!" He gulped and hesitated.

Grandpa whispered in his ear, "It will be all right. Just tell us your story, Robbie."

Robbie stirred uneasily. "I was so scared when I fell. I cried for you, Mother. All I could see were rocks getting bigger. I don't know what happened next, but when I opened my eyes, everything was dark, and I hurt really bad. I couldn't move or see, but I could hear.

"Somewhere in the dark I heard someone ask, 'Where did you come from?'

"I wasn't sure the voice was talking to me, but when I tried to answer, I couldn't make a sound. Then I heard a second voice ask, 'Who are you talking to, Wart?'

"By now, I had heard two different voices, but I still couldn't see anyone. I did want to see the second voice, though, because that one liked to laugh.

"The first voice said, 'Look who dropped in!'"

"And the second voice said, 'Why, it's the little Cotton boy!'"

"The first voice said, 'I know who he is, Rudy, but what are we going to do with him?'"

"Maybe I should have been scared, but I wasn't. That second voice sounded so happy; somehow I knew everything was going to be all right.

"The jolly voice said, 'Well, make him comfortable while I see whether he stays or not.'

"Someone picked me up, and I realized again that I hurt all over, but my leg was the worst. I wanted to ask where we were going, but I couldn't talk. Someone moved me very gently, and it should have been nice, but all I really wanted was you, Mother."

Destry instinctively rose, crossed the room, and knelt beside her son. She could not stop the tears from sliding down her cheeks.

Robbie continued. "The first voice said, 'I think you could use some water.' The man must have left, but he was back so soon that I couldn't be sure. 'Here!' he said, lifting my head. 'Drink some of this.'

"The water he pressed to my lips was so cold it hurt my teeth, but with each sip, I began to feel better.

"Just then the jolly voice shouted, 'Wart, what are you doing?'"

"The man giving me water answered, 'I'm just giving him a drink.'"

"'Well, all right!' the jolly one said, 'but don't make him too comfortable; the boss says he has to go back.'

"The man with the water said, 'That's too bad. You know he'd fit right in, even though he is pretty beat up.'

"The jolly man said, 'I know, Wart, but orders are orders. Why don't I take him back? You go on to the party.'

"The first voice said, 'You'd better hurry. The celebration is about to begin, and we don't want to be late!'

"Again, someone picked me up, and this time I felt like I was floating. I still couldn't see anything, but I felt much better than I had before drinking the water. Whoever was carrying me was a big man, almost like Uncle Ned, and while he was carrying me, he said, 'I can't take you back looking like this! Maybe some of the leaves from this tree will help.' He gently laid me on the ground, and in a minute he was rubbing something scratchy all over my body. Whatever he put on me began to burn like fire.

"'Hey, stop it!' I yelled. 'That burns!'

"I wanted to cry, but this didn't seem like the kind of place where anyone ever cried. So I shouted again, 'Please, get it off!'

"The jolly voice just said, 'Steady, lad.'

"If the burning wasn't bad enough, the man began to pull what felt like a big scab off my body. It kind of hurt, but it kind of felt good too. As he peeled something off my face, the darkness around me became lighter, and when he was done, I could see!

"I couldn't understand where I was. Everything was so green, like spring, only more so. And there, standing in the tall grass, was a huge man as big as Uncle Ned, laughing as he watched me.

"'Where am I?' I asked. 'And who are you?'

"He just smiled and said, 'It doesn't really matter who I am or where you are, because you can't stay. I have to take you home. My boss heard your request.'

"'What request?' I asked. 'I couldn't talk until now.'

"The big man looked very serious. 'My boss listens to people's hearts. He knows what they need even before they know it themselves. He knows you want your mother, and he knows she needs you too.'"

Destry held a hand to her trembling mouth as tears continued to stream down her cheeks.

"The big man suddenly laughed and picked me up like I was a twig. 'Now to get you home,' he said.

"One moment we were in a place of bright colors and warmth, and the next everything was brown and cold. I shivered and cuddled closer to the man for warmth. 'My leg still hurts,' I complained.

"The big man looked at me soberly. 'I'm sorry, lad. I can't do anything about that.'

"'Why not?' I asked.

"He shook his head. 'Pain and suffering help us remember. Now, if you felt no pain, this would all seem like a dream to you, wouldn't it?'

"'I suppose,' I said. 'I sure never had a dream hurt this much.'

"At that very moment we rounded a bend and saw our farm. 'Your leg is broken, Robbie,' the big man said. 'It will heal in time, but I think your broken leg will help your mother heal too.'

"'Is my mother sick?' I asked.

"The big man grinned. 'She's not sick in the way you are thinking, Robbie, but she's not ready to believe everything you've just been through.' He stopped on the far side of the barn and set me on the ground. 'This is as far as I go.'

"'Why can't you take me to the house?' I begged.

"The big man actually looked sad for the first time. 'No one can see me in your world, Robbie, only you—and that will only last a few more moments. You need to keep this adventure to yourself, at least until Christmas. Your mother would never understand right now, but there will come a time when she will, and you'll know when you can tell her.'

"'But my leg hurts,' I cried. 'How will I get to the house?'

"The big man grinned and said, 'Your dog is almost back from the mountain. He's going to start barking and bring your mother on the run. She's going to take good care of you, Robbie. She loves you so much! Now, I have to go, but I will see you again someday, and that is a promise!'

"I blinked, and the man was gone. Before I knew it, Mother was hovering over me, crying and scolding. She thought I had fallen from the barn loft. I wanted to tell you, Mother, but the angel who brought me home didn't think you'd believe me."

Philip suddenly stood and crossed the room. Pulling a broken knife from his pocket, he held it out for his son to see. "I've been meaning to ask you, Robbie: Is this knife yours?"

Robbie's eyes grew big and round. "Yes, it is!" he said excitedly. "Where did you find it?"

Philip was now visibly shaken. "The day you broke your leg, I was watching your grandfather's sheep not far from Promontory Point. Several lambs had strayed, and I wanted to check the rocks below the cliff. While I was down there, I discovered this knife, bent and broken, and the rocks covered with blood.

Destry pulled her son from Bill's lap and held him close. "Why didn't you tell me?" she sobbed.

"The man said you wouldn't believe me, Mother, and I didn't think you would, either," Robbie said timidly.

Destry began to weep without restraint. Holding Robbie tight, she whispered, "I feel so ashamed, but you were probably right!"

"Do you believe me now?" Robbie asked.

Destry glanced around the room. Mary sat quietly by the fire, her snow-white hair a vivid reminder of the trials she had endured and the miracles surrounding them. Looking quickly at Philip's father, a man she had both feared and refused to accept, she now failed to even notice his missing hand. All she could see was the love in his tear-moistened eyes.

Doubt and fear had always kept Destry from exercising the faith she tried to profess. Wanting desperately to start a new chapter in her life, she hugged her tiny son and whispered, "Yes, Robbie, I believe I do!"

CHAPTER 65

Life beyond the Fire

The following morning dawned clear, and a hint of warmth softened the frosty air. There was a flurry of activity as Philip's brothers helped him load the sleigh. Destry carefully wrapped a blanket around Robbie's coat and muffler, and Philip placed him on the front seat, where he would ride between his parents. Both Philip and Destry were beginning to realize their little boy was becoming a young man, and they did not want to miss another moment of his journey.

When everyone had said their goodbyes, Philip urged the horses into a trot. Destry watched Philip's family over her shoulder until the sleigh rounded a bend and they disappeared from view. Reaching the Greenway, Philip turned the horses west, and they began to glide quickly over the snow. Destry spoke little as she considered her Christmas—all the stories she had heard and family she had met. She thought about Philip's father, whose commitment to country and duty had cost him his hand. She was sorry now that she had refused to see him all these years. He was so gentle with Robbie, and he loved his family so much. It was easy to understand why Robbie adored him.

Her mind turned to Philip's mother, the spry little woman with snow-white hair. Destry's cheeks flushed as she thought of all Mary had endured, and yet now, no one could possibly know how much she had suffered. Life had tried to destroy Bill and Mary Cotton, but God had other plans. By trusting in their loving Heavenly Father, Philip's parents had been able to move beyond sorrow and loss and still make good things happen in their lives.

Destry placed one arm around her son. For once she did not feel the need to protect him; she simply wanted to be close to this unique individual God had allowed into her life. She marveled at Robbie's simple faith. He was far more confident than she that all things would work together for good. After his fall, while still in terrible pain, blind, and mute, Robbie had somehow known everything would turn out all right. Destry really wanted to trust the Lord like that. She had spent years attempting to control every situation in life, clinging to her son, trying to protect him from every danger, yet in one afternoon, Robbie's life had nearly been taken. It made her realize God was a far better guardian than she could ever be.

Destry closed her eyes and began to thank the Lord for saving her son. She praised God for giving her—no, for giving her entire family—another chance. Instinctively, she wrapped her arms around Robbie, determined not to waste this new opportunity. Life was not to be lived in fear. She understood bad things would still happen, but she also realized God had the power to overcome evil with good. She could waste her life by looking back at mistakes and living with regret, or she could look forward with faith, hope, and love. In her mind, Destry could still see Philip's parents standing in the snow outside their home, smiling and waving goodbye.

Suddenly reaching for Philip's hand, Destry surprised everyone, including herself, when she whispered, "Can we come back next year?"